"No excellent soul
is exempt from a
mixture of madness."
-Aristotle.

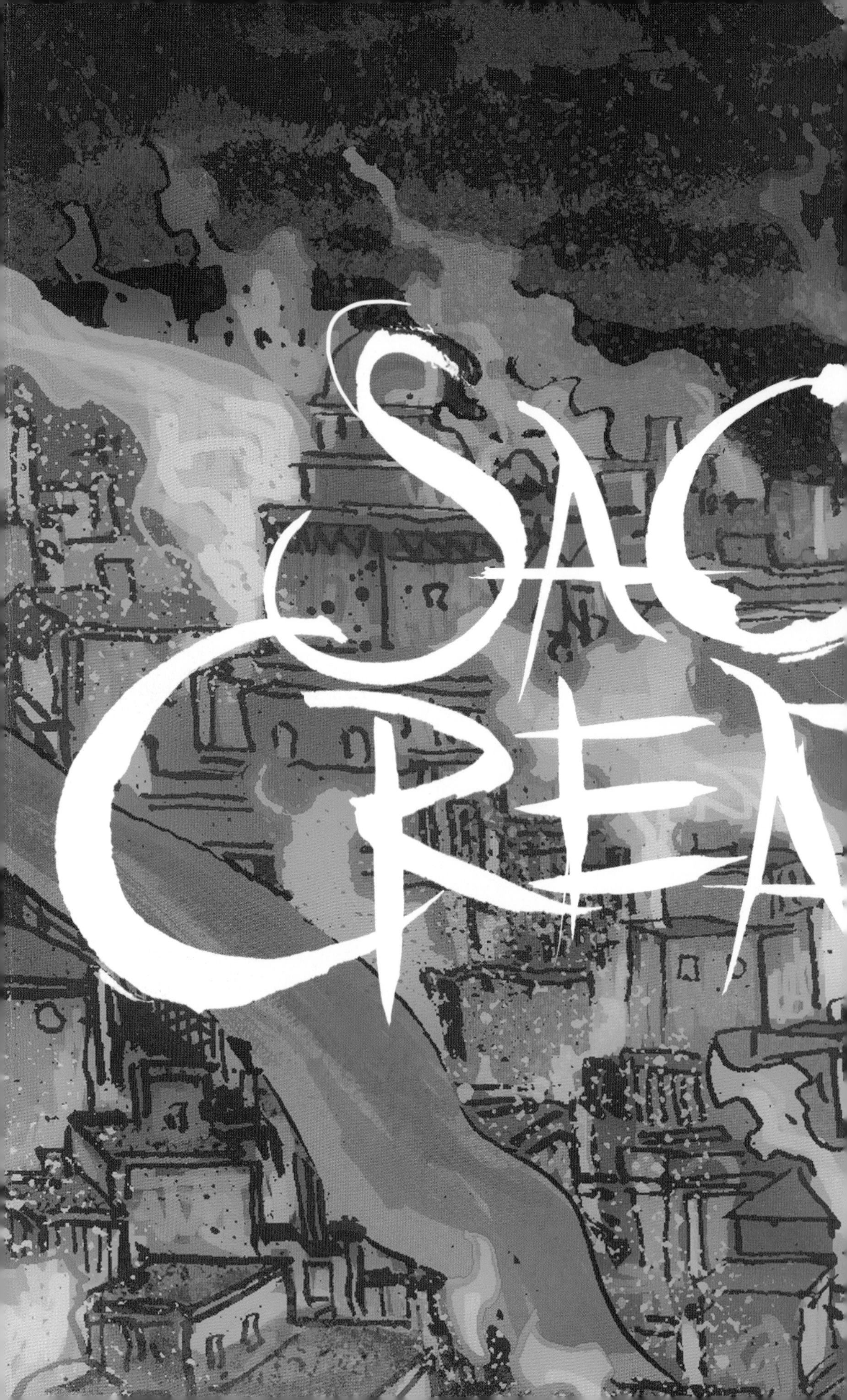

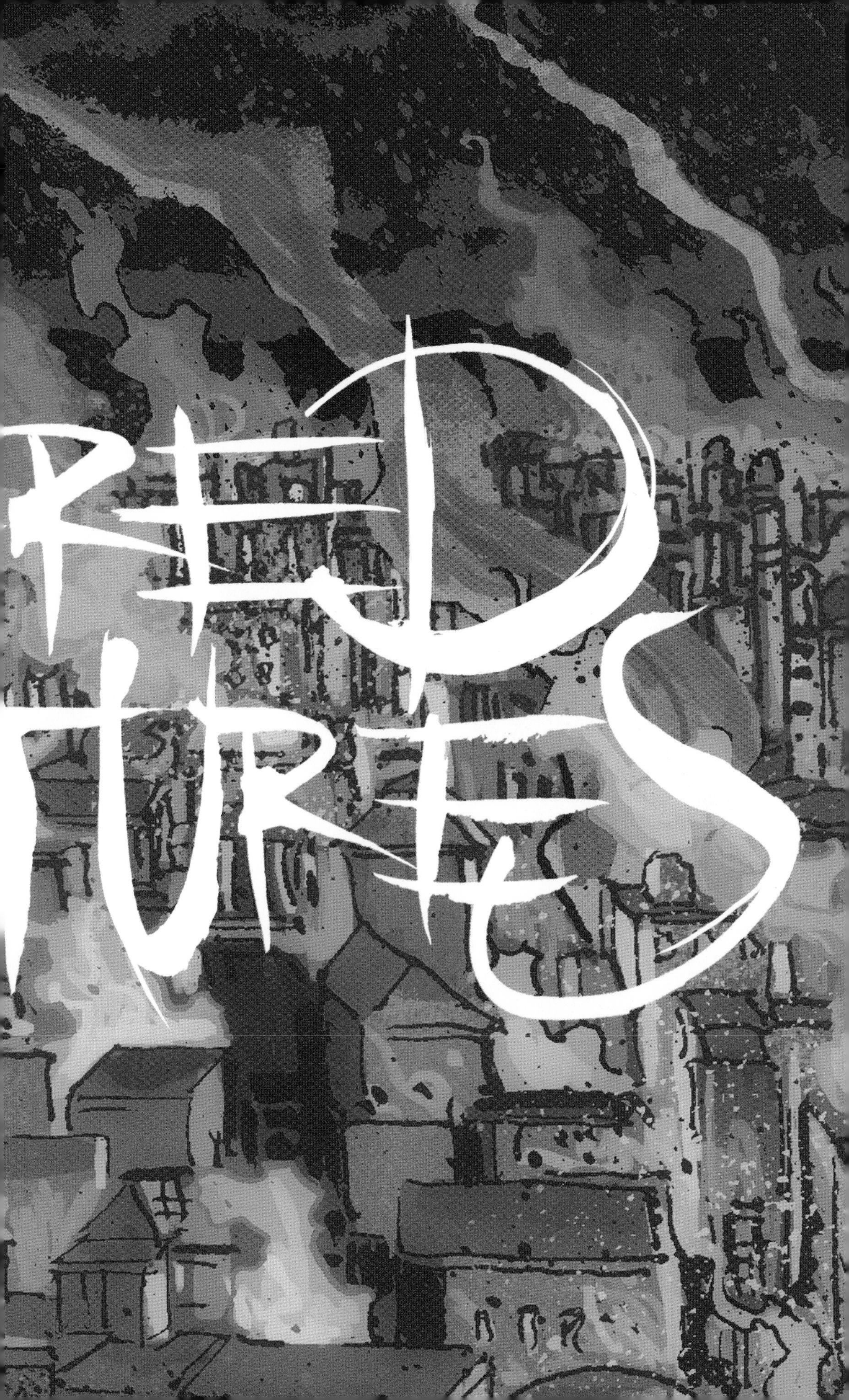
RED
FURIES

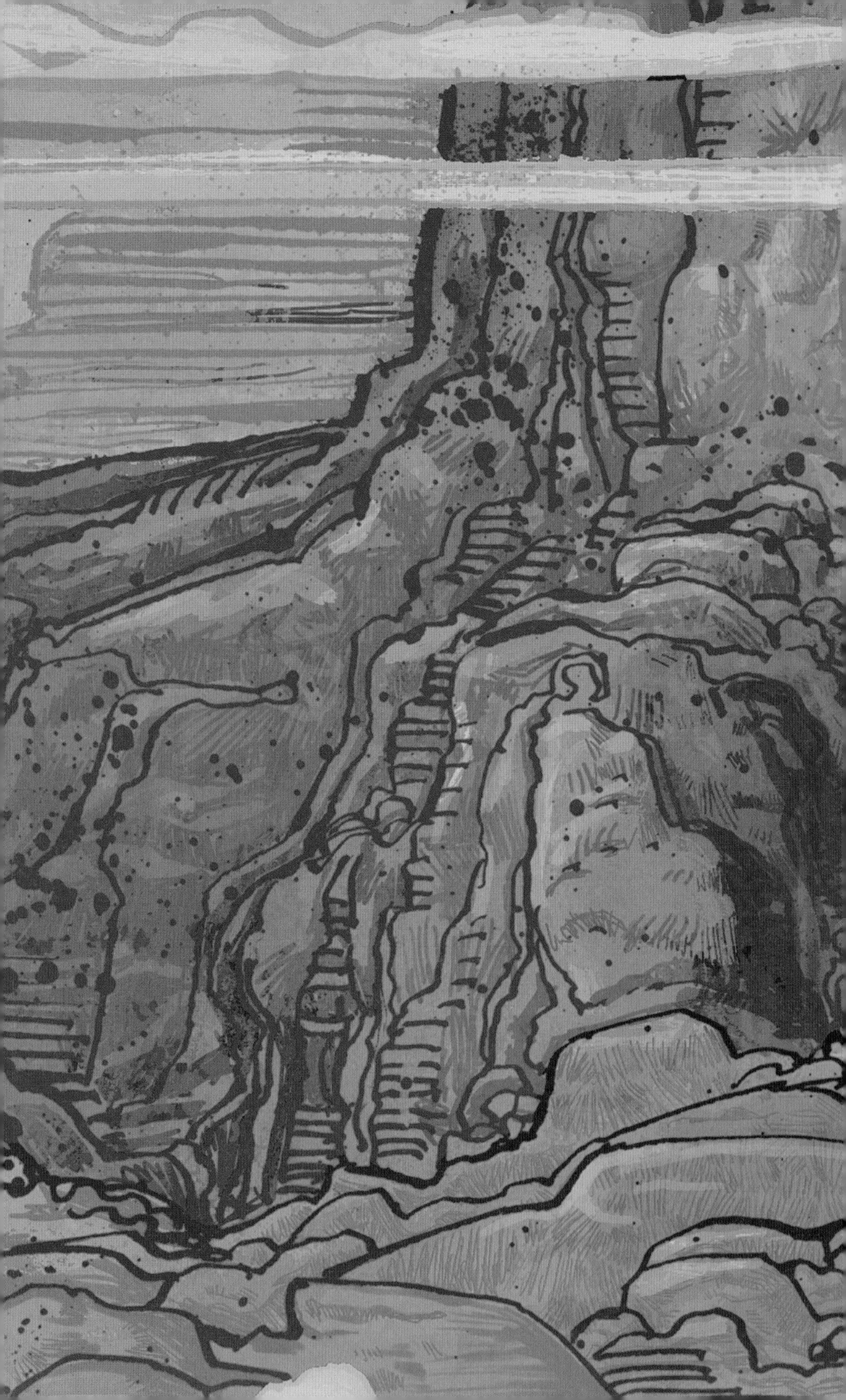

SACRED CREATURES
Volume One

A MIXTURE OF MADNESS

CREDITS

Pablo Raimondi and Klaus Janson
WRITERS

CONTEMPORARY SCENES
Pablo Raimondi
ARTIST
Chris Chuckry, Brian Reber
and Hi-Fi Studio
COLORISTS

ANCIENT PAST SCENES
Klaus Janson
ARTIST
Dean White
COLORIST

Tom Orzechowski and Clem Robins
LETTERERS

COVER ART
Pablo Raimondi and Dean White

Collected Edition edited and
designed by Pablo Raimondi

SACRED CREATURES created by
Pablo Raimondi and Klaus Janson

IMAGE COMICS, INC. • **Robert Kirkman:** Chief Operating Officer • **Erik Larsen:** Chief Financial Officer • **Todd McFarlane:** President • **Marc Silvestri:** Chief Executive Officer • **Jim Valentino:** Vice President • **Eric Stephenson:** Publisher / Chief Creative Officer • **Corey Hart:** Director of Sales • **Jeff Boison:** Director of Publishing Planning & Book Trade Sales • **Chris Ross:** Director of Digital Sales • **Jeff Stang:** Director of Specialty Sales • **Kat Salazar:** Director of PR & Marketing • **Drew Gill:** Art Director • **Heather Doornink:** Production Director • **Nicole Lapalme:** Controller • IMAGECOMICS.COM

SACRED CREATURES, VOL. 1: A MIXTURE OF MADNESS. First printing. May 2018. Published by Image Comics, Inc. Office of publication: 2701 NW Vaughn St., Suite 780, Portland, OR 97210. Copyright © 2018 Pablo Raimondi & Klaus Janson. All rights reserved. Contains material originally published in single magazine form as SACRED CREATURES #1-6. "Sacred Creatures," its logos, and the likenesses of all characters herein are trademarks of Pablo Raimondi & Klaus Janson, unless otherwise noted. "Image" and the Image Comics logos are registered trademarks of Image Comics, Inc. No part of this publication may be reproduced or transmitted, in any form or by any means (except for short excerpts for journalistic or review purposes), without the express written permission of Pablo Raimondi & Klaus Janson, or Image Comics, Inc. All names, characters, events, and locales in this publication are entirely fictional. Any resemblance to actual persons (living or dead), events, or places, without satiric intent, is coincidental. Printed in the USA. For information regarding the CPSIA on this printed material call: 203-595-3636 and provide reference #RICH-789143. For international rights, contact: foreignlicensing@imagecomics.com. ISBN: 978-1-5343-0496-3.

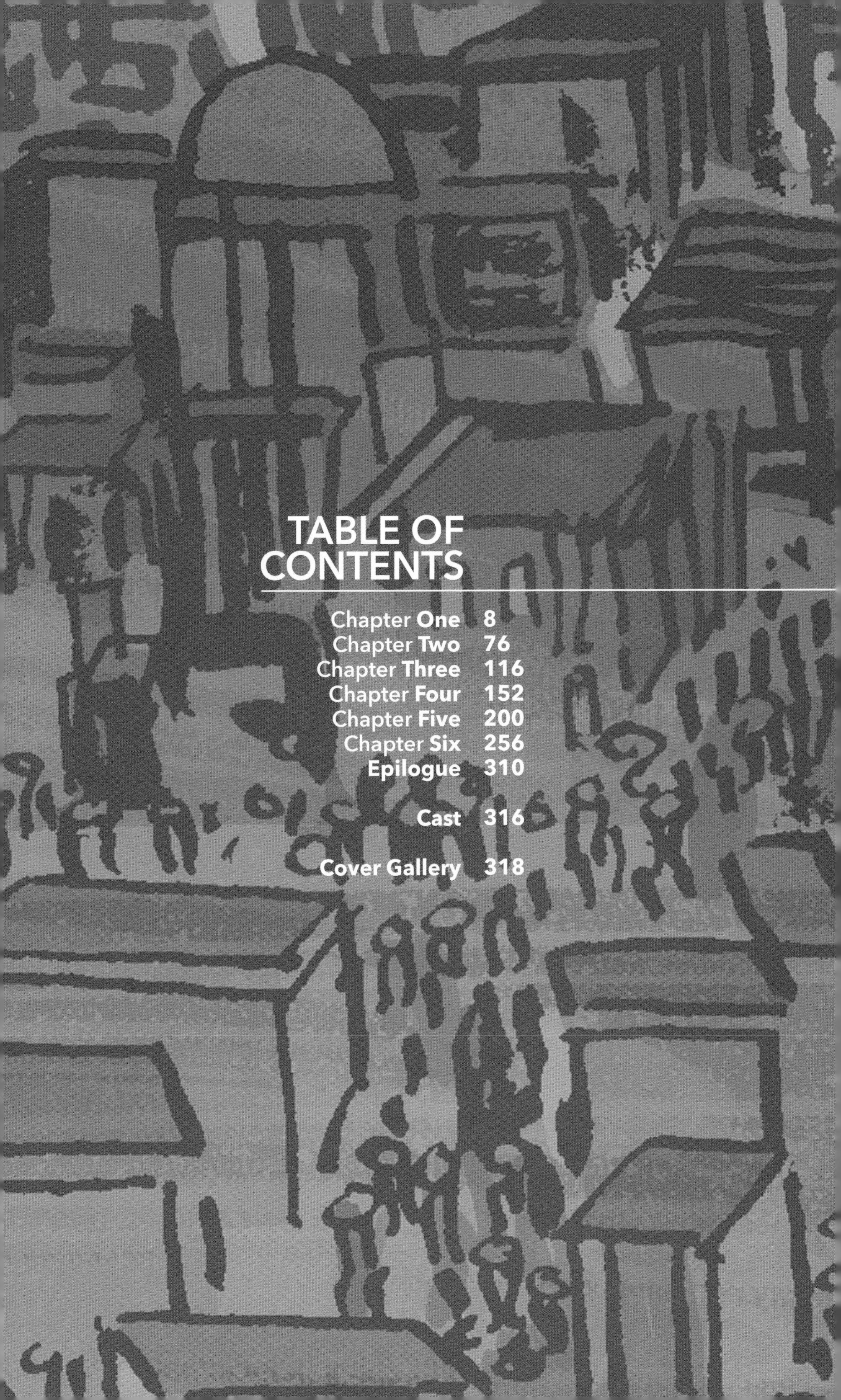

TABLE OF CONTENTS

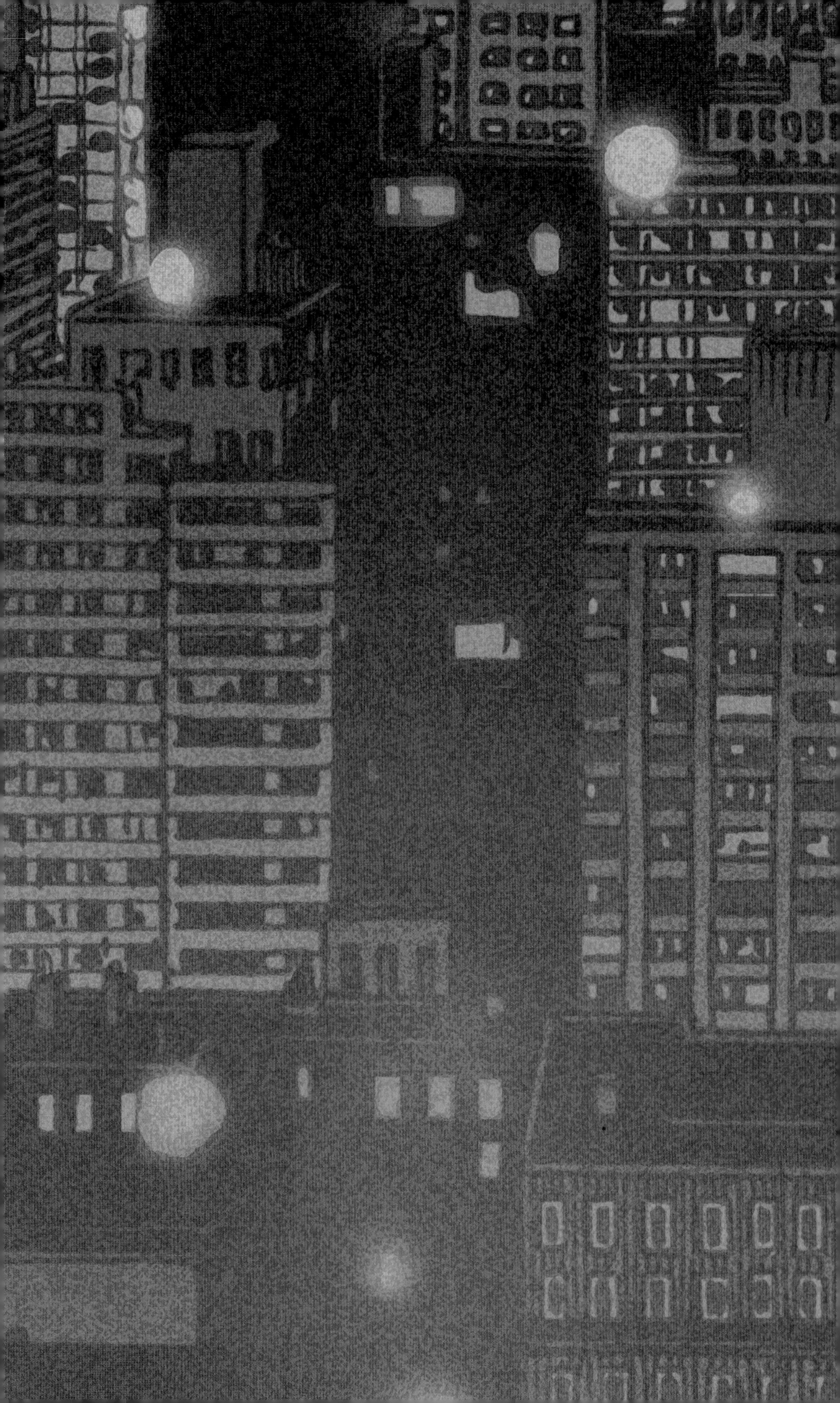

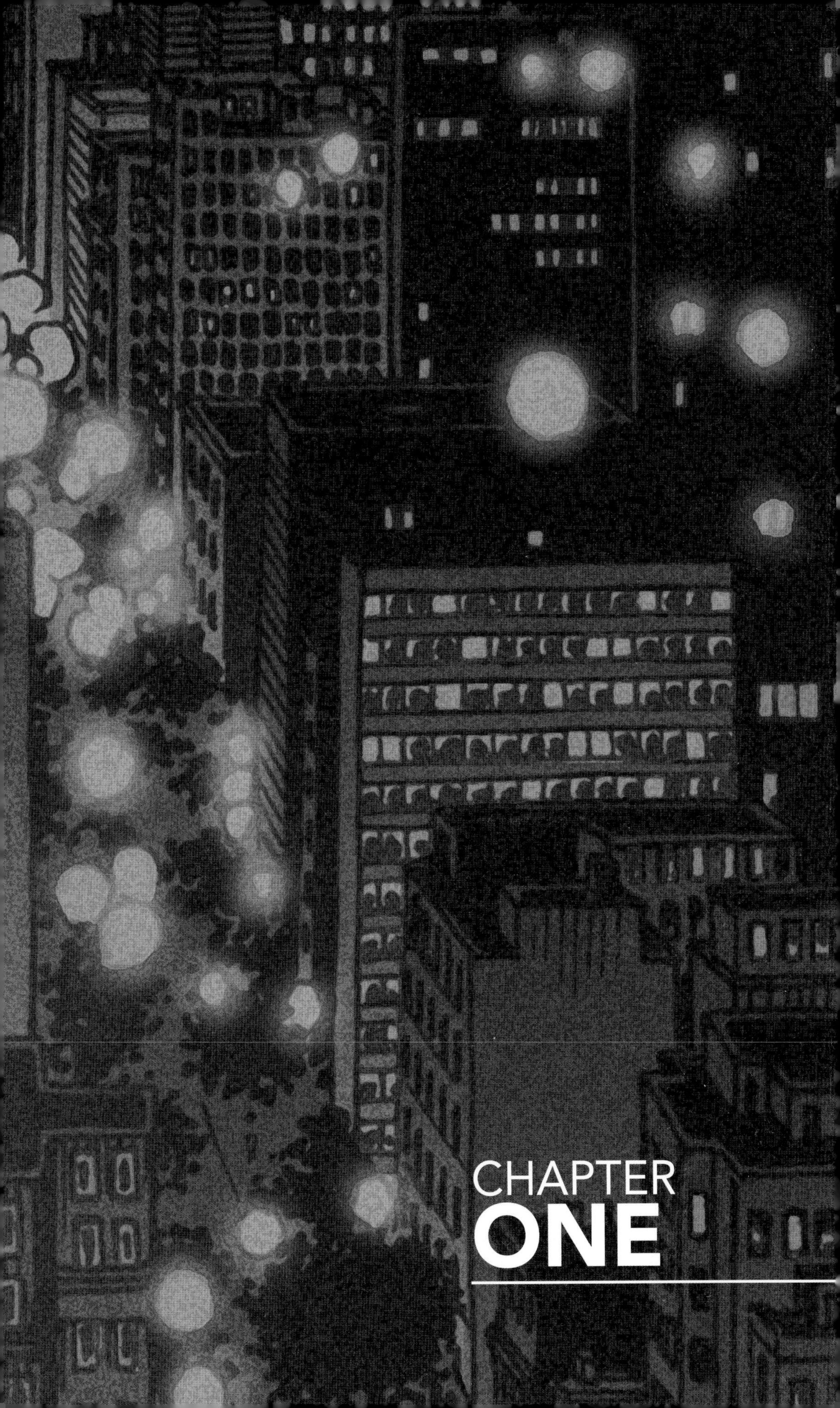

CHAPTER ONE

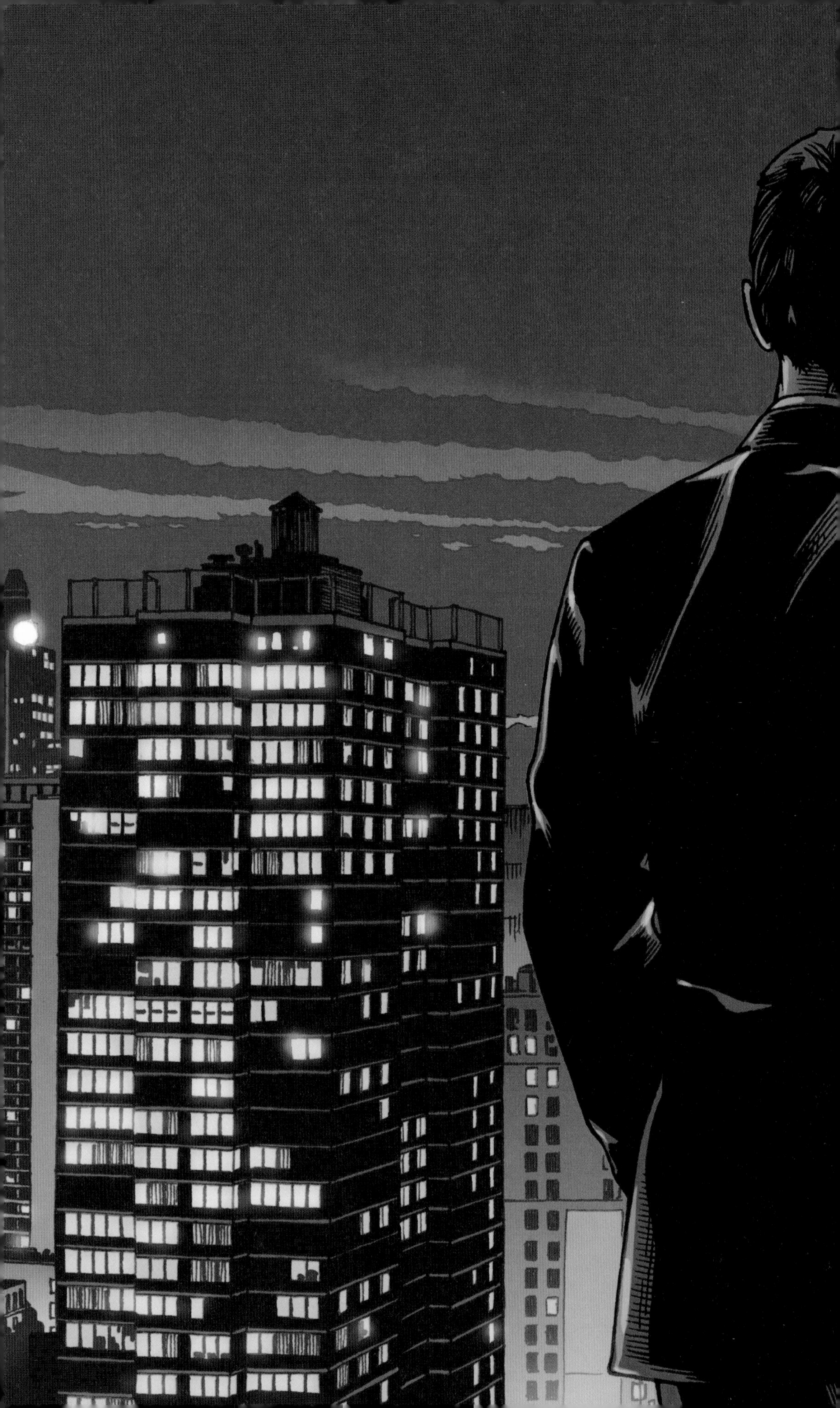

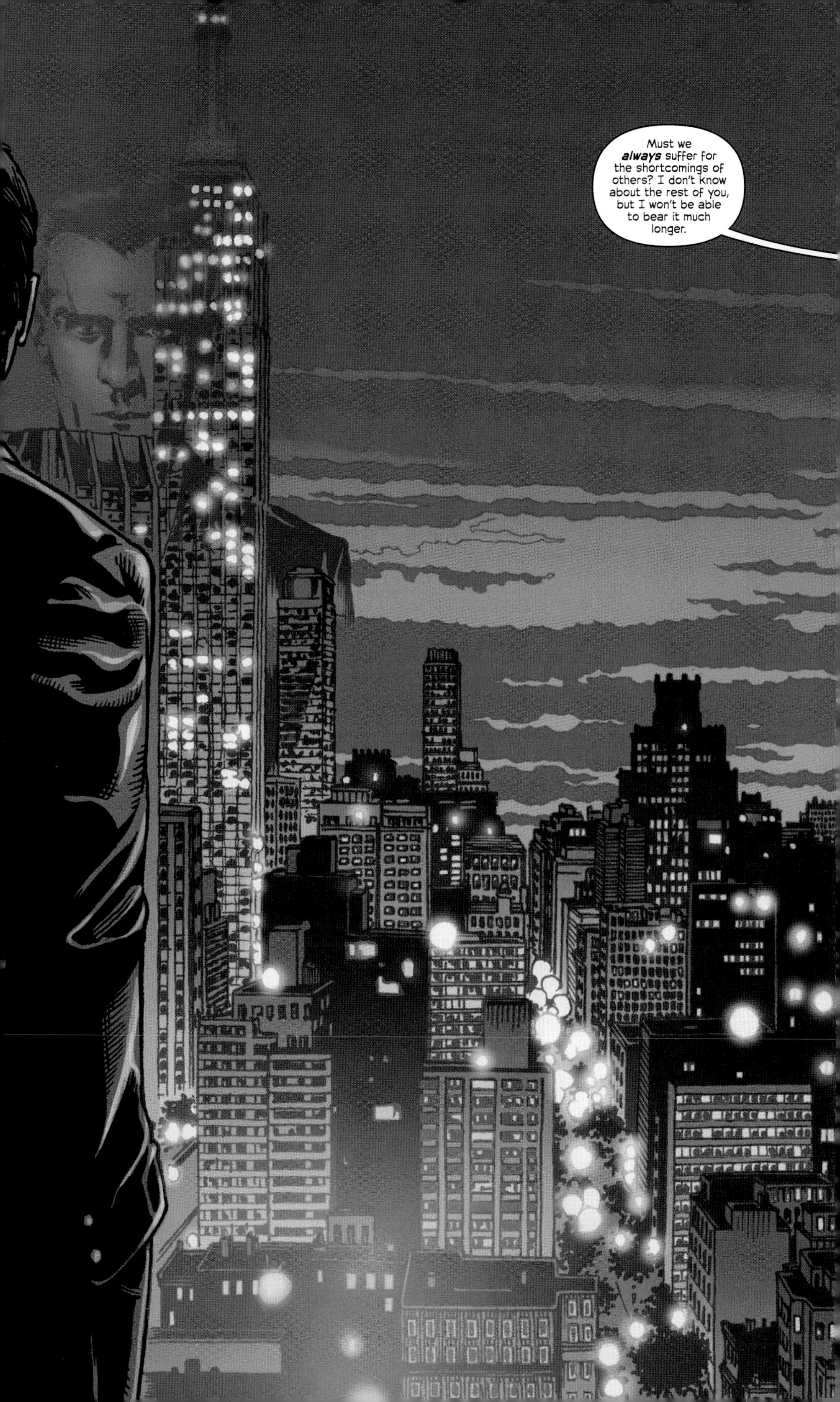
Must we **always** suffer for the shortcomings of others? I don't know about the rest of you, but I won't be able to bear it much longer.

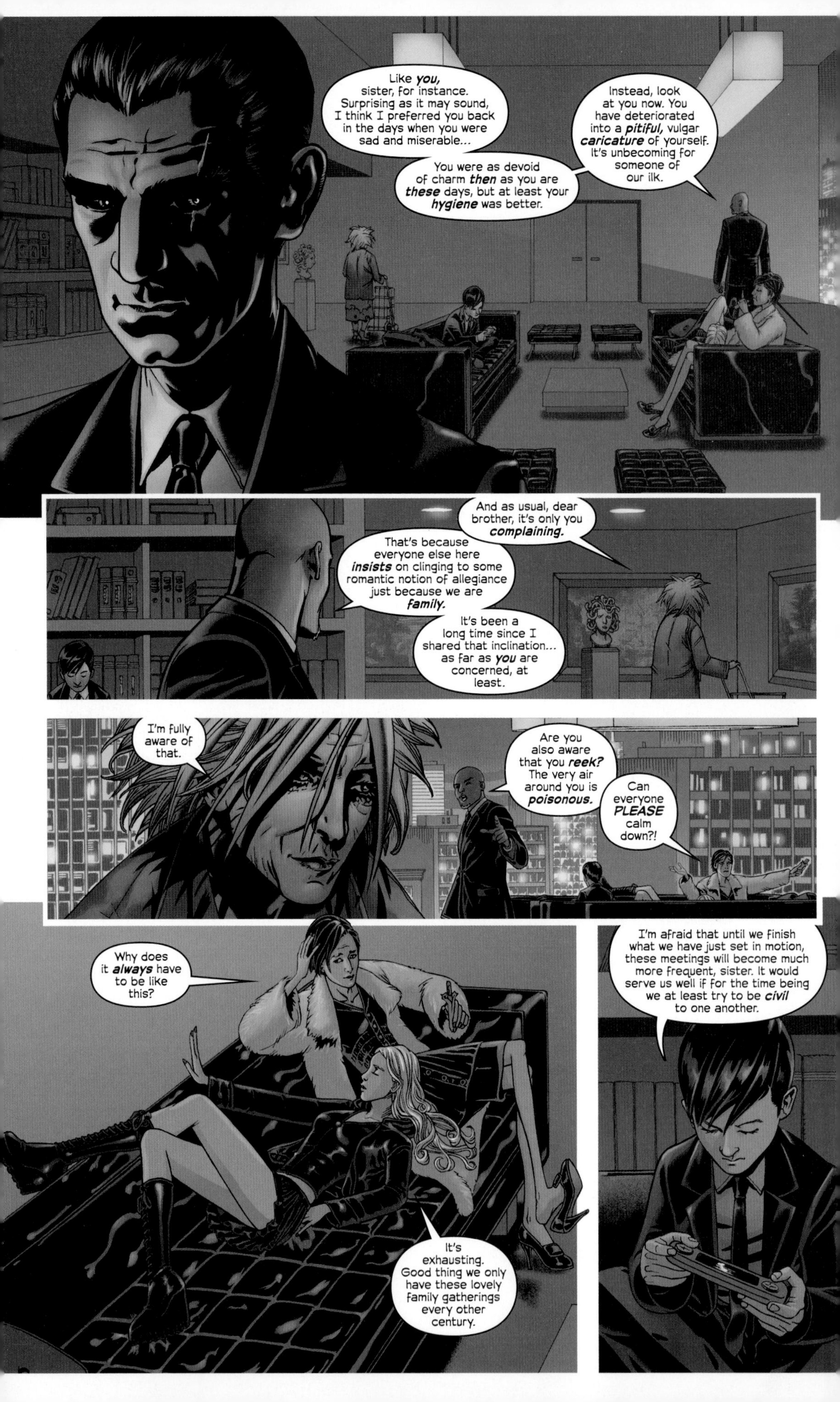

Like *you,* sister, for instance. Surprising as it may sound, I think I preferred you back in the days when you were sad and miserable...
You were as devoid of charm *then* as you are *these* days, but at least your *hygiene* was better.
Instead, look at you now. You have deteriorated into a *pitiful,* vulgar *caricature* of yourself. It's unbecoming for someone of our ilk.
And as usual, dear brother, it's only you *complaining.*
That's because everyone else here *insists* on clinging to some romantic notion of allegiance just because we are *family.*
It's been a long time since I shared that inclination... as far as *you* are concerned, at least.
I'm fully aware of that.
Are you also aware that you *reek?* The very air around you is *poisonous.*
Can everyone *PLEASE* calm down?!
Why does it *always* have to be like this?
It's exhausting. Good thing we only have these lovely family gatherings every other century.
I'm afraid that until we finish what we have just set in motion, these meetings will become much more frequent, sister. It would serve us well if for the time being we at least try to be *civil* to one another.

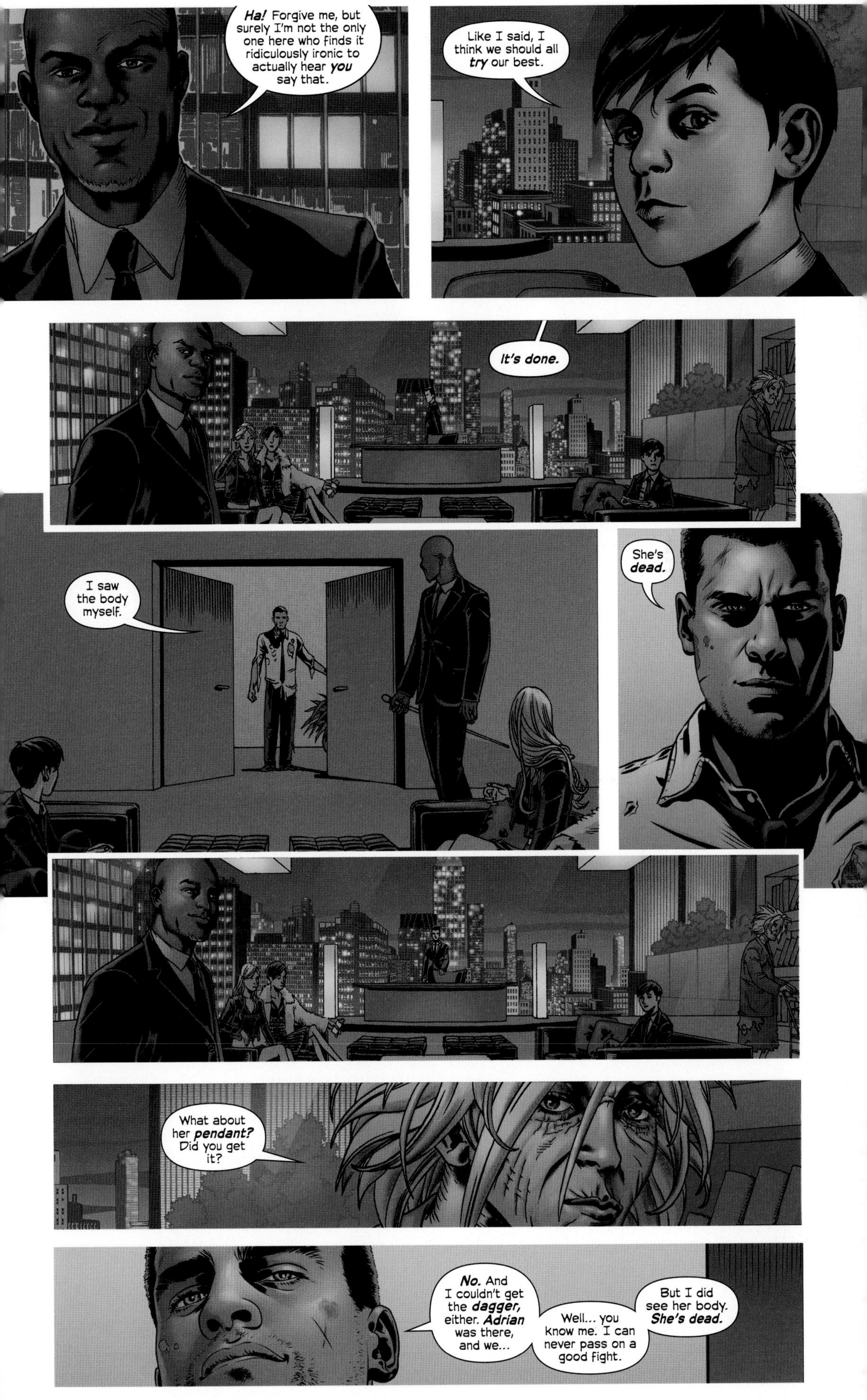

Ha! Forgive me, but surely I'm not the only one here who finds it ridiculously ironic to actually hear **you** say that.
Like I said, I think we should all **try** our best.
It's done.
I saw the body myself.
She's **dead.**
What about her **pendant?** Did you get it?
No. And I couldn't get the **dagger,** either. **Adrian** was there, and we...
Well... you know me. I can never pass on a good fight.
But I did see her body. **She's dead.**

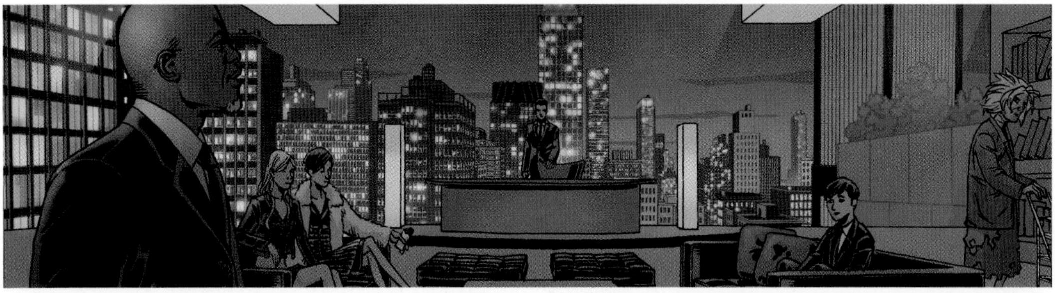

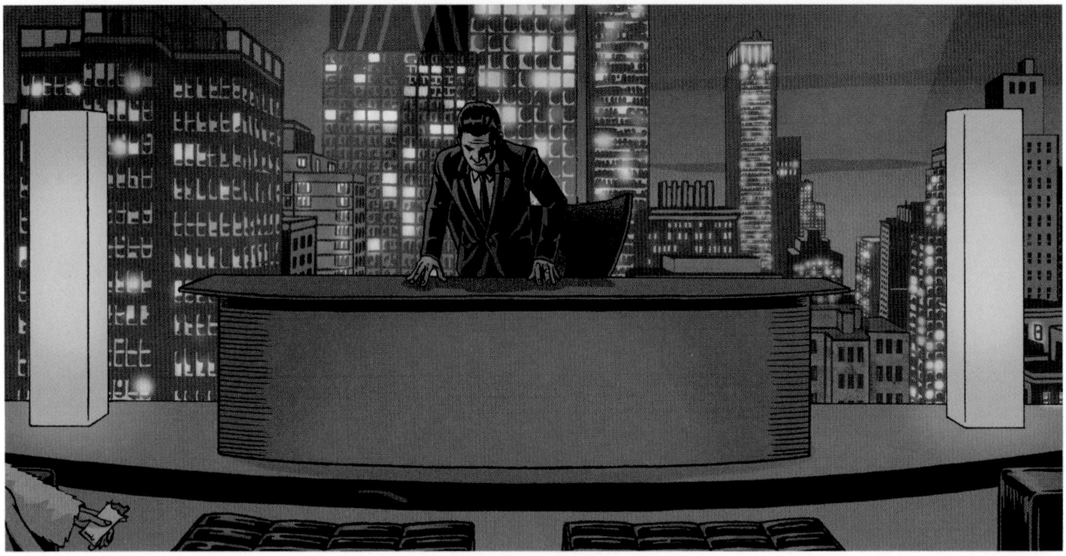

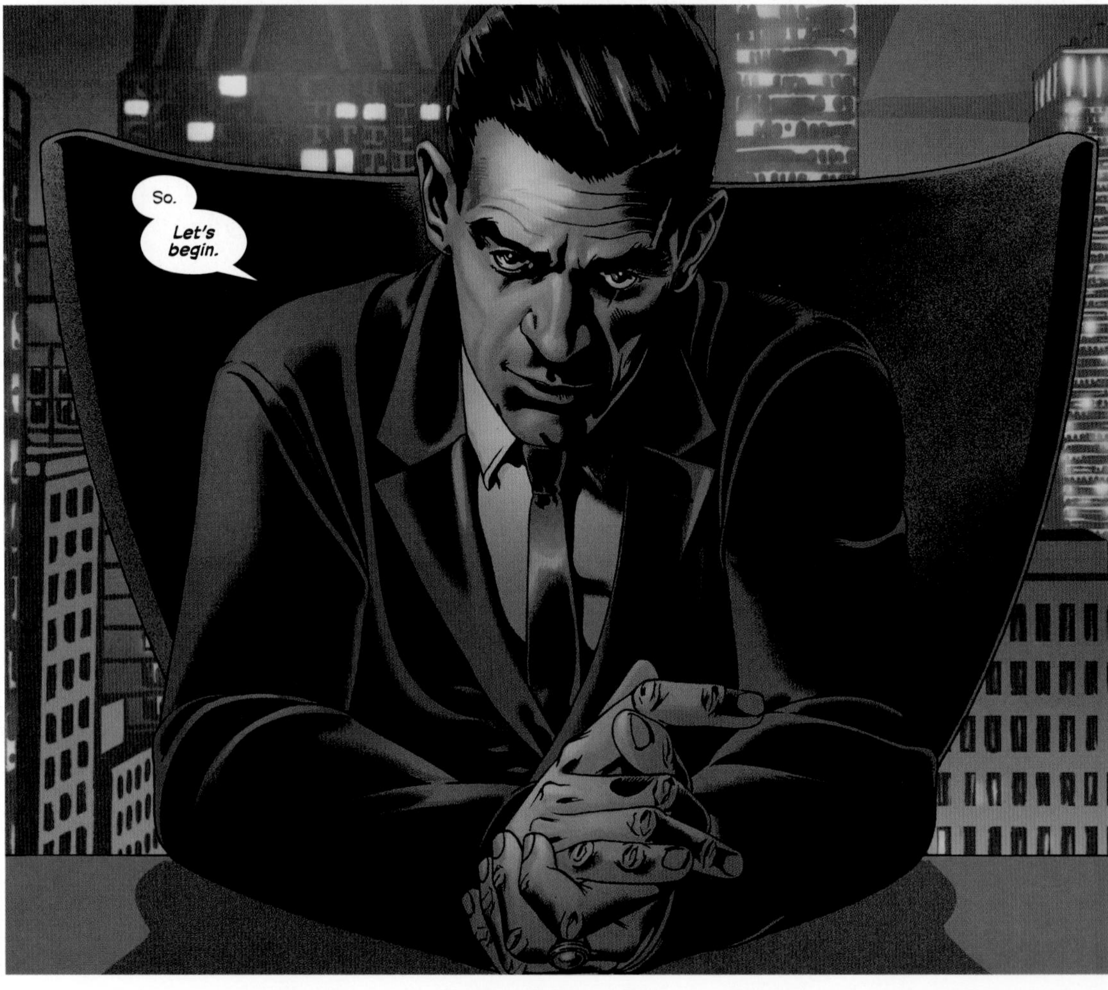
So.
Let's begin.

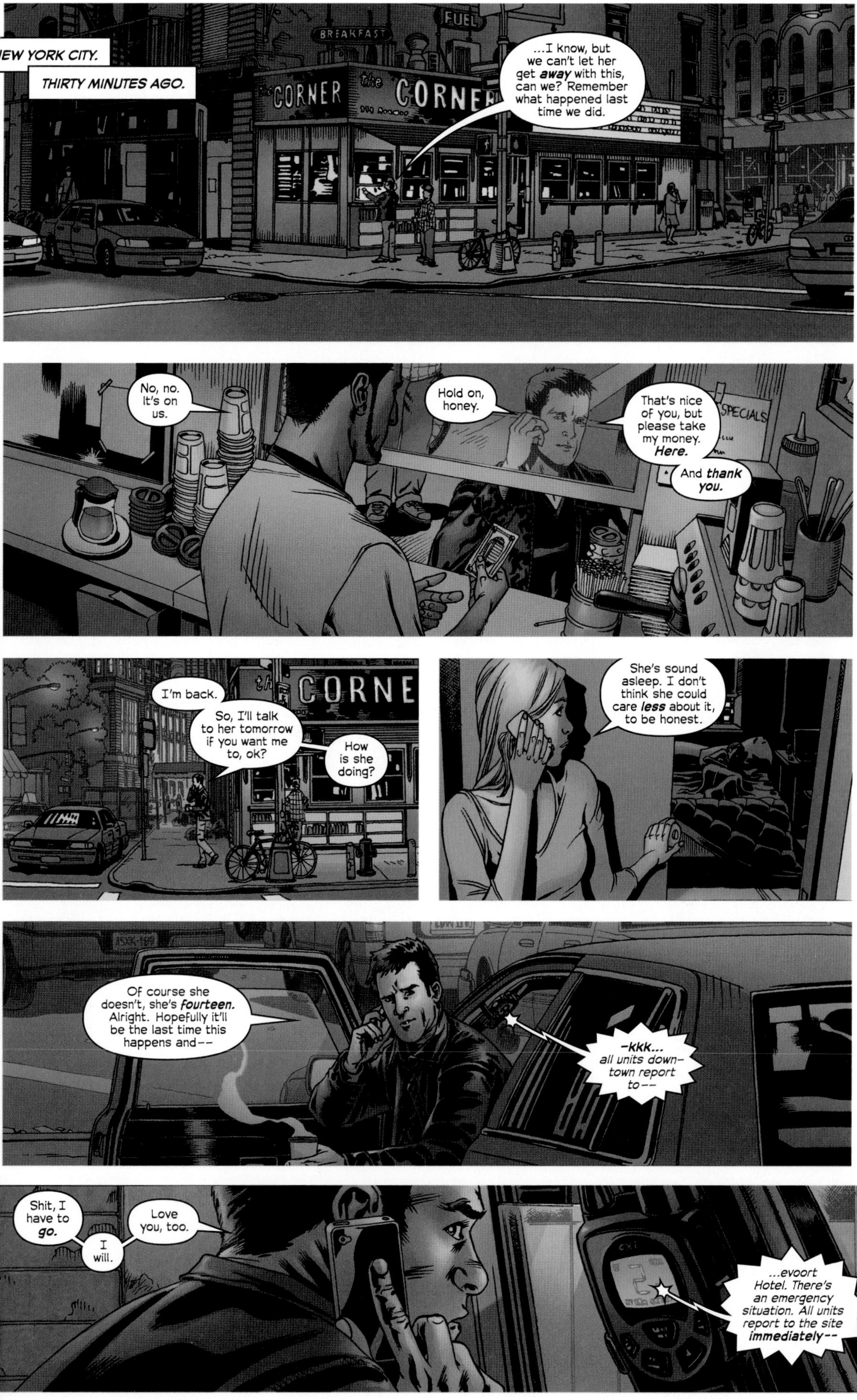
NEW YORK CITY.
THIRTY MINUTES AGO.
BREAKFAST
FUEL
the CORNER
the CORNER
...I know, but we can't let her get *away* with this, can we? Remember what happened last time we did.
No, no. It's on us.
Hold on, honey.
That's nice of you, but please take my money. *Here.*
And *thank you.*
SPECIALS
I'm back.
So, I'll talk to her tomorrow if you want me to, ok?
How is she doing?
She's sound asleep. I don't think she could care *less* about it, to be honest.
Of course she doesn't, she's *fourteen.* Alright. Hopefully it'll be the last time this happens and--
-kkk... all units down-town report to--
Shit, I have to *go.*
I will.
Love you, too.
*...evoort Hotel. There's an emergency situation. All units report to the site **immediately**--*

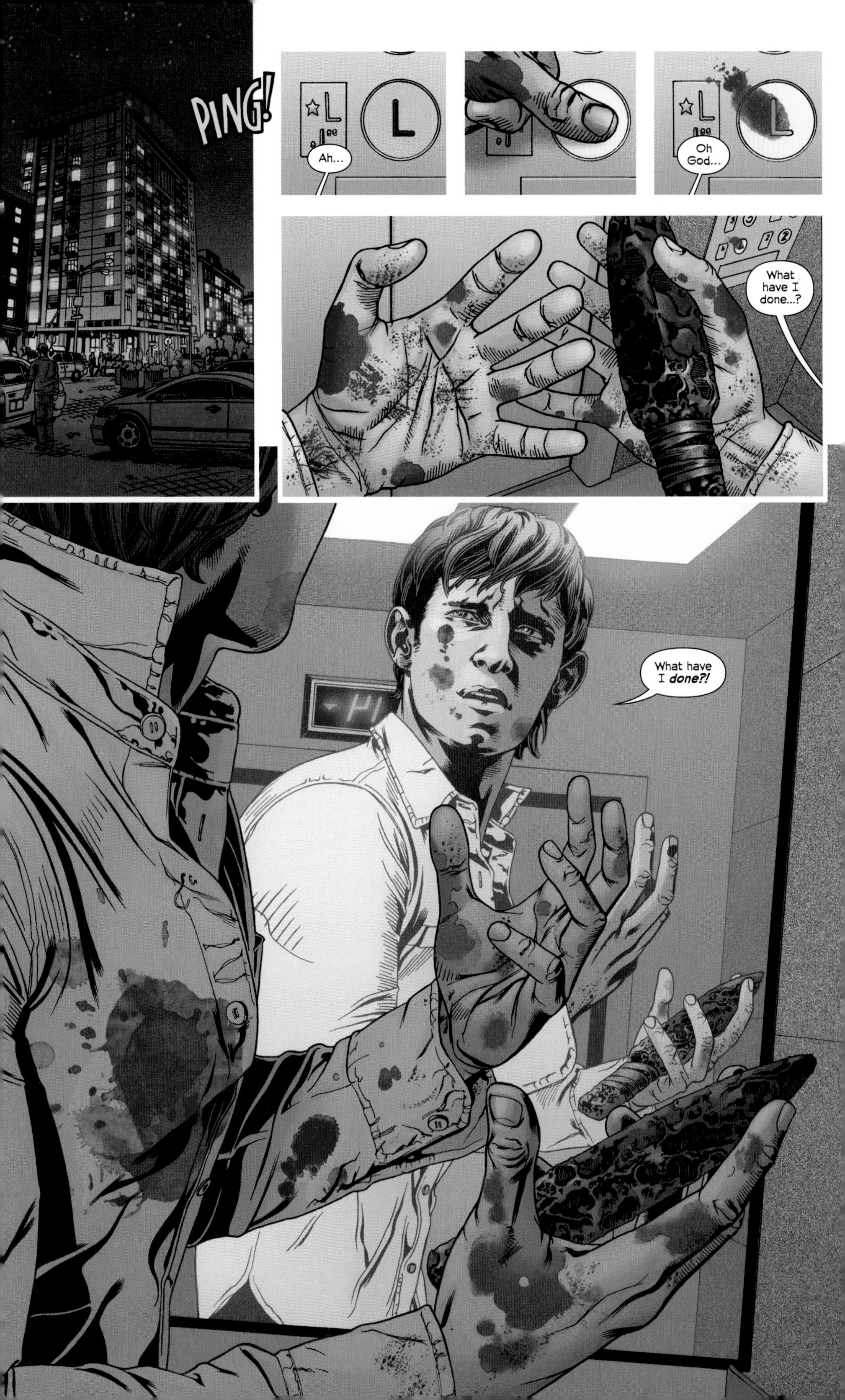
PING!
Ah...
Oh God...
What have I done...?
What have I *done?!*

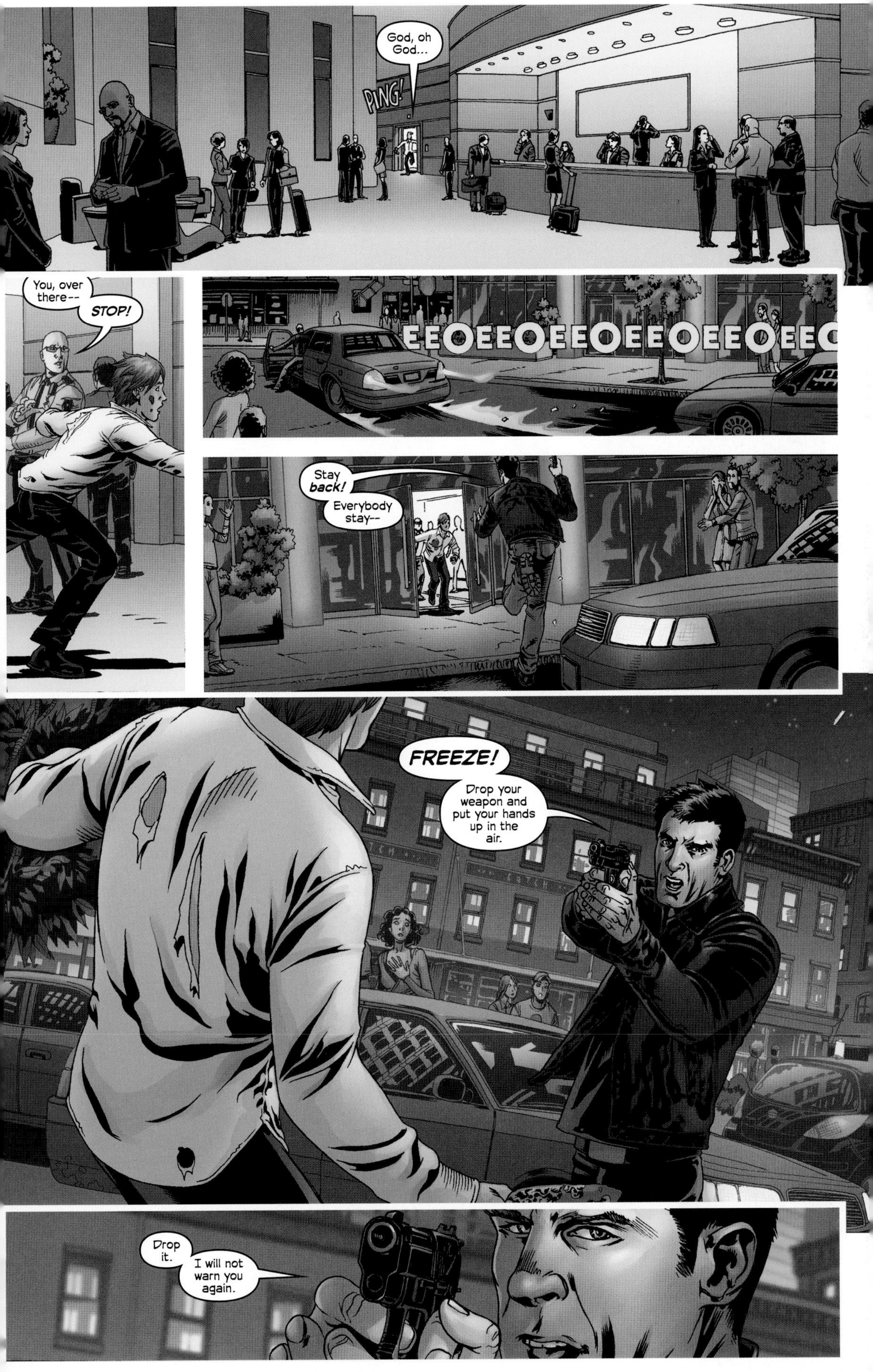
God, oh God...
PING!
You, over there-- STOP!
EEOEEOEEOEEOEEOEEO
Stay back!
Everybody stay--
FREEZE!
Drop your weapon and put your hands up in the air.
Drop it.
I will not warn you again.

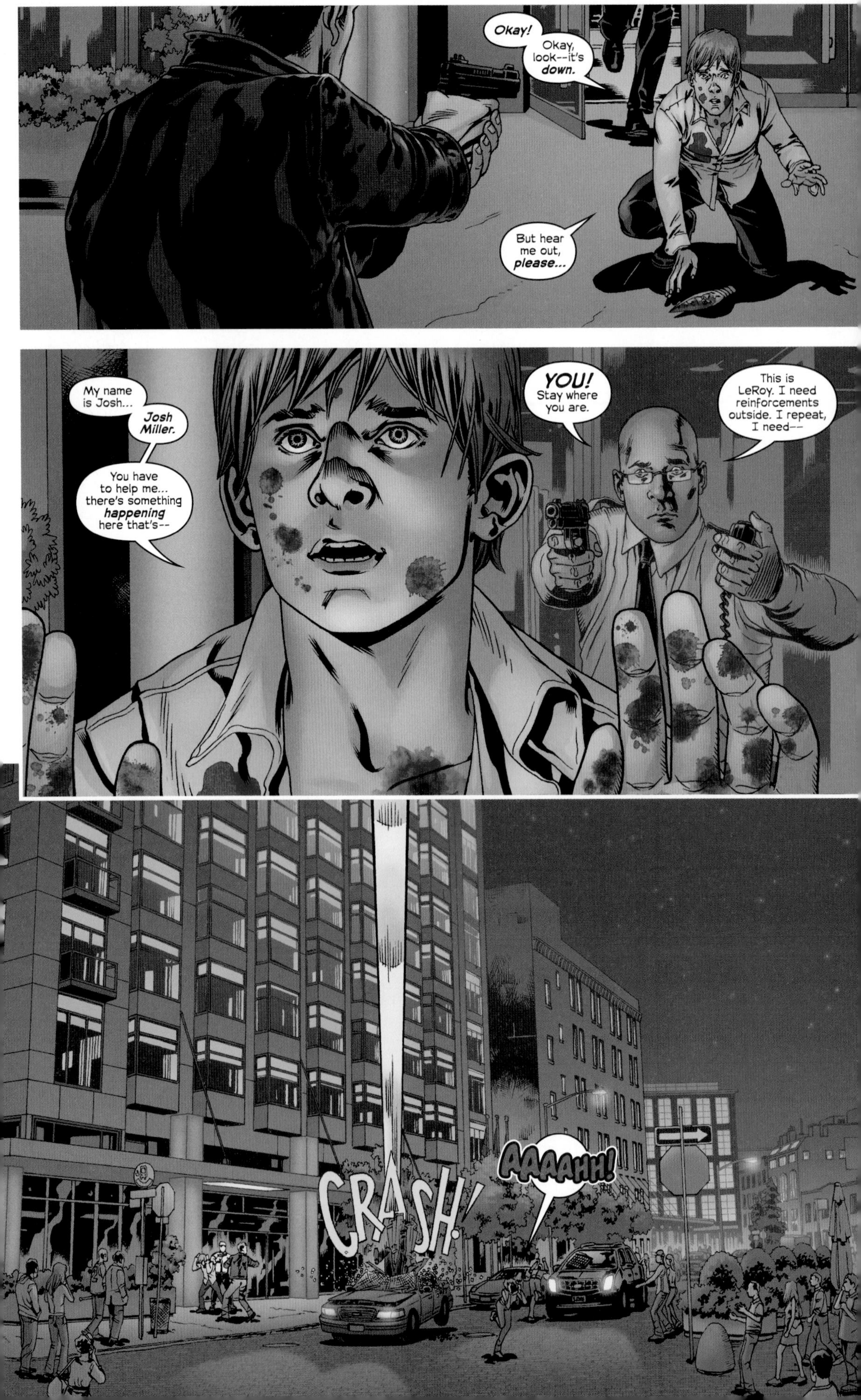
Okay!
Okay, look--it's down.
But hear me out, please...
My name is Josh... Josh Miller.
You have to help me... there's something happening here that's--
YOU! Stay where you are.
This is LeRoy. I need reinforcements outside. I repeat, I need--
CRASH!
AAAAHH!

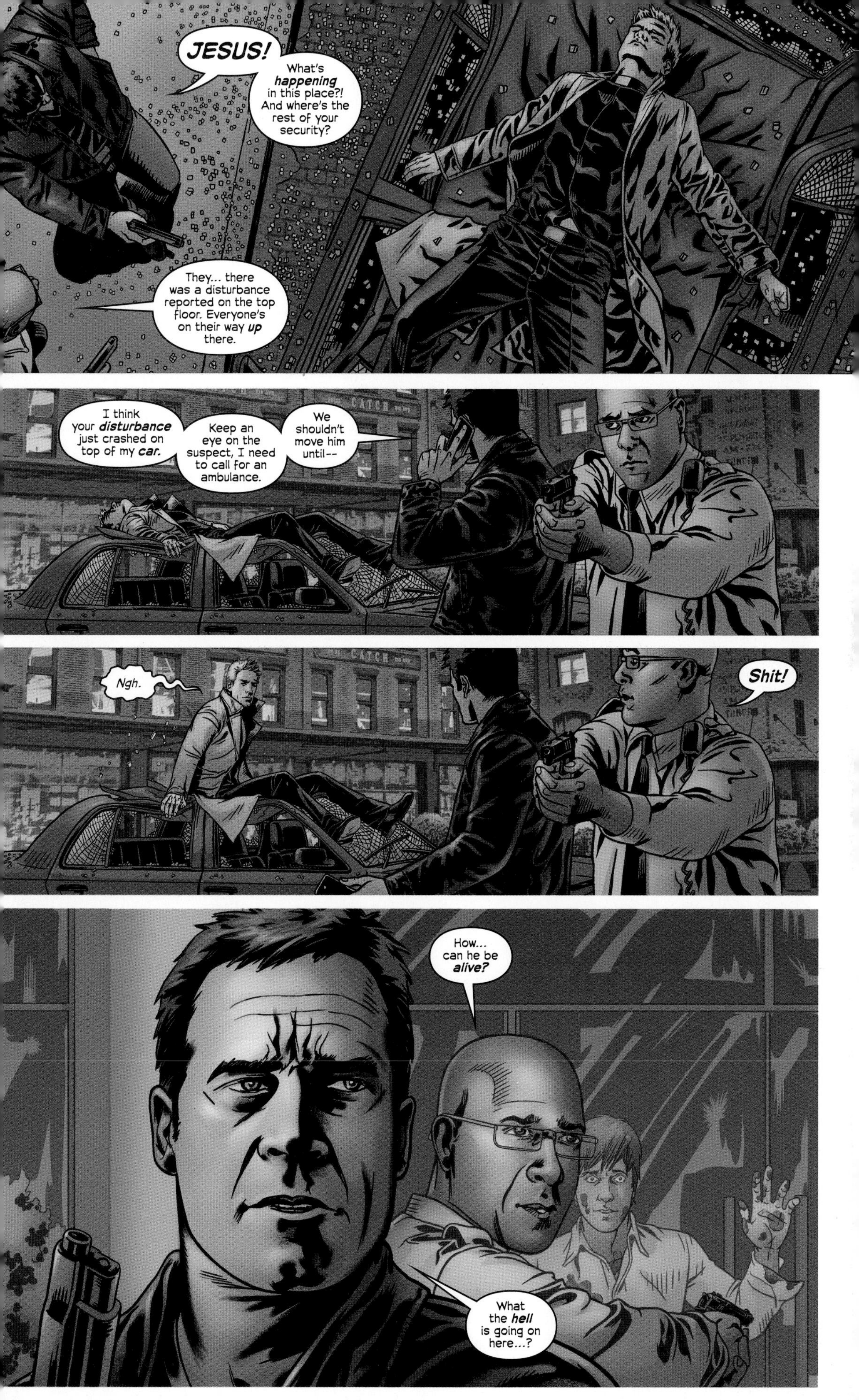
JESUS!
What's happening in this place?! And where's the rest of your security?
They... there was a disturbance reported on the top floor. Everyone's on their way up there.
I think your disturbance just crashed on top of my car.
Keep an eye on the suspect, I need to call for an ambulance.
We shouldn't move him until--
CATCH
Ngh.
Shit!
How... can he be alive?
What the hell is going on here...?

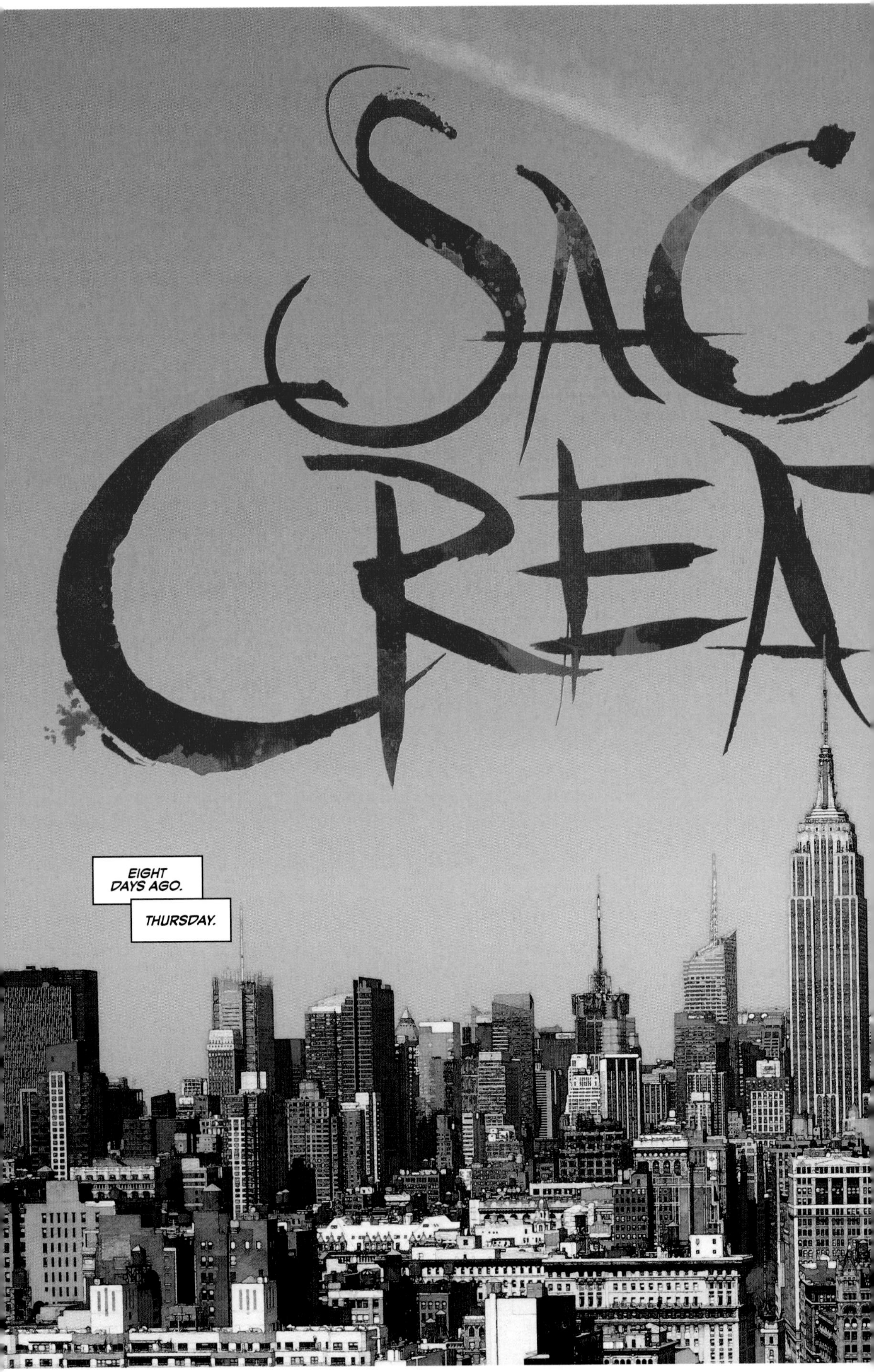
SAC
CREA
EIGHT DAYS AGO.
THURSDAY.

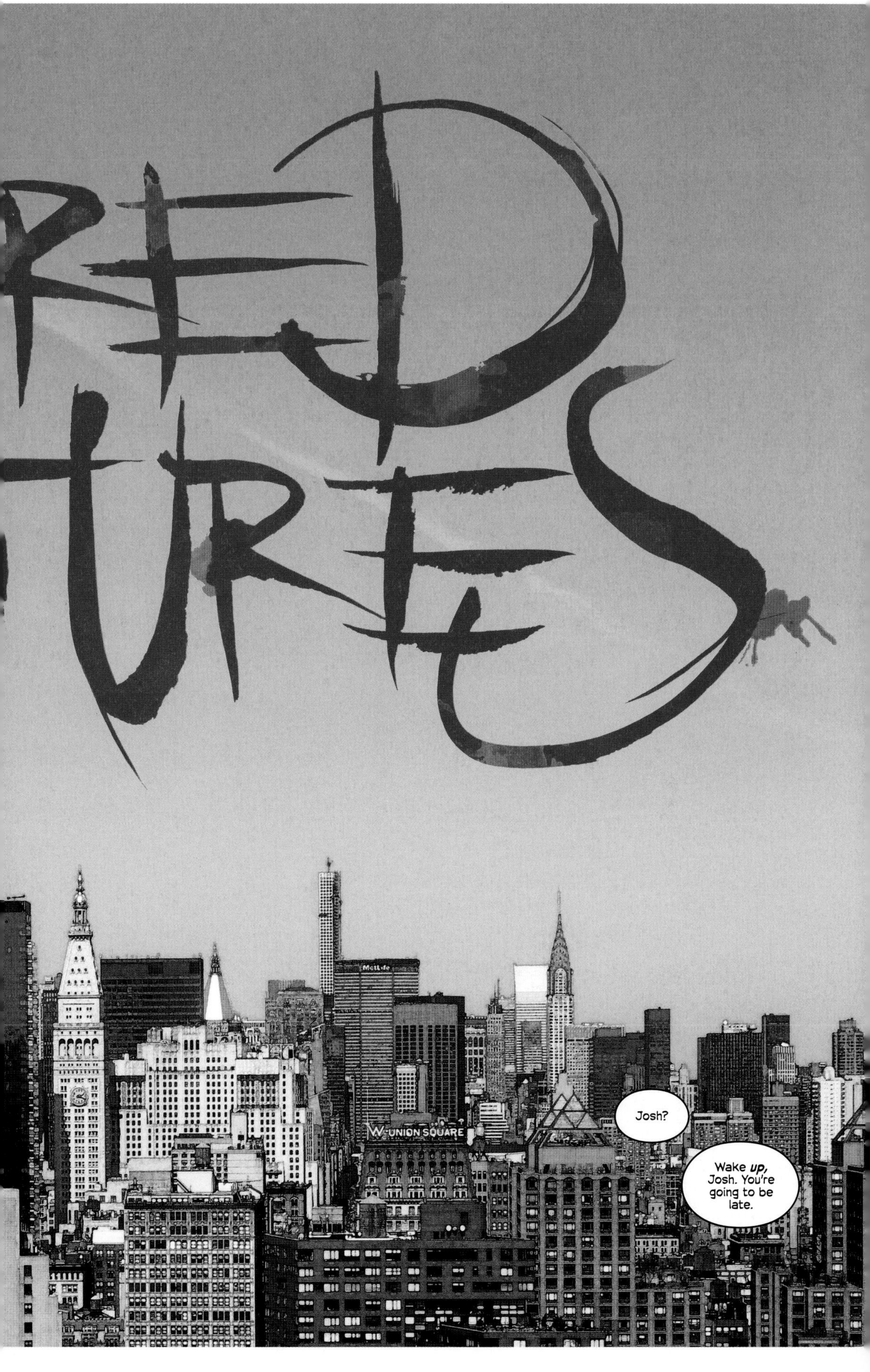

MetLife
W UNION SQUARE
Josh?
Wake *up,* Josh. You're going to be late.

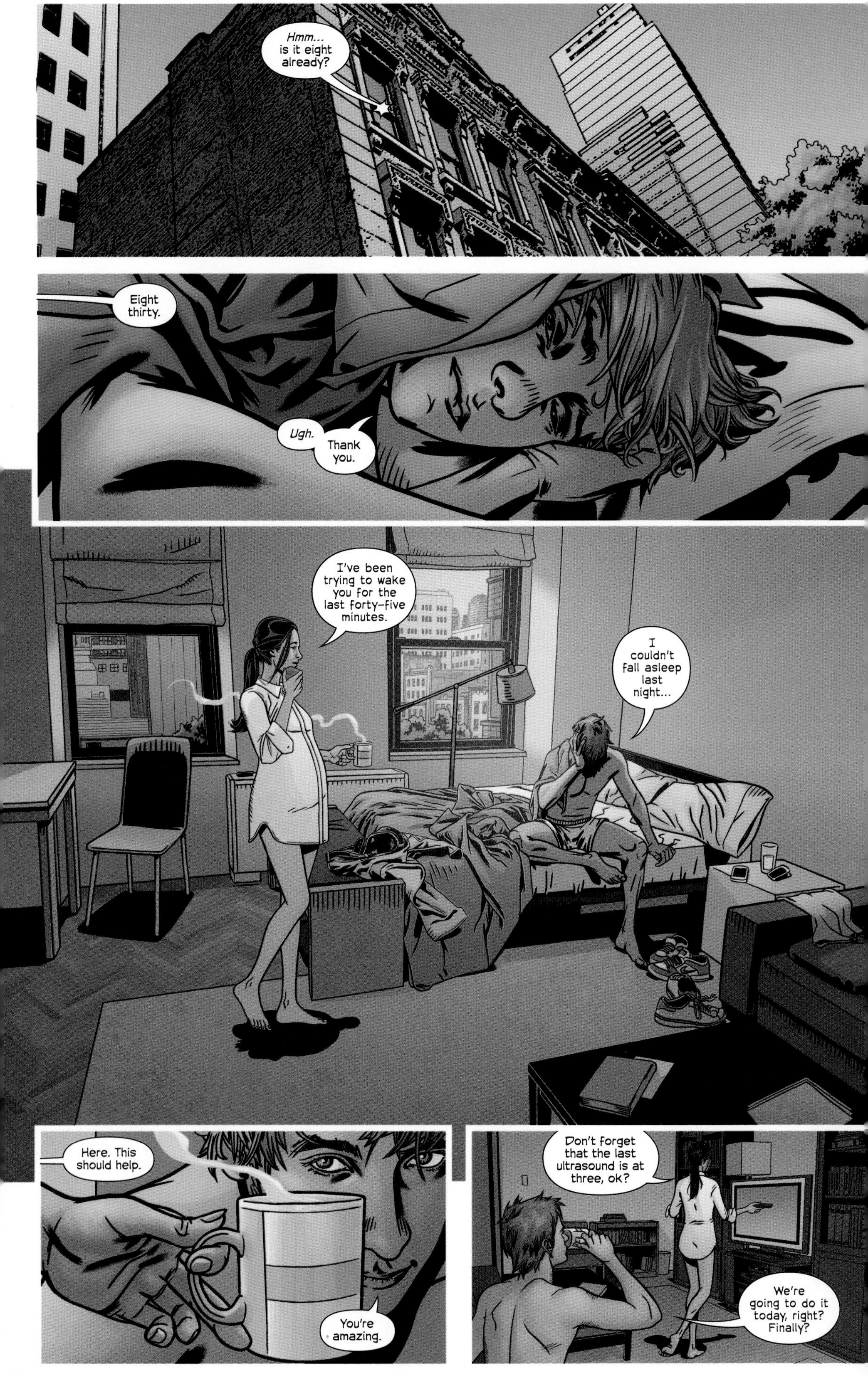
Hmm... is it eight already?
Eight thirty.
Ugh. Thank you.
I've been trying to wake you for the last forty-five minutes.
I couldn't fall asleep last night...
Here. This should help.
You're amazing.
Don't forget that the last ultrasound is at three, ok?
We're going to do it today, right? Finally?

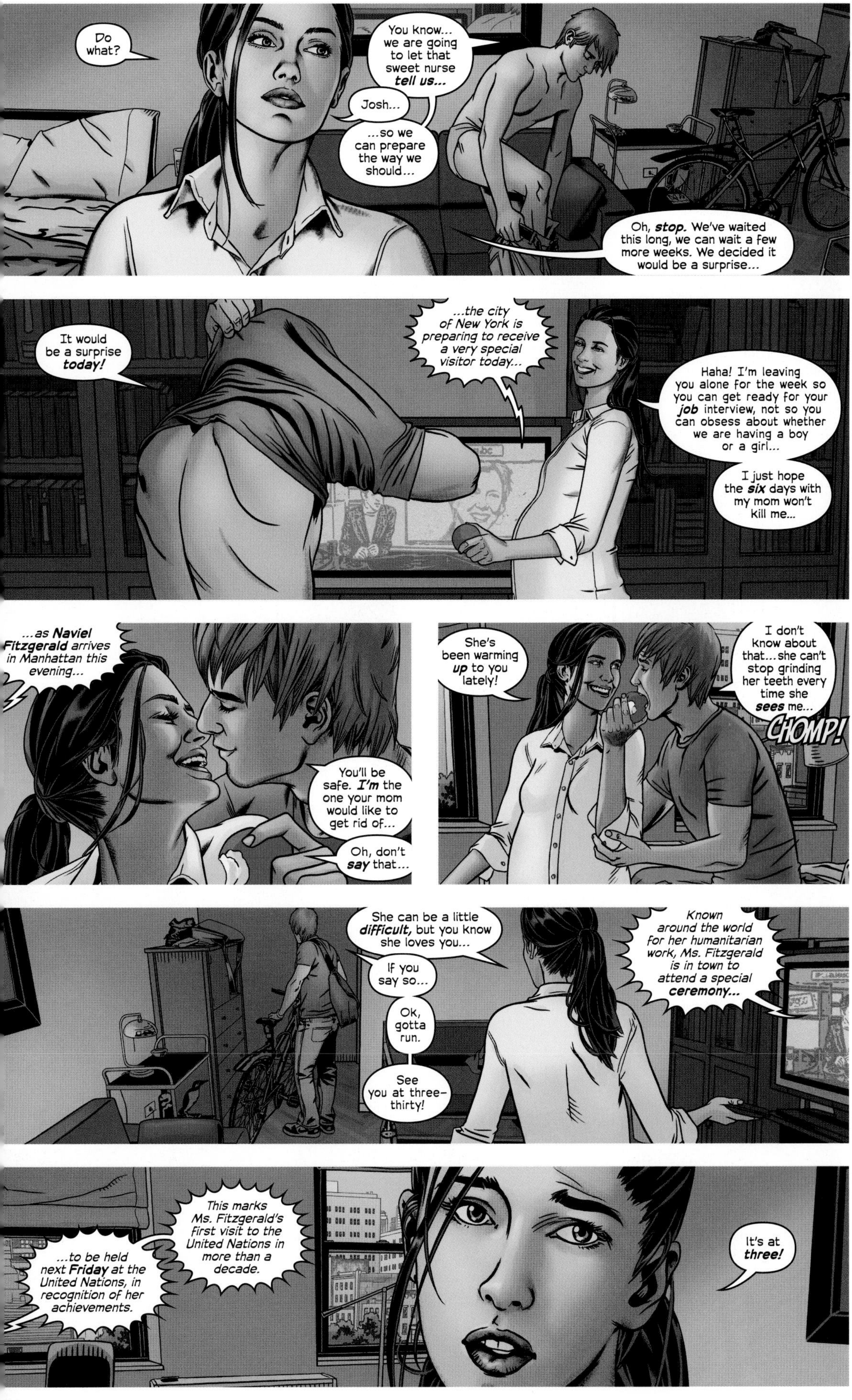
Do what?
You know... we are going to let that sweet nurse tell us...
Josh...
...so we can prepare the way we should...
Oh, stop. We've waited this long, we can wait a few more weeks. We decided it would be a surprise...
It would be a surprise today!
...the city of New York is preparing to receive a very special visitor today...
Haha! I'm leaving you alone for the week so you can get ready for your job interview, not so you can obsess about whether we are having a boy or a girl...
I just hope the six days with my mom won't kill me...
...as Naviel Fitzgerald arrives in Manhattan this evening...
You'll be safe. I'm the one your mom would like to get rid of...
Oh, don't say that...
She's been warming up to you lately!
I don't know about that...she can't stop grinding her teeth every time she sees me...
CHOMP!
She can be a little difficult, but you know she loves you...
If you say so...
Ok, gotta run.
See you at three-thirty!
Known around the world for her humanitarian work, Ms. Fitzgerald is in town to attend a special ceremony...
...to be held next Friday at the United Nations, in recognition of her achievements.
This marks Ms. Fitzgerald's first visit to the United Nations in more than a decade.
It's at three!

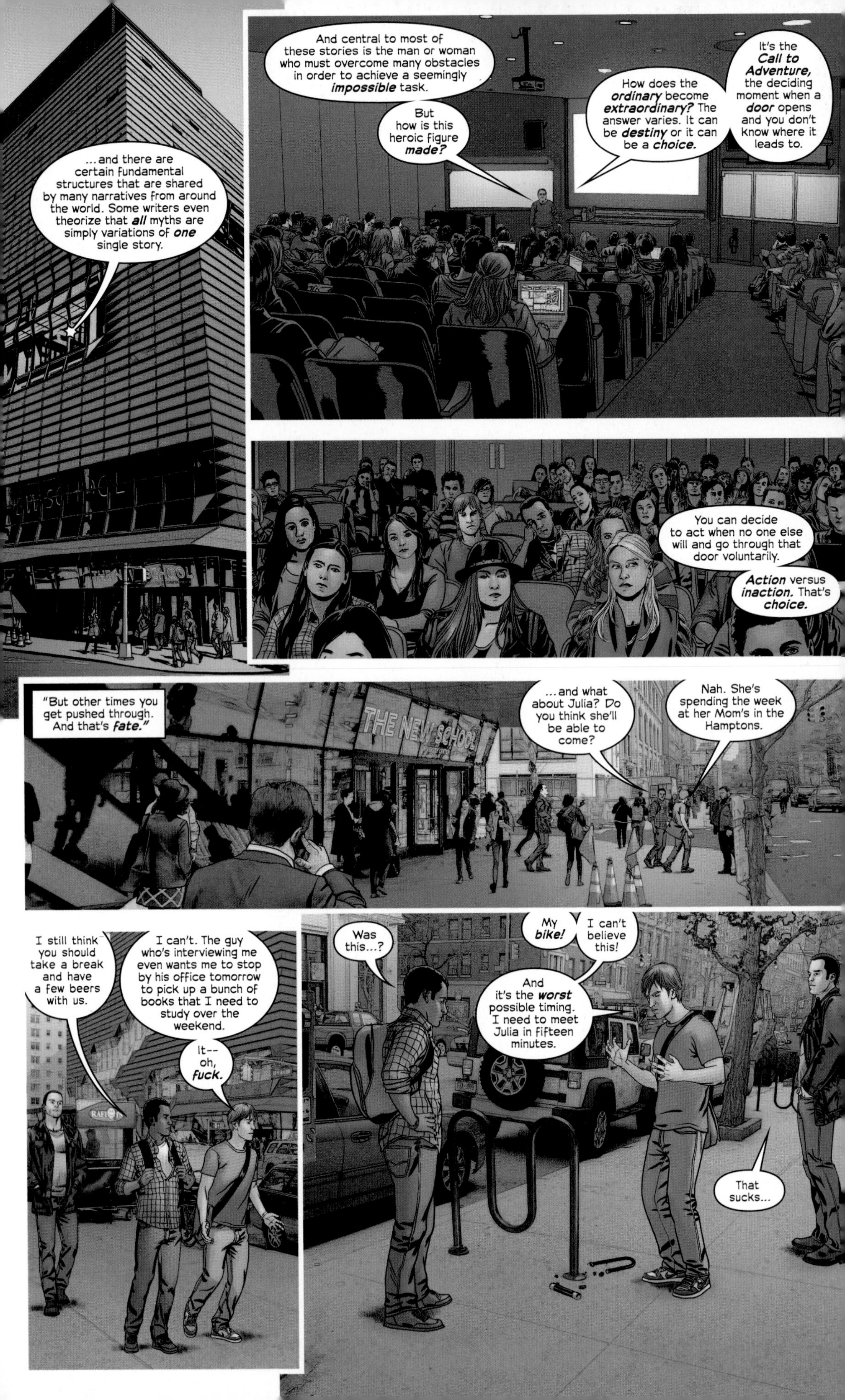
...and there are certain fundamental structures that are shared by many narratives from around the world. Some writers even theorize that *all* myths are simply variations of *one* single story.
And central to most of these stories is the man or woman who must overcome many obstacles in order to achieve a seemingly *impossible* task.
But how is this heroic figure *made?*
How does the *ordinary* become *extraordinary?* The answer varies. It can be *destiny* or it can be a *choice.*
It's the *Call to Adventure,* the deciding moment when a *door* opens and you don't know where it leads to.
You can decide to act when no one else will and go through that door voluntarily.
Action versus *inaction.* That's *choice.*
"But other times you get pushed through. And that's *fate.*"
...and what about Julia? Do you think she'll be able to come?
Nah. She's spending the week at her Mom's in the Hamptons.
I still think you should take a break and have a few beers with us.
I can't. The guy who's interviewing me even wants me to stop by his office tomorrow to pick up a bunch of books that I need to study over the weekend.
It-- oh, *fuck.*
Was this...?
My *bike!*
I can't believe this!
And it's the *worst* possible timing. I need to meet Julia in fifteen minutes.
That sucks...

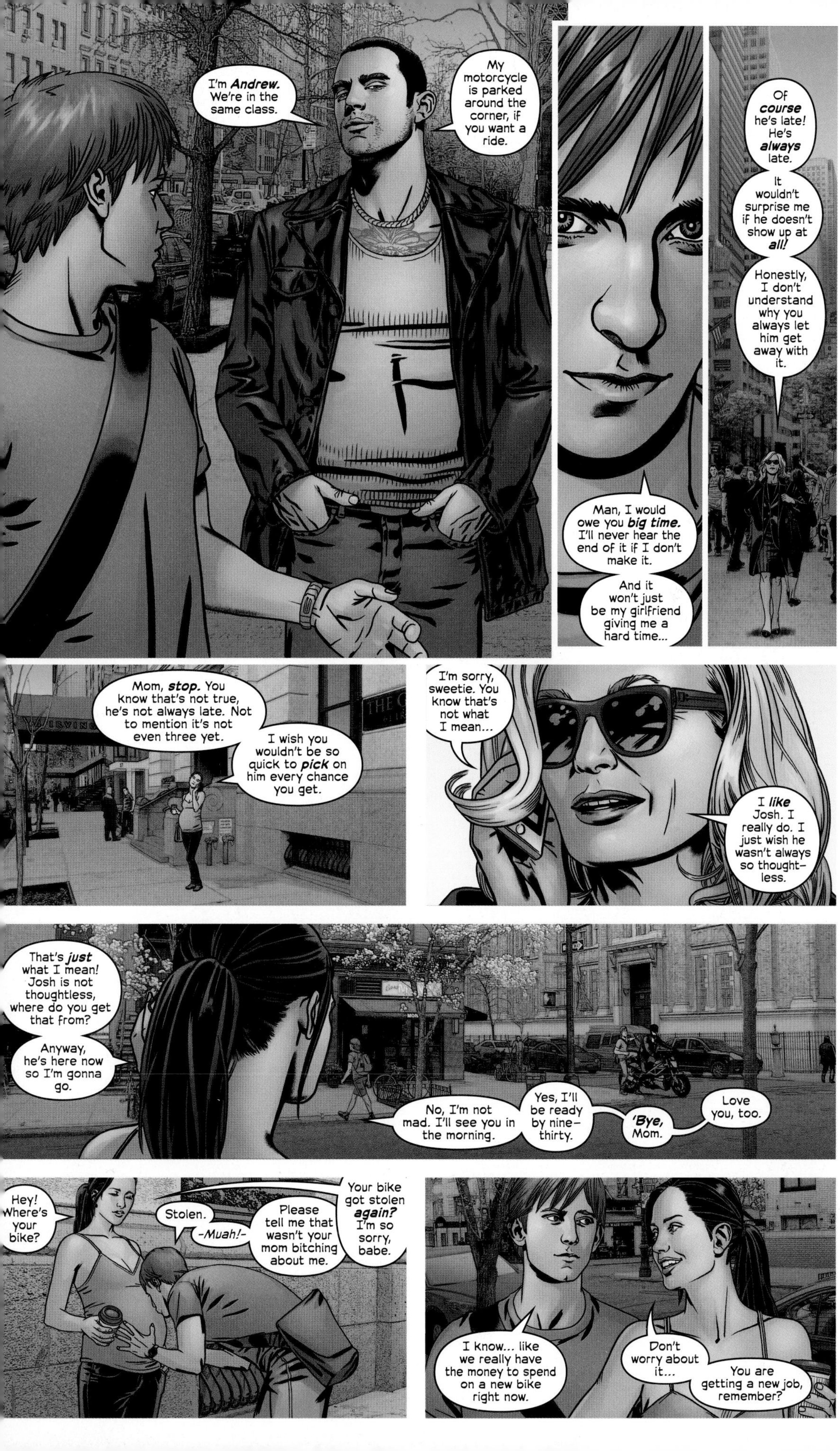
I'm *Andrew.* We're in the same class.
My motorcycle is parked around the corner, if you want a ride.
Man, I would owe you *big time.* I'll never hear the end of it if I don't make it.
And it won't just be my girlfriend giving me a hard time...
Of *course* he's late! He's *always* late.
It wouldn't surprise me if he doesn't show up at *all!*
Honestly, I don't understand why you always let him get away with it.
Mom, *stop.* You know that's not true, he's not always late. Not to mention it's not even three yet.
I wish you wouldn't be so quick to *pick* on him every chance you get.
I'm sorry, sweetie. You know that's not what I mean...
I *like* Josh. I really do. I just wish he wasn't always so thought-less.
That's *just* what I mean! Josh is not thoughtless, where do you get that from?
Anyway, he's here now so I'm gonna go.
No, I'm not mad. I'll see you in the morning.
Yes, I'll be ready by nine-thirty.
'Bye, Mom.
Love you, too.
Hey! Where's your bike?
Stolen.
-Muah!-
Please tell me that wasn't your mom bitching about me.
Your bike got stolen *again?* I'm so sorry, babe.
I know... like we really have the money to spend on a new bike right now.
Don't worry about it...
You are getting a new job, remember?

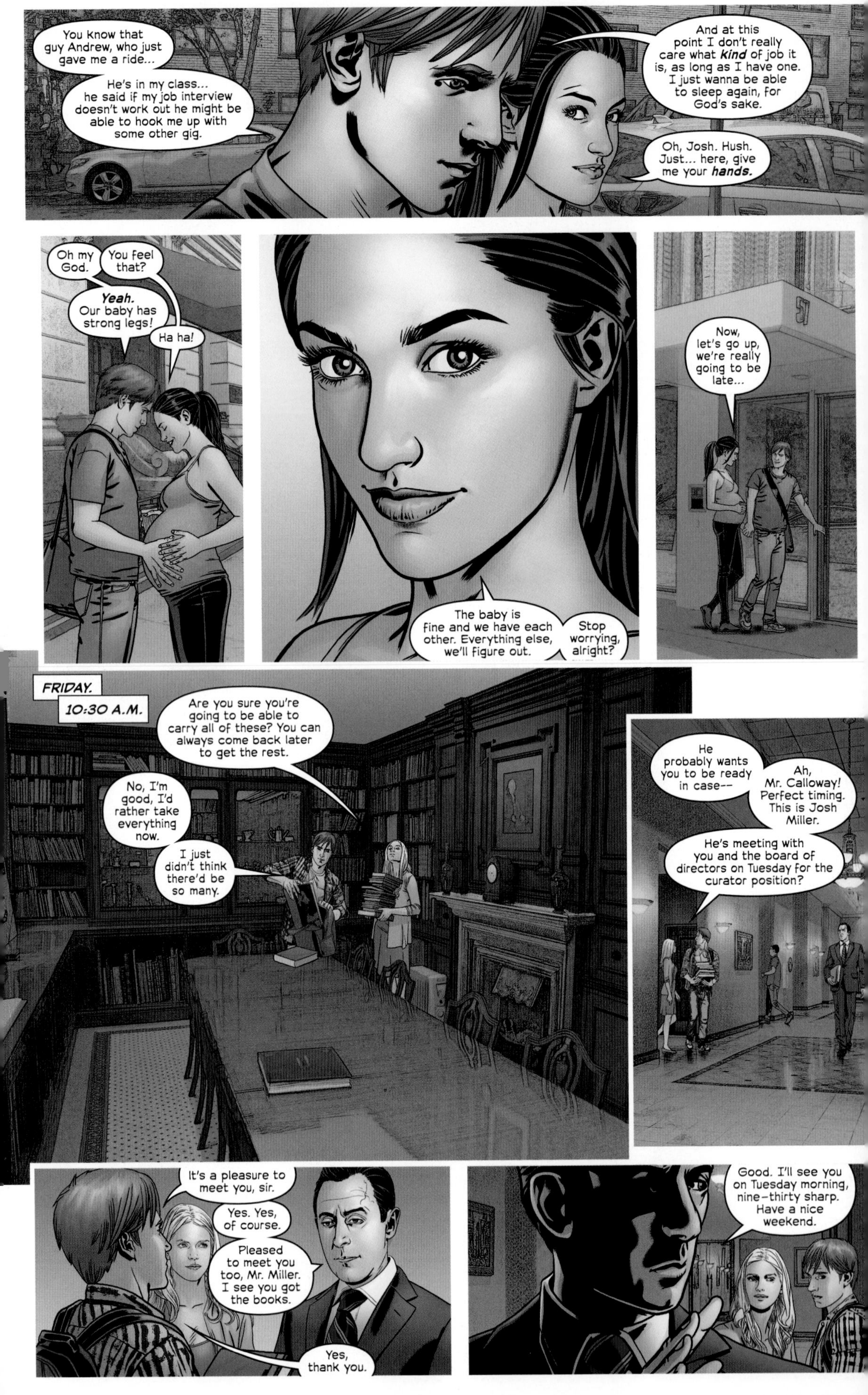
You know that guy Andrew, who just gave me a ride...
He's in my class... he said if my job interview doesn't work out he might be able to hook me up with some other gig.
And at this point I don't really care what *kind* of job it is, as long as I have one. I just wanna be able to sleep again, for God's sake.
Oh, Josh. Hush. Just... here, give me your *hands.*
Oh my God.
You feel that?
Yeah. Our baby has strong legs!
Ha ha!
The baby is fine and we have each other. Everything else, we'll figure out.
Stop worrying, alright?
Now, let's go up, we're really going to be late...
FRIDAY.
10:30 A.M.
Are you sure you're going to be able to carry all of these? You can always come back later to get the rest.
No, I'm good, I'd rather take everything now.
I just didn't think there'd be so many.
He probably wants you to be ready in case--
Ah, Mr. Calloway! Perfect timing. This is Josh Miller.
He's meeting with you and the board of directors on Tuesday for the curator position?
It's a pleasure to meet you, sir.
Yes. Yes, of course.
Pleased to meet you too, Mr. Miller. I see you got the books.
Yes, thank you.
Good. I'll see you on Tuesday morning, nine-thirty sharp. Have a nice weekend.

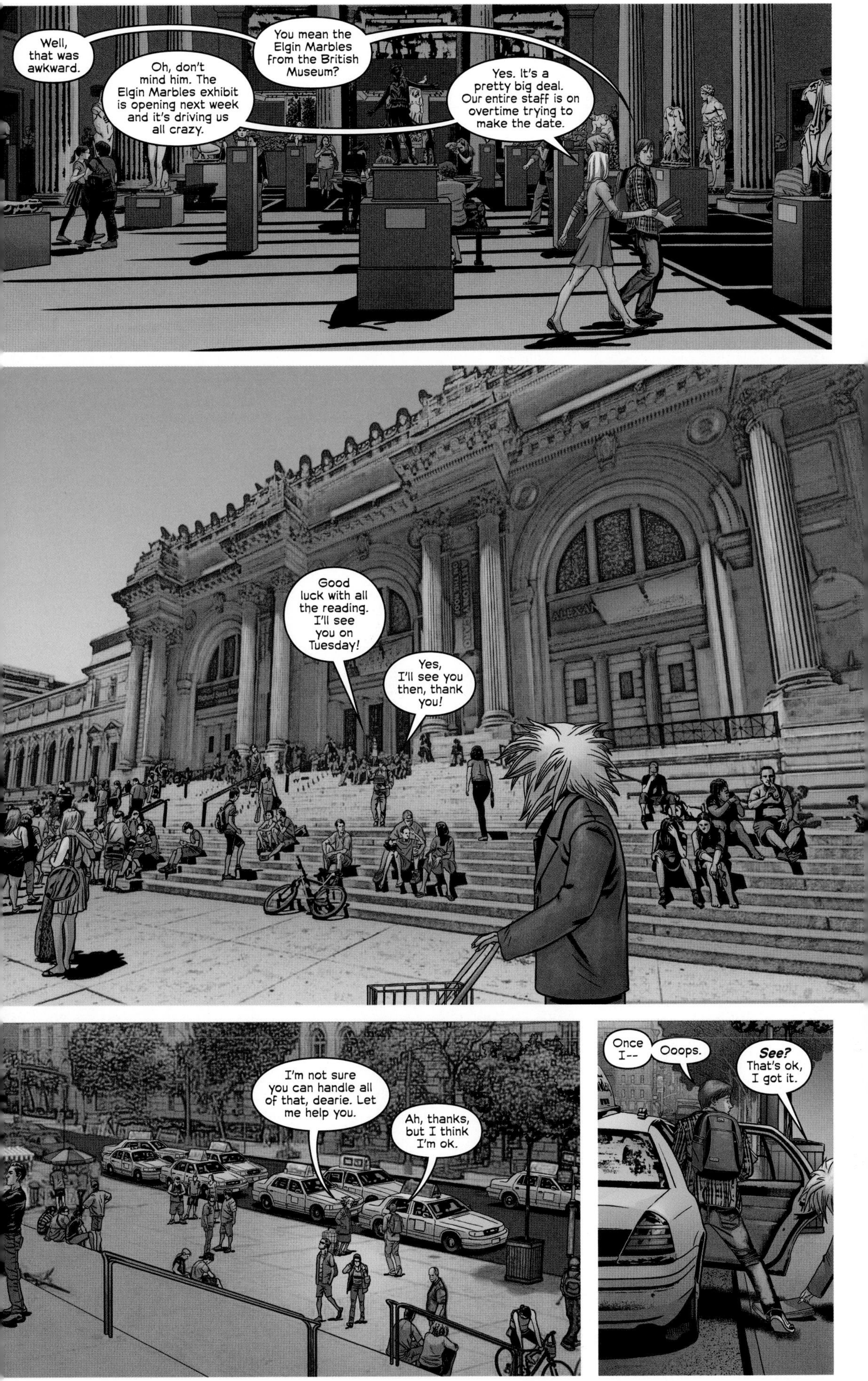
Well, that was awkward.
Oh, don't mind him. The Elgin Marbles exhibit is opening next week and it's driving us all crazy.
You mean the Elgin Marbles from the British Museum?
Yes. It's a pretty big deal. Our entire staff is on overtime trying to make the date.
Good luck with all the reading. I'll see you on Tuesday!
Yes, I'll see you then, thank you!
I'm not sure you can handle all of that, dearie. Let me help you.
Ah, thanks, but I think I'm ok.
Once I--
Ooops.
See? That's ok, I got it.

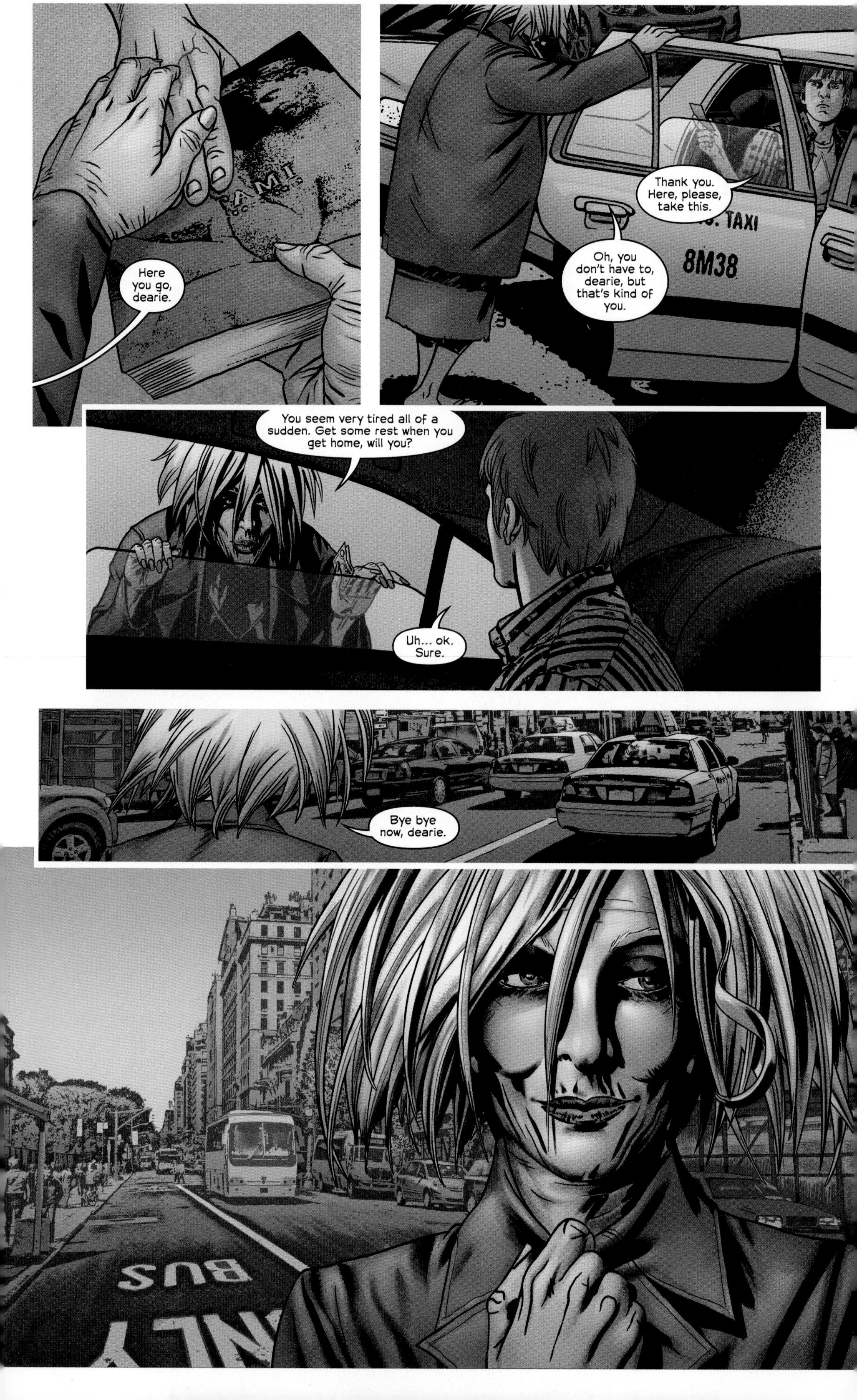

Here you go, dearie.
Thank you. Here, please, take this.
Oh, you don't have to, dearie, but that's kind of you.
TAXI
8M38
You seem very tired all of a sudden. Get some rest when you get home, will you?
Uh... ok. Sure.
Bye bye now, dearie.
BUS

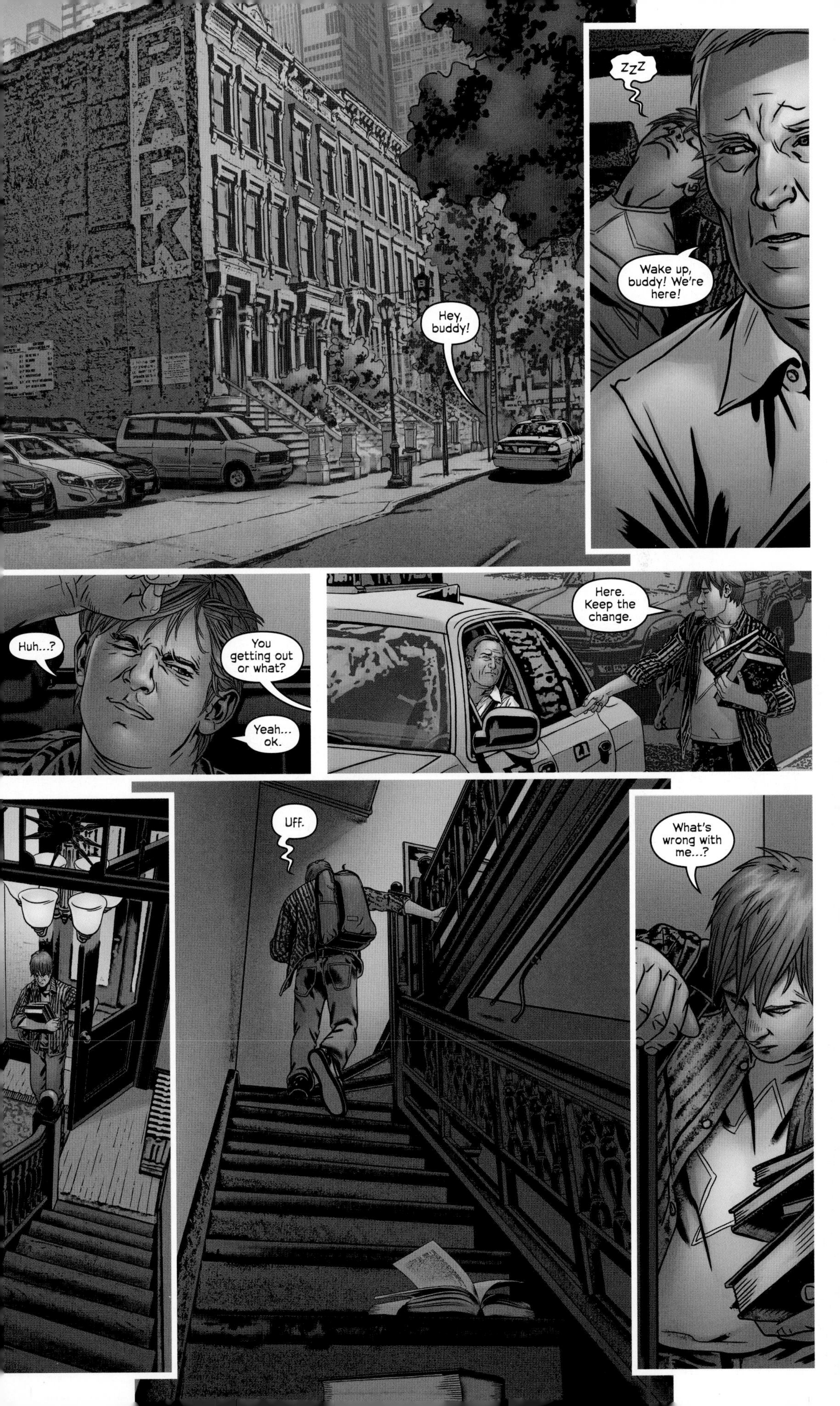

Hey, buddy!
ZZZ
Wake up, buddy! We're here!
Huh...?
You getting out or what?
Yeah... ok.
Here. Keep the change.
Uff.
What's wrong with me...?

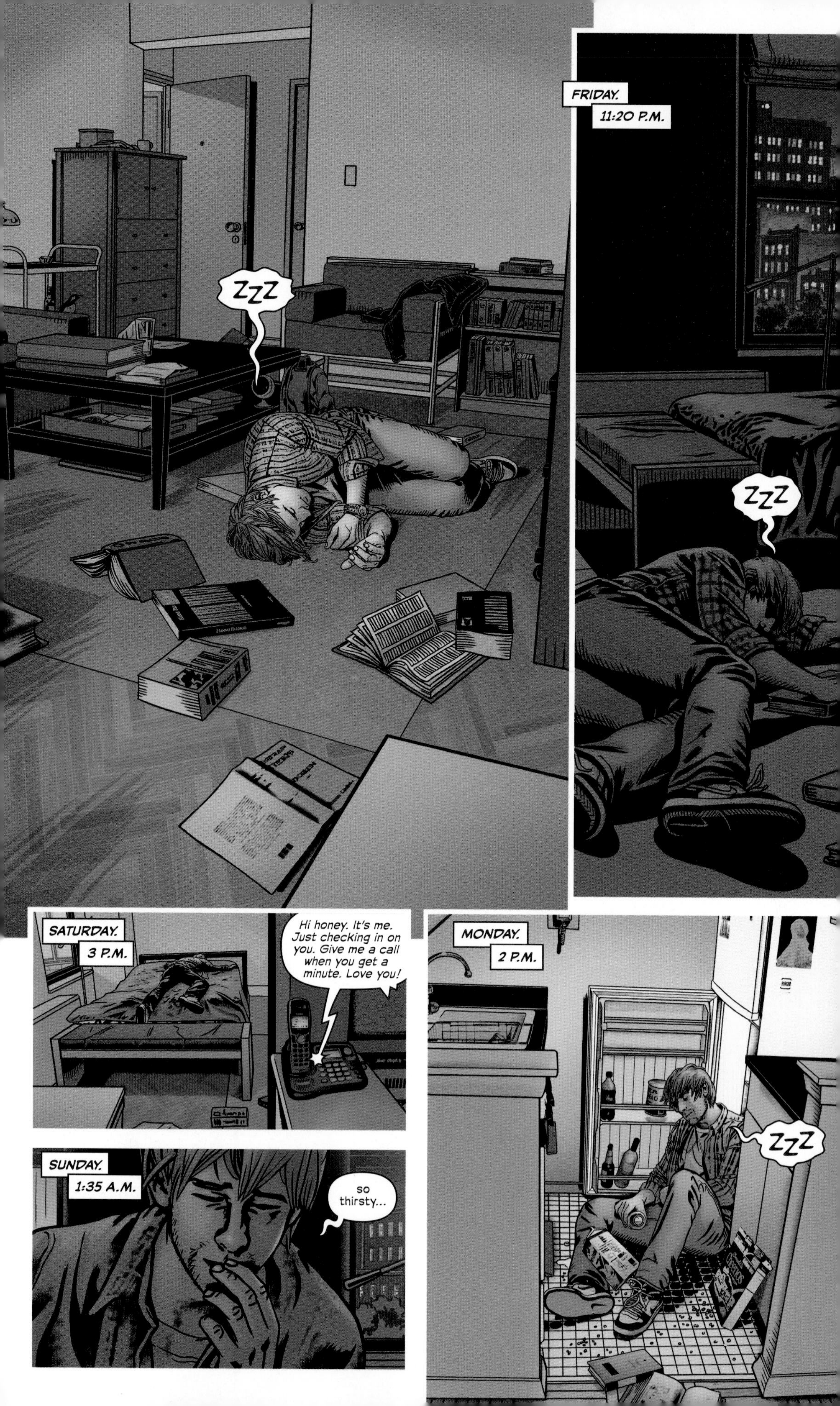

ZZZ
FRIDAY.
11:20 P.M.
ZZZ
SATURDAY.
3 P.M.
Hi honey. It's me. Just checking in on you. Give me a call when you get a minute. Love you!
SUNDAY.
1:35 A.M.
so thirsty...
MONDAY.
2 P.M.
ZZZ

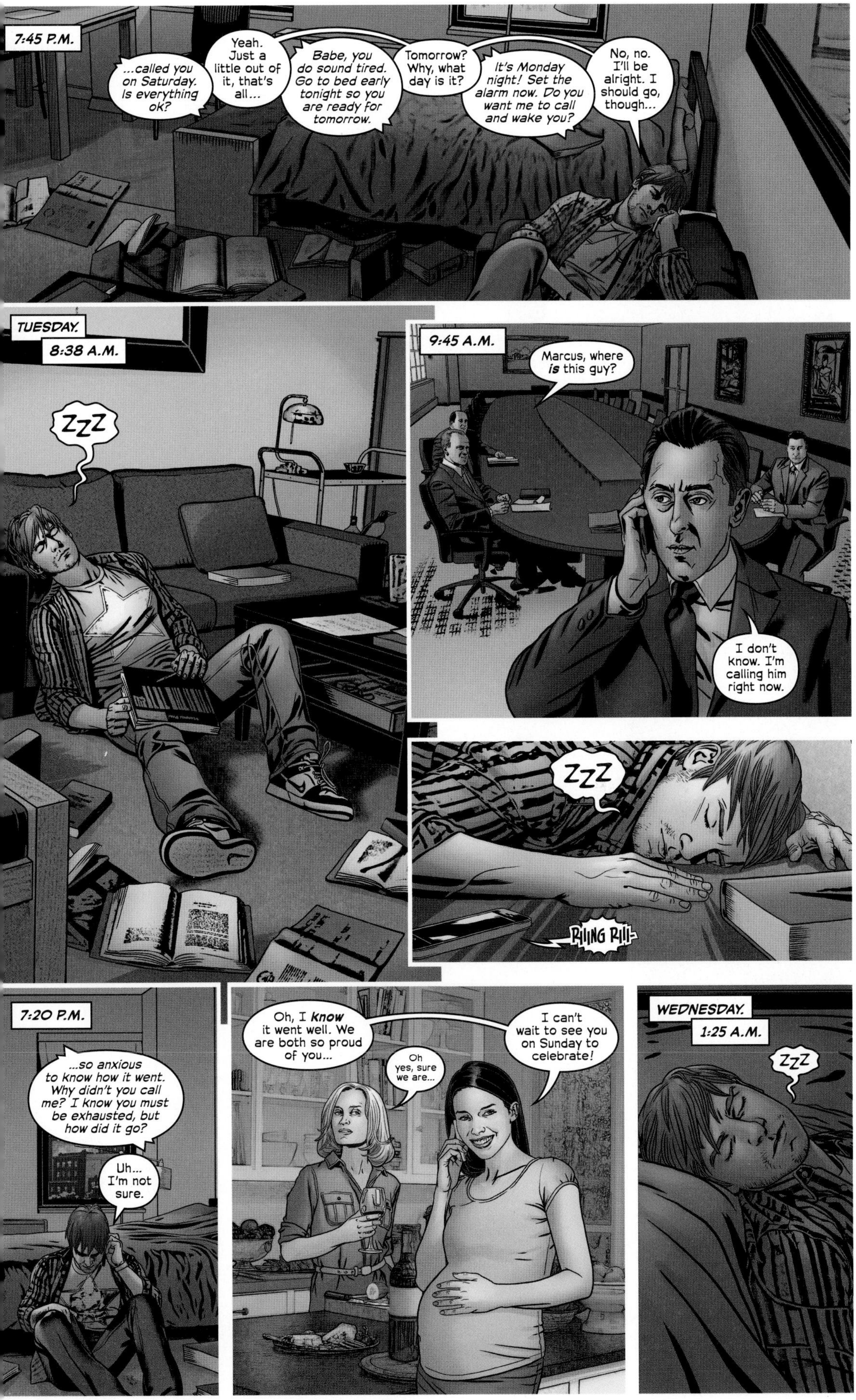
7:45 P.M.
...called you on Saturday. Is everything ok?
Yeah. Just a little out of it, that's all...
Babe, you do sound tired. Go to bed early tonight so you are ready for tomorrow.
Tomorrow? Why, what day is it?
It's Monday night! Set the alarm now. Do you want me to call and wake you?
No, no. I'll be alright. I should go, though...
TUESDAY.
8:38 A.M.
ZZZ
9:45 A.M.
Marcus, where *is* this guy?
I don't know. I'm calling him right now.
ZZZ
RIIING RIII-
7:20 P.M.
...so anxious to know how it went. Why didn't you call me? I know you must be exhausted, but how did it go?
Uh... I'm not sure.
Oh, I **know** it went well. We are both so proud of you...
Oh yes, sure we are...
I can't wait to see you on Sunday to celebrate!
WEDNESDAY.
1:25 A.M.
ZZZ

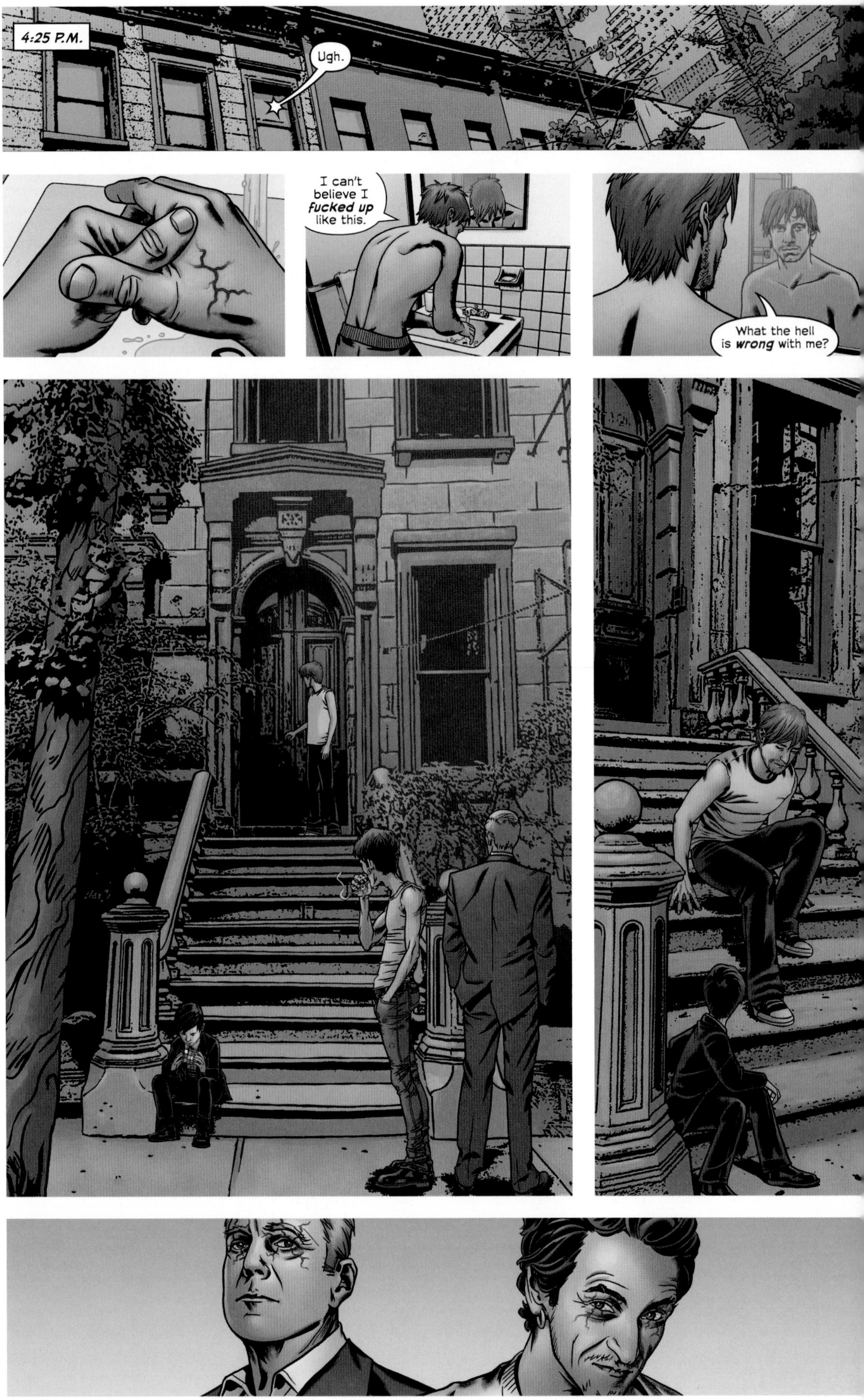
4:25 P.M.
Ugh.
I can't believe I fucked up like this.
What the hell is wrong with me?

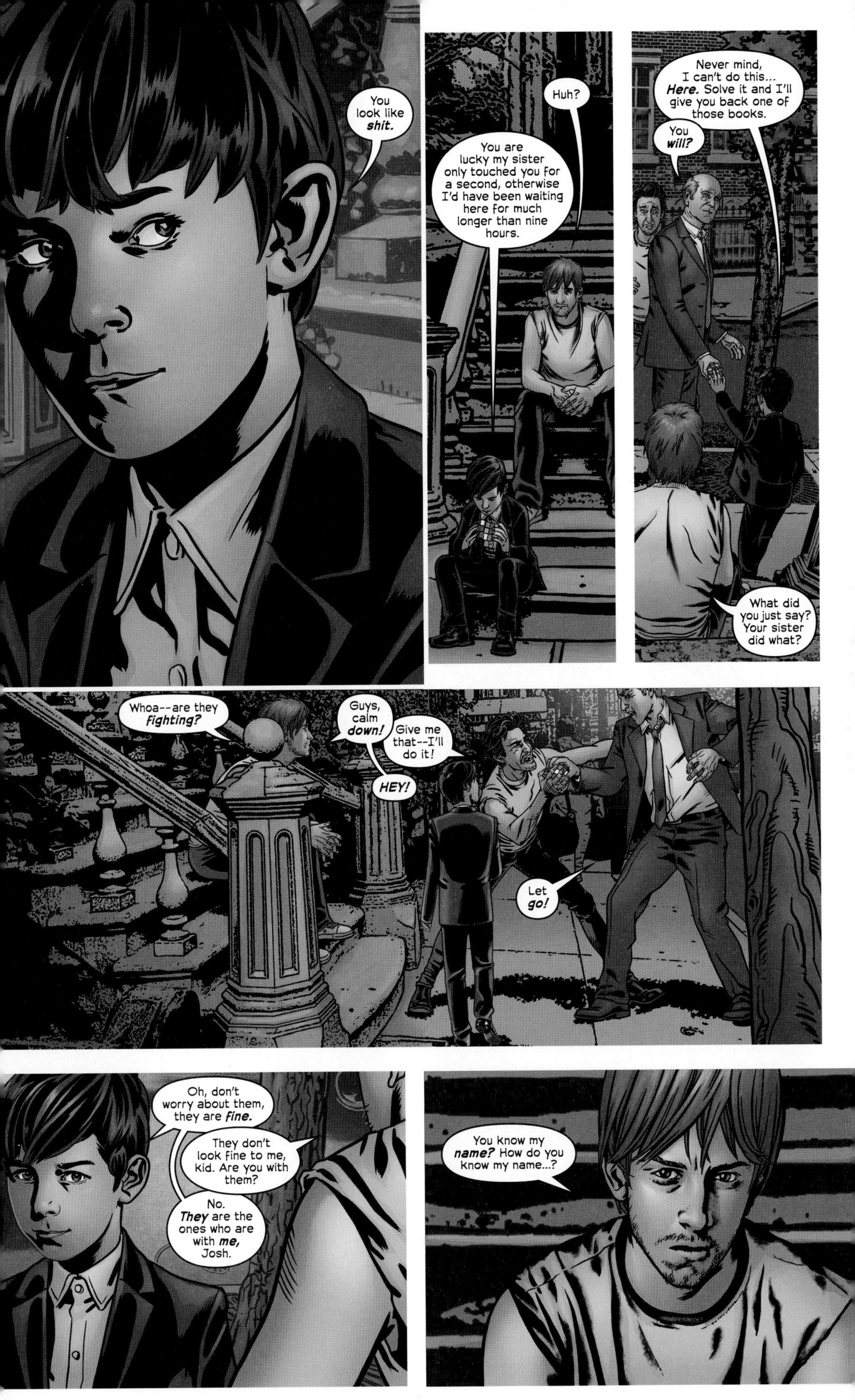
You look like *shit.*
Huh?
You are lucky my sister only touched you for a second, otherwise I'd have been waiting here for much longer than nine hours.
Never mind, I can't do this... *Here.* Solve it and I'll give you back one of those books.
You *will?*
What did you just say? Your sister did what?
Whoa--are they *fighting?*
Guys, calm *down!*
Give me that--I'll do it!
HEY!
Let *go!*
Oh, don't worry about them, they are *fine.*
They don't look fine to me, kid. Are you with them?
No. *They* are the ones who are with *me,* Josh.
You know my *name?* How do you know my name...?

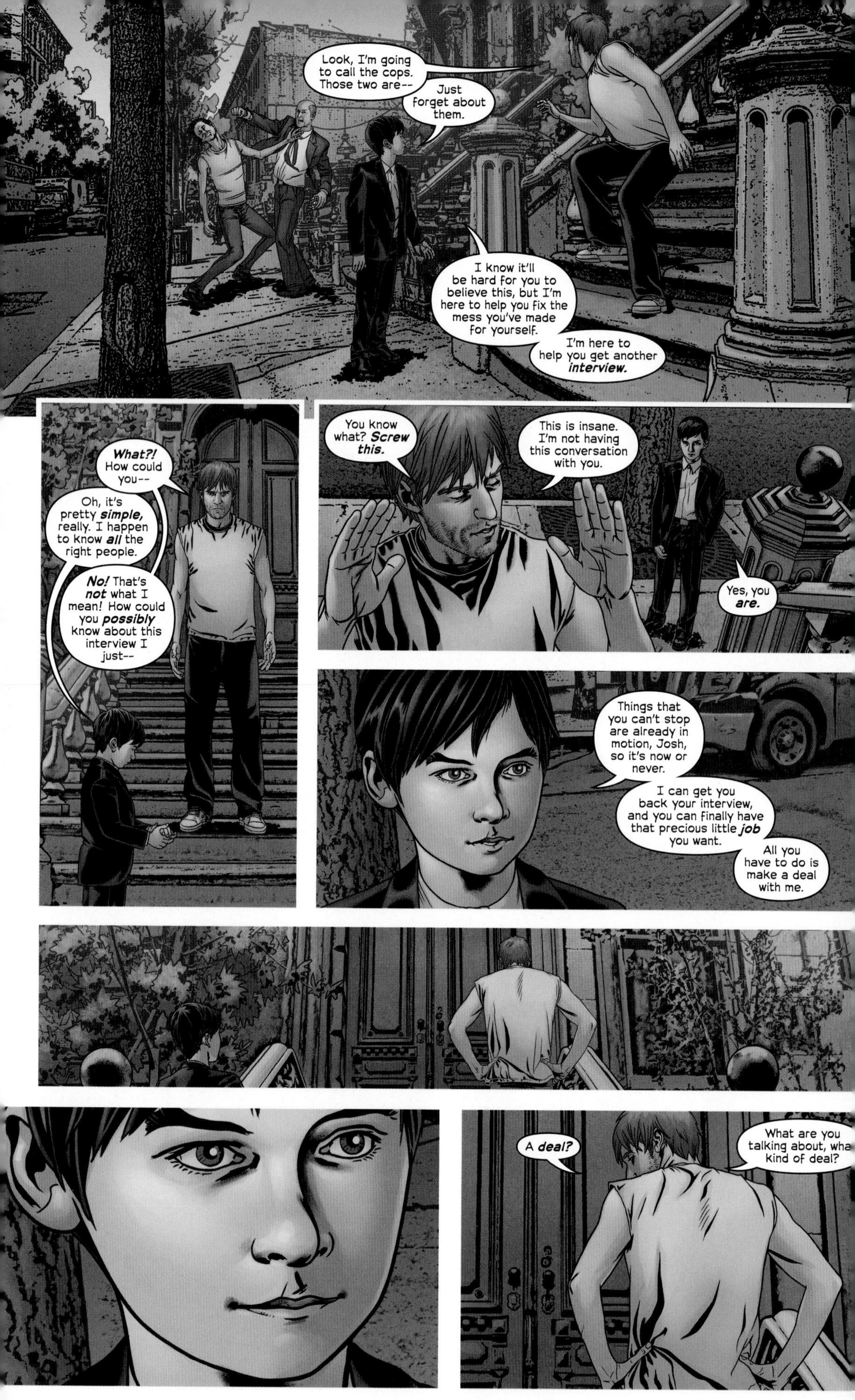

Look, I'm going to call the cops. Those two are--
Just forget about them.
I know it'll be hard for you to believe this, but I'm here to help you fix the mess you've made for yourself.
I'm here to help you get another *interview.*
What?! How could you--
Oh, it's pretty ***simple,*** really. I happen to know ***all*** the right people.
No! That's ***not*** what I mean! How could you ***possibly*** know about this interview I just--
You know what? ***Screw this.***
This is insane. I'm not having this conversation with you.
Yes, you ***are.***
Things that you can't stop are already in motion, Josh, so it's now or never.
I can get you back your interview, and you can finally have that precious little ***job*** you want.
All you have to do is make a deal with me.
A ***deal?***
What are you talking about, wha kind of deal?

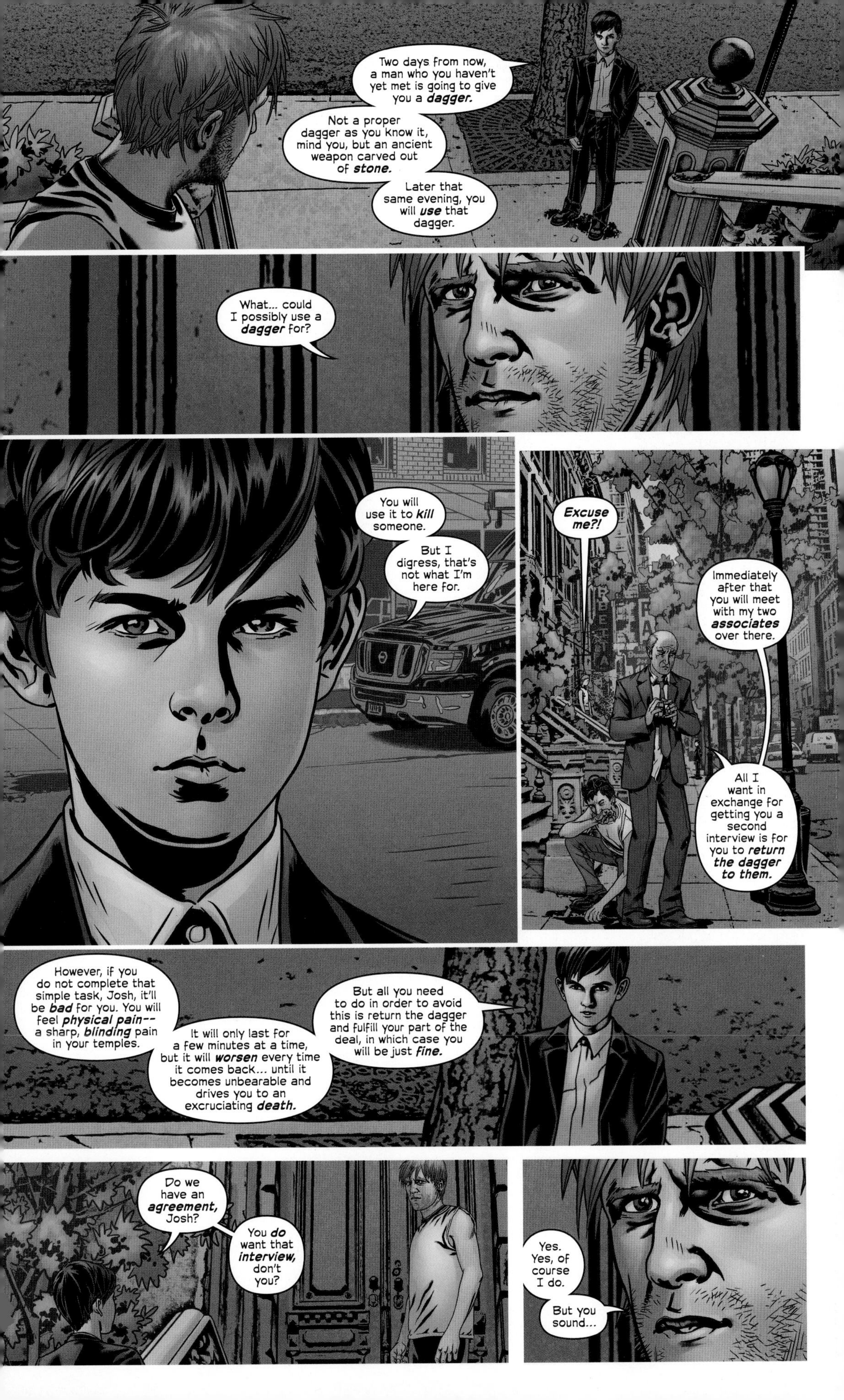

Two days from now, a man who you haven't yet met is going to give you a dagger.
Not a proper dagger as you know it, mind you, but an ancient weapon carved out of stone.
Later that same evening, you will use that dagger.
What... could I possibly use a dagger for?
You will use it to kill someone.
But I digress, that's not what I'm here for.
Excuse me?!
Immediately after that you will meet with my two associates over there.
All I want in exchange for getting you a second interview is for you to return the dagger to them.
However, if you do not complete that simple task, Josh, it'll be bad for you. You will feel physical pain-- a sharp, blinding pain in your temples.
It will only last for a few minutes at a time, but it will worsen every time it comes back... until it becomes unbearable and drives you to an excruciating death.
But all you need to do in order to avoid this is return the dagger and fulfill your part of the deal, in which case you will be just fine.
Do we have an agreement, Josh?
You do want that interview, don't you?
Yes. Yes, of course I do.
But you sound...

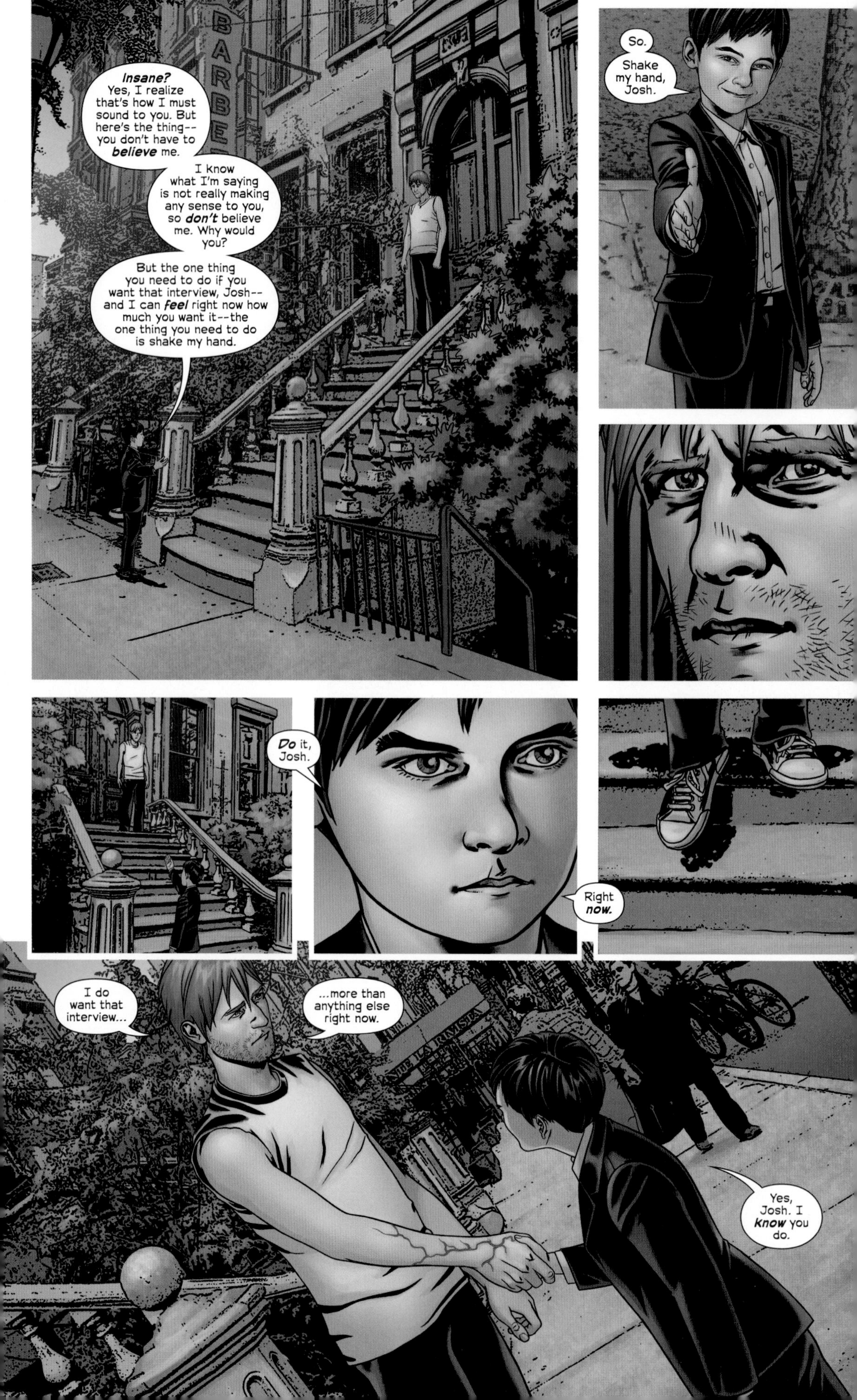

BARBE
Insane? Yes, I realize that's how I must sound to you. But here's the thing--you don't have to ***believe*** me.
I know what I'm saying is not really making any sense to you, so ***don't*** believe me. Why would you?
But the one thing you need to do if you want that interview, Josh--and I can ***feel*** right now how much you want it--the one thing you need to do is shake my hand.
So.
Shake my hand, Josh.
Do it, Josh.
Right ***now.***
I do want that interview...
...more than anything else right now.
Yes, Josh. I ***know*** you do.

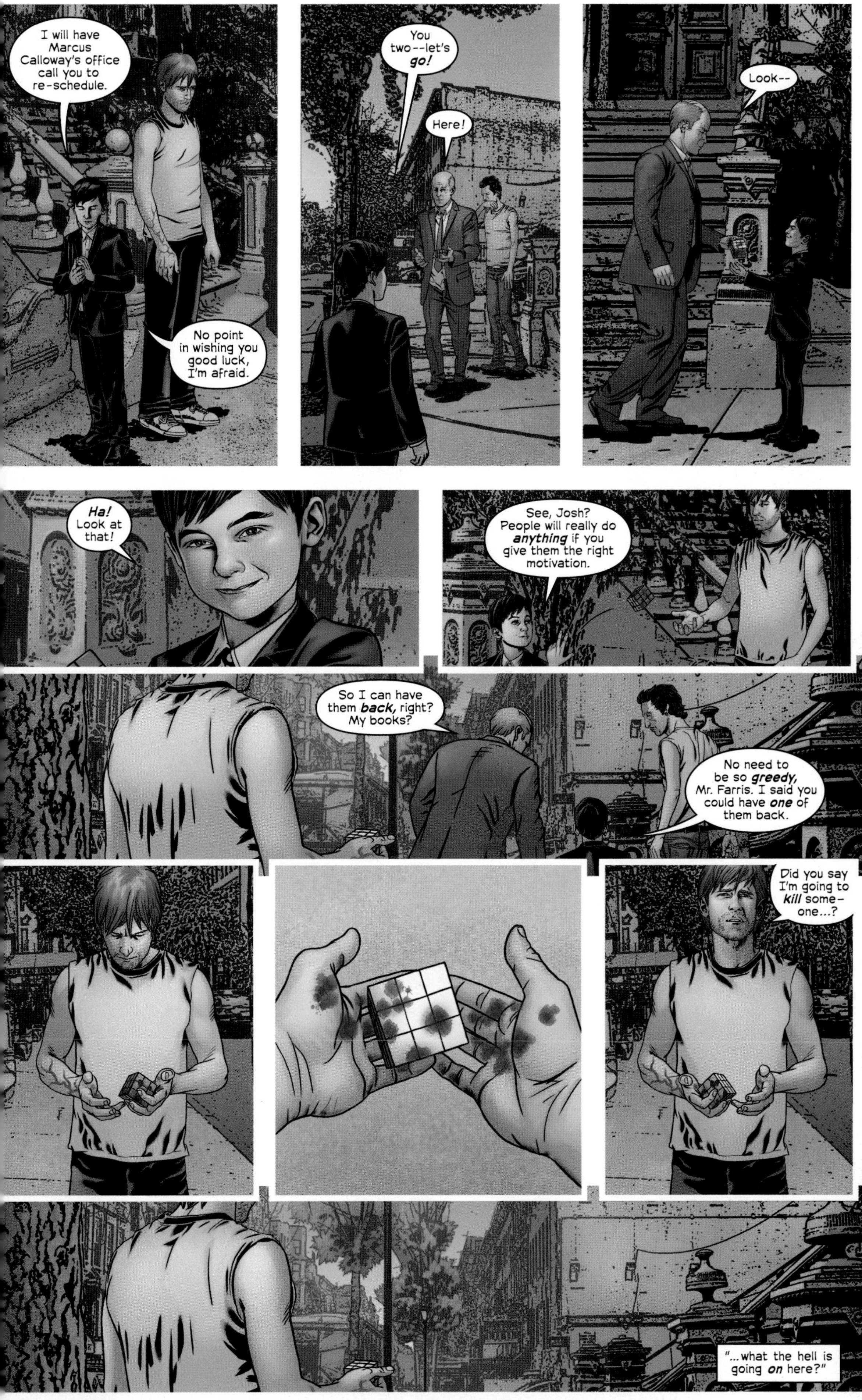
I will have Marcus Calloway's office call you to re-schedule.
No point in wishing you good luck, I'm afraid.
You two--let's go!
Here!
Look--
Ha! Look at that!
See, Josh? People will really do anything if you give them the right motivation.
So I can have them back, right? My books?
No need to be so greedy, Mr. Farris. I said you could have one of them back.
Did you say I'm going to kill some-one...?
"...what the hell is going on here?"

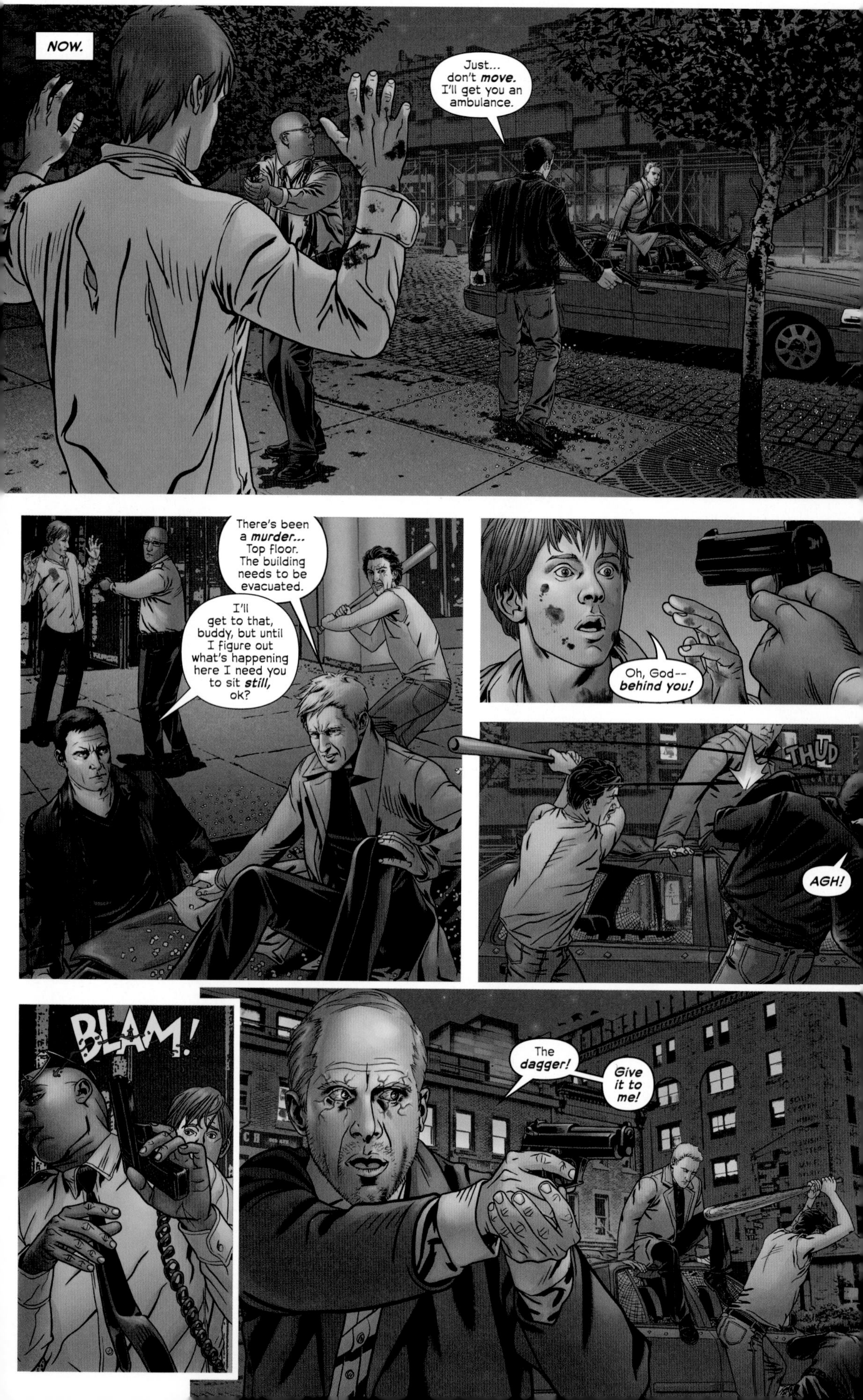
NOW.
Just... don't move. I'll get you an ambulance.
There's been a murder... Top floor. The building needs to be evacuated.
I'll get to that, buddy, but until I figure out what's happening here I need you to sit still, ok?
Oh, God-- behind you!
THUD
AGH!
BLAM!
The dagger!
Give it to me!

It's--it's there, on the *ground...*

ENOUGH!

I realize you are under someone else's control right now, but I can't help you. For this, I'm *sorry.*

Akk--

Stay right there! Don't make me *shoot* you!

No.

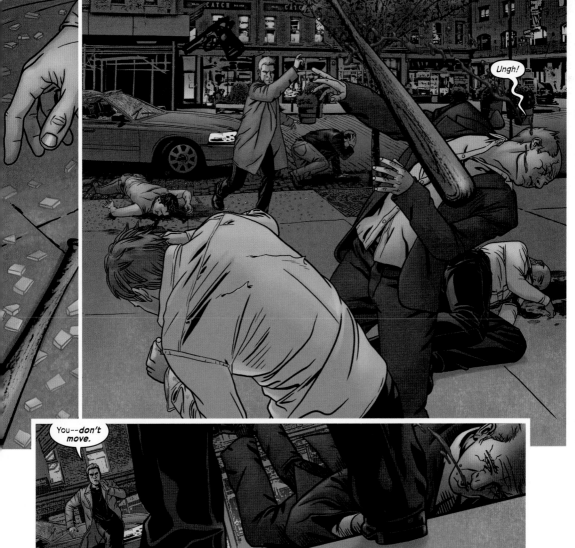

Ungh!

You--*don't* move.

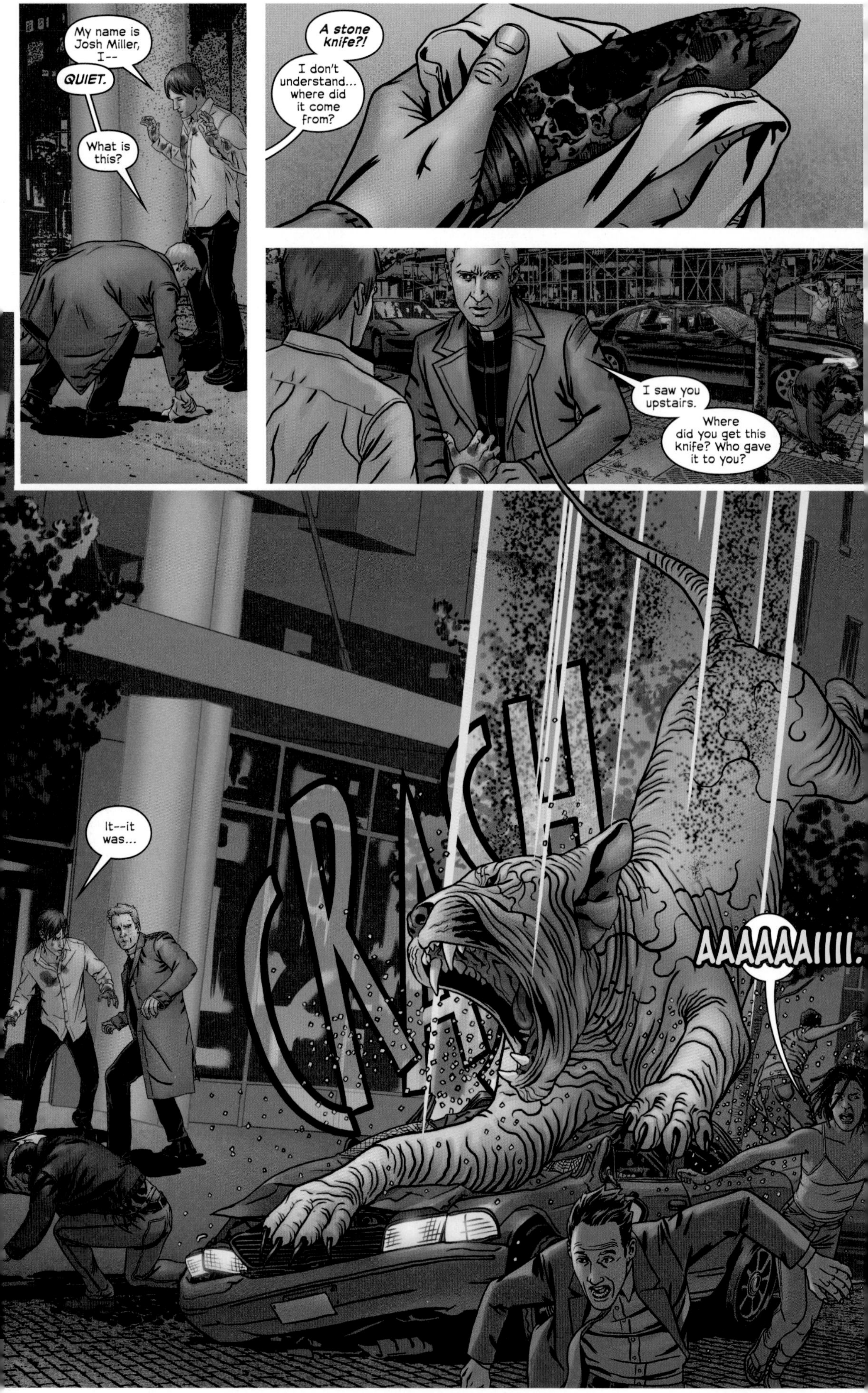
My name is Josh Miller, I--
QUIET.
What is this?
A stone knife?!
I don't understand... where did it come from?
I saw you upstairs.
Where did you get this knife? Who gave it to you?
It--it was...
CRASH
AAAAAIIIII.

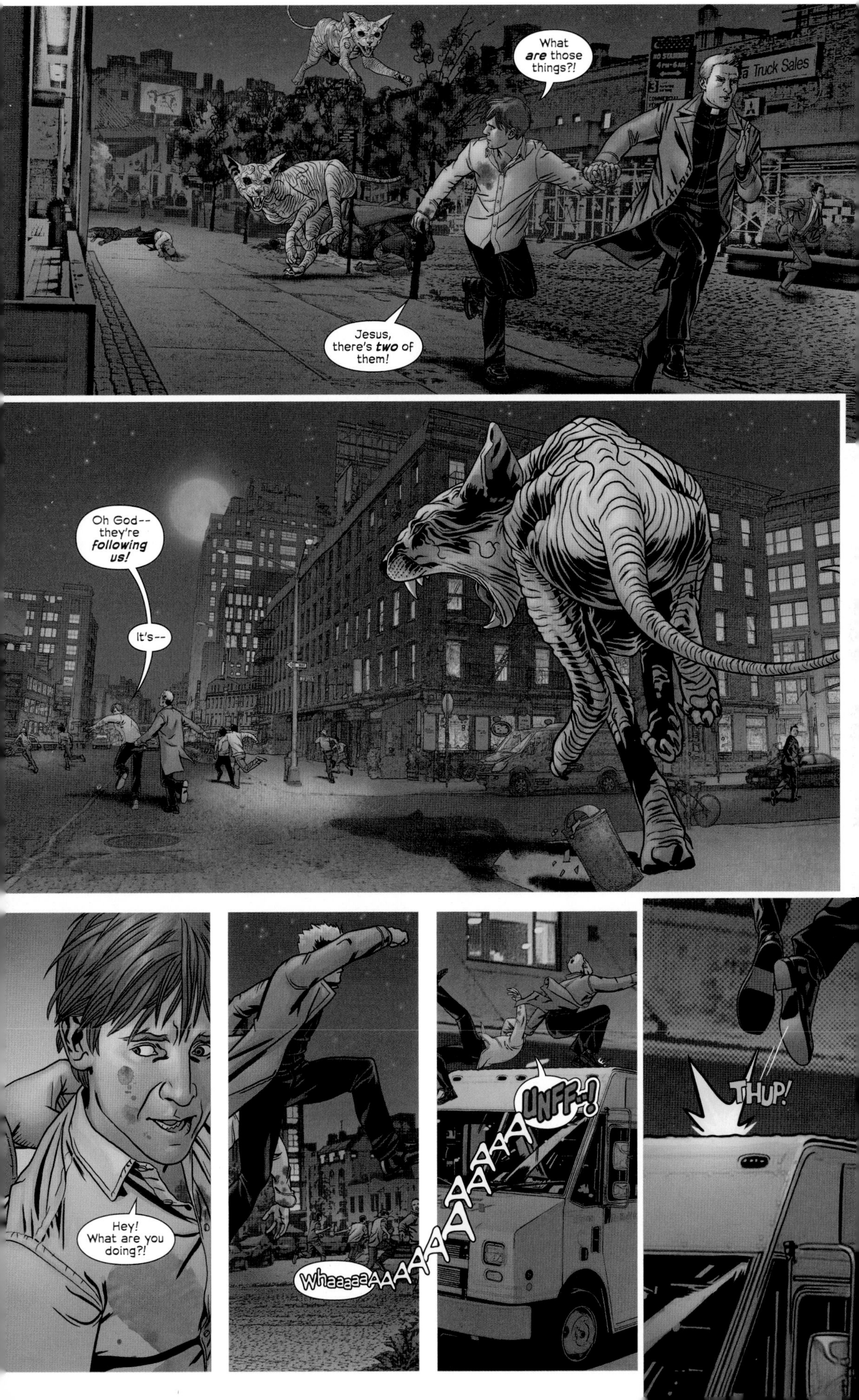
What are those things?!
Jesus, there's two of them!
Oh God-- they're following us!
It's--
Hey! What are you doing?!
WhaaaaAAAAAAAAAAA
UNFF--!
THUP!

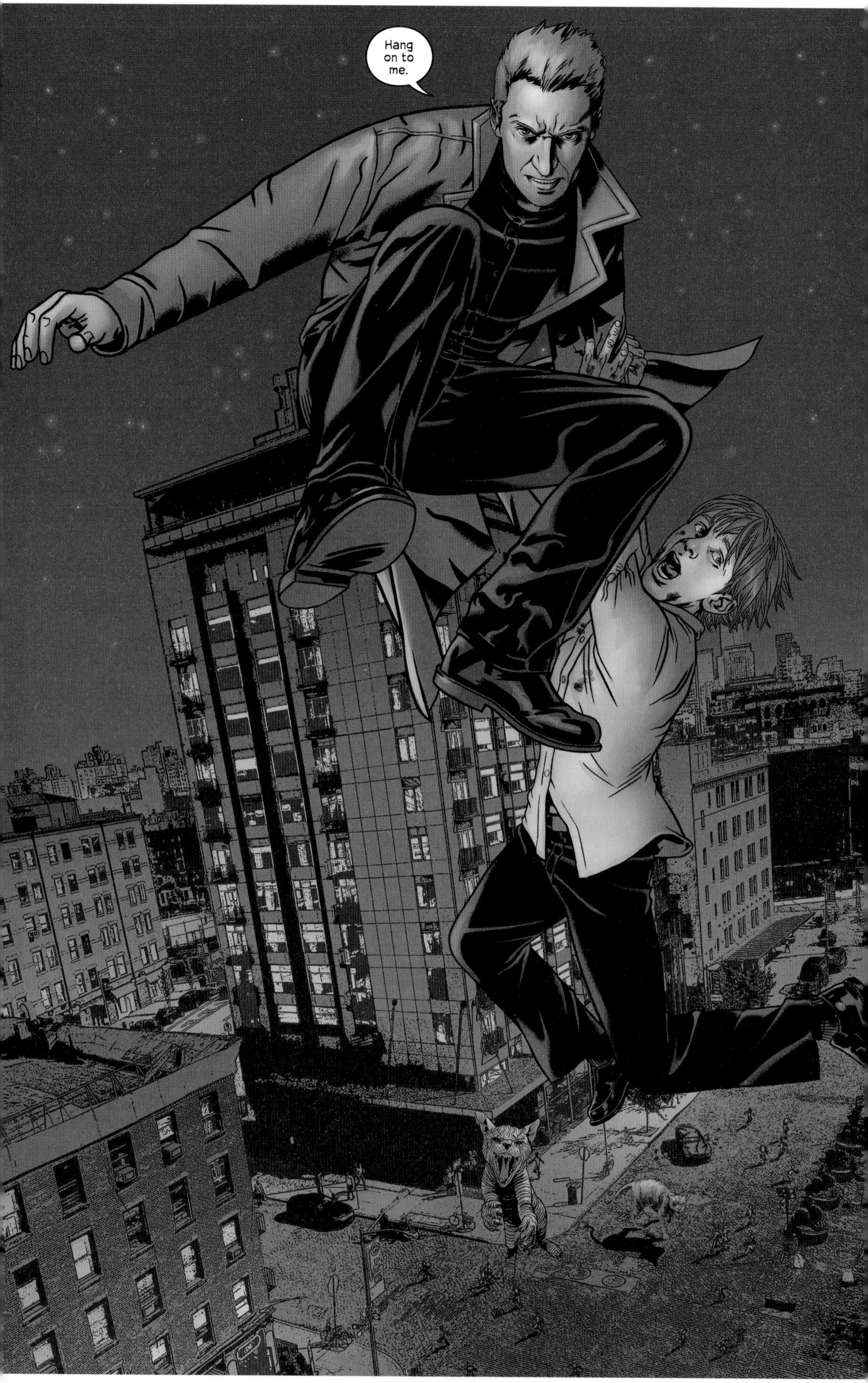
Hang on to me.

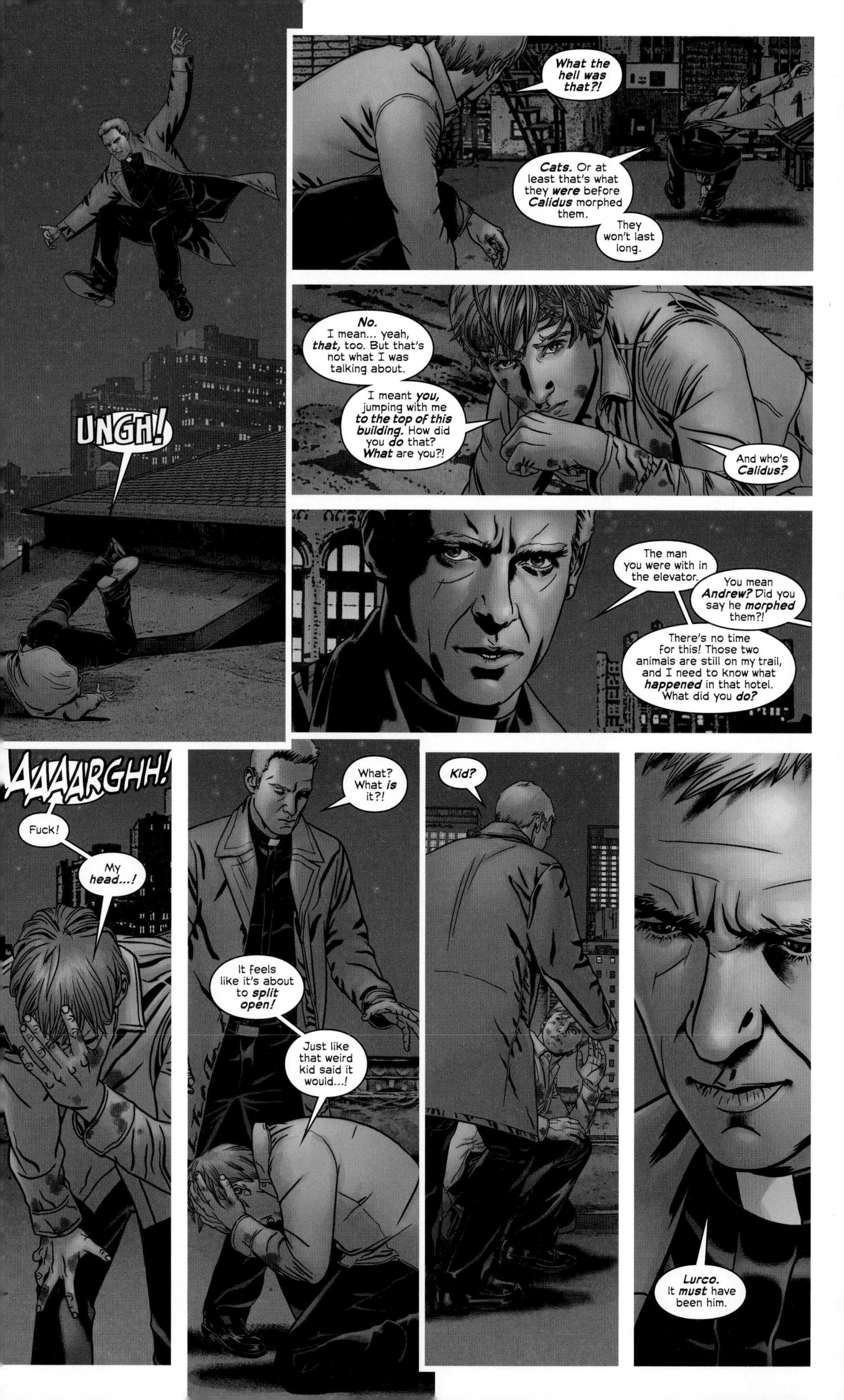
What the hell was that?!
Cats. Or at least that's what they were before Calidus morphed them.
They won't last long.
UNGH!
No.
I mean... yeah, that, too. But that's not what I was talking about.
I meant you, jumping with me to the top of this building. How did you do that? What are you?!
And who's Calidus?
The man you were with in the elevator.
You mean Andrew? Did you say he morphed them?!
There's no time for this! Those two animals are still on my trail, and I need to know what happened in that hotel. What did you do?
AAAARGHH!
Fuck!
My head...!
What? What is it?!
It feels like it's about to split open!
Just like that weird kid said it would...!
Kid?
Lurco.
It must have been him.

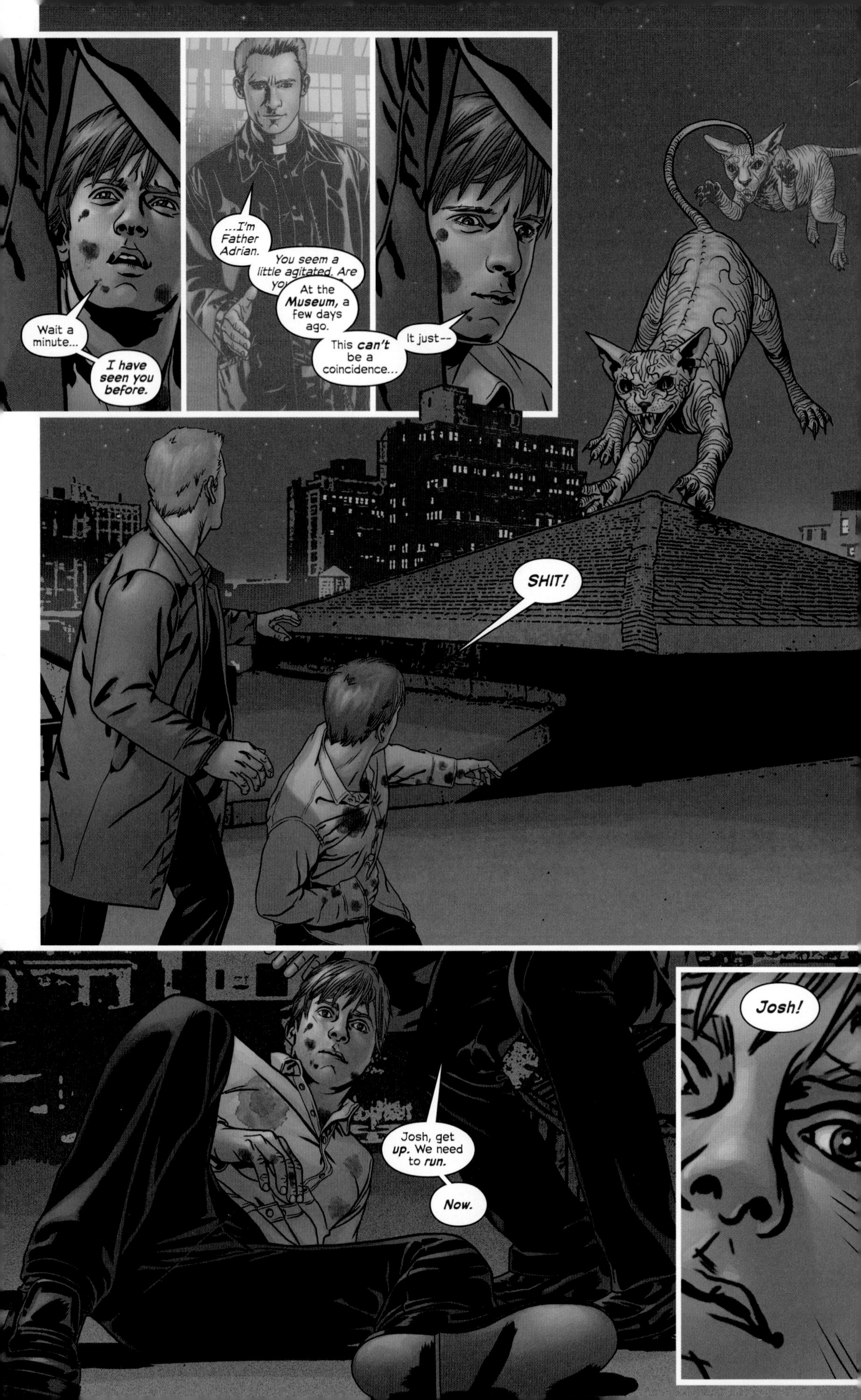

Wait a minute...
I have seen you before.
...I'm Father Adrian.
You seem a little agitated. Are
At the Museum, a few days ago.
This can't be a coincidence...
It just--
SHIT!
Josh, get up. We need to run.
Now.
Josh!

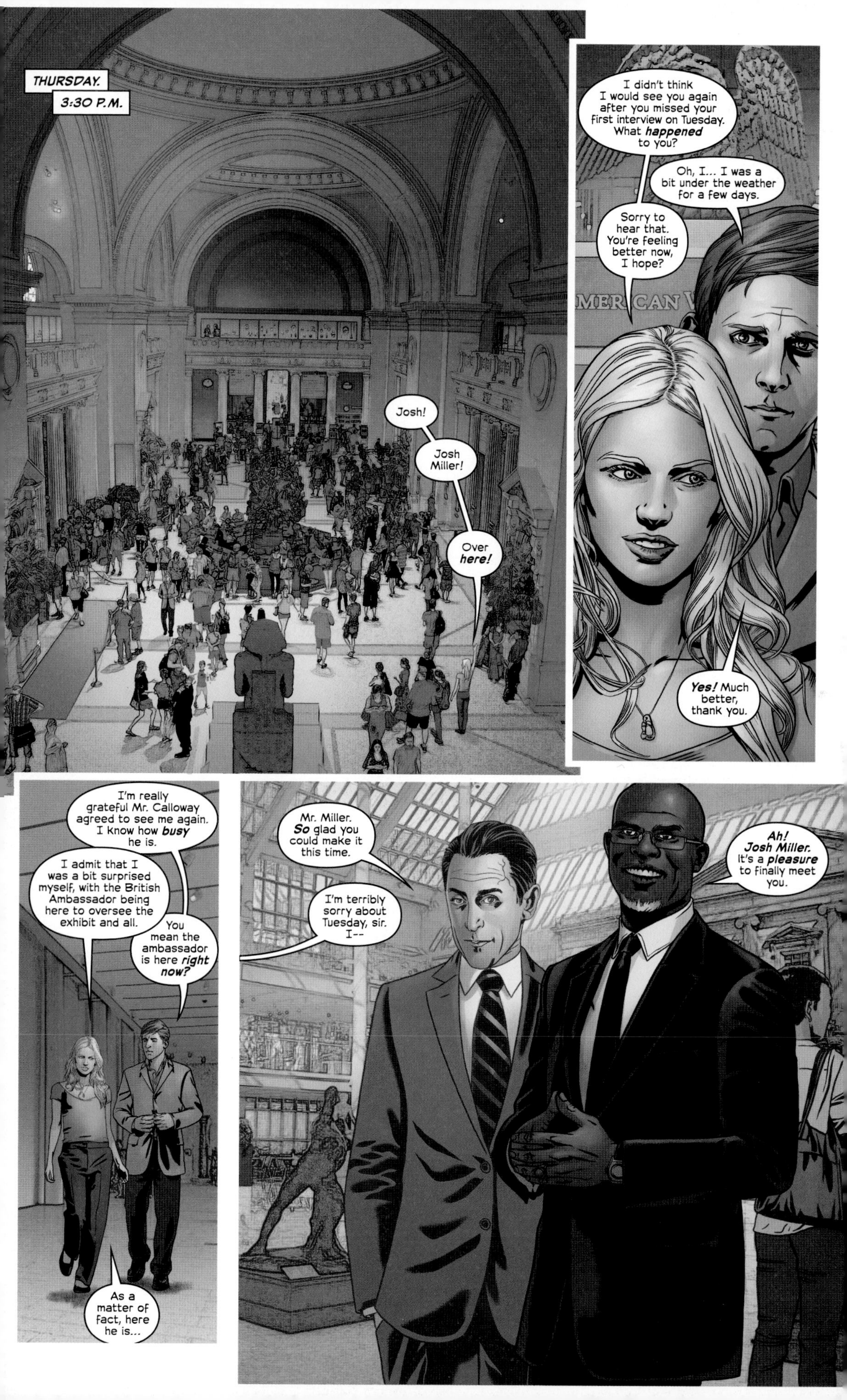
THURSDAY.
3:30 P.M.
Josh!
Josh Miller!
Over here!
I didn't think I would see you again after you missed your first interview on Tuesday. What happened to you?
Oh, I... I was a bit under the weather for a few days.
Sorry to hear that. You're feeling better now, I hope?
Yes! Much better, thank you.
I'm really grateful Mr. Calloway agreed to see me again. I know how busy he is.
I admit that I was a bit surprised myself, with the British Ambassador being here to oversee the exhibit and all.
You mean the ambassador is here right now?
As a matter of fact, here he is...
Mr. Miller. So glad you could make it this time.
I'm terribly sorry about Tuesday, sir. I--
Ah! Josh Miller. It's a pleasure to finally meet you.

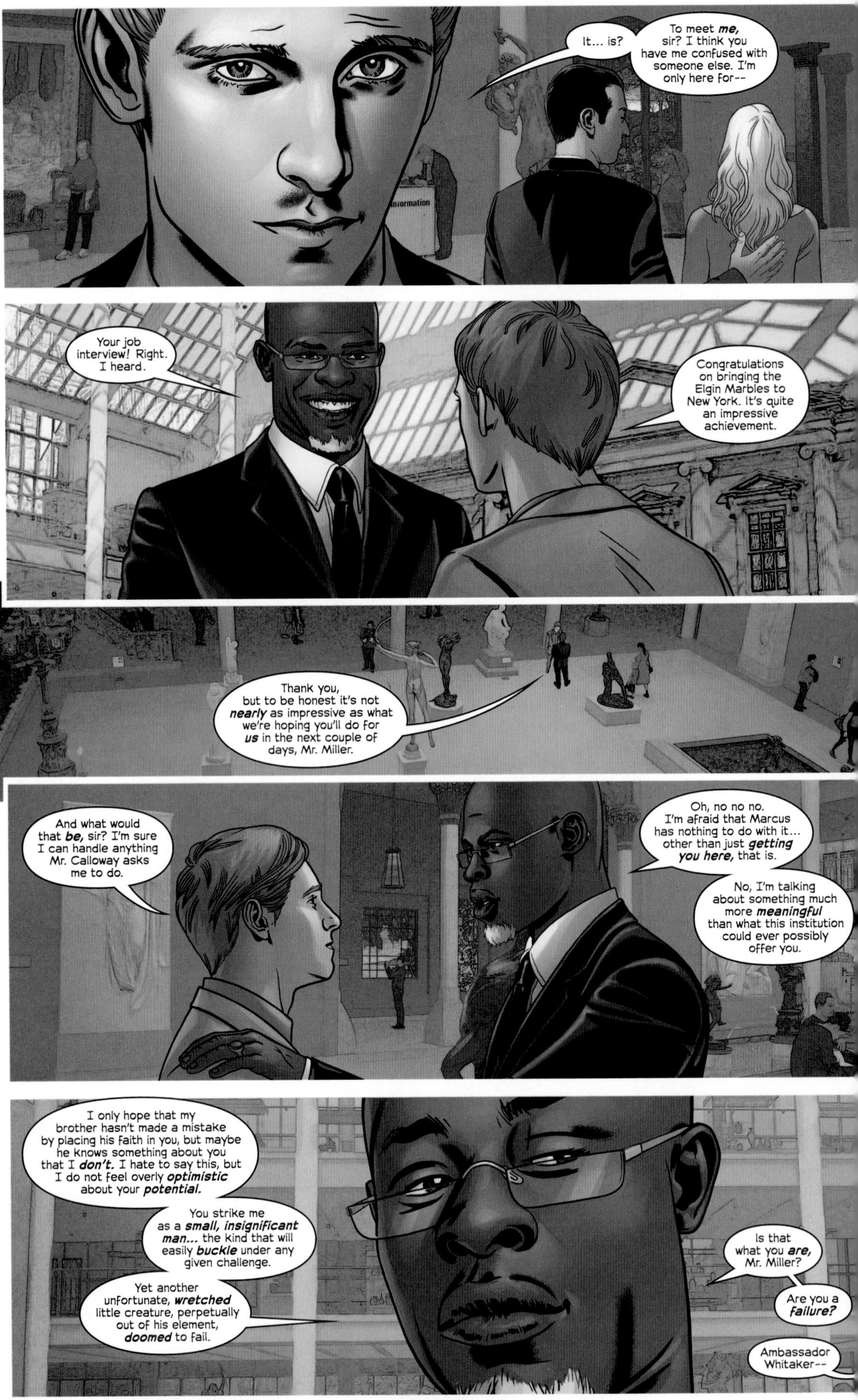
It... is?
To meet *me,* sir? I think you have me confused with someone else. I'm only here for--
Your job interview! Right. I heard.
Congratulations on bringing the Elgin Marbles to New York. It's quite an impressive achievement.
Thank you, but to be honest it's not *nearly* as impressive as what we're hoping you'll do for *us* in the next couple of days, Mr. Miller.
And what would that *be,* sir? I'm sure I can handle anything Mr. Calloway asks me to do.
Oh, no no no. I'm afraid that Marcus has nothing to do with it... other than just *getting you here,* that is.
No, I'm talking about something much more *meaningful* than what this institution could ever possibly offer you.
I only hope that my brother hasn't made a mistake by placing his faith in you, but maybe he knows something about you that I *don't.* I hate to say this, but I do not feel overly *optimistic* about your *potential.*
You strike me as a *small, insignificant man...* the kind that will easily *buckle* under any given challenge.
Yet another unfortunate, *wretched* little creature, perpetually out of his element, *doomed* to fail.
Is that what you *are,* Mr. Miller?
Are you a *failure?*
Ambassador Whitaker--

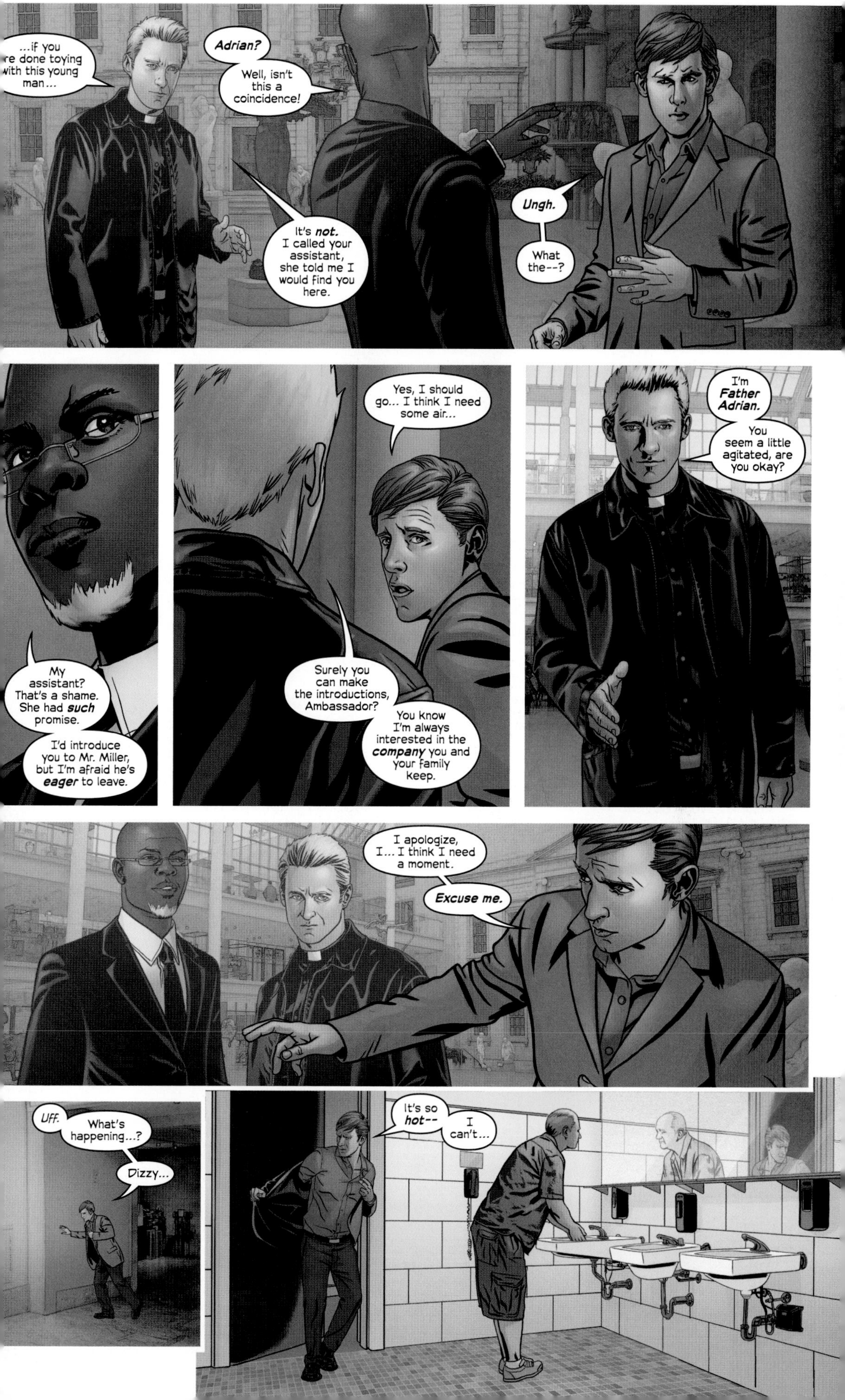
...if you
re done toying
with this young
man...
Adrian?
Well, isn't
this a
coincidence!
It's not.
I called your
assistant,
she told me I
would find you
here.
Ungh.
What
the--?
My
assistant?
That's a shame.
She had such
promise.
I'd introduce
you to Mr. Miller,
but I'm afraid he's
eager to leave.
Yes, I should
go... I think I need
some air...
Surely you
can make
the introductions,
Ambassador?
You know
I'm always
interested in the
company you and
your family
keep.
I'm
Father
Adrian.
You
seem a little
agitated, are
you okay?
I apologize,
I... I think I need
a moment.
Excuse me.
Uff.
What's
happening...?
Dizzy...
It's so
hot--
I
can't...

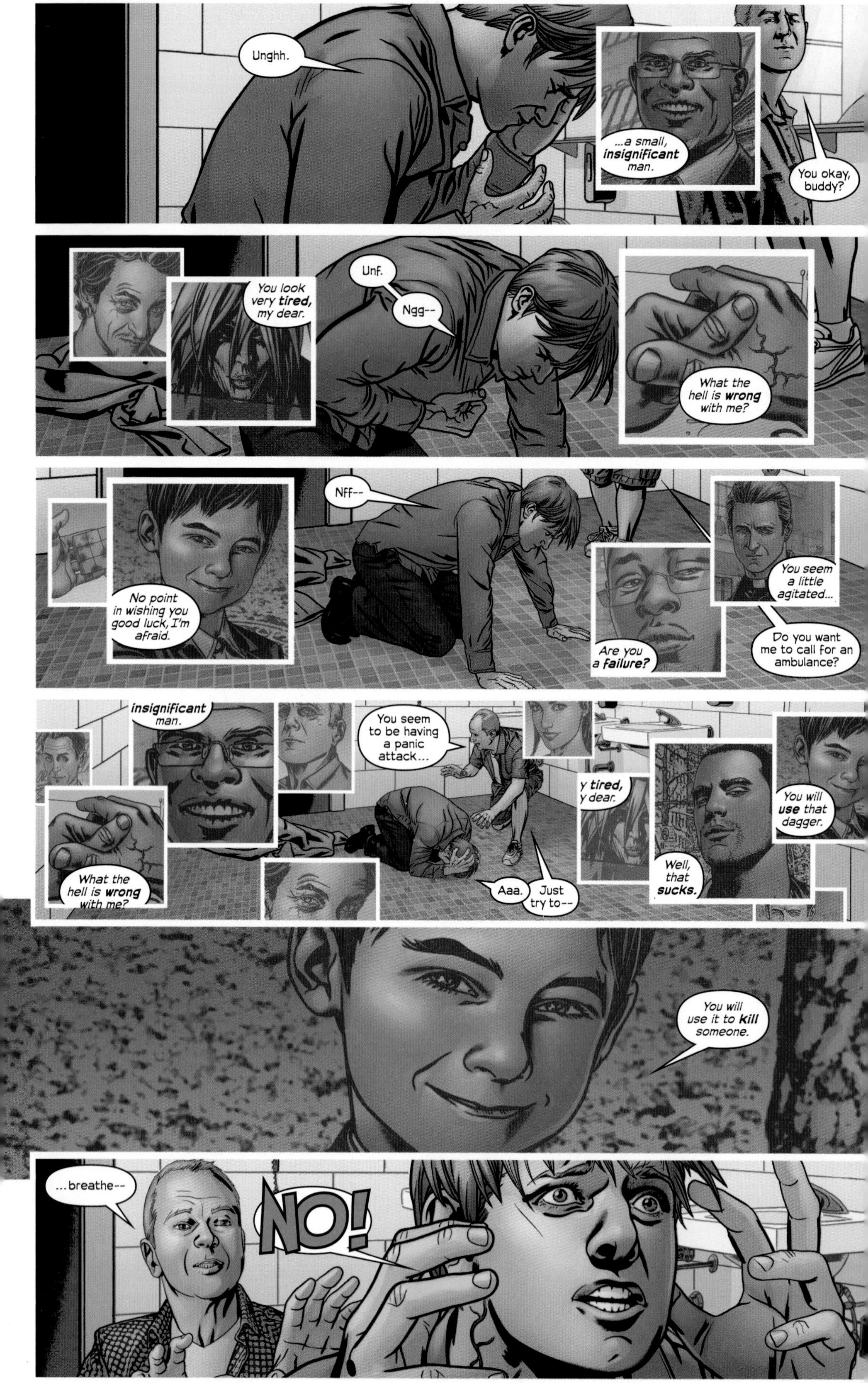
Unghh.
...a small, **insignificant** man.
You okay, buddy?
You look very **tired,** my dear.
Unf.
Ngg--
What the hell is **wrong** with me?
Nff--
No point in wishing you good luck, I'm afraid.
Are you a **failure?**
You seem a little agitated...
Do you want me to call for an ambulance?
insignificant man.
You seem to be having a panic attack...
What the hell is **wrong** with me?
y **tired,** y dear.
Aaa.
Just try to--
Well, that **sucks.**
You will **use** that dagger.
You will use it to **kill** someone.
...breathe--
NO!

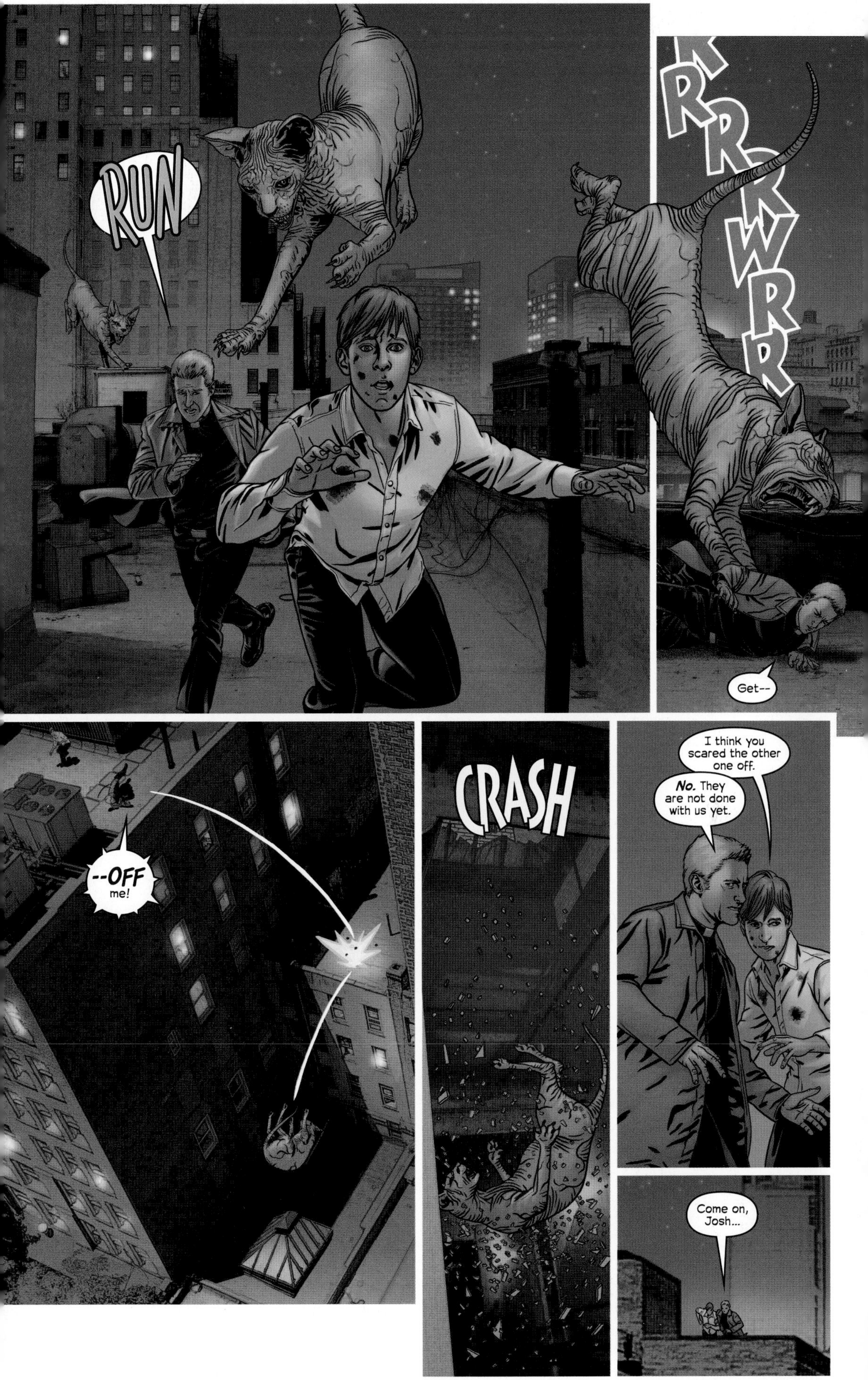
RUN
RRRRWRR
Get--
--OFF me!
CRASH
I think you scared the other one off.
No. They are not done with us yet.
Come on, Josh...

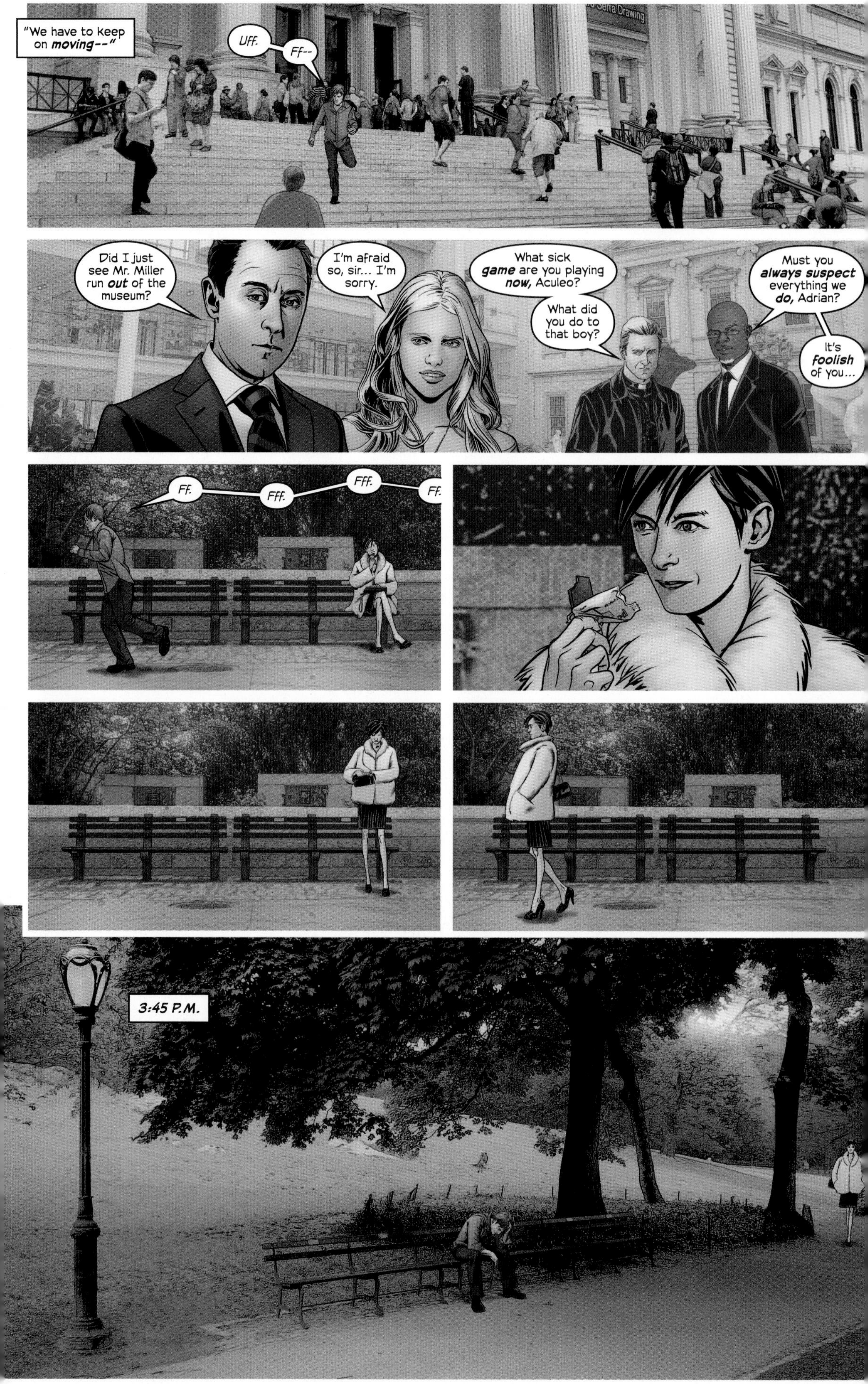
"We have to keep on *moving*--"
Uff.
Ff--
Did I just see Mr. Miller run *out* of the museum?
I'm afraid so, sir... I'm sorry.
What sick *game* are you playing *now,* Aculeo?
What did you do to that boy?
Must you *always suspect* everything we *do,* Adrian?
It's *foolish* of you...
Ff.
Fff.
Fff.
Ff.
3:45 P.M.

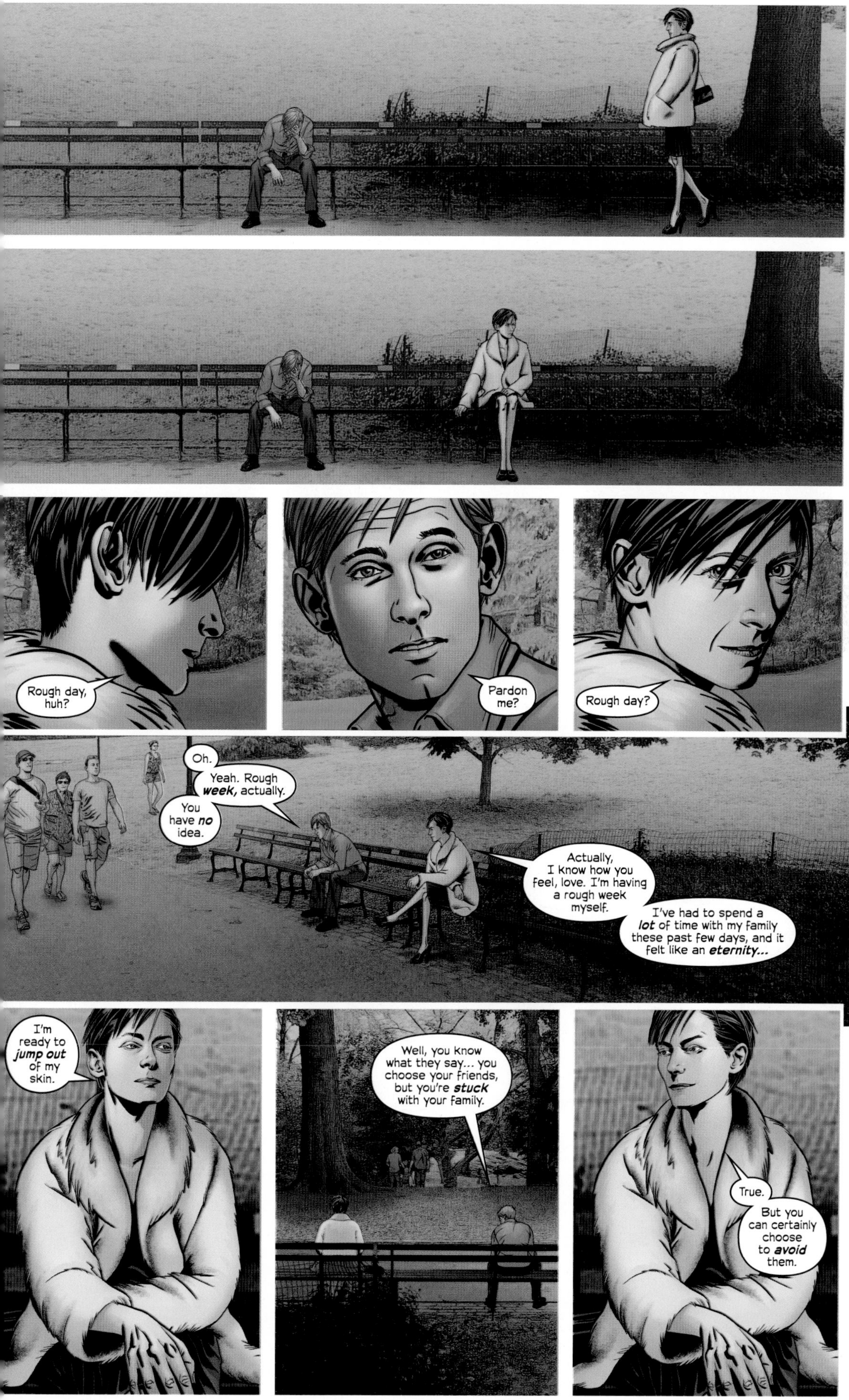
Rough day, huh?
Pardon me?
Rough day?
Oh.
Yeah. Rough *week,* actually.
You have *no* idea.
Actually, I know how you feel, love. I'm having a rough week myself.
I've had to spend a *lot* of time with my family these past few days, and it felt like an *eternity...*
I'm ready to *jump out* of my skin.
Well, you know what they say... you choose your friends, but you're *stuck* with your family.
True.
But you can certainly choose to *avoid* them.

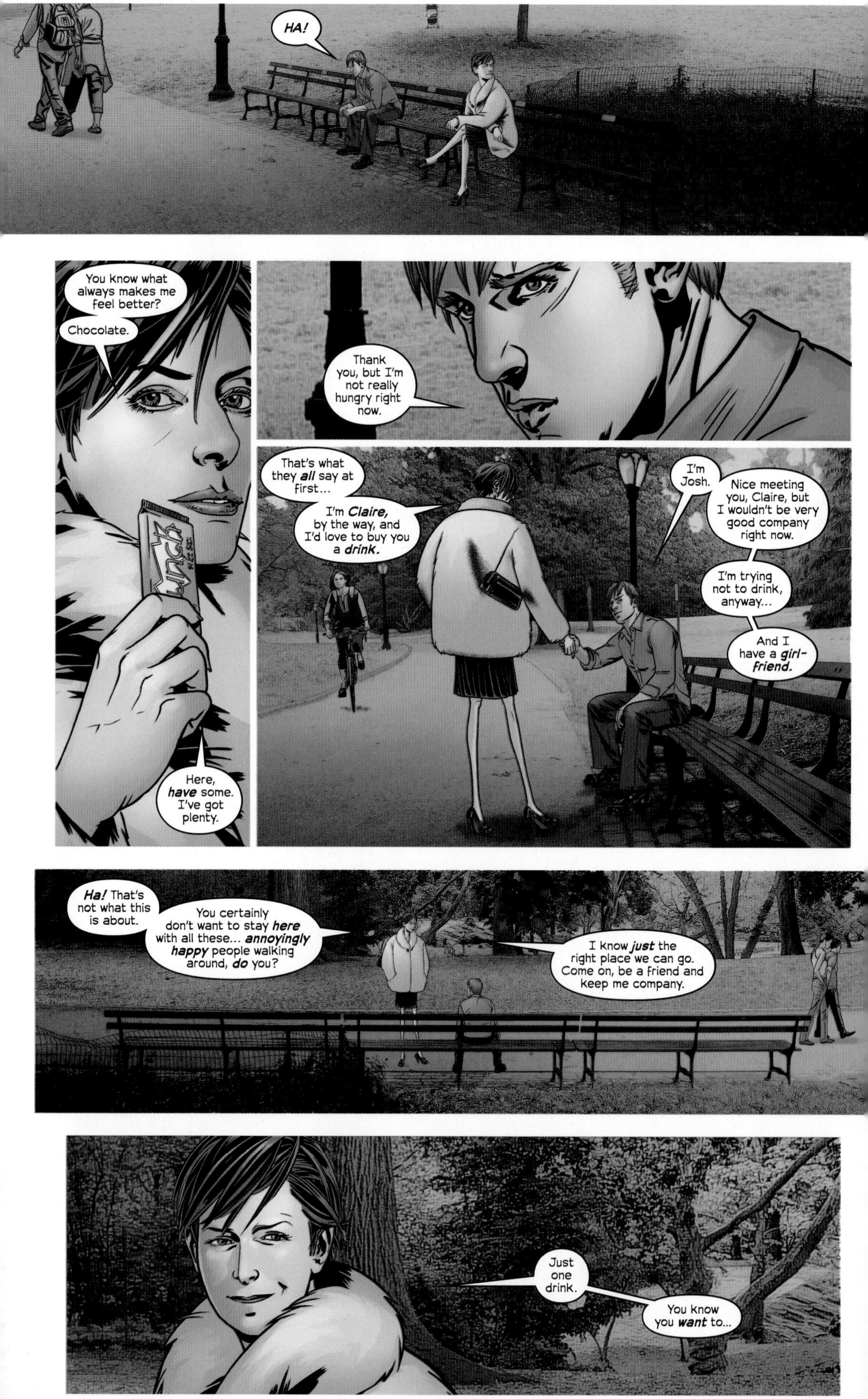
HA!
You know what always makes me feel better?
Chocolate.
Here, have some. I've got plenty.
Thank you, but I'm not really hungry right now.
That's what they all say at first...
I'm Claire, by the way, and I'd love to buy you a drink.
I'm Josh.
Nice meeting you, Claire, but I wouldn't be very good company right now.
I'm trying not to drink, anyway...
And I have a girl-friend.
Ha! That's not what this is about.
You certainly don't want to stay here with all these... annoyingly happy people walking around, do you?
I know just the right place we can go. Come on, be a friend and keep me company.
Just one drink.
You know you want to...

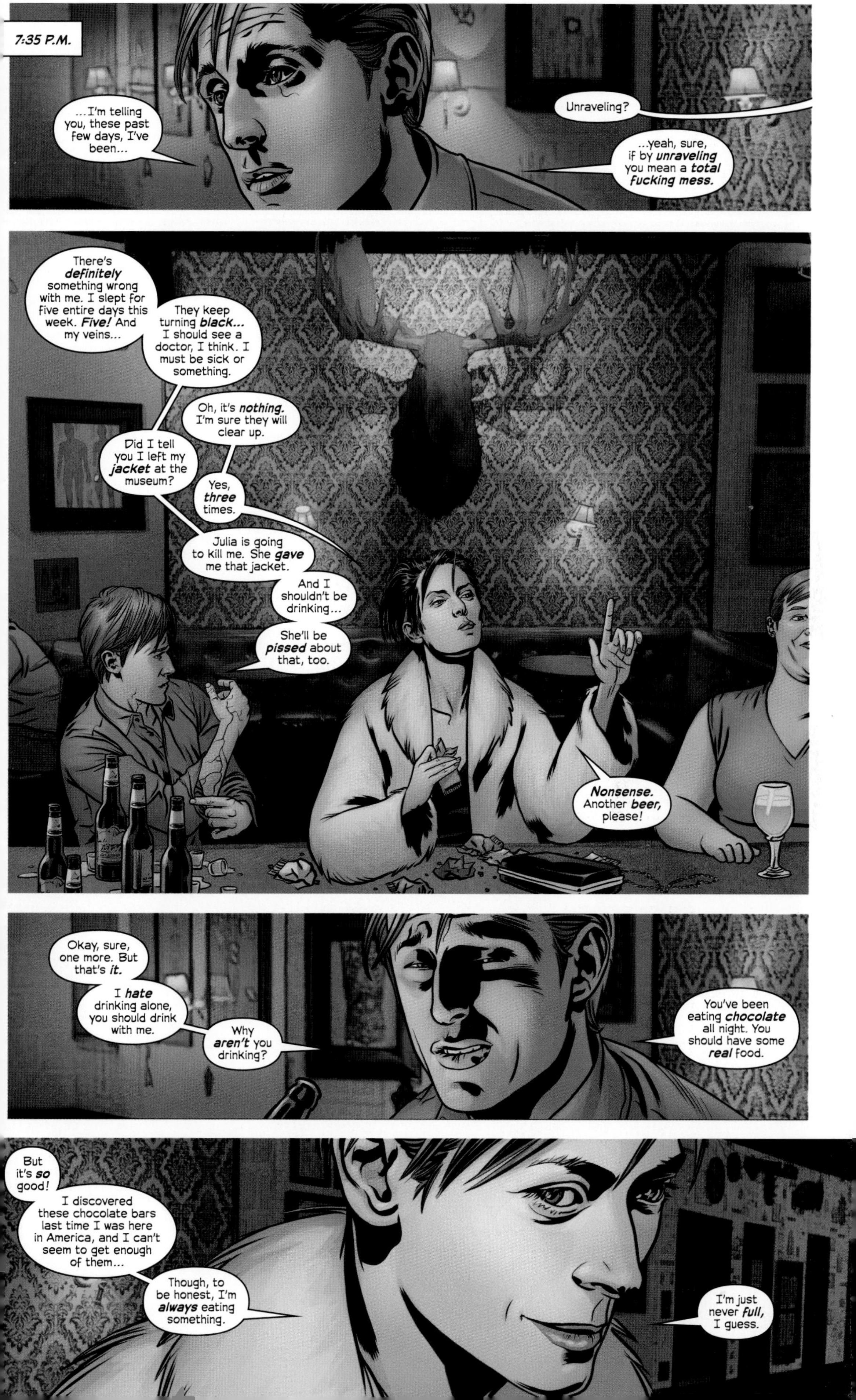
7:35 P.M.
...I'm telling you, these past few days, I've been...
Unraveling?
...yeah, sure, if by *unraveling* you mean a *total fucking mess.*
There's *definitely* something wrong with me. I slept for five entire days this week. *Five!* And my veins...
They keep turning *black...* I should see a doctor, I think. I must be sick or something.
Oh, it's *nothing.* I'm sure they will clear up.
Did I tell you I left my *jacket* at the museum?
Yes, *three* times.
Julia is going to kill me. She *gave* me that jacket.
And I shouldn't be drinking...
She'll be *pissed* about that, too.
Nonsense. Another *beer,* please!
Okay, sure, one more. But that's *it.*
I *hate* drinking alone, you should drink with me.
Why *aren't* you drinking?
You've been eating *chocolate* all night. You should have some *real* food.
But it's *so* good!
I discovered these chocolate bars last time I was here in America, and I can't seem to get enough of them...
Though, to be honest, I'm *always* eating something.
I'm just never *full,* I guess.

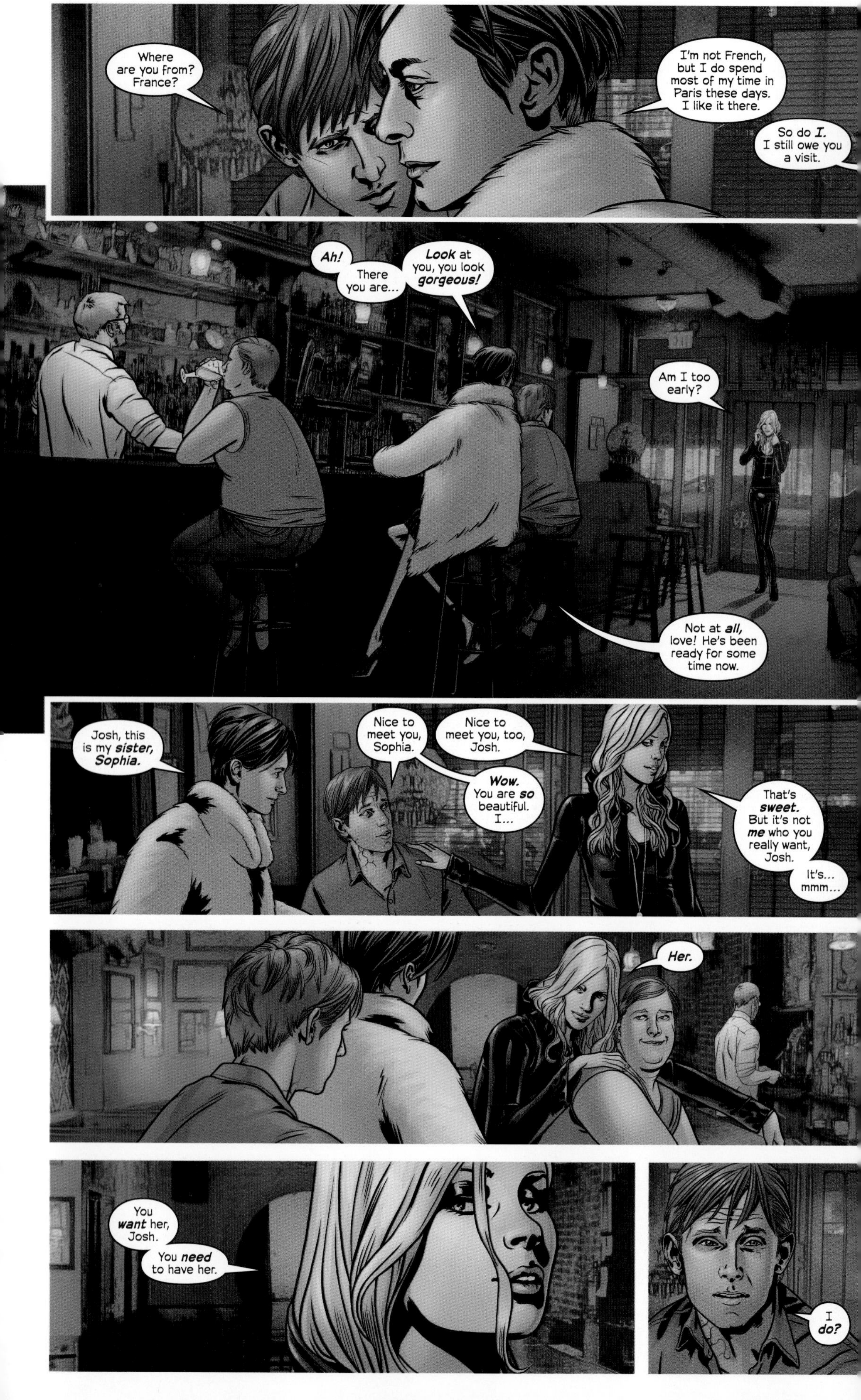
Where are you from? France?
I'm not French, but I do spend most of my time in Paris these days. I like it there.
So do *I.* I still owe you a visit.
Ah! There you are...
Look at you, you look *gorgeous!*
Am I too early?
Not at *all,* love! He's been ready for some time now.
Josh, this is my *sister, Sophia.*
Nice to meet you, Sophia.
Nice to meet you, too, Josh.
Wow. You are *so* beautiful. I...
That's *sweet.* But it's not *me* who you really want, Josh.
It's... mmm...
Her.
You *want* her, Josh.
You *need* to have her.
I *do?*

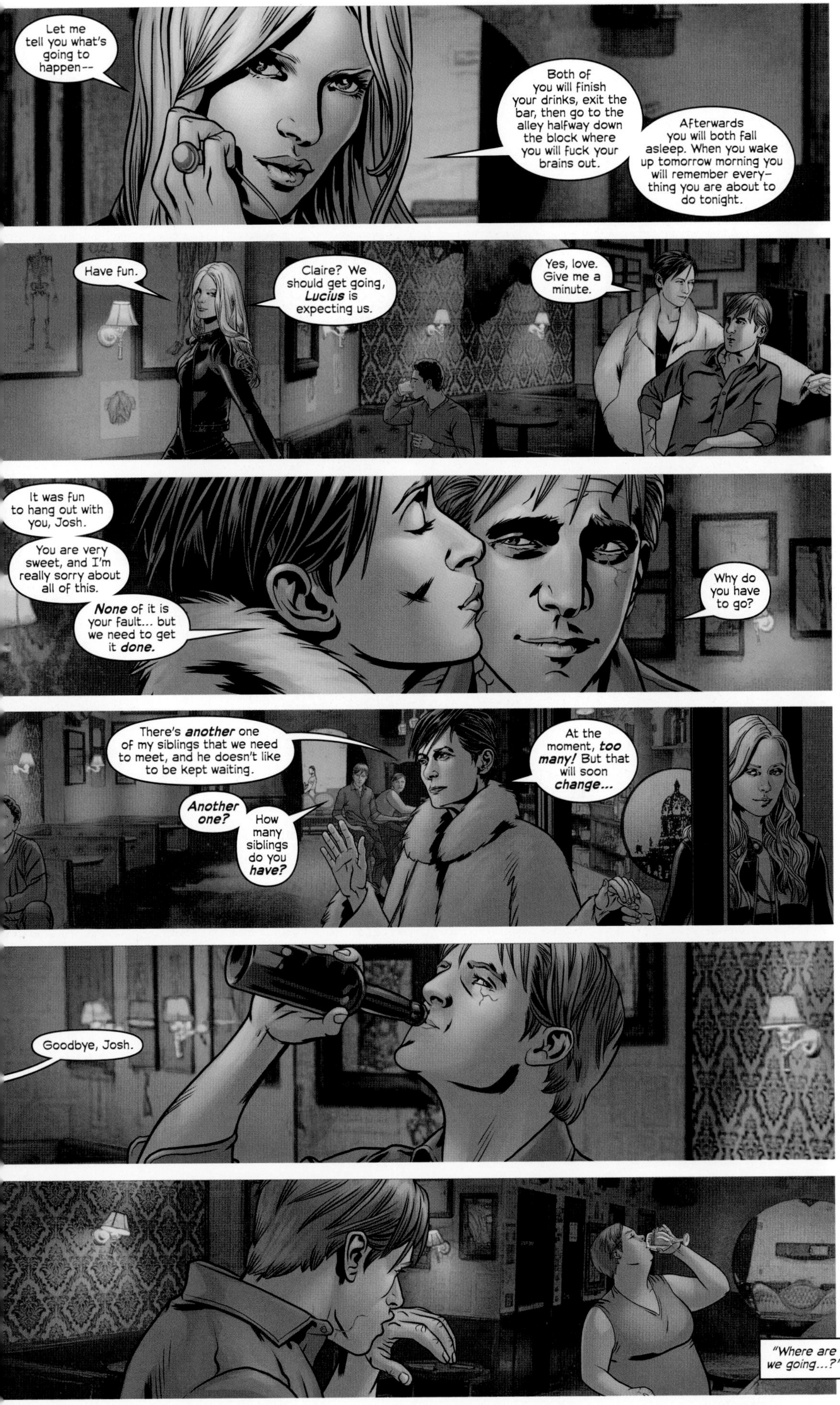
Let me tell you what's going to happen--
Both of you will finish your drinks, exit the bar, then go to the alley halfway down the block where you will fuck your brains out.
Afterwards you will both fall asleep. When you wake up tomorrow morning you will remember everything you are about to do tonight.
Have fun.
Claire? We should get going, *Lucius* is expecting us.
Yes, love. Give me a minute.
It was fun to hang out with you, Josh.
You are very sweet, and I'm really sorry about all of this.
None of it is your fault... but we need to get it *done.*
Why do you have to go?
There's *another* one of my siblings that we need to meet, and he doesn't like to be kept waiting.
Another one?
How many siblings do you *have?*
At the moment, *too many!* But that will soon *change...*
Goodbye, Josh.
"Where are we going...?"

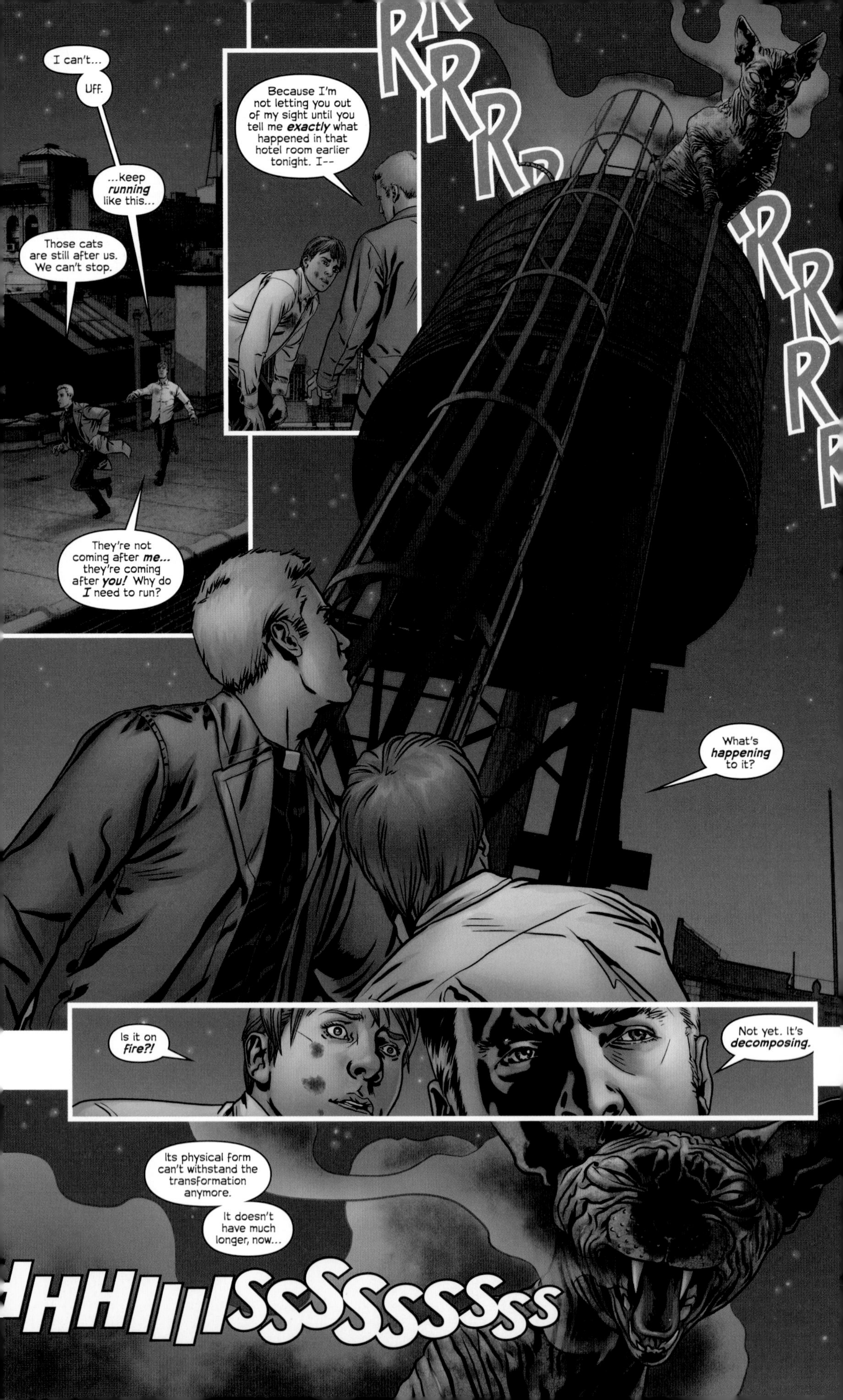

I can't...
UFF.
...keep *running* like this...
Those cats are still after us. We can't stop.
They're not coming after *me...* they're coming after *you!* Why do *I* need to run?
Because I'm not letting you out of my sight until you tell me *exactly* what happened in that hotel room earlier tonight. I--
RRRRR
RRRRR
What's *happening* to it?
Is it on *fire?!*
Not yet. It's *decomposing.*
Its physical form can't withstand the transformation anymore.
It doesn't have much longer, now...
HHIIIISSSSSSSss

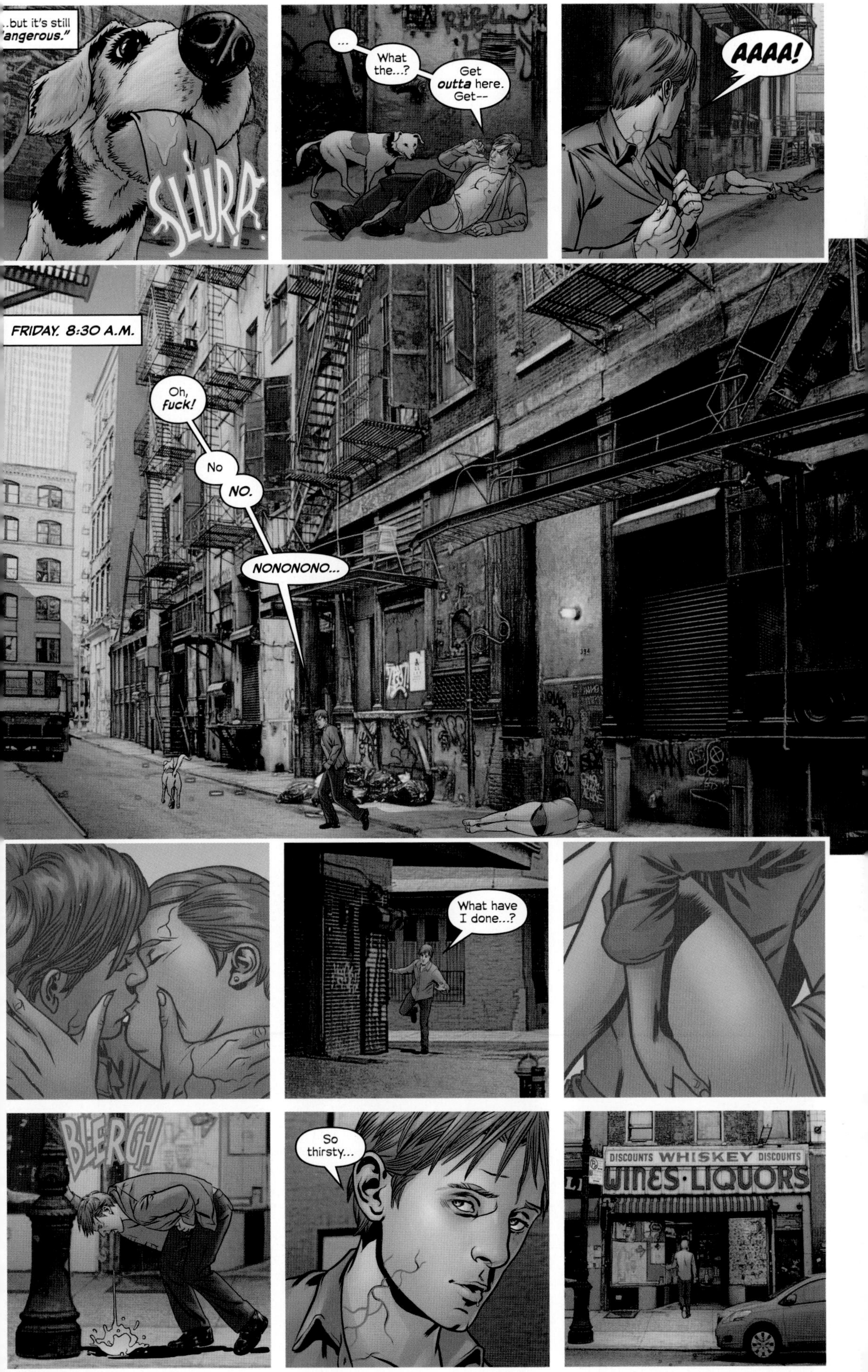
..but it's still
"angerous."
SLURP
...
What
the...?
Get
outta here.
Get--
AAAA!
FRIDAY. 8:30 A.M.
Oh,
fuck!
No
NO.
NONONONO...
What have
I done...?
BLERGH
So
thirsty...
DISCOUNTS WHISKEY DISCOUNTS
WINES·LIQUORS

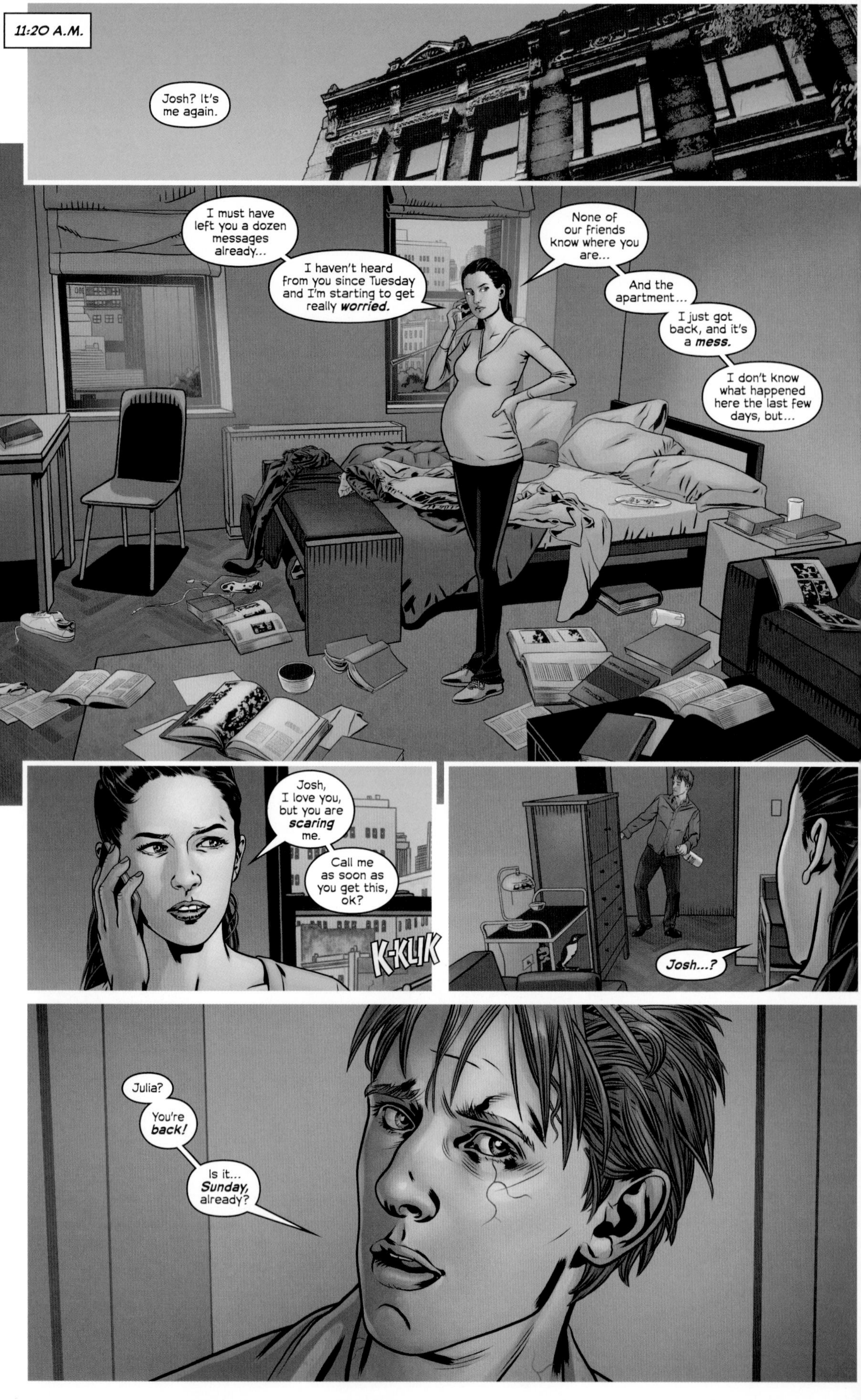
11:20 A.M.
Josh? It's me again.
I must have left you a dozen messages already...
I haven't heard from you since Tuesday and I'm starting to get really *worried.*
None of our friends know where you are...
And the apartment...
I just got back, and it's a *mess.*
I don't know what happened here the last few days, but...
Josh, I love you, but you are *scaring* me.
Call me as soon as you get this, ok?
K-KLIK
Josh...?
Julia?
You're *back!*
Is it... *Sunday,* already?

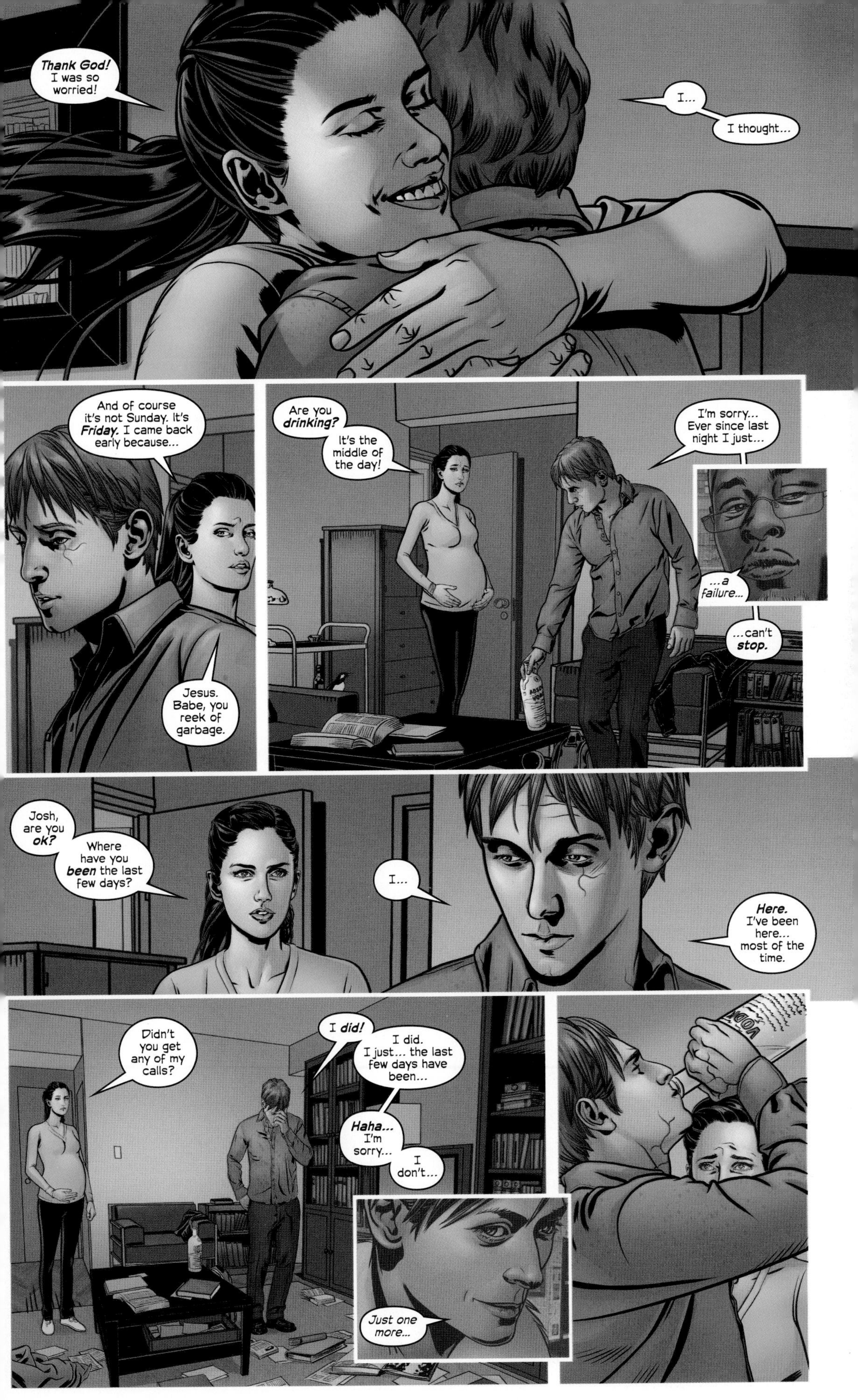

Thank God! I was so worried!
I...
I thought...
And of course it's not Sunday. It's Friday. I came back early because...
Jesus. Babe, you reek of garbage.
Are you drinking? It's the middle of the day!
I'm sorry... Ever since last night I just...
...a failure...
...can't stop.
Josh, are you ok?
Where have you been the last few days?
I...
Here. I've been here... most of the time.
Didn't you get any of my calls?
I did!
I did. I just... the last few days have been...
Haha... I'm sorry...
I don't...
Just one more...

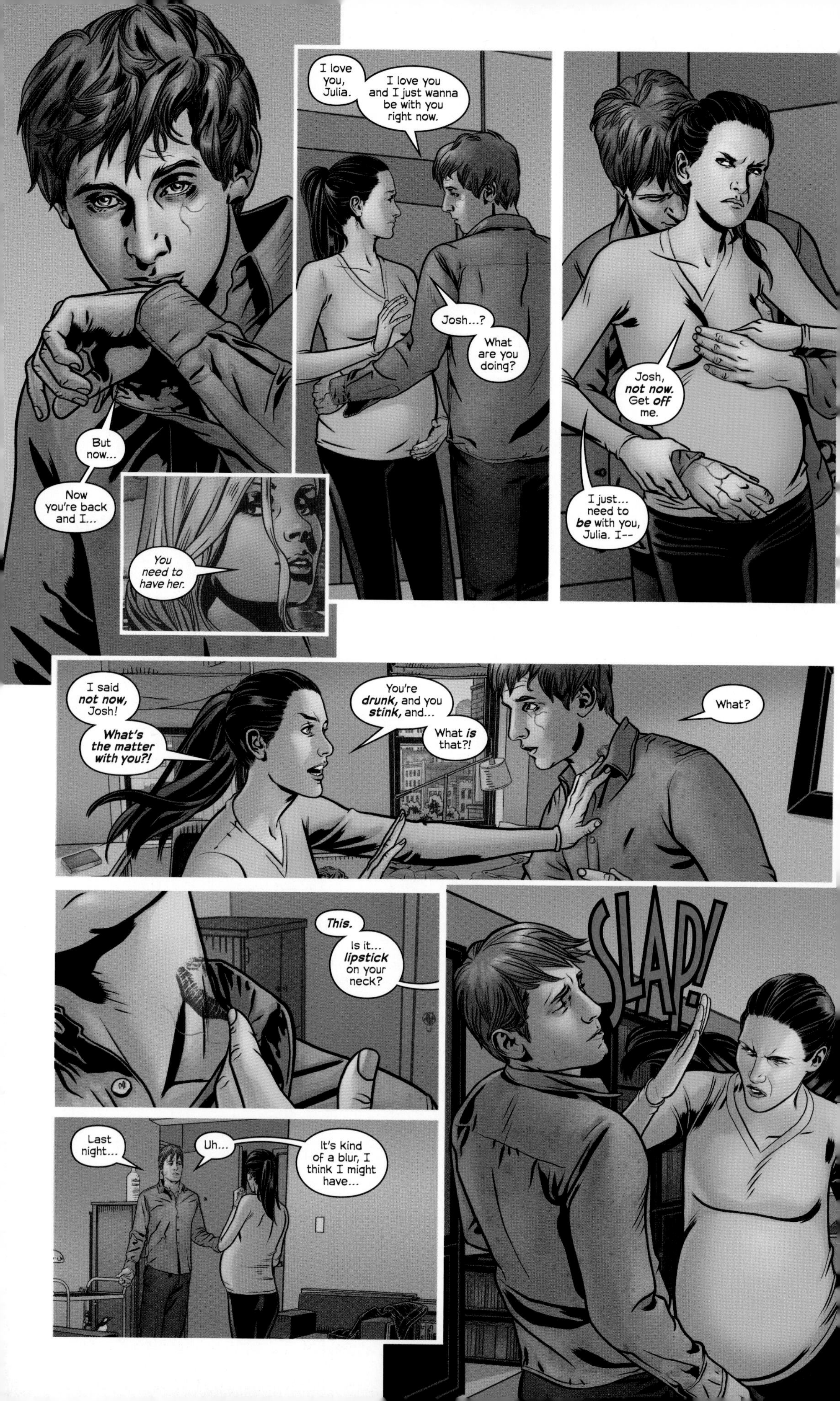
But now...
Now you're back and I...
You need to have her.
I love you, Julia.
I love you and I just wanna be with you right now.
Josh...?
What are you doing?
Josh, not now. Get off me.
I just... need to be with you, Julia. I--
I said not now, Josh!
What's the matter with you?!
You're drunk, and you stink, and...
What is that?!
What?
This.
Is it... lipstick on your neck?
Last night...
Uh...
It's kind of a blur, I think I might have...
SLAP!

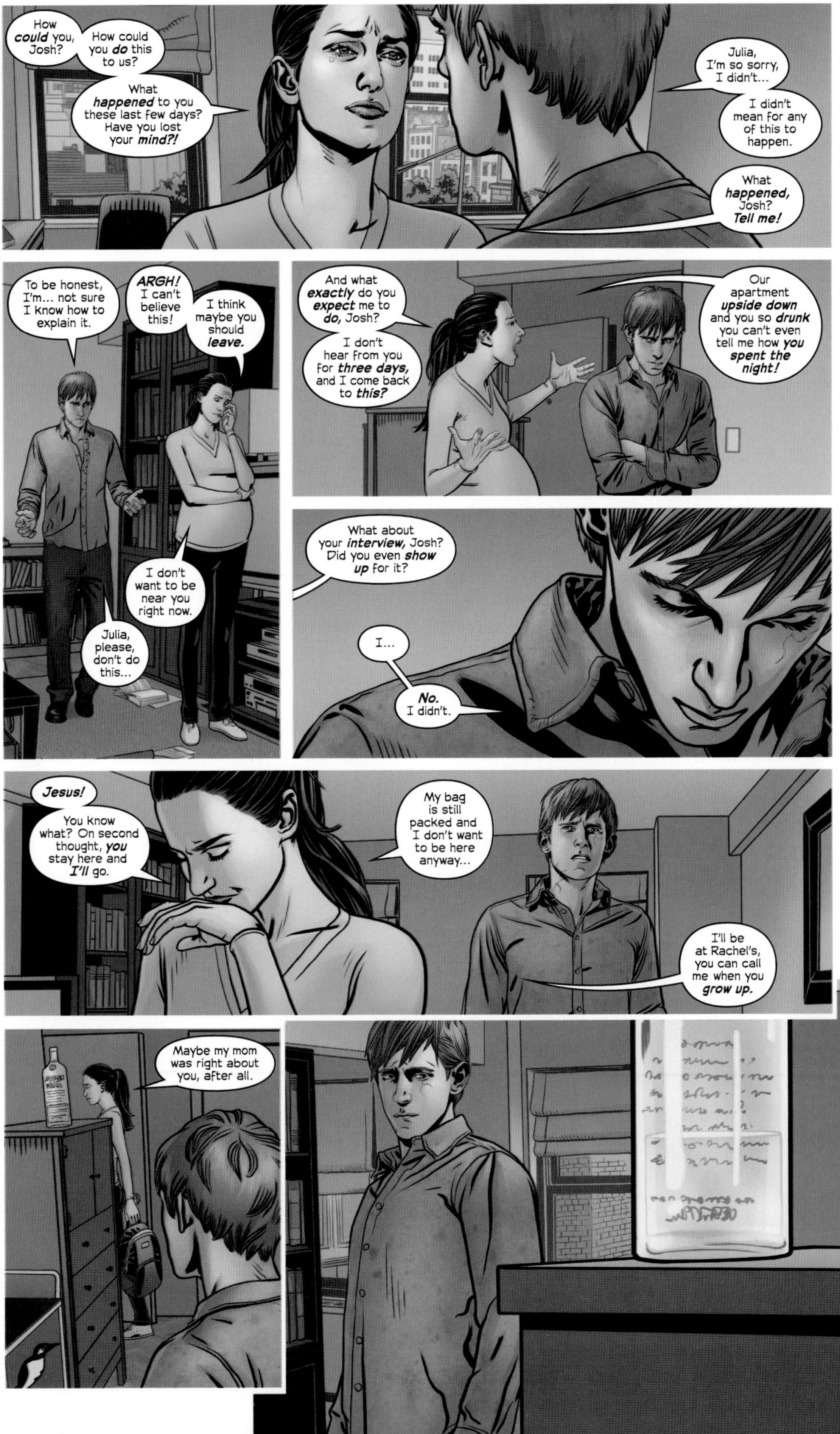
How could you, Josh?
How could you do this to us?
What happened to you these last few days? Have you lost your mind?!
Julia, I'm so sorry, I didn't...
I didn't mean for any of this to happen.
What happened, Josh? Tell me!
To be honest, I'm... not sure I know how to explain it.
ARGH! I can't believe this!
I think maybe you should leave.
I don't want to be near you right now.
Julia, please, don't do this...
And what exactly do you expect me to do, Josh?
I don't hear from you for three days, and I come back to this?
Our apartment upside down and you so drunk you can't even tell me how you spent the night!
What about your interview, Josh? Did you even show up for it?
I...
No. I didn't.
Jesus!
You know what? On second thought, you stay here and I'll go.
My bag is still packed and I don't want to be here anyway...
I'll be at Rachel's, you can call me when you grow up.
Maybe my mom was right about you, after all.

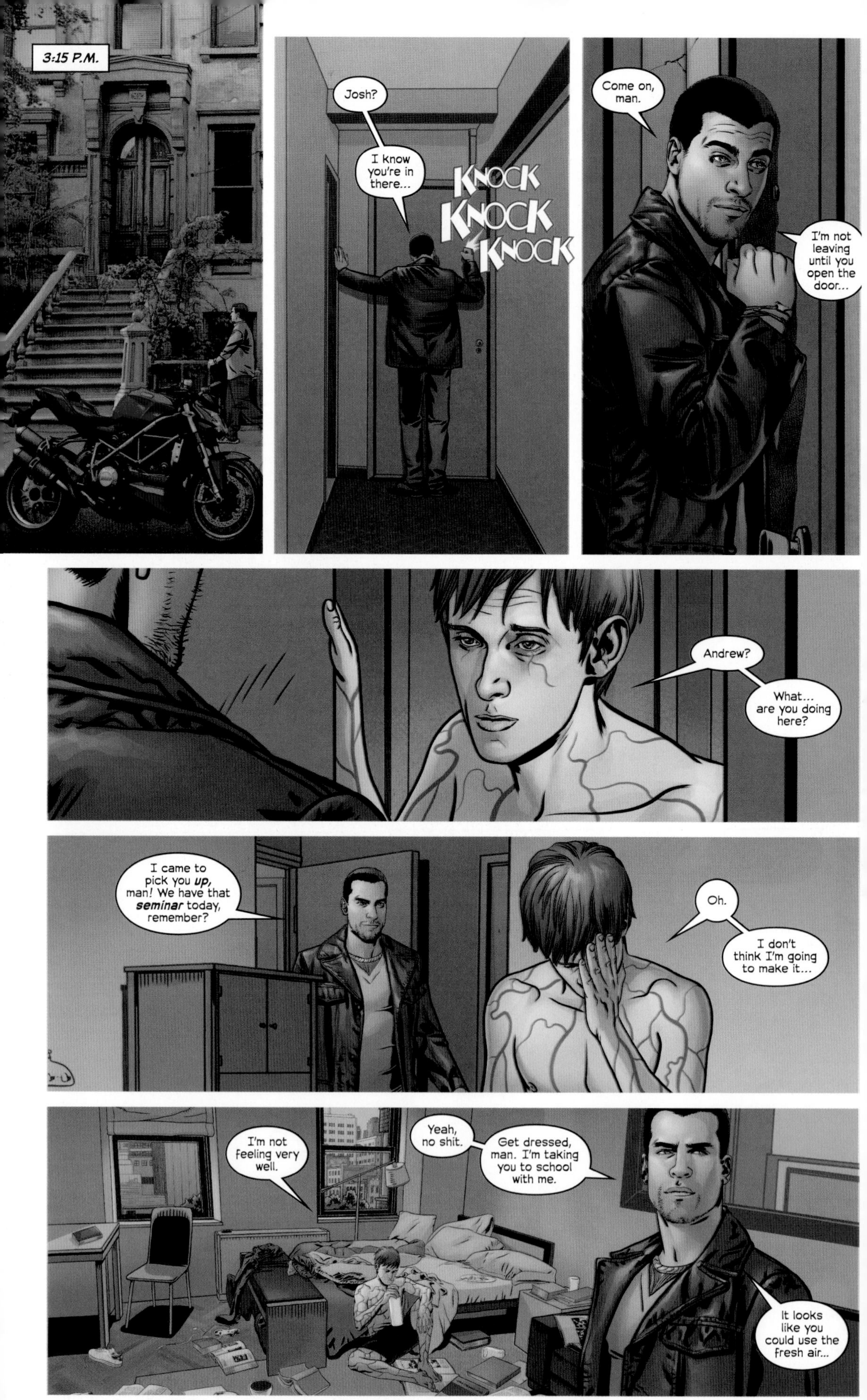
3:15 P.M.
Josh?
I know you're in there...
KNOCK
KNOCK
KNOCK
Come on, man.
I'm not leaving until you open the door...
Andrew?
What... are you doing here?
I came to pick you *up*, man! We have that *seminar* today, remember?
Oh.
I don't think I'm going to make it...
I'm not feeling very well.
Yeah, no shit.
Get dressed, man. I'm taking you to school with me.
It looks like you could use the fresh air...

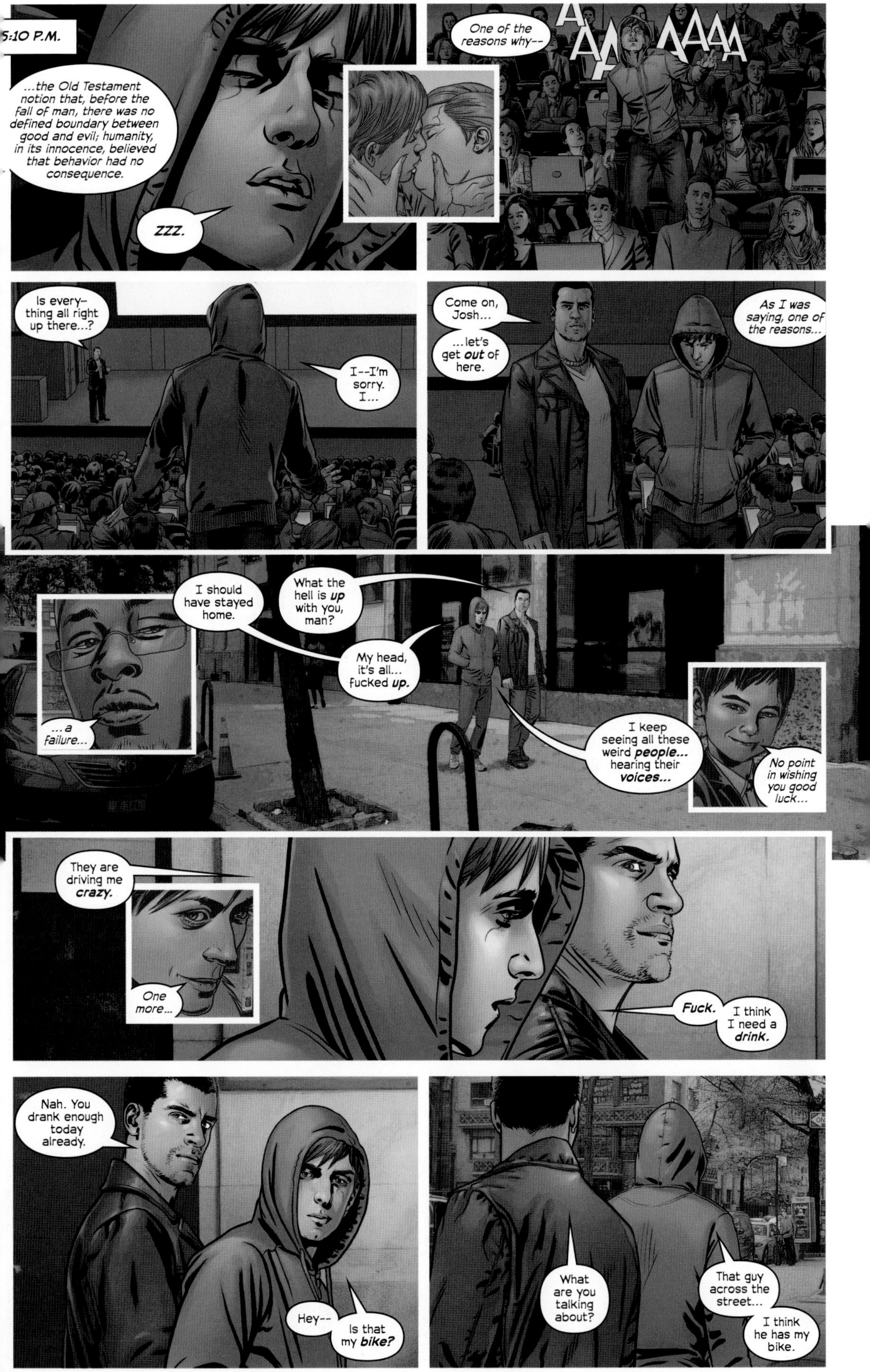
5:10 P.M.
...the Old Testament notion that, before the fall of man, there was no defined boundary between good and evil; humanity, in its innocence, believed that behavior had no consequence.
ZZZ.
One of the reasons why--
AAAAAAA
Is every-thing all right up there...?
I--I'm sorry. I...
Come on, Josh...
...let's get out of here.
As I was saying, one of the reasons...
I should have stayed home.
...a failure...
What the hell is up with you, man?
My head, it's all... fucked up.
I keep seeing all these weird people... hearing their voices...
No point in wishing you good luck...
They are driving me crazy.
One more...
Fuck.
I think I need a drink.
Nah. You drank enough today already.
Hey--
Is that my bike?
What are you talking about?
That guy across the street...
I think he has my bike.

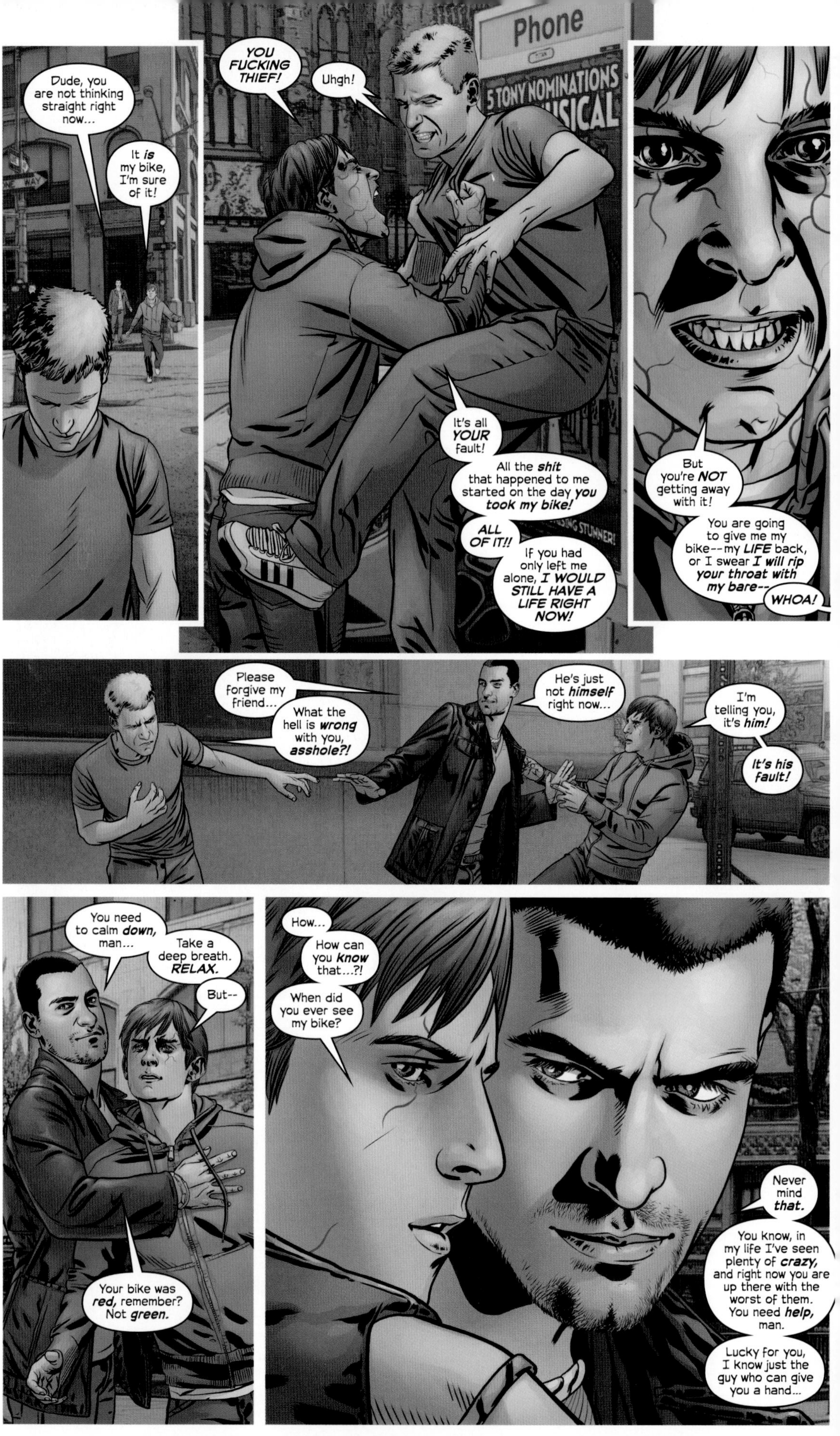
Dude, you are not thinking straight right now...
It *is* my bike, I'm sure of it!
ONE WAY
YOU FUCKING THIEF!
Uhgh!
Phone
5 TONY NOMINATIONS
MUSICAL
It's all YOUR fault!
All the *shit* that happened to me started on the day *you took my bike!*
ALL OF IT!!
If you had only left me alone, I WOULD STILL HAVE A LIFE RIGHT NOW!
But you're NOT getting away with it!
You are going to give me my bike--my *LIFE* back, or I swear *I will rip your throat with my bare--*
WHOA!
Please forgive my friend...
What the hell is *wrong* with you, *asshole?!*
He's just not *himself* right now...
I'm telling you, it's *him!*
It's his fault!
You need to calm *down,* man...
Take a deep breath. *RELAX.*
But--
Your bike was *red,* remember? Not *green.*
How...
How can you *know* that...?!
When did you ever see my bike?
Never mind *that.*
You know, in my life I've seen plenty of *crazy,* and right now you are up there with the worst of them. You need *help,* man.
Lucky for you, I know just the guy who can give you a hand...

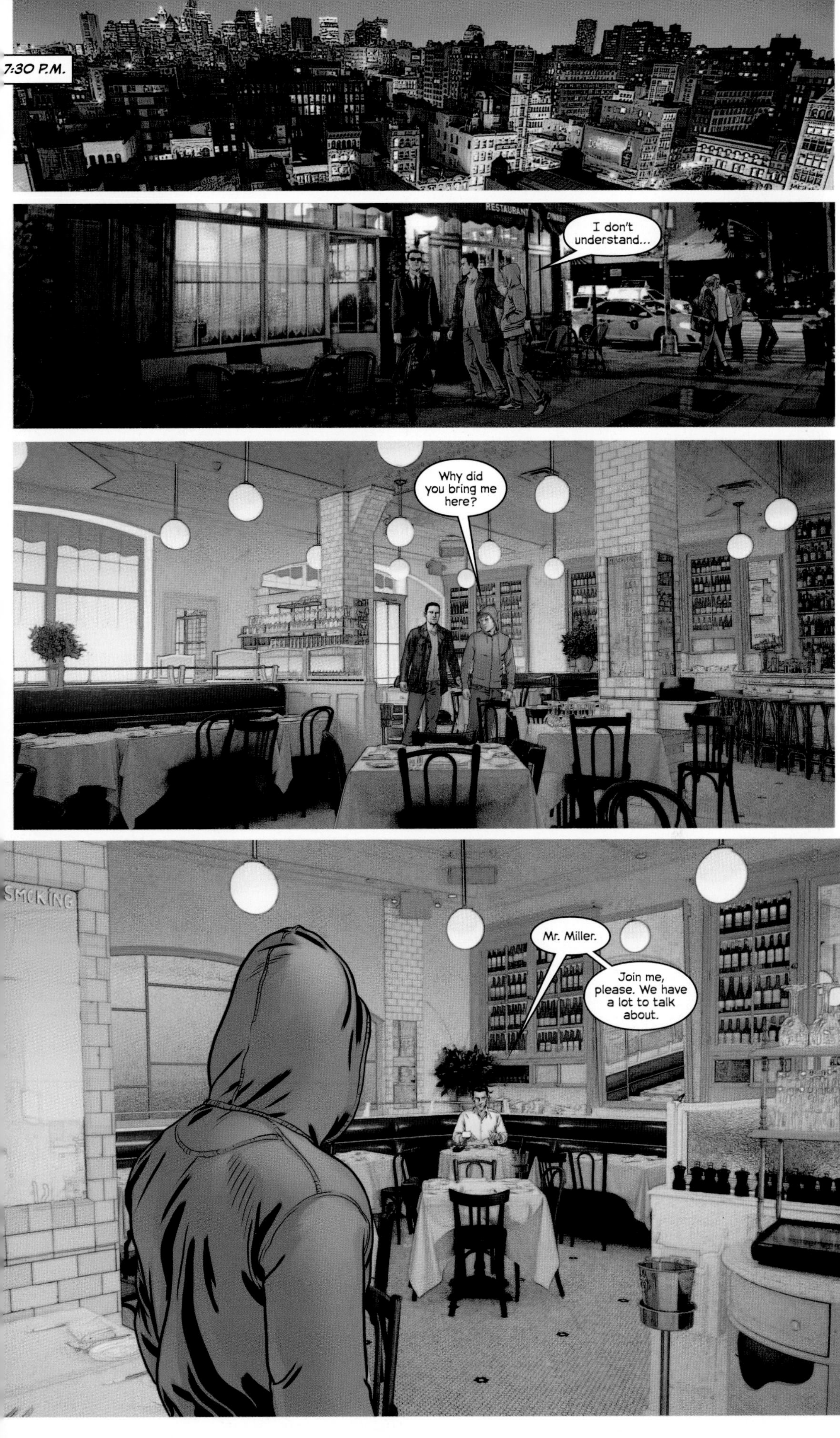
7:30 P.M.
RESTAURANT
I don't understand...
Why did you bring me here?
Mr. Miller.
Join me, please. We have a lot to talk about.

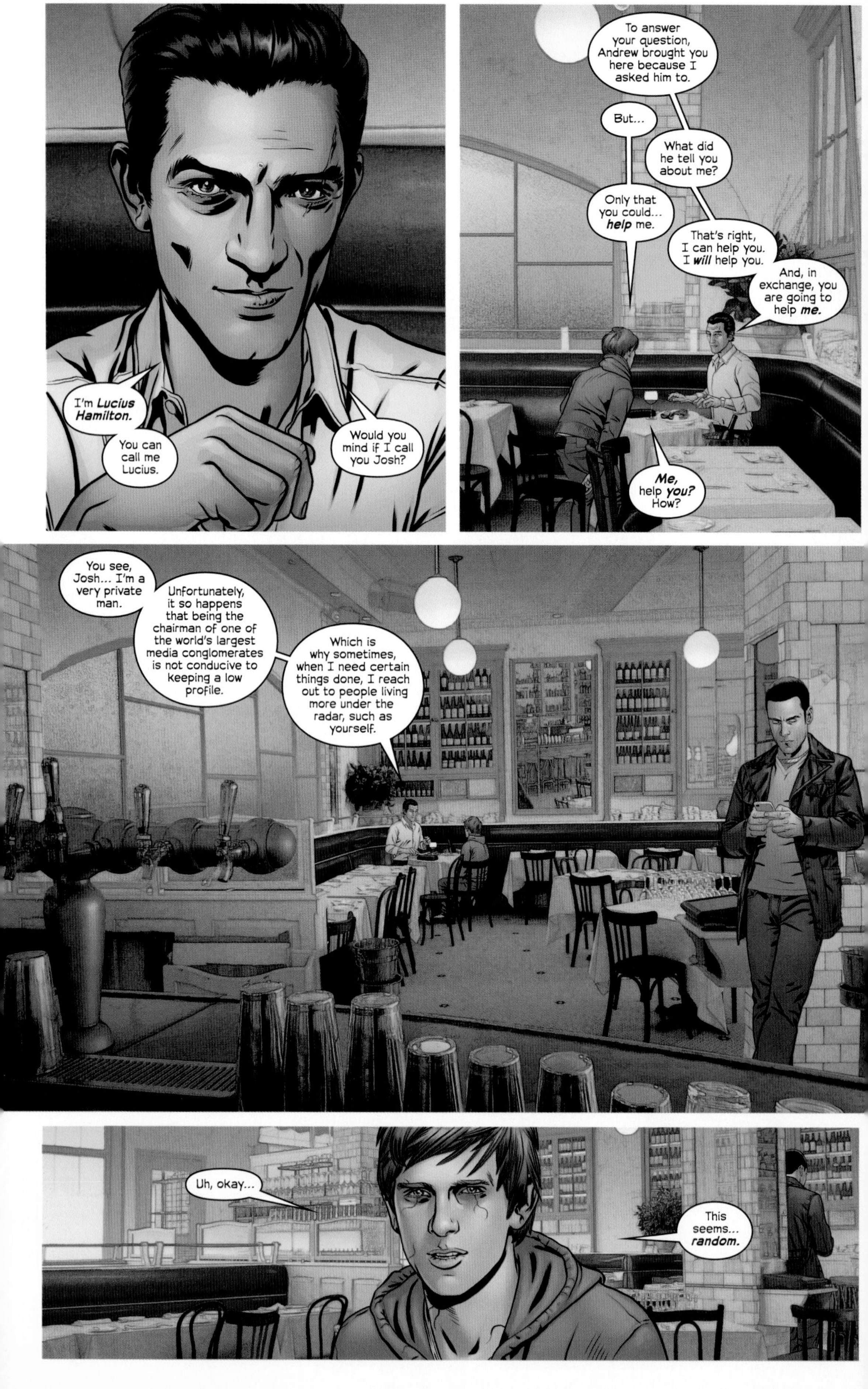

I'm *Lucius Hamilton.*
You can call me Lucius.
Would you mind if I call you Josh?
To answer your question, Andrew brought you here because I asked him to.
But...
What did he tell you about me?
Only that you could... *help* me.
That's right, I can help you. I *will* help you.
And, in exchange, you are going to help *me.*
Me, help *you?* How?
You see, Josh... I'm a very private man.
Unfortunately, it so happens that being the chairman of one of the world's largest media conglomerates is not conducive to keeping a low profile.
Which is why sometimes, when I need certain things done, I reach out to people living more under the radar, such as yourself.
Uh, okay...
This seems... *random.*

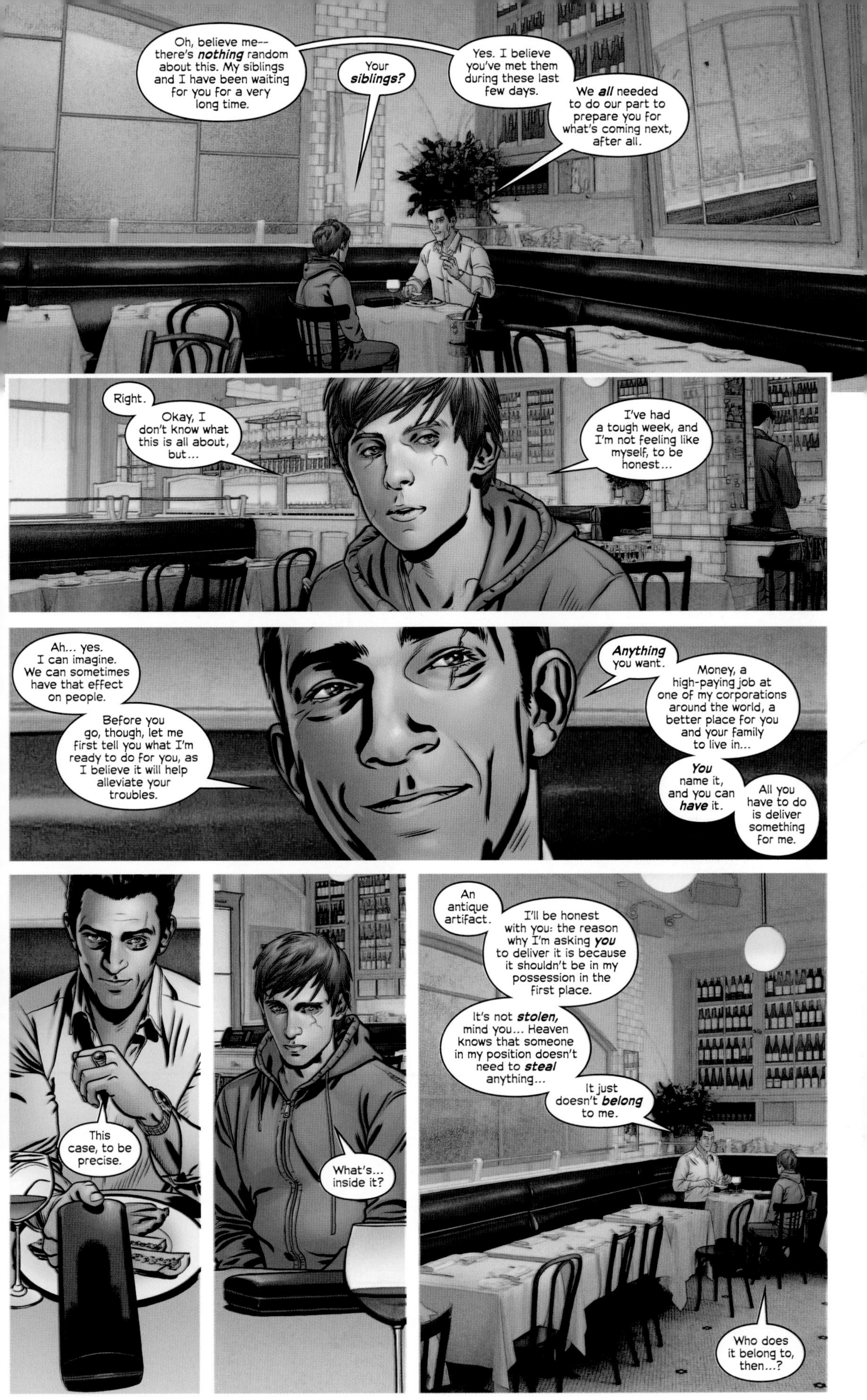
Oh, believe me-- there's ***nothing*** random about this. My siblings and I have been waiting for you for a very long time.
Your ***siblings?***
Yes. I believe you've met them during these last few days.
We ***all*** needed to do our part to prepare you for what's coming next, after all.
Right.
Okay, I don't know what this is all about, but...
I've had a tough week, and I'm not feeling like myself, to be honest...
Ah... yes. I can imagine. We can sometimes have that effect on people.
Before you go, though, let me first tell you what I'm ready to do for you, as I believe it will help alleviate your troubles.
Anything you want.
Money, a high-paying job at one of my corporations around the world, a better place for you and your family to live in...
You name it, and you can ***have*** it.
All you have to do is deliver something for me.
This case, to be precise.
What's... inside it?
An antique artifact.
I'll be honest with you: the reason why I'm asking ***you*** to deliver it is because it shouldn't be in my possession in the first place.
It's not ***stolen,*** mind you... Heaven knows that someone in my position doesn't need to ***steal*** anything...
It just doesn't ***belong*** to me.
Who does it belong to, then...?

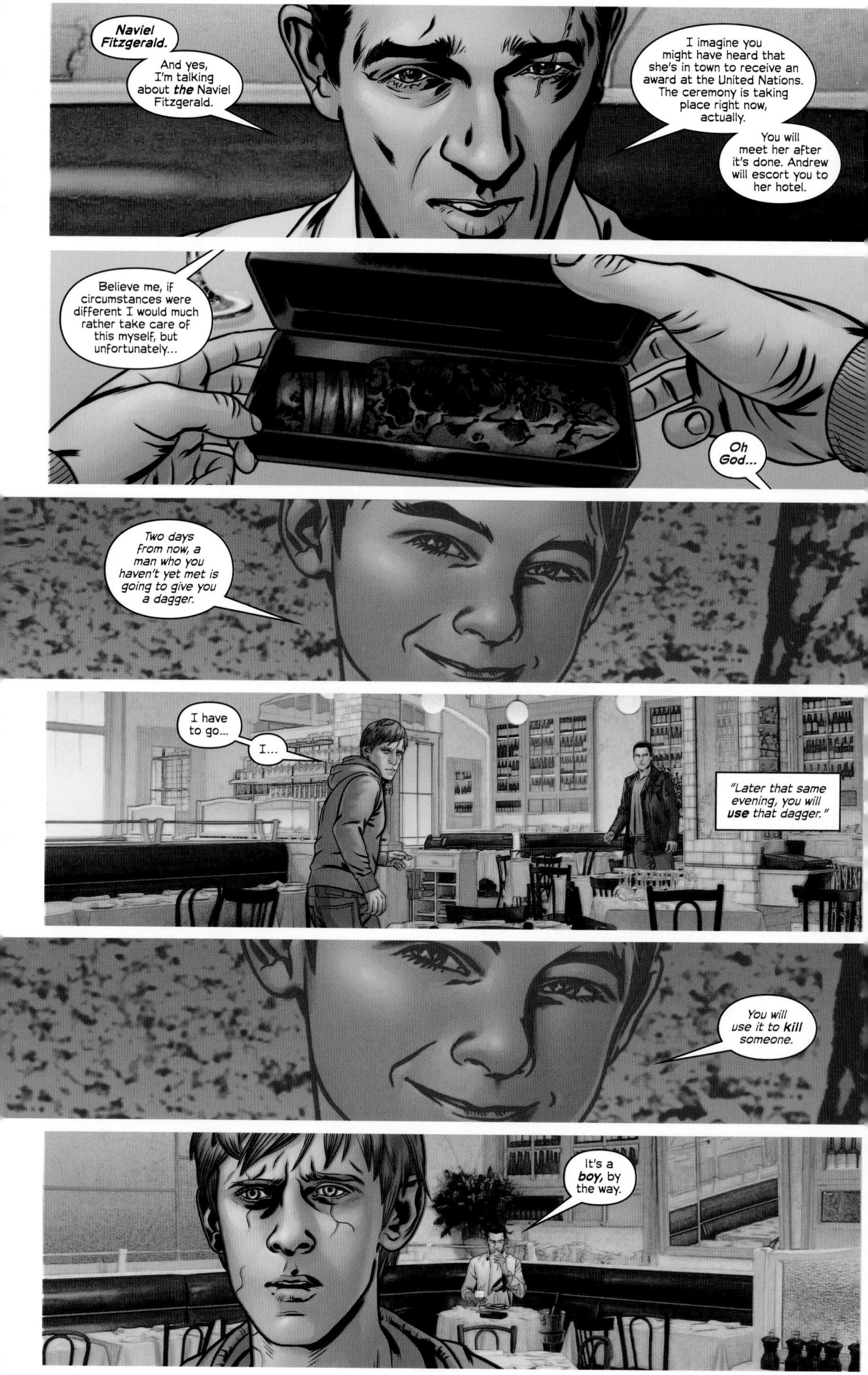

Naviel Fitzgerald.
And yes, I'm talking about the Naviel Fitzgerald.
I imagine you might have heard that she's in town to receive an award at the United Nations. The ceremony is taking place right now, actually.
You will meet her after it's done. Andrew will escort you to her hotel.
Believe me, if circumstances were different I would much rather take care of this myself, but unfortunately...
Oh God...
Two days from now, a man who you haven't yet met is going to give you a dagger.
I have to go...
I...
"Later that same evening, you will use that dagger."
You will use it to kill someone.
It's a boy, by the way.

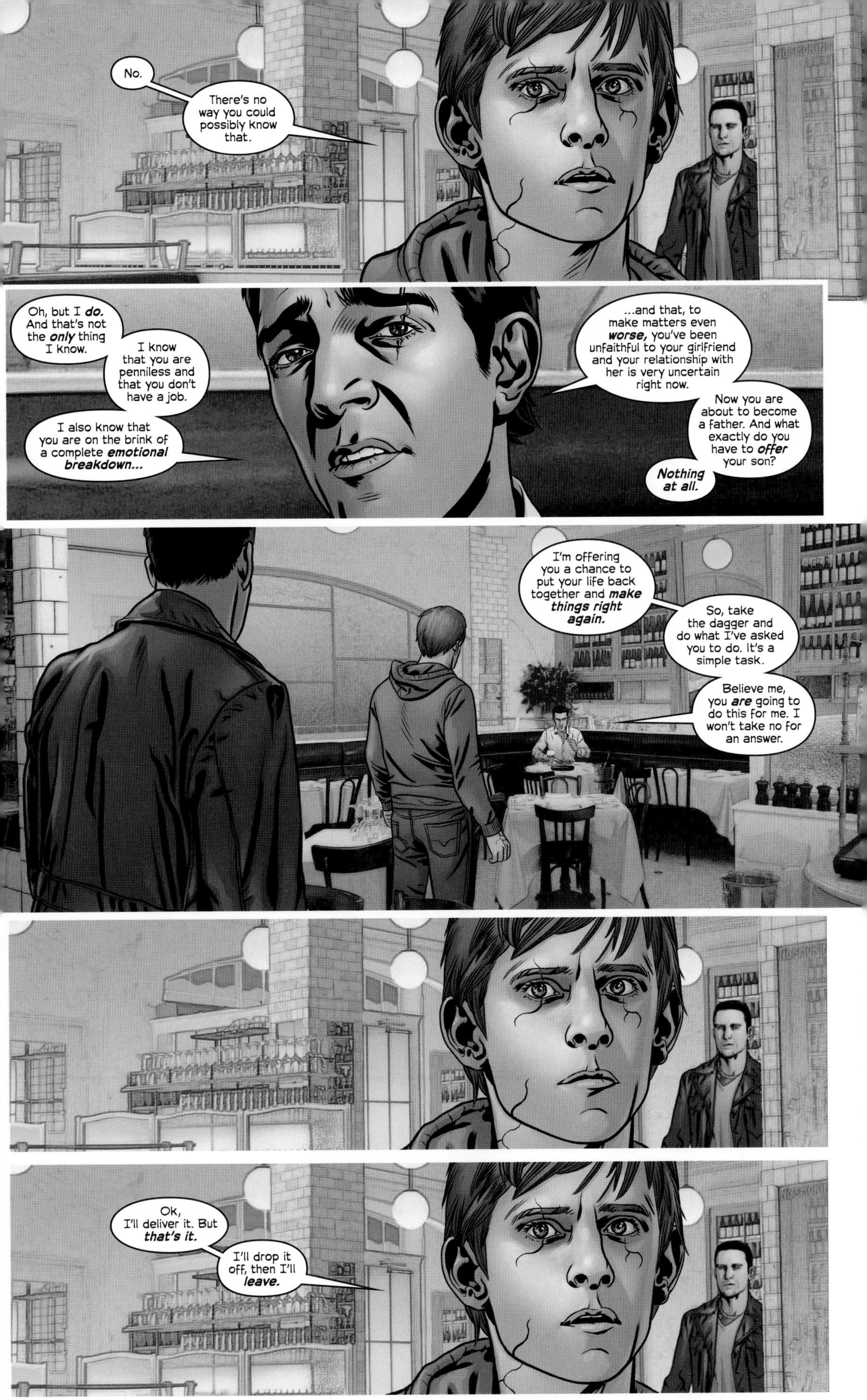
No.
There's no way you could possibly know that.
Oh, but I *do.* And that's not the *only* thing I know.
I know that you are penniless and that you don't have a job.
I also know that you are on the brink of a complete *emotional breakdown...*
...and that, to make matters even *worse,* you've been unfaithful to your girlfriend and your relationship with her is very uncertain right now.
Now you are about to become a father. And what exactly do you have to *offer* your son?
Nothing at all.
I'm offering you a chance to put your life back together and *make things right again.*
So, take the dagger and do what I've asked you to do. It's a simple task.
Believe me, you *are* going to do this for me. I won't take no for an answer.
Ok, I'll deliver it. But *that's it.*
I'll drop it off, then I'll *leave.*

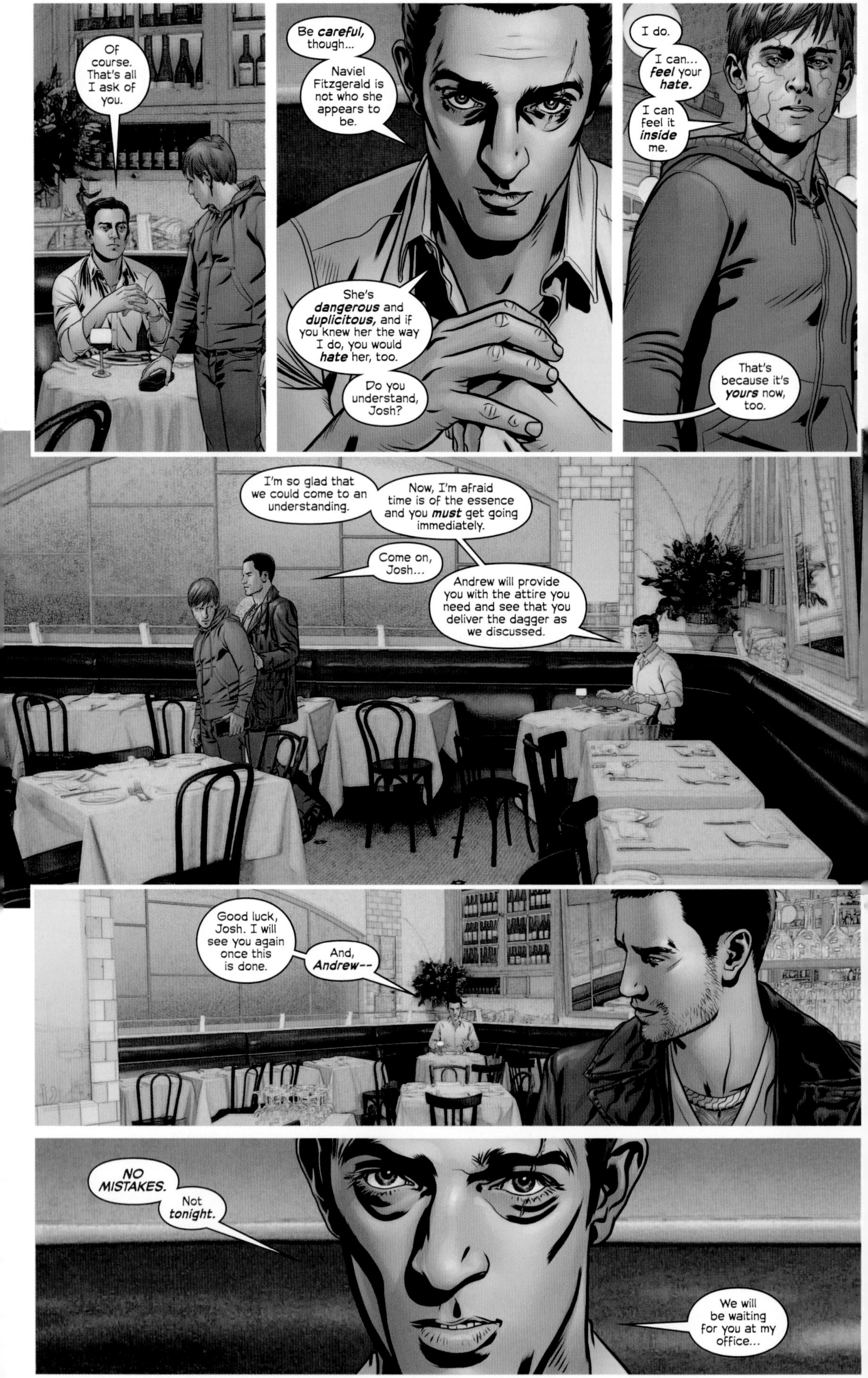
Of course. That's all I ask of you.
Be *careful,* though...
Naviel Fitzgerald is not who she appears to be.
She's *dangerous* and *duplicitous,* and if you knew her the way I do, you would *hate* her, too.
Do you understand, Josh?
I do.
I can... *feel* your *hate.*
I can feel it *inside* me.
That's because it's *yours* now, too.
I'm so glad that we could come to an understanding.
Now, I'm afraid time is of the essence and you *must* get going immediately.
Come on, Josh...
Andrew will provide you with the attire you need and see that you deliver the dagger as we discussed.
Good luck, Josh. I will see you again once this is done.
And, *Andrew--*
NO MISTAKES.
Not *tonight.*
We will be waiting for you at my office...

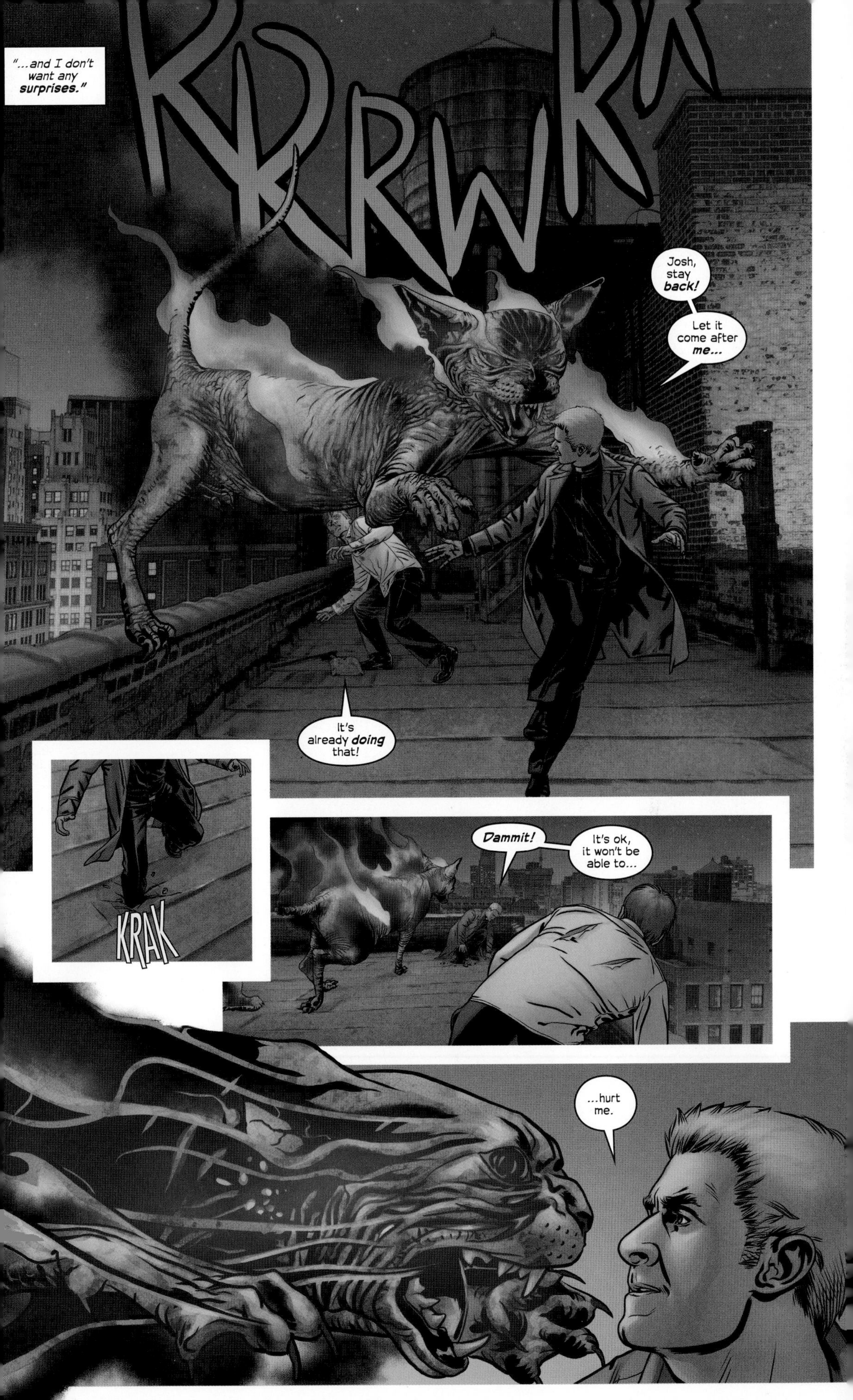
"...and I don't want any surprises."
KRRWKRA
Josh, stay back!
Let it come after me...
It's already doing that!
KRAK
Dammit!
It's ok, it won't be able to...
...hurt me.

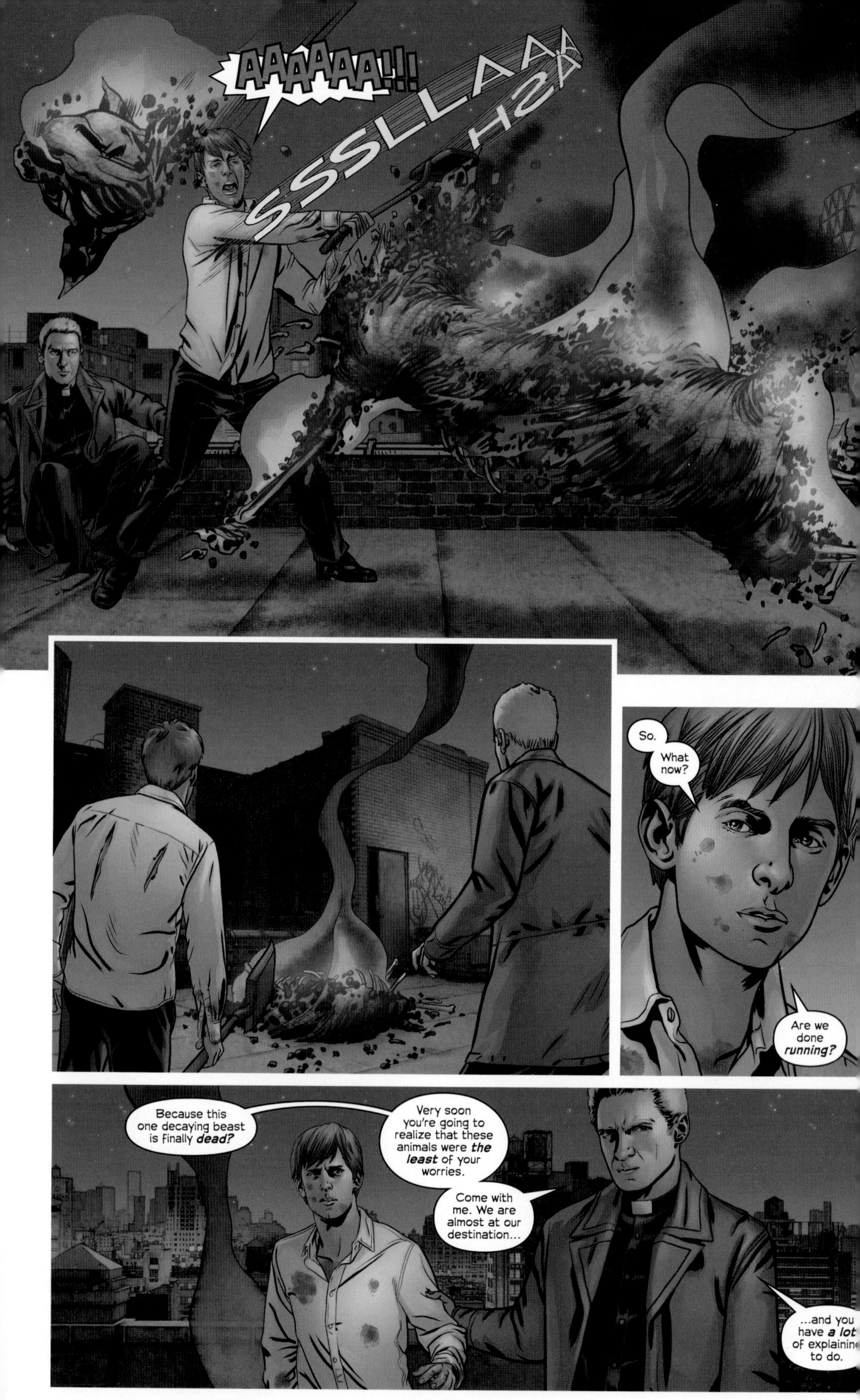
AAAAAA!!!
SSSLLAAAASH
So.
What now?
Are we done *running?*
Because this one decaying beast is finally *dead?*
Very soon you're going to realize that these animals were *the least* of your worries.
Come with me. We are almost at our destination...
...and you have *a lot* of explaining to do.

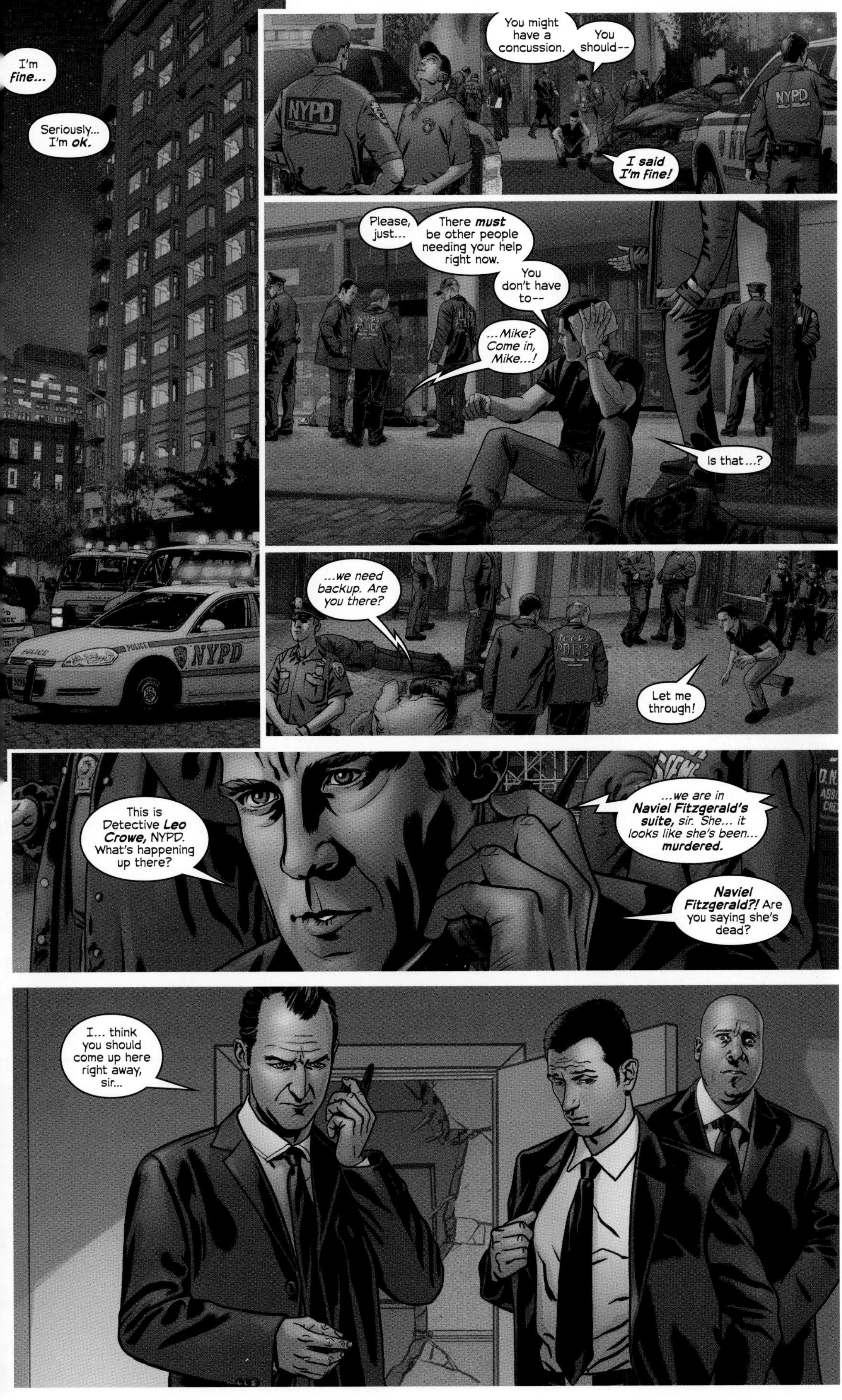
I'm *fine...*
Seriously... I'm **ok.**
You might have a concussion.
You should--
I said I'm fine!
Please, just...
There ***must*** be other people needing your help right now.
You don't have to--
...Mike? Come in, Mike...!
Is that...?
...we need backup. Are you there?
Let me through!
This is Detective ***Leo Crowe,*** NYPD. What's happening up there?
*...we are in **Naviel Fitzgerald's suite,** sir. She... it looks like she's been... **murdered.***
Naviel Fitzgerald?! Are you saying she's dead?
I... think you should come up here right away, sir...

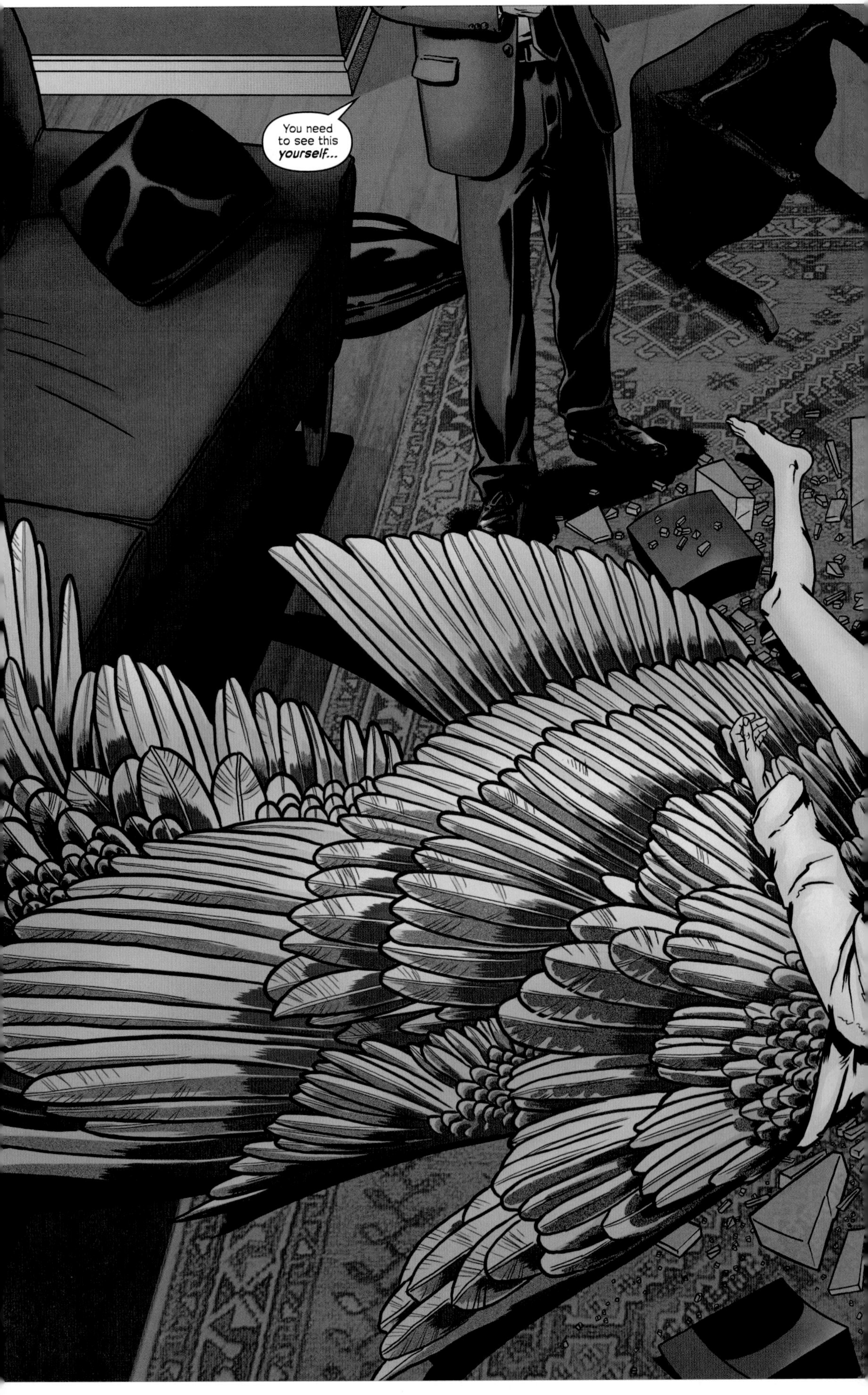
You need to see this *yourself*...

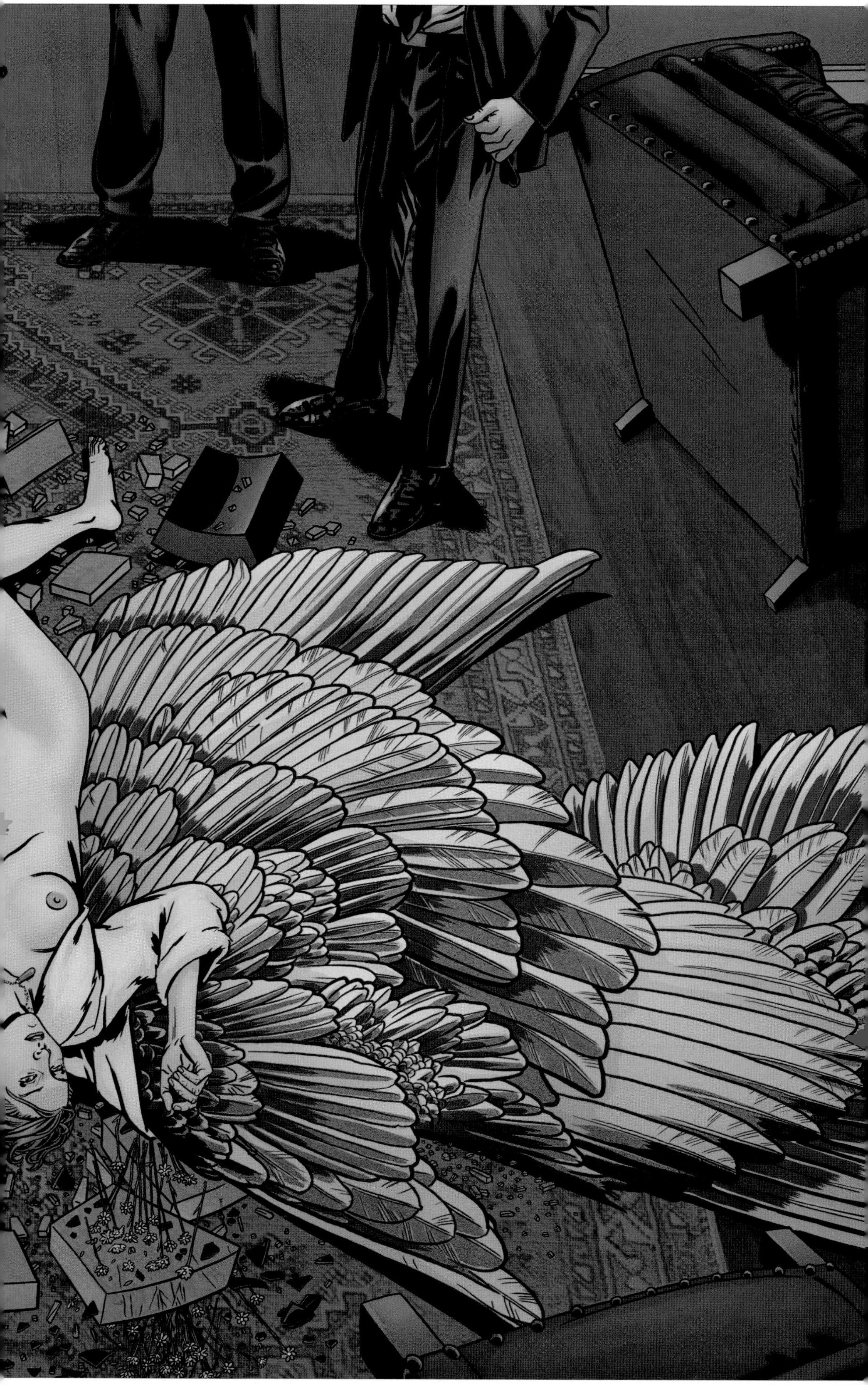

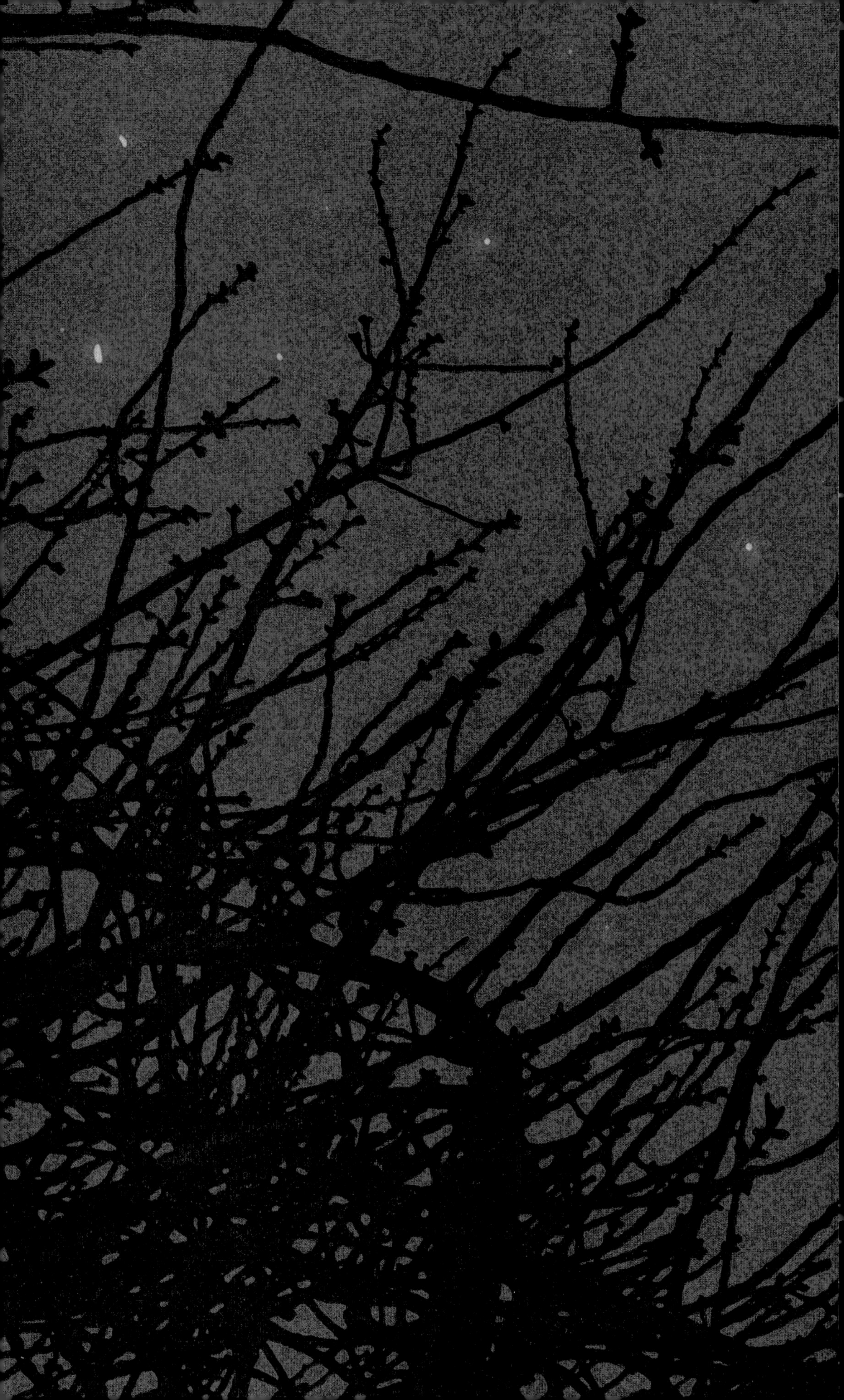

CHAPTER
TWO

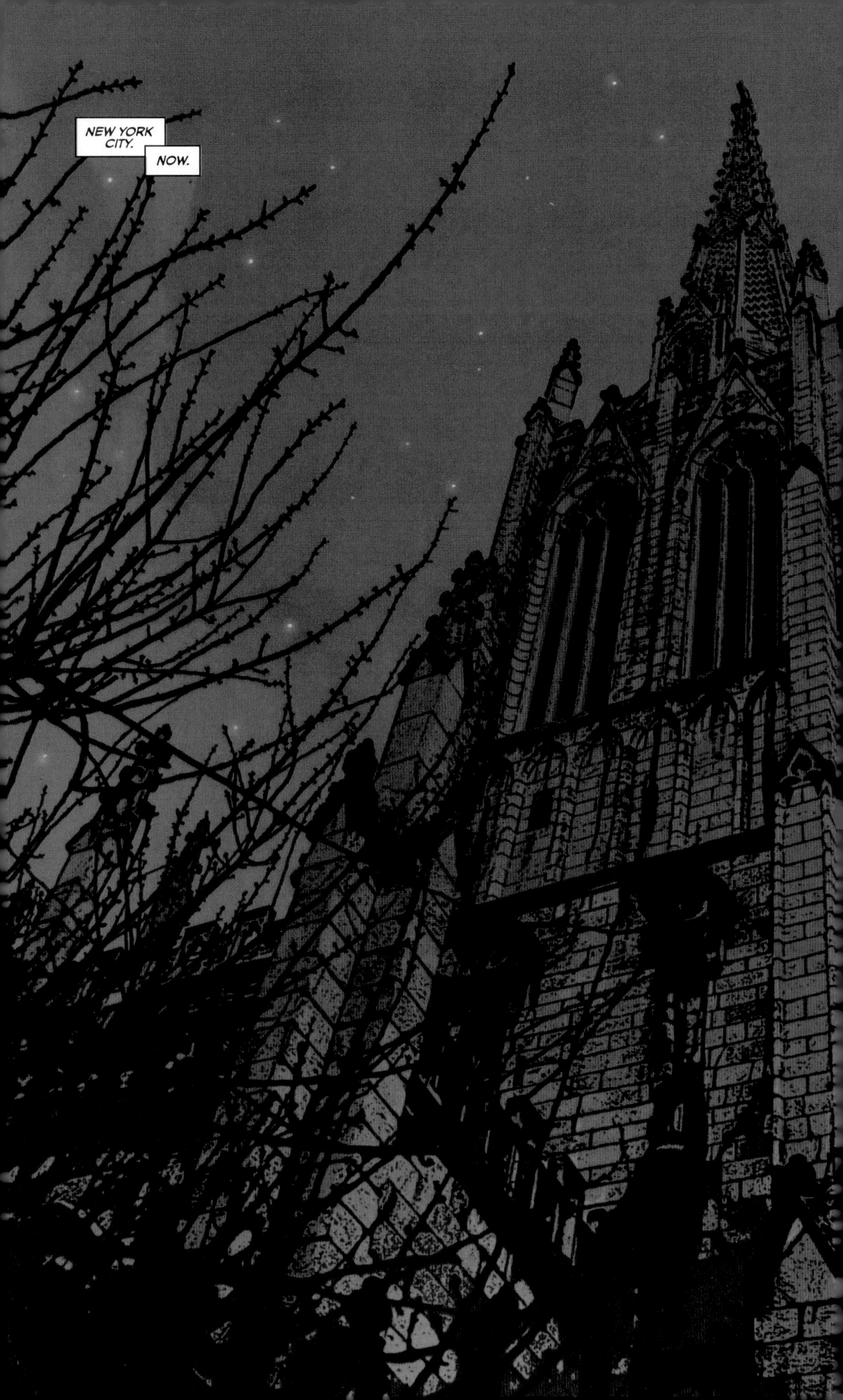
NEW YORK CITY.
NOW.

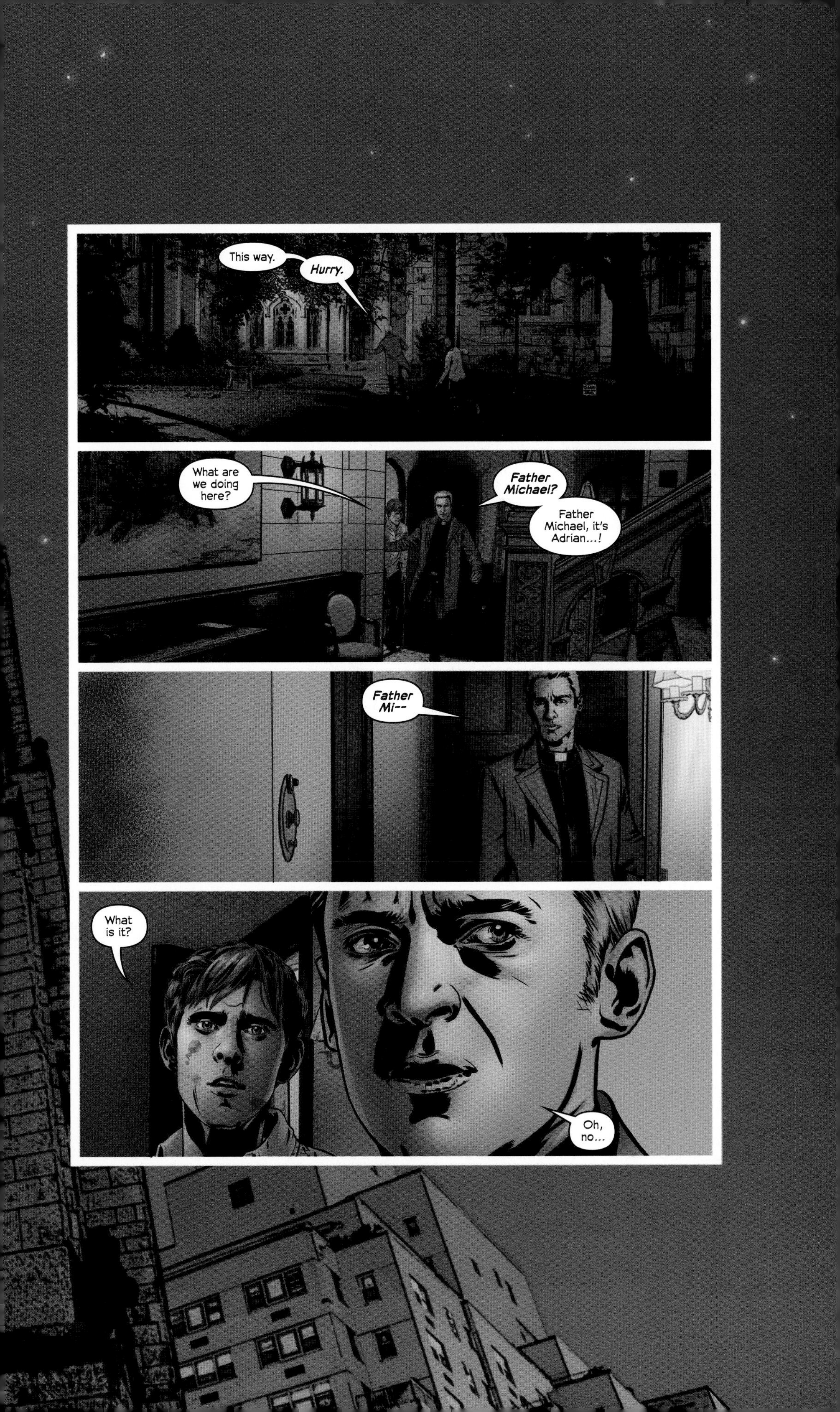
This way.
Hurry.
What are we doing here?
Father Michael?
Father Michael, it's Adrian...!
Father Mi--
What is it?
Oh, no...

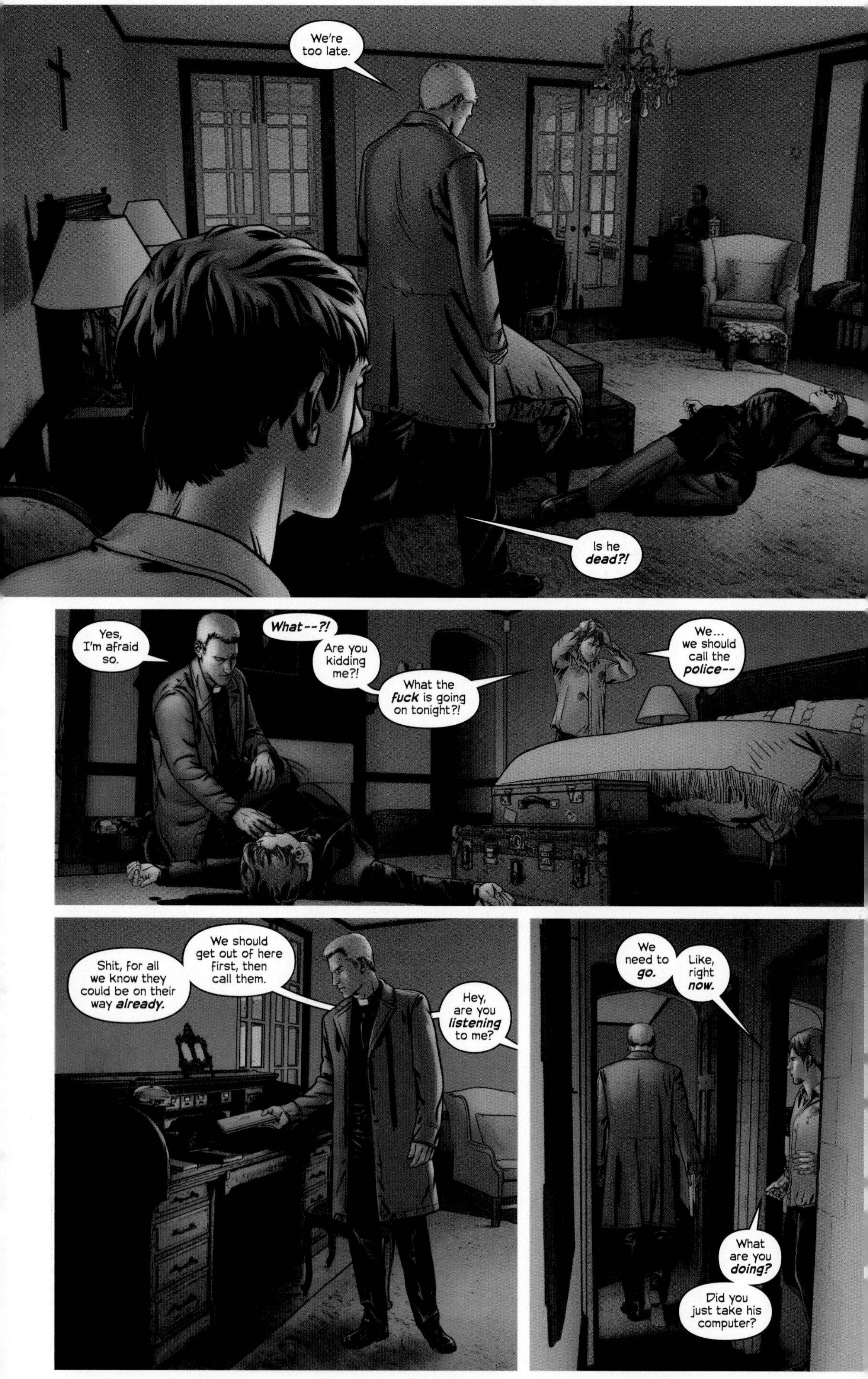
We're too late.
Is he *dead?!*
Yes, I'm afraid so.
What--?!
Are you kidding me?!
What the *fuck* is going on tonight?!
We... we should call the *police--*
We should get out of here first, then call them.
Shit, for all we know they could be on their way *already.*
Hey, are you *listening* to me?
We need to *go.*
Like, right *now.*
What are you *doing?*
Did you just take his computer?

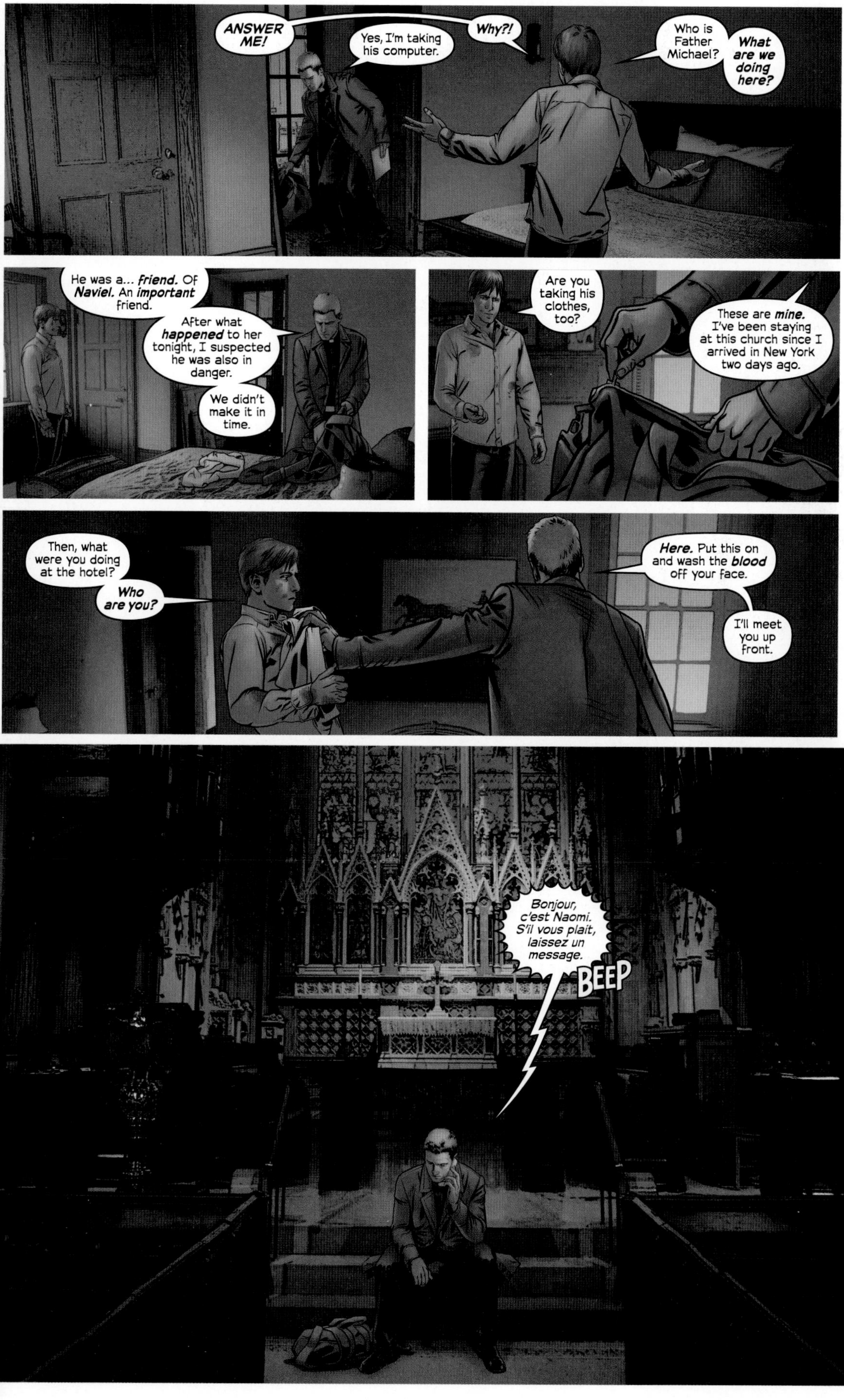
ANSWER ME!
Yes, I'm taking his computer.
Why?!
Who is Father Michael?
What are we doing here?
He was a... friend. Of Naviel. An important friend.
After what happened to her tonight, I suspected he was also in danger.
We didn't make it in time.
Are you taking his clothes, too?
These are mine. I've been staying at this church since I arrived in New York two days ago.
Then, what were you doing at the hotel?
Who are you?
Here. Put this on and wash the blood off your face.
I'll meet you up front.
Bonjour, c'est Naomi. S'il vous plait, laissez un message.
BEEP

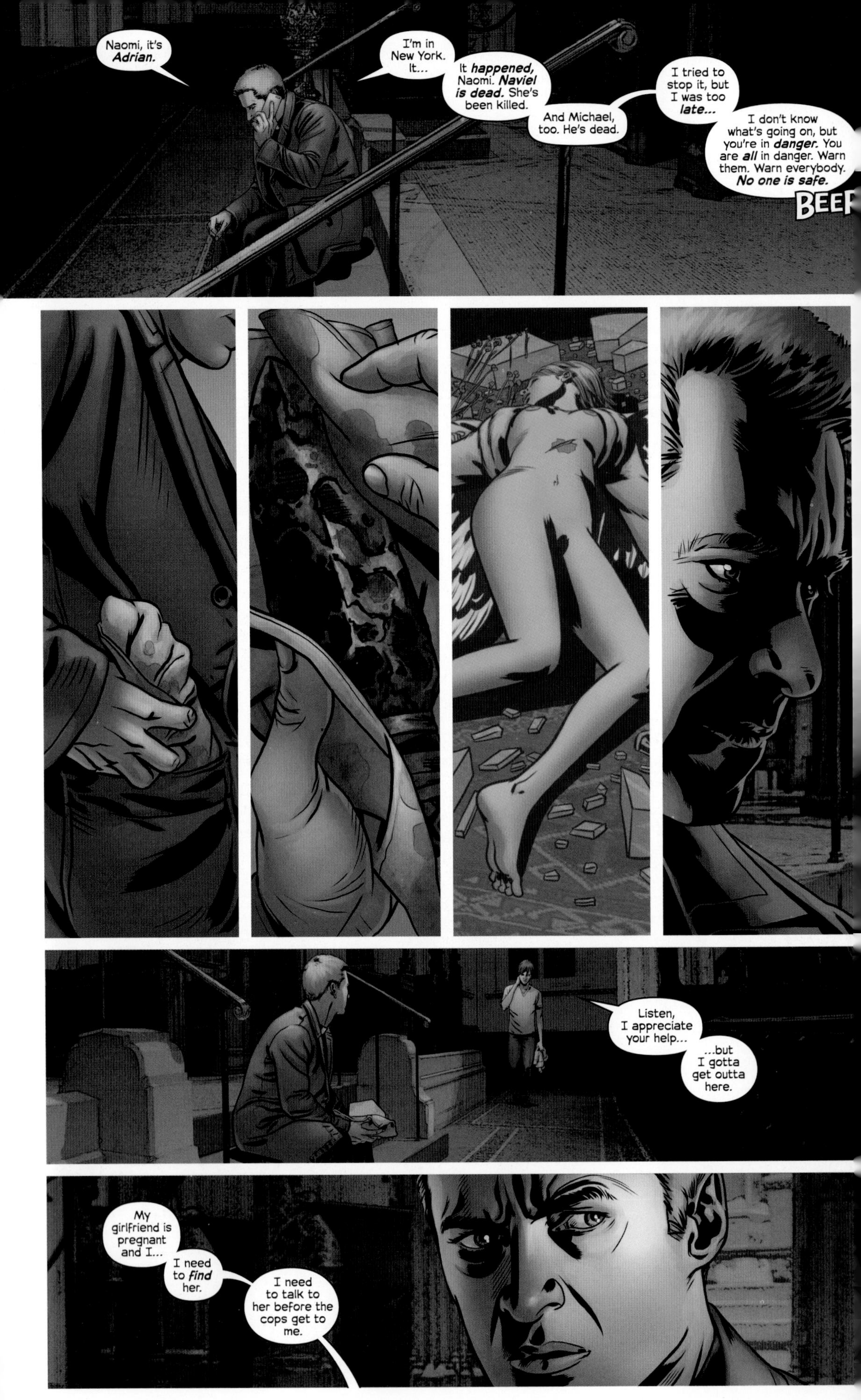
Naomi, it's *Adrian.*
I'm in New York. It...
It ***happened,*** Naomi. ***Naviel is dead.*** She's been killed.
And Michael, too. He's dead.
I tried to stop it, but I was too ***late...***
I don't know what's going on, but you're in ***danger.*** You are ***all*** in danger. Warn them. Warn everybody. ***No one is safe.***
BEEP
Listen, I appreciate your help...
...but I gotta get outta here.
My girlfriend is pregnant and I...
I need to ***find*** her.
I need to talk to her before the cops get to me.

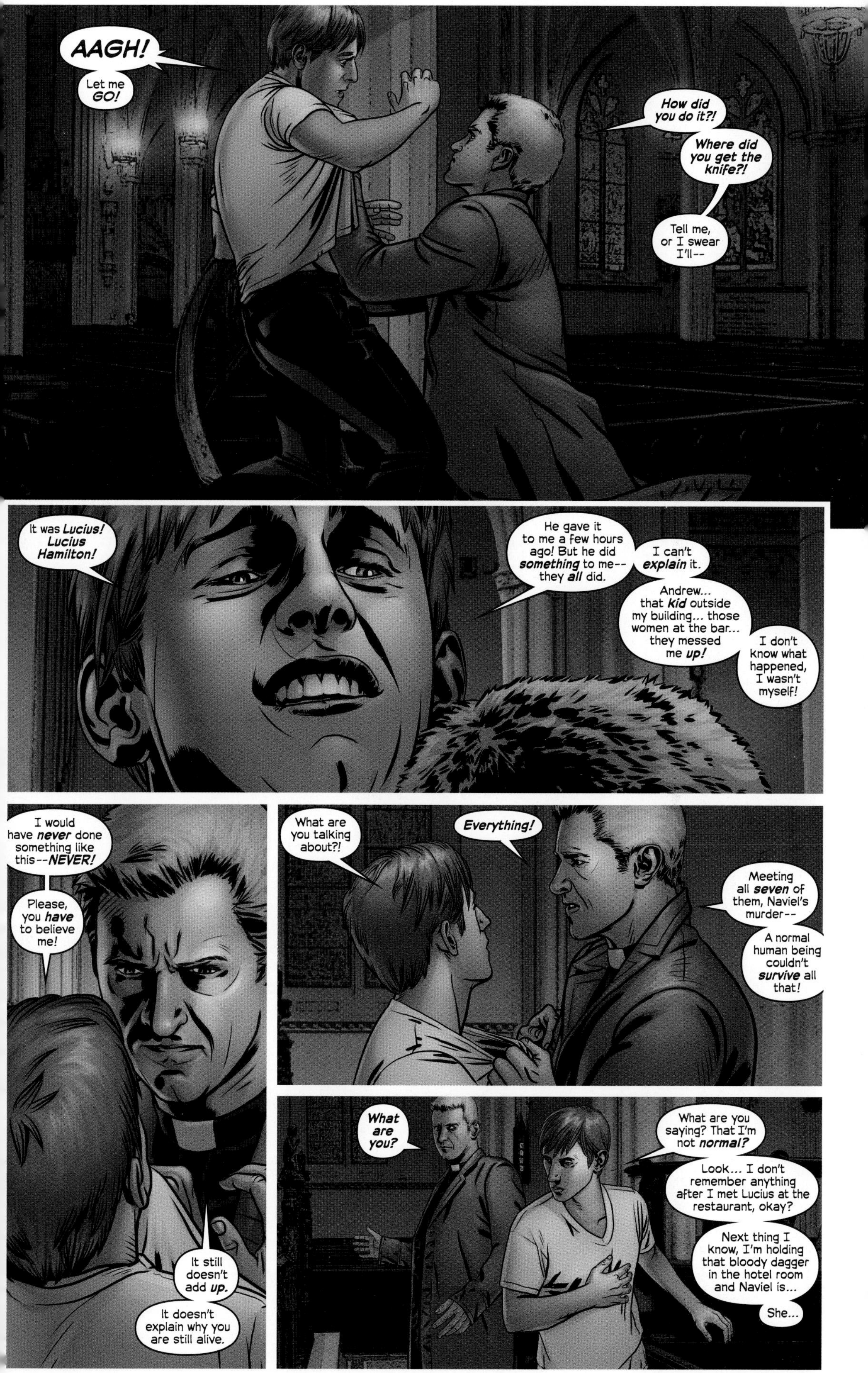
AAGH!
Let me GO!
How did you do it?!
Where did you get the knife?!
Tell me, or I swear I'll--
It was Lucius! Lucius Hamilton!
He gave it to me a few hours ago! But he did something to me-- they all did.
I can't explain it.
Andrew... that kid outside my building... those women at the bar... they messed me up!
I don't know what happened, I wasn't myself!
I would have never done something like this--NEVER!
Please, you have to believe me!
It still doesn't add up.
It doesn't explain why you are still alive.
What are you talking about?!
Everything!
Meeting all seven of them, Naviel's murder--
A normal human being couldn't survive all that!
What are you?
What are you saying? That I'm not normal?
Look... I don't remember anything after I met Lucius at the restaurant, okay?
Next thing I know, I'm holding that bloody dagger in the hotel room and Naviel is...
She...

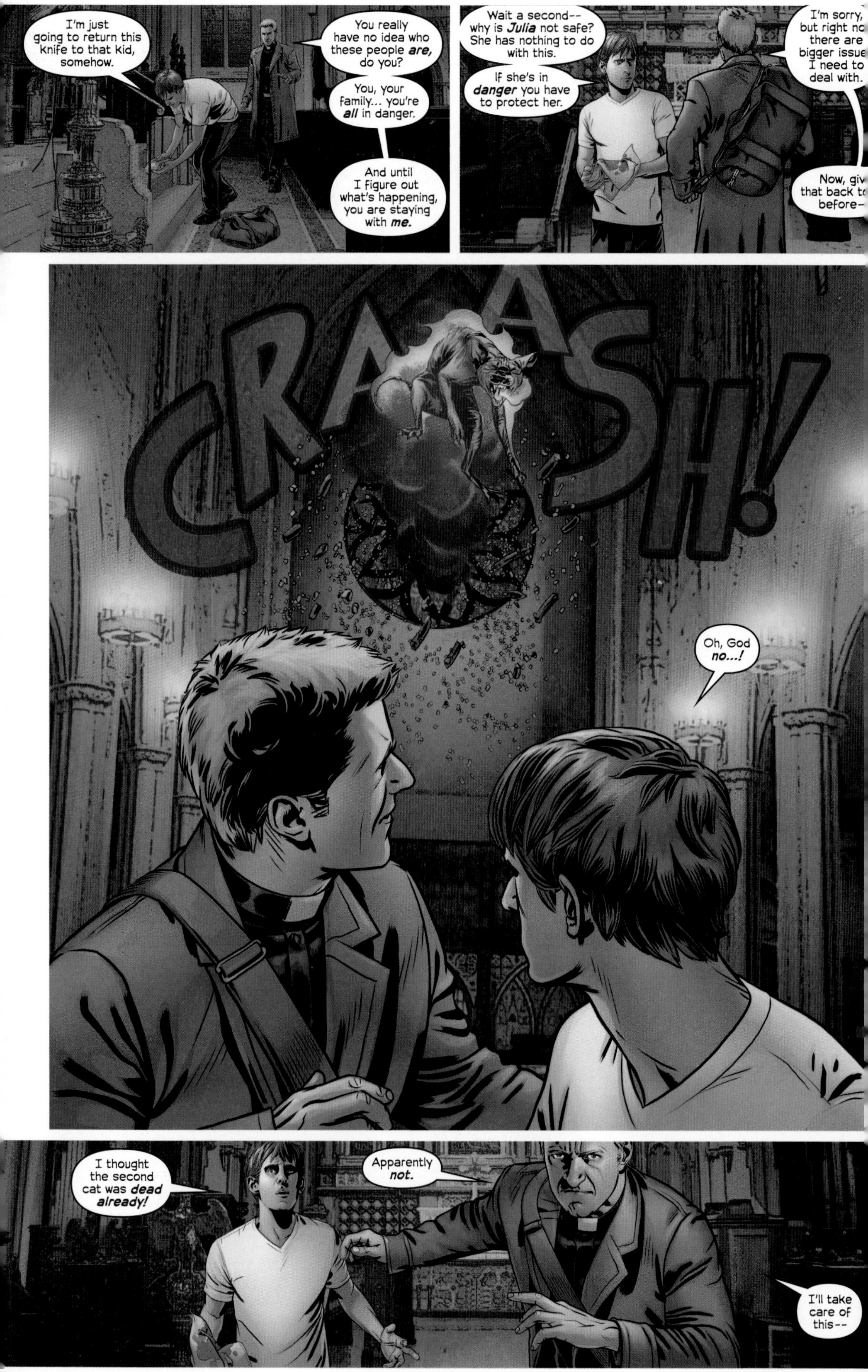
I'm just going to return this knife to that kid, somehow.
You really have no idea who these people *are*, do you?
You, your family... you're *all* in danger.
And until I figure out what's happening, you are staying with *me.*
Wait a second-- why is *Julia* not safe? She has nothing to do with this.
If she's in *danger* you have to protect her.
I'm sorry, but right no there are bigger issue I need to deal with.
Now, giv that back t before-
CRASH!
Oh, God *no...!*
I thought the second cat was *dead already!*
Apparently *not.*
I'll take care of this--

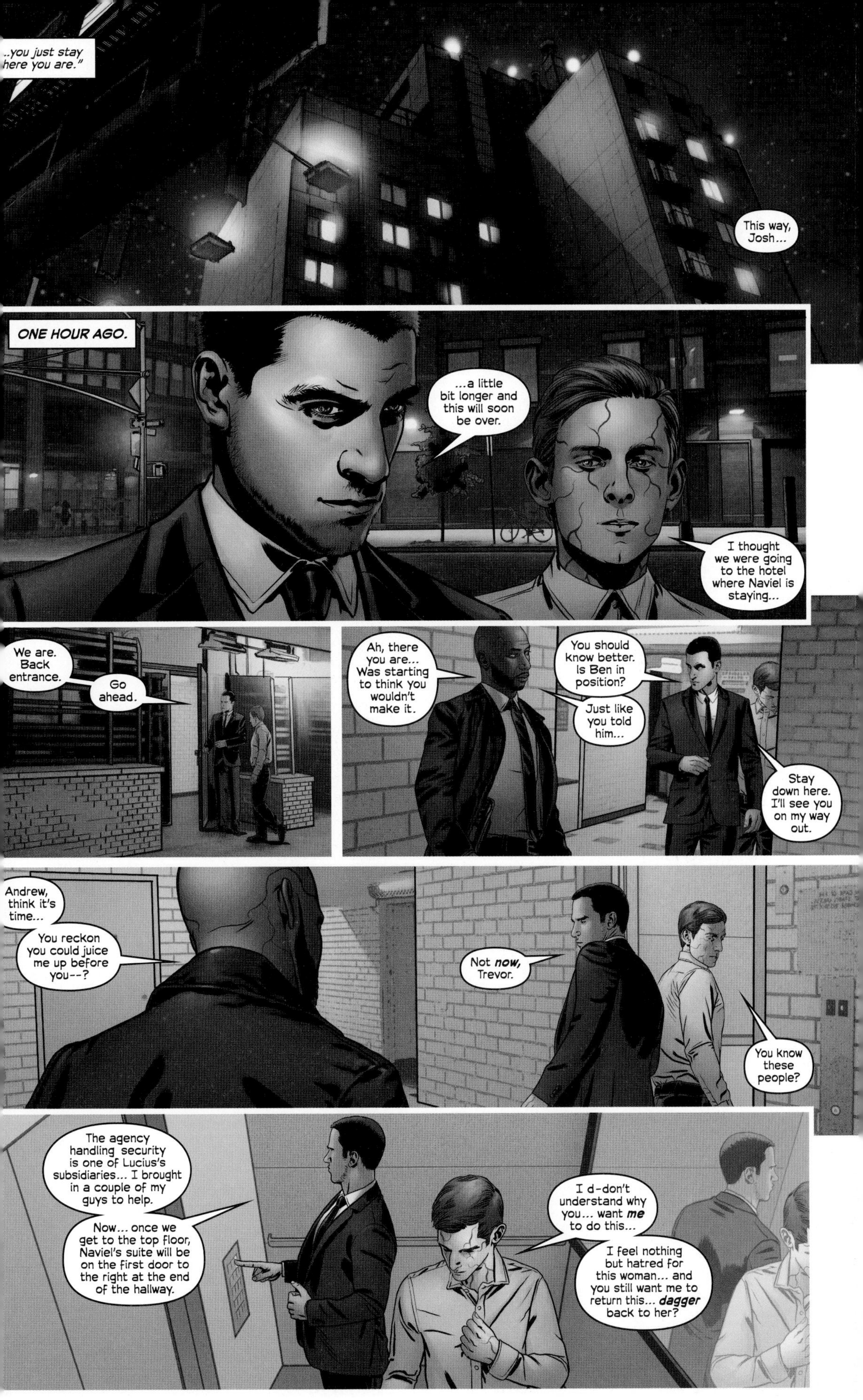

..you just stay here you are."
This way, Josh...
ONE HOUR AGO.
...a little bit longer and this will soon be over.
I thought we were going to the hotel where Naviel is staying...
We are. Back entrance.
Go ahead.
Ah, there you are... Was starting to think you wouldn't make it.
You should know better. Is Ben in position?
Just like you told him...
Stay down here. I'll see you on my way out.
Andrew, think it's time...
You reckon you could juice me up before you--?
Not *now,* Trevor.
You know these people?
The agency handling security is one of Lucius's subsidiaries... I brought in a couple of my guys to help.
Now... once we get to the top floor, Naviel's suite will be on the first door to the right at the end of the hallway.
I d-don't understand why you... want *me* to do this...
I feel nothing but hatred for this woman... and you still want me to return this... *dagger* back to her?

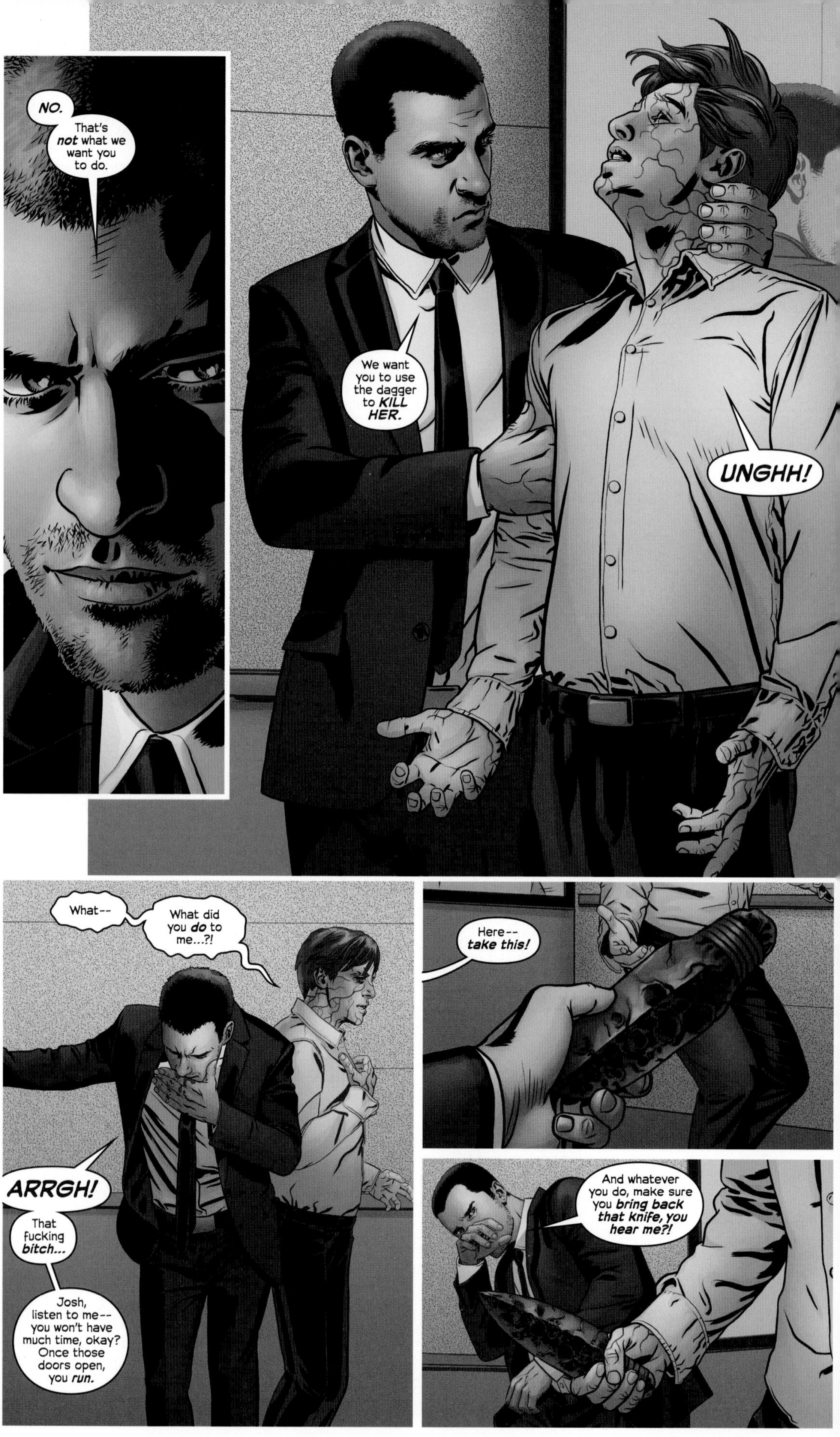
NO.
That's *not* what we want you to do.
We want you to use the dagger to *KILL HER.*
UNGHH!
What--
What did you *do* to me...?!
ARRGH!
That fucking *bitch...*
Josh, listen to me-- you won't have much time, okay? Once those doors open, you *run.*
Here-- *take this!*
And whatever you do, make sure you *bring back that knife, you hear me?!*

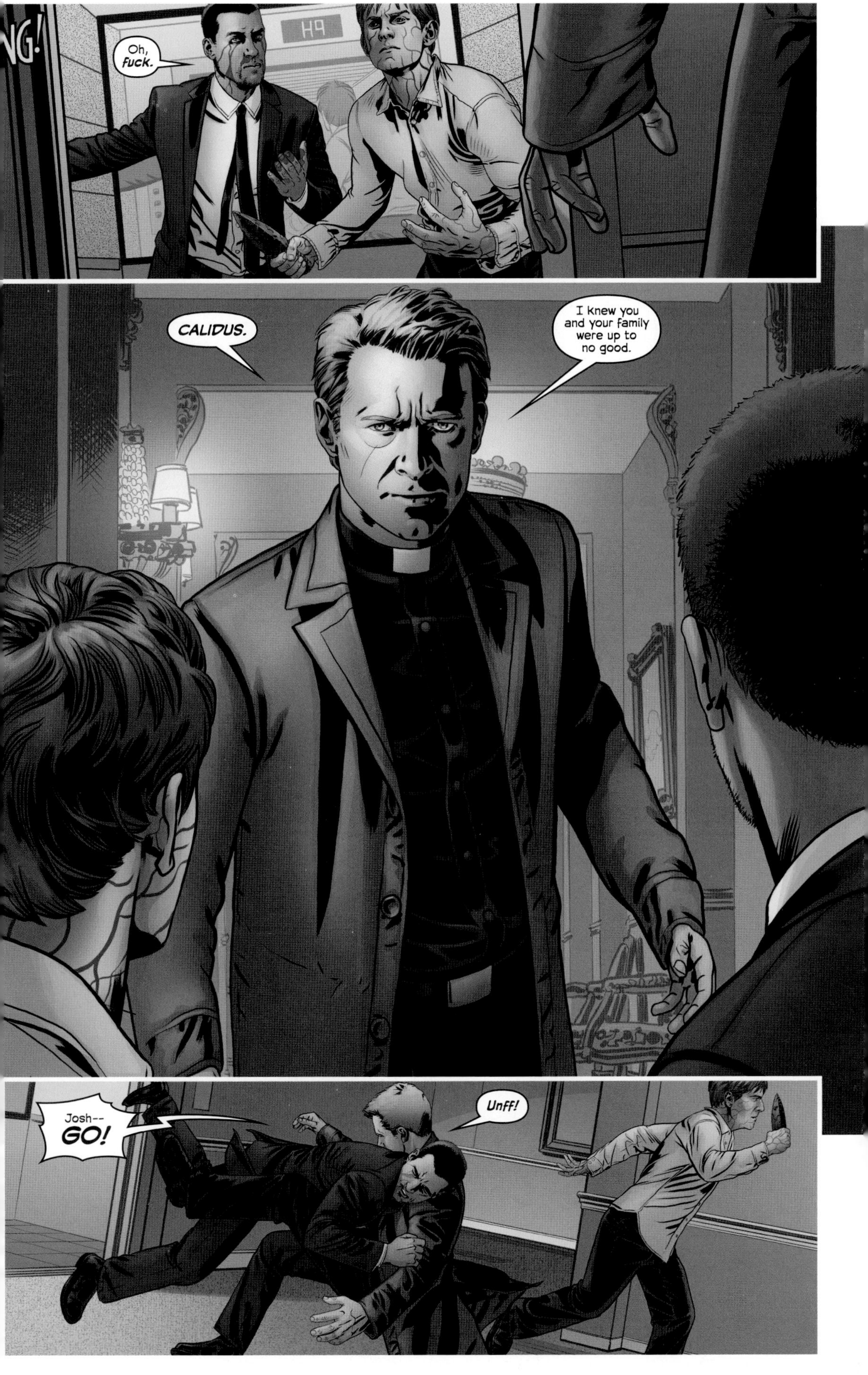
NG!
Oh, fuck.
CALIDUS.
I knew you and your family were up to no good.
Josh-- GO!
Unff!

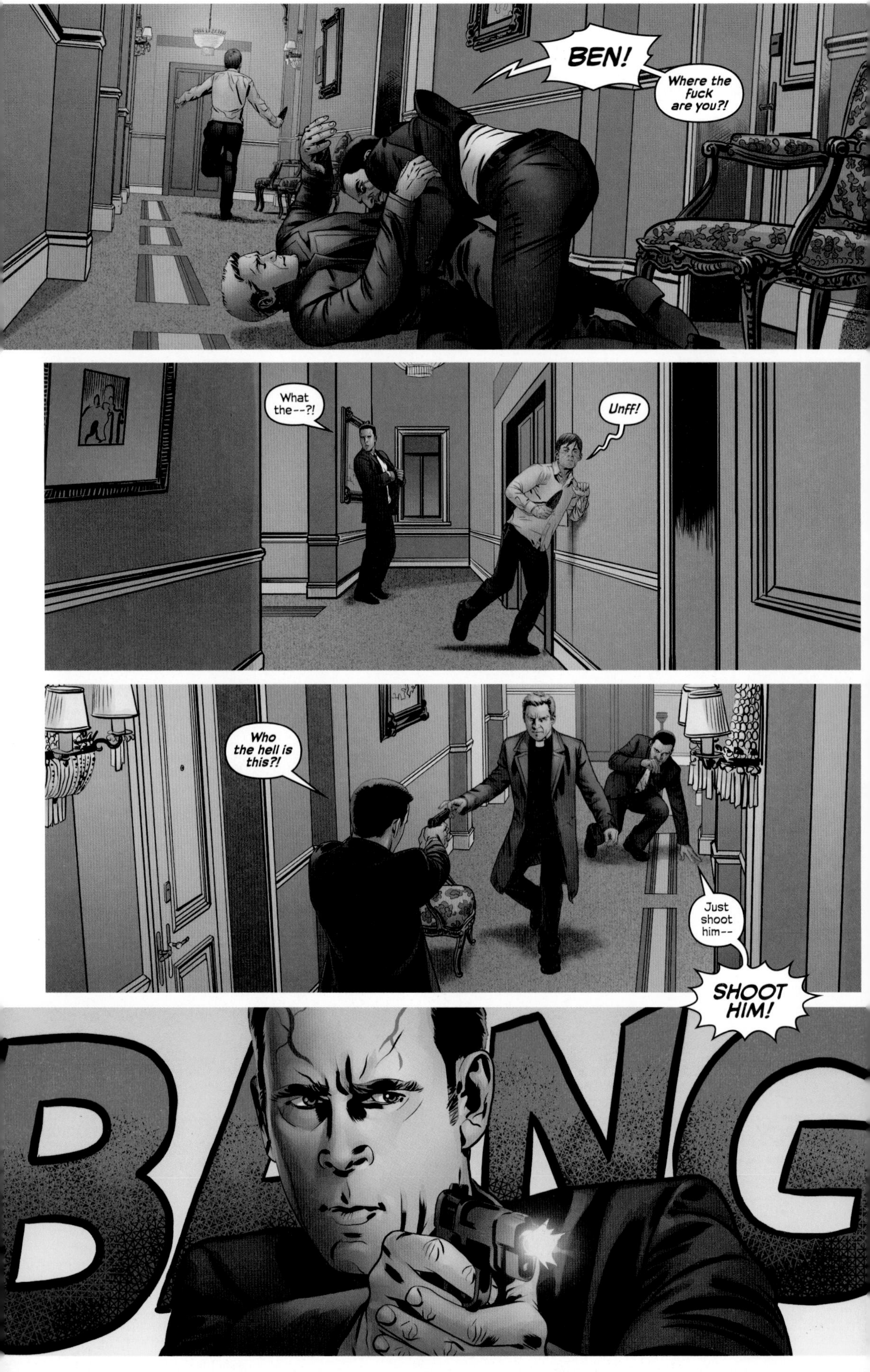
BEN!
Where the fuck are you?!
What the--?!
Unff!
Who the hell is this?!
Just shoot him--
SHOOT HIM!
BANG

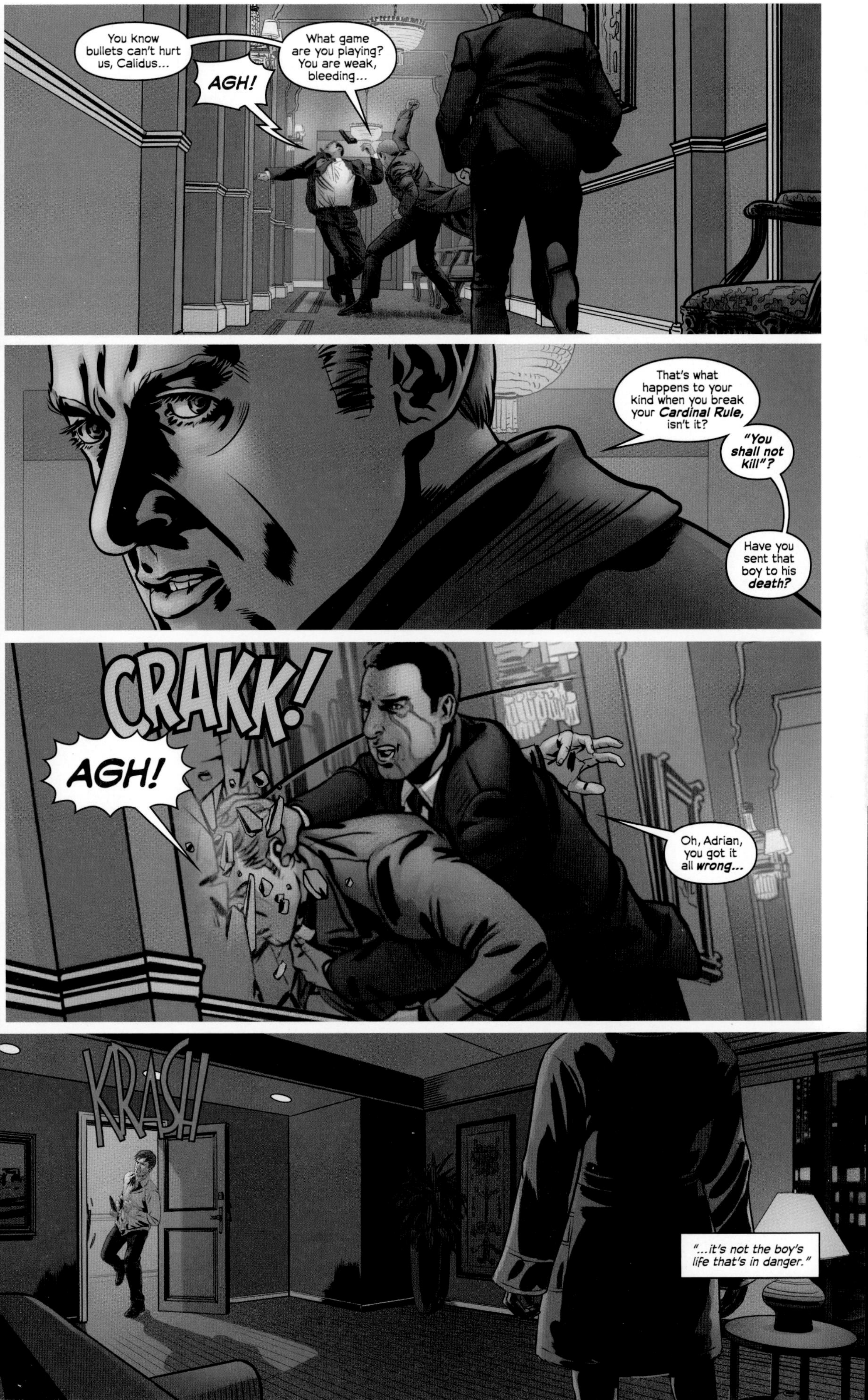
You know bullets can't hurt us, Calidus...
AGH!
What game are you playing? You are weak, bleeding...
That's what happens to your kind when you break your *Cardinal Rule,* isn't it?
"You shall not kill"?
Have you sent that boy to his *death?*
CRAKK!
AGH!
Oh, Adrian, you got it all *wrong...*
KRASH
"...it's not the boy's life that's in danger."

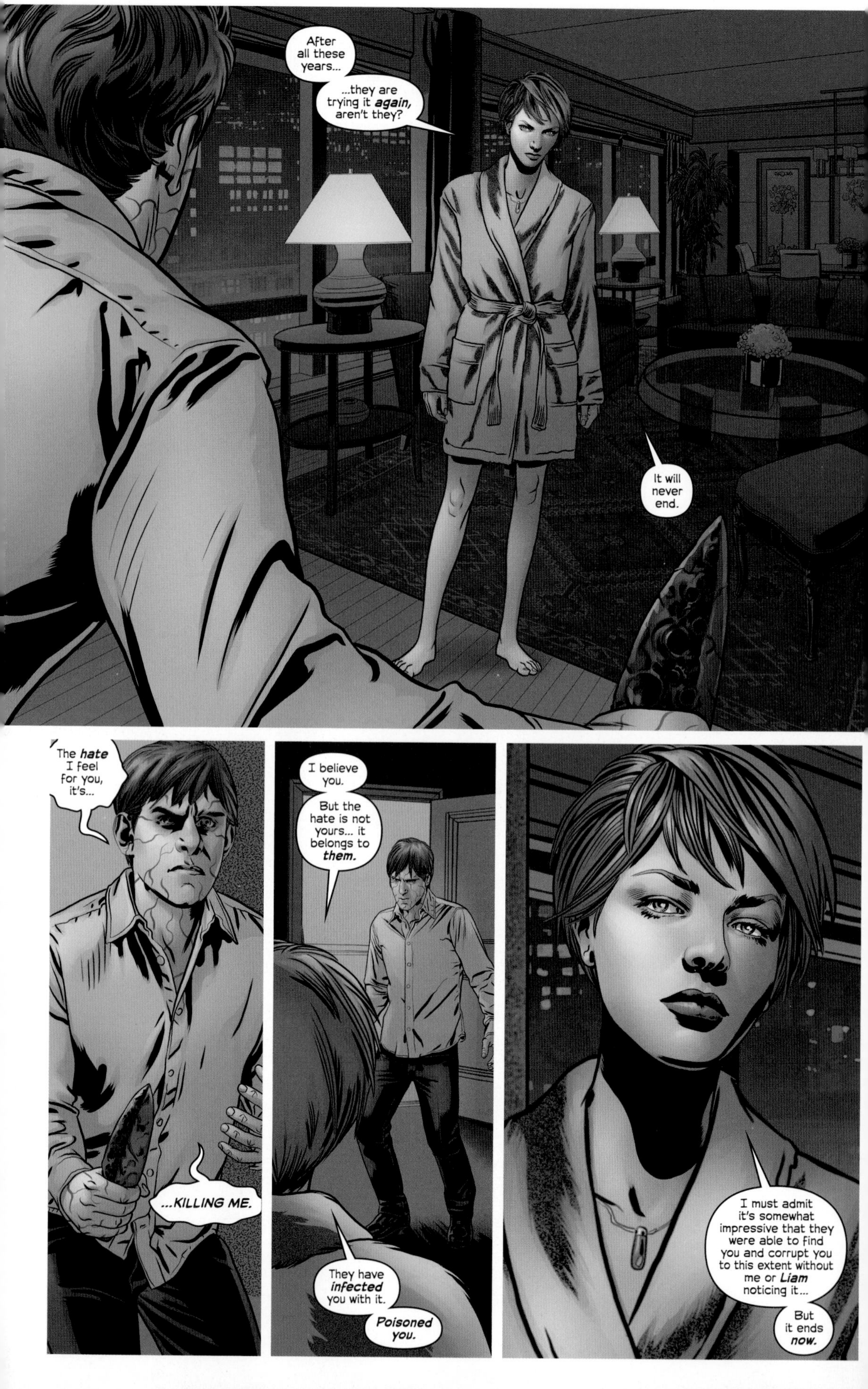
After all these years...
...they are trying it *again,* aren't they?
It will never end.
The *hate* I feel for you, it's...
...KILLING ME.
I believe you.
But the hate is not yours... it belongs to *them.*
They have *infected* you with it.
Poisoned you.
I must admit it's somewhat impressive that they were able to find you and corrupt you to this extent without me or *Liam* noticing it...
But it ends *now.*

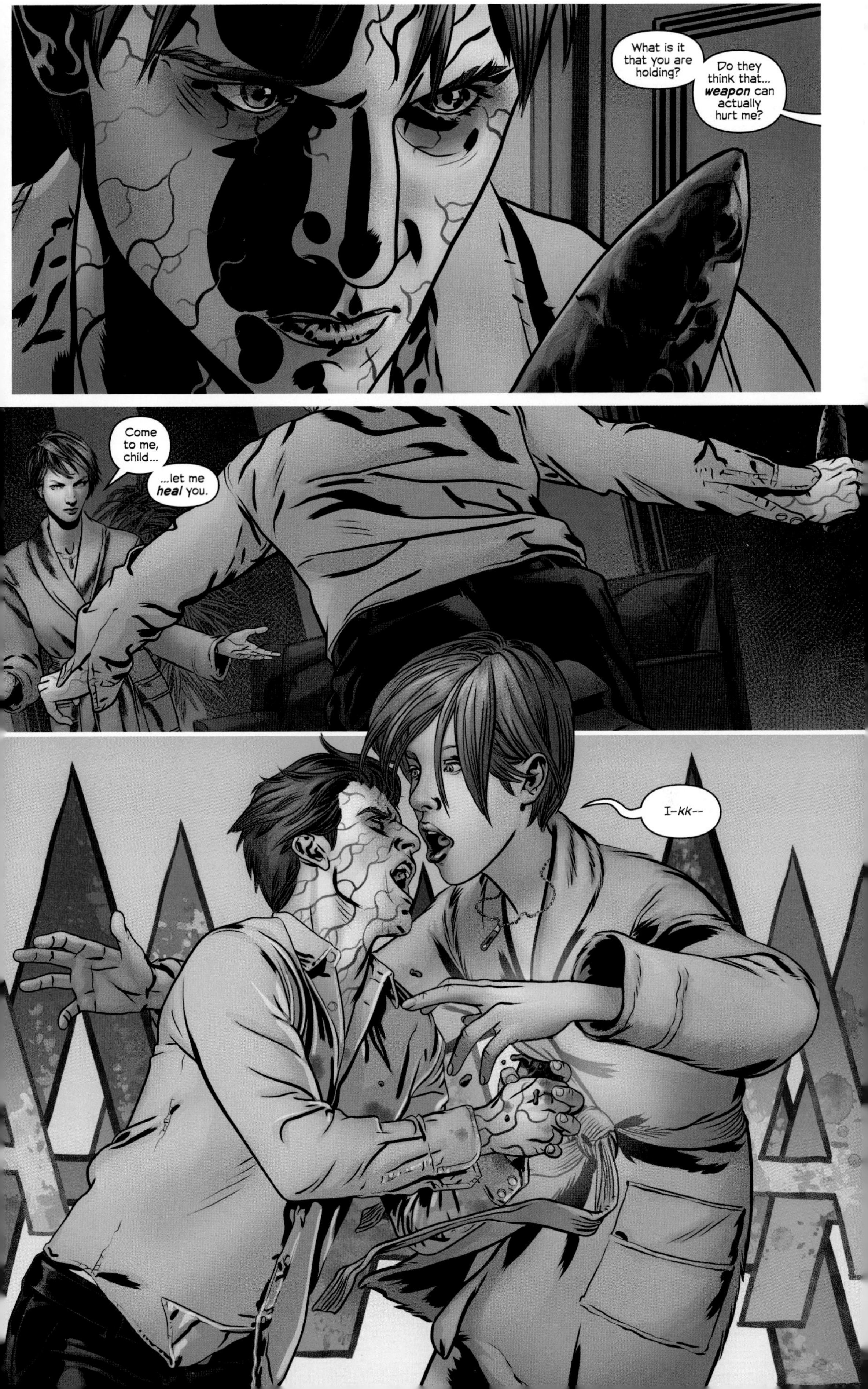
What is it that you are holding?
Do they think that... *weapon* can actually hurt me?
Come to me, child...
...let me *heal* you.
I-KK--

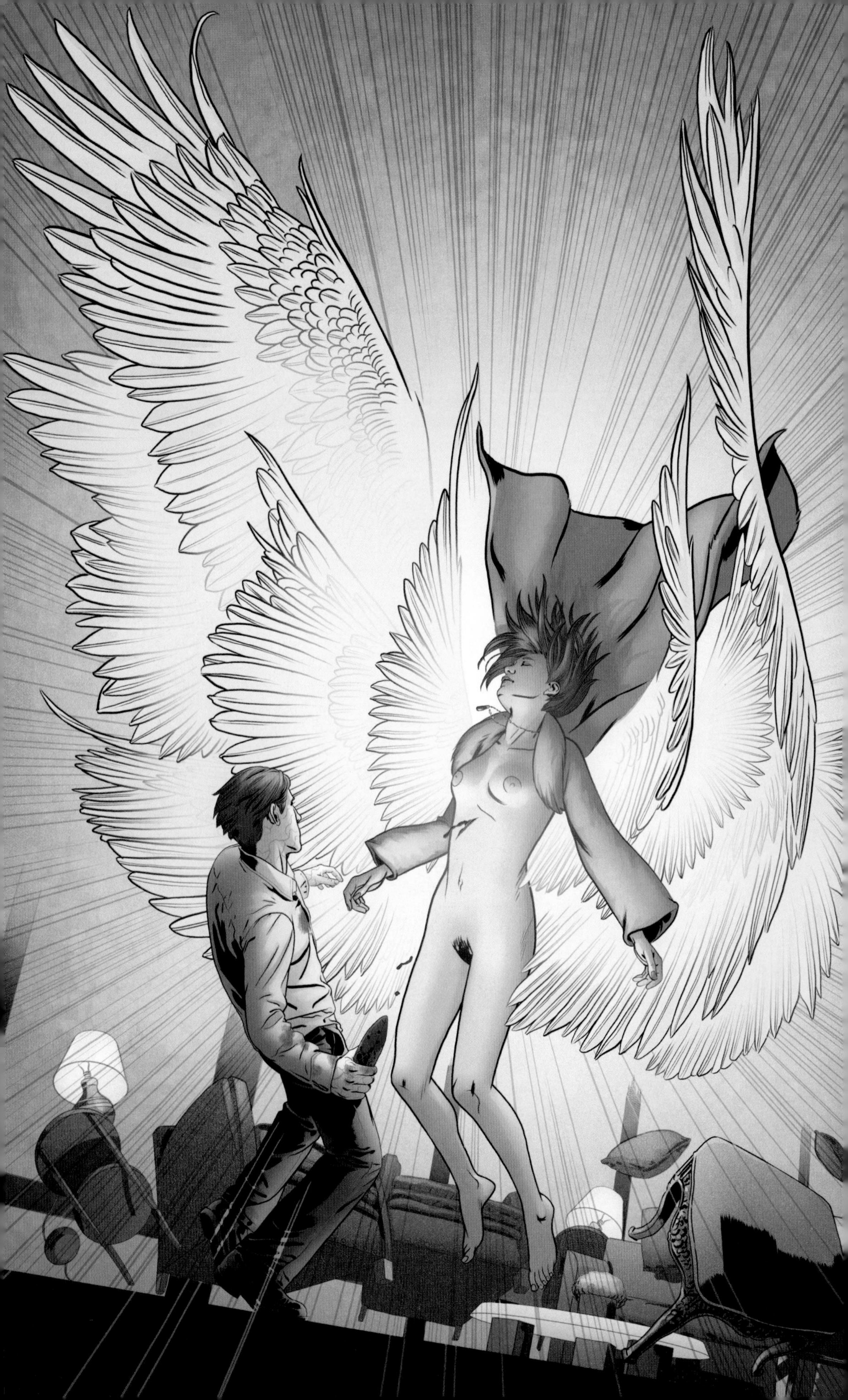

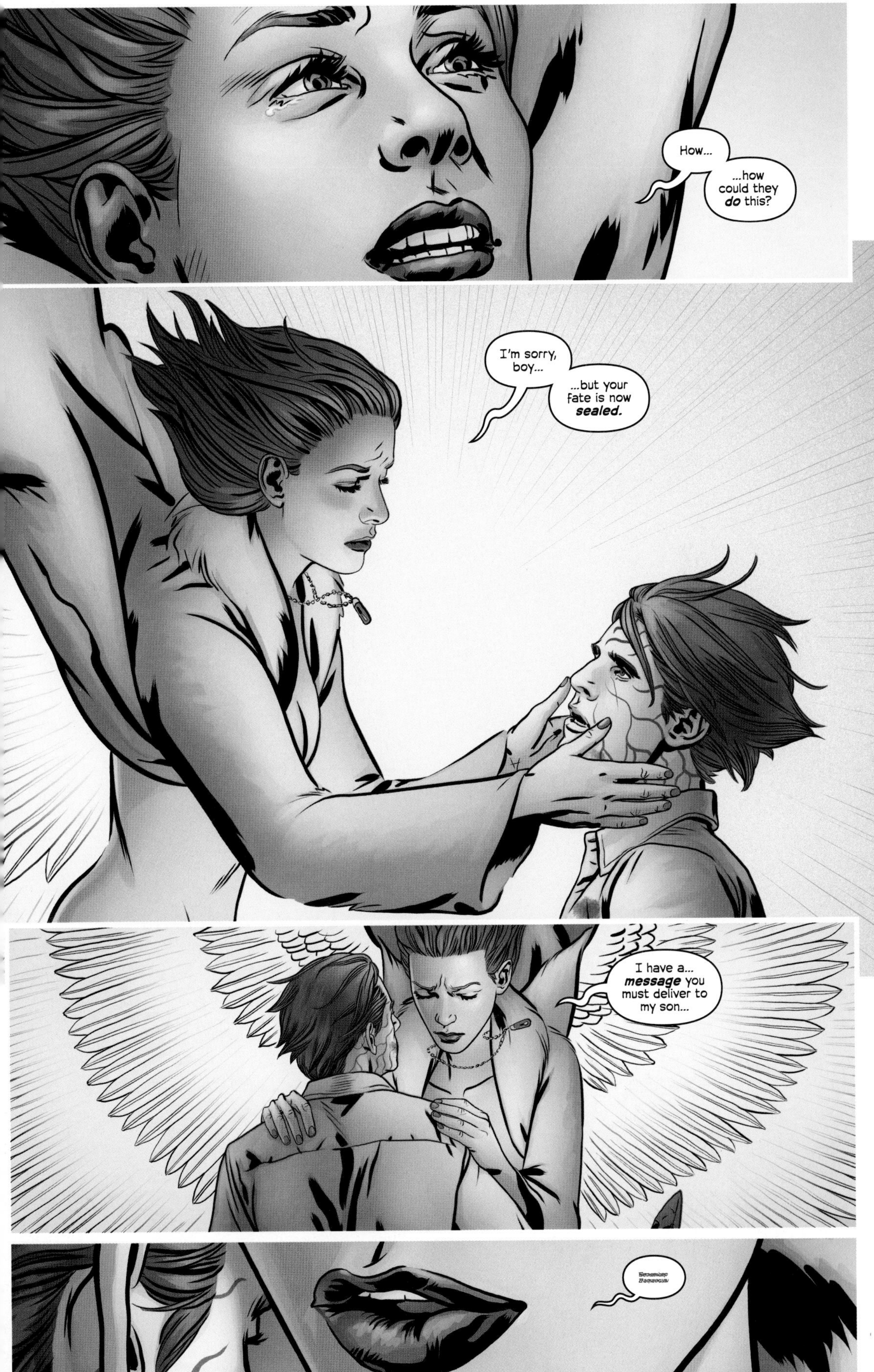
How...
...how could they *do* this?
I'm sorry, boy...
...but your fate is now ***sealed.***
I have a... ***message*** you must deliver to my son...

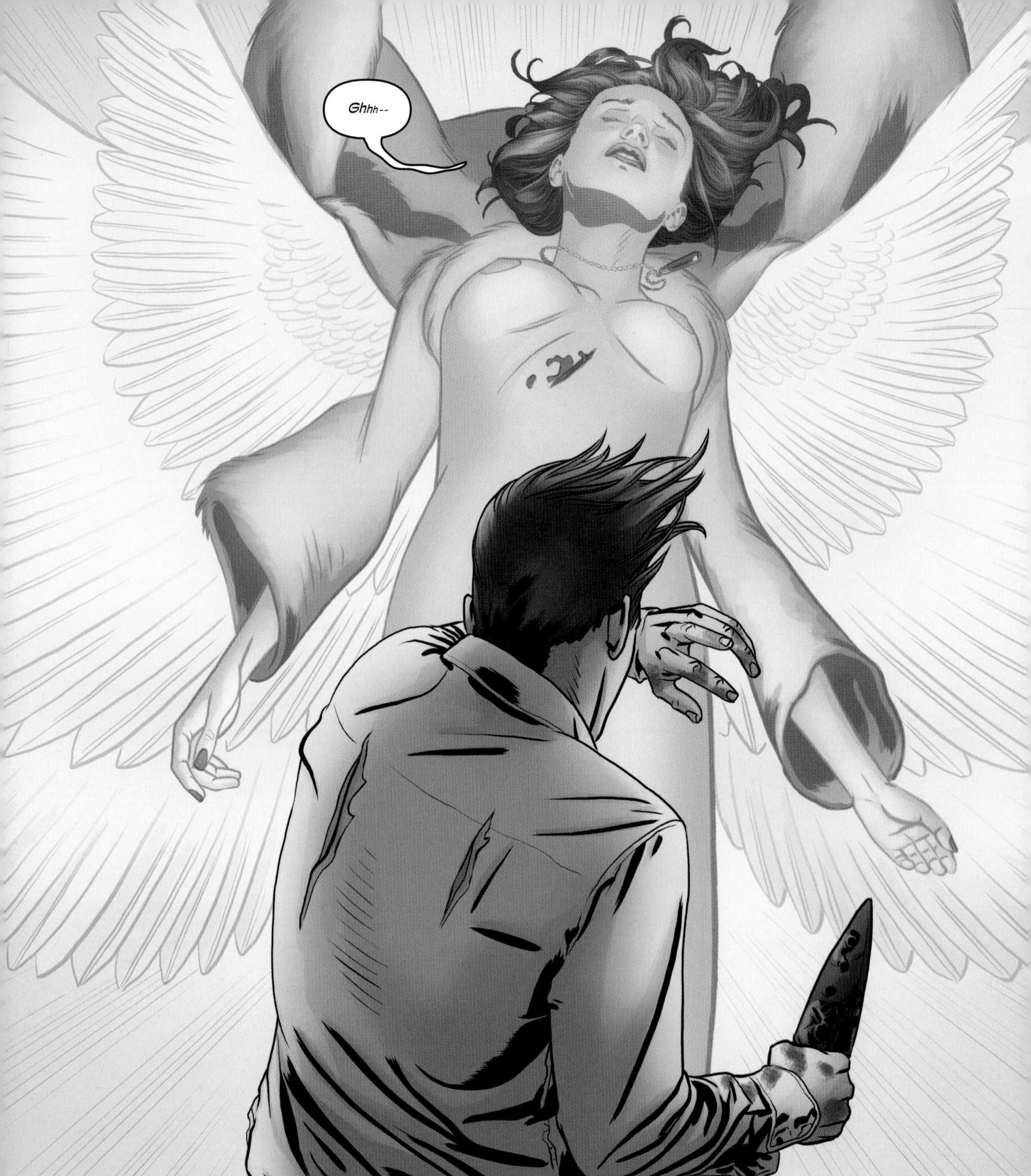
Ghhh--
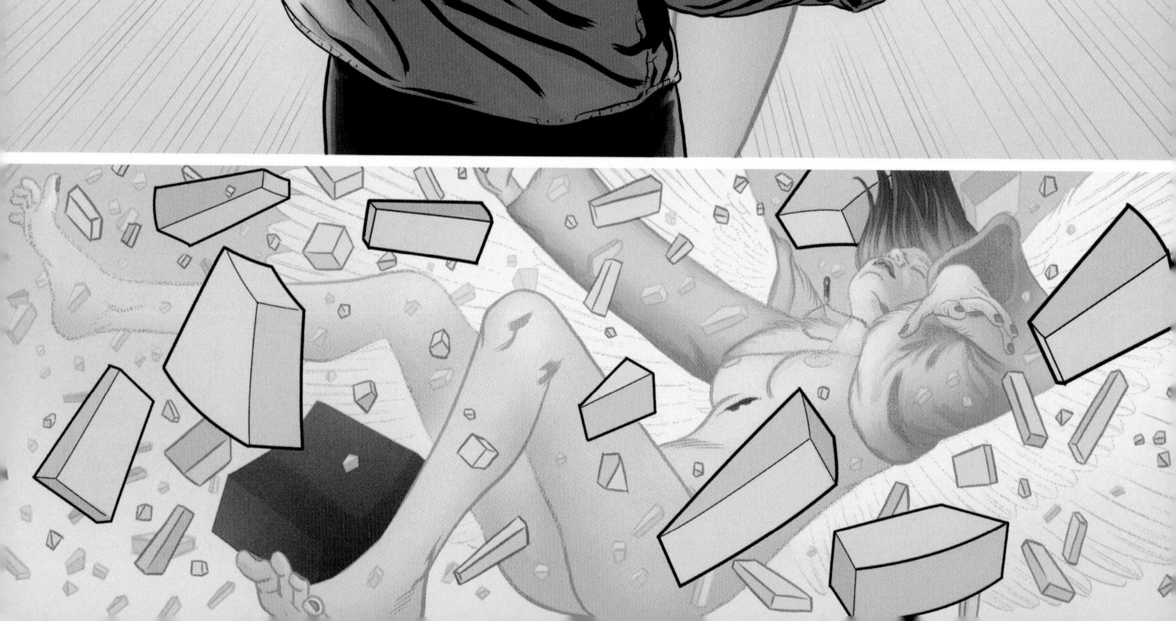

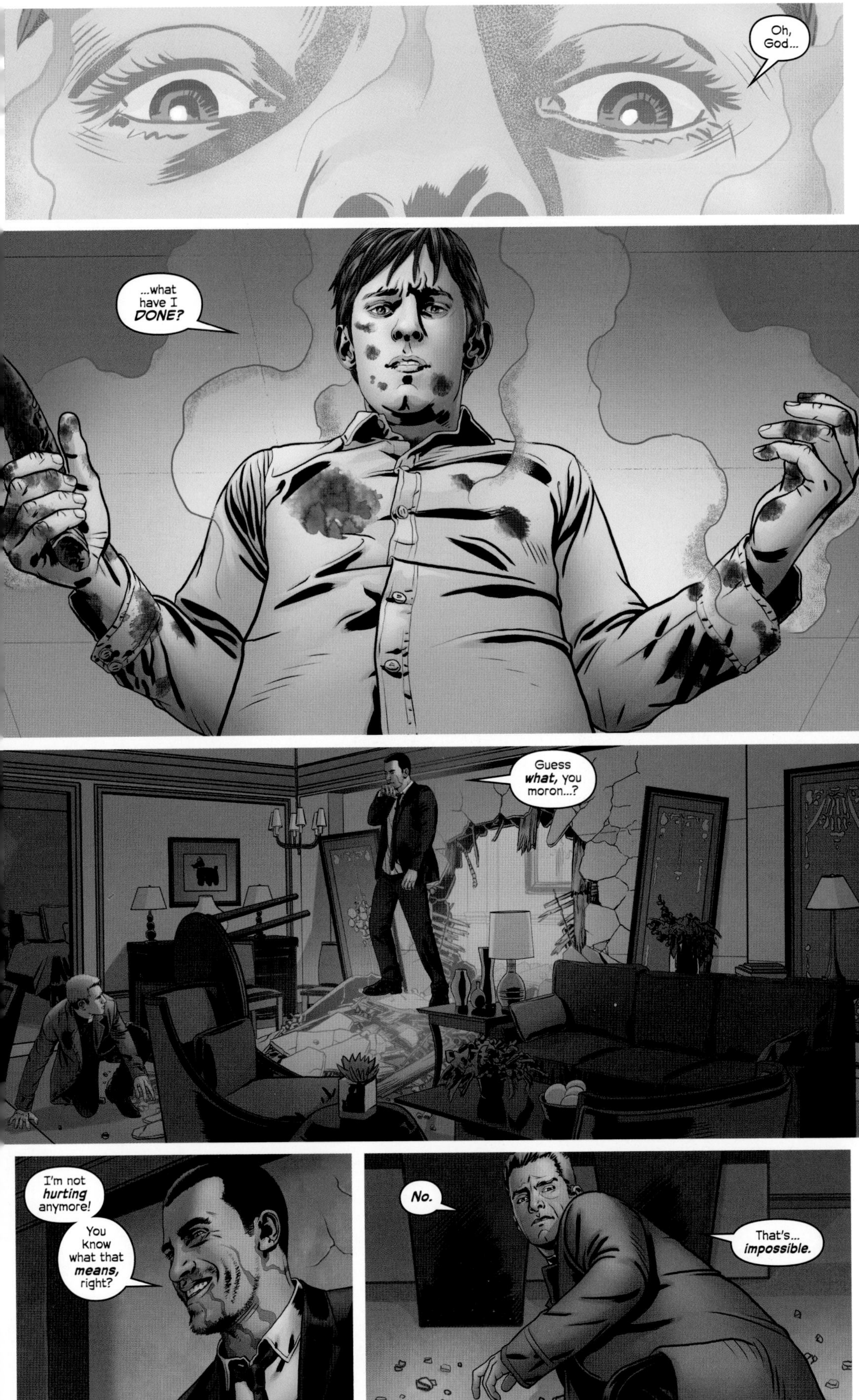
Oh, God...
...what have I *DONE?*
Guess *what,* you moron...?
I'm not *hurting* anymore!
You know what that *means,* right?
No.
That's... *impossible.*

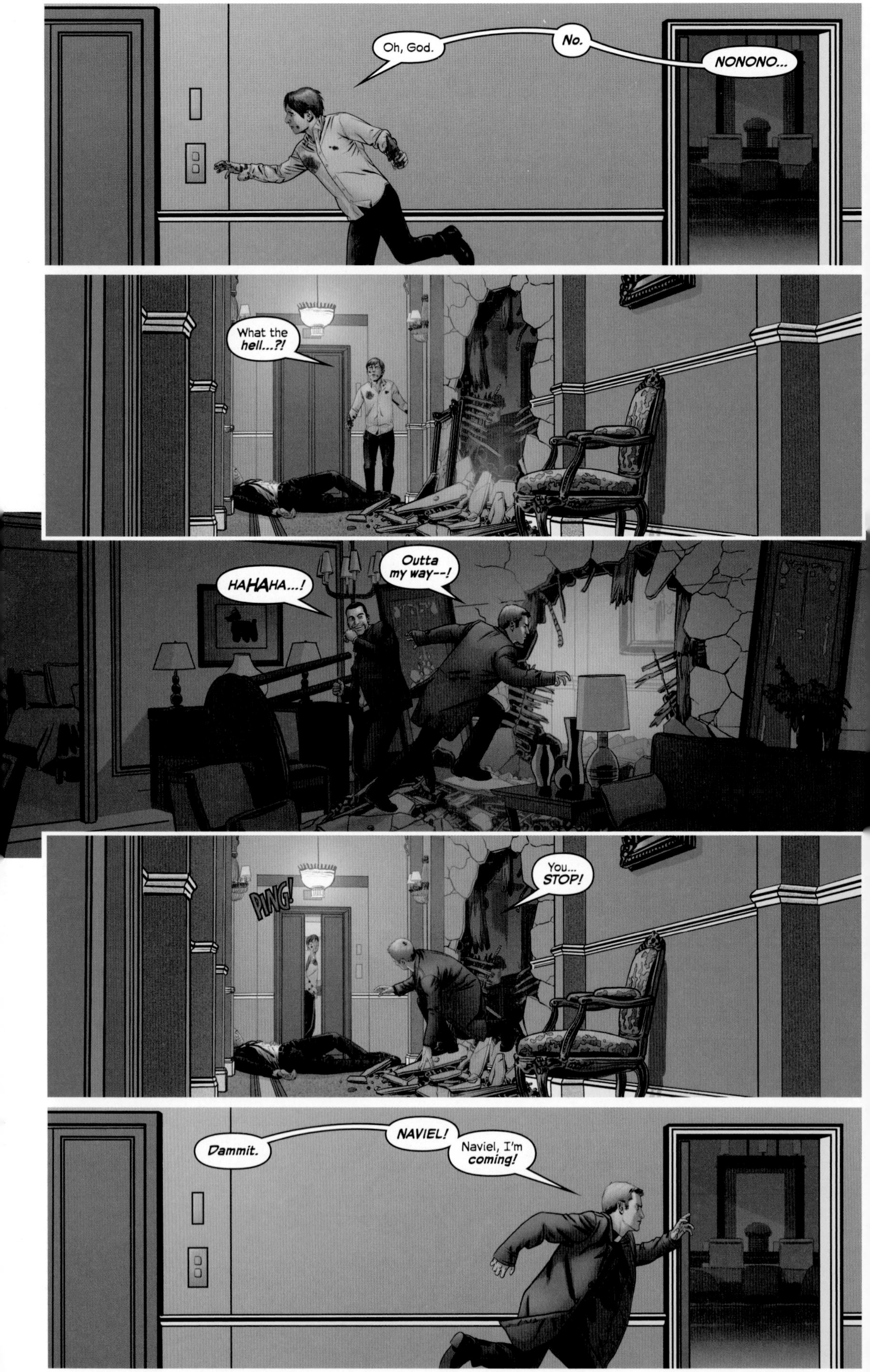
Oh, God.
No.
NONONO...
What the hell...?!
HAHAHA...!
Outta my way--!
PING!
You... STOP!
Dammit.
NAVIEL!
Naviel, I'm coming!

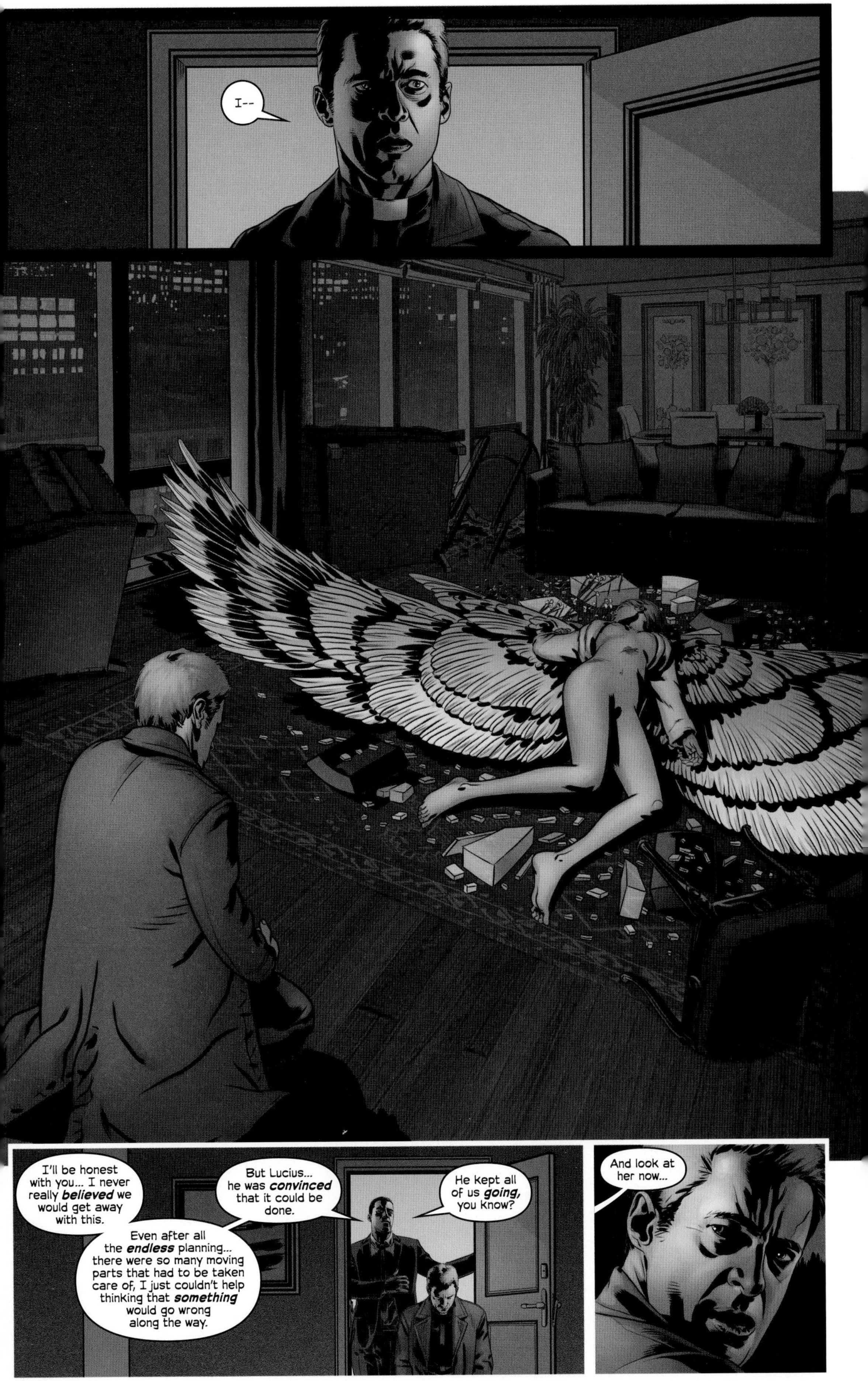
I--
I'll be honest with you... I never really **believed** we would get away with this.
Even after all the **endless** planning... there were so many moving parts that had to be taken care of, I just couldn't help thinking that **something** would go wrong along the way.
But Lucius... he was **convinced** that it could be done.
He kept all of us **going,** you know?
And look at her now...

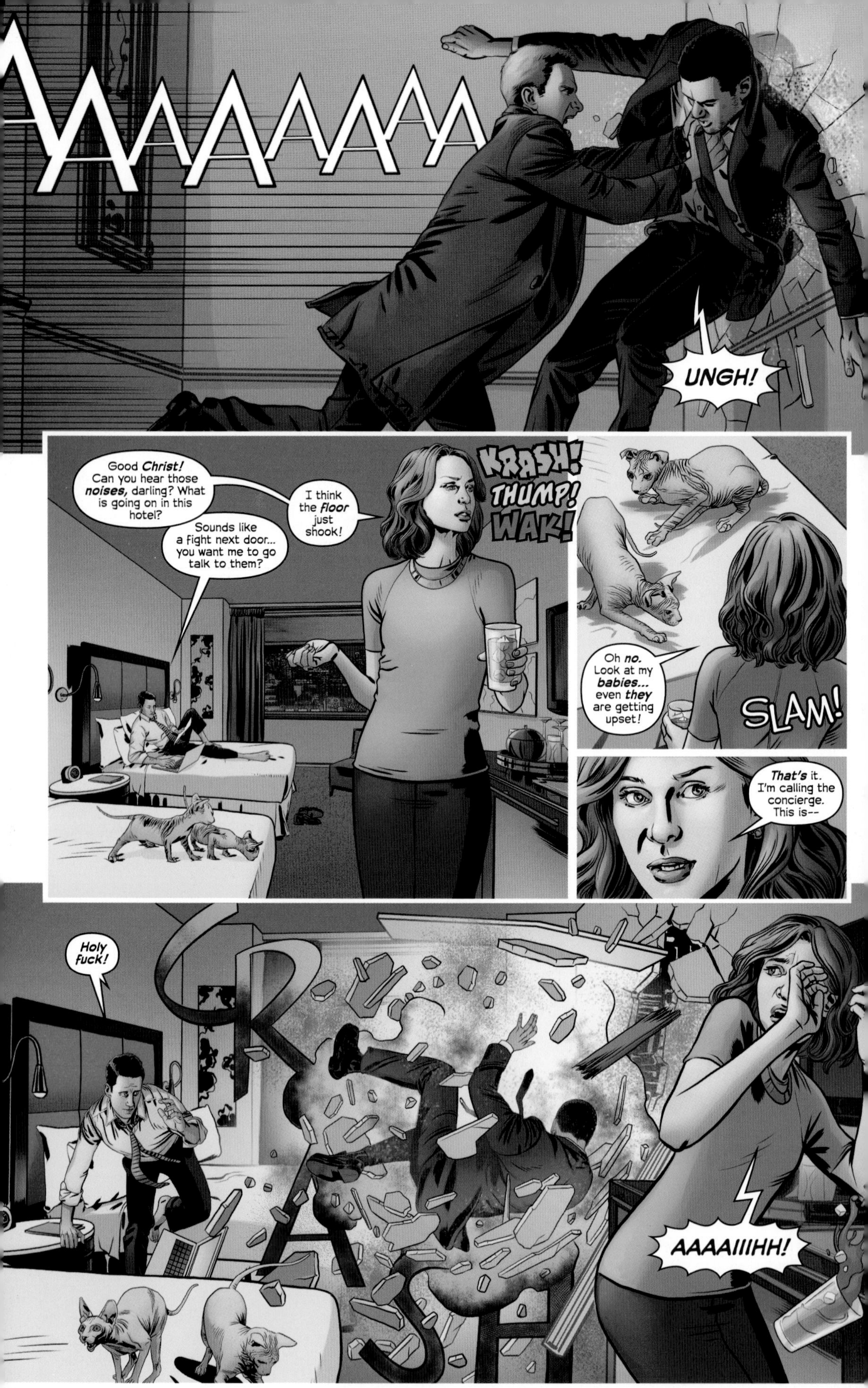
AAAAAAA
UNGH!
Good Christ! Can you hear those noises, darling? What is going on in this hotel?
I think the floor just shook!
Sounds like a fight next door... you want me to go talk to them?
KRASH! THUMP! WAK!
Oh no. Look at my babies... even they are getting upset!
SLAM!
That's it. I'm calling the concierge. This is--
Holy fuck!
AAAAIIIHH!

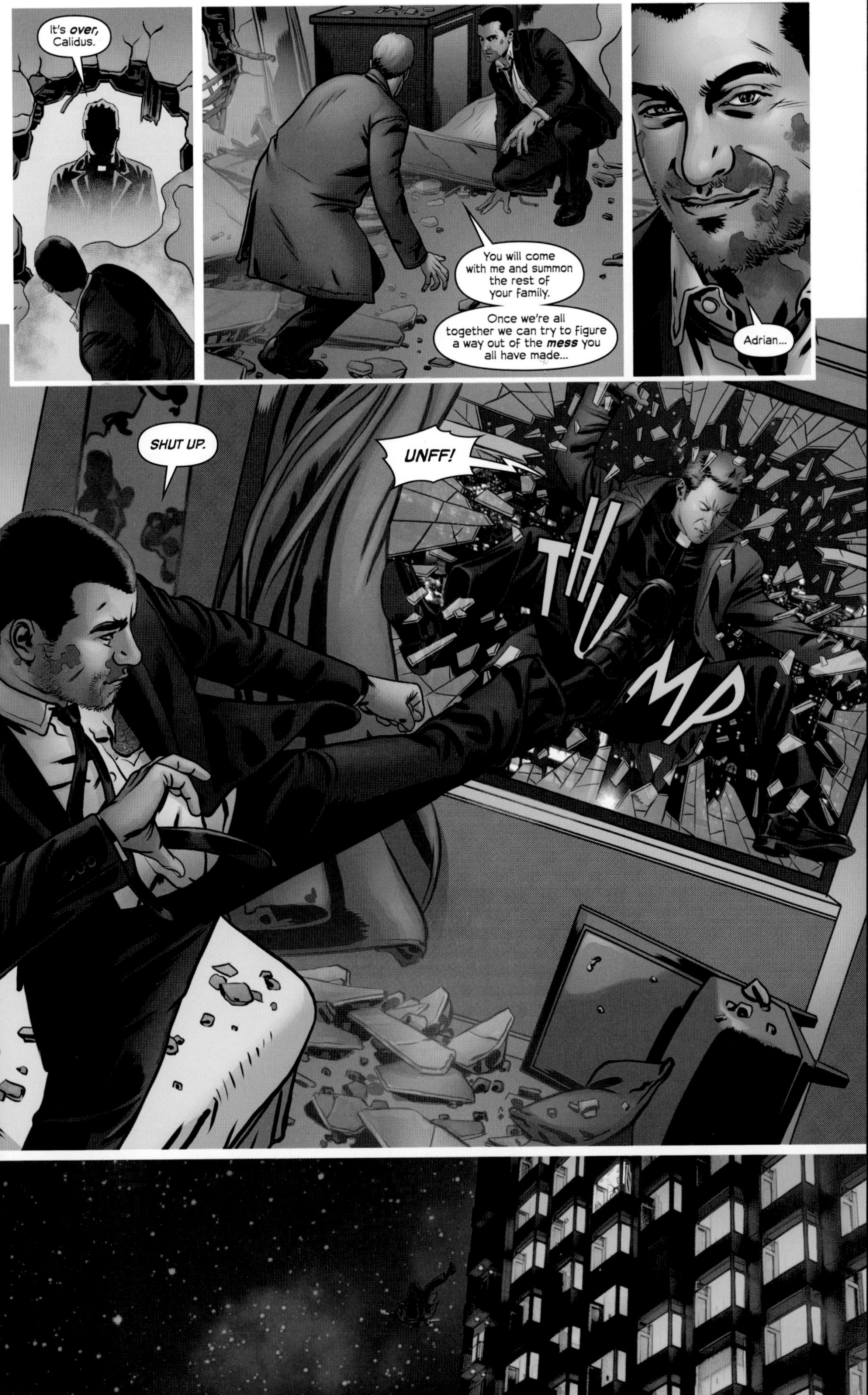
It's *over,* Calidus.
You will come with me and summon the rest of your family.
Once we're all together we can try to figure a way out of the *mess* you all have made...
Adrian...
SHUT UP.
UNFF!
THUMP

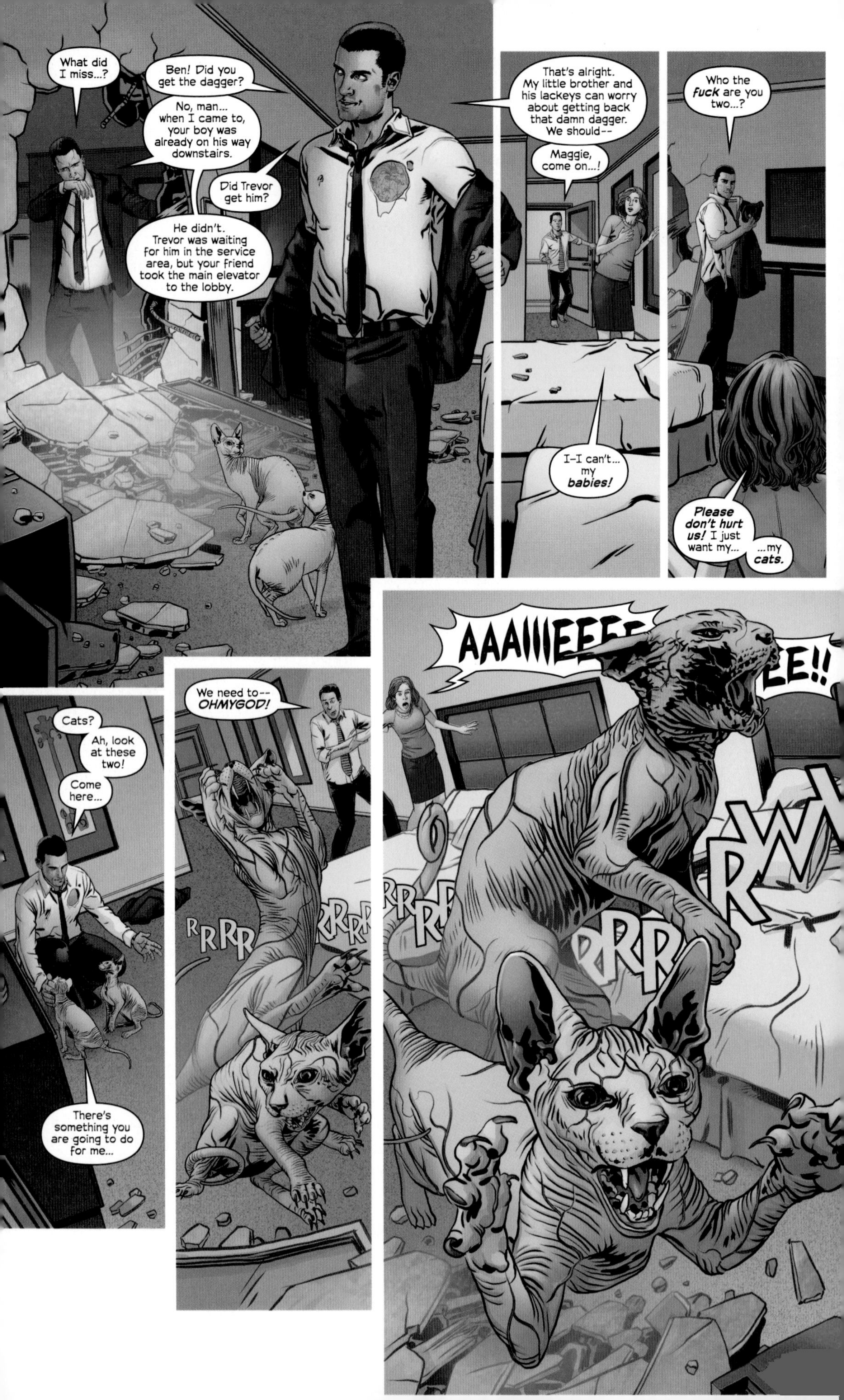
What did I miss...?
Ben! Did you get the dagger?
No, man... when I came to, your boy was already on his way downstairs.
Did Trevor get him?
He didn't. Trevor was waiting for him in the service area, but your friend took the main elevator to the lobby.
That's alright. My little brother and his lackeys can worry about getting back that damn dagger. We should--
Maggie, come on...!
I-I can't... my *babies!*
Who the *fuck* are you two...?
Please don't hurt us! I just want my...
...my *cats.*
Cats?
Ah, look at these two!
Come here...
There's something you are going to do for me...
We need to-- *OHMYGOD!*
RRRR
RRRR
AAAIIIEEEEEE!!
RRRR
RRRR
RWW

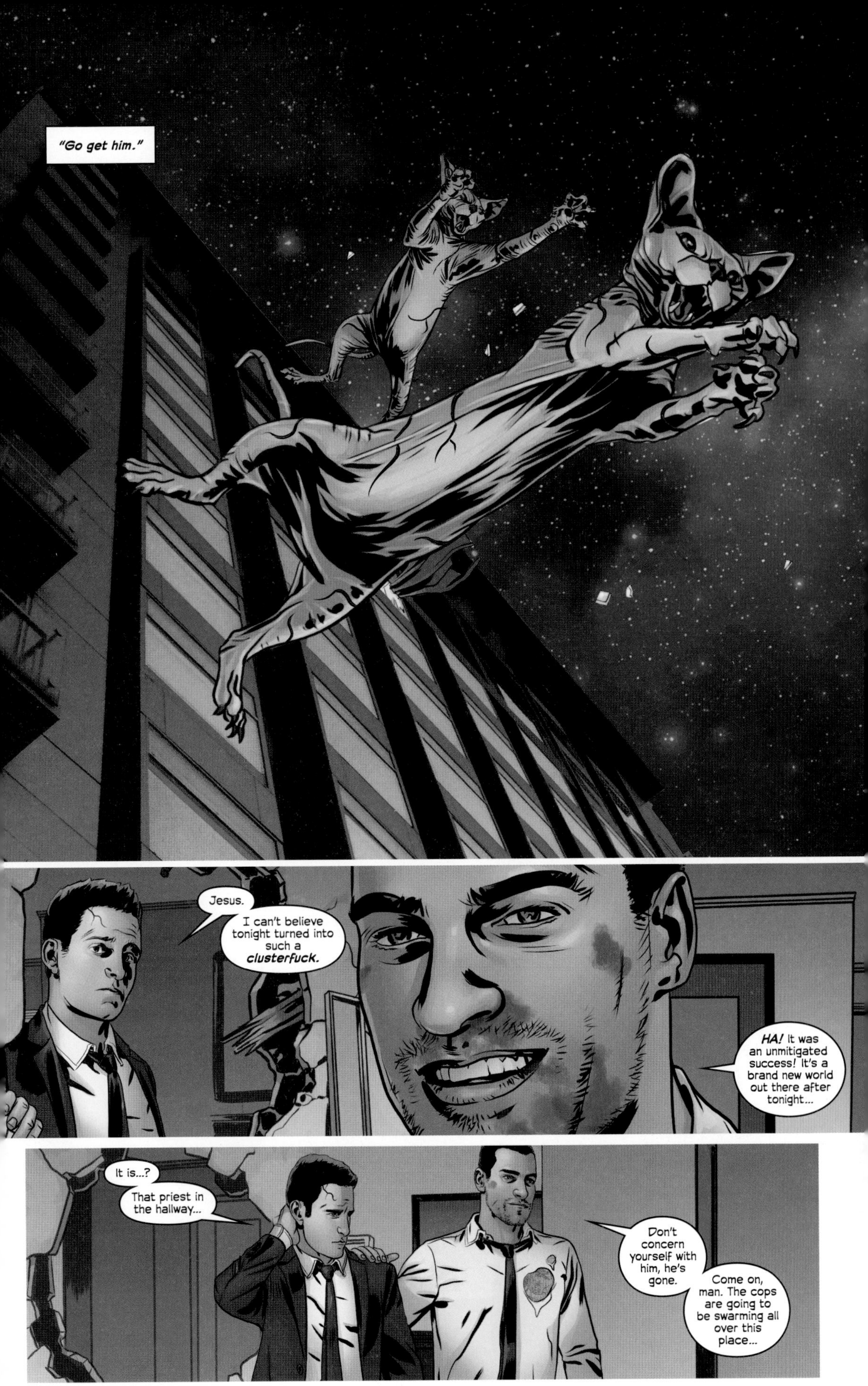
"Go get him."
Jesus.
I can't believe tonight turned into such a *clusterfuck.*
HA! It was an unmitigated success*!* It's a brand new world out there after tonight...
It is...?
That priest in the hallway...
Don't concern yourself with him, he's gone.
Come on, man. The cops are going to be swarming all over this place...

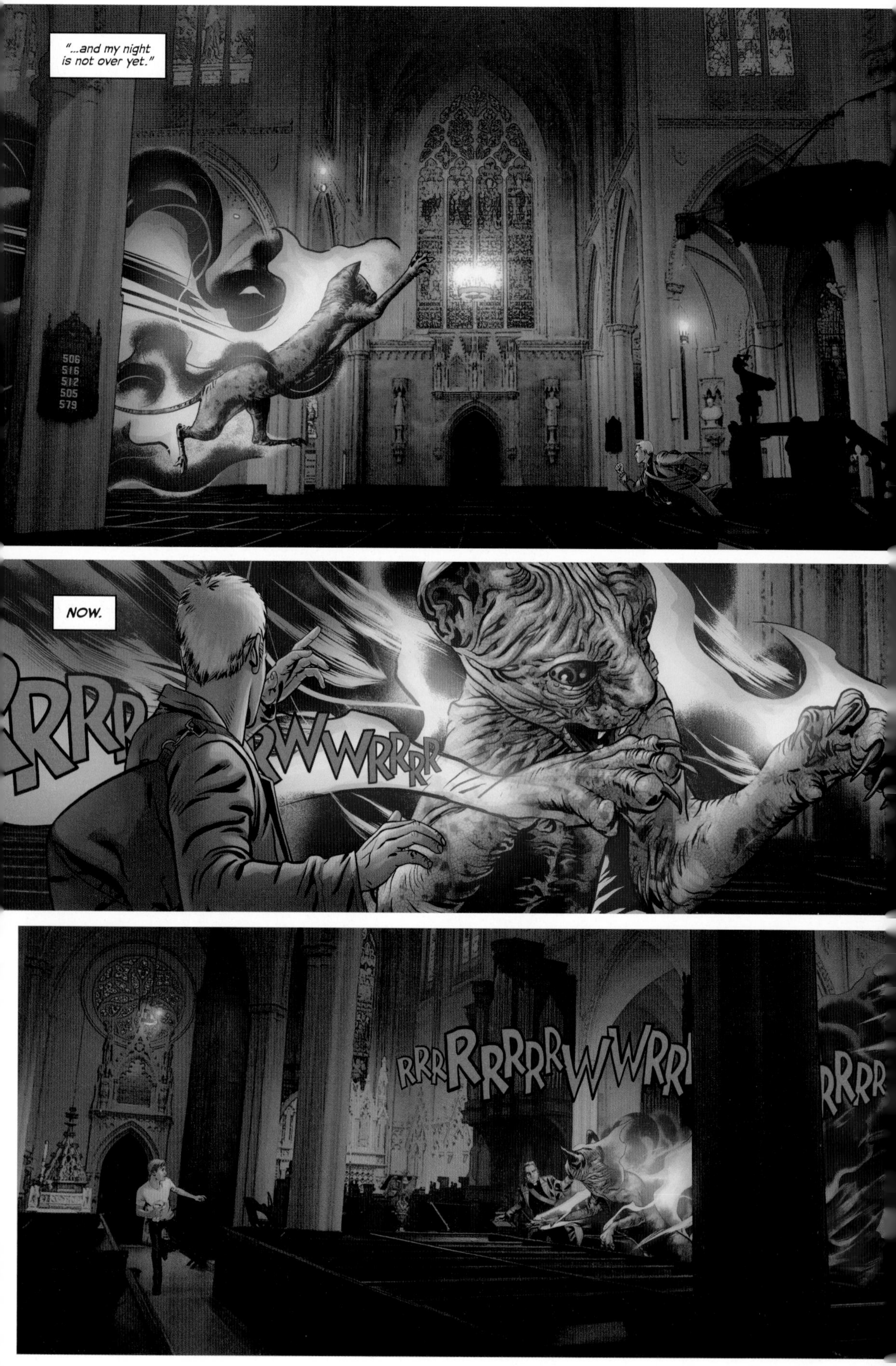
"...and my night is not over yet."
506
516
512
505
579
NOW.
RRRRWWWRRRR
RRRRRRRRWWRR
RRRR

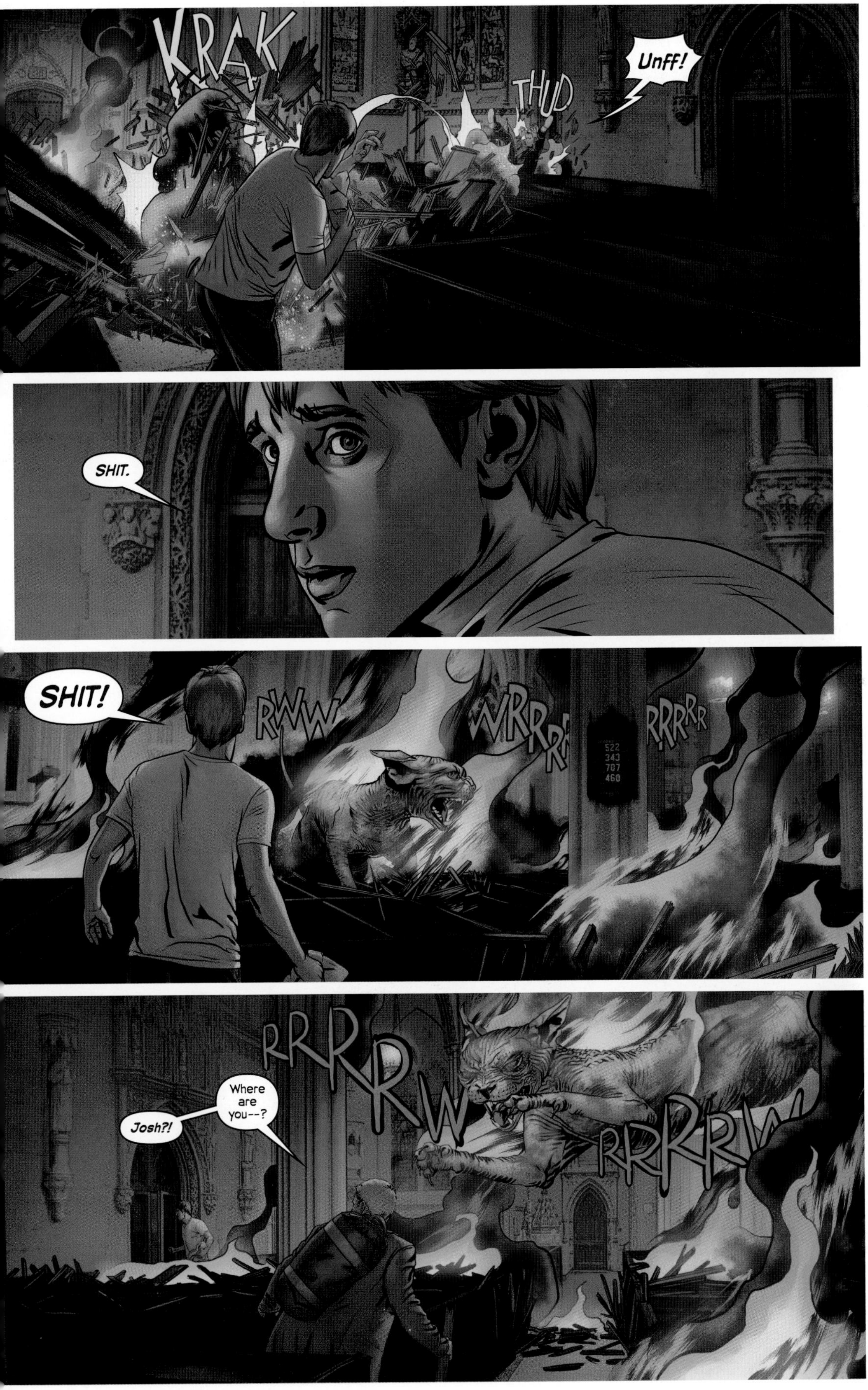
KRAK
THUD
Unff!
SHIT.
SHIT!
RWW
WRRRR
RRRRR
522
343
707
460
RRRRRW
Josh?!
Where are you--?
RRRRRW

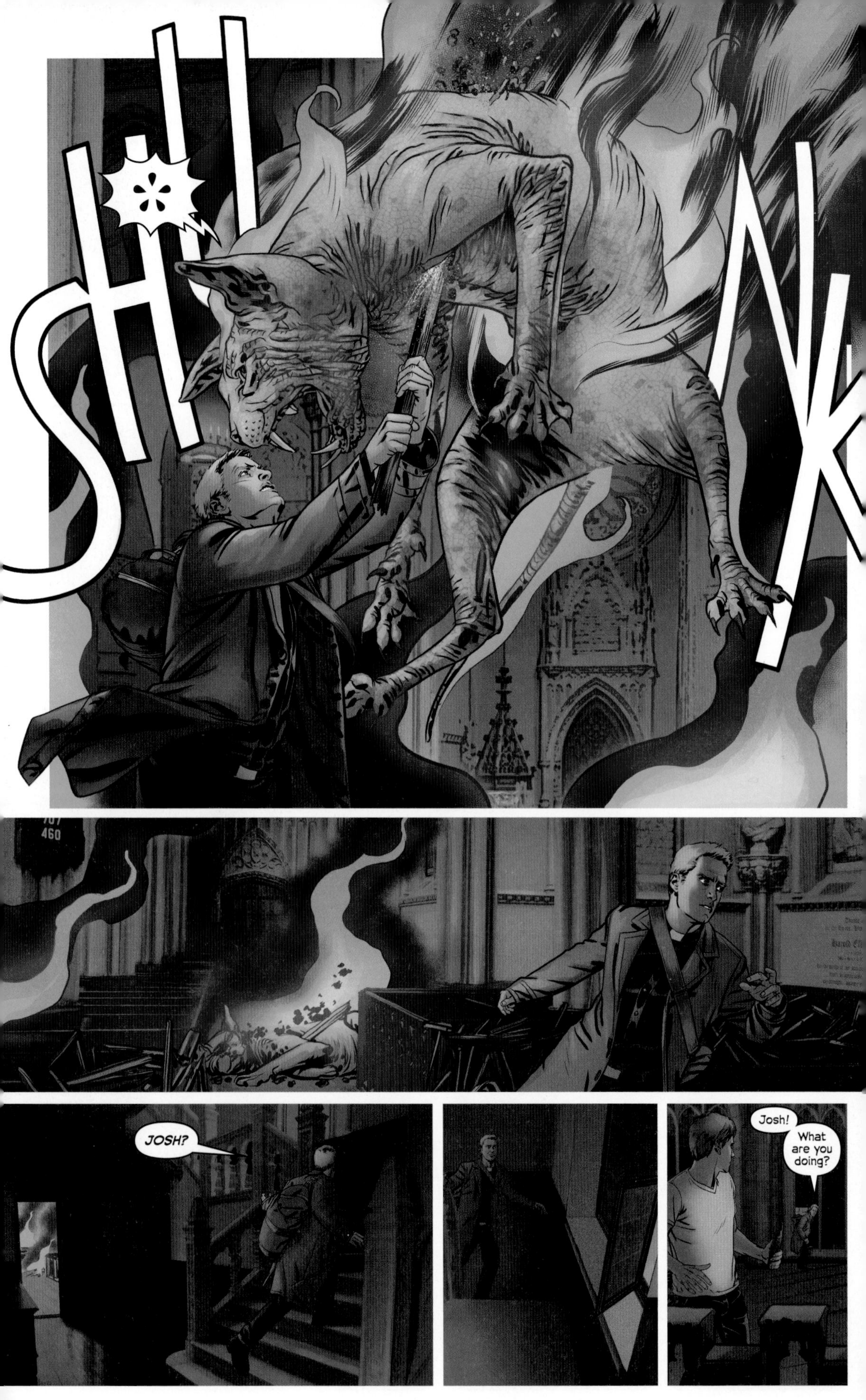
SHHNK
!
707
460
JOSH?
Josh!
What are you doing?

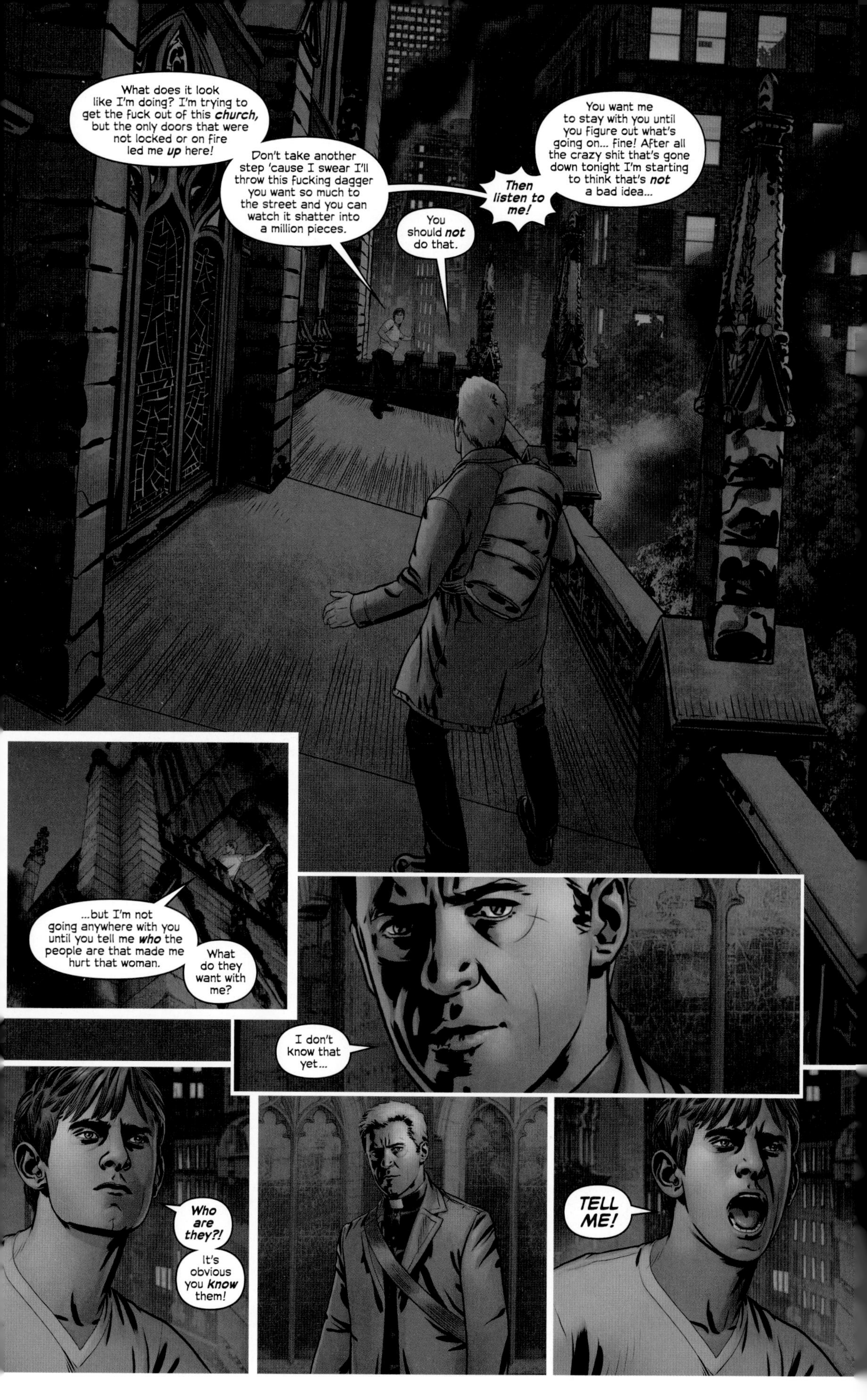
What does it look like I'm doing? I'm trying to get the fuck out of this *church,* but the only doors that were not locked or on fire led me *up* here!
Don't take another step 'cause I swear I'll throw this fucking dagger you want so much to the street and you can watch it shatter into a million pieces.
You should *not* do that.
Then listen to me!
You want me to stay with you until you figure out what's going on... fine! After all the crazy shit that's gone down tonight I'm starting to think that's *not* a bad idea...
...but I'm not going anywhere with you until you tell me *who* the people are that made me hurt that woman.
What do they want with me?
I don't know that yet...
Who are they?!
It's obvious you *know* them!
TELL ME!

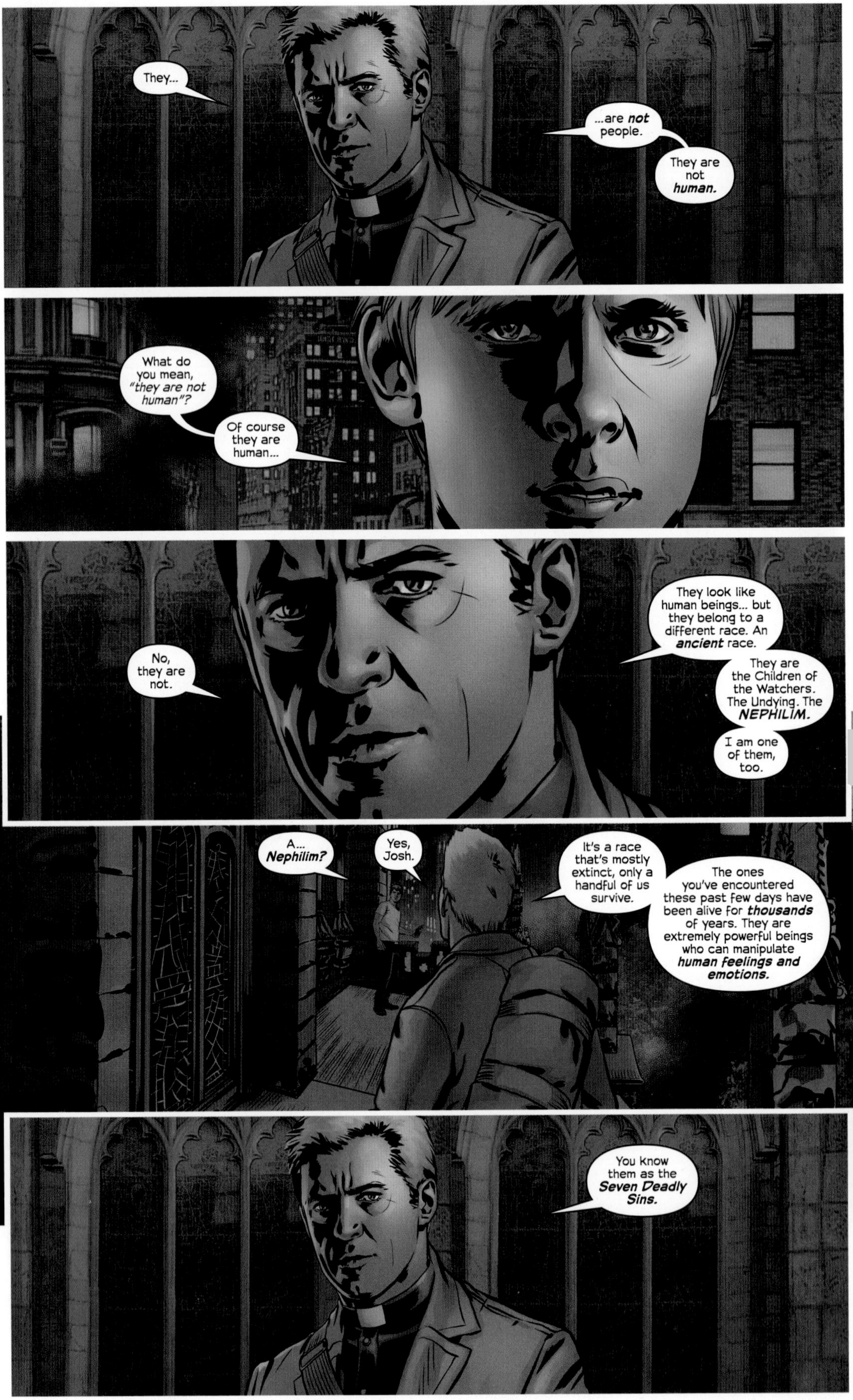
They...
...are *not* people.
They are not *human.*
What do you mean, *"they are not human"?*
Of course they are human...
No, they are not.
They look like human beings... but they belong to a different race. An *ancient* race.
They are the Children of the Watchers. The Undying. The *NEPHILIM.*
I am one of them, too.
A... *Nephilim?*
Yes, Josh.
It's a race that's mostly extinct, only a handful of us survive.
The ones you've encountered these past few days have been alive for *thousands* of years. They are extremely powerful beings who can manipulate *human feelings and emotions.*
You know them as the *Seven Deadly Sins.*

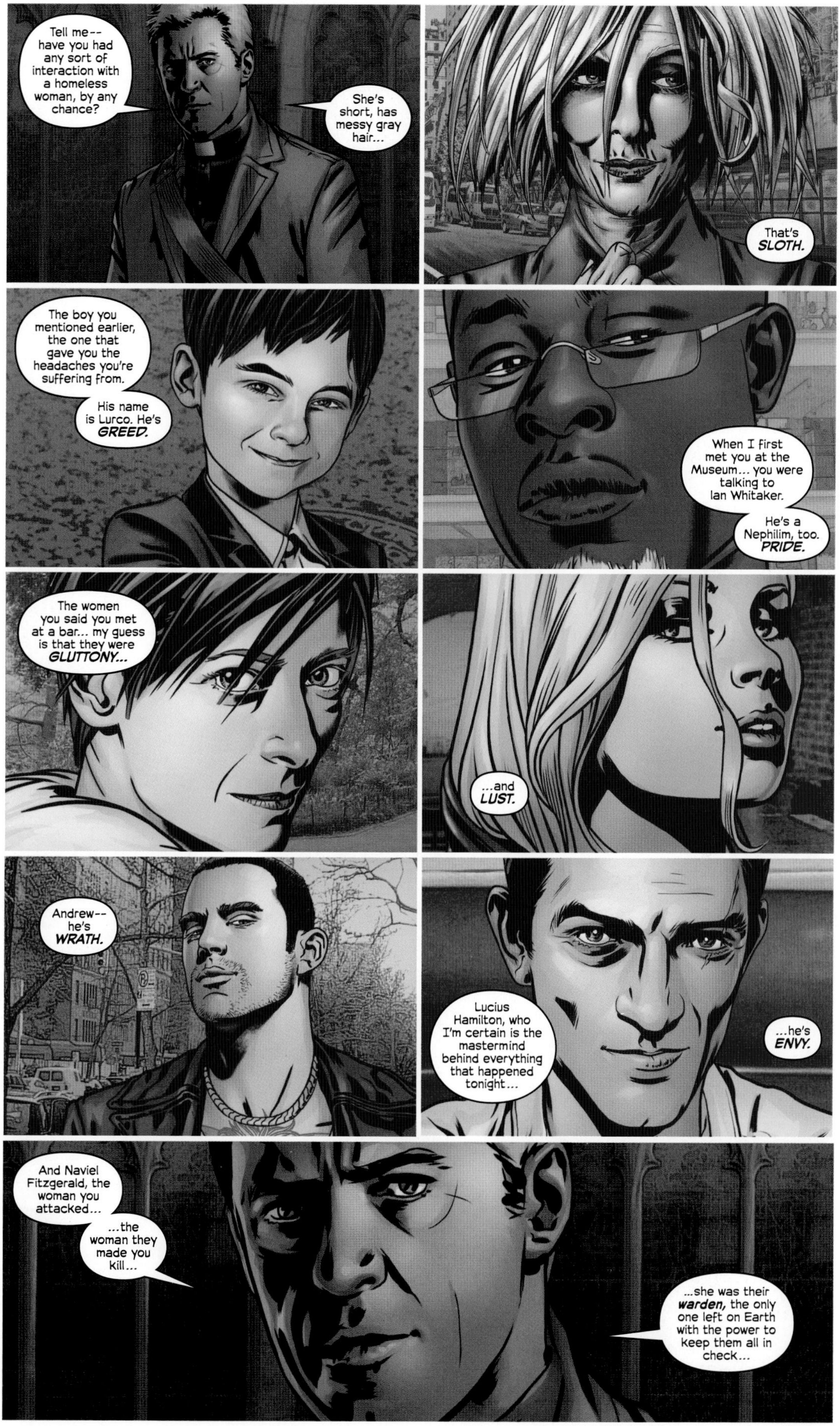

Tell me-- have you had any sort of interaction with a homeless woman, by any chance?
She's short, has messy gray hair...
That's *SLOTH.*
The boy you mentioned earlier, the one that gave you the headaches you're suffering from.
His name is Lurco. He's *GREED.*
When I first met you at the Museum... you were talking to Ian Whitaker.
He's a Nephilim, too. *PRIDE.*
The women you said you met at a bar... my guess is that they were *GLUTTONY...*
...and *LUST.*
Andrew-- he's *WRATH.*
Lucius Hamilton, who I'm certain is the mastermind behind everything that happened tonight...
...he's *ENVY.*
And Naviel Fitzgerald, the woman you attacked...
...the woman they made you kill...
...she was their *warden,* the only one left on Earth with the power to keep them all in check...

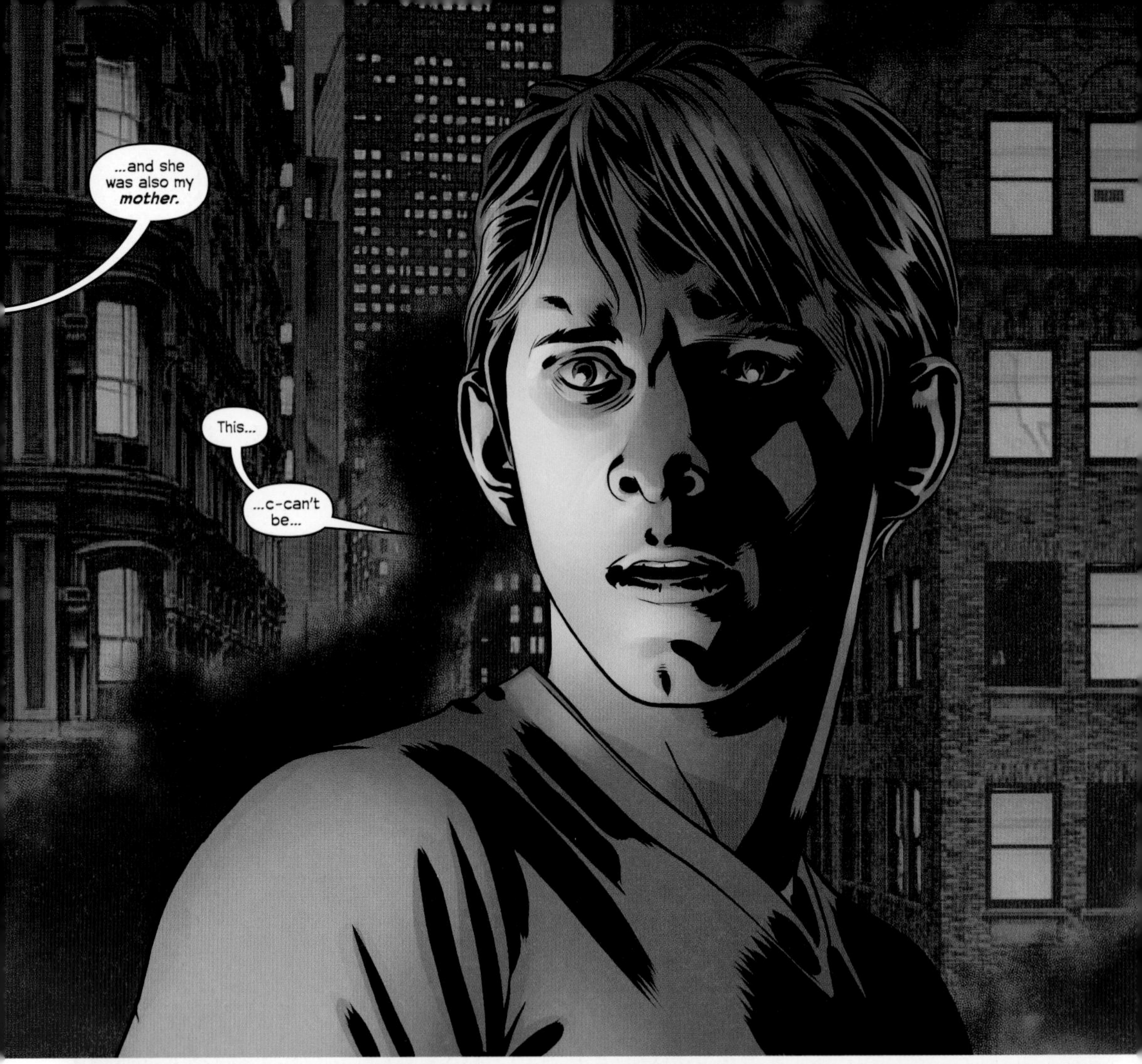
...and she was also my *mother.*
This...
...c-can't be...

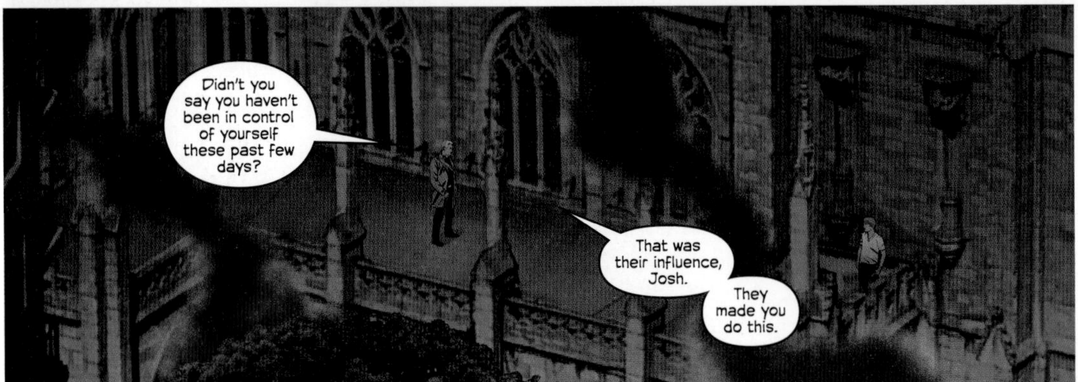
Didn't you say you haven't been in control of yourself these past few days?
That was their influence, Josh.
They made you do this.

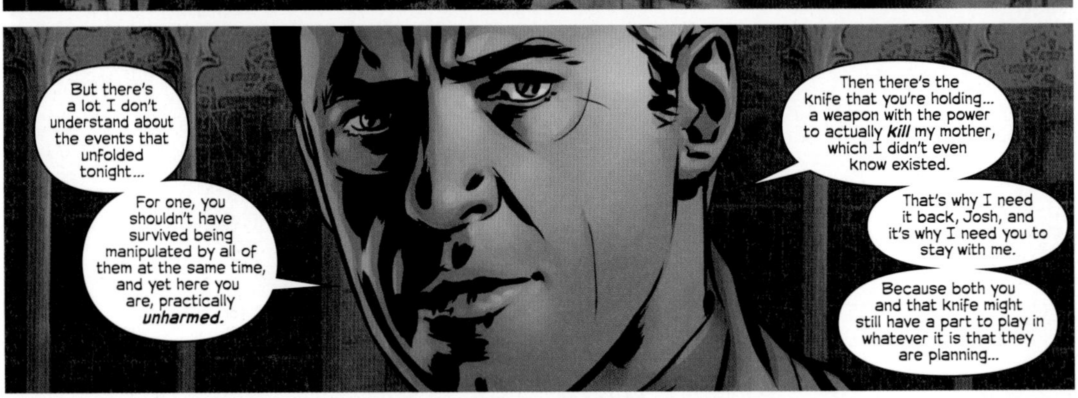
But there's a lot I don't understand about the events that unfolded tonight...
For one, you shouldn't have survived being manipulated by all of them at the same time, and yet here you are, practically *unharmed.*
Then there's the knife that you're holding... a weapon with the power to actually *kill* my mother, which I didn't even know existed.
That's why I need it back, Josh, and it's why I need you to stay with me.
Because both you and that knife might still have a part to play in whatever it is that they are planning...

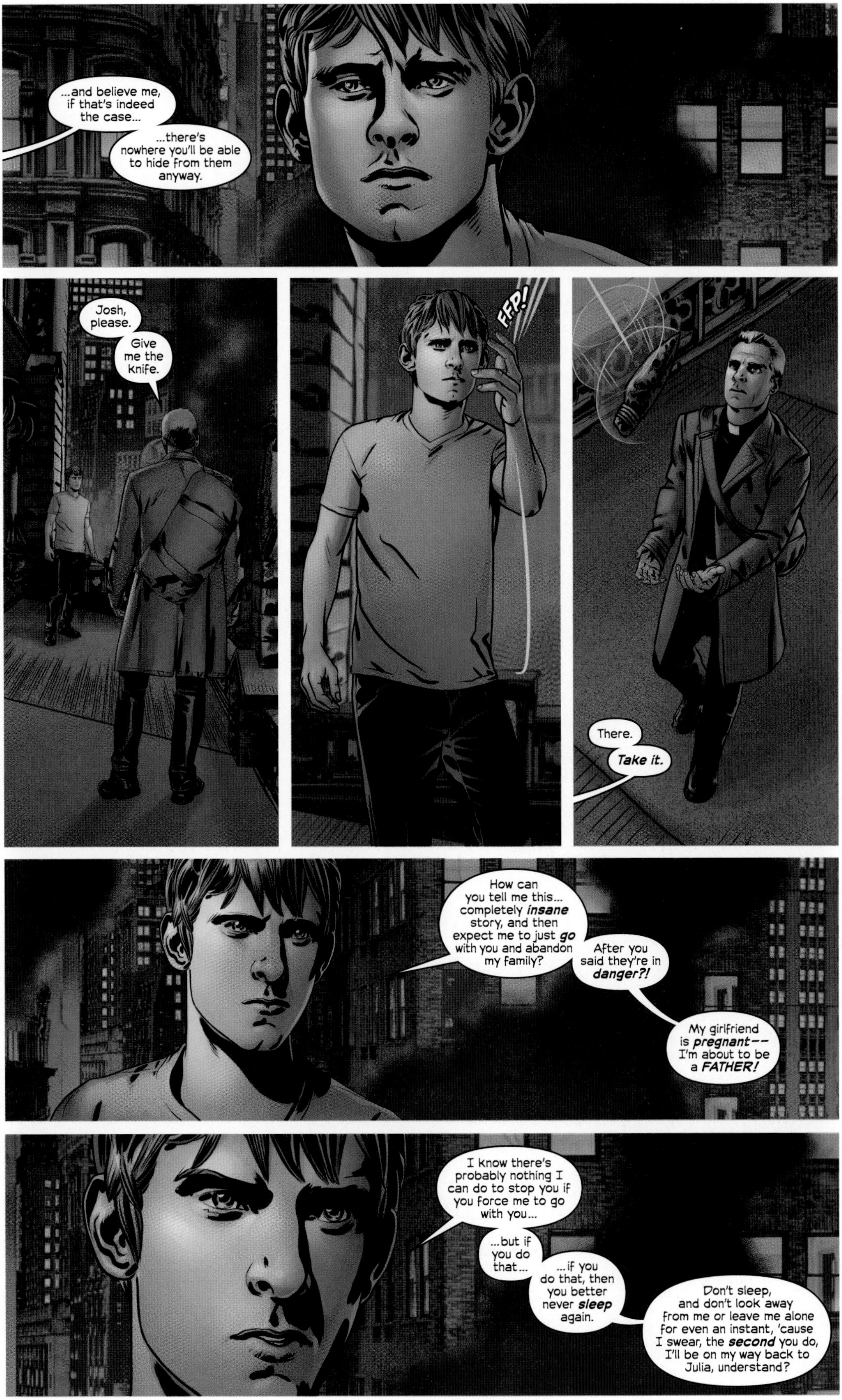
...and believe me, if that's indeed the case...
...there's nowhere you'll be able to hide from them anyway.
Josh, please.
Give me the knife.
FFP!
There.
Take it.
How can you tell me this... completely *insane* story, and then expect me to just *go* with you and abandon my family?
After you said they're in *danger?!*
My girlfriend is *pregnant*-- I'm about to be a *FATHER!*
I know there's probably nothing I can do to stop you if you force me to go with you...
...but if you do that...
...if you do that, then you better never *sleep* again.
Don't sleep, and don't look away from me or leave me alone for even an instant, 'cause I swear, the *second* you do, I'll be on my way back to Julia, understand?

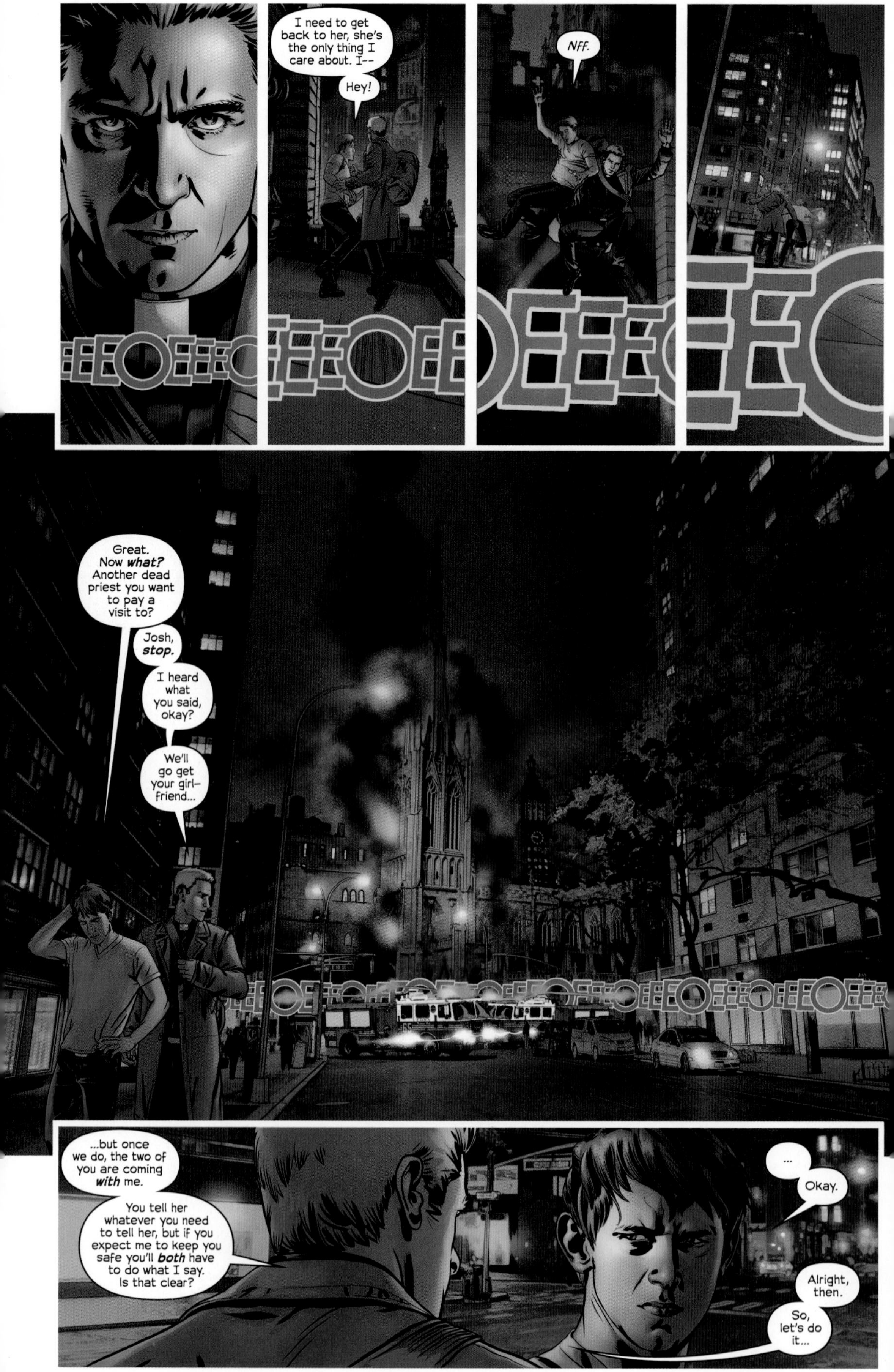
I need to get back to her, she's the only thing I care about. I--
Hey!
NFF.
Great. Now what? Another dead priest you want to pay a visit to?
Josh, stop.
I heard what you said, okay?
We'll go get your girl-friend...
...but once we do, the two of you are coming with me.
You tell her whatever you need to tell her, but if you expect me to keep you safe you'll both have to do what I say. Is that clear?
...
Okay.
Alright, then.
So, let's do it...

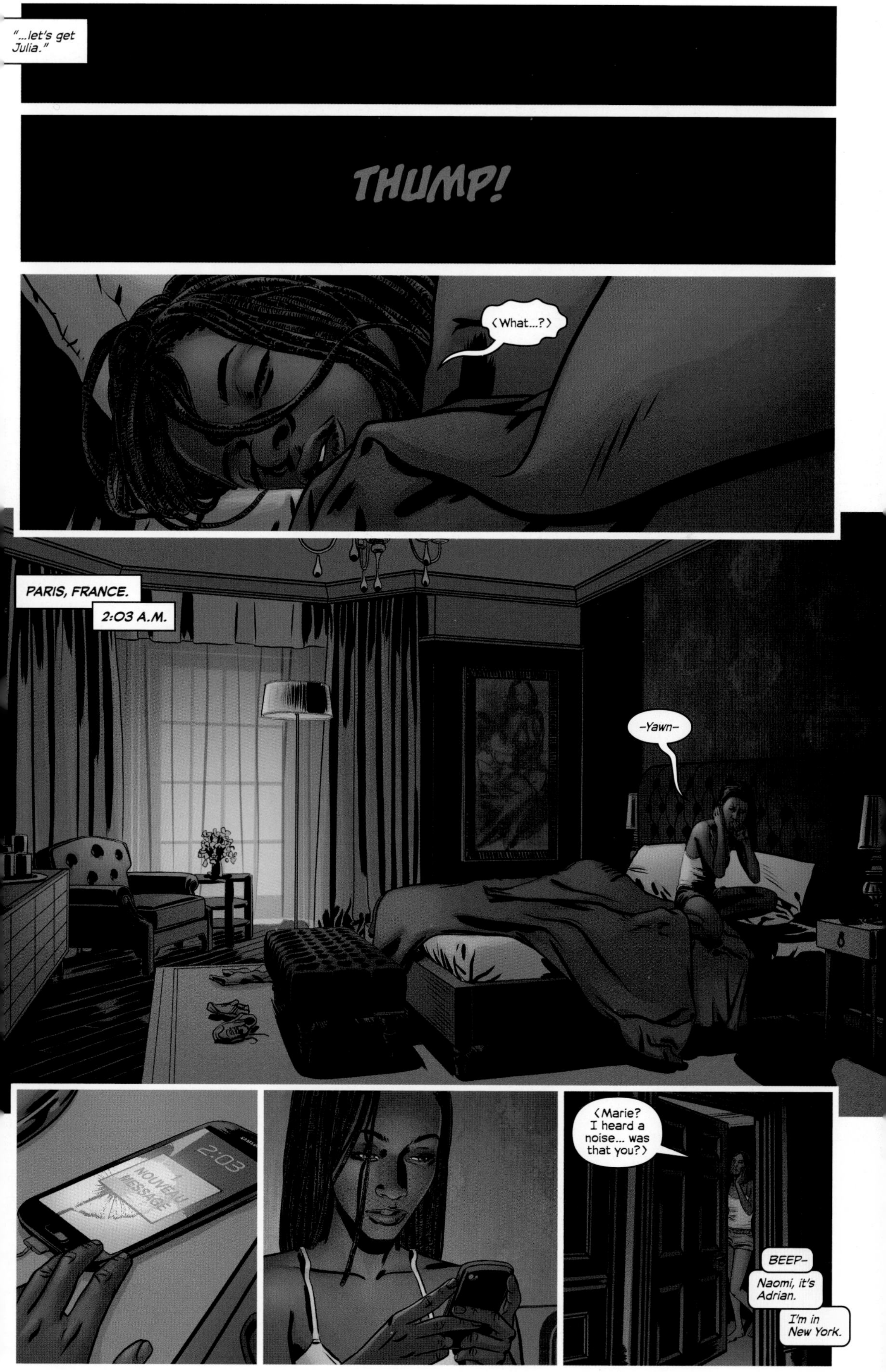
"...let's get Julia."
THUMP!
‹What...?›
PARIS, FRANCE.
2:03 A.M.
-Yawn-
2:03
1 NOUVEAU MESSAGE
‹Marie? I heard a noise... was that you?›
BEEP-
Naomi, it's Adrian.
I'm in New York.

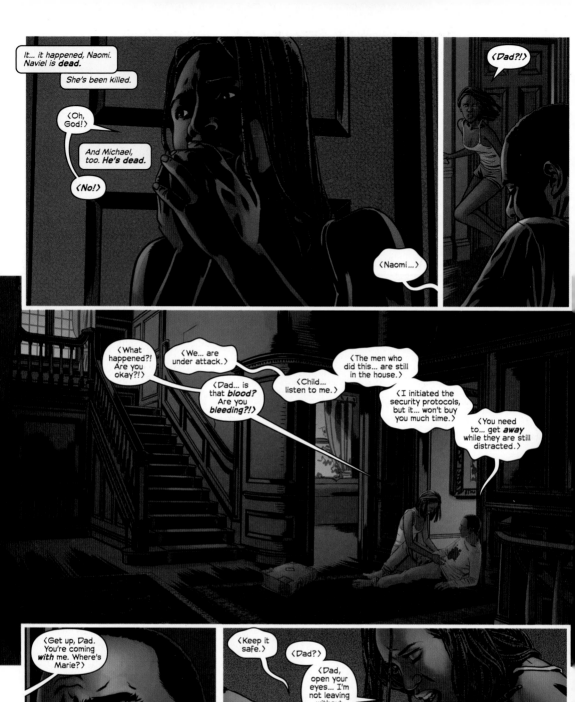

It... it happened, Naomi. Naviel is **dead.**

She's been killed.

⟨Oh, God!⟩

And Michael, too. **He's dead.**

⟨No!⟩

⟨Dad?!⟩

⟨Naomi...⟩

⟨What happened?! Are you okay?!⟩

⟨We... are under attack.⟩

⟨Dad... is that **blood?** Are you **bleeding?!**⟩

⟨Child... listen to me.⟩

⟨The men who did this... are still in the house.⟩

⟨I initiated the security protocols, but it... won't buy you much time.⟩

⟨You need to... get **away** while they are still distracted.⟩

⟨Get up, Dad. You're coming **with** me. Where's Marie?⟩

⟨It's... too late for me, sweetheart. But you...⟩

⟨You must... take **the book.** Take it... and run.⟩

⟨Keep it safe.⟩

⟨Dad?⟩

⟨Dad, open your eyes... I'm not leaving without you.⟩

I tried to stop it...

⟨DAD!⟩

...but I was too **late.**

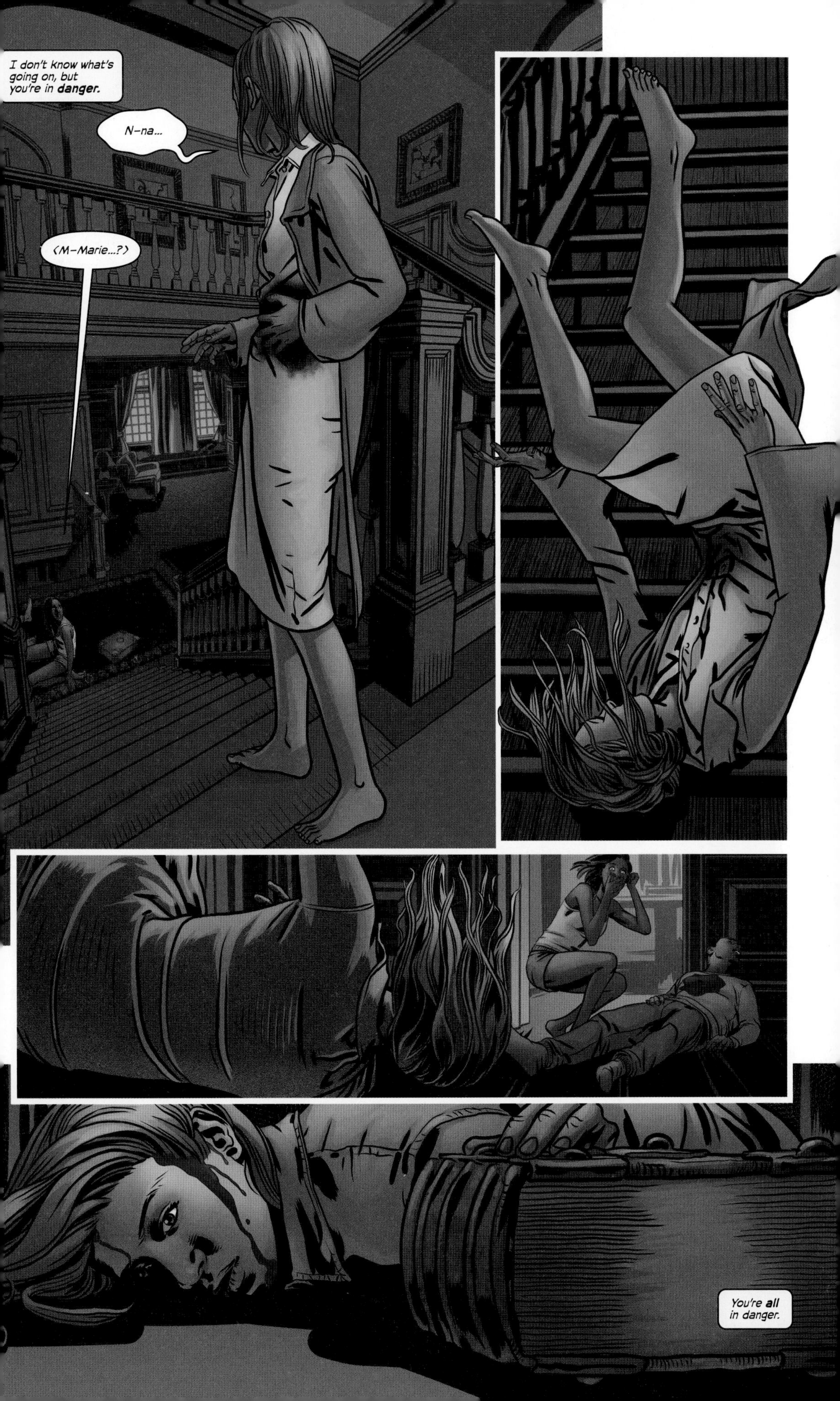

I don't know what's going on, but you're in **danger.**
N-na...
‹M-Marie...?›
You're **all** in danger.

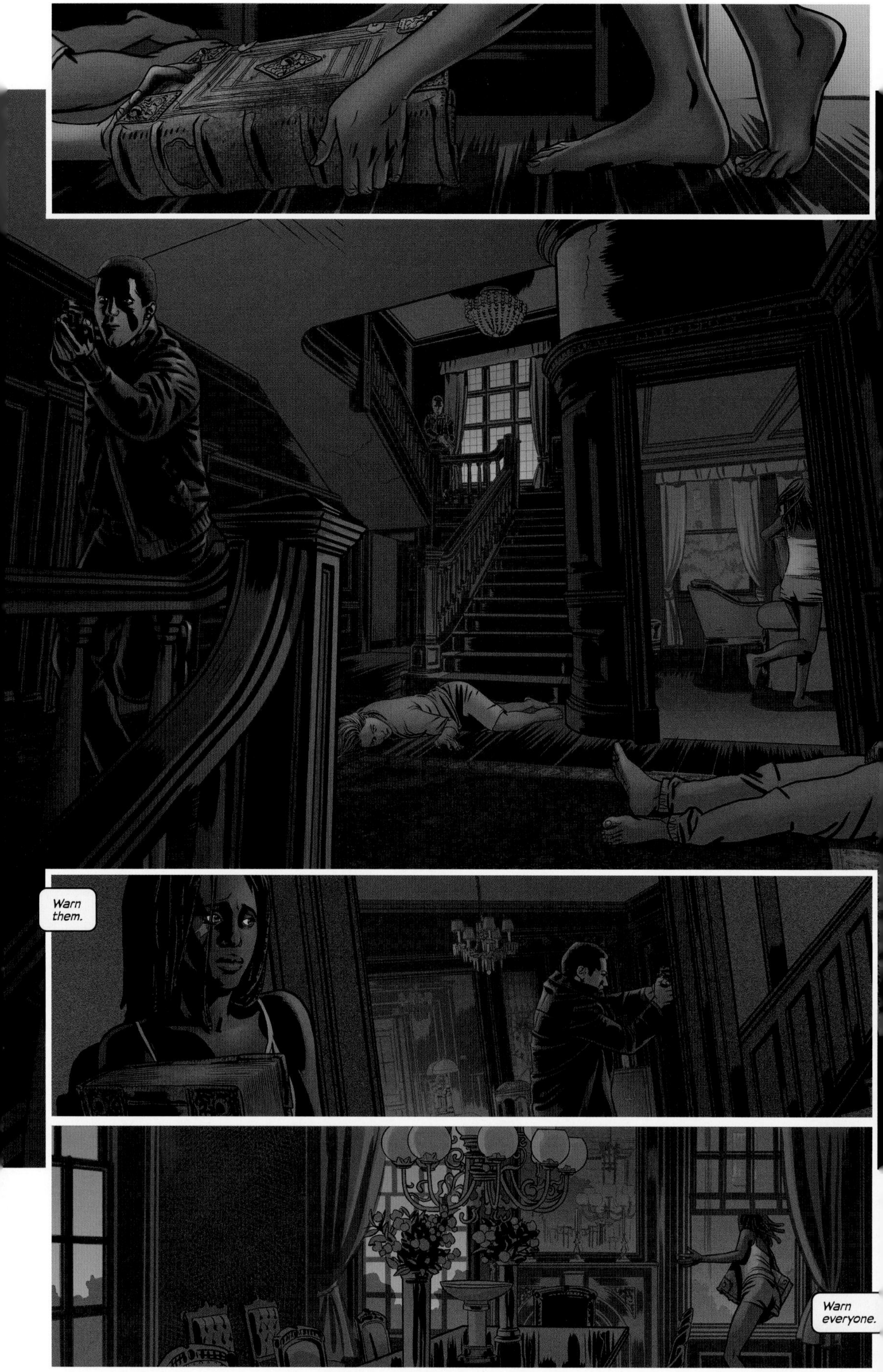
Warn them.
Warn everyone.

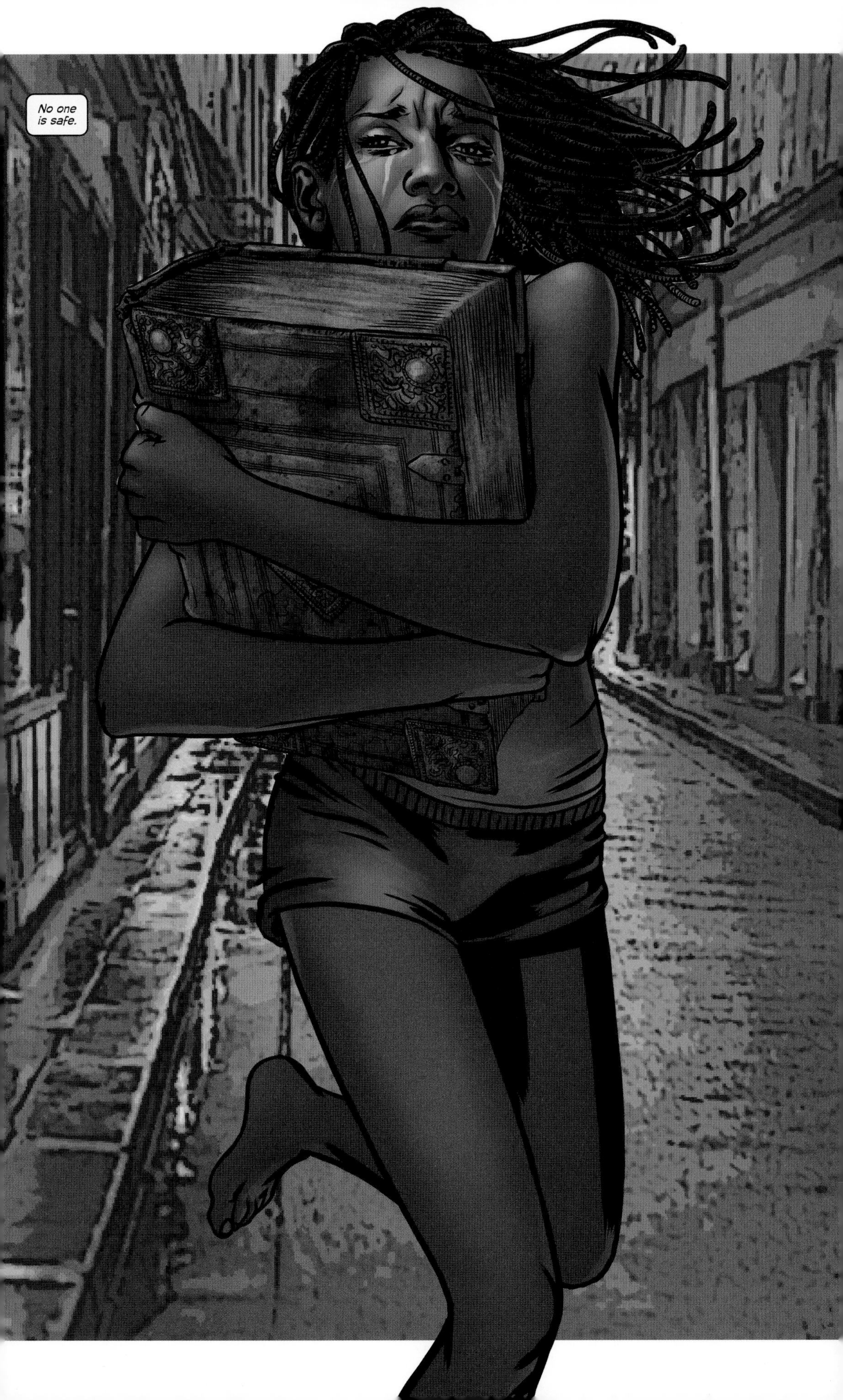
No one is safe.

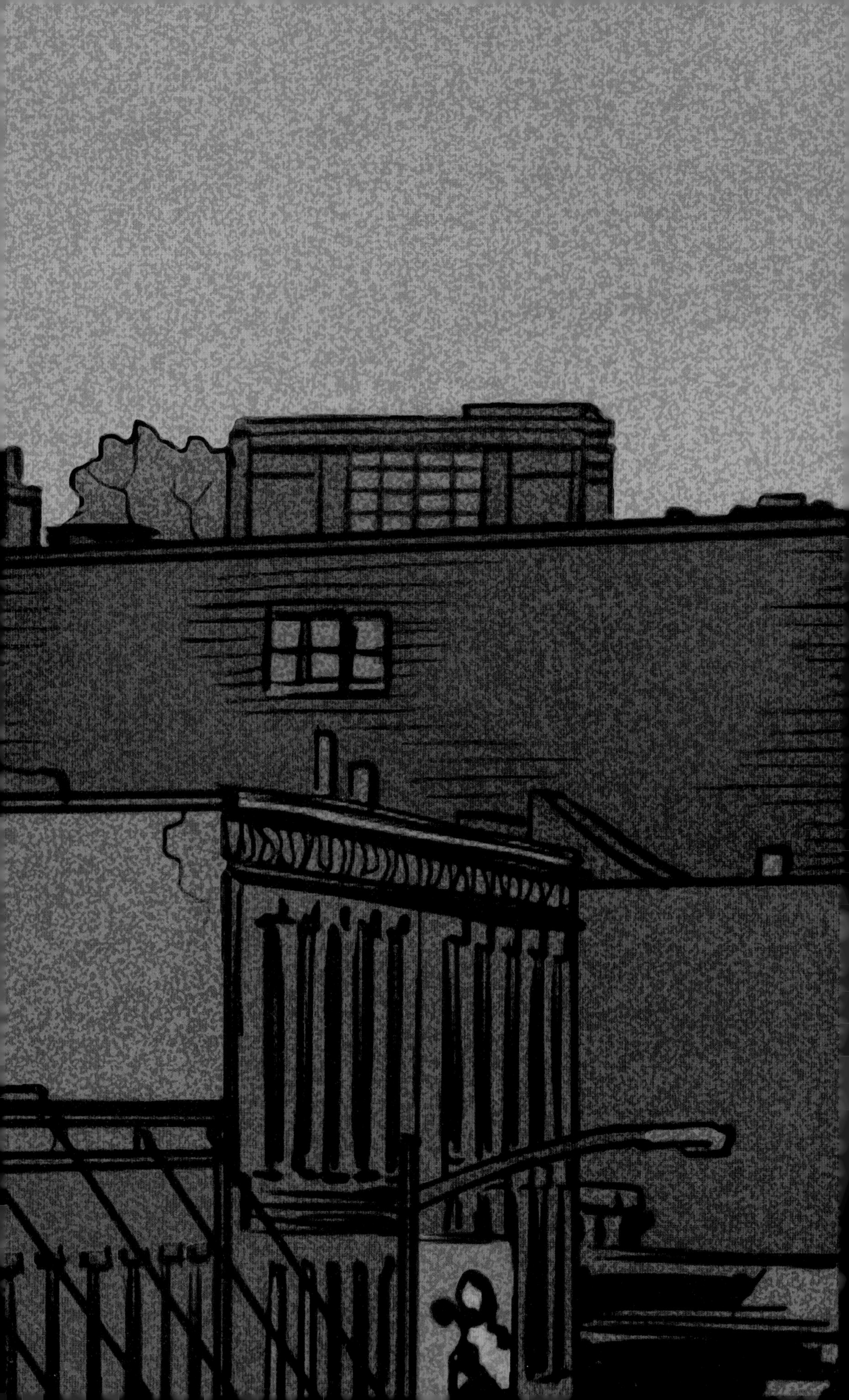

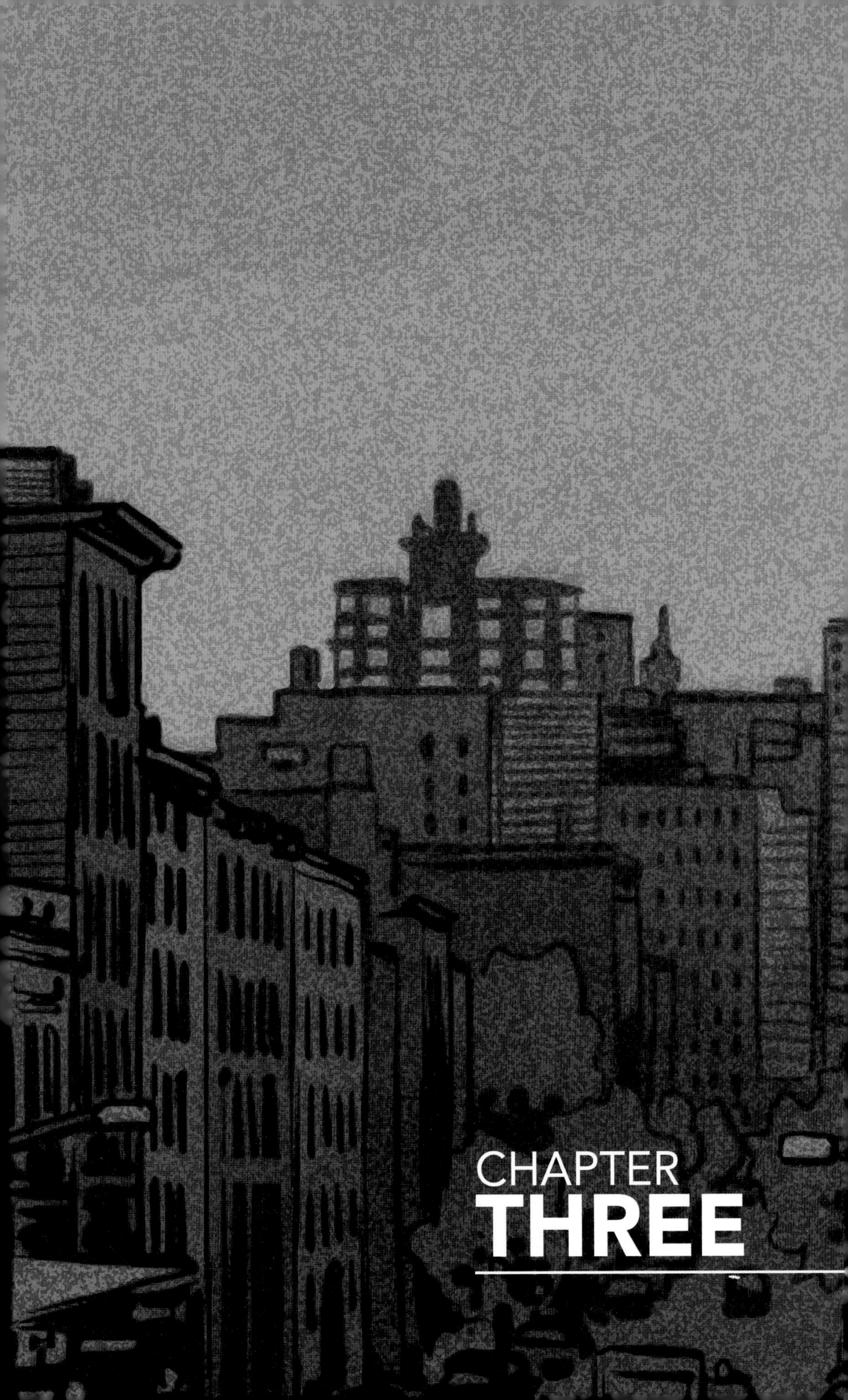

CHAPTER THREE

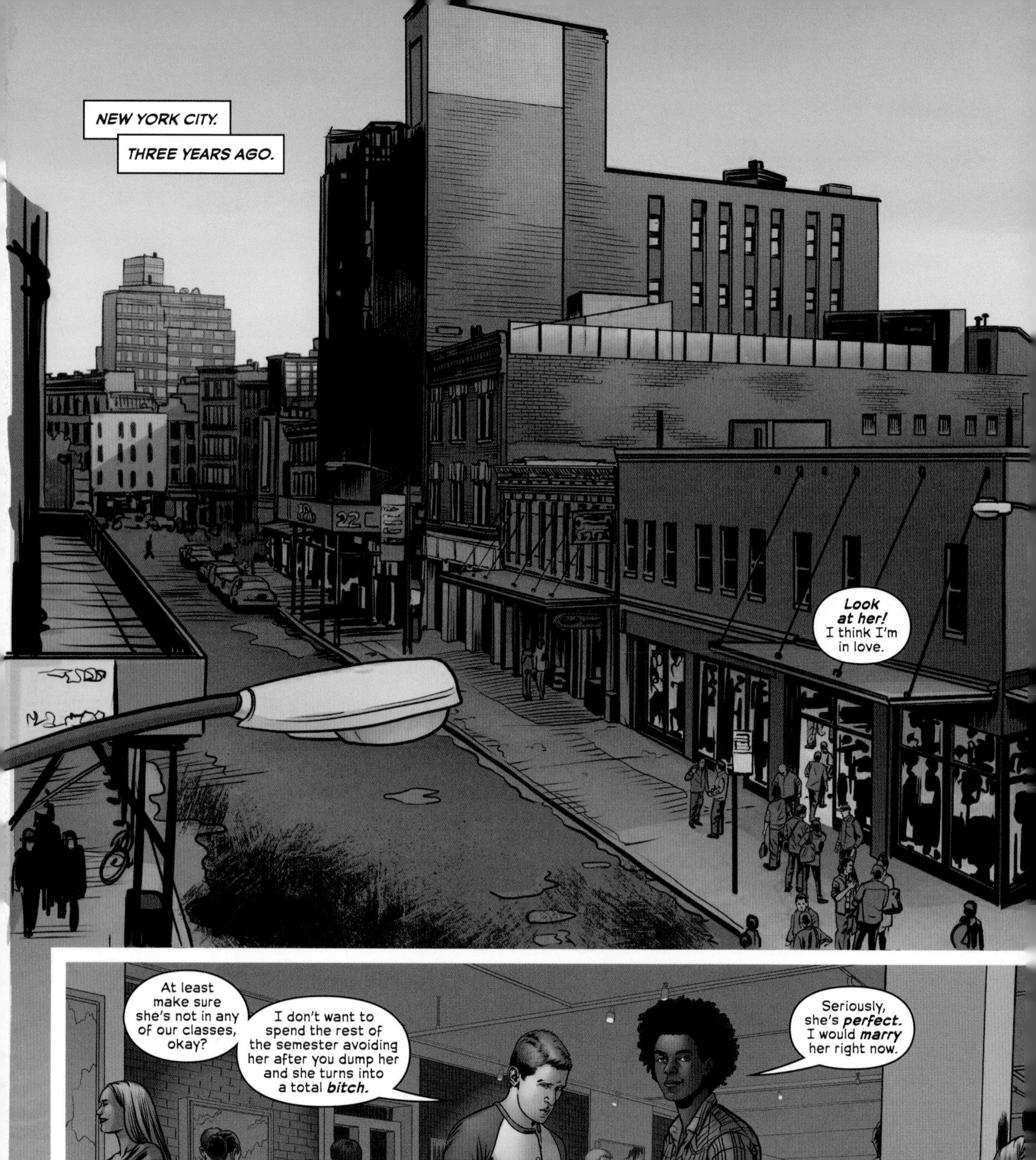
NEW YORK CITY.
THREE YEARS AGO.
Look at her! I think I'm in love.

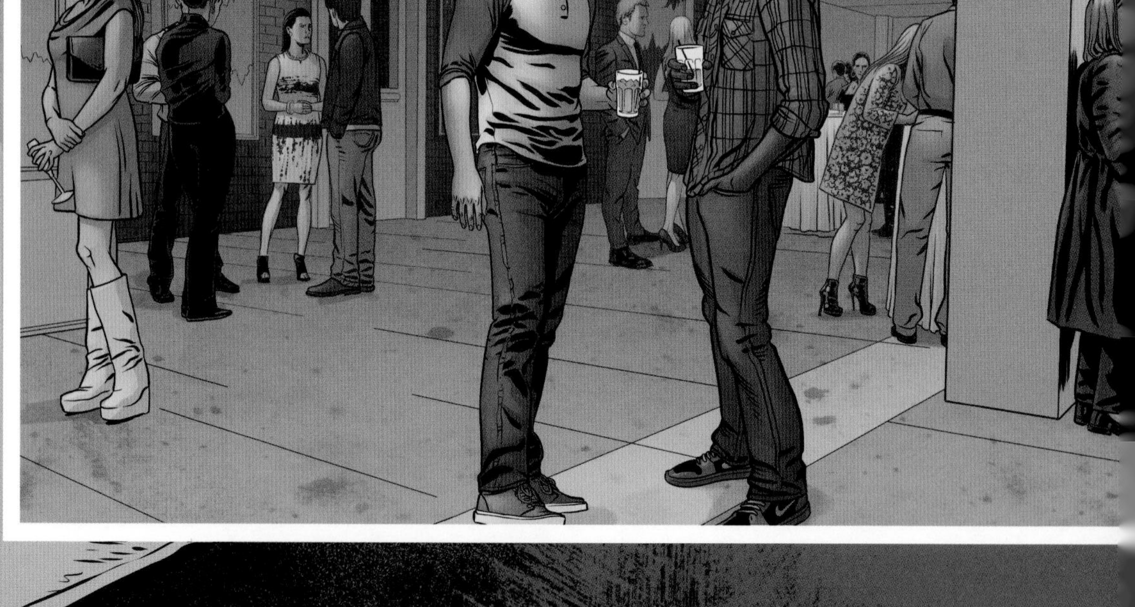
At least make sure she's not in any of our classes, okay?
I don't want to spend the rest of the semester avoiding her after you dump her and she turns into a total *bitch.*
Seriously, she's *perfect.* I would *marry* her right now.

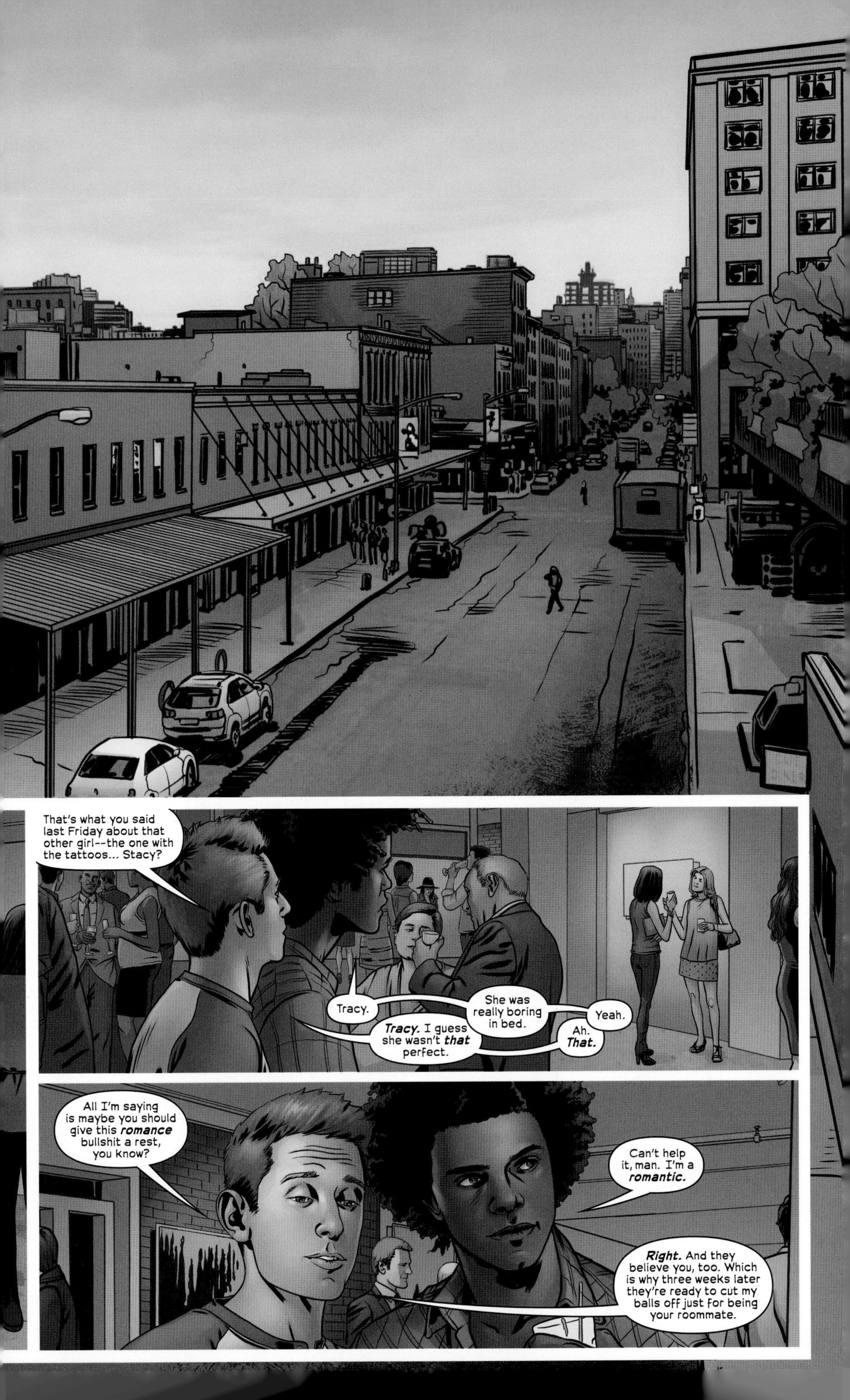
That's what you said last Friday about that other girl--the one with the tattoos... Stacy?
Tracy.
Tracy. I guess she wasn't *that* perfect.
She was really boring in bed.
Ah. *That.*
Yeah.
All I'm saying is maybe you should give this *romance* bullshit a rest, you know?
Can't help it, man. I'm a *romantic.*
Right. And they believe you, too. Which is why three weeks later they're ready to cut my balls off just for being your roommate.

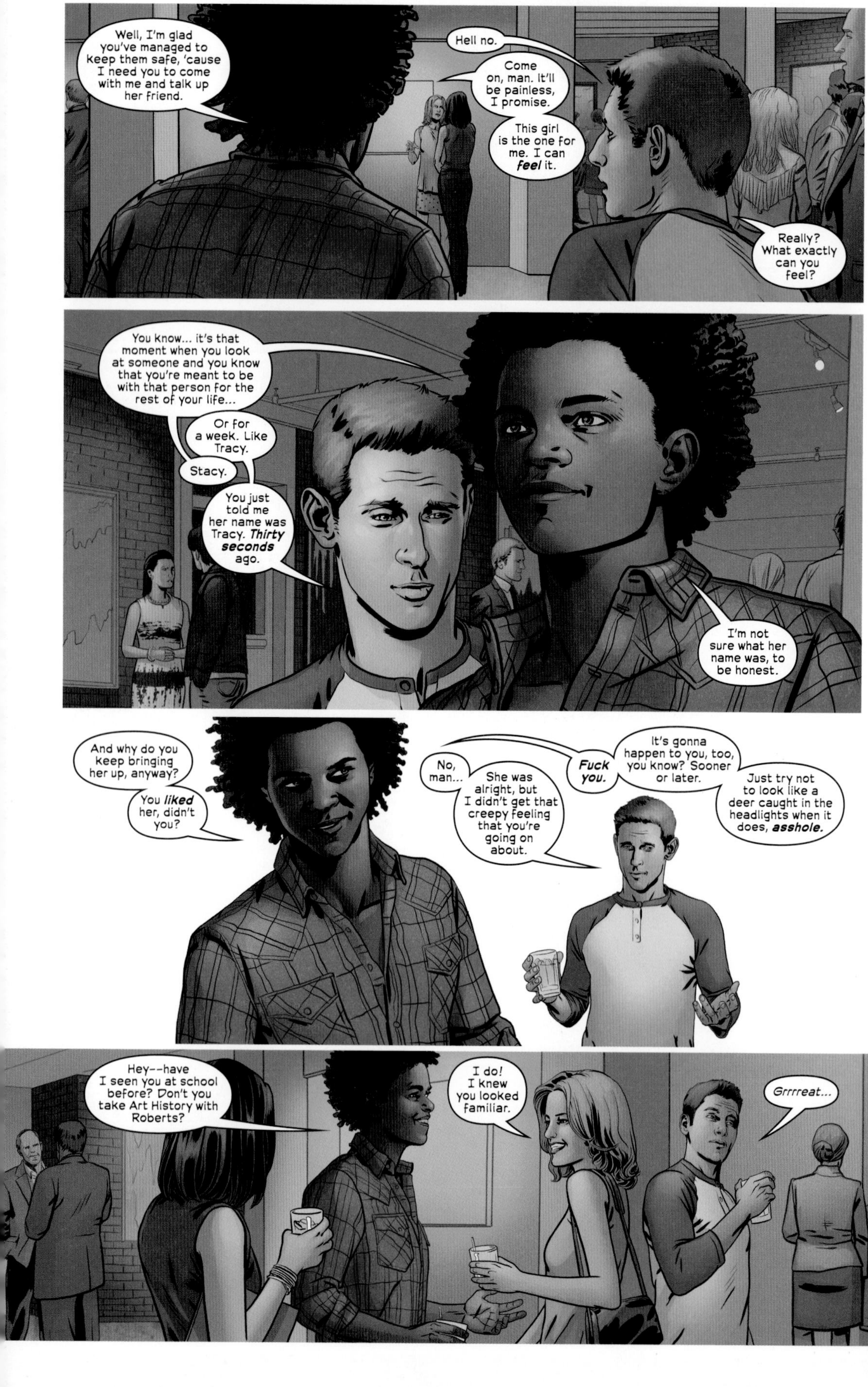
Well, I'm glad you've managed to keep them safe, 'cause I need you to come with me and talk up her friend.
Hell no.
Come on, man. It'll be painless, I promise.
This girl is the one for me. I can *feel* it.
Really? What exactly can you feel?
You know... it's that moment when you look at someone and you know that you're meant to be with that person for the rest of your life...
Or for a week. Like Tracy.
Stacy.
You just told me her name was Tracy. *Thirty seconds* ago.
I'm not sure what her name was, to be honest.
And why do you keep bringing her up, anyway?
You *liked* her, didn't you?
No, man...
She was alright, but I didn't get that creepy feeling that you're going on about.
Fuck you.
It's gonna happen to you, too, you know? Sooner or later.
Just try not to look like a deer caught in the headlights when it does, *asshole.*
Hey--have I seen you at school before? Don't you take Art History with Roberts?
I do! I knew you looked familiar.
Grrrreat...

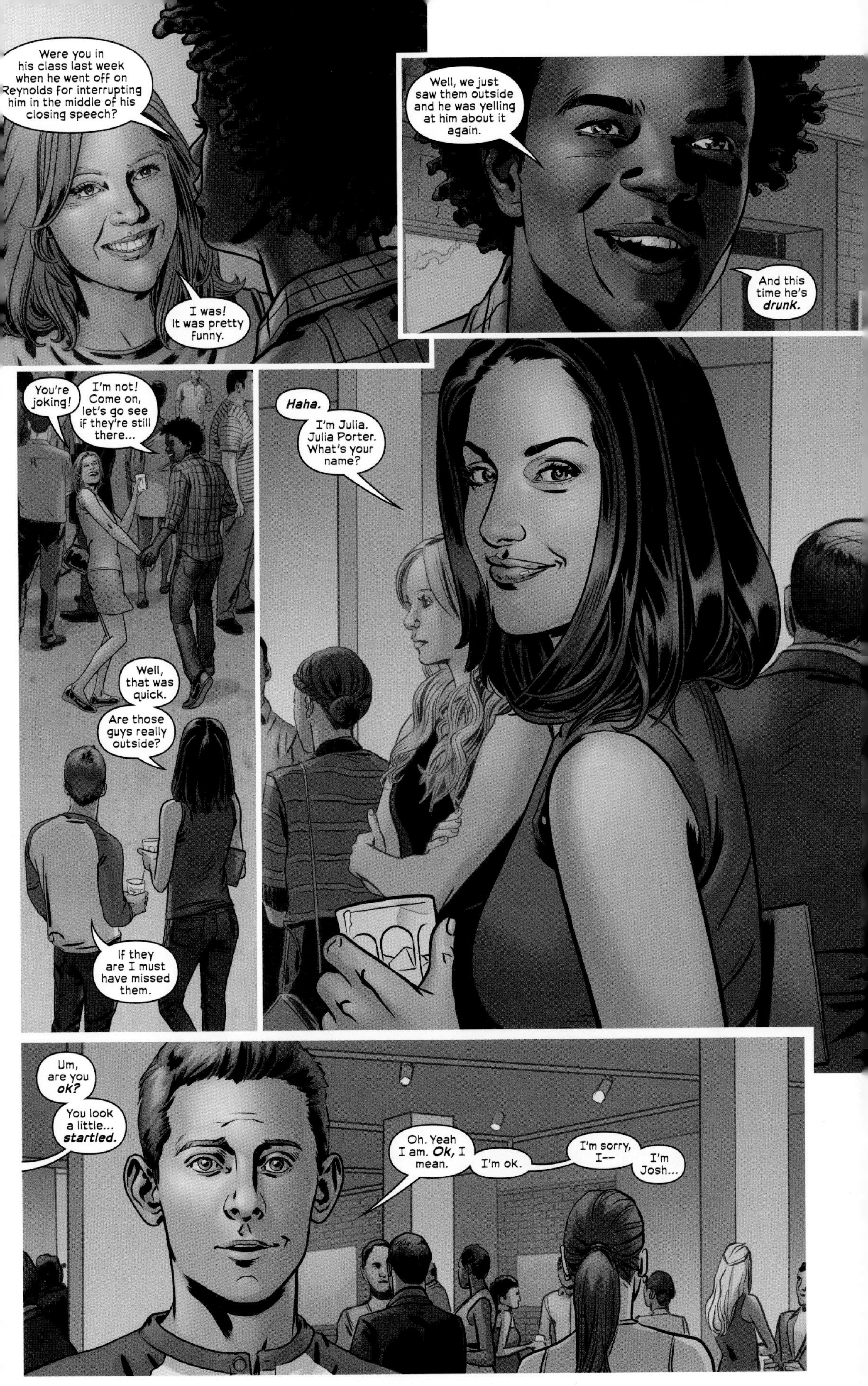
Were you in his class last week when he went off on Reynolds for interrupting him in the middle of his closing speech?
I was! It was pretty funny.
Well, we just saw them outside and he was yelling at him about it again.
And this time he's *drunk.*
You're joking!
I'm not! Come on, let's go see if they're still there...
Well, that was quick.
Are those guys really outside?
If they are I must have missed them.
Haha.
I'm Julia. Julia Porter. What's your name?
Um, are you *ok?*
You look a little... *startled.*
Oh. Yeah I am. *Ok,* I mean.
I'm ok.
I'm sorry, I--
I'm Josh...

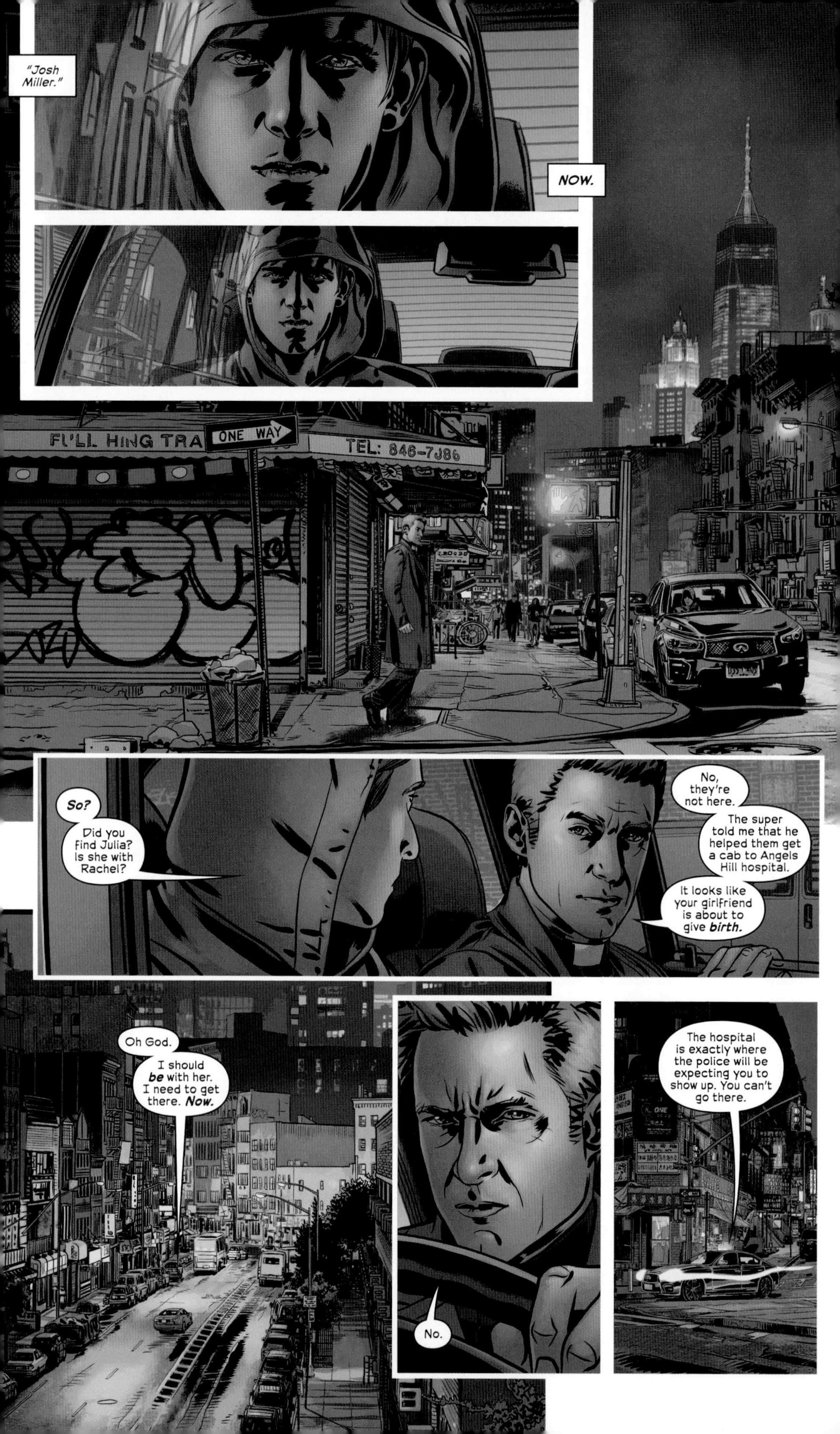

"Josh Miller."
NOW.
FU'LL HING TRA
ONE WAY
TEL: 846-7J86
So?
Did you find Julia? Is she with Rachel?
No, they're not here.
The super told me that he helped them get a cab to Angels Hill hospital.
It looks like your girlfriend is about to give *birth.*
Oh God.
I should *be* with her. I need to get there. *Now.*
No.
The hospital is exactly where the police will be expecting you to show up. You can't go there.

I don't care. I need to see her!

And do what?

Julia is safe at the hospital. All you're going to do is get yourself caught.

Who?!

Lucius Hamilton.

I want him to explain to me how he managed to manipulate you into doing what you did tonight, and where it was that he got that--

NO.

You're going to come with me instead. There's someone I need to see.

No fucking way!

Josh-- come back here!

JOSH!

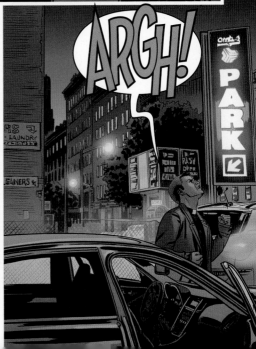

ARGH!

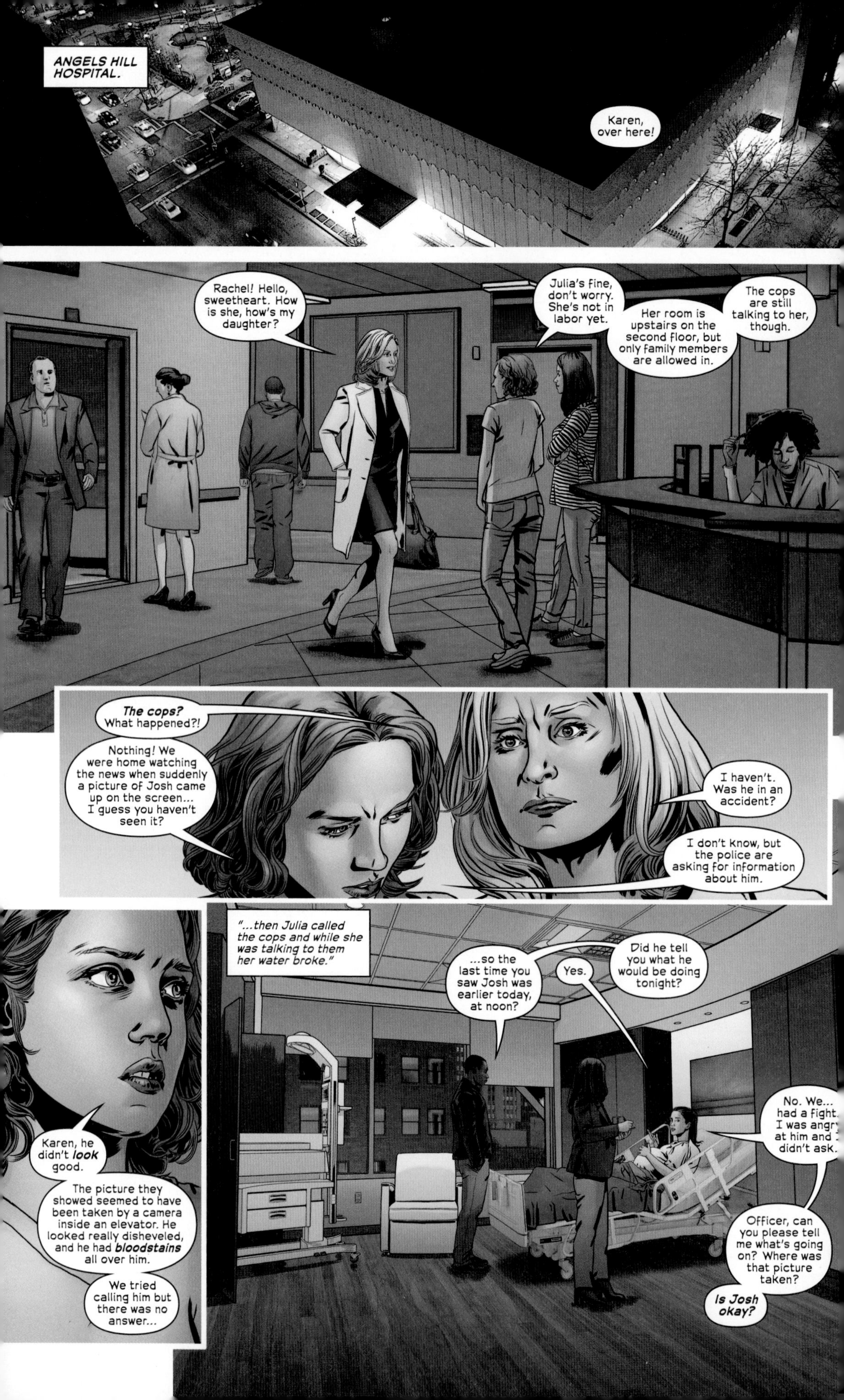
ANGELS HILL HOSPITAL.
Karen, over here!
Rachel! Hello, sweetheart. How is she, how's my daughter?
Julia's fine, don't worry. She's not in labor yet.
Her room is upstairs on the second floor, but only family members are allowed in.
The cops are still talking to her, though.
The cops? What happened?!
Nothing! We were home watching the news when suddenly a picture of Josh came up on the screen... I guess you haven't seen it?
I haven't. Was he in an accident?
I don't know, but the police are asking for information about him.
Karen, he didn't look good.
The picture they showed seemed to have been taken by a camera inside an elevator. He looked really disheveled, and he had bloodstains all over him.
We tried calling him but there was no answer...
"...then Julia called the cops and while she was talking to them her water broke."
...so the last time you saw Josh was earlier today, at noon?
Yes.
Did he tell you what he would be doing tonight?
No. We... had a fight. I was angry at him and I didn't ask.
Officer, can you please tell me what's going on? Where was that picture taken?
Is Josh okay?

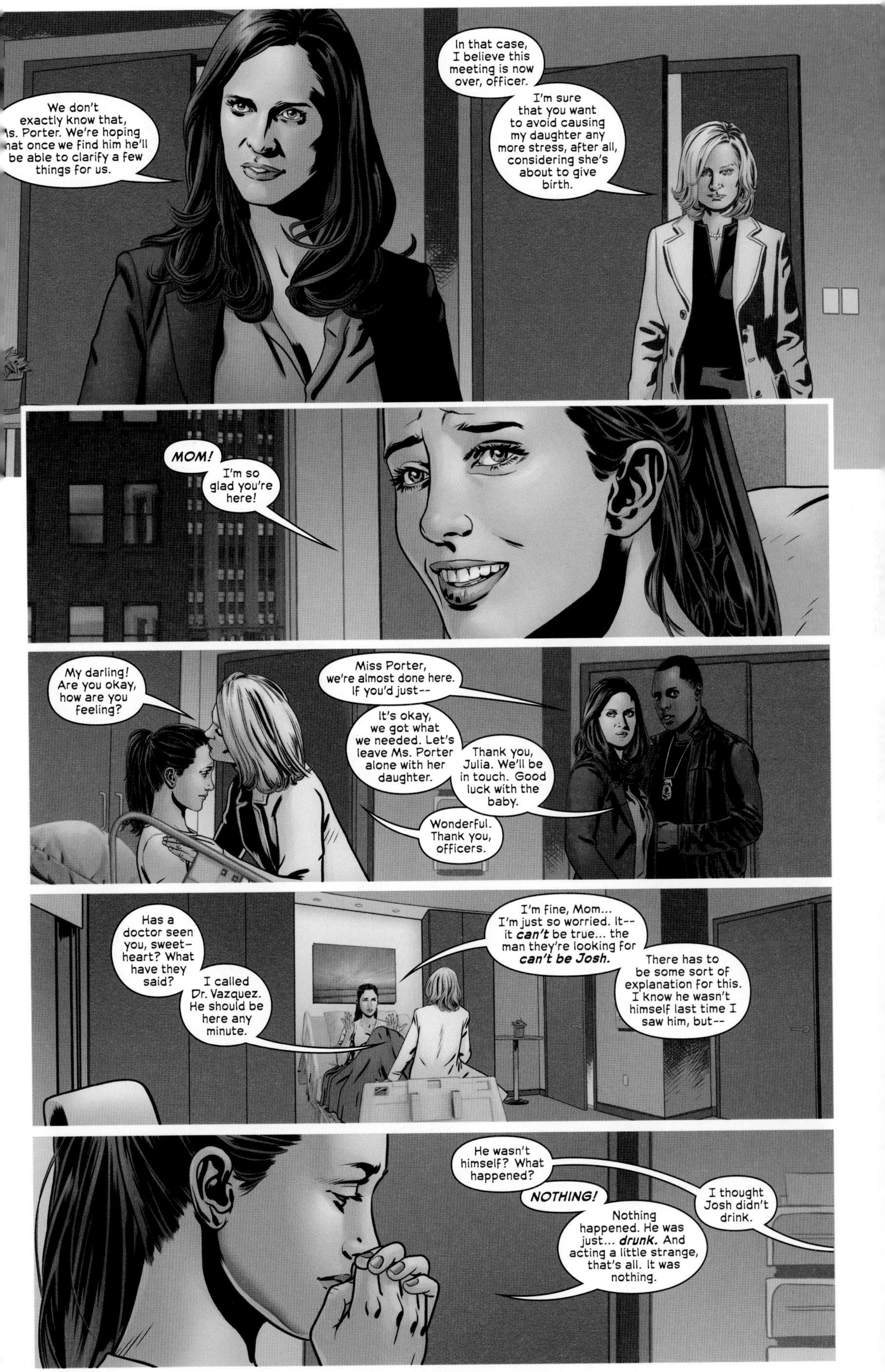
We don't exactly know that, Ms. Porter. We're hoping that once we find him he'll be able to clarify a few things for us.
In that case, I believe this meeting is now over, officer.
I'm sure that you want to avoid causing my daughter any more stress, after all, considering she's about to give birth.
MOM! I'm so glad you're here!
My darling! Are you okay, how are you feeling?
Miss Porter, we're almost done here. If you'd just--
It's okay, we got what we needed. Let's leave Ms. Porter alone with her daughter.
Thank you, Julia. We'll be in touch. Good luck with the baby.
Wonderful. Thank you, officers.
Has a doctor seen you, sweet-heart? What have they said?
I called Dr. Vazquez. He should be here any minute.
I'm fine, Mom... I'm just so worried. It-- it *can't* be true... the man they're looking for ***can't be Josh.***
There has to be some sort of explanation for this. I know he wasn't himself last time I saw him, but--
He wasn't himself? What happened?
I thought Josh didn't drink.
NOTHING!
Nothing happened. He was just... *drunk.* And acting a little strange, that's all. It was nothing.

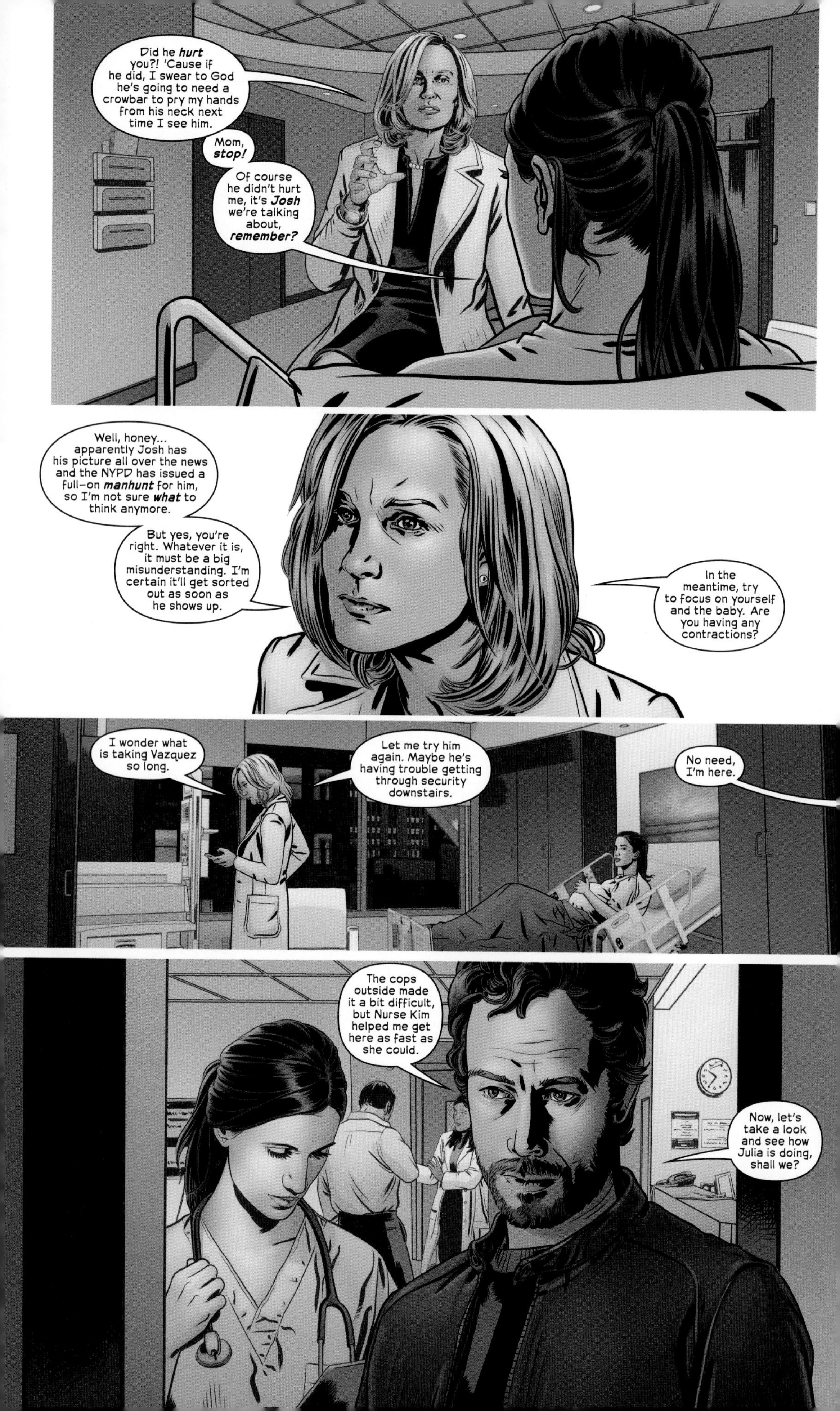
Did he *hurt* you?! 'Cause if he did, I swear to God he's going to need a crowbar to pry my hands from his neck next time I see him.
Mom, *stop!*
Of course he didn't hurt me, it's *Josh* we're talking about, *remember?*
Well, honey... apparently Josh has his picture all over the news and the NYPD has issued a full-on *manhunt* for him, so I'm not sure *what* to think anymore.
But yes, you're right. Whatever it is, it must be a big misunderstanding. I'm certain it'll get sorted out as soon as he shows up.
In the meantime, try to focus on yourself and the baby. Are you having any contractions?
I wonder what is taking Vazquez so long.
Let me try him again. Maybe he's having trouble getting through security downstairs.
No need, I'm here.
The cops outside made it a bit difficult, but Nurse Kim helped me get here as fast as she could.
Now, let's take a look and see how Julia is doing, shall we?

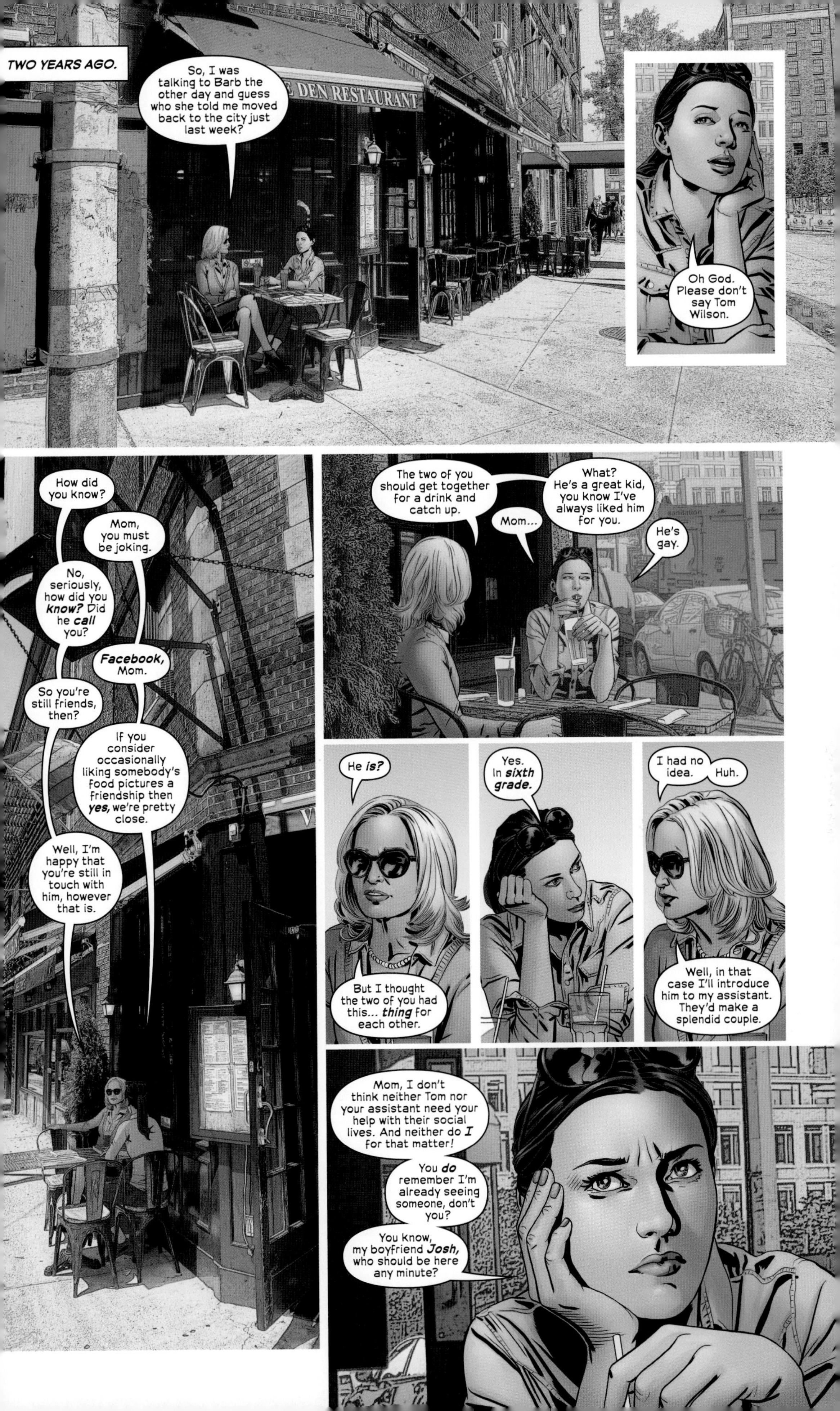

TWO YEARS AGO.
So, I was talking to Barb the other day and guess who she told me moved back to the city just last week?
DEN RESTAURANT
Oh God. Please don't say Tom Wilson.
How did you know?
Mom, you must be joking.
No, seriously, how did you know? Did he call you?
Facebook, Mom.
So you're still friends, then?
If you consider occasionally liking somebody's food pictures a friendship then yes, we're pretty close.
Well, I'm happy that you're still in touch with him, however that is.
The two of you should get together for a drink and catch up.
Mom...
What? He's a great kid, you know I've always liked him for you.
He's gay.
He is?
But I thought the two of you had this... thing for each other.
Yes. In sixth grade.
I had no idea.
Huh.
Well, in that case I'll introduce him to my assistant. They'd make a splendid couple.
Mom, I don't think neither Tom nor your assistant need your help with their social lives. And neither do I for that matter!
You do remember I'm already seeing someone, don't you?
You know, my boyfriend Josh, who should be here any minute?

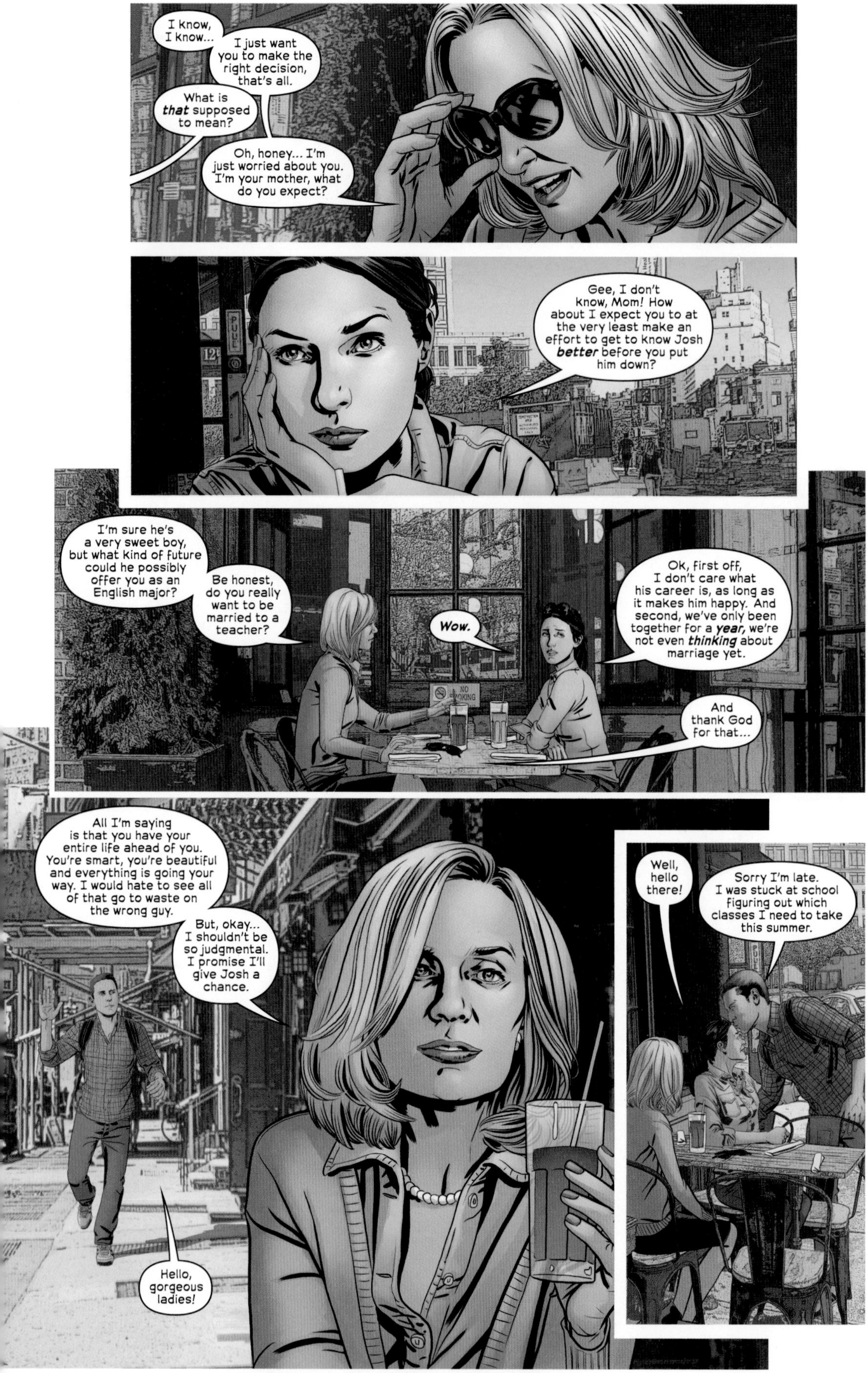
I know, I know...
I just want you to make the right decision, that's all.
What is *that* supposed to mean?
Oh, honey... I'm just worried about you. I'm your mother, what do you expect?
Gee, I don't know, Mom! How about I expect you to at the very least make an effort to get to know Josh *better* before you put him down?
I'm sure he's a very sweet boy, but what kind of future could he possibly offer you as an English major?
Be honest, do you really want to be married to a teacher?
Wow.
Ok, first off, I don't care what his career is, as long as it makes him happy. And second, we've only been together for a *year,* we're not even *thinking* about marriage yet.
And thank God for that...
All I'm saying is that you have your entire life ahead of you. You're smart, you're beautiful and everything is going your way. I would hate to see all of that go to waste on the wrong guy.
But, okay... I shouldn't be so judgmental. I promise I'll give Josh a chance.
Hello, gorgeous ladies!
Well, hello there!
Sorry I'm late. I was stuck at school figuring out which classes I need to take this summer.

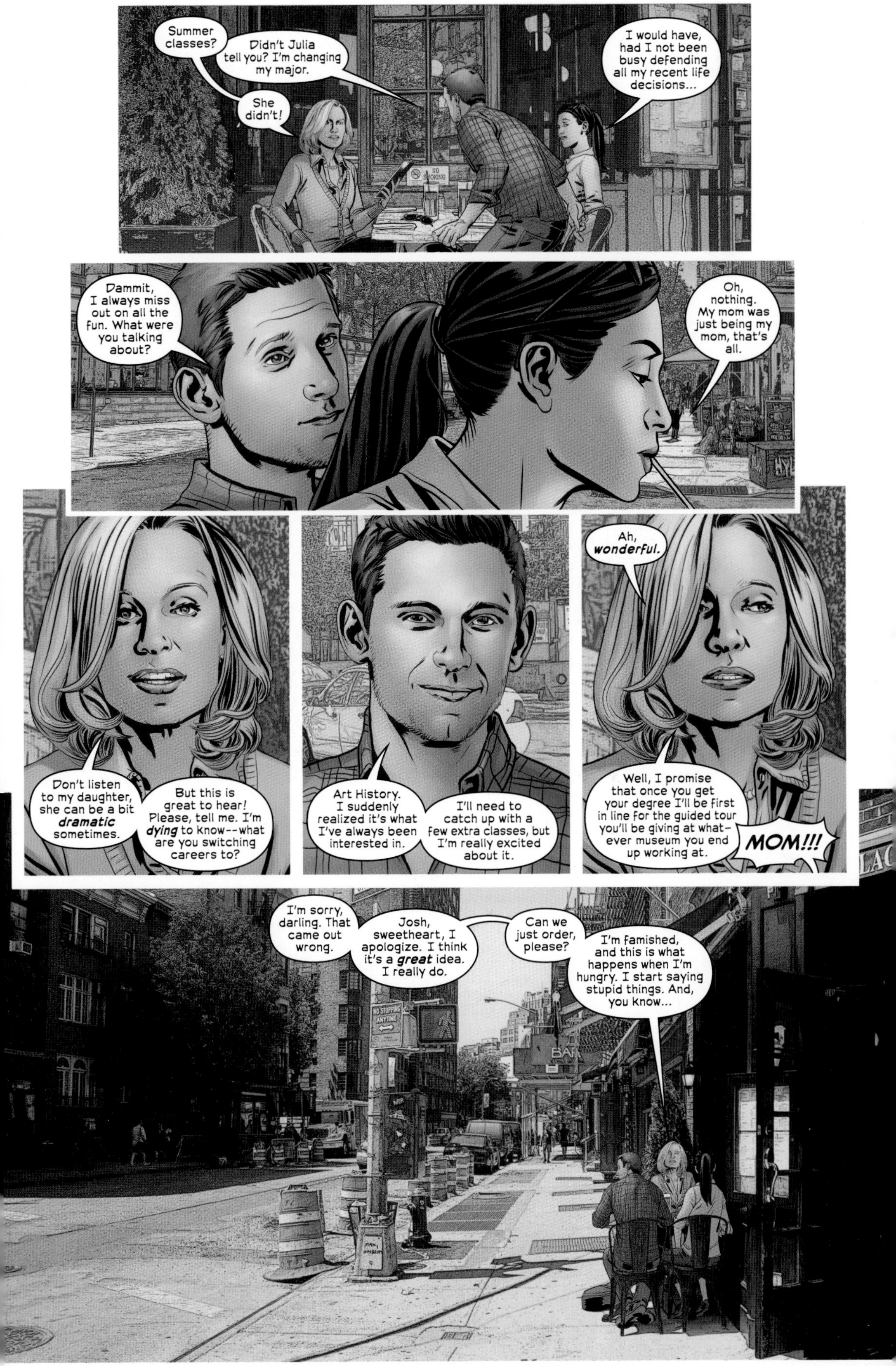
Summer classes?
Didn't Julia tell you? I'm changing my major.
She didn't!
I would have, had I not been busy defending all my recent life decisions...
NO SMOKING
Dammit, I always miss out on all the fun. What were you talking about?
Oh, nothing. My mom was just being my mom, that's all.
Don't listen to my daughter, she can be a bit *dramatic* sometimes.
But this is great to hear! Please, tell me. I'm *dying* to know--what are you switching careers to?
Art History. I suddenly realized it's what I've always been interested in.
I'll need to catch up with a few extra classes, but I'm really excited about it.
Ah, *wonderful.*
Well, I promise that once you get your degree I'll be first in line for the guided tour you'll be giving at whatever museum you end up working at.
MOM!!!
I'm sorry, darling. That came out wrong.
Josh, sweetheart, I apologize. I think it's a *great* idea. I really do.
Can we just order, please?
I'm famished, and this is what happens when I'm hungry. I start saying stupid things. And, you know...
NO STOPPING ANYTIME

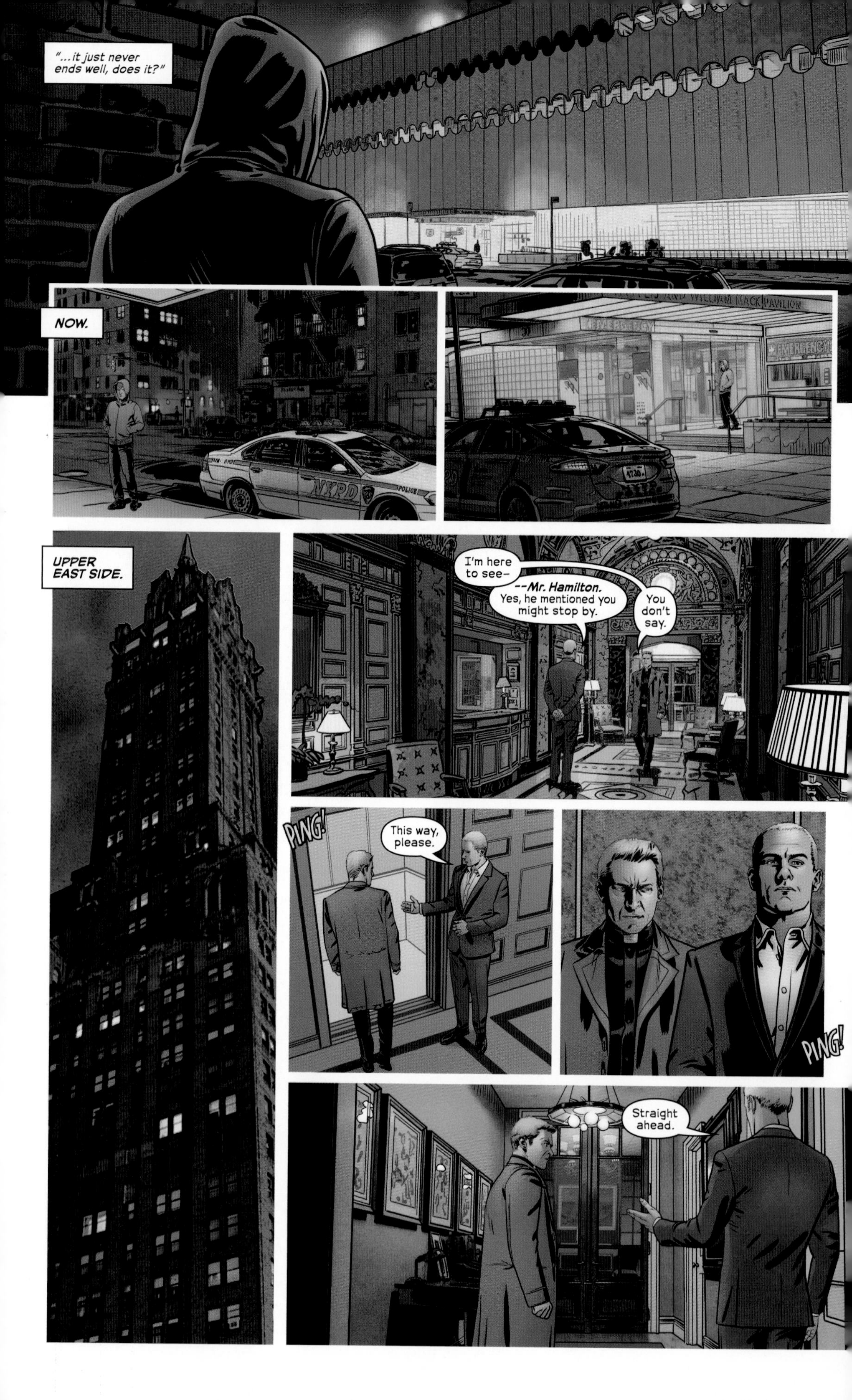
"...it just never ends well, does it?"
NOW.
EMERGENCY
PAVILION
NYPD
POLICE
UPPER EAST SIDE.
I'm here to see–
--Mr. Hamilton. Yes, he mentioned you might stop by.
You don't say.
PING!
This way, please.
PING!
Straight ahead.

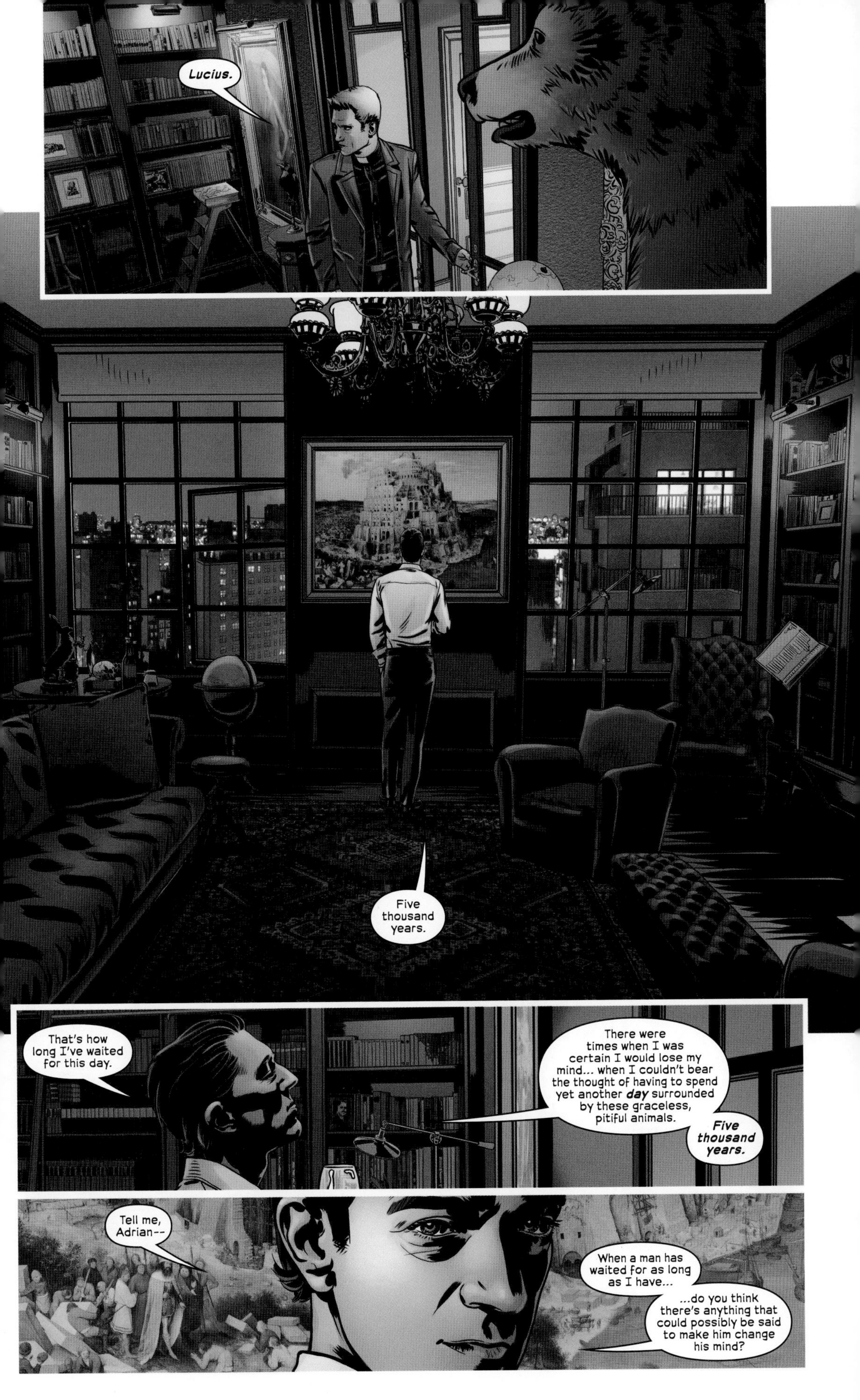
Lucius.
Five thousand years.
That's how long I've waited for this day.
There were times when I was certain I would lose my mind... when I couldn't bear the thought of having to spend yet another *day* surrounded by these graceless, pitiful animals.
Five thousand years.
Tell me, Adrian--
When a man has waited for as long as I have...
...do you think there's anything that could possibly be said to make him change his mind?

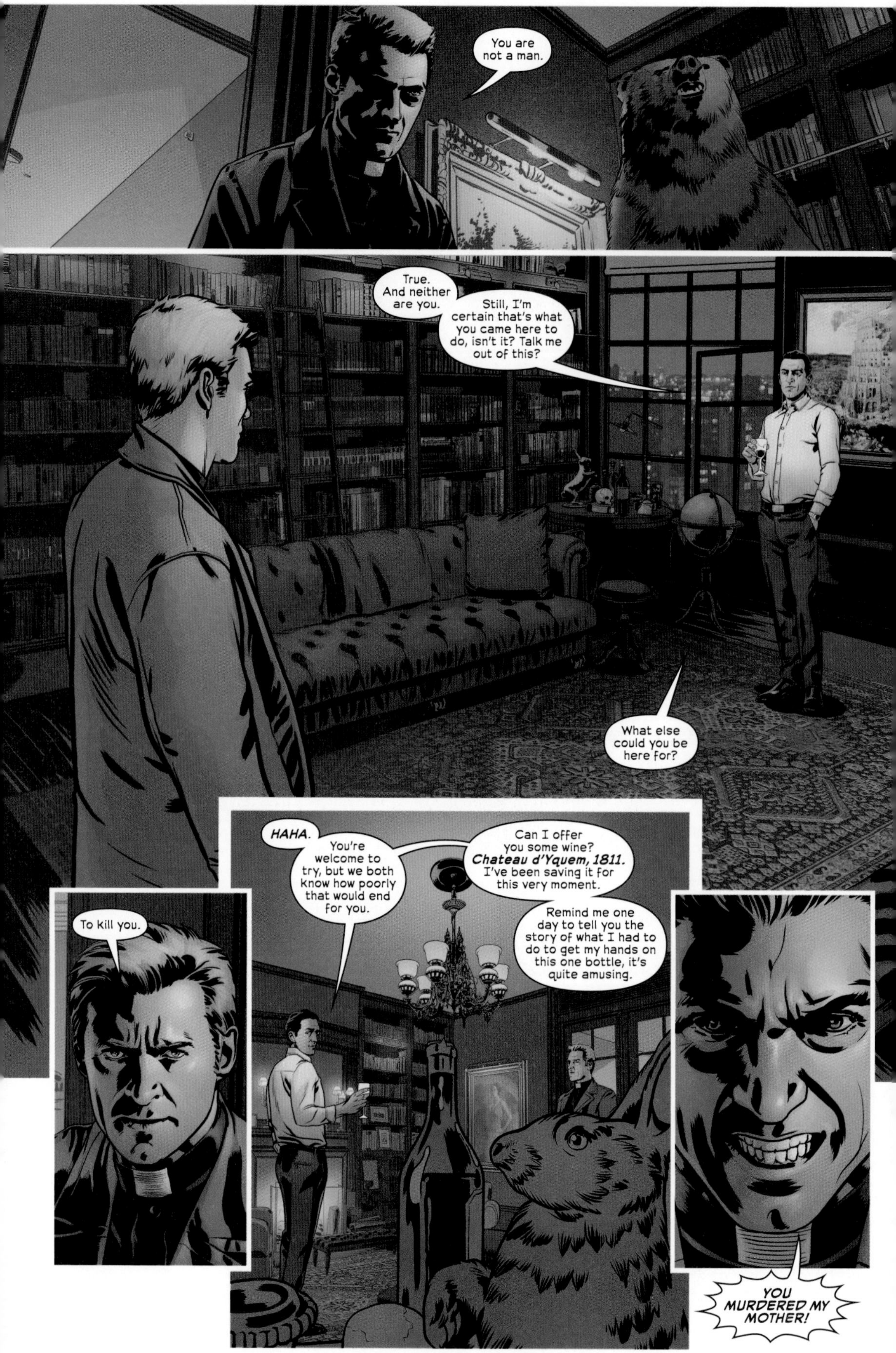
You are not a man.
True. And neither are you.
Still, I'm certain that's what you came here to do, isn't it? Talk me out of this?
What else could you be here for?
To kill you.
HAHA.
You're welcome to try, but we both know how poorly that would end for you.
Can I offer you some wine? Chateau d'Yquem, 1811. I've been saving it for this very moment.
Remind me one day to tell you the story of what I had to do to get my hands on this one bottle, it's quite amusing.
YOU MURDERED MY MOTHER!

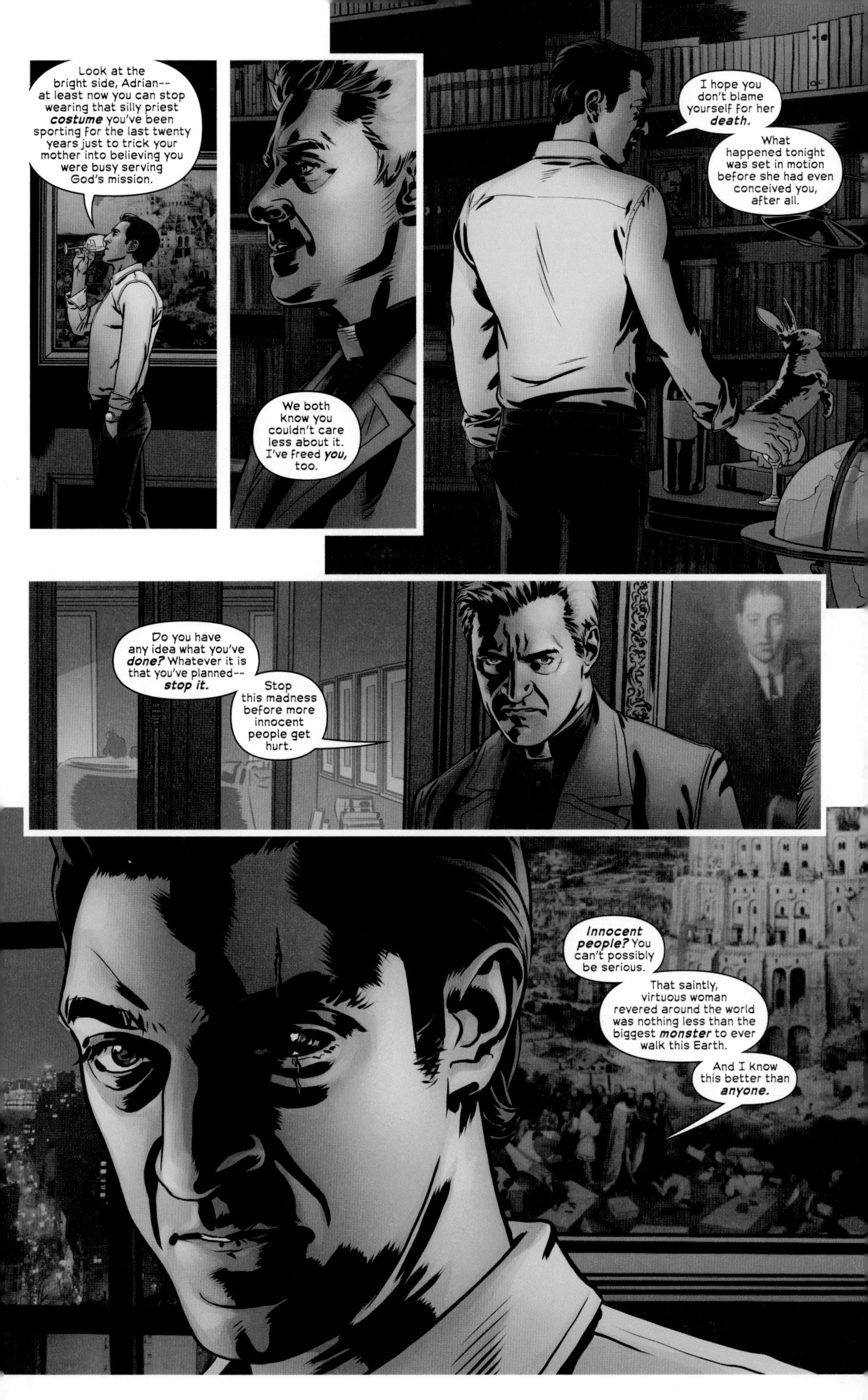

Look at the bright side, Adrian-- at least now you can stop wearing that silly priest **costume** you've been sporting for the last twenty years just to trick your mother into believing you were busy serving God's mission.
We both know you couldn't care less about it. I've freed **you,** too.
I hope you don't blame yourself for her **death.**
What happened tonight was set in motion before she had even conceived you, after all.
Do you have any idea what you've **done?** Whatever it is that you've planned-- **stop it.**
Stop this madness before more innocent people get hurt.
Innocent people? You can't possibly be serious.
That saintly, virtuous woman revered around the world was nothing less than the biggest ***monster*** to ever walk this Earth.
And I know this better than ***anyone.***

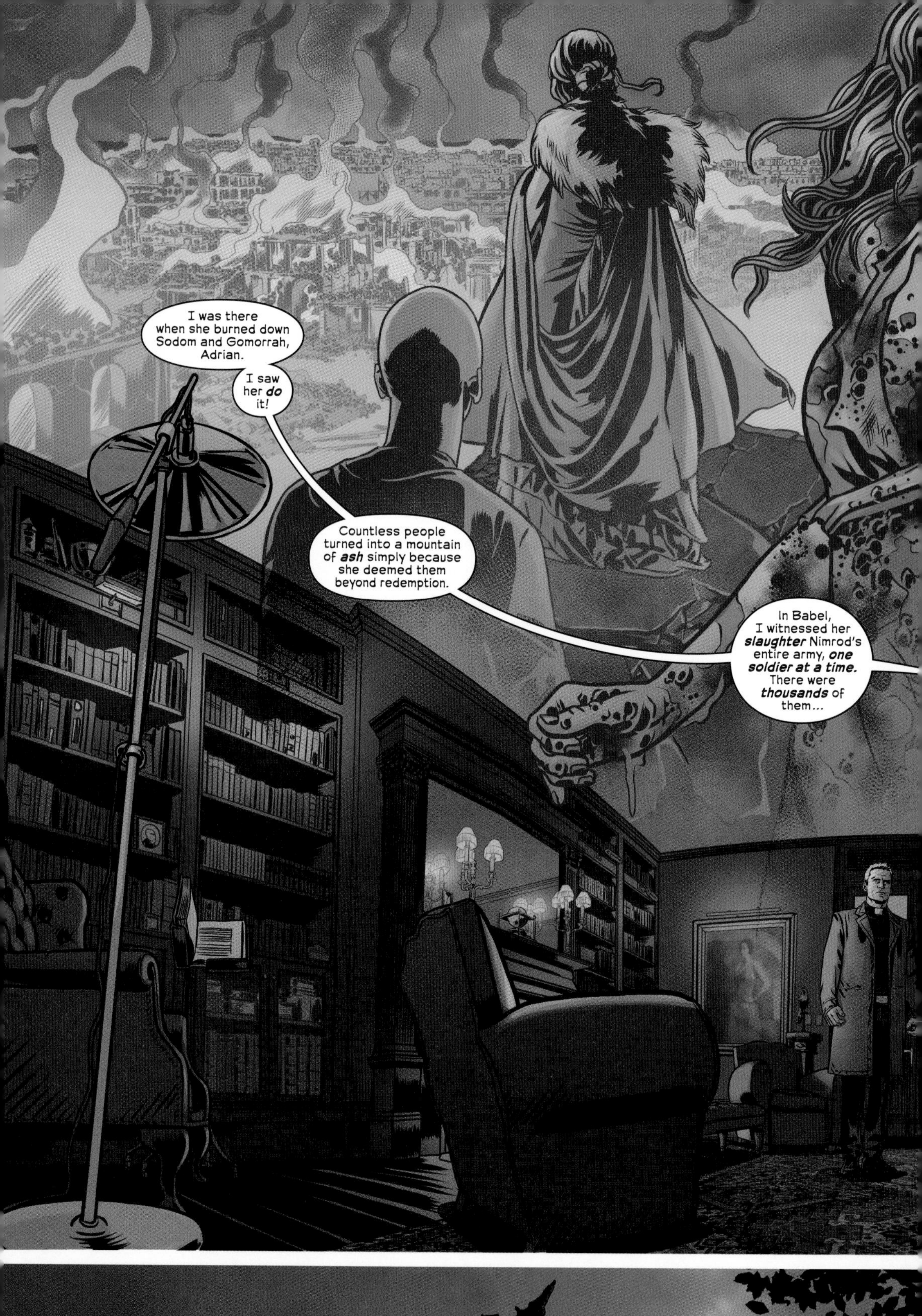
I was there when she burned down Sodom and Gomorrah, Adrian.
I saw her *do* it!
Countless people turned into a mountain of *ash* simply because she deemed them beyond redemption.
In Babel, I witnessed her *slaughter* Nimrod's entire army, *one soldier at a time.* There were *thousands* of them...

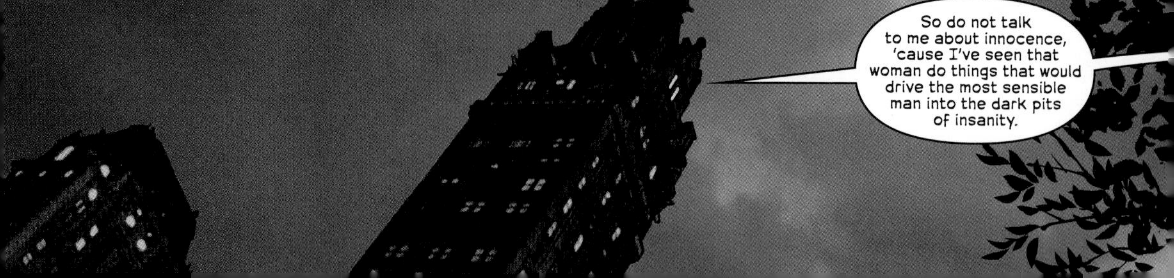
So do not talk to me about innocence, 'cause I've seen that woman do things that would drive the most sensible man into the dark pits of insanity.

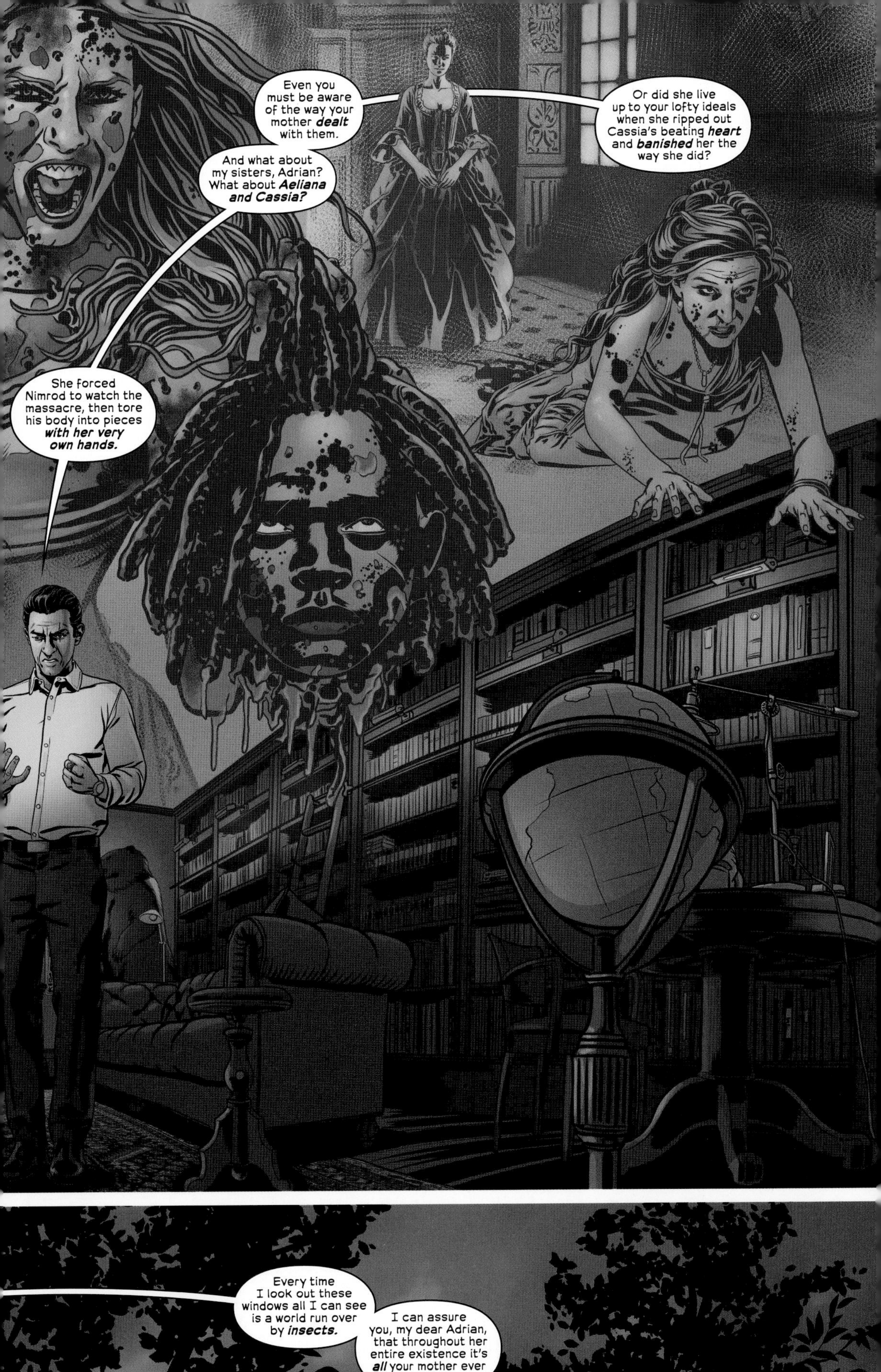
Even you must be aware of the way your mother ***dealt*** with them.
And what about my sisters, Adrian? What about ***Aeliana and Cassia?***
Or did she live up to your lofty ideals when she ripped out Cassia's beating ***heart*** and ***banished*** her the way she did?
She forced Nimrod to watch the massacre, then tore his body into pieces ***with her very own hands.***

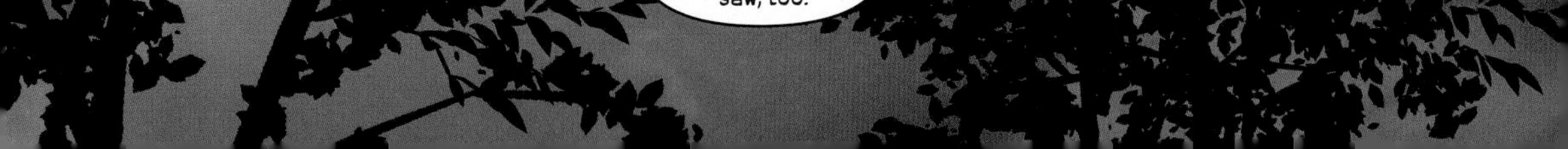
Every time I look out these windows all I can see is a world run over by ***insects.***
I can assure you, my dear Adrian, that throughout her entire existence it's ***all*** your mother ever saw, too.

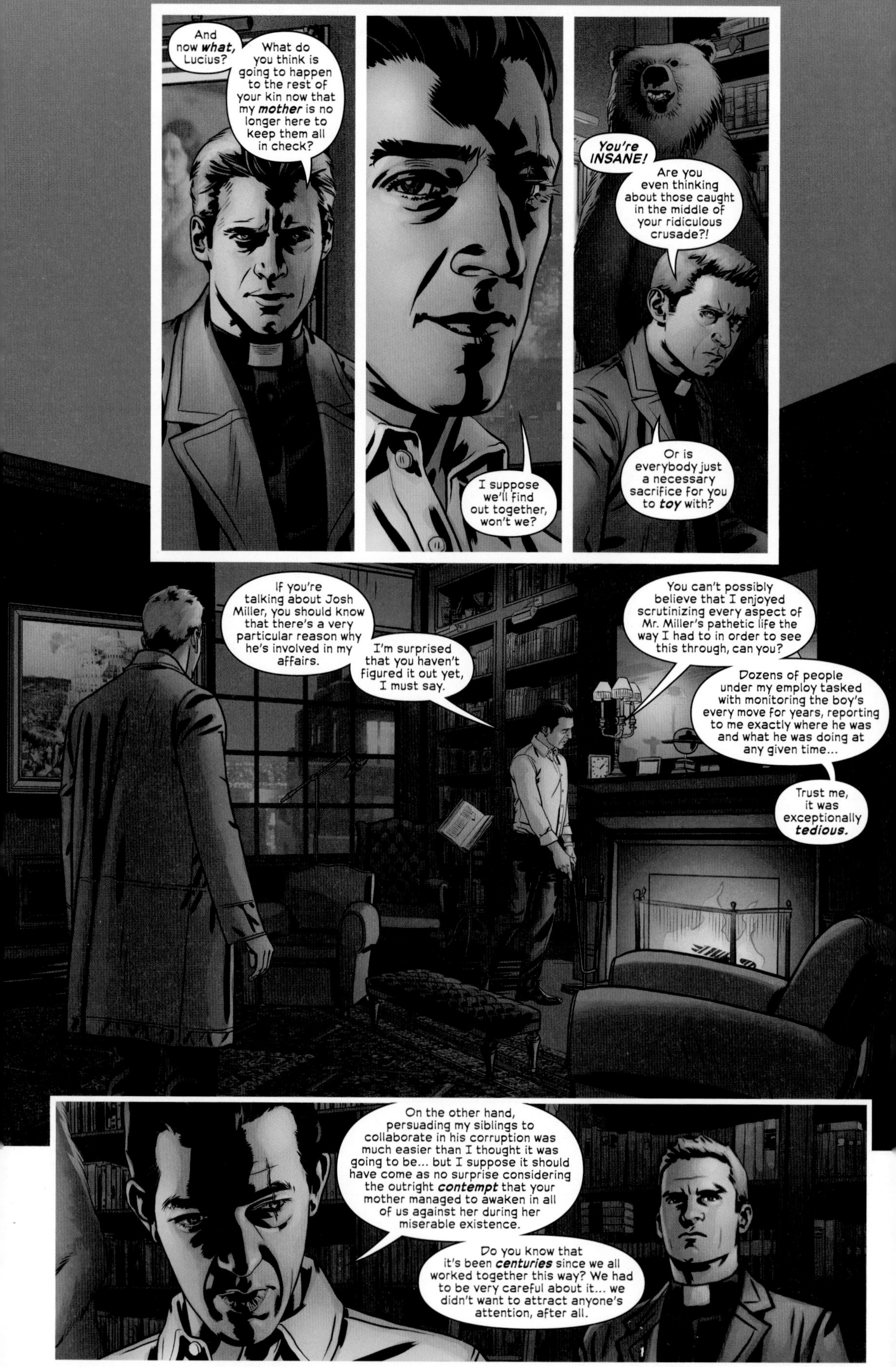
And now *what,* Lucius?
What do you think is going to happen to the rest of your kin now that my *mother* is no longer here to keep them all in check?
I suppose we'll find out together, won't we?
You're INSANE!
Are you even thinking about those caught in the middle of your ridiculous crusade?!
Or is everybody just a necessary sacrifice for you to *toy* with?
If you're talking about Josh Miller, you should know that there's a very particular reason why he's involved in my affairs.
I'm surprised that you haven't figured it out yet, I must say.
You can't possibly believe that I enjoyed scrutinizing every aspect of Mr. Miller's pathetic life the way I had to in order to see this through, can you?
Dozens of people under my employ tasked with monitoring the boy's every move for years, reporting to me exactly where he was and what he was doing at any given time...
Trust me, it was exceptionally *tedious.*
On the other hand, persuading my siblings to collaborate in his corruption was much easier than I thought it was going to be... but I suppose it should have come as no surprise considering the outright *contempt* that your mother managed to awaken in all of us against her during her miserable existence.
Do you know that it's been *centuries* since we all worked together this way? We had to be very careful about it... we didn't want to attract anyone's attention, after all.

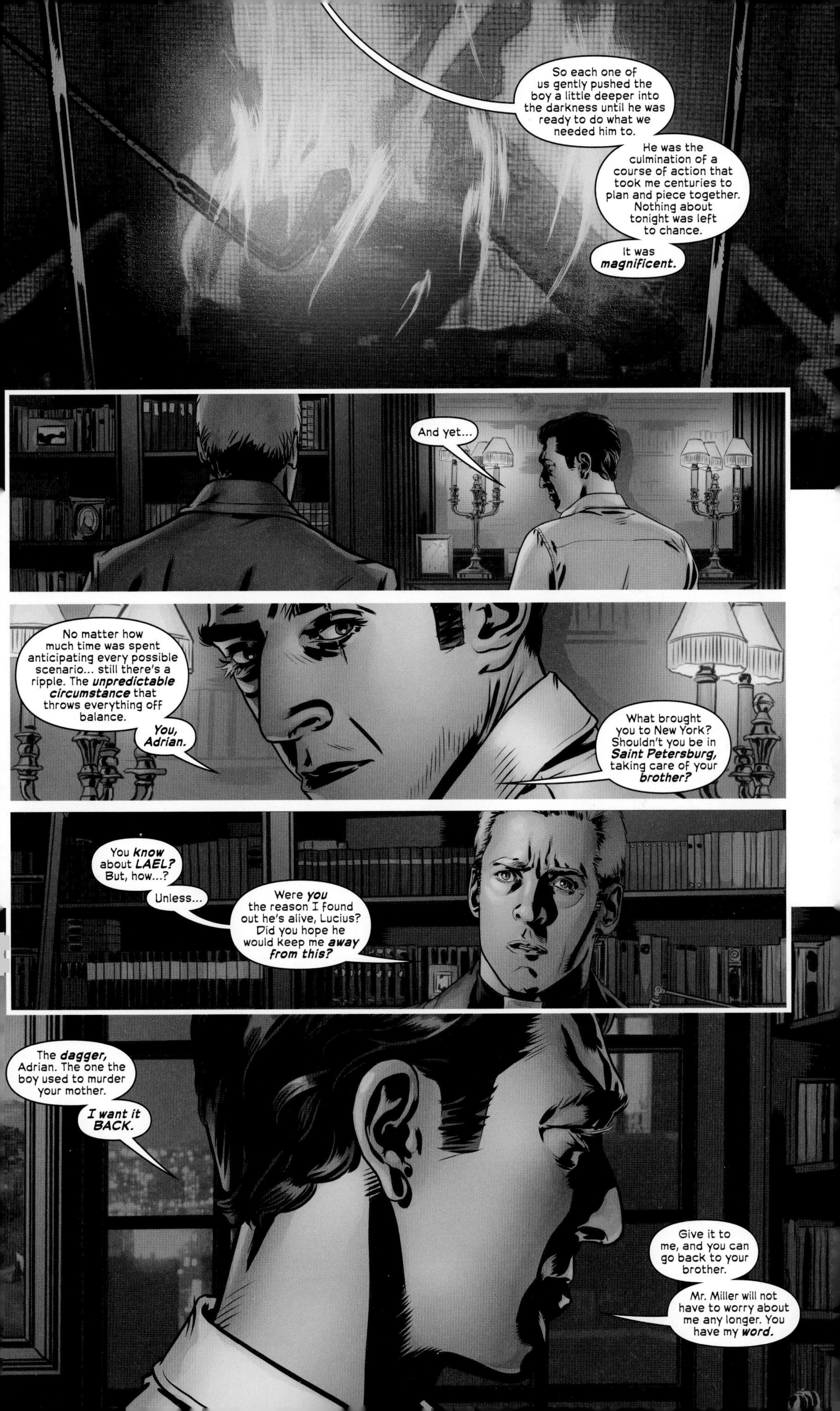

So each one of us gently pushed the boy a little deeper into the darkness until he was ready to do what we needed him to.
He was the culmination of a course of action that took me centuries to plan and piece together. Nothing about tonight was left to chance.
It was ***magnificent.***
And yet...
No matter how much time was spent anticipating every possible scenario... still there's a ripple. The ***unpredictable circumstance*** that throws everything off balance.
You, Adrian.
What brought you to New York? Shouldn't you be in ***Saint Petersburg,*** taking care of your ***brother?***
You ***know*** about ***LAEL?*** But, how...?
Unless...
Were ***you*** the reason I found out he's alive, Lucius? Did you hope he would keep me ***away from this?***
The ***dagger,*** Adrian. The one the boy used to murder your mother.
I want it BACK.
Give it to me, and you can go back to your brother.
Mr. Miller will not have to worry about me any longer. You have my ***word.***

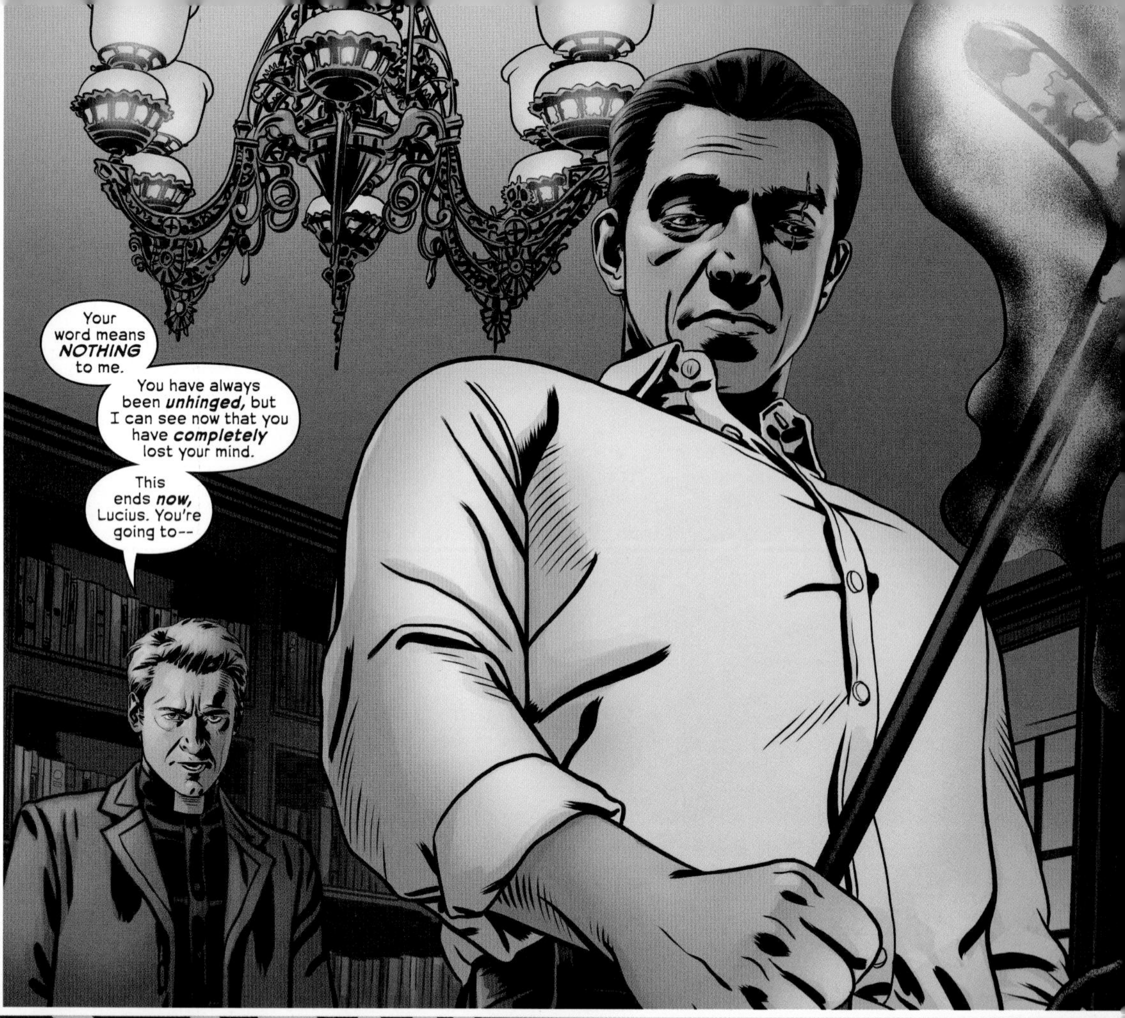
Your word means NOTHING to me.
You have always been unhinged, but I can see now that you have completely lost your mind.
This ends now, Lucius. You're going to--

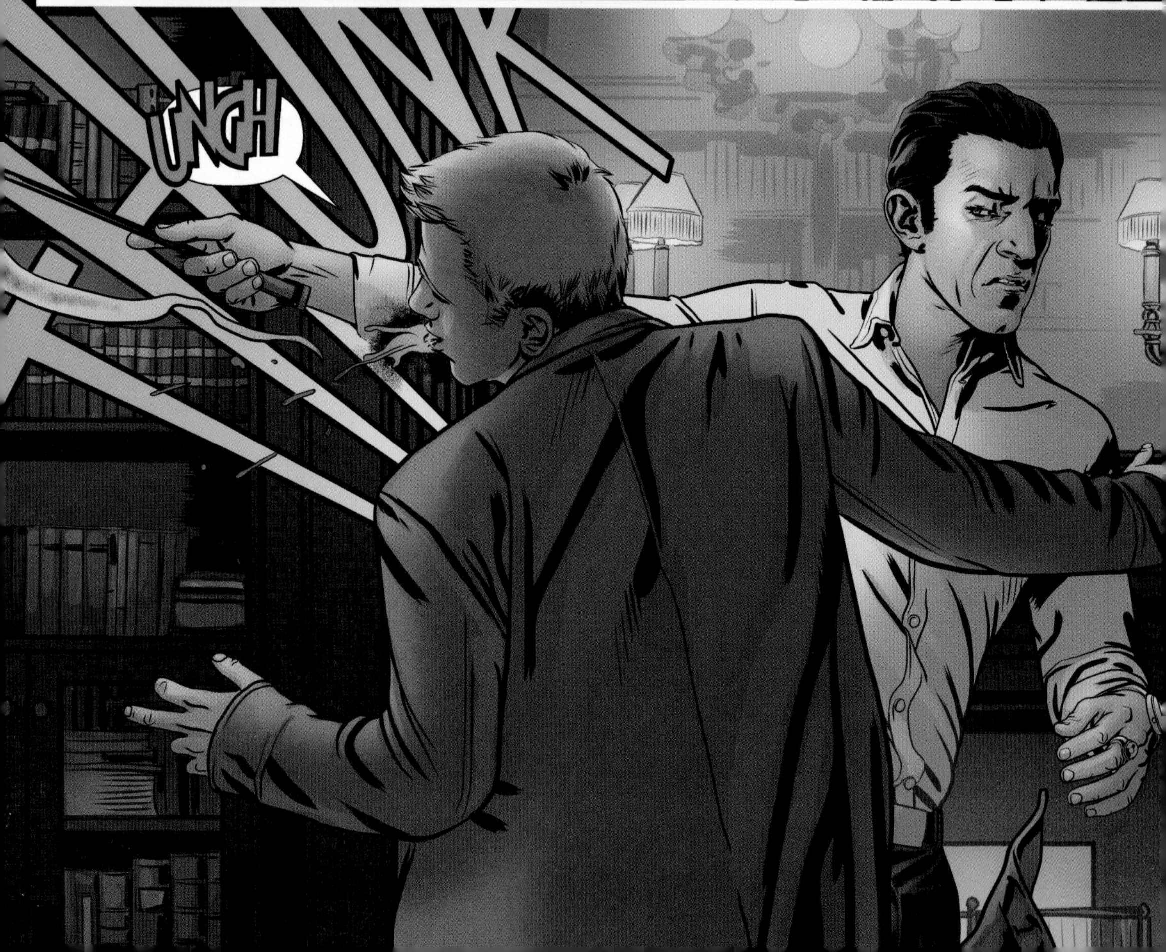
UNGH

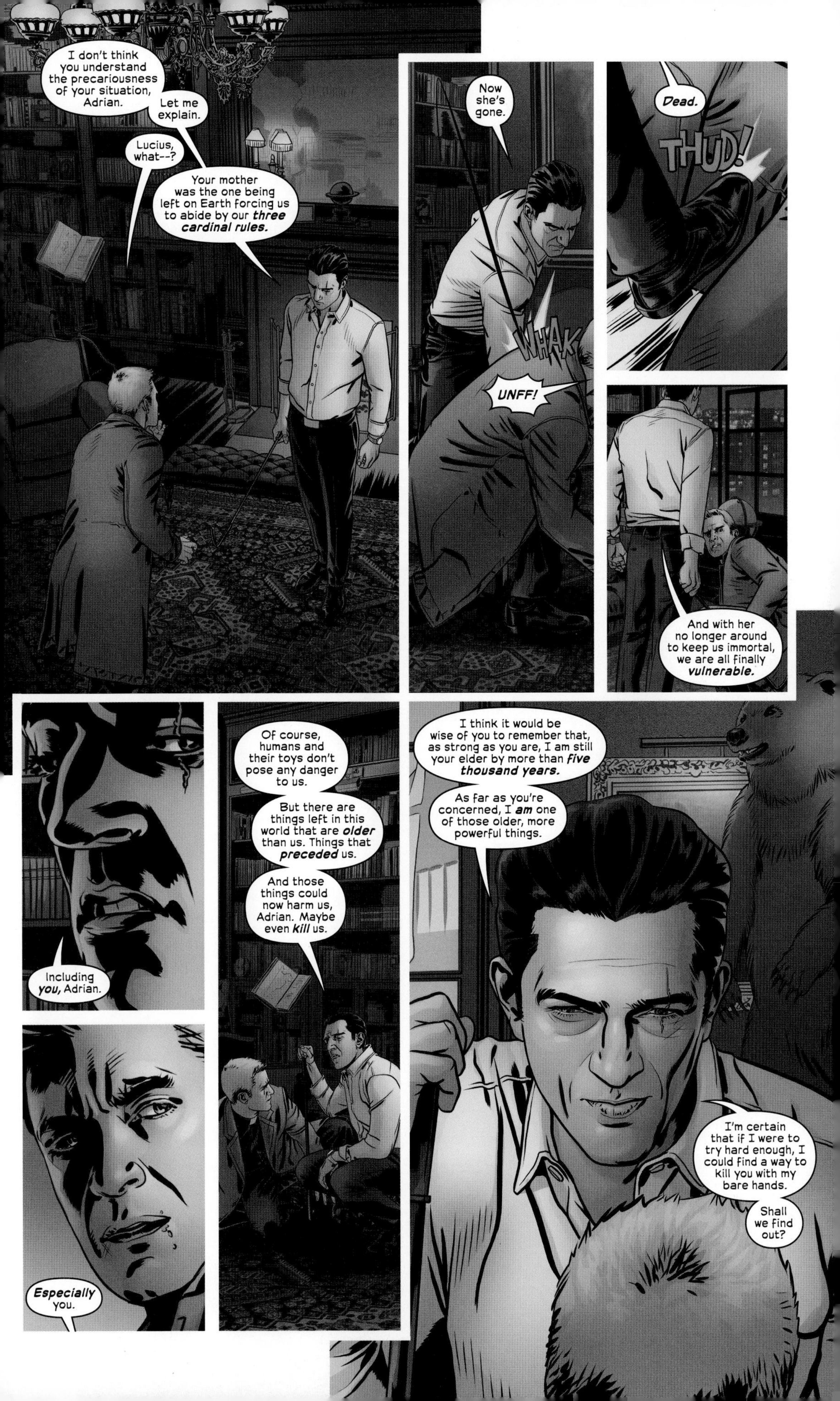
I don't think you understand the precariousness of your situation, Adrian.
Let me explain.
Lucius, what--?
Your mother was the one being left on Earth forcing us to abide by our *three cardinal rules.*
Now she's gone.
WHAK
UNFF!
Dead.
THUD!
And with her no longer around to keep us immortal, we are all finally *vulnerable.*
Including *you,* Adrian.
Especially you.
Of course, humans and their toys don't pose any danger to us.
But there are things left in this world that are *older* than us. Things that *preceded* us.
And those things could now harm us, Adrian. Maybe even *kill* us.
I think it would be wise of you to remember that, as strong as you are, I am still your elder by more than *five thousand years.*
As far as you're concerned, I *am* one of those older, more powerful things.
I'm certain that if I were to try hard enough, I could find a way to kill you with my bare hands.
Shall we find out?

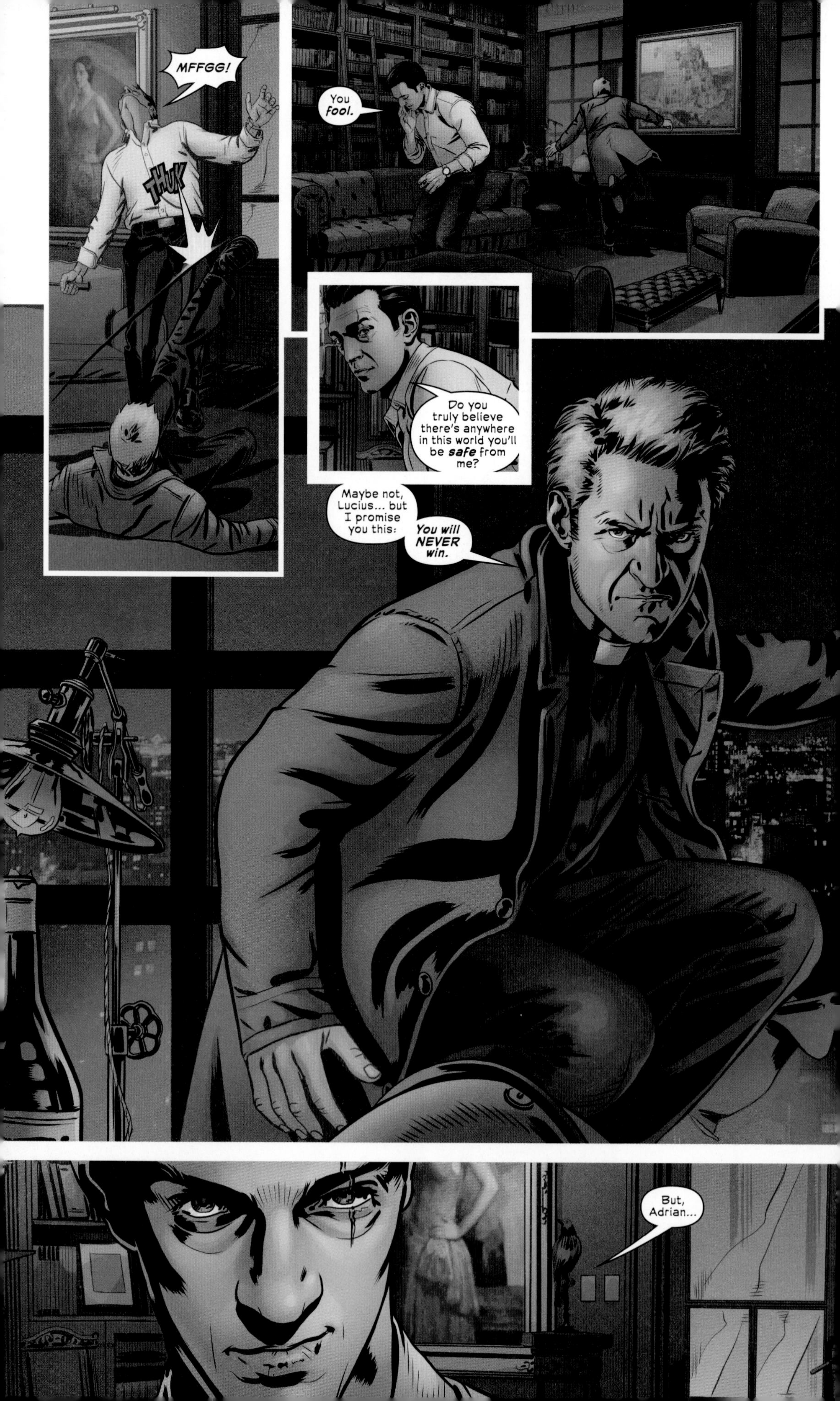
MFFGG!
THUK
You fool.
Do you truly believe there's anywhere in this world you'll be safe from me?
Maybe not, Lucius... but I promise you this:
You will NEVER win.
But, Adrian...

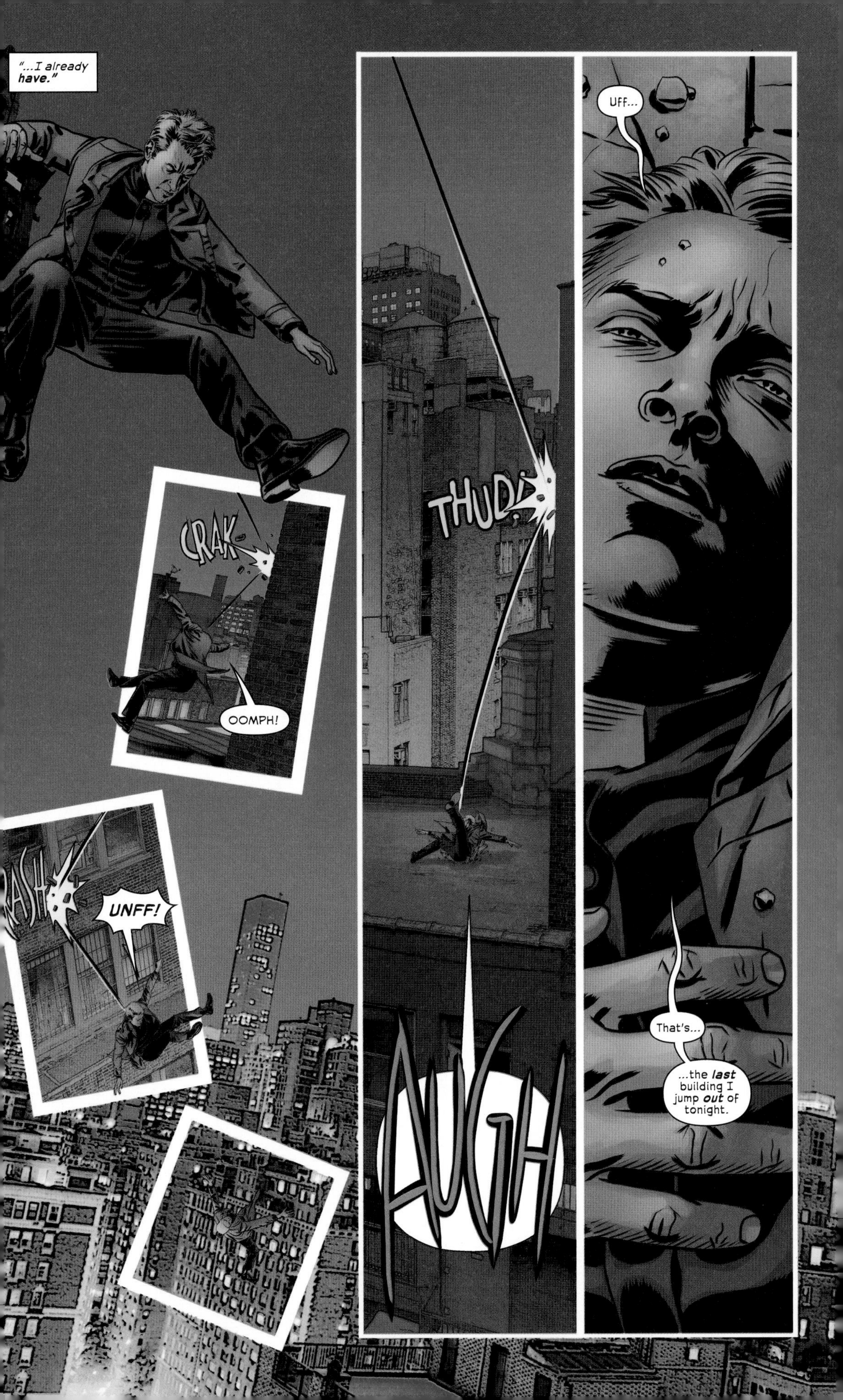
"...I already have."
CRAK
OOMPH!
RASH
UNFF!
THUD!
AUGH
UFF...
That's...
...the last building I jump out of tonight.

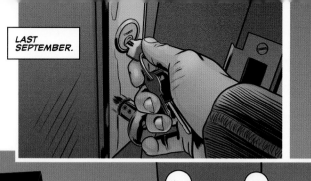

LAST SEPTEMBER.

Julia?

Hey.

Hi.

I'm... so sorry about last night.

I hate that I had to leave for work in the middle of our conversation...

Are you mad at me?

Well, to be honest, you were kind of a jerk.

I was? I'm sorry, I didn't mean to.

I don't even know how we ended up arguing about it.

I guess I just didn't see this coming.

I wasn't expecting this either, Josh, but there's no need to *panic.*

I didn't panic, ok?

I just want to make sure that we do this the right way, that's all.

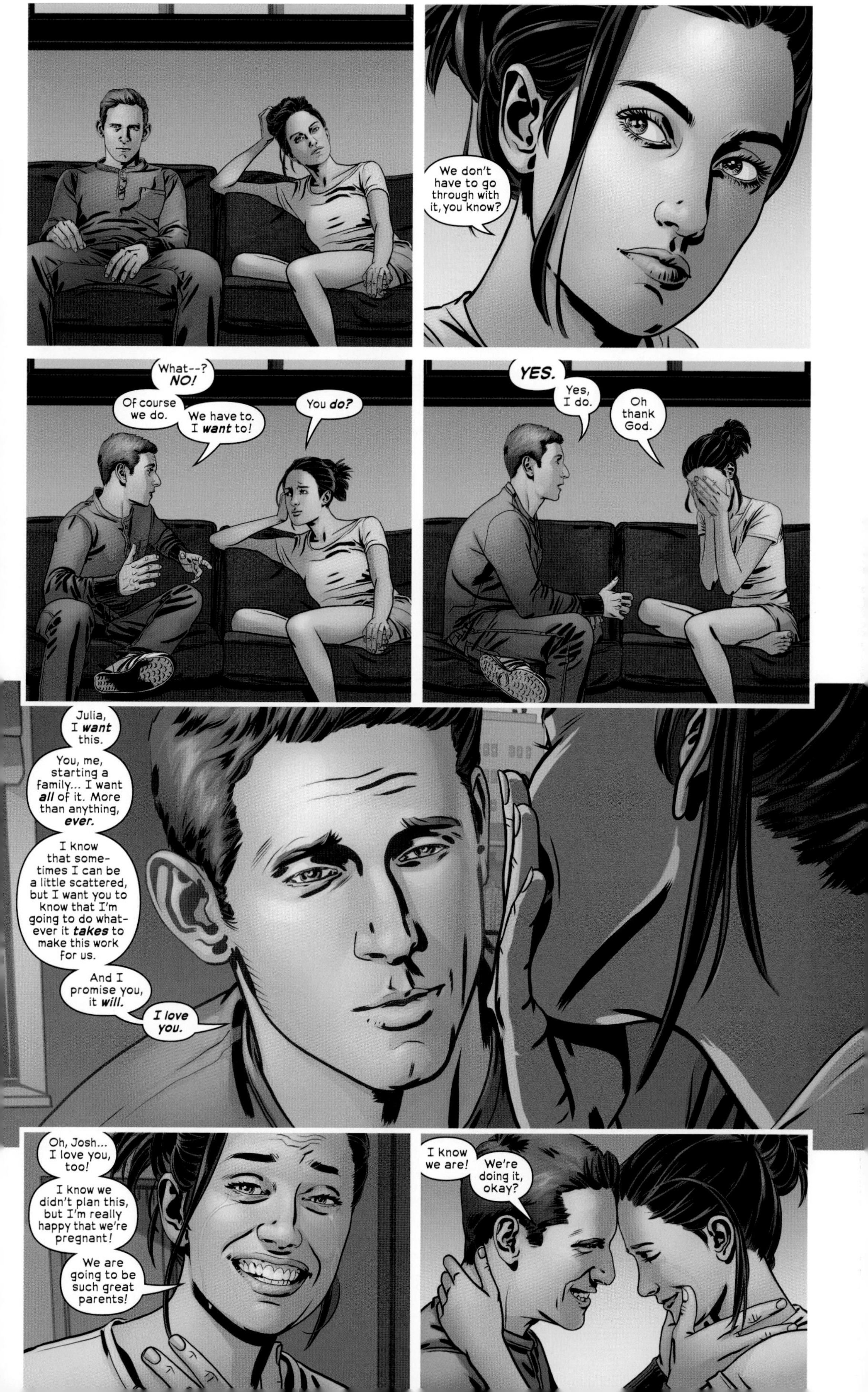

We don't have to go through with it, you know?
What--? NO!
Of course we do.
We have to. I *want* to!
You *do?*
YES.
Yes, I do.
Oh thank God.
Julia, I *want* this.
You, me, starting a family... I want *all* of it. More than anything, *ever.*
I know that some-times I can be a little scattered, but I want you to know that I'm going to do what-ever it *takes* to make this work for us.
And I promise you, it *will.*
I love you.
Oh, Josh... I love you, too!
I know we didn't plan this, but I'm really happy that we're pregnant!
We are going to be such great parents!
I know we are!
We're doing it, okay?

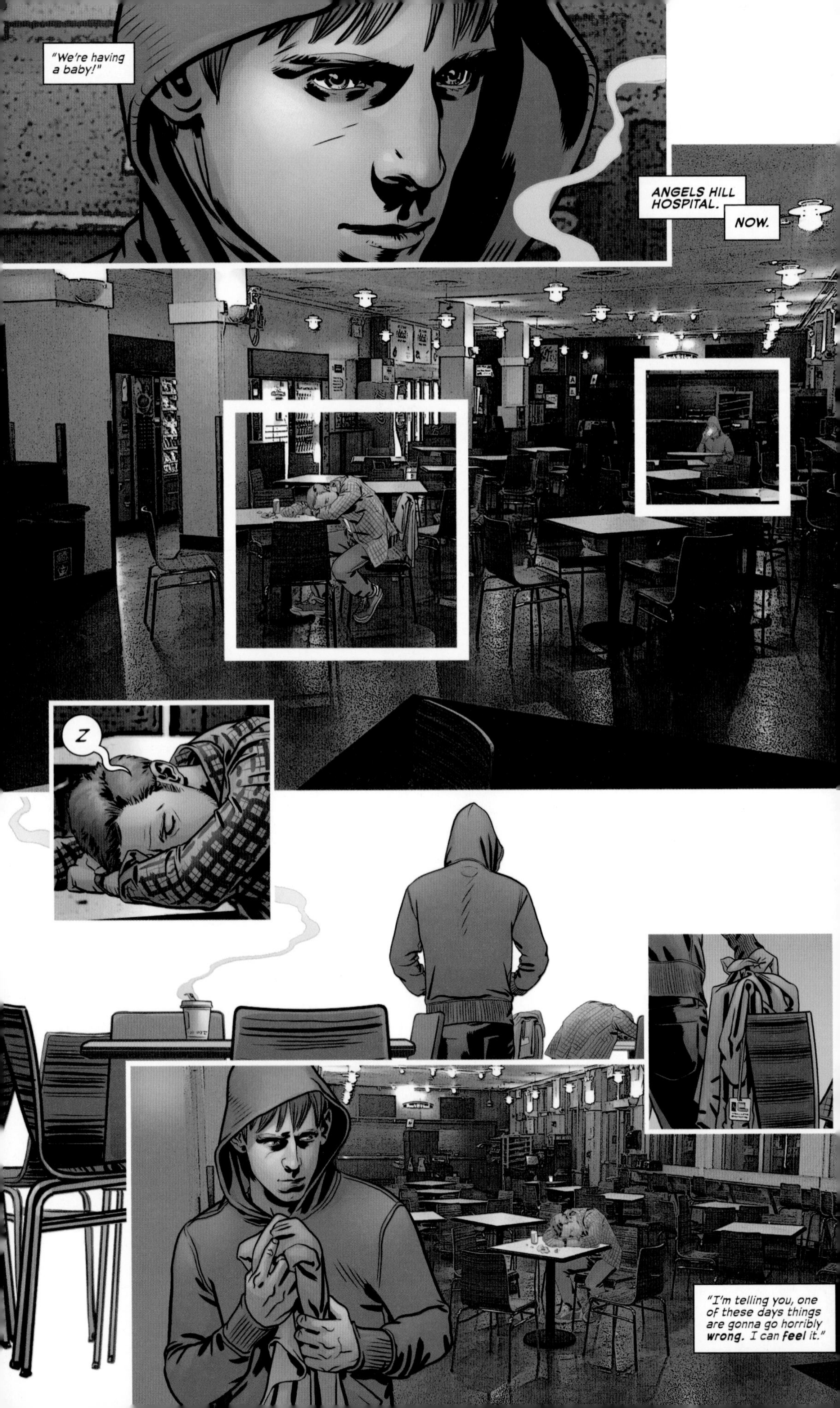
"We're having a baby!"
ANGELS HILL HOSPITAL.
NOW.
Z
"I'm telling you, one of these days things are gonna go horribly wrong. I can feel it."

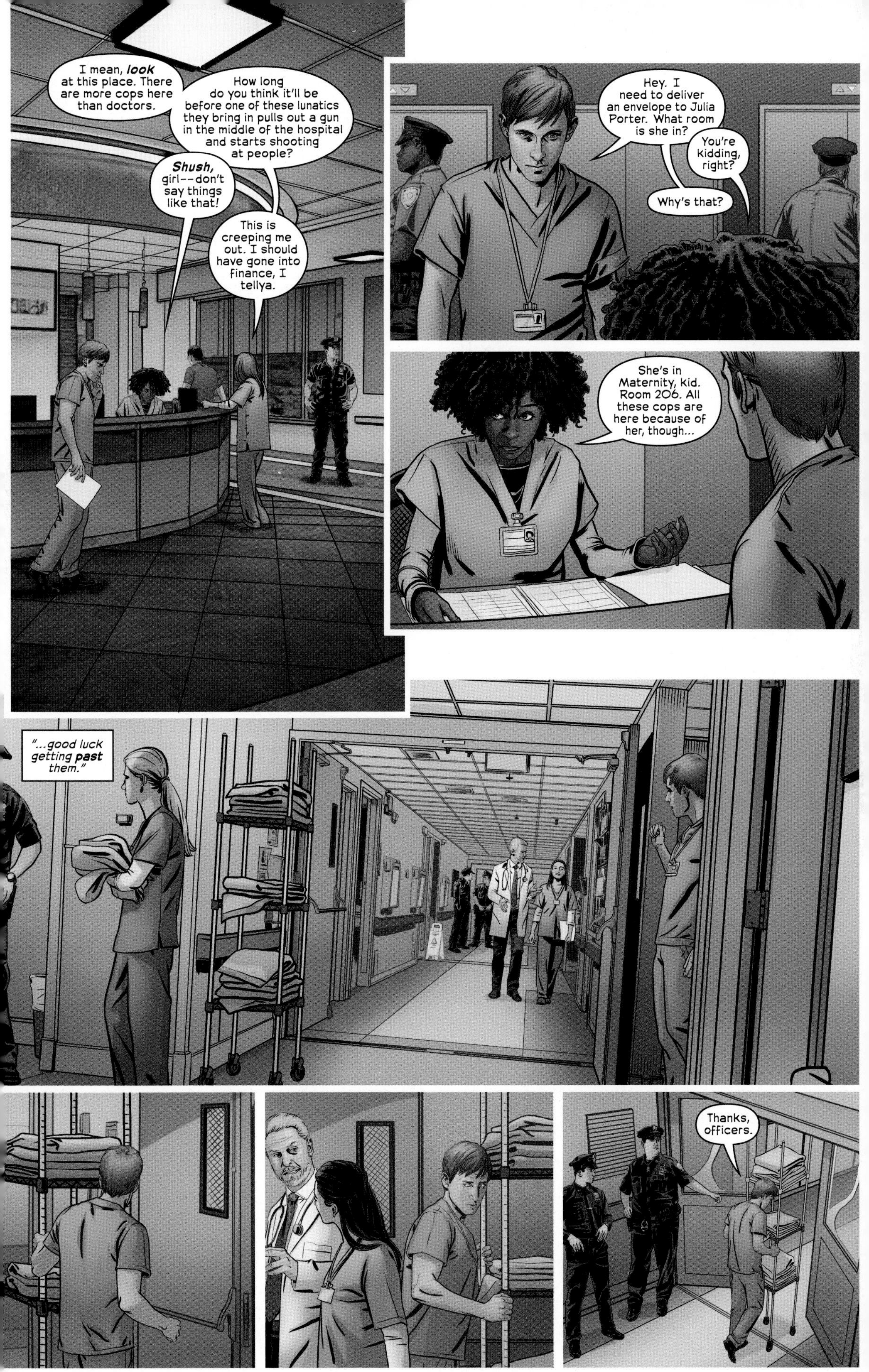
I mean, **look** at this place. There are more cops here than doctors.
How long do you think it'll be before one of these lunatics they bring in pulls out a gun in the middle of the hospital and starts shooting at people?
Shush, girl--don't say things like that!
This is creeping me out. I should have gone into finance, I tellya.
Hey. I need to deliver an envelope to Julia Porter. What room is she in?
You're kidding, right?
Why's that?
She's in Maternity, kid. Room 206. All these cops are here because of her, though...
*"...good luck getting **past** them."*
Thanks, officers.

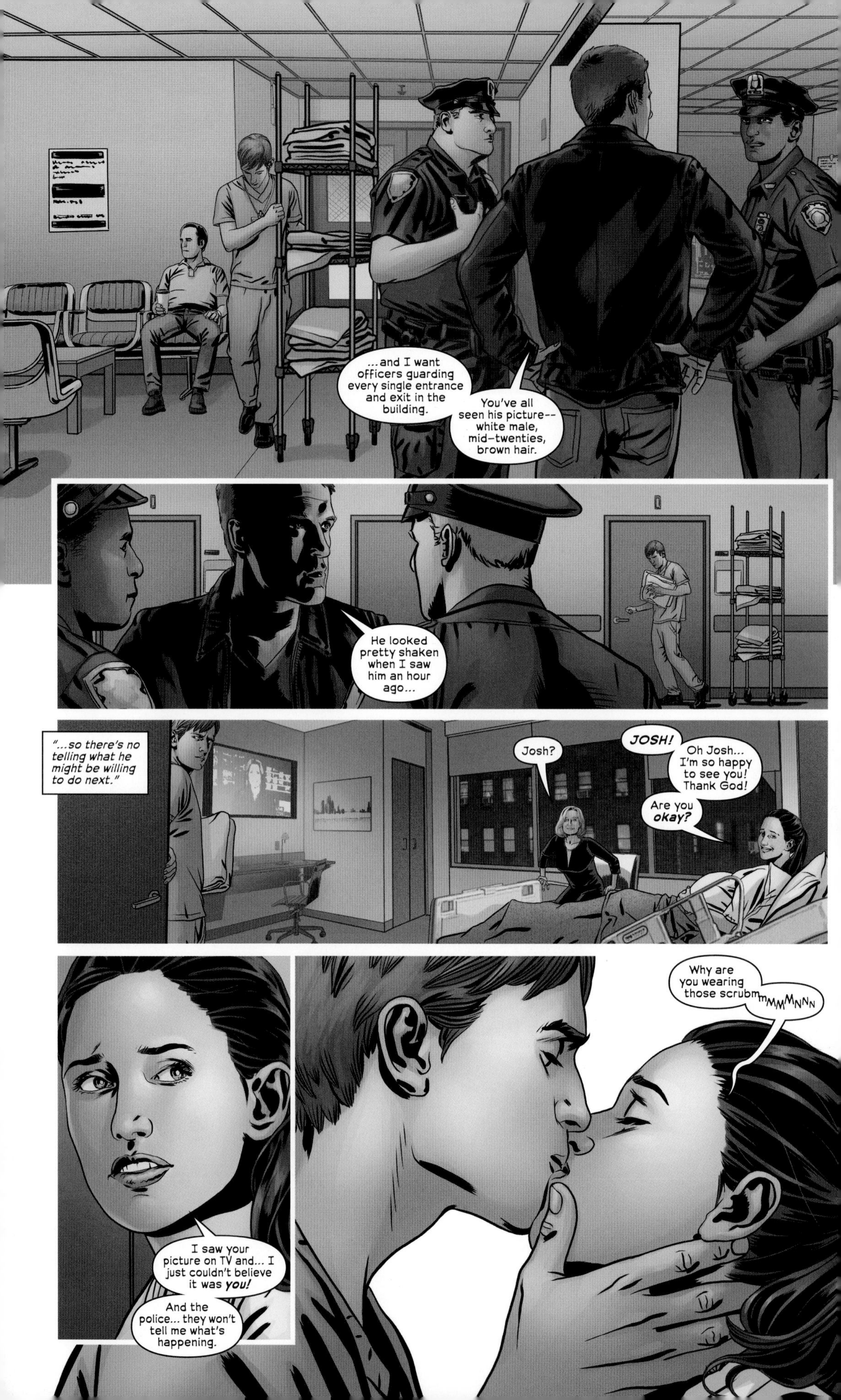
...and I want officers guarding every single entrance and exit in the building.
You've all seen his picture-- white male, mid-twenties, brown hair.
He looked pretty shaken when I saw him an hour ago...
"...so there's no telling what he might be willing to do next."
Josh?
JOSH!
Oh Josh... I'm so happy to see you! Thank God!
Are you okay?
I saw your picture on TV and... I just couldn't believe it was you!
And the police... they won't tell me what's happening.
Why are you wearing those scrubmmMMMNNN

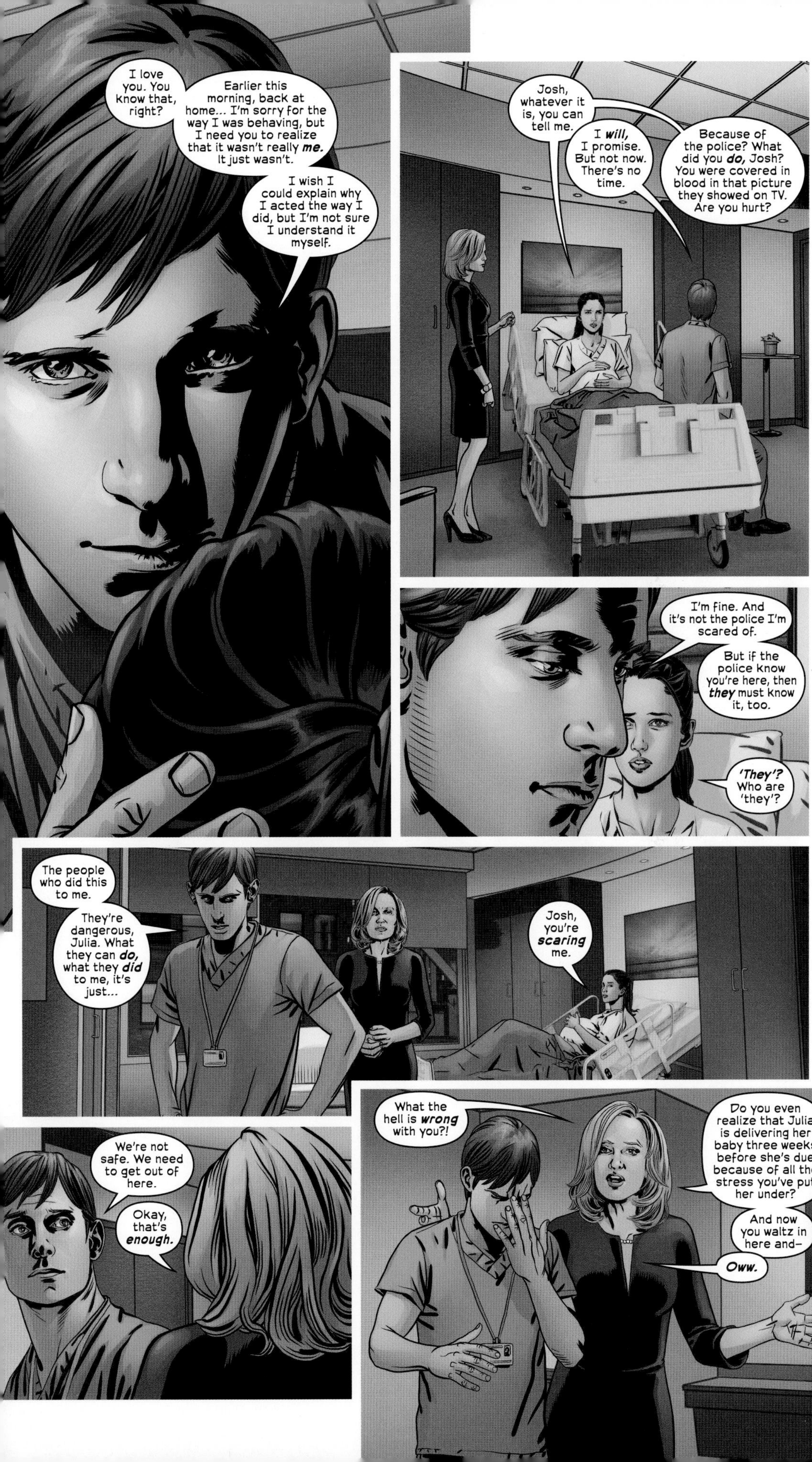

I love you. You know that, right?
Earlier this morning, back at home... I'm sorry for the way I was behaving, but I need you to realize that it wasn't really *me.* It just wasn't.
I wish I could explain why I acted the way I did, but I'm not sure I understand it myself.
Josh, whatever it is, you can tell me.
I *will,* I promise. But not now. There's no time.
Because of the police? What did you *do,* Josh? You were covered in blood in that picture they showed on TV. Are you hurt?
I'm fine. And it's not the police I'm scared of.
But if the police know you're here, then *they* must know it, too.
'They'? Who are 'they'?
The people who did this to me.
They're dangerous, Julia. What they can *do,* what they *did* to me, it's just...
Josh, you're *scaring* me.
We're not safe. We need to get out of here.
Okay, that's *enough.*
What the hell is *wrong* with you?!
Do you even realize that Julia is delivering her baby three weeks before she's due because of all the stress you've put her under?
And now you waltz in here and–
Oww.

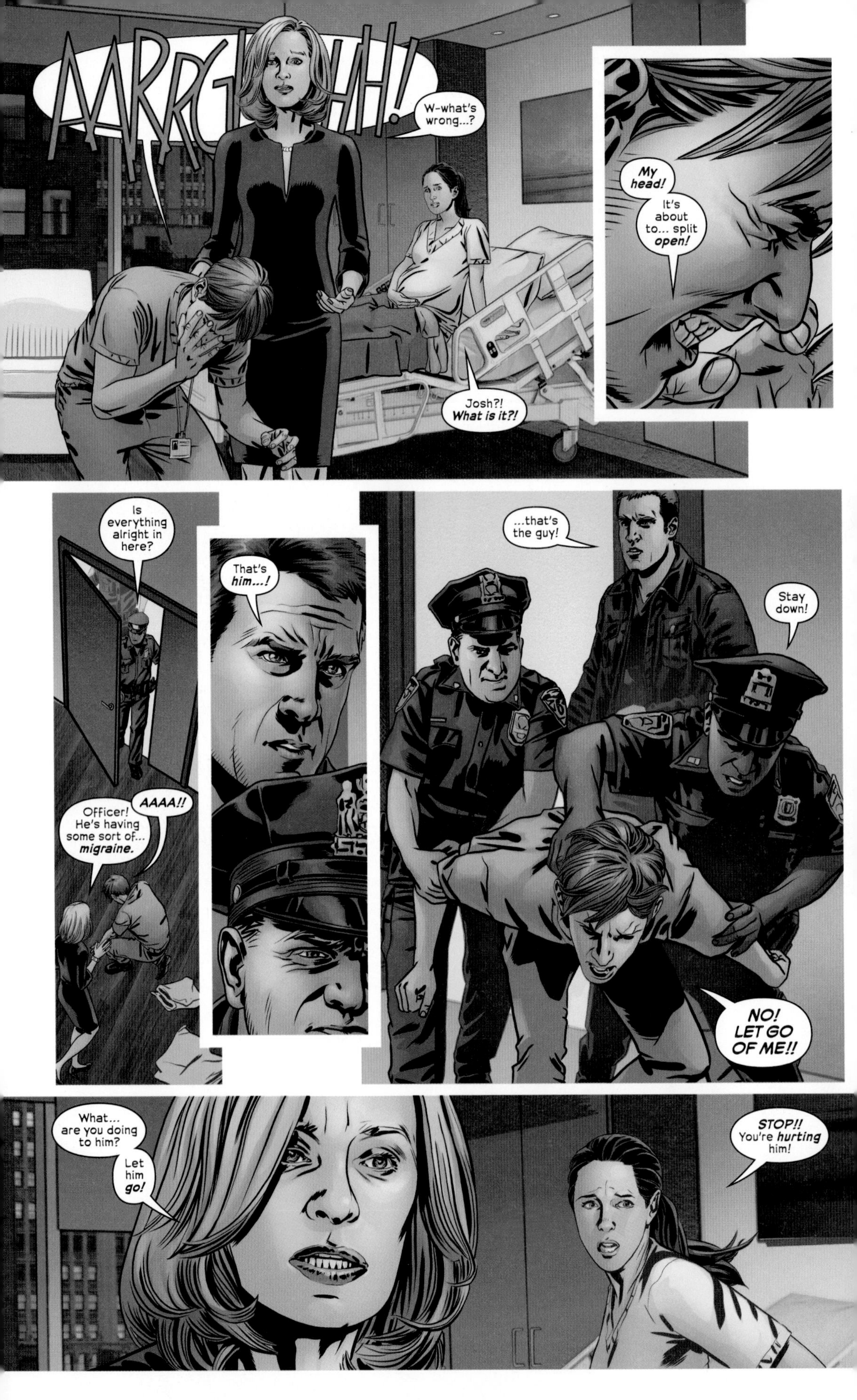
AARRGHHH!
W-what's wrong...?
Josh?! What is it?!
My head!
It's about to... split open!
Is everything alright in here?
Officer! He's having some sort of... migraine.
AAAA!!
That's him...!
...that's the guy!
Stay down!
NO! LET GO OF ME!!
What... are you doing to him?
Let him go!
STOP!! You're hurting him!

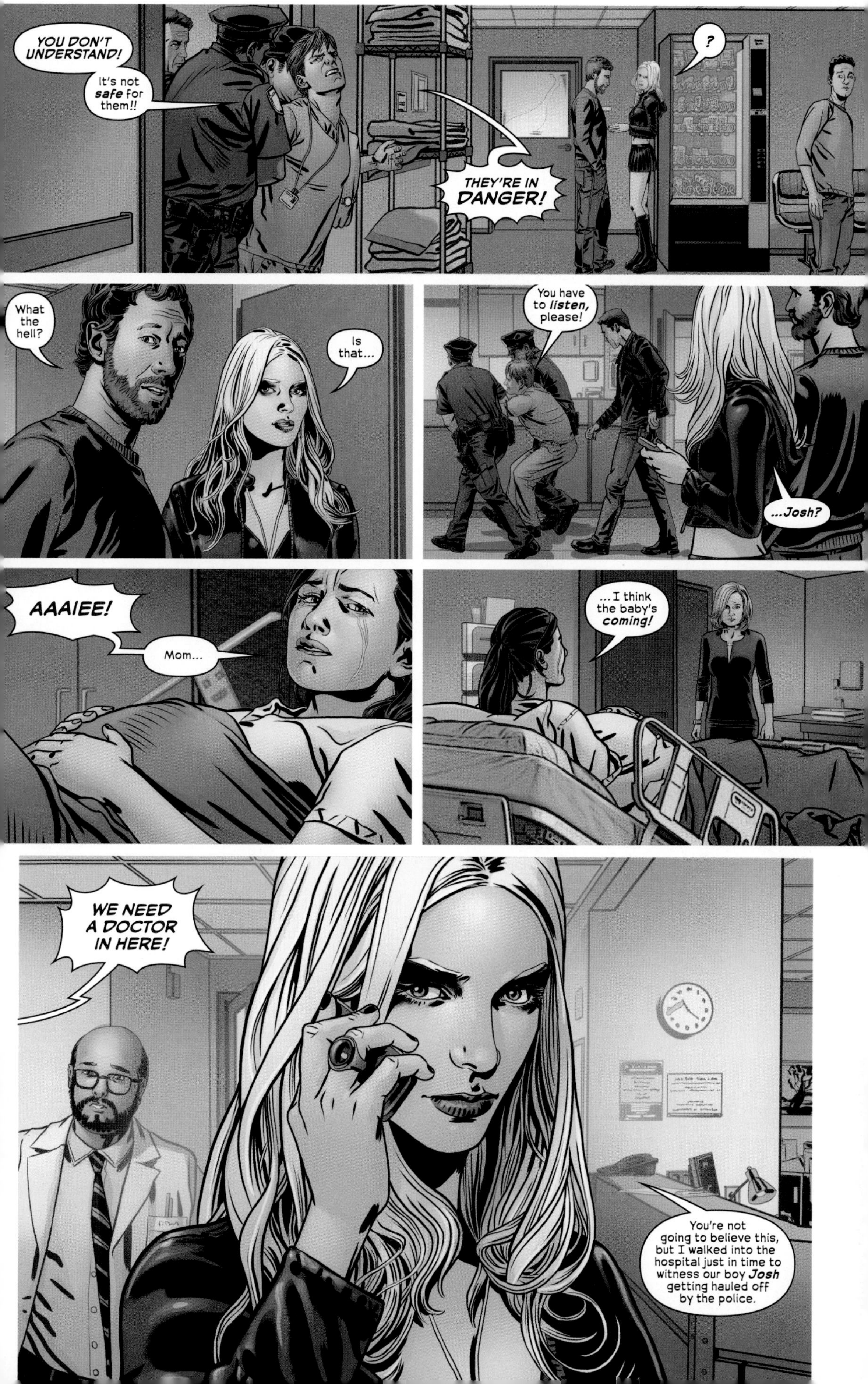
YOU DON'T UNDERSTAND!
It's not safe for them!!
THEY'RE IN DANGER!
?
What the hell?
Is that...
You have to listen, please!
...Josh?
AAAIEE!
Mom...
...I think the baby's coming!
WE NEED A DOCTOR IN HERE!
You're not going to believe this, but I walked into the hospital just in time to witness our boy Josh getting hauled off by the police.

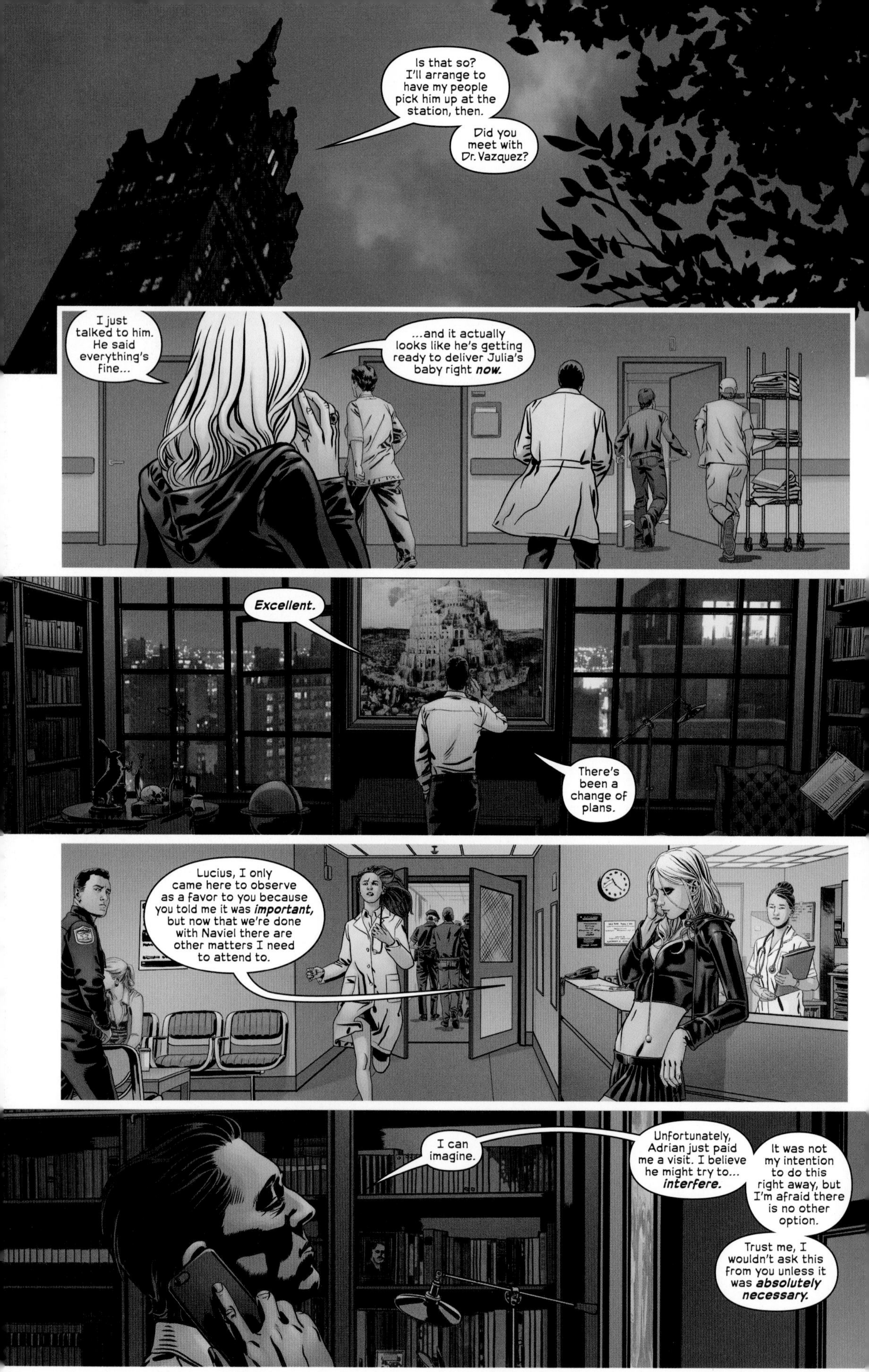
Is that so? I'll arrange to have my people pick him up at the station, then.
Did you meet with Dr. Vazquez?
I just talked to him. He said everything's fine...
...and it actually looks like he's getting ready to deliver Julia's baby right *now.*
Excellent.
There's been a change of plans.
Lucius, I only came here to observe as a favor to you because you told me it was *important,* but now that we're done with Naviel there are other matters I need to attend to.
I can imagine.
Unfortunately, Adrian just paid me a visit. I believe he might try to... *interfere.*
It was not my intention to do this right away, but I'm afraid there is no other option.
Trust me, I wouldn't ask this from you unless it was *absolutely necessary.*

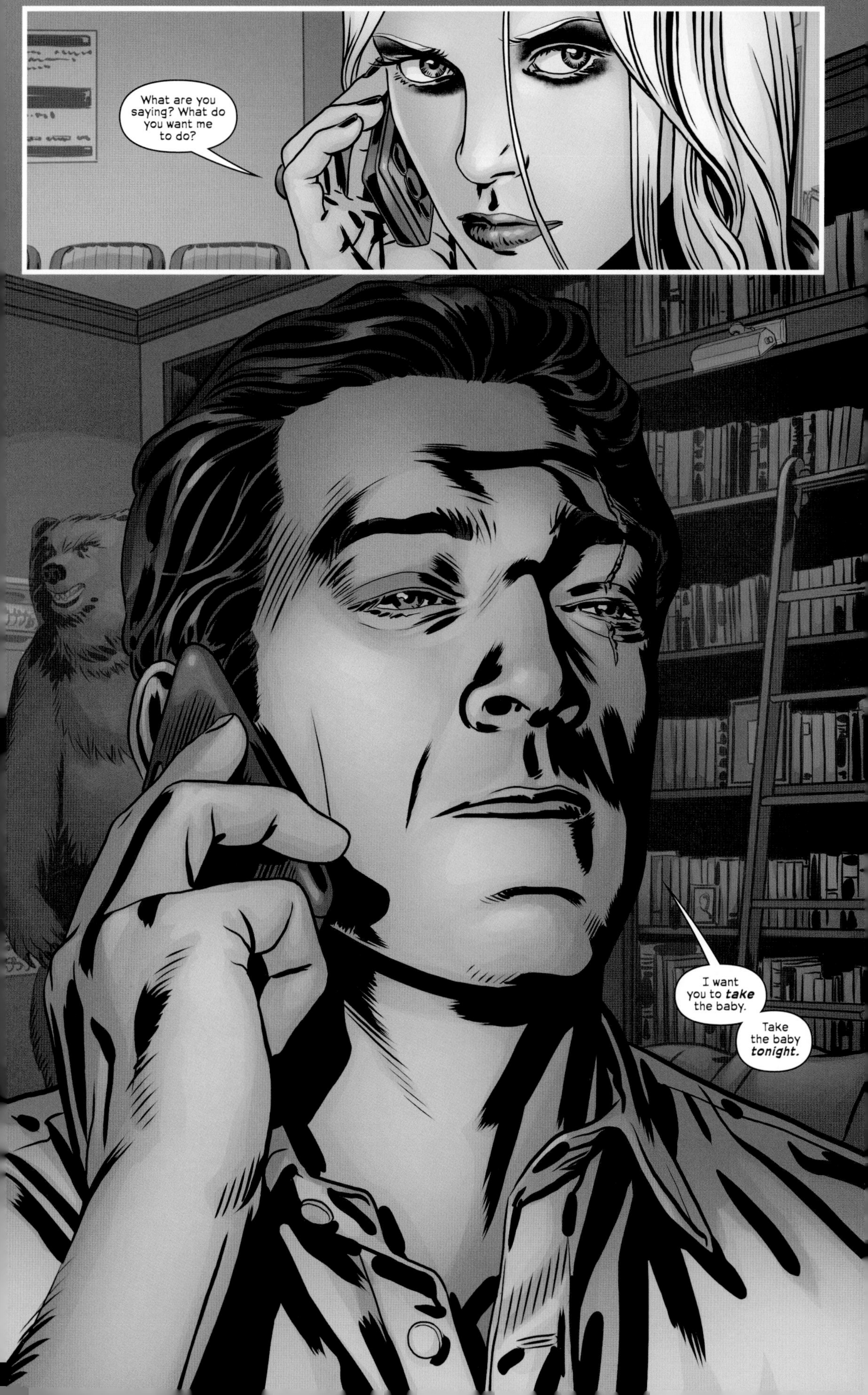

What are you saying? What do you want me to do?
I want you to *take* the baby.
Take the baby *tonight.*

CHAPTER
FOUR

3,650 B.C.
Sodom and Gomorrah.

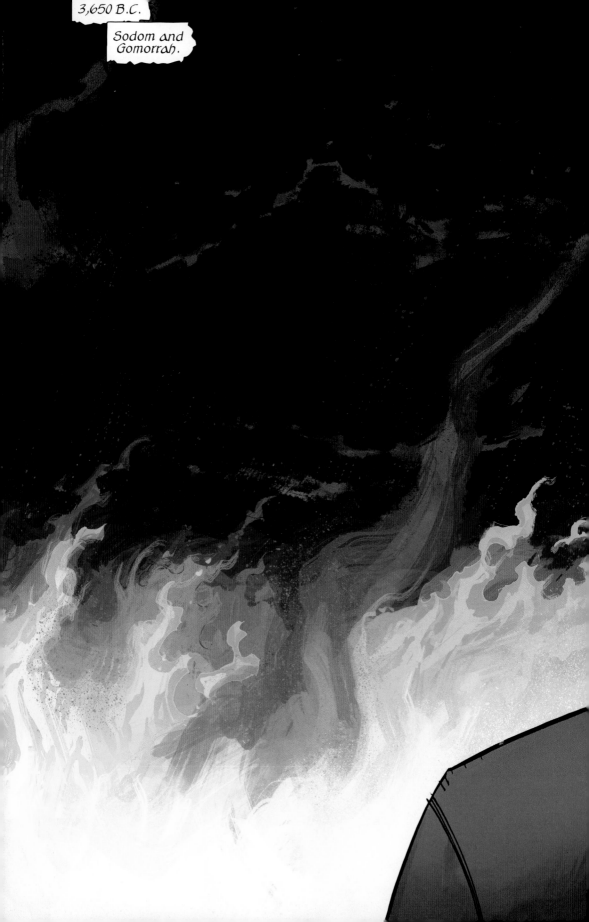

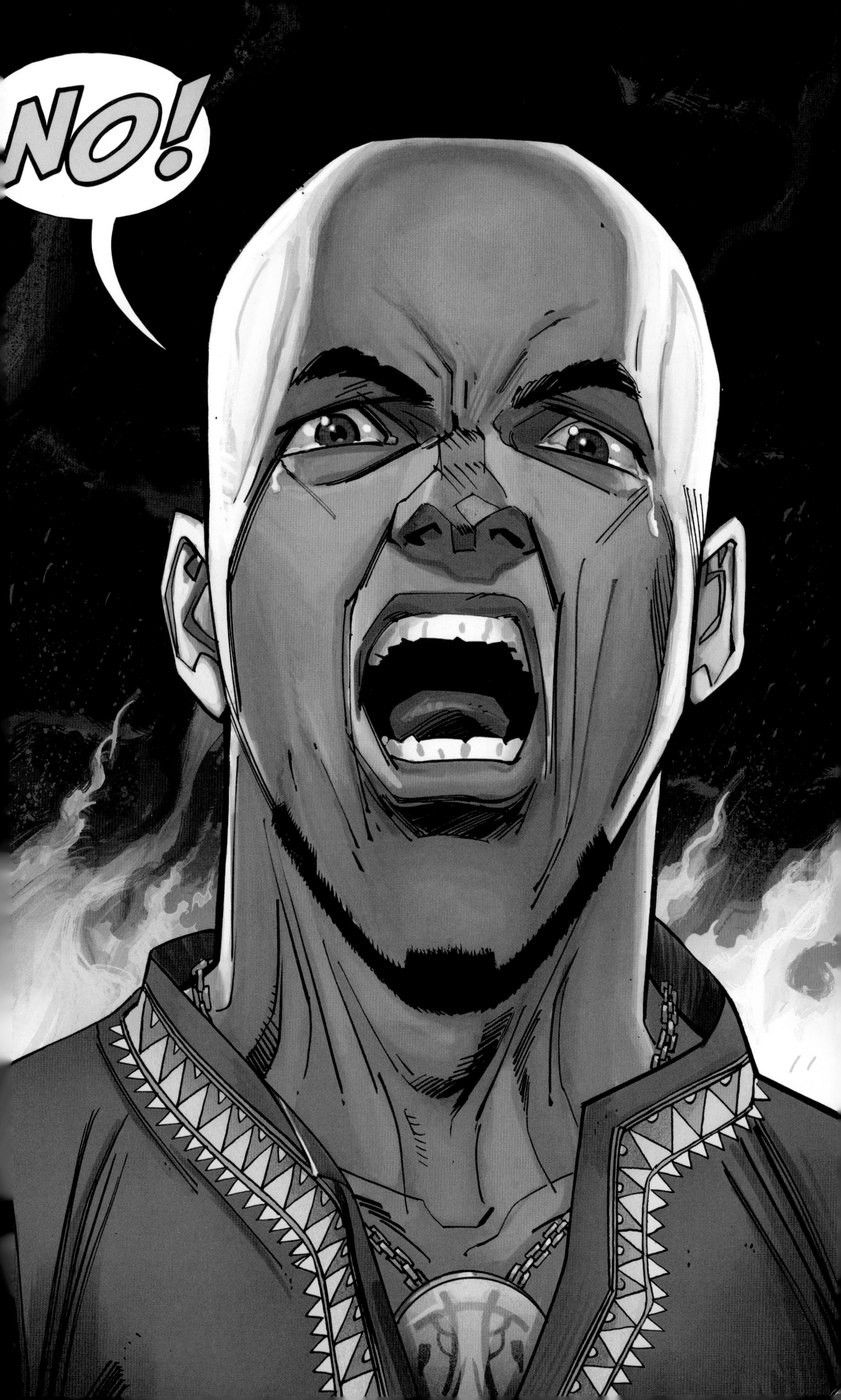
NO!

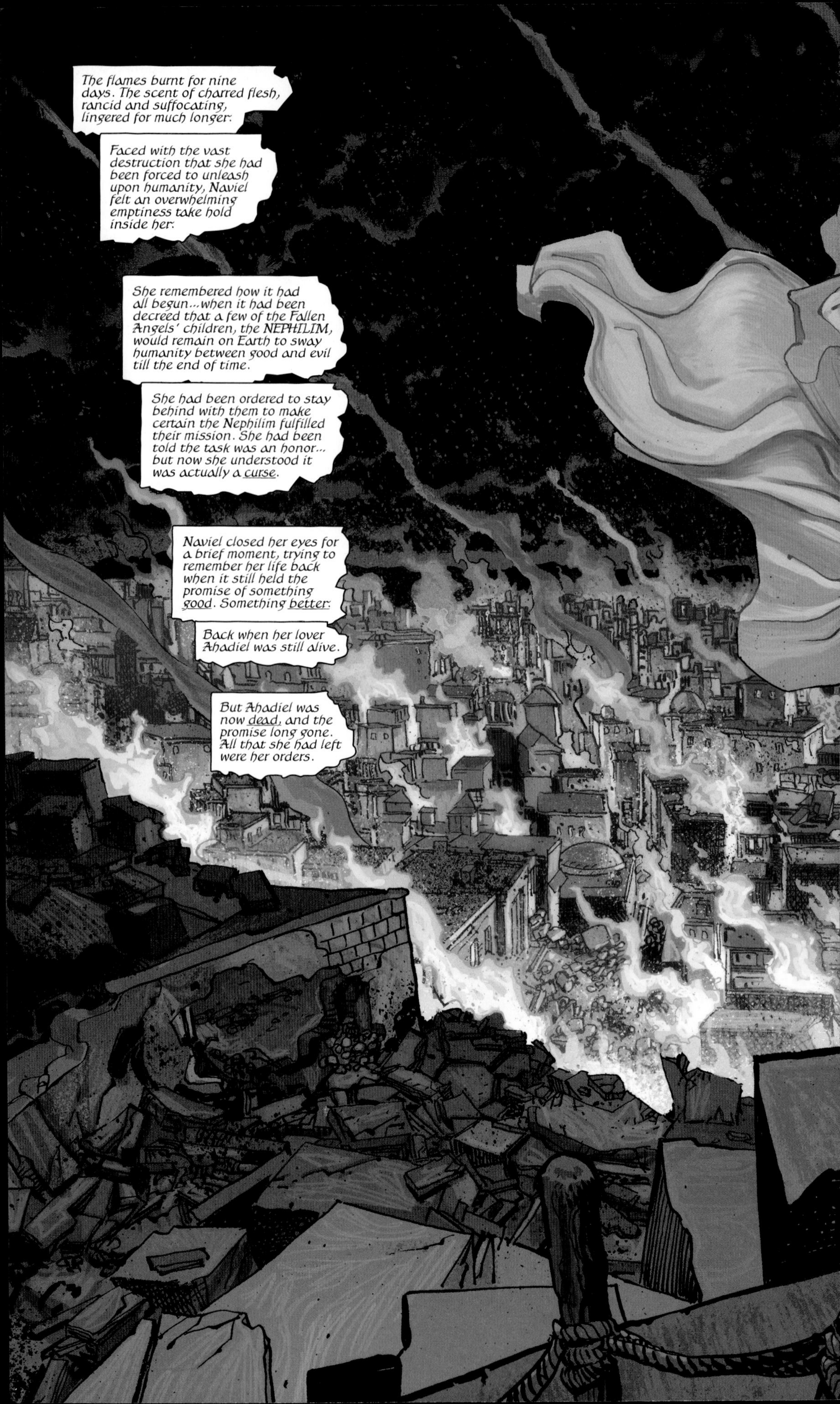
The flames burnt for nine days. The scent of charred flesh, rancid and suffocating, lingered for much longer.
Faced with the vast destruction that she had been forced to unleash upon humanity, Naviel felt an overwhelming emptiness take hold inside her.
She remembered how it had all begun... when it had been decreed that a few of the Fallen Angels' children, the NEPHILIM, would remain on Earth to sway humanity between good and evil till the end of time.
She had been ordered to stay behind with them to make certain the Nephilim fulfilled their mission. She had been told the task was an honor... but now she understood it was actually a curse.
Naviel closed her eyes for a brief moment, trying to remember her life back when it still held the promise of something good. Something better.
Back when her lover Ahadiel was still alive.
But Ahadiel was now dead, and the promise long gone. All that she had left were her orders.

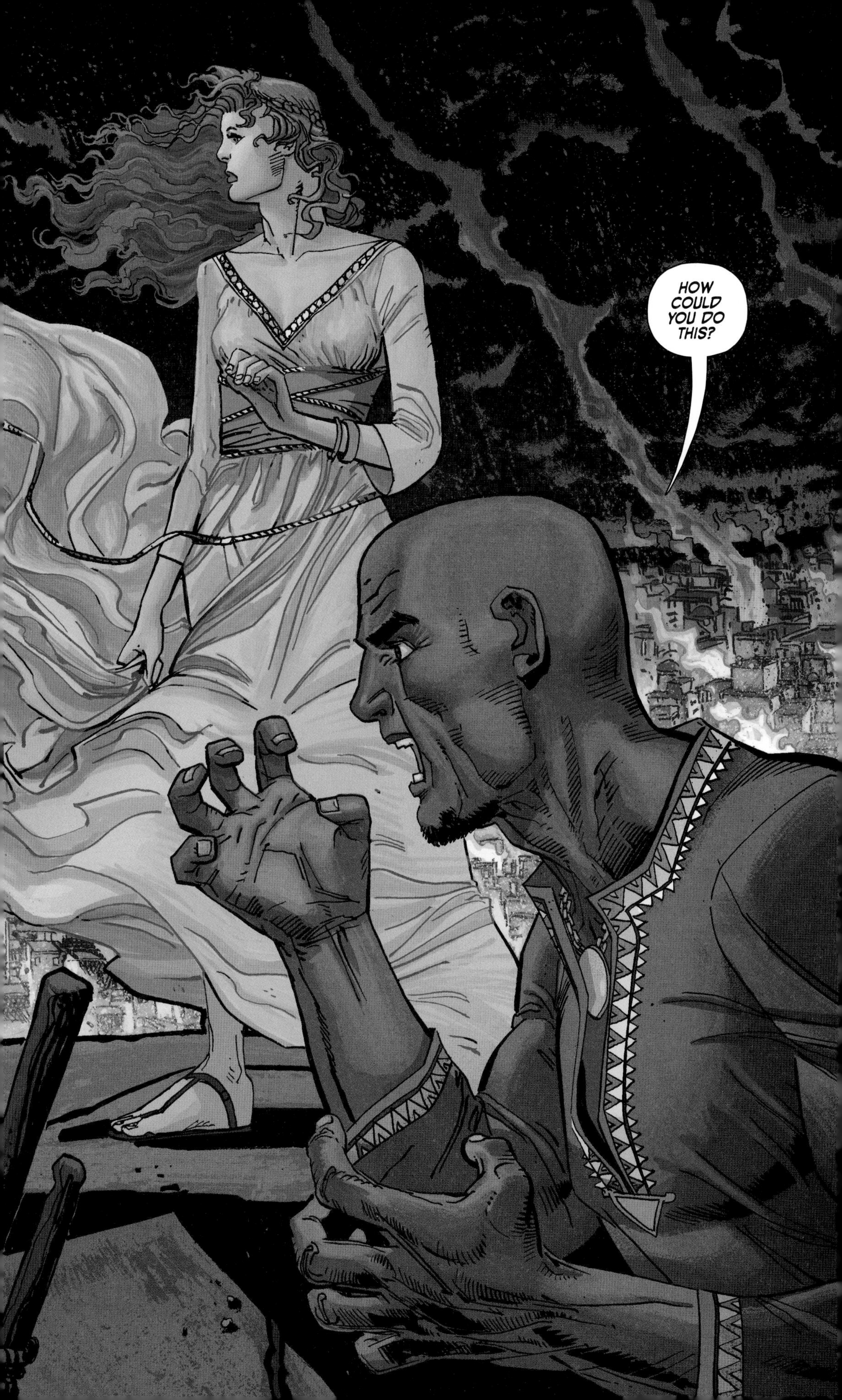
HOW COULD YOU DO THIS?

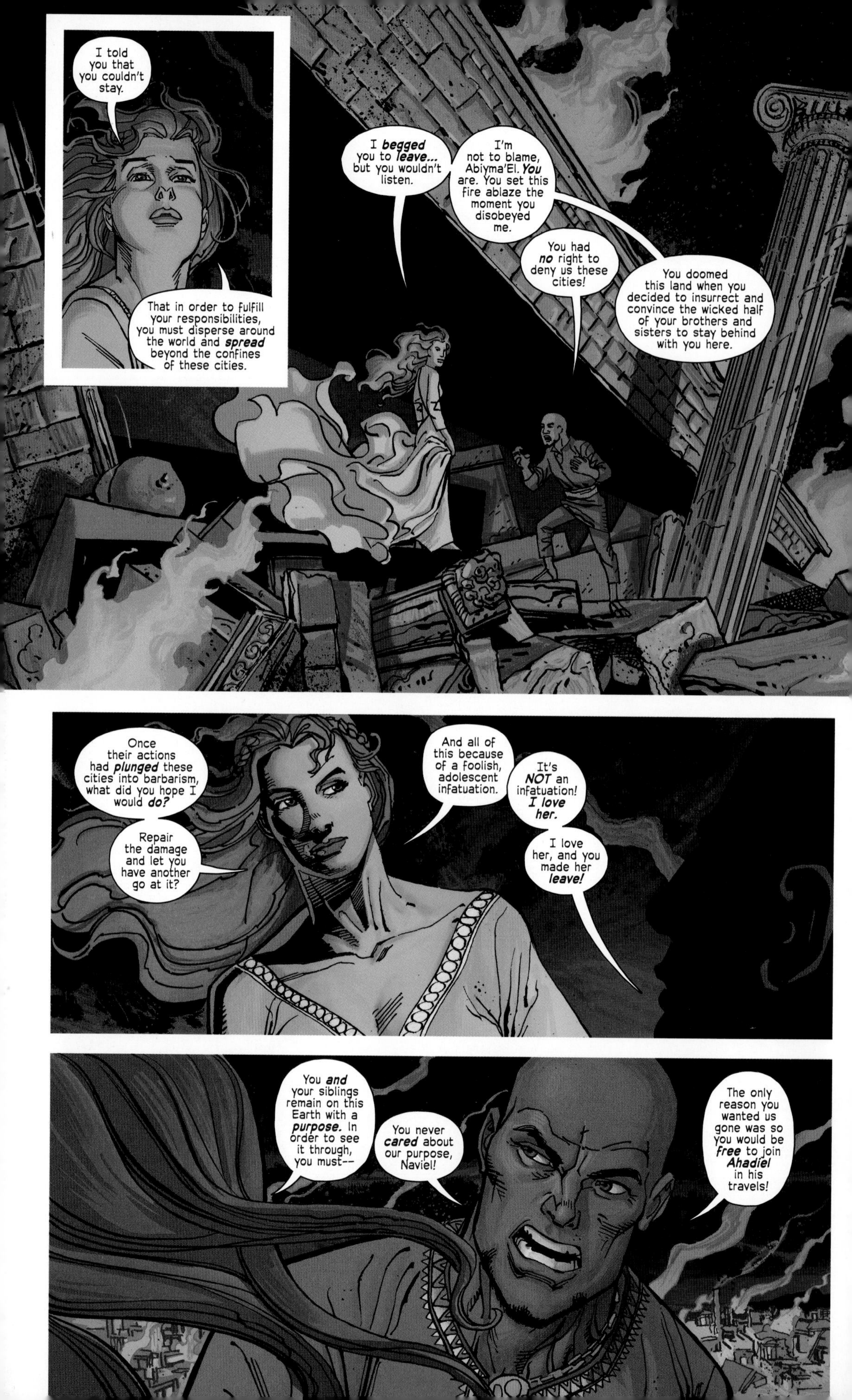

I told you that you couldn't stay.
That in order to fulfill your responsibilities, you must disperse around the world and **spread** beyond the confines of these cities.
I **begged** you to **leave...** but you wouldn't listen.
I'm not to blame, Abiyma'El. **You** are. You set this fire ablaze the moment you disobeyed me.
You had **no** right to deny us these cities!
You doomed this land when you decided to insurrect and convince the wicked half of your brothers and sisters to stay behind with you here.
Once their actions had **plunged** these cities into barbarism, what did you hope I would **do?**
Repair the damage and let you have another go at it?
And all of this because of a foolish, adolescent infatuation.
It's **NOT** an infatuation! **I love her.**
I love her, and you made her **leave!**
You **and** your siblings remain on this Earth with a **purpose.** In order to see it through, you must--
You never **cared** about our purpose, Naviel!
The only reason you wanted us gone was so you would be **free** to join **Ahadiel** in his travels!

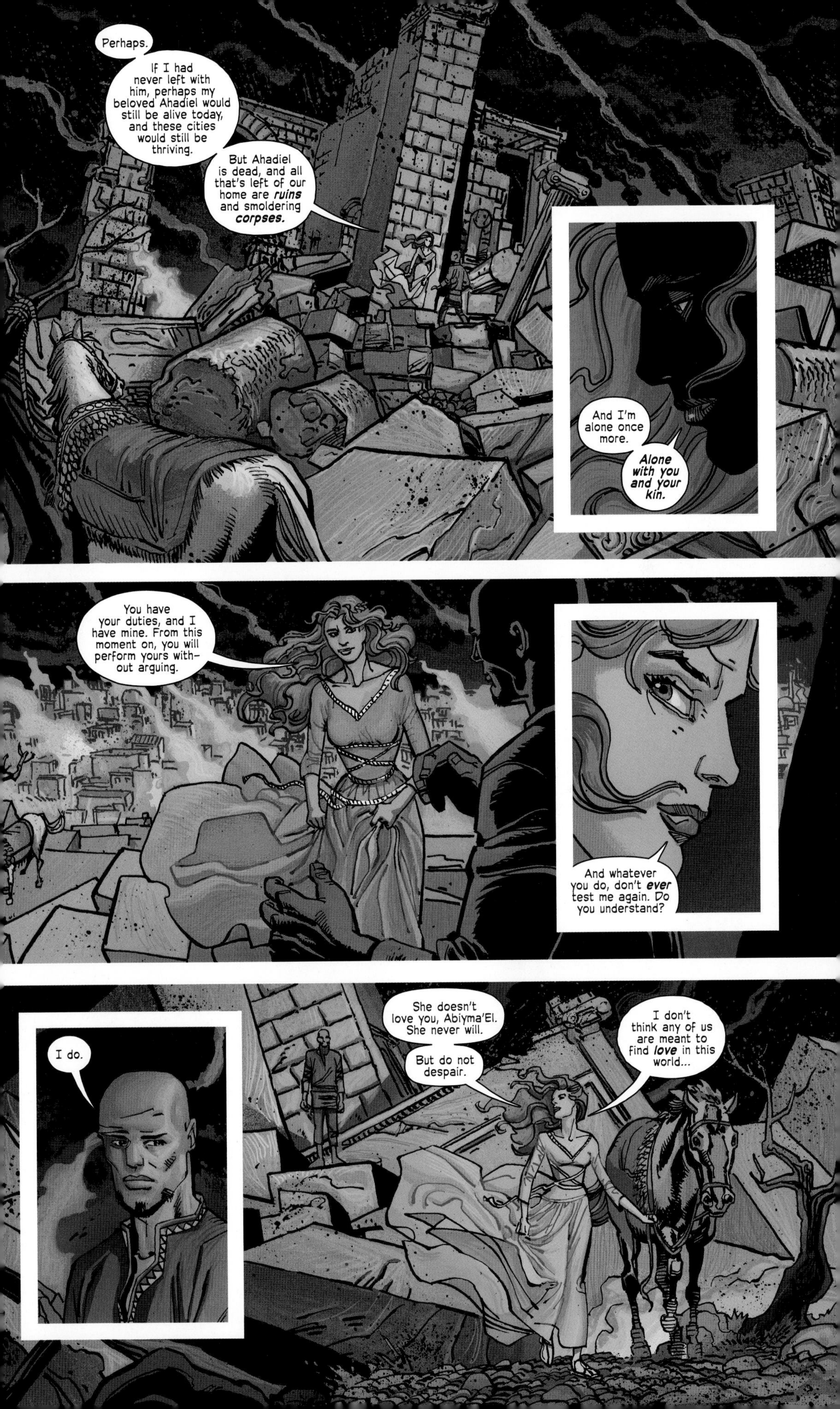
Perhaps.
If I had never left with him, perhaps my beloved Ahadiel would still be alive today, and these cities would still be thriving.
But Ahadiel is dead, and all that's left of our home are *ruins* and smoldering *corpses.*
And I'm alone once more.
Alone with you and your kin.
You have your duties, and I have mine. From this moment on, you will perform yours with-out arguing.
And whatever you do, don't *ever* test me again. Do you understand?
I do.
She doesn't love you, Abiyma'El. She never will.
But do not despair.
I don't think any of us are meant to find *love* in this world...

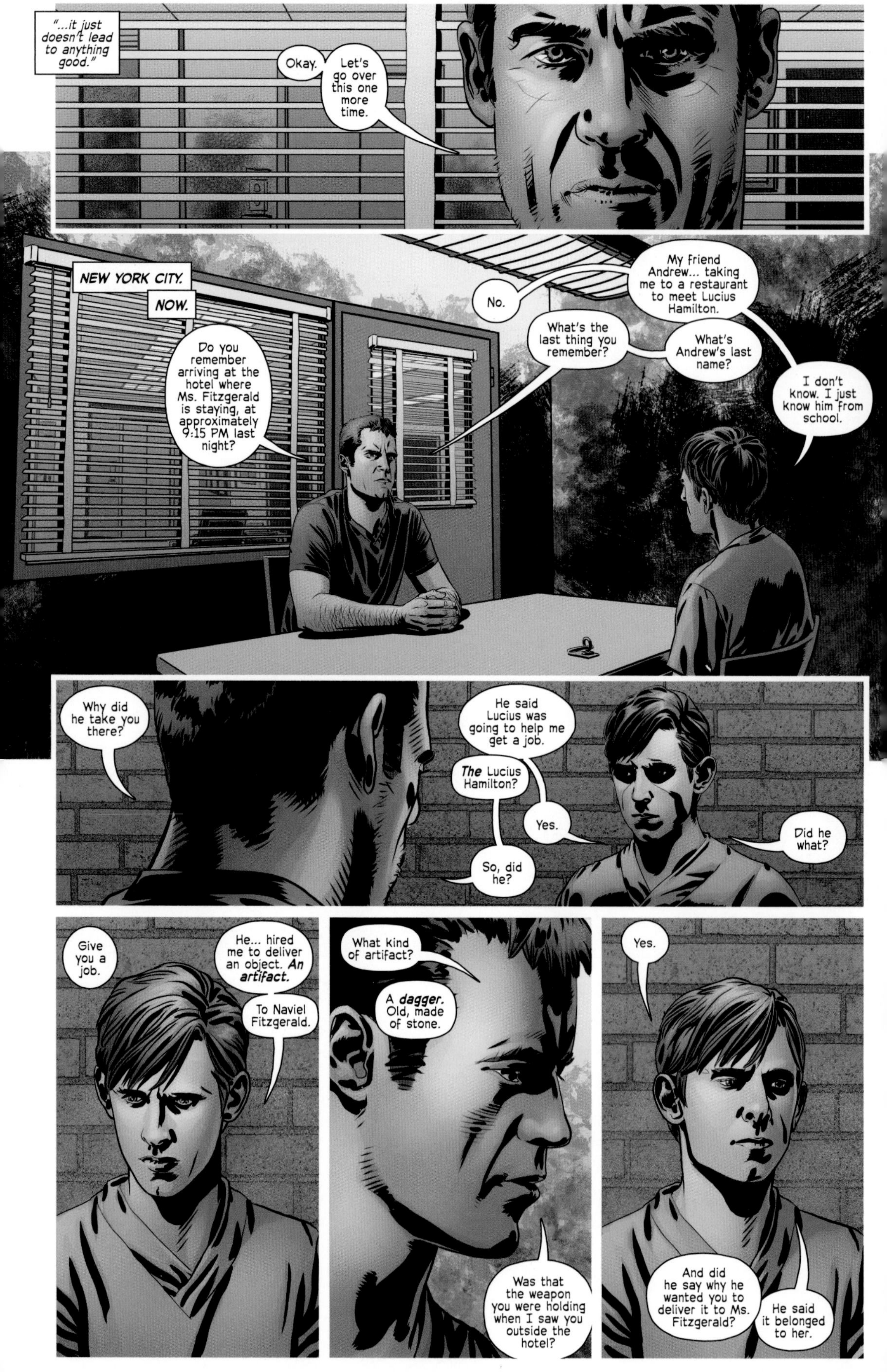
"...it just doesn't lead to anything good."
Okay.
Let's go over this one more time.
NEW YORK CITY.
NOW.
Do you remember arriving at the hotel where Ms. Fitzgerald is staying, at approximately 9:15 PM last night?
No.
What's the last thing you remember?
My friend Andrew... taking me to a restaurant to meet Lucius Hamilton.
What's Andrew's last name?
I don't know. I just know him from school.
Why did he take you there?
He said Lucius was going to help me get a job.
The Lucius Hamilton?
Yes.
So, did he?
Did he what?
Give you a job.
He... hired me to deliver an object. *An artifact.*
To Naviel Fitzgerald.
What kind of artifact?
A *dagger.* Old, made of stone.
Was that the weapon you were holding when I saw you outside the hotel?
Yes.
And did he say why he wanted you to deliver it to Ms. Fitzgerald?
He said it belonged to her.

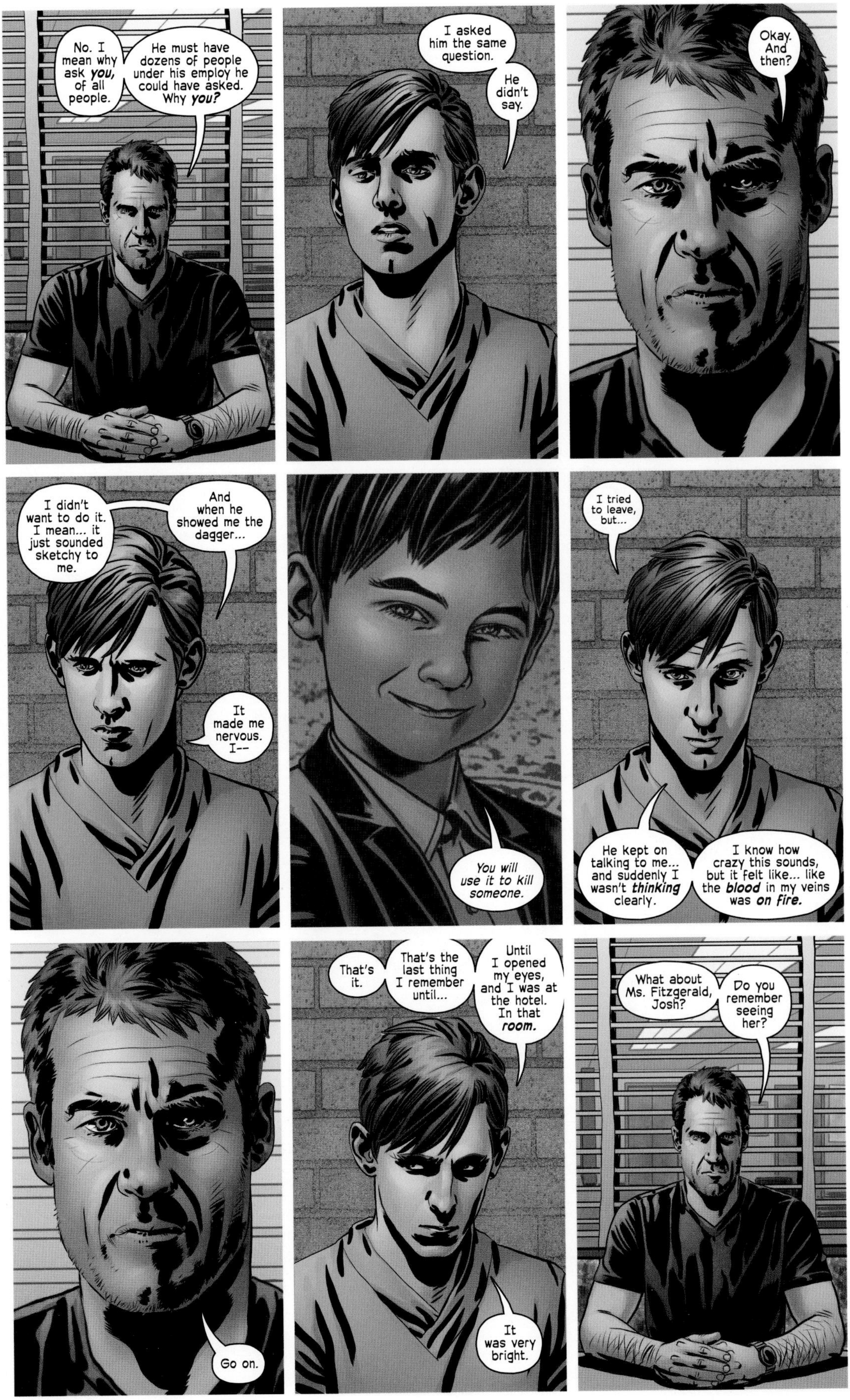
No. I mean why ask *you,* of all people.
He must have dozens of people under his employ he could have asked. Why *you?*
I asked him the same question.
He didn't say.
Okay. And then?
I didn't want to do it. I mean... it just sounded sketchy to me.
And when he showed me the dagger...
It made me nervous. I--
You will use it to kill someone.
I tried to leave, but...
He kept on talking to me... and suddenly I wasn't ***thinking*** clearly.
I know how crazy this sounds, but it felt like... like the ***blood*** in my veins was ***on fire.***
Go on.
That's it.
That's the last thing I remember until...
Until I opened my eyes, and I was at the hotel. In that ***room.***
It was very bright.
What about Ms. Fitzgerald, Josh?
Do you remember seeing her?

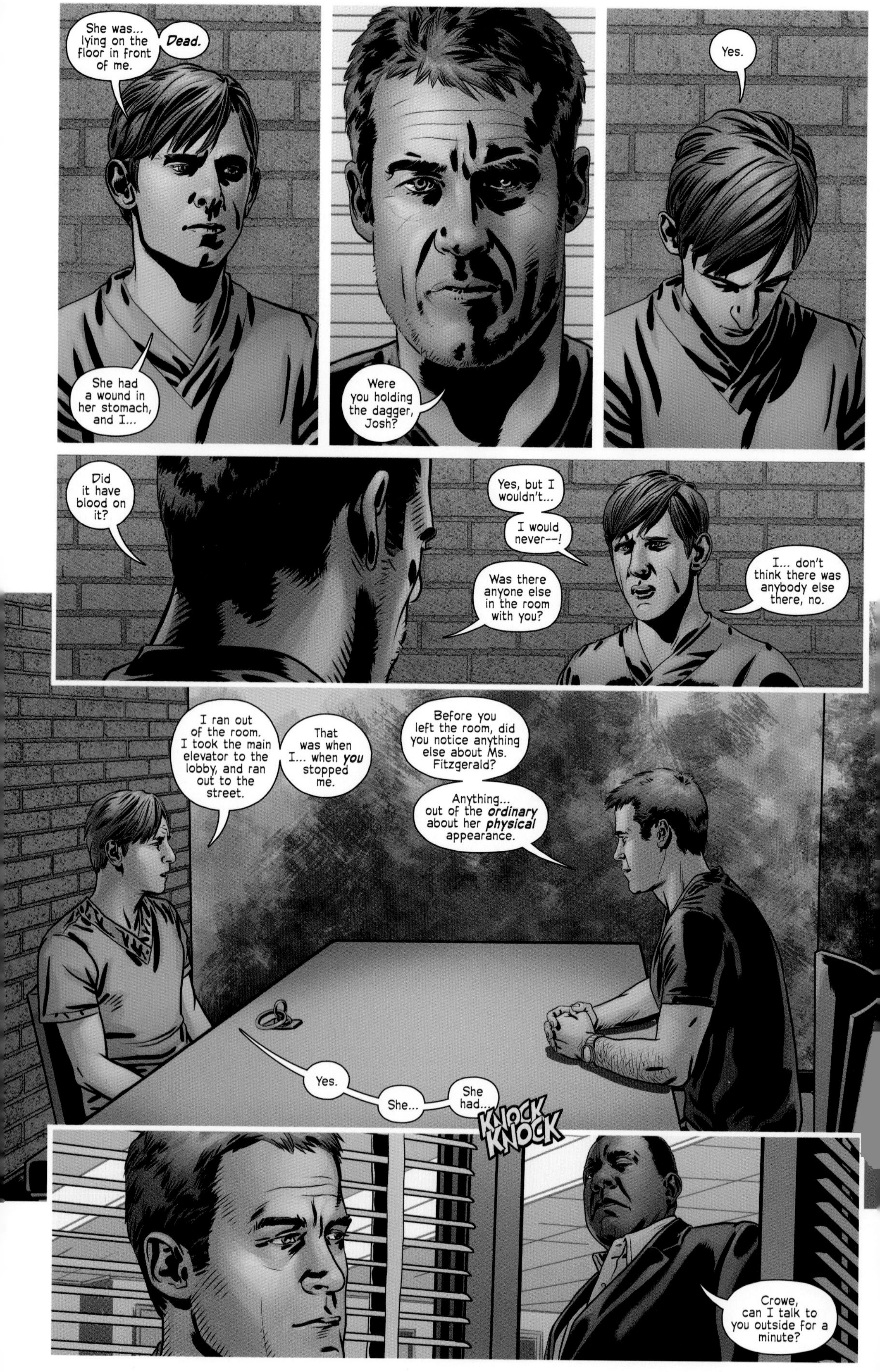

She was... lying on the floor in front of me.
Dead.
She had a wound in her stomach, and I...
Were you holding the dagger, Josh?
Yes.
Did it have blood on it?
Yes, but I wouldn't...
I would never--!
Was there anyone else in the room with you?
I... don't think there was anybody else there, no.
I ran out of the room. I took the main elevator to the lobby, and ran out to the street.
That was when I... when you stopped me.
Before you left the room, did you notice anything else about Ms. Fitzgerald?
Anything... out of the ordinary about her physical appearance.
Yes.
She...
She had...
KNOCK KNOCK
Crowe, can I talk to you outside for a minute?

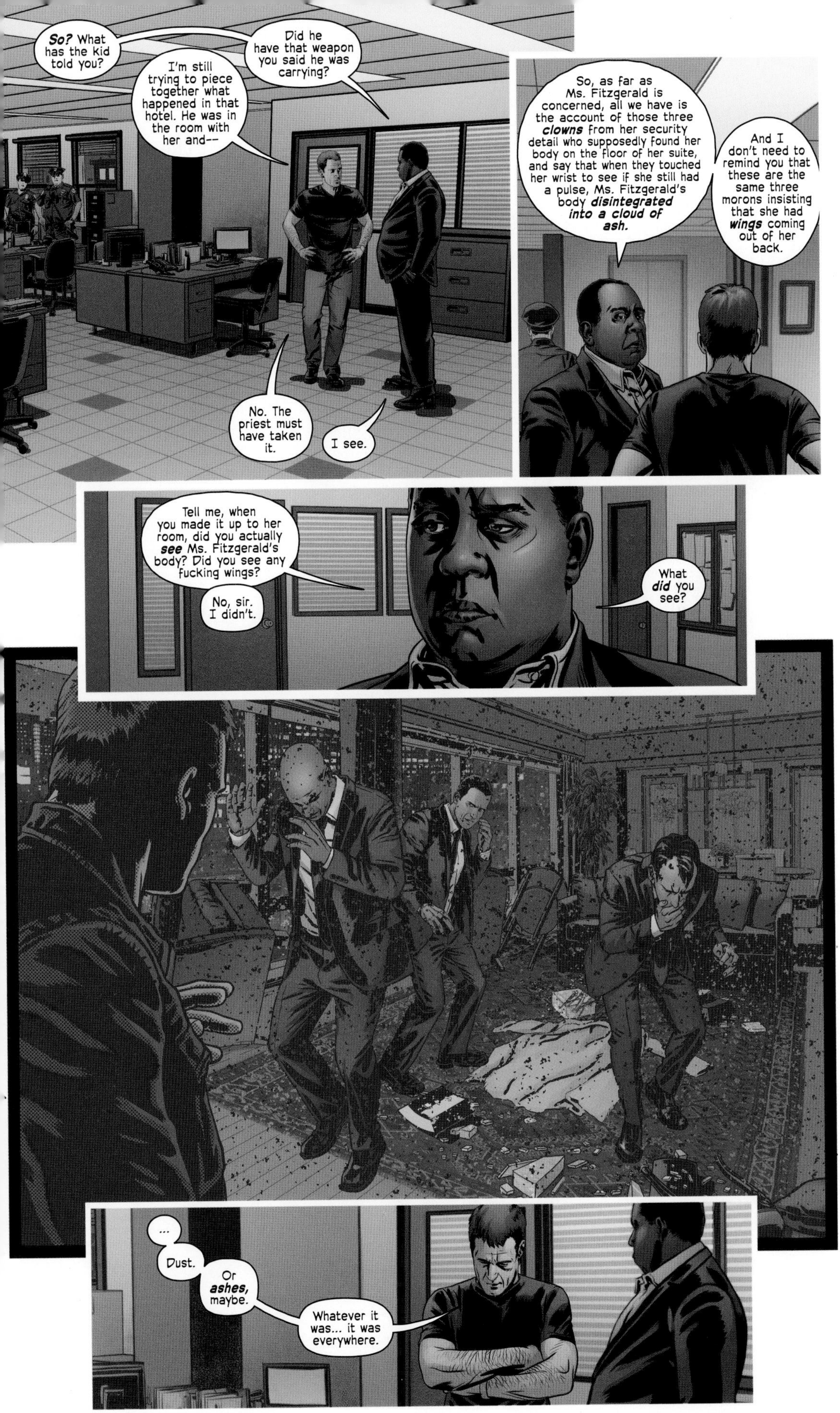

So? What has the kid told you?
Did he have that weapon you said he was carrying?
I'm still trying to piece together what happened in that hotel. He was in the room with her and--
No. The priest must have taken it.
I see.
So, as far as Ms. Fitzgerald is concerned, all we have is the account of those three ***clowns*** from her security detail who supposedly found her body on the floor of her suite, and say that when they touched her wrist to see if she still had a pulse, Ms. Fitzgerald's body ***disintegrated into a cloud of ash.***
And I don't need to remind you that these are the same three morons insisting that she had ***wings*** coming out of her back.
Tell me, when you made it up to her room, did you actually ***see*** Ms. Fitzgerald's body? Did you see any fucking wings?
No, sir. I didn't.
What ***did*** you see?
...
Dust.
Or ***ashes,*** maybe.
Whatever it was... it was everywhere.

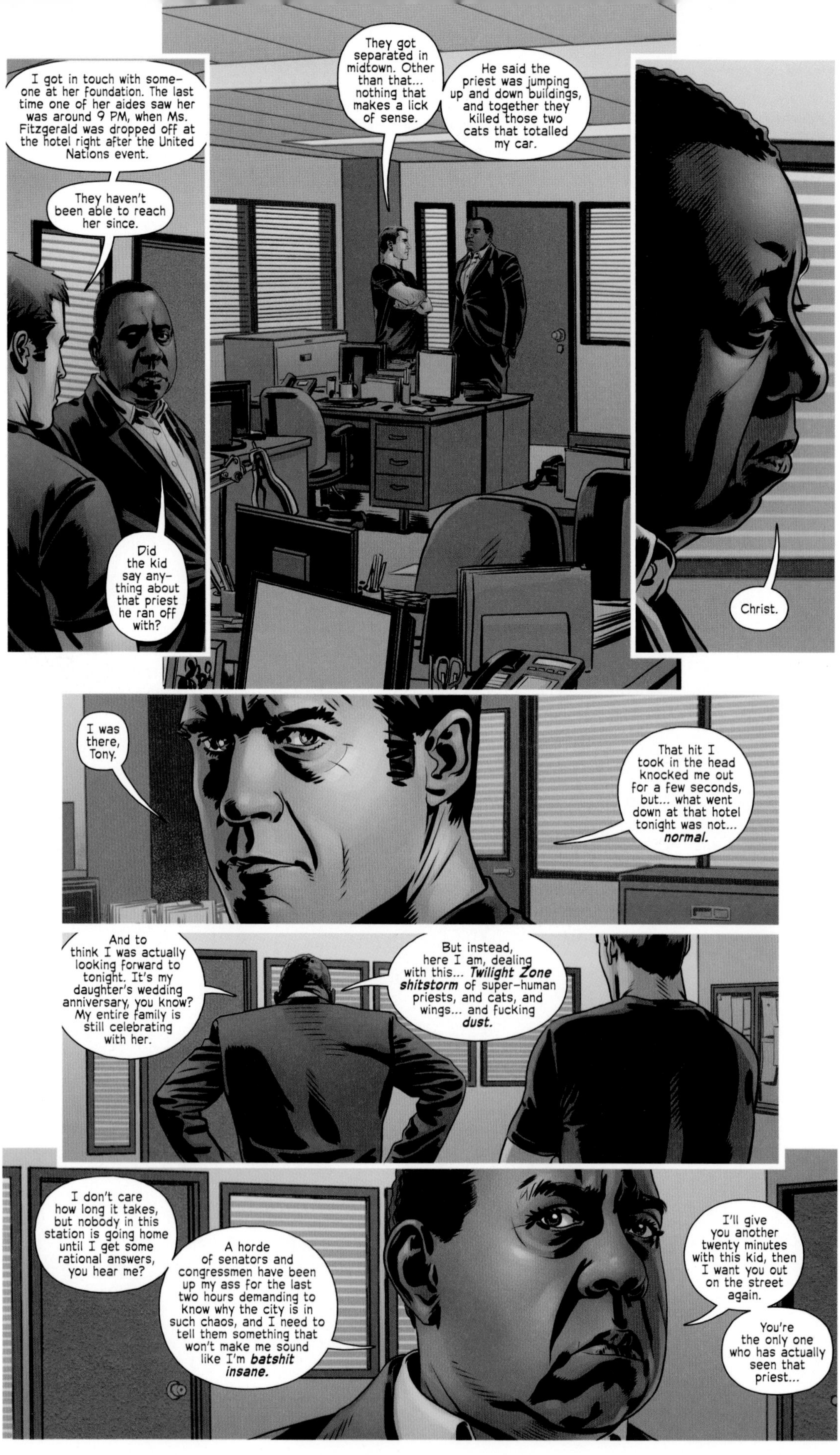
I got in touch with someone at her foundation. The last time one of her aides saw her was around 9 PM, when Ms. Fitzgerald was dropped off at the hotel right after the United Nations event.
They haven't been able to reach her since.
Did the kid say anything about that priest he ran off with?
They got separated in midtown. Other than that... nothing that makes a lick of sense.
He said the priest was jumping up and down buildings, and together they killed those two cats that totalled my car.
Christ.
I was there, Tony.
That hit I took in the head knocked me out for a few seconds, but... what went down at that hotel tonight was not... ***normal.***
And to think I was actually looking forward to tonight. It's my daughter's wedding anniversary, you know? My entire family is still celebrating with her.
But instead, here I am, dealing with this... ***Twilight Zone shitstorm*** of super-human priests, and cats, and wings... and fucking ***dust.***
I don't care how long it takes, but nobody in this station is going home until I get some rational answers, you hear me?
A horde of senators and congressmen have been up my ass for the last two hours demanding to know why the city is in such chaos, and I need to tell them something that won't make me sound like I'm ***batshit insane.***
I'll give you another twenty minutes with this kid, then I want you out on the street again.
You're the only one who has actually seen that priest...

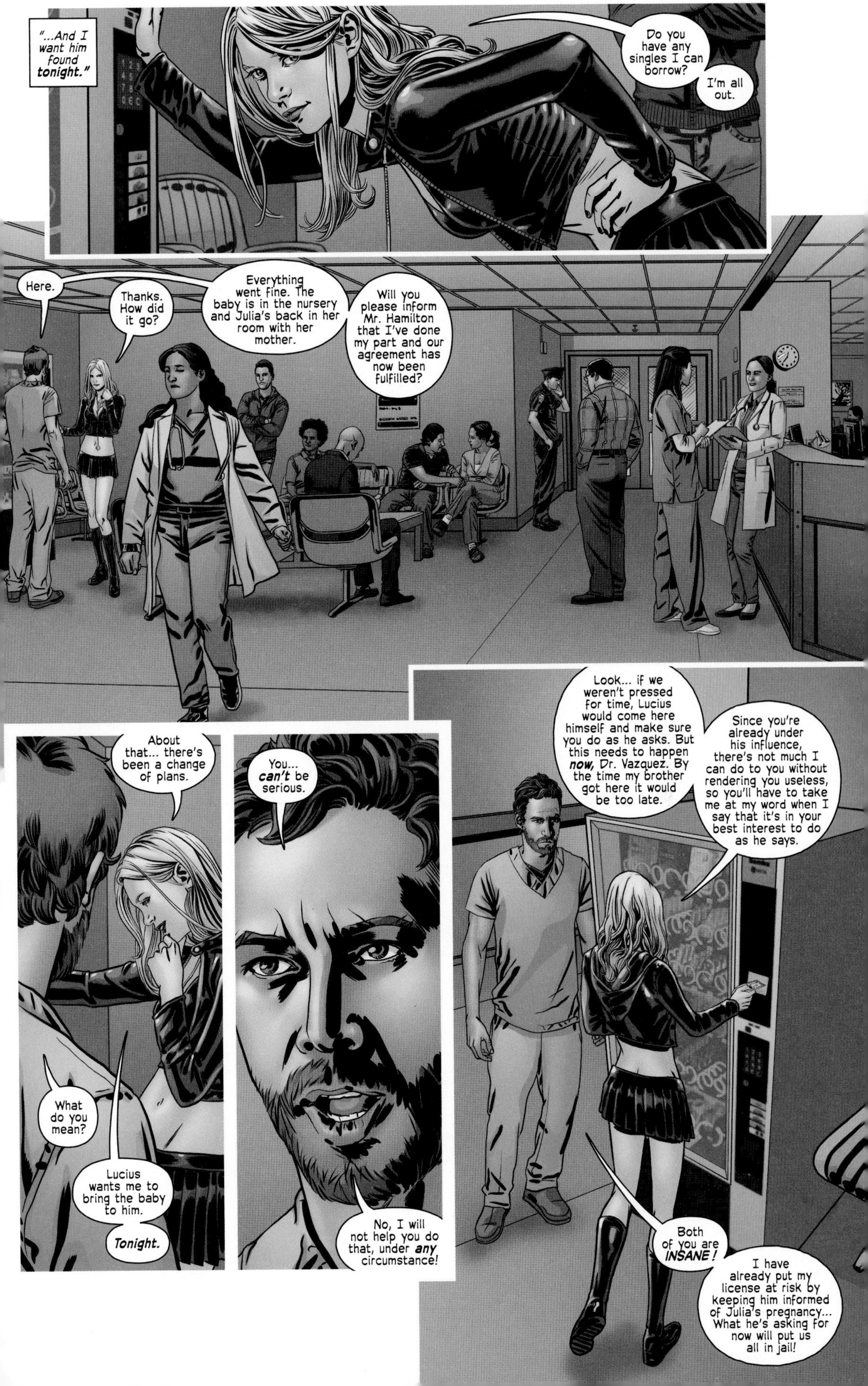
"...And I want him found tonight."
Do you have any singles I can borrow?
I'm all out.
Here.
Thanks. How did it go?
Everything went fine. The baby is in the nursery and Julia's back in her room with her mother.
Will you please inform Mr. Hamilton that I've done my part and our agreement has now been fulfilled?
About that... there's been a change of plans.
What do you mean?
Lucius wants me to bring the baby to him.
Tonight.
You... can't be serious.
No, I will not help you do that, under any circumstance!
Look... if we weren't pressed for time, Lucius would come here himself and make sure you do as he asks. But this needs to happen now, Dr. Vazquez. By the time my brother got here it would be too late.
Since you're already under his influence, there's not much I can do to you without rendering you useless, so you'll have to take me at my word when I say that it's in your best interest to do as he says.
Both of you are INSANE!
I have already put my license at risk by keeping him informed of Julia's pregnancy... What he's asking for now will put us all in jail!

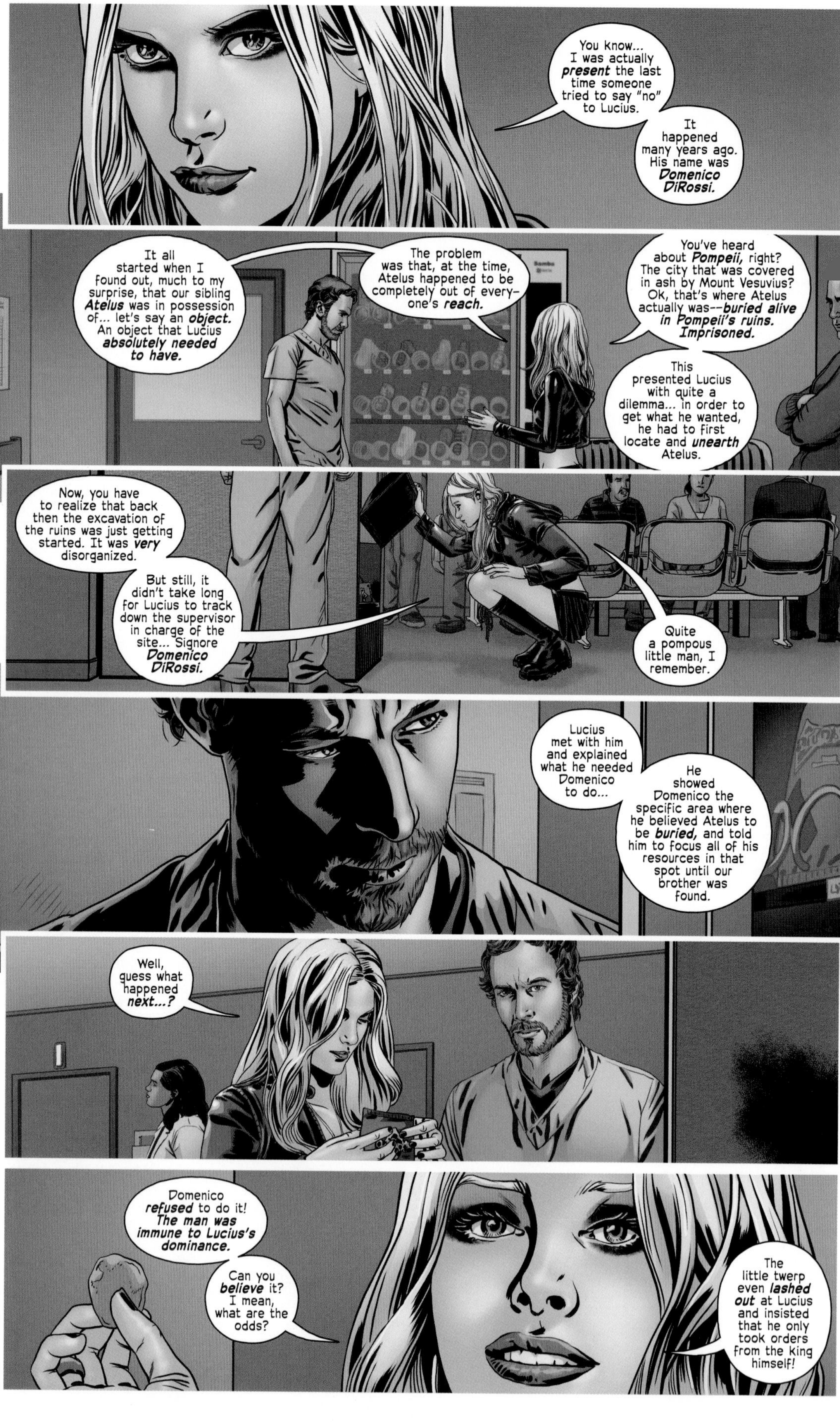

You know... I was actually *present* the last time someone tried to say "no" to Lucius.
It happened many years ago. His name was *Domenico DiRossi.*
It all started when I found out, much to my surprise, that our sibling *Atelus* was in possession of... let's say an *object.* An object that Lucius *absolutely needed to have.*
The problem was that, at the time, Atelus happened to be completely out of every-one's *reach.*
You've heard about *Pompeii,* right? The city that was covered in ash by Mount Vesuvius? Ok, that's where Atelus actually was--*buried alive in Pompeii's ruins. Imprisoned.*
This presented Lucius with quite a dilemma... in order to get what he wanted, he had to first locate and *unearth* Atelus.
Now, you have to realize that back then the excavation of the ruins was just getting started. It was *very* disorganized.
But still, it didn't take long for Lucius to track down the supervisor in charge of the site... Signore *Domenico DiRossi.*
Quite a pompous little man, I remember.
Lucius met with him and explained what he needed Domenico to do...
He showed Domenico the specific area where he believed Atelus to be *buried,* and told him to focus all of his resources in that spot until our brother was found.
Well, guess what happened *next...?*
Domenico *refused* to do it! ***The man was immune to Lucius's dominance.***
Can you *believe* it? I mean, what are the odds?
The little twerp even ***lashed out*** at Lucius and insisted that he only took orders from the King himself!

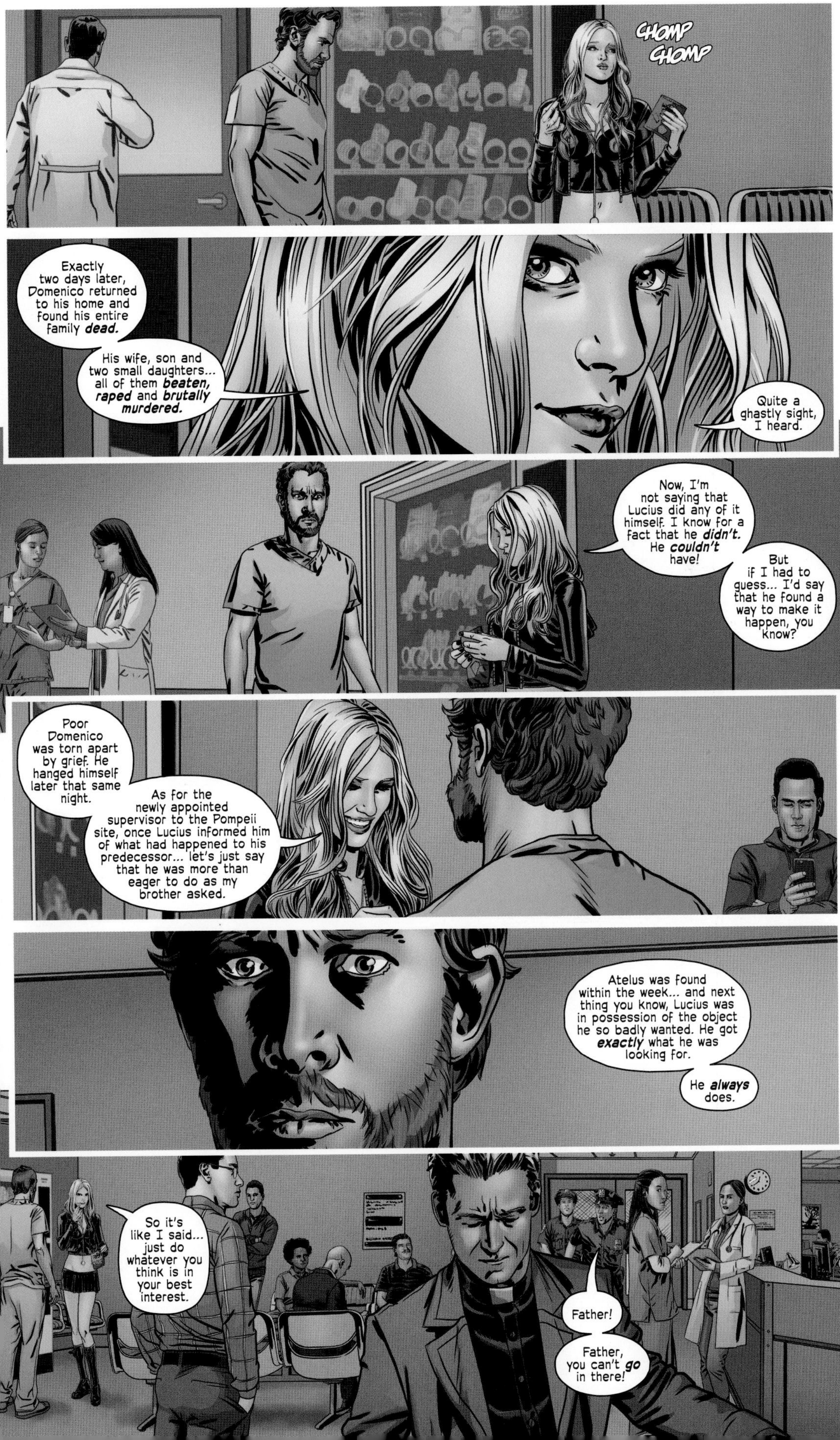
CHOMP CHOMP
Exactly two days later, Domenico returned to his home and found his entire family *dead.*
His wife, son and two small daughters... all of them *beaten, raped* and *brutally murdered.*
Quite a ghastly sight, I heard.
Now, I'm not saying that Lucius did any of it himself. I know for a fact that he *didn't.* He *couldn't* have!
But if I had to guess... I'd say that he found a way to make it happen, you know?
Poor Domenico was torn apart by grief. He hanged himself later that same night.
As for the newly appointed supervisor to the Pompeii site, once Lucius informed him of what had happened to his predecessor... let's just say that he was more than eager to do as my brother asked.
Atelus was found within the week... and next thing you know, Lucius was in possession of the object he so badly wanted. He got *exactly* what he was looking for.
He *always* does.
So it's like I said... just do whatever you think is in your best interest.
Father!
Father, you can't *go* in there!

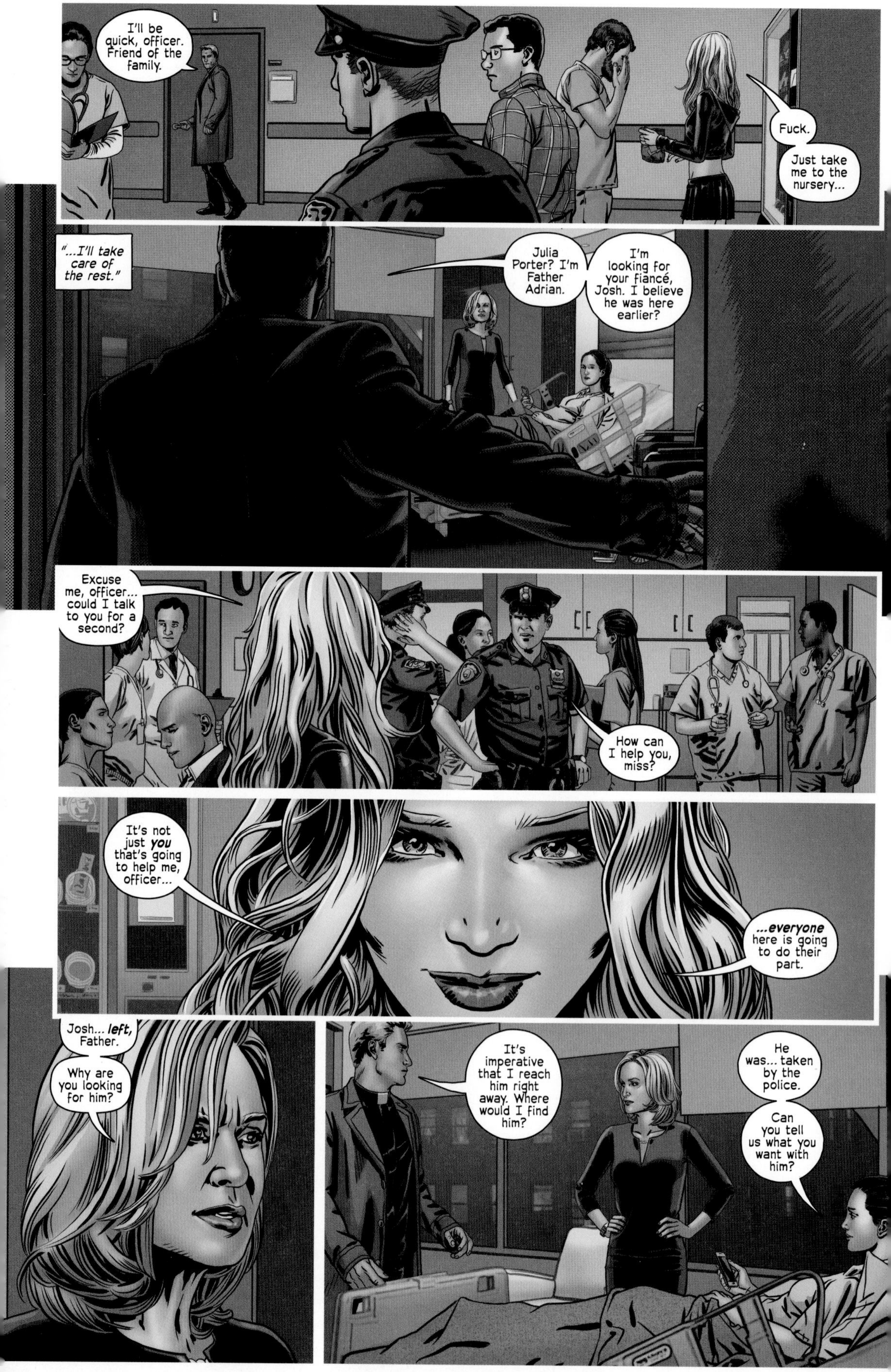

I'll be quick, officer. Friend of the family.
Fuck.
Just take me to the nursery...
"...I'll take care of the rest."
Julia Porter? I'm Father Adrian.
I'm looking for your fiancé, Josh. I believe he was here earlier?
Excuse me, officer... could I talk to you for a second?
How can I help you, miss?
It's not just *you* that's going to help me, officer...
...everyone here is going to do their part.
Josh... *left,* Father.
Why are you looking for him?
It's imperative that I reach him right away. Where would I find him?
He was... taken by the police.
Can you tell us what you want with him?

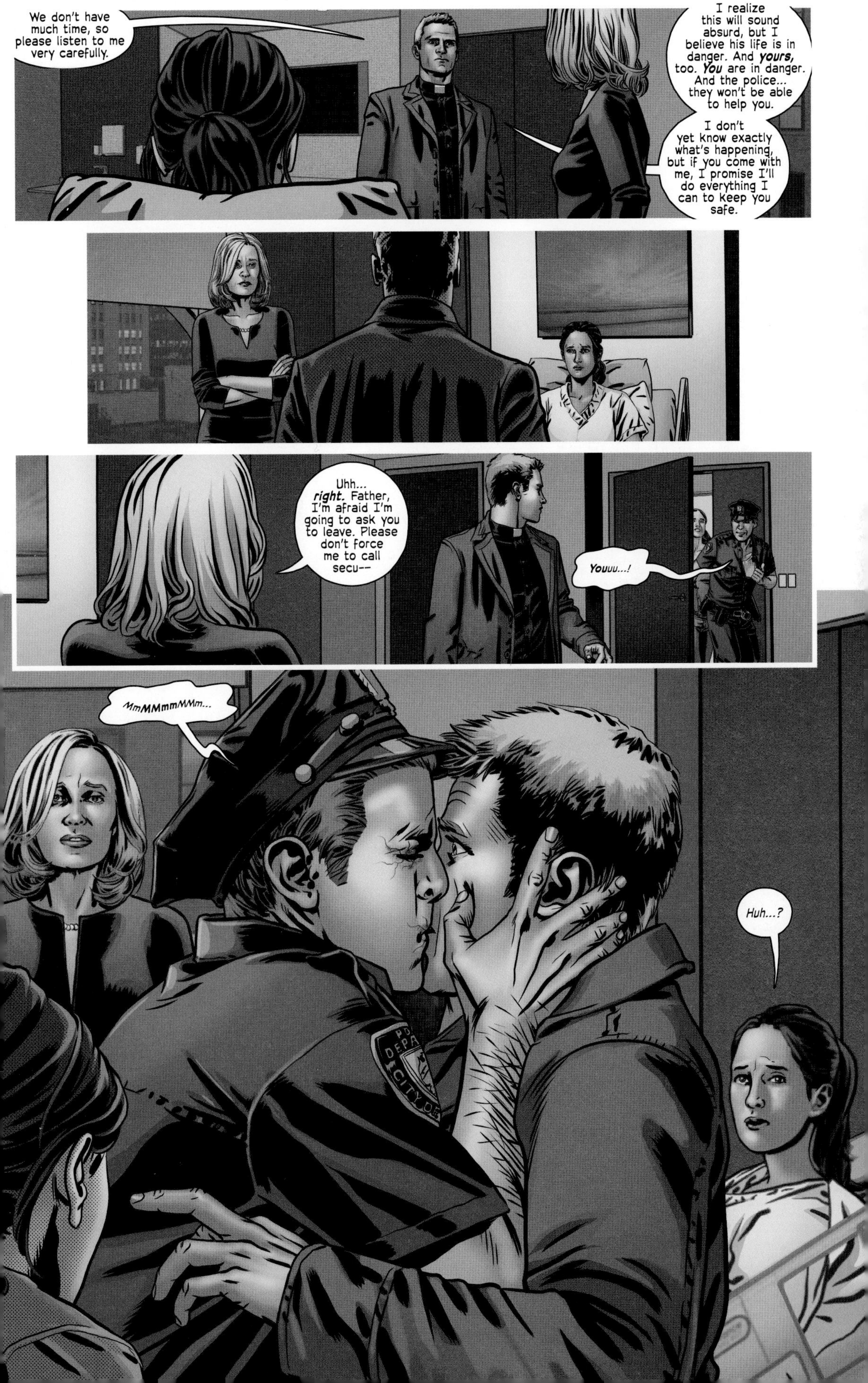
We don't have much time, so please listen to me very carefully.
I realize this will sound absurd, but I believe his life is in danger. And yours, too. You are in danger. And the police... they won't be able to help you.
I don't yet know exactly what's happening, but if you come with me, I promise I'll do everything I can to keep you safe.
Uhh... right. Father, I'm afraid I'm going to ask you to leave. Please don't force me to call secu--
Youuu...!
MmMMmmMMm...
Huh...?

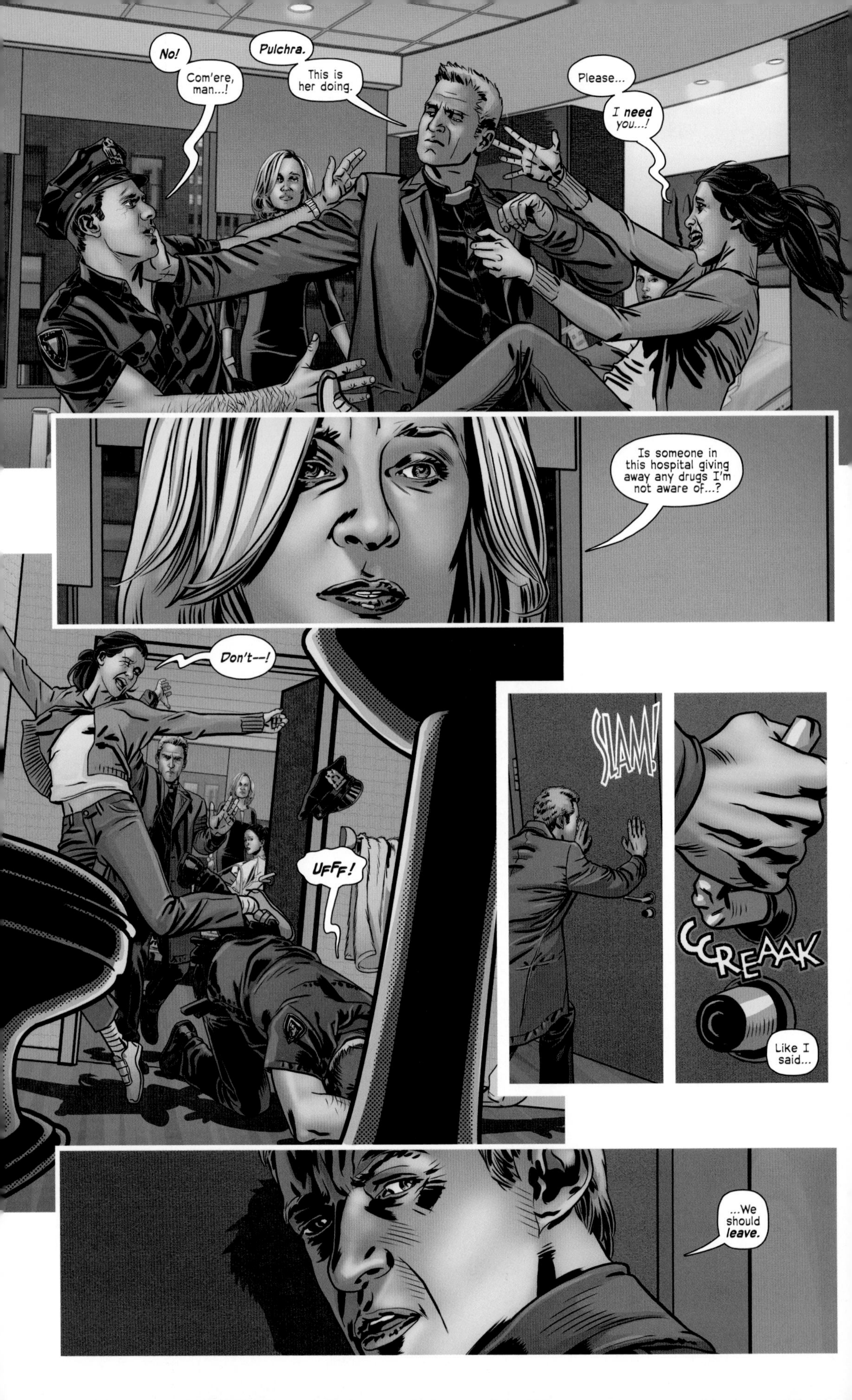
No!
Com'ere, man...!
Pulchra.
This is her doing.
Please...
I need you...!
Is someone in this hospital giving away any drugs I'm not aware of...?
Don't--!
UFFF!
SLAM!
CCREAAK
Like I said...
...We should leave.

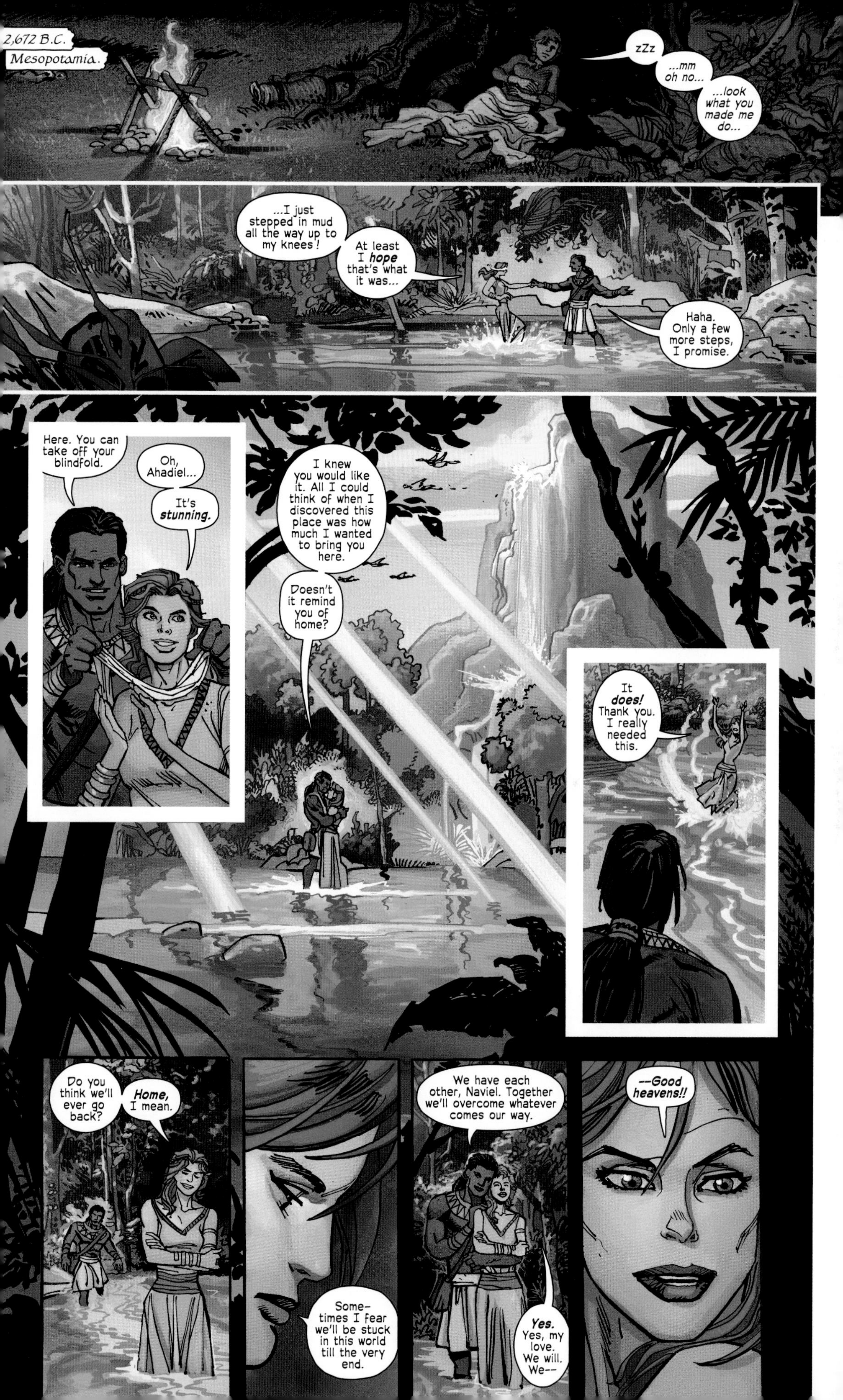
2,672 B.C.
Mesopotamia.
zZz
...mm oh no...
...look what you made me do...
...I just stepped in mud all the way up to my knees!
At least I hope that's what it was...
Haha. Only a few more steps, I promise.
Here. You can take off your blindfold.
Oh, Ahadiel...
It's stunning.
I knew you would like it. All I could think of when I discovered this place was how much I wanted to bring you here.
Doesn't it remind you of home?
It does! Thank you. I really needed this.
Do you think we'll ever go back?
Home, I mean.
Some-times I fear we'll be stuck in this world till the very end.
We have each other, Naviel. Together we'll overcome whatever comes our way.
Yes. Yes, my love. We will. We--
--Good heavens!!

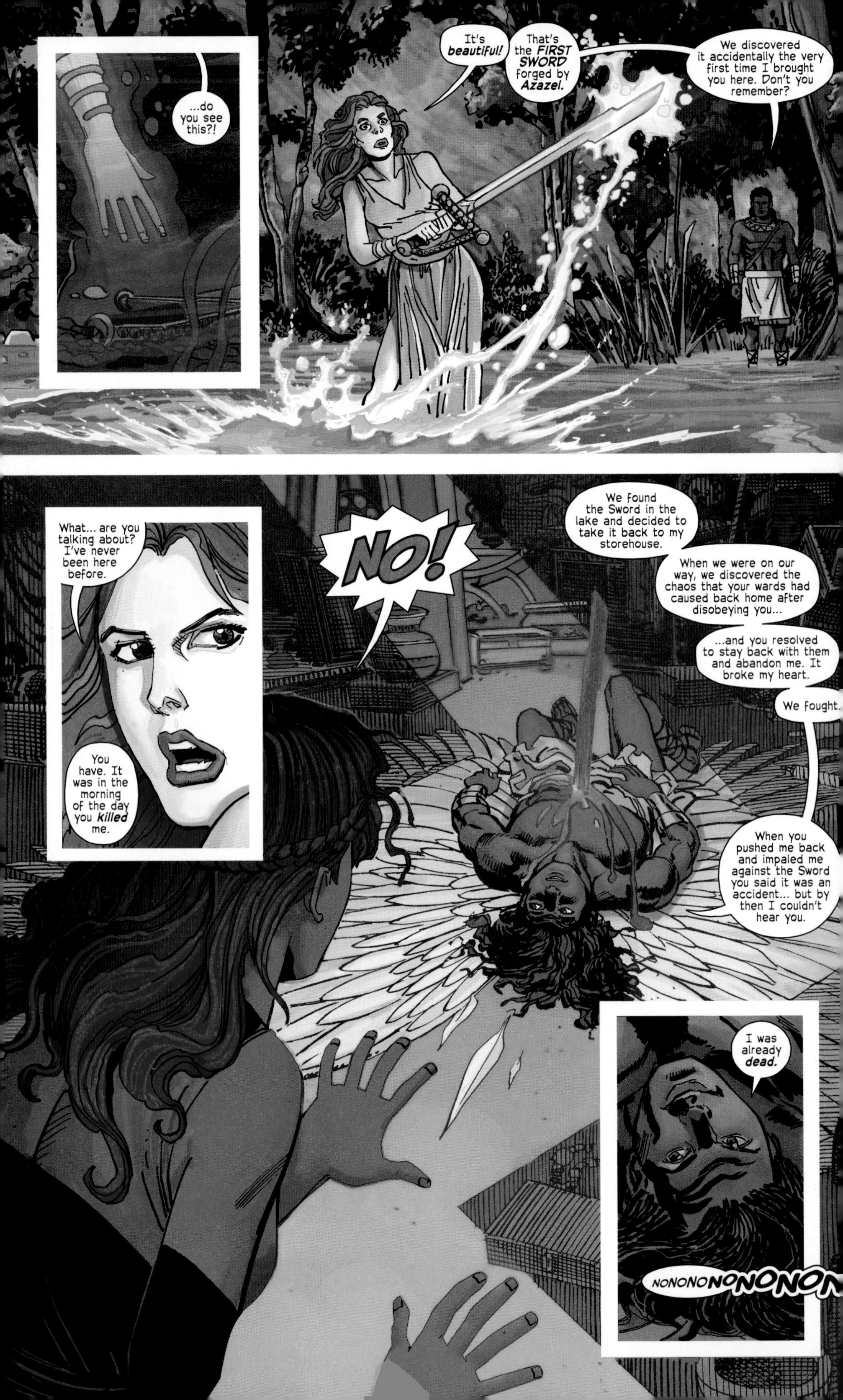
...do you see this?!
It's beautiful!
That's the FIRST SWORD forged by Azazel.
We discovered it accidentally the very first time I brought you here. Don't you remember?
What... are you talking about? I've never been here before.
You have. It was in the morning of the day you killed me.
NO!
We found the Sword in the lake and decided to take it back to my storehouse.
When we were on our way, we discovered the chaos that your wards had caused back home after disobeying you...
...and you resolved to stay back with them and abandon me. It broke my heart.
We fought.
When you pushed me back and impaled me against the Sword you said it was an accident... but by then I couldn't hear you.
I was already dead.
NONONONONONONON

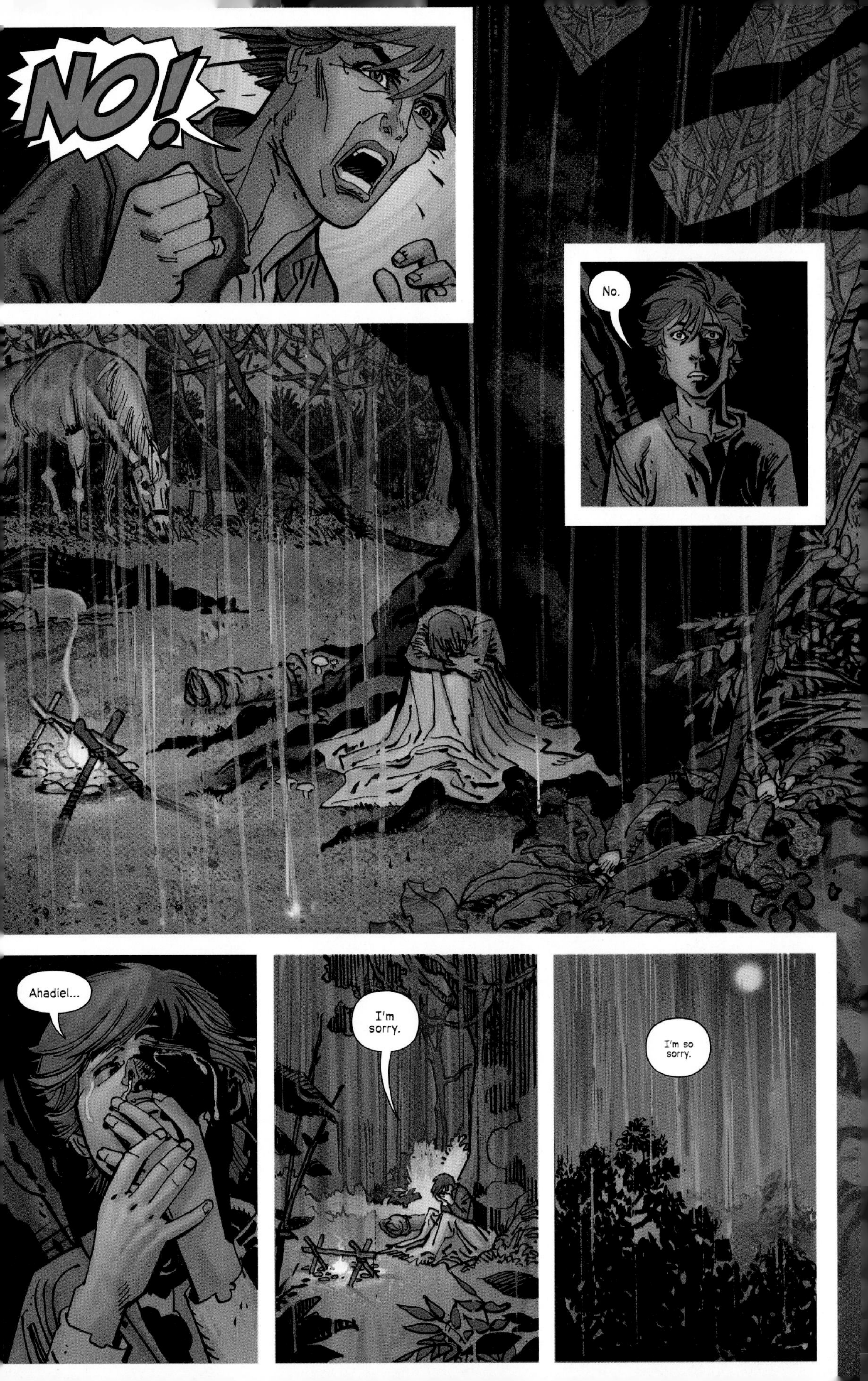
NO!
No.
Ahadiel...
I'm sorry.
I'm so sorry.

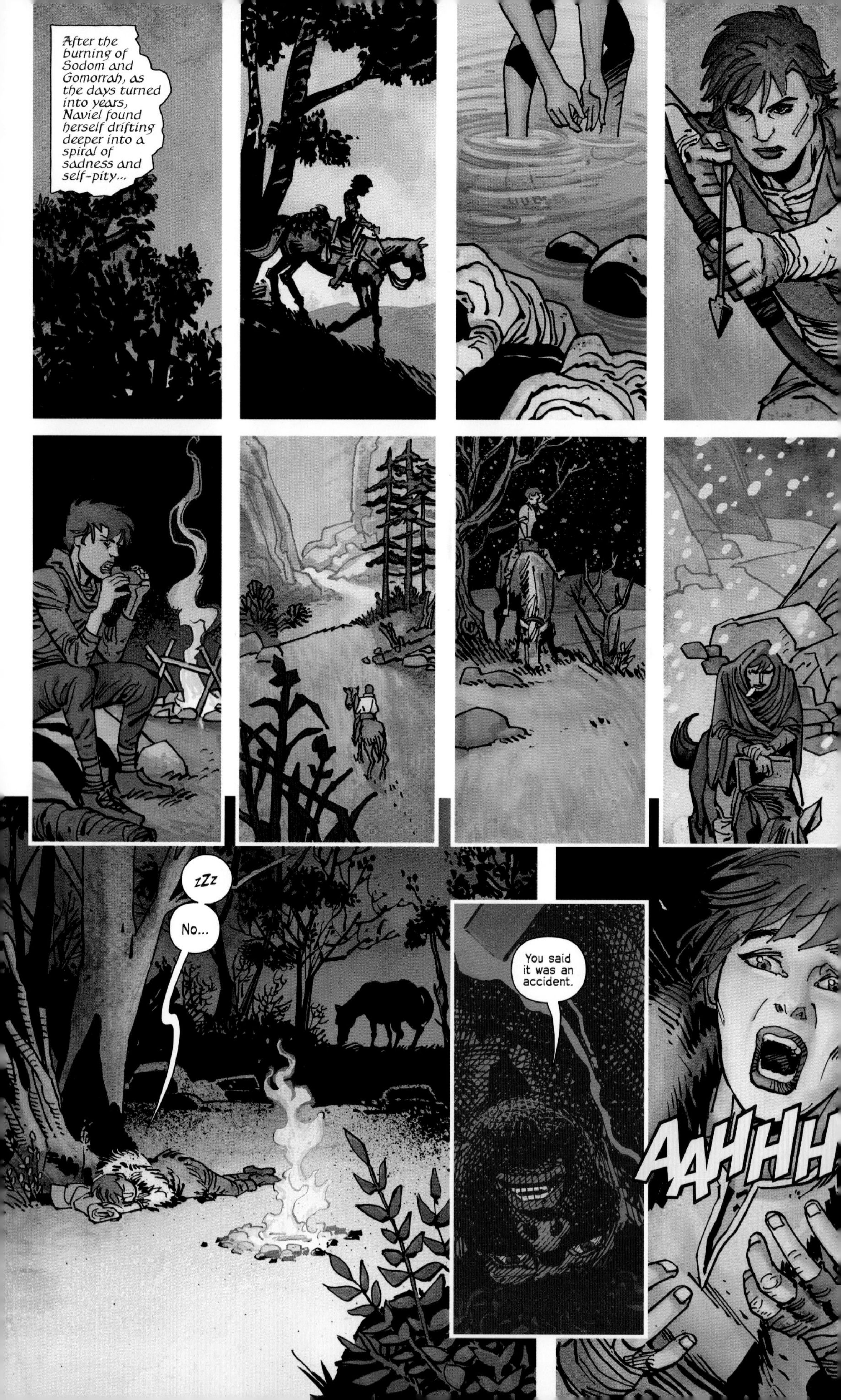
After the burning of Sodom and Gomorrah, as the days turned into years, Naviel found herself drifting deeper into a spiral of sadness and self-pity...
zZz
No...
You said it was an accident.
AAHHH

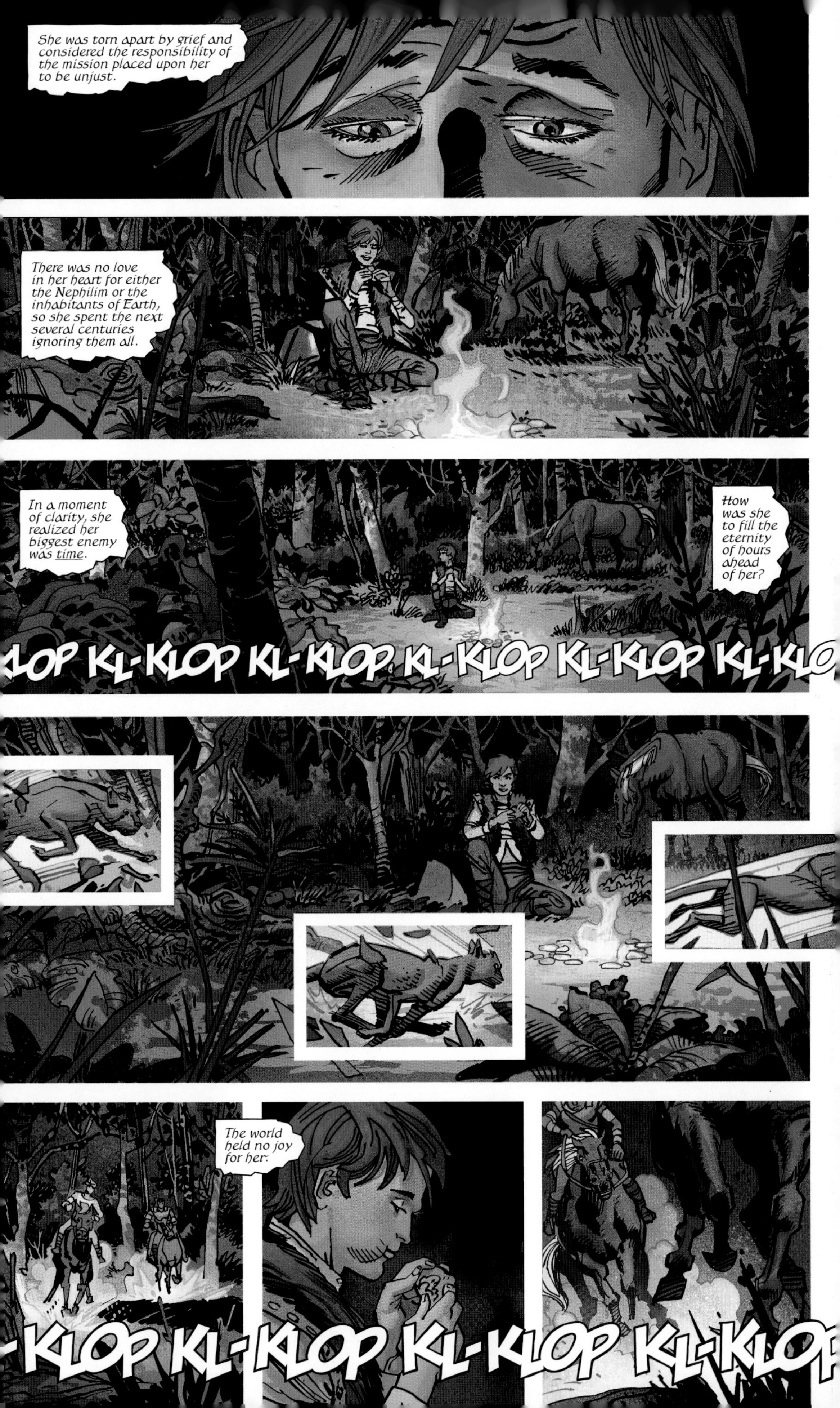

She was torn apart by grief and considered the responsibility of the mission placed upon her to be unjust.
There was no love in her heart for either the Nephilim or the inhabitants of Earth, so she spent the next several centuries ignoring them all.
In a moment of clarity, she realized her biggest enemy was time.
How was she to fill the eternity of hours ahead of her?
KLOP KL-KLOP KL-KLOP KL-KLOP KL-KLOP KL-KLO
The world held no joy for her.
-KLOP KL-KLOP KL-KLOP KL-KLOP

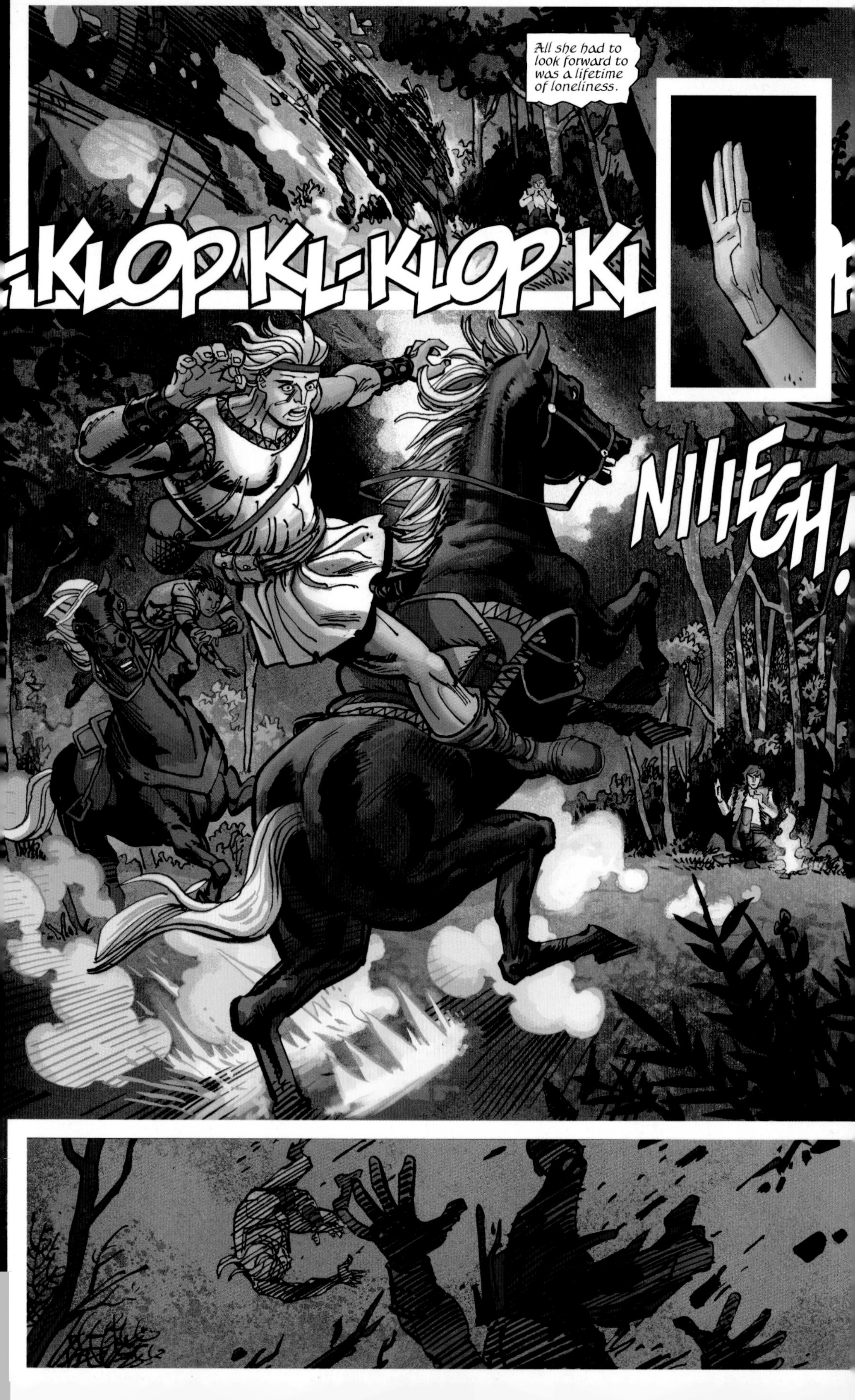
All she had to look forward to was a lifetime of loneliness.
KLOP KL-KLOP KL
NIIIEGH!

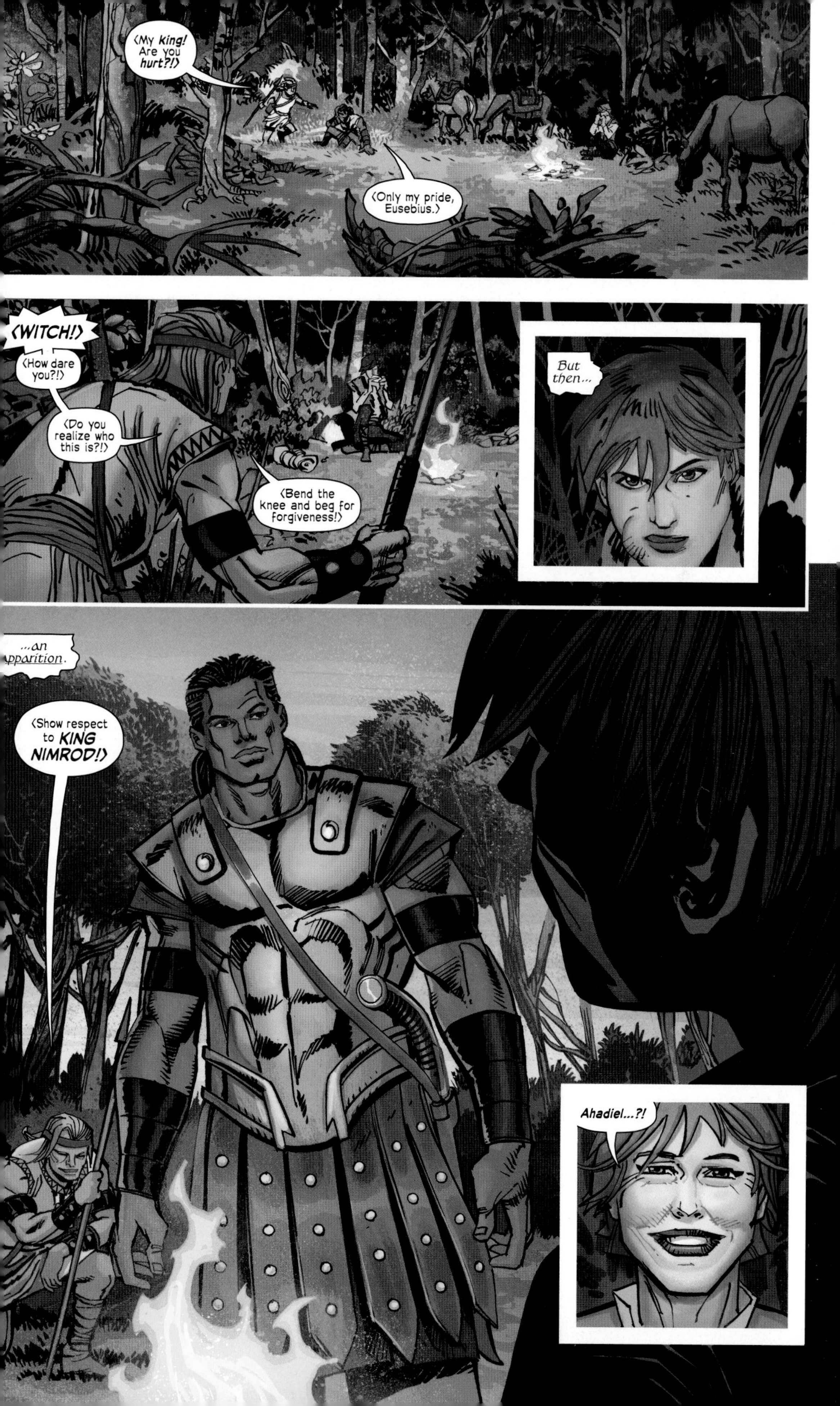

‹My king! Are you hurt?!›
‹Only my pride, Eusebius.›
‹WITCH!›
‹How dare you?!›
‹Do you realize who this is?!›
‹Bend the knee and beg for forgiveness!›
But then...
...an apparition.
‹Show respect to KING NIMROD!›
Ahadiel...?!

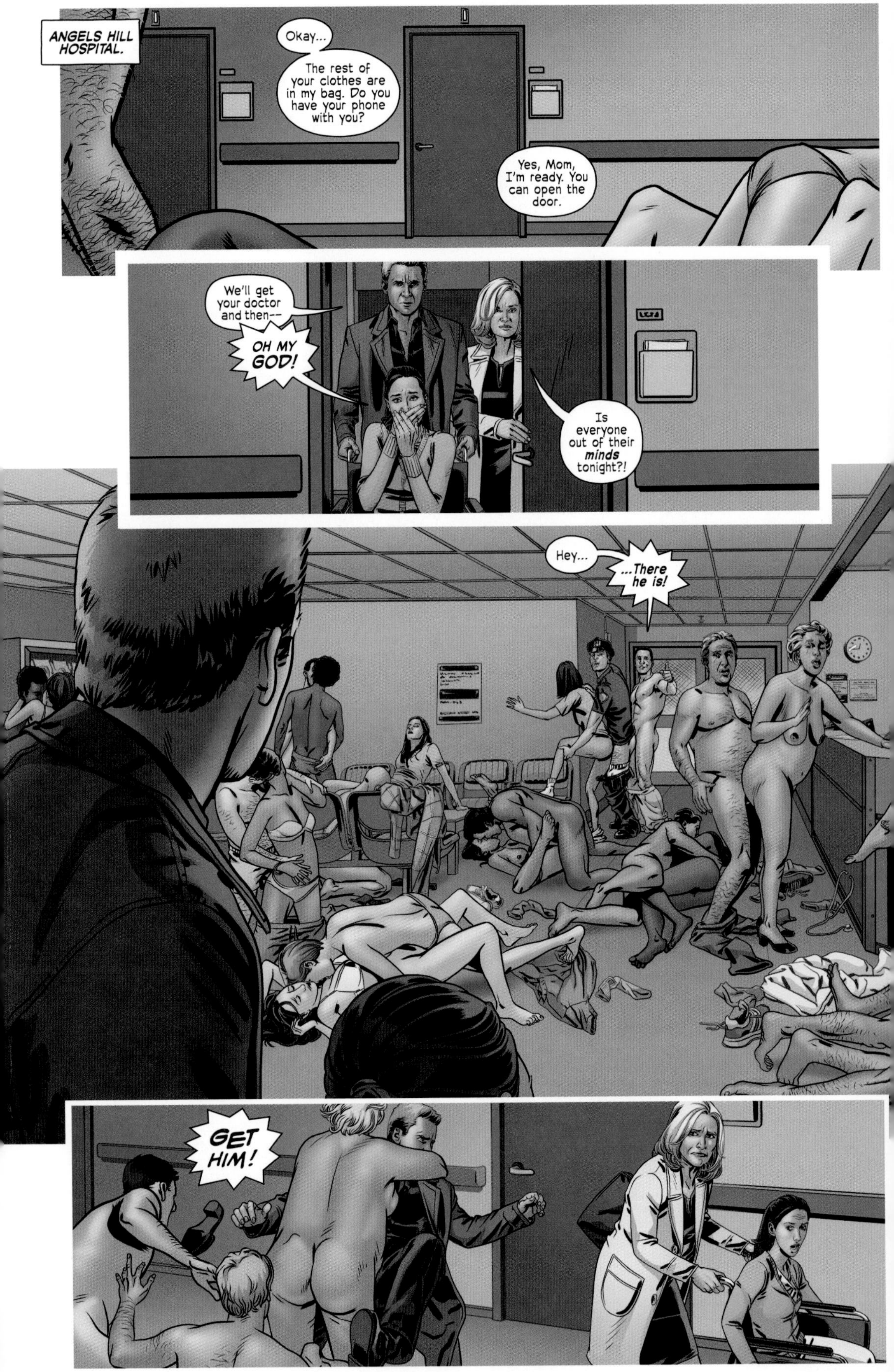
ANGELS HILL HOSPITAL.
Okay...
The rest of your clothes are in my bag. Do you have your phone with you?
Yes, Mom, I'm ready. You can open the door.
We'll get your doctor and then--
OH MY GOD!
Is everyone out of their *minds* tonight?!
Hey...
...There he is!
GET HIM!

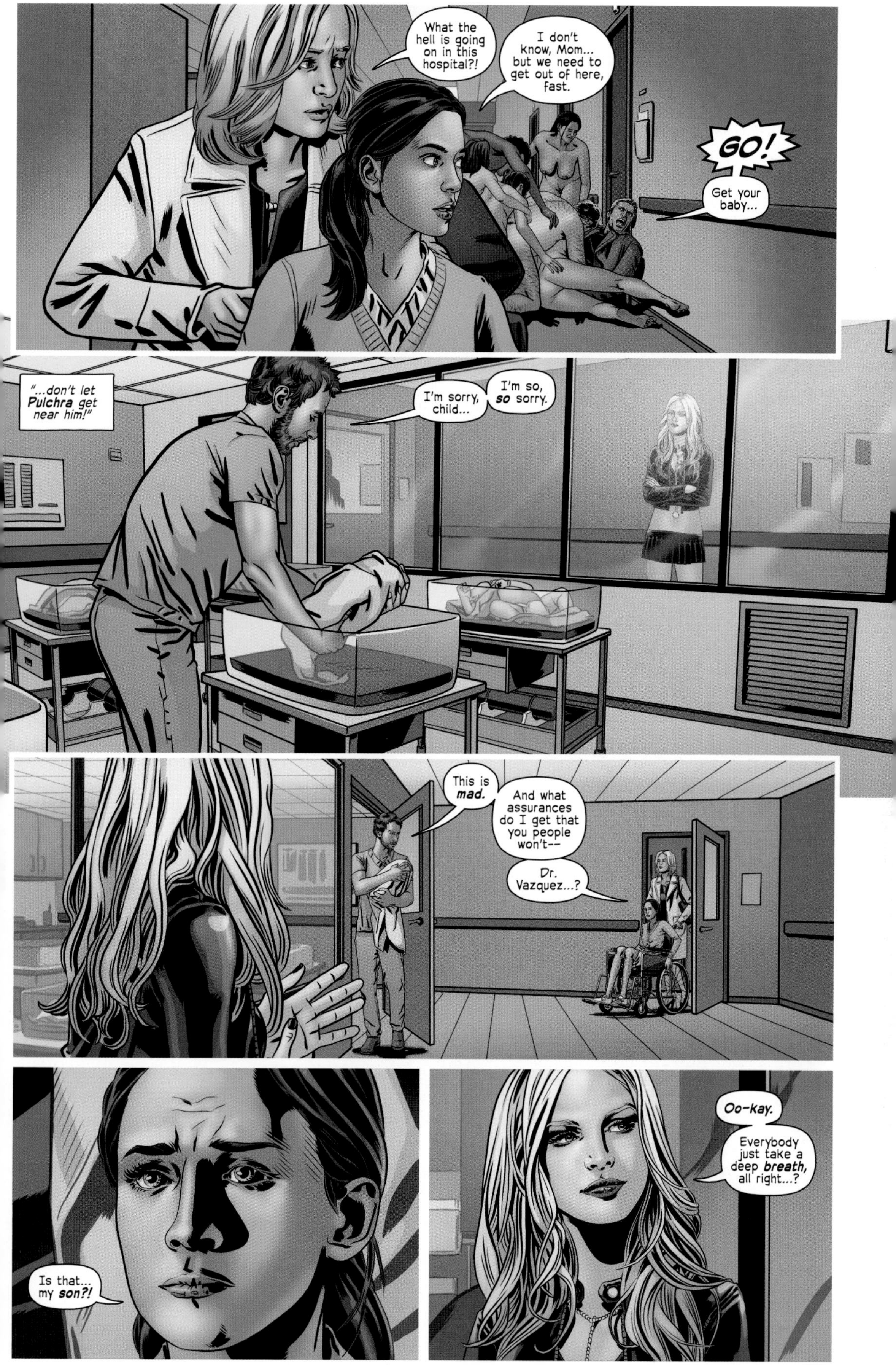
What the hell is going on in this hospital?!
I don't know, Mom... but we need to get out of here, fast.
GO!
Get your baby...
"...don't let Pulchra get near him!"
I'm sorry, child...
I'm so, so sorry.
This is mad.
And what assurances do I get that you people won't--
Dr. Vazquez...?
Is that... my son?!
Oo-kay.
Everybody just take a deep breath, all right...?

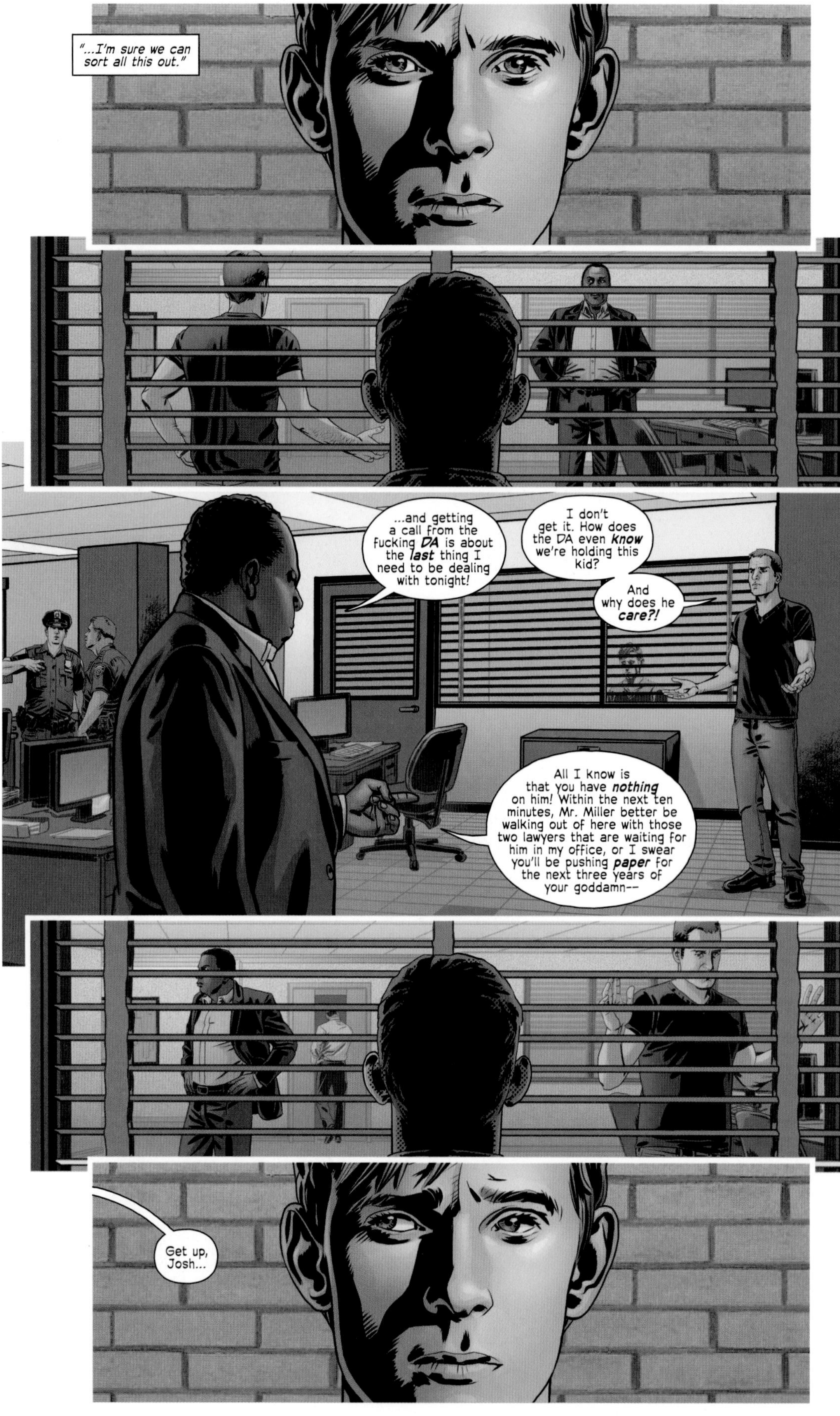
"...I'm sure we can sort all this out."
...and getting a call from the fucking *DA* is about the *last* thing I need to be dealing with tonight!
I don't get it. How does the DA even *know* we're holding this kid?
And why does he *care?!*
All I know is that you have *nothing* on him! Within the next ten minutes, Mr. Miller better be walking out of here with those two lawyers that are waiting for him in my office, or I swear you'll be pushing *paper* for the next three years of your goddamn--
Get up, Josh...

"...It appears you have some very powerful friends looking out for you."

I don't mean to sound ungrateful, but who are you people?

Just follow us, please.

I'm not going anywhere with you until you tell me--

Hey, Josh.

Long time no see.

HELL NO!

Come on...

Are we really gonna do this?!

Don't worry, boss--

Don't--

NO!

We got it!

Officers!

Those men, behind me...

They have guns!

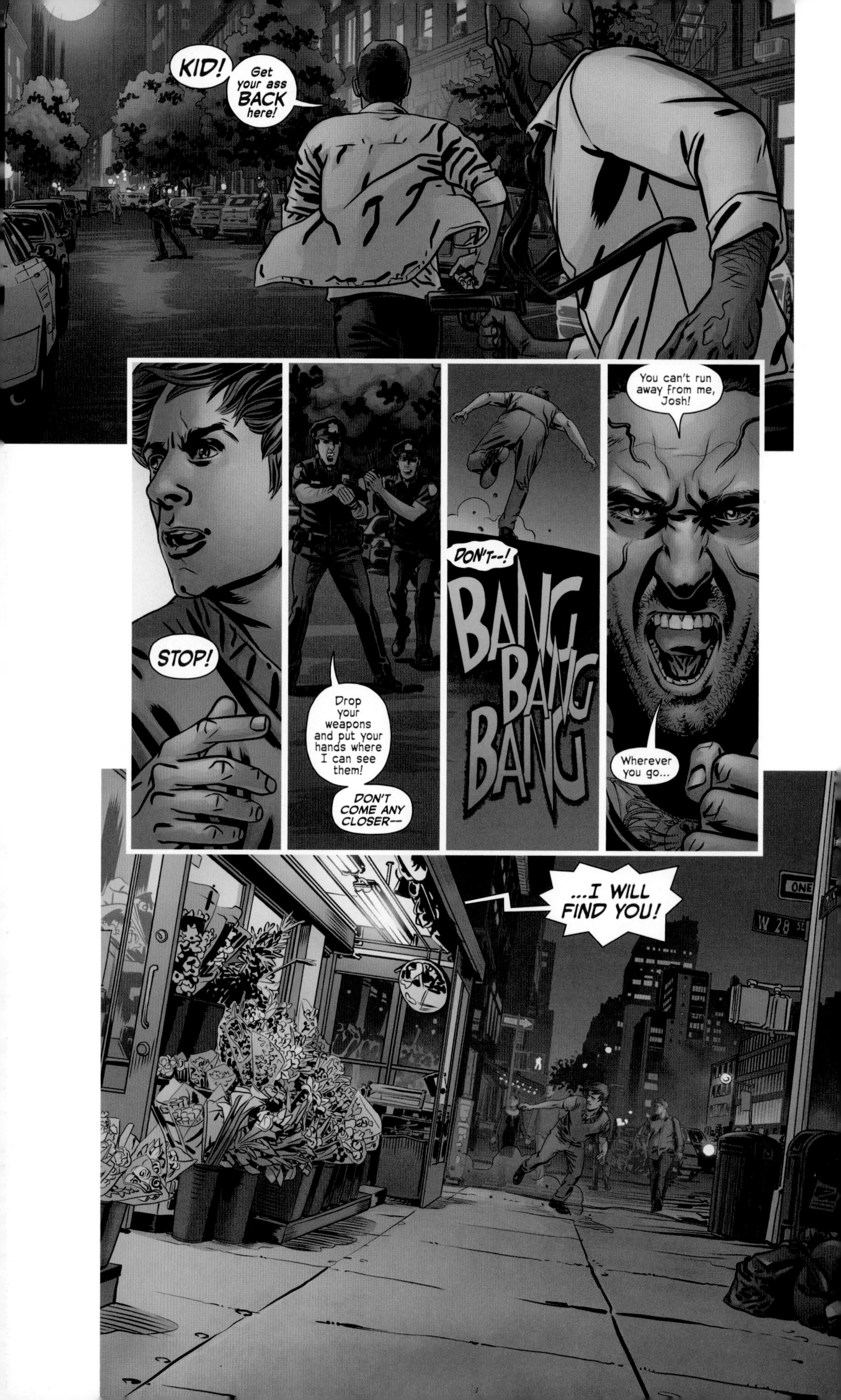
KID!
Get your ass BACK here!
STOP!
Drop your weapons and put your hands where I can see them!
DON'T COME ANY CLOSER--
DON'T--!
BANG BANG BANG
You can't run away from me, Josh!
Wherever you go...
...I WILL FIND YOU!
ONE
W 28

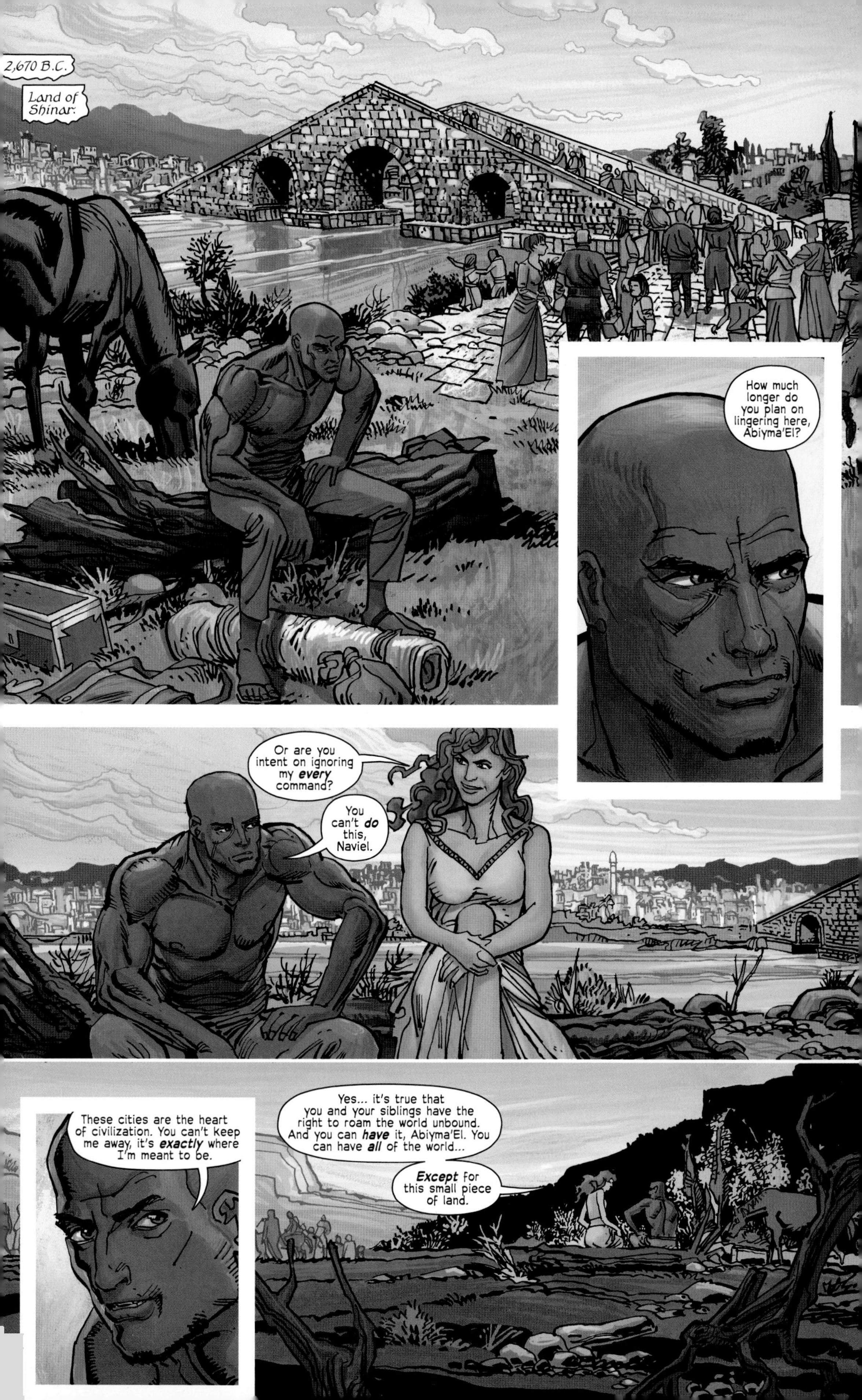
2,670 B.C.
Land of Shinar.
How much longer do you plan on lingering here, Abiyma'El?
Or are you intent on ignoring my *every* command?
You can't *do* this, Naviel.
These cities are the heart of civilization. You can't keep me away, it's *exactly* where I'm meant to be.
Yes... it's true that you and your siblings have the right to roam the world unbound. And you can *have* it, Abiyma'El. You can have *all* of the world...
Except for this small piece of land.

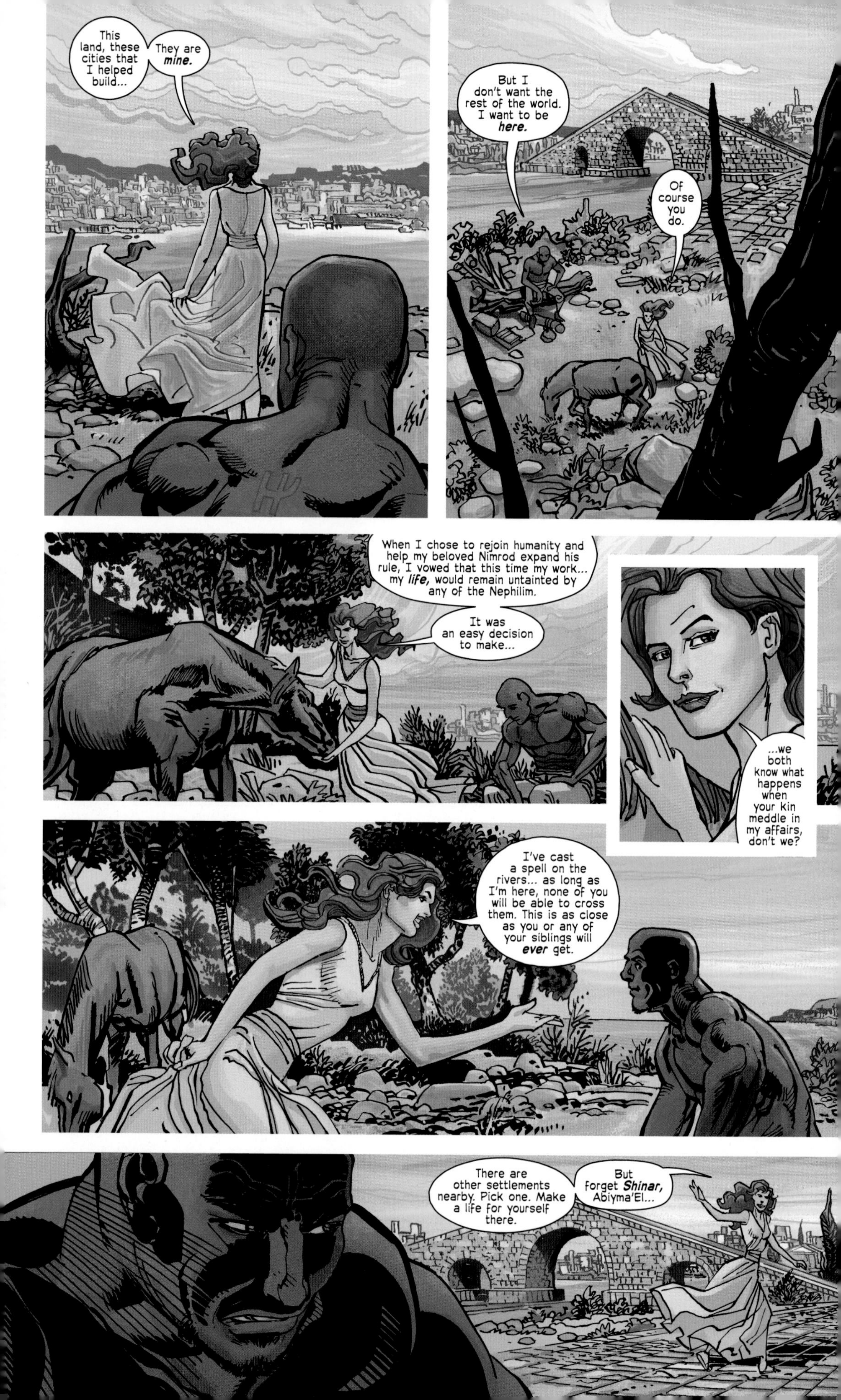

This land, these cities that I helped build...
They are *mine.*
But I don't want the rest of the world. I want to be *here.*
Of course you do.
When I chose to rejoin humanity and help my beloved Nimrod expand his rule, I vowed that this time my work... my *life,* would remain untainted by any of the Nephilim.
It was an easy decision to make...
...we both know what happens when your kin meddle in my affairs, don't we?
I've cast a spell on the rivers... as long as I'm here, none of you will be able to cross them. This is as close as you or any of your siblings will *ever* get.
There are other settlements nearby. Pick one. Make a life for yourself there.
But forget *Shinar,* Abiyma'El...

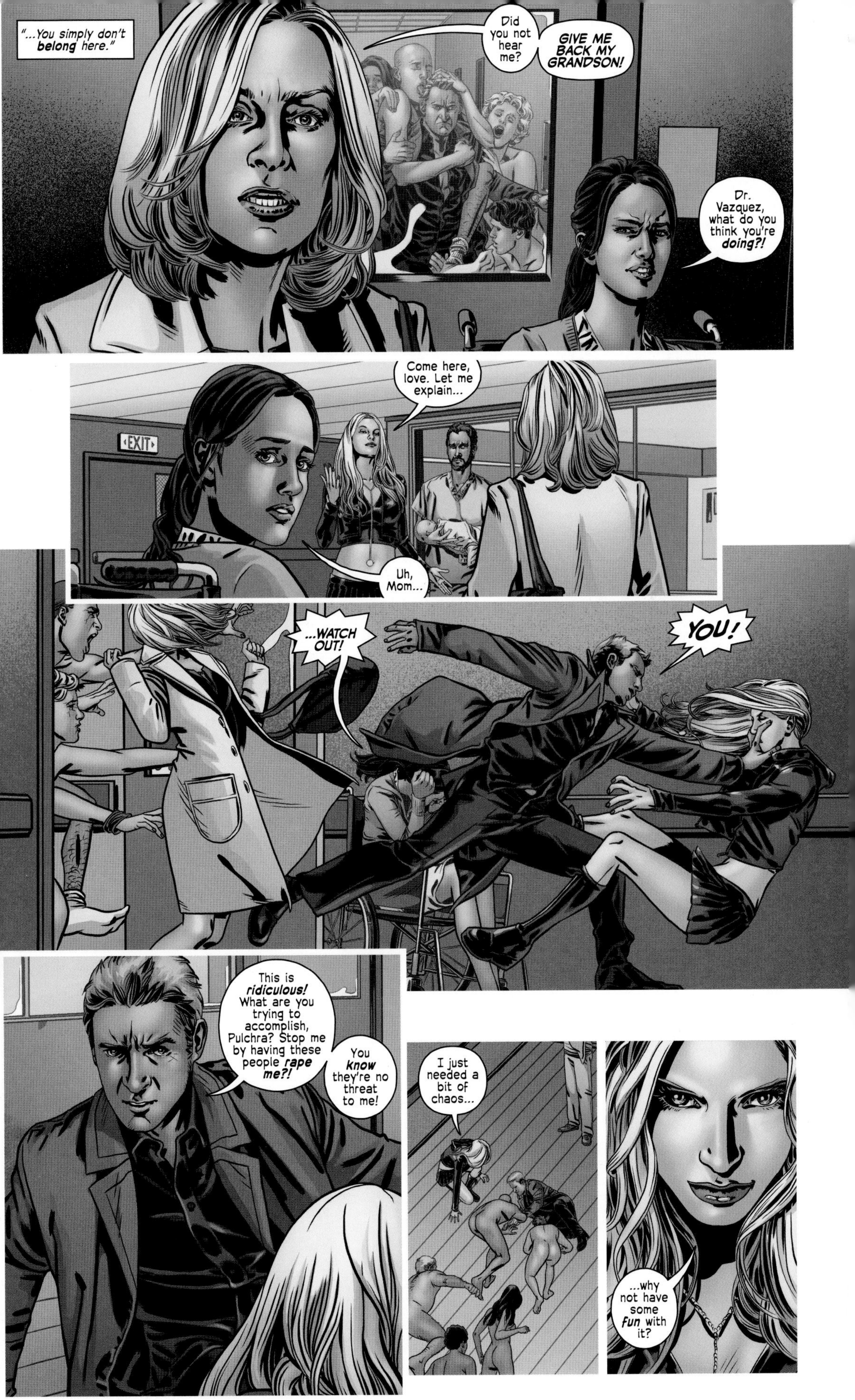
"...You simply don't belong here."
Did you not hear me?
GIVE ME BACK MY GRANDSON!
Dr. Vazquez, what do you think you're doing?!
Come here, love. Let me explain...
Uh, Mom...
...WATCH OUT!
YOU!
This is ridiculous! What are you trying to accomplish, Pulchra? Stop me by having these people rape me?!
You know they're no threat to me!
I just needed a bit of chaos...
...why not have some fun with it?

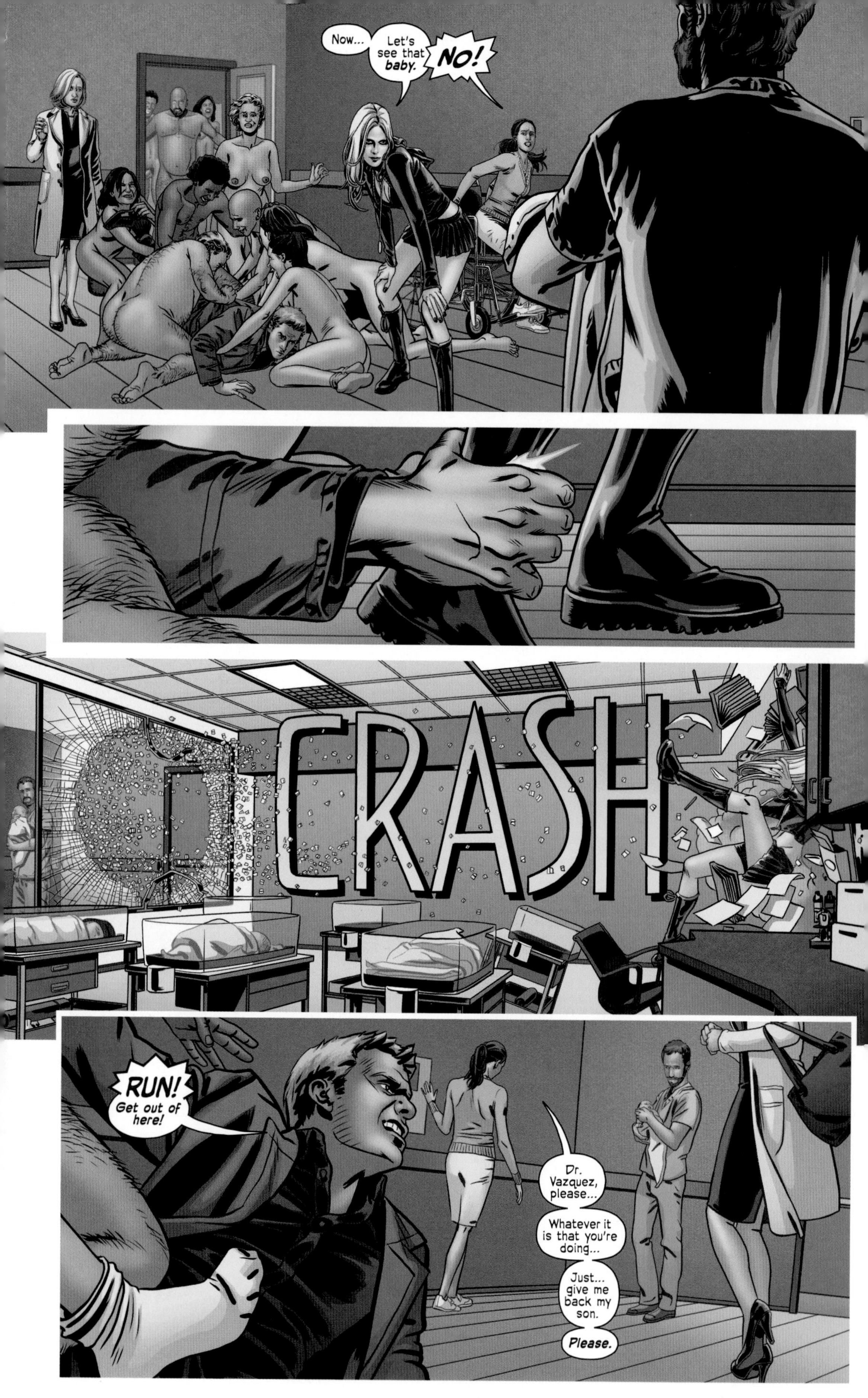

Now...
Let's see that baby.
NO!
CRASH
RUN! Get out of here!
Dr. Vazquez, please...
Whatever it is that you're doing...
Just... give me back my son.
Please.

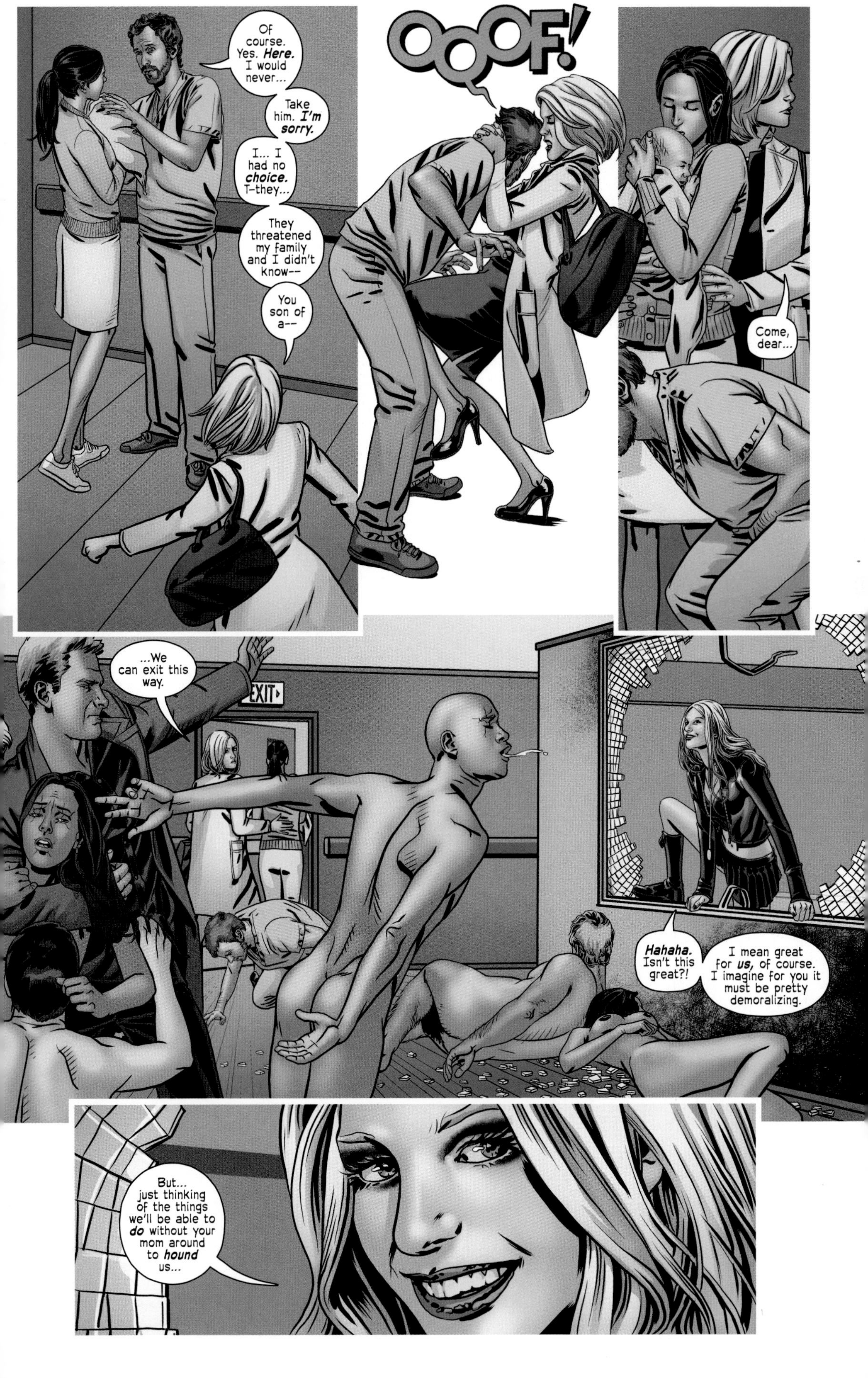
Of course. Yes. *Here.* I would never...
Take him. *I'm sorry.*
I... I had no *choice.* T-they...
They threatened my family and I didn't know--
You son of a--
OOOF!
Come, dear...
...We can exit this way.
EXIT
Hahaha. Isn't this great?!
I mean great for *us,* of course. I imagine for you it must be pretty demoralizing.
But... just thinking of the things we'll be able to *do* without your mom around to *hound* us...

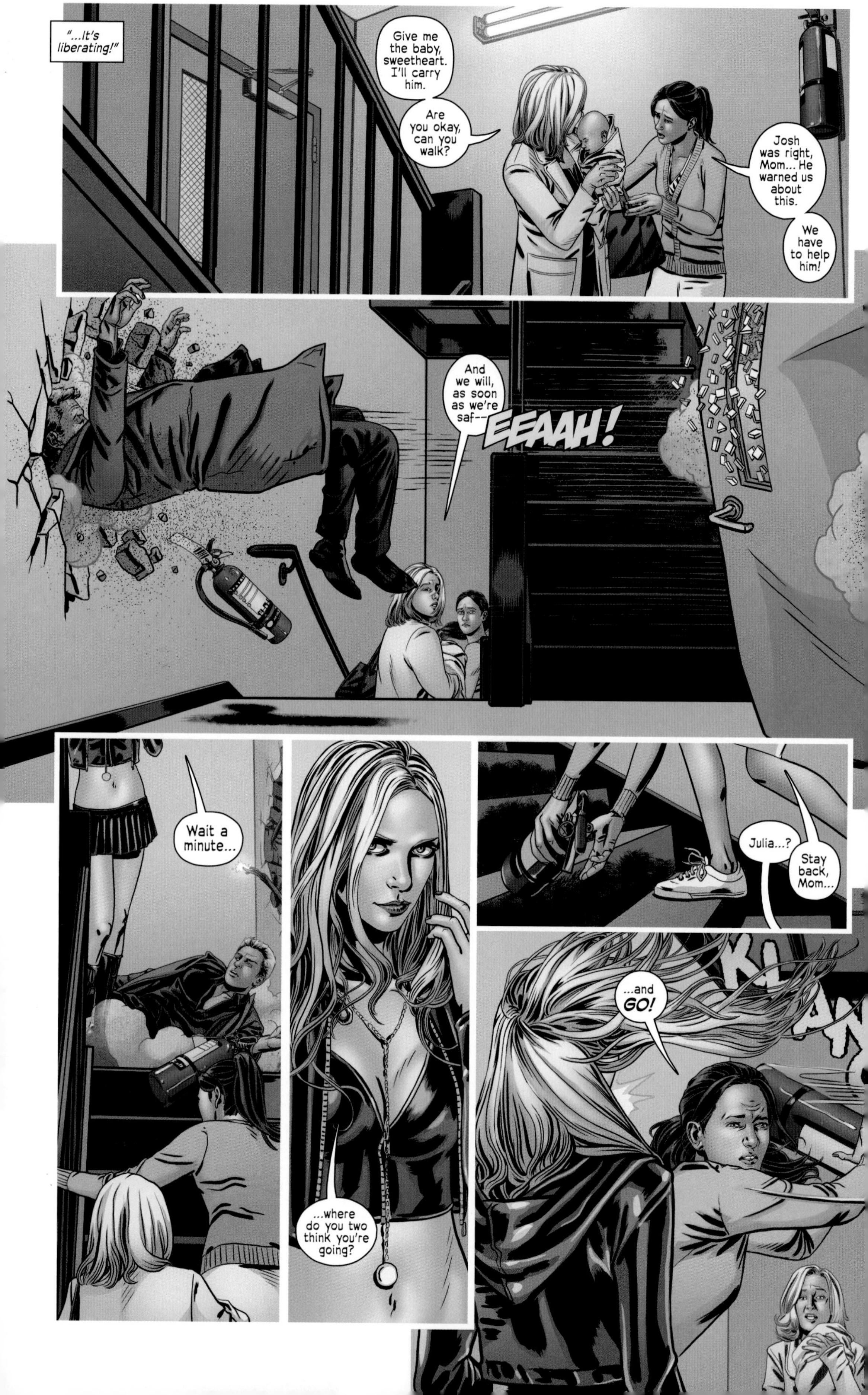
"...It's liberating!"
Give me the baby, sweetheart. I'll carry him.
Are you okay, can you walk?
Josh was right, Mom... He warned us about this.
We have to help him!
And we will, as soon as we're saf--
EEAAH!
Wait a minute...
...where do you two think you're going?
Julia...?
Stay back, Mom...
...and GO!

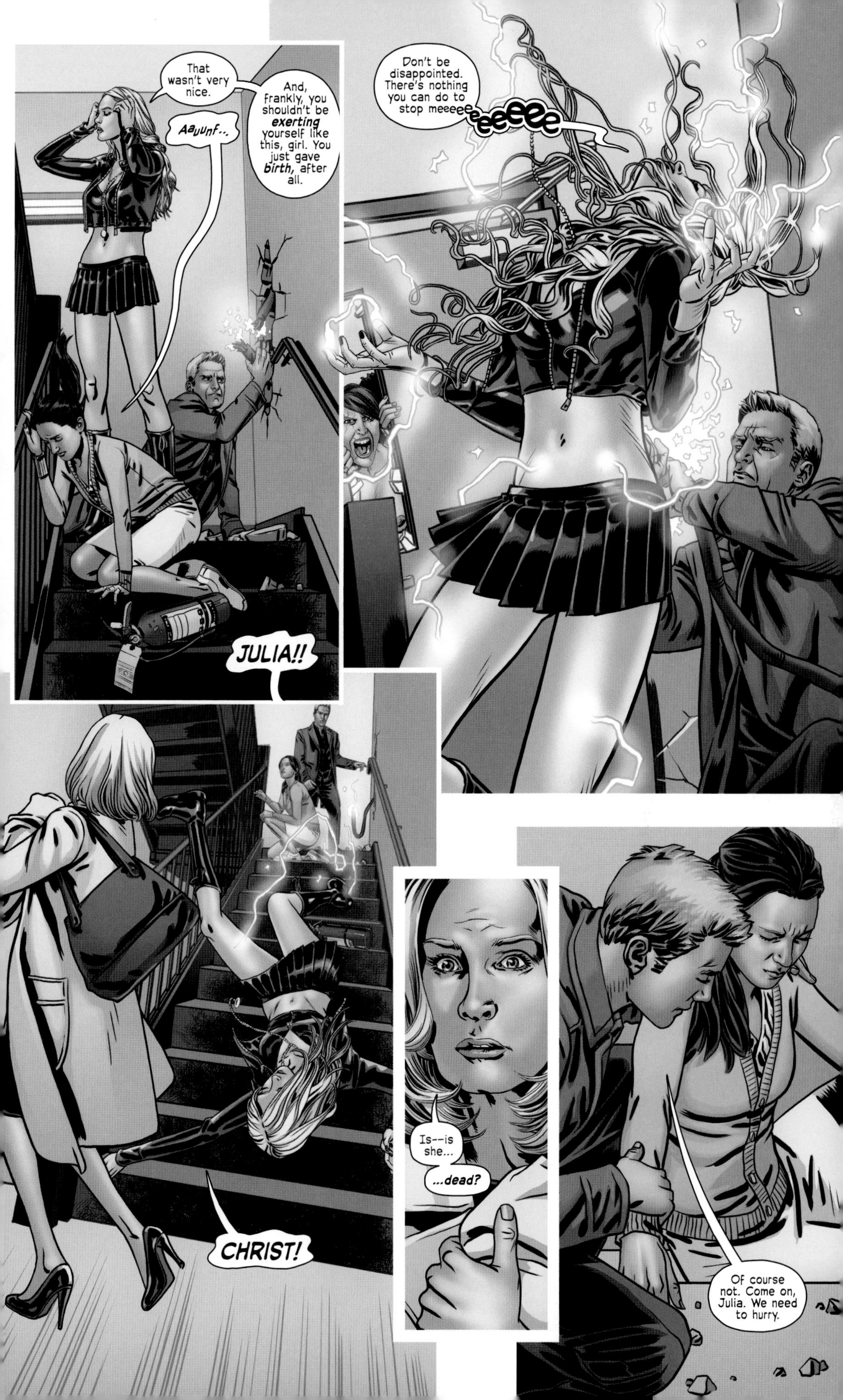
That wasn't very nice.
And, frankly, you shouldn't be *exerting* yourself like this, girl. You just gave *birth*, after all.
Aauunf...
JULIA!!
Don't be disappointed. There's nothing you can do to stop meeeeeeeee
CHRIST!
Is--is she...
...dead?
Of course not. Come on, Julia. We need to hurry.

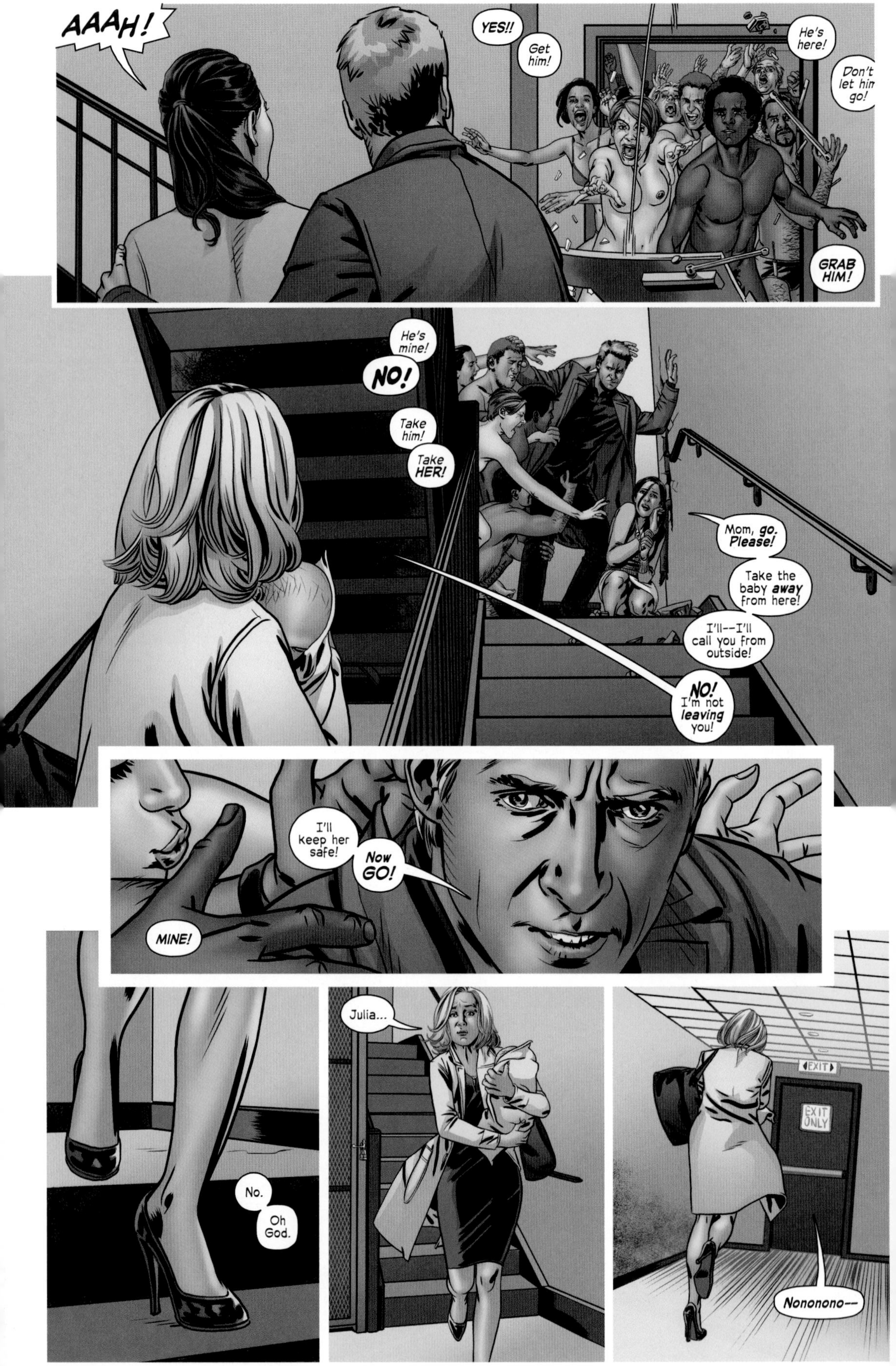
AAAH!
YES!!
Get him!
He's here!
Don't let him go!
GRAB HIM!
He's mine!
NO!
Take him!
Take HER!
Mom, go. Please!
Take the baby away from here!
I'll--I'll call you from outside!
NO! I'm not leaving you!
I'll keep her safe!
Now GO!
MINE!
No.
Oh God.
Julia...
EXIT
EXIT ONLY
Nononono--

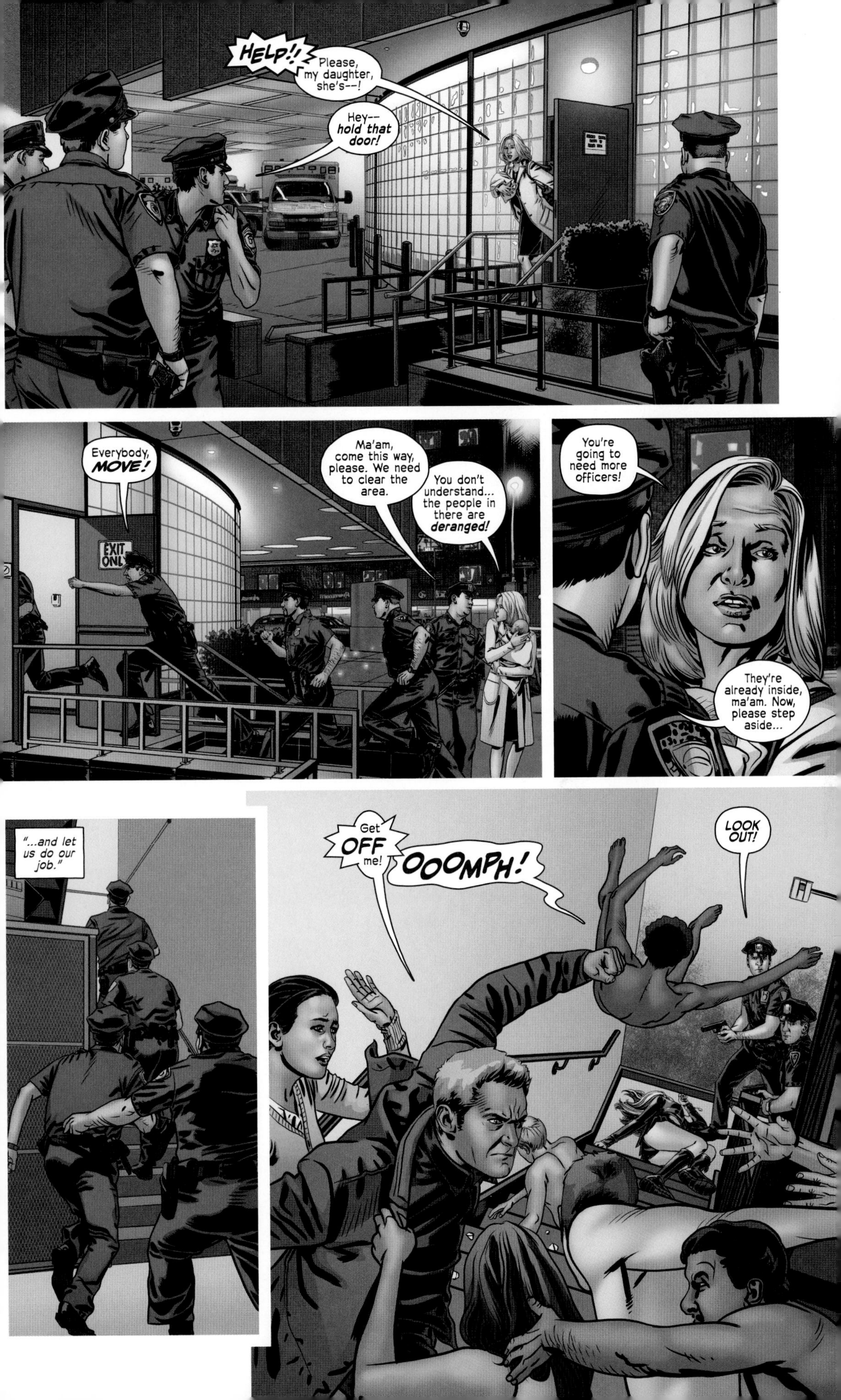

HELP!!
Please, my daughter, she's--!
Hey-- hold that door!
Everybody, MOVE!
EXIT ONLY
Ma'am, come this way, please. We need to clear the area.
You don't understand... the people in there are deranged!
You're going to need more officers!
They're already inside, ma'am. Now, please step aside...
"...and let us do our job."
Get OFF me!
OOOMPH!
LOOK OUT!

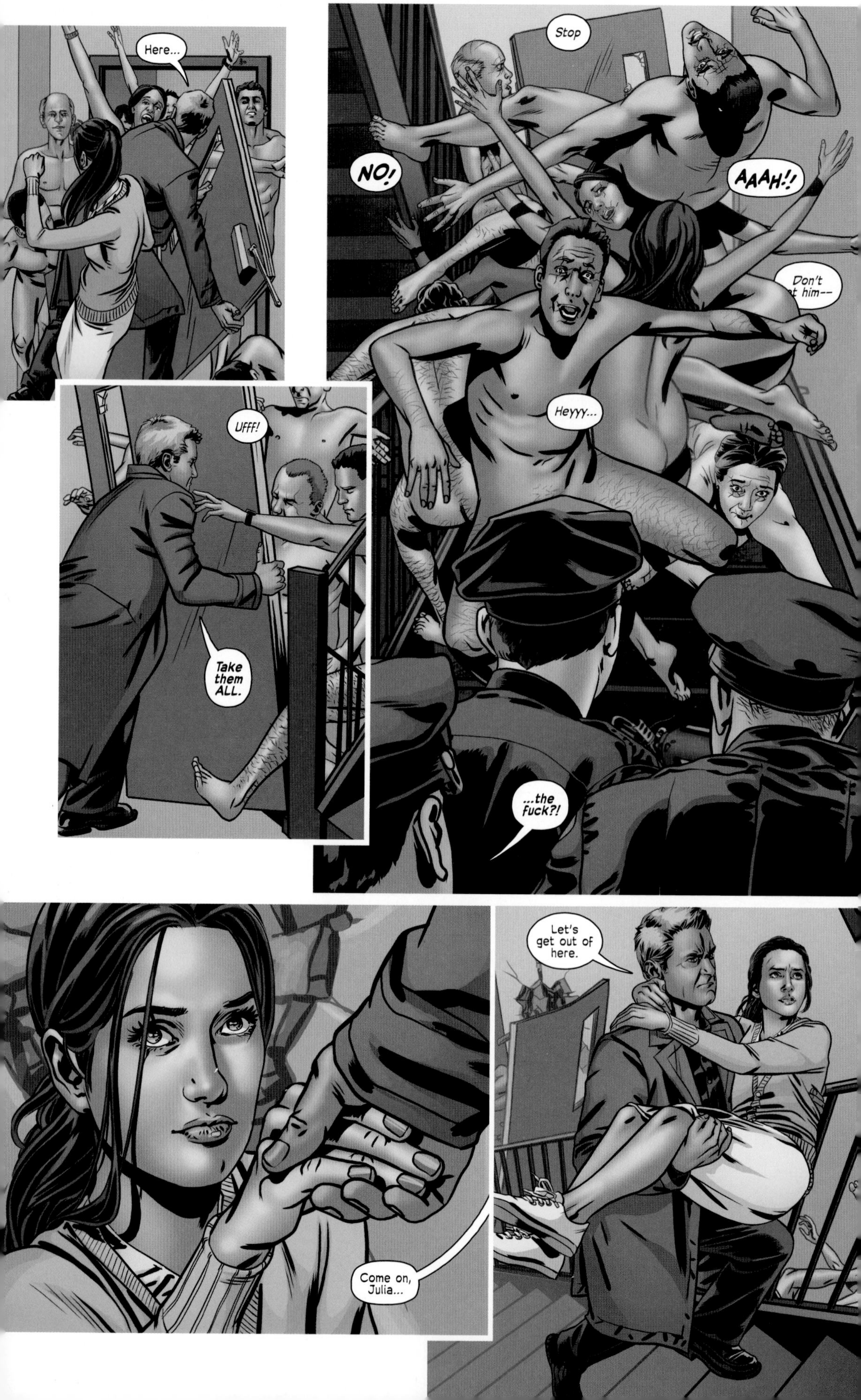
Here...
UFFF!
Take them ALL.
Stop
NO!
AAAH!!
Don't
t him--
Heyyy...
...the fuck?!
Come on, Julia...
Let's get out of here.

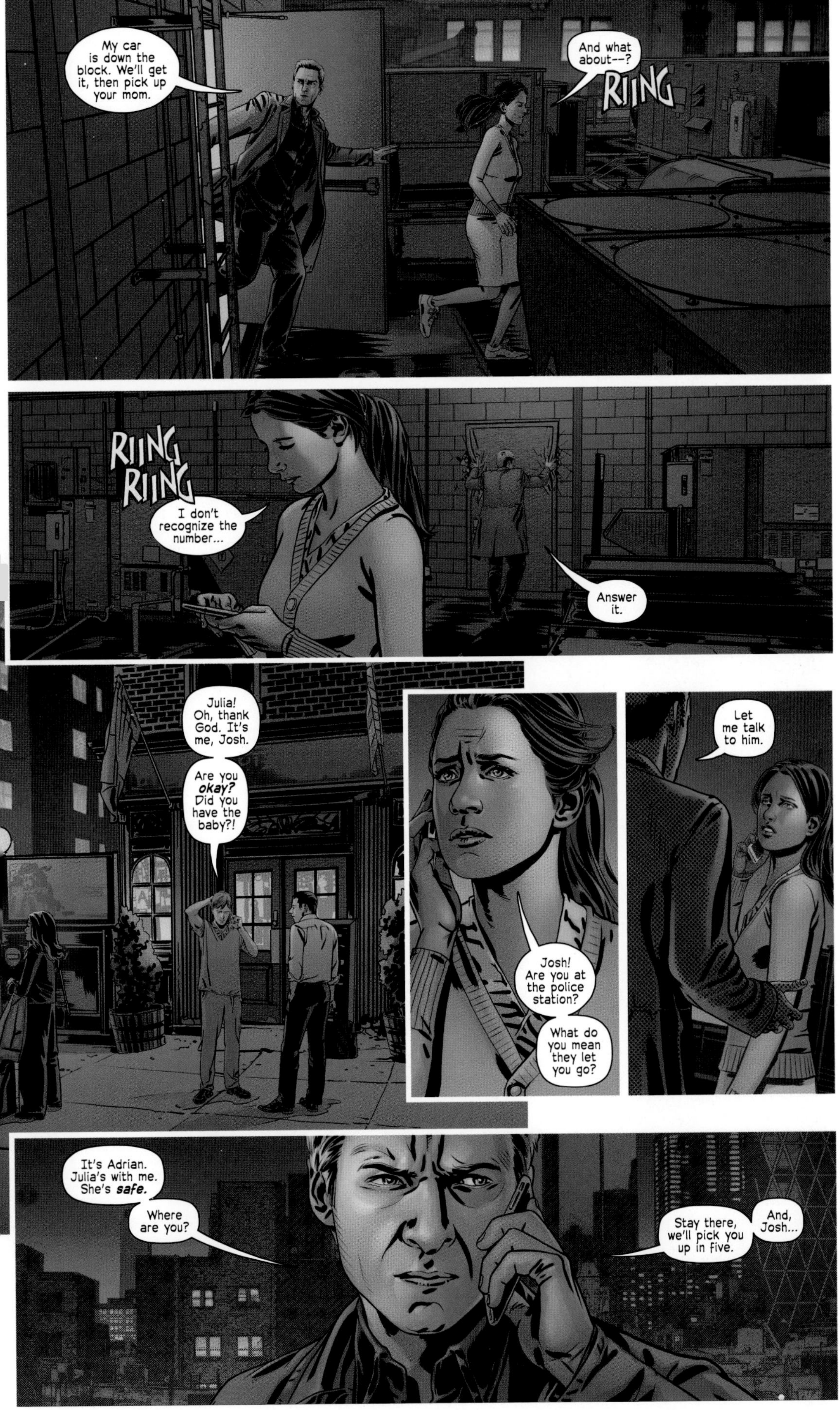
My car is down the block. We'll get it, then pick up your mom.
And what about--?
RIING
RIING
RIING
I don't recognize the number...
Answer it.
Julia! Oh, thank God. It's me, Josh.
Are you *okay?* Did you have the baby?!
Josh! Are you at the police station?
What do you mean they let you go?
Let me talk to him.
It's Adrian. Julia's with me. She's *safe.*
Where are you?
Stay there, we'll pick you up in five.
And, Josh...

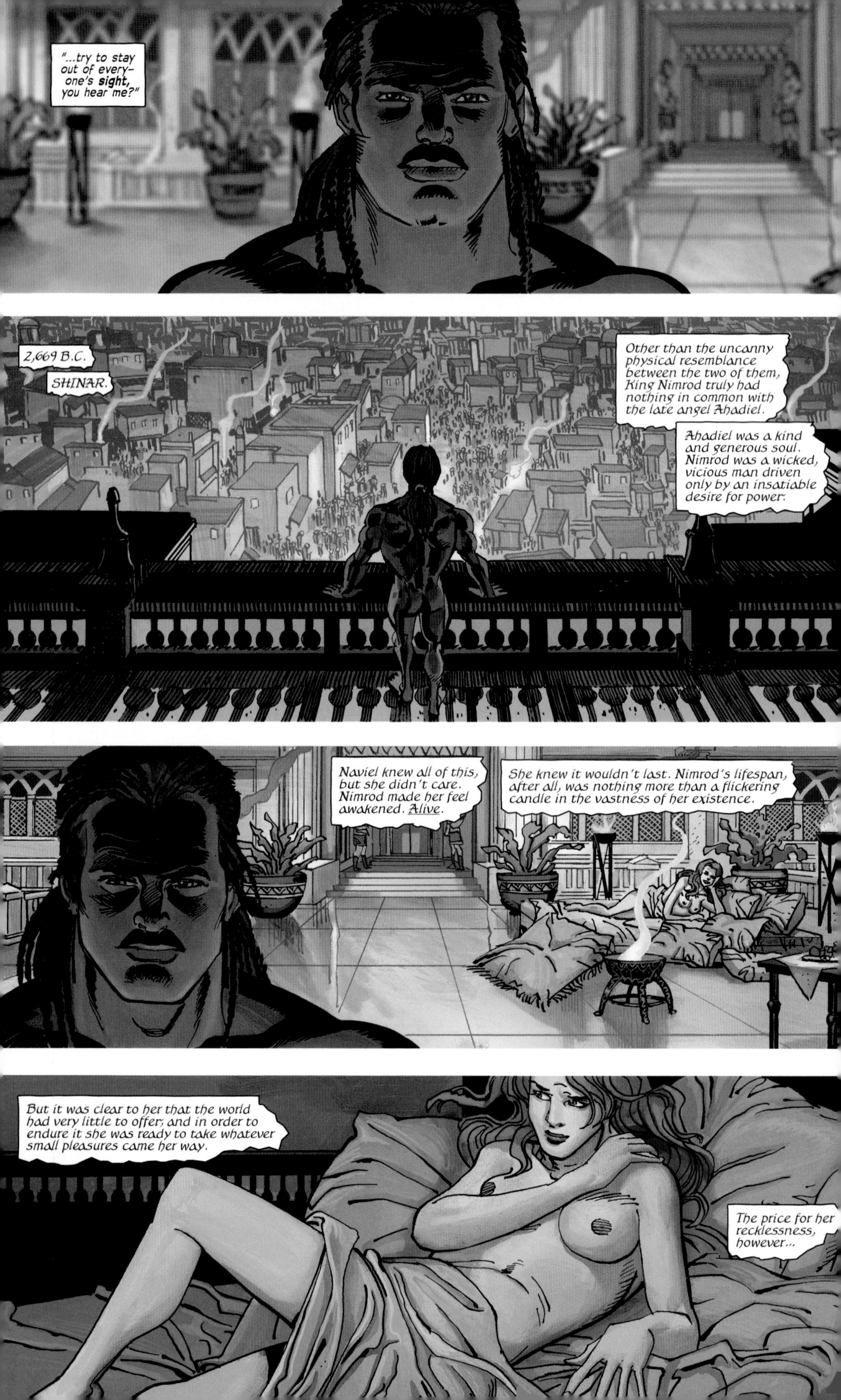
"...try to stay out of every-one's **sight,** you hear me?"
2,669 B.C.
SHINAR.
Other than the uncanny physical resemblance between the two of them, King Nimrod truly had nothing in common with the late angel Ahadiel.
Ahadiel was a kind and generous soul. Nimrod was a wicked, vicious man driven only by an insatiable desire for power.
Naviel knew all of this, but she didn't care. Nimrod made her feel awakened. Alive.
She knew it wouldn't last. Nimrod's lifespan, after all, was nothing more than a flickering candle in the vastness of her existence.
But it was clear to her that the world had very little to offer, and in order to endure it she was ready to take whatever small pleasures came her way.
The price for her recklessness, however...

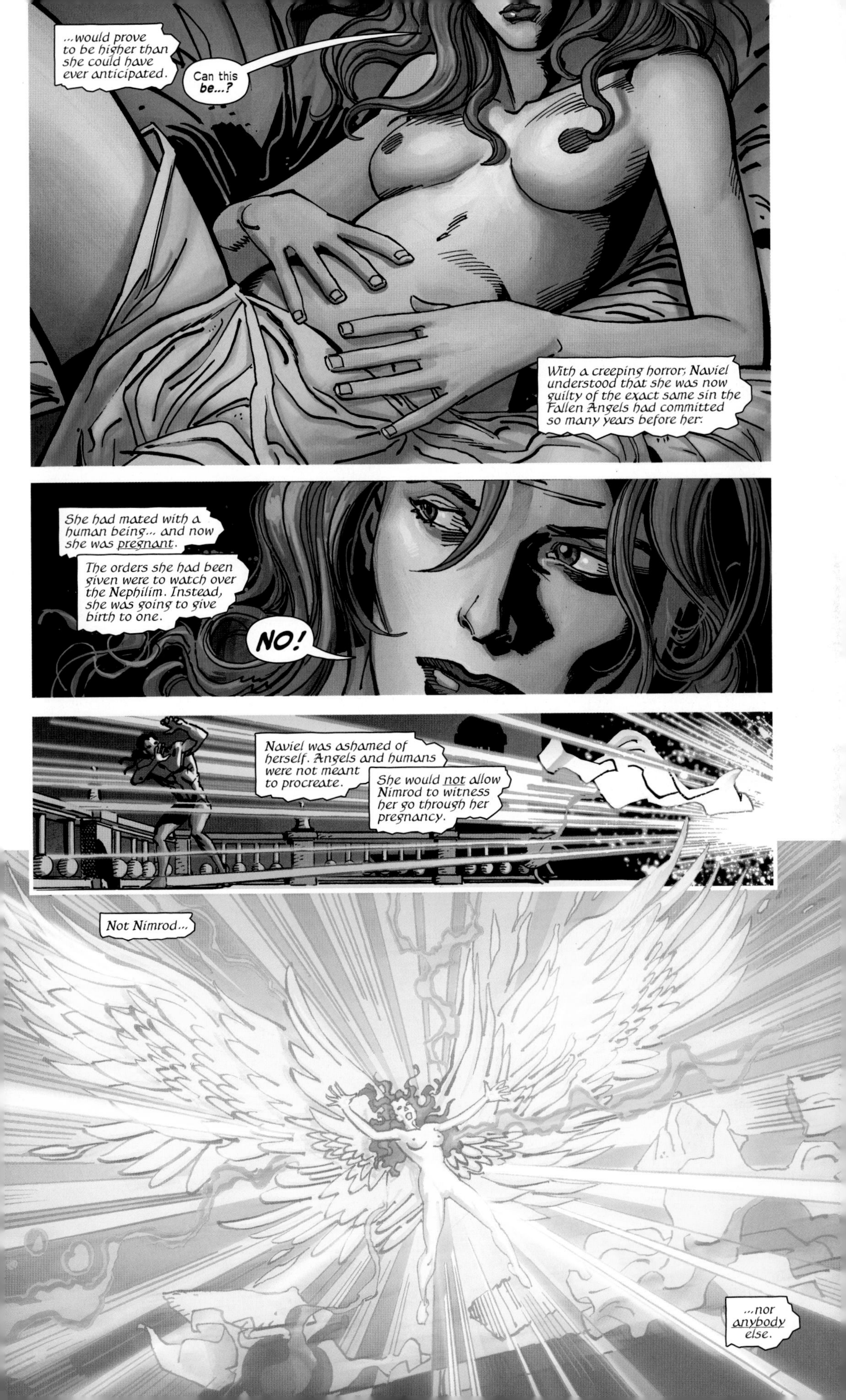
...would prove to be higher than she could have ever anticipated.
Can this be...?
With a creeping horror, Naviel understood that she was now guilty of the exact same sin the Fallen Angels had committed so many years before her.
She had mated with a human being... and now she was pregnant.
The orders she had been given were to watch over the Nephilim. Instead, she was going to give birth to one.
NO!
Naviel was ashamed of herself. Angels and humans were not meant to procreate.
She would not allow Nimrod to witness her go through her pregnancy.
Not Nimrod...
...nor anybody else.

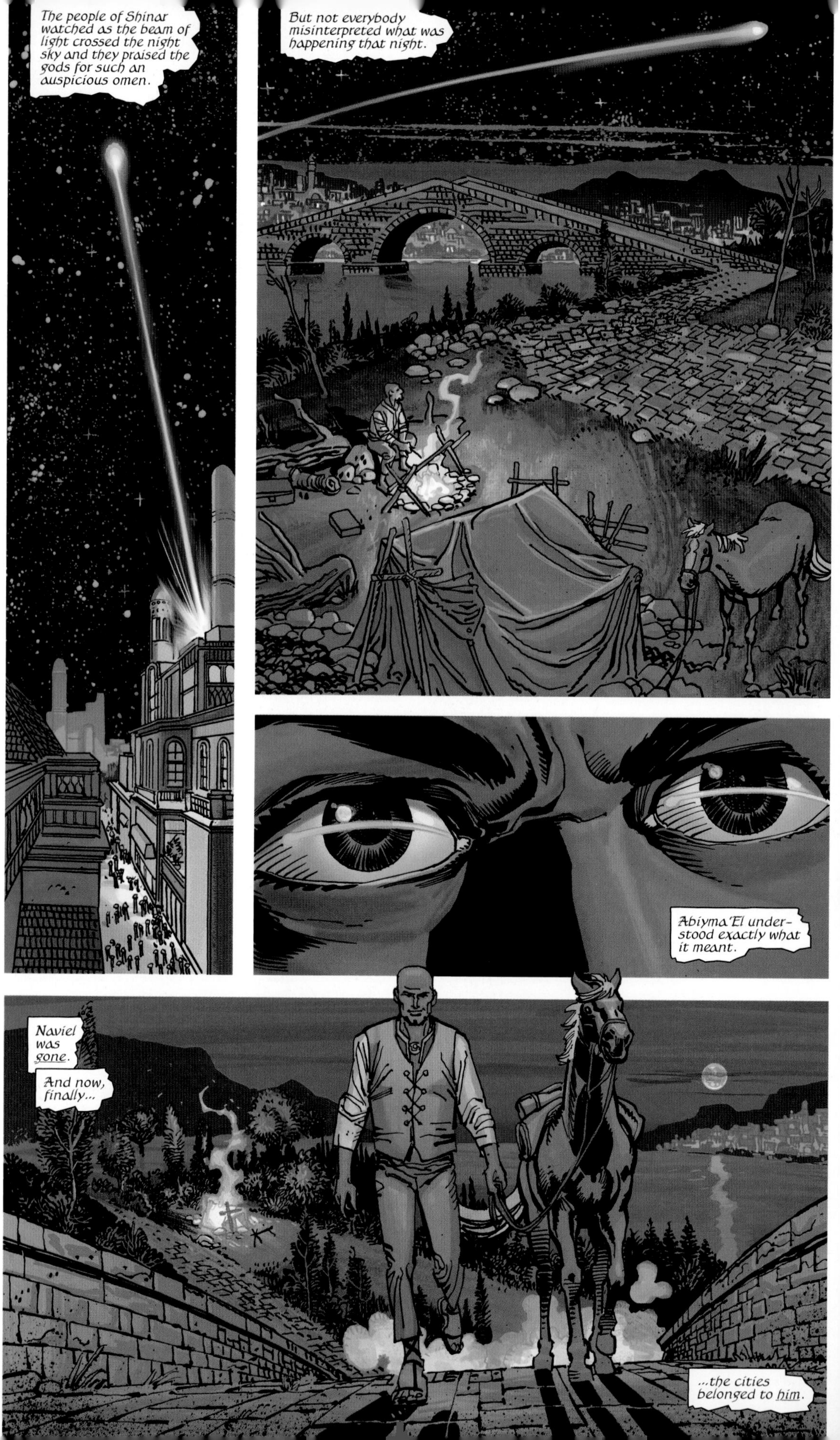
The people of Shinar watched as the beam of light crossed the night sky and they praised the gods for such an auspicious omen.
But not everybody misinterpreted what was happening that night.
Abiyma'El understood exactly what it meant.
Naviel was gone.
And now, finally...
...the cities belonged to him.

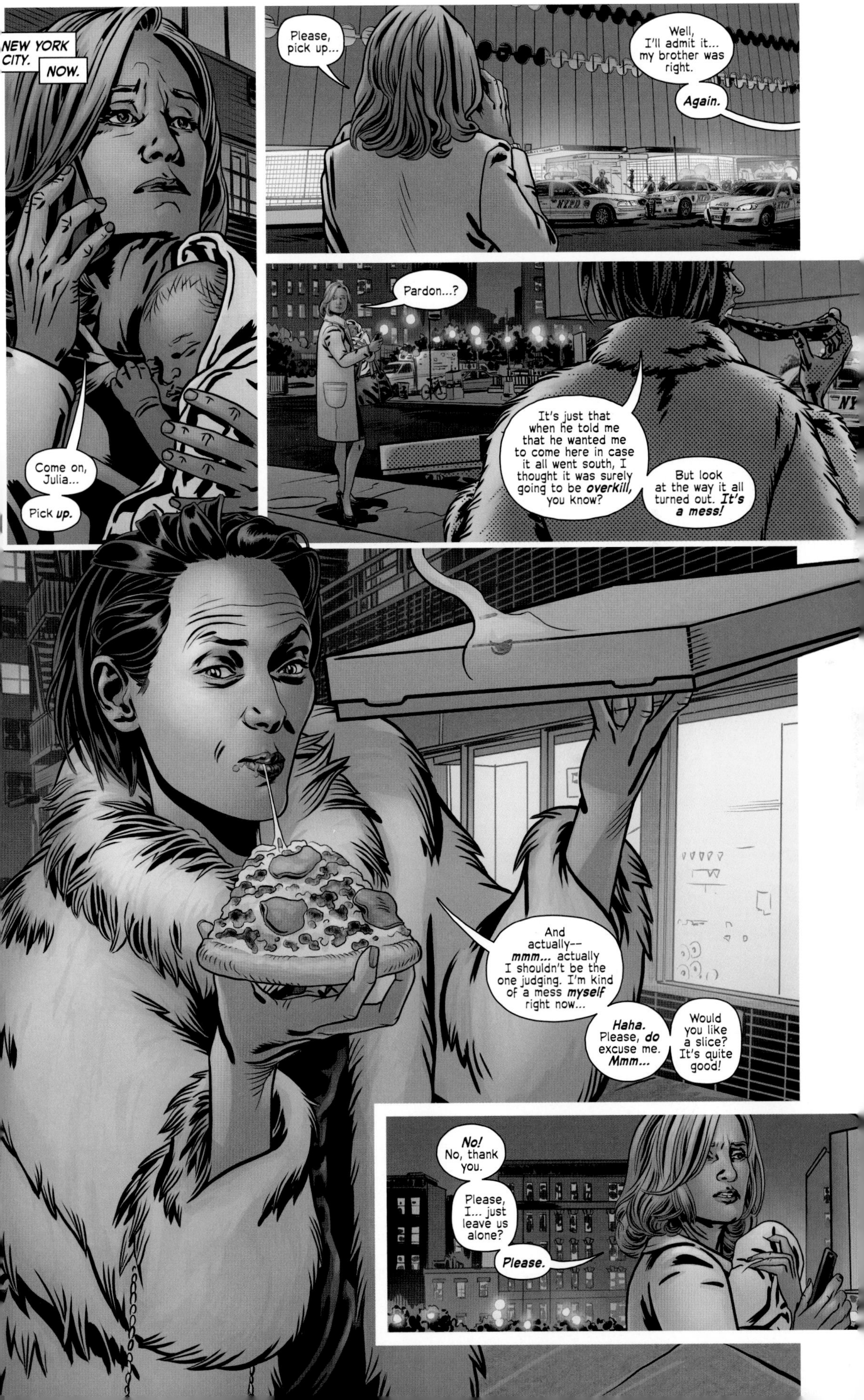
NEW YORK CITY.
NOW.
Come on, Julia...
Pick *up.*
Please, pick up...
Well, I'll admit it... my brother was right.
Again.
Pardon...?
It's just that when he told me that he wanted me to come here in case it all went south, I thought it was surely going to be *overkill,* you know?
But look at the way it all turned out. *It's a mess!*
And actually-- *mmm...* actually I shouldn't be the one judging. I'm kind of a mess *myself* right now...
Haha. Please, *do* excuse me. *Mmm...*
Would you like a slice? It's quite good!
No! No, thank you.
Please, I... just leave us alone?
Please.

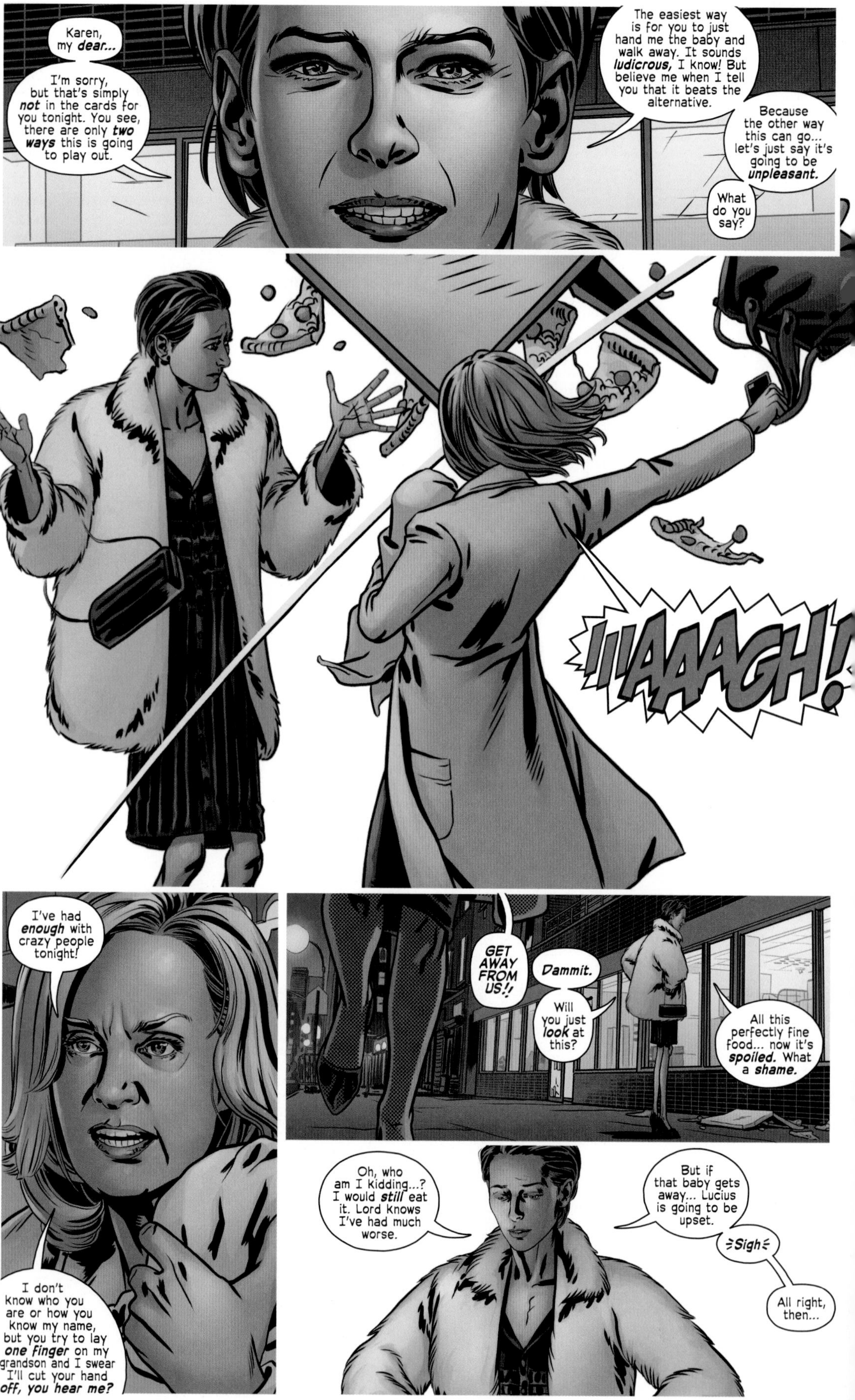
Karen, my *dear...*
I'm sorry, but that's simply ***not*** in the cards for you tonight. You see, there are only ***two ways*** this is going to play out.
The easiest way is for you to just hand me the baby and walk away. It sounds ***ludicrous,*** I know! But believe me when I tell you that it beats the alternative.
Because the other way this can go... let's just say it's going to be ***unpleasant.***
What do you say?
!!AAAGH!!
I've had ***enough*** with crazy people tonight!
I don't know who you are or how you know my name, but you try to lay ***one finger*** on my grandson and I swear I'll cut your hand ***off, you hear me?***
GET AWAY FROM US!!
Dammit.
Will you just ***look*** at this?
All this perfectly fine food... now it's ***spoiled.*** What a ***shame.***
Oh, who am I kidding...? I would ***still*** eat it. Lord knows I've had much worse.
But if that baby gets away... Lucius is going to be upset.
Sigh
All right, then...

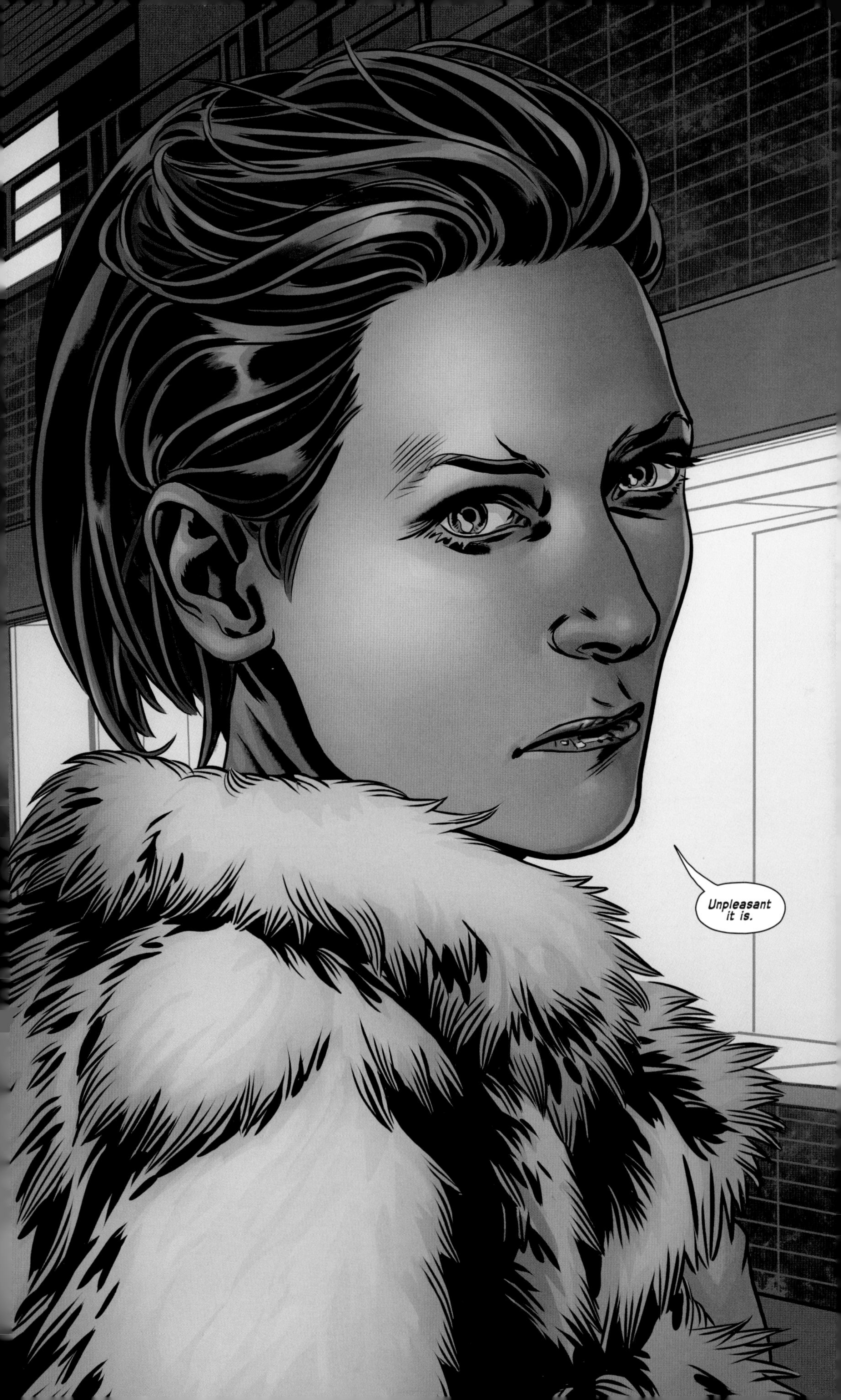
Unpleasant it is.

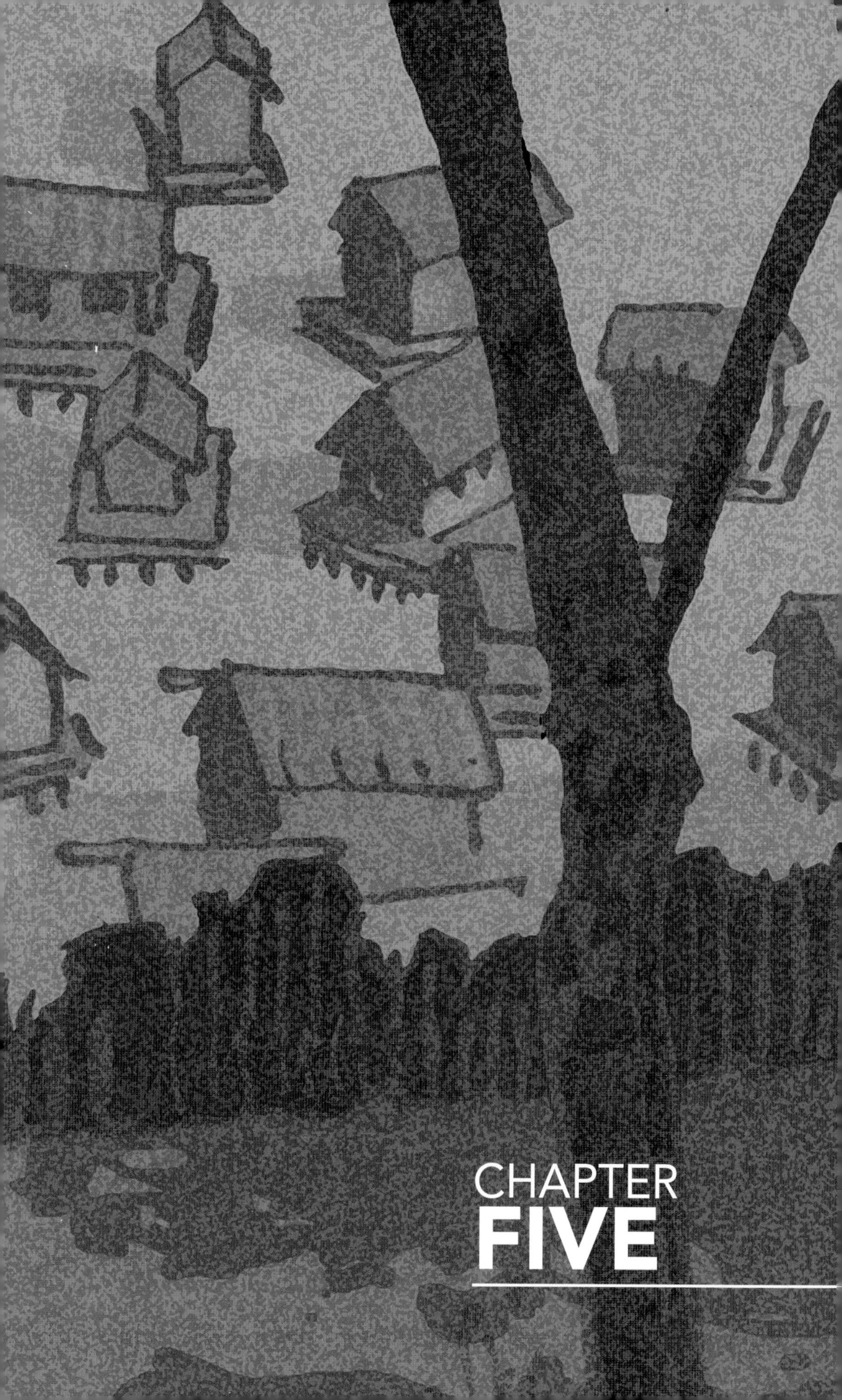

CHAPTER FIVE

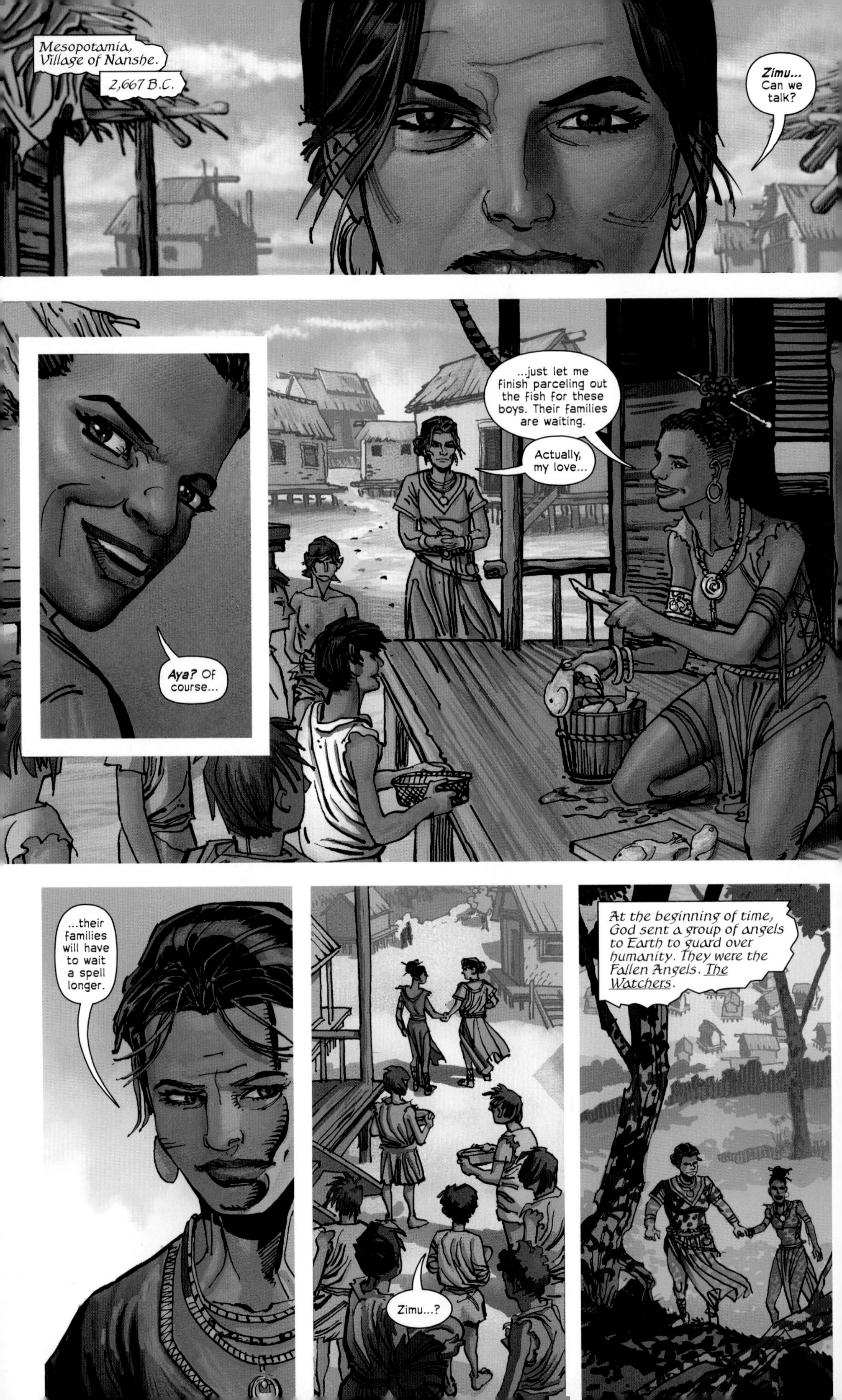
Mesopotamia, Village of Nanshe.
2,667 B.C.
Zimu... Can we talk?
Aya? Of course...
...just let me finish parceling out the fish for these boys. Their families are waiting.
Actually, my love...
...their families will have to wait a spell longer.
Zimu...?
At the beginning of time, God sent a group of angels to Earth to guard over humanity. They were the Fallen Angels. The Watchers.

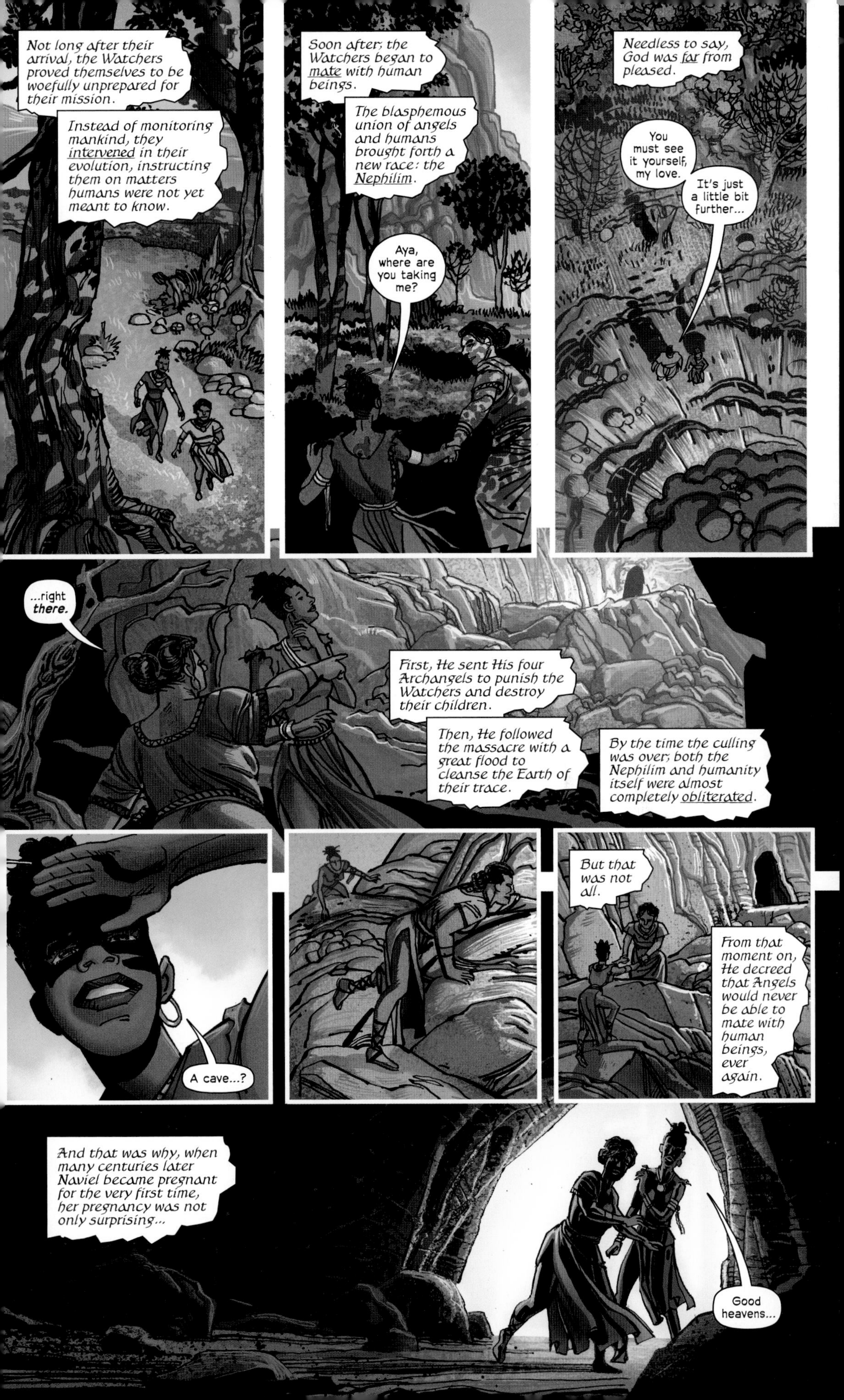

Not long after their arrival, the Watchers proved themselves to be woefully unprepared for their mission.
Instead of monitoring mankind, they intervened in their evolution, instructing them on matters humans were not yet meant to know.
Soon after, the Watchers began to mate with human beings.
The blasphemous union of angels and humans brought forth a new race: the Nephilim.
Aya, where are you taking me?
Needless to say, God was far from pleased.
You must see it yourself, my love.
It's just a little bit further...
...right there.
First, He sent His four Archangels to punish the Watchers and destroy their children.
Then, He followed the massacre with a great flood to cleanse the Earth of their trace.
By the time the culling was over, both the Nephilim and humanity itself were almost completely obliterated.
A cave...?
But that was not all.
From that moment on, He decreed that Angels would never be able to mate with human beings, ever again.
And that was why, when many centuries later Naviel became pregnant for the very first time, her pregnancy was not only surprising...
Good heavens...

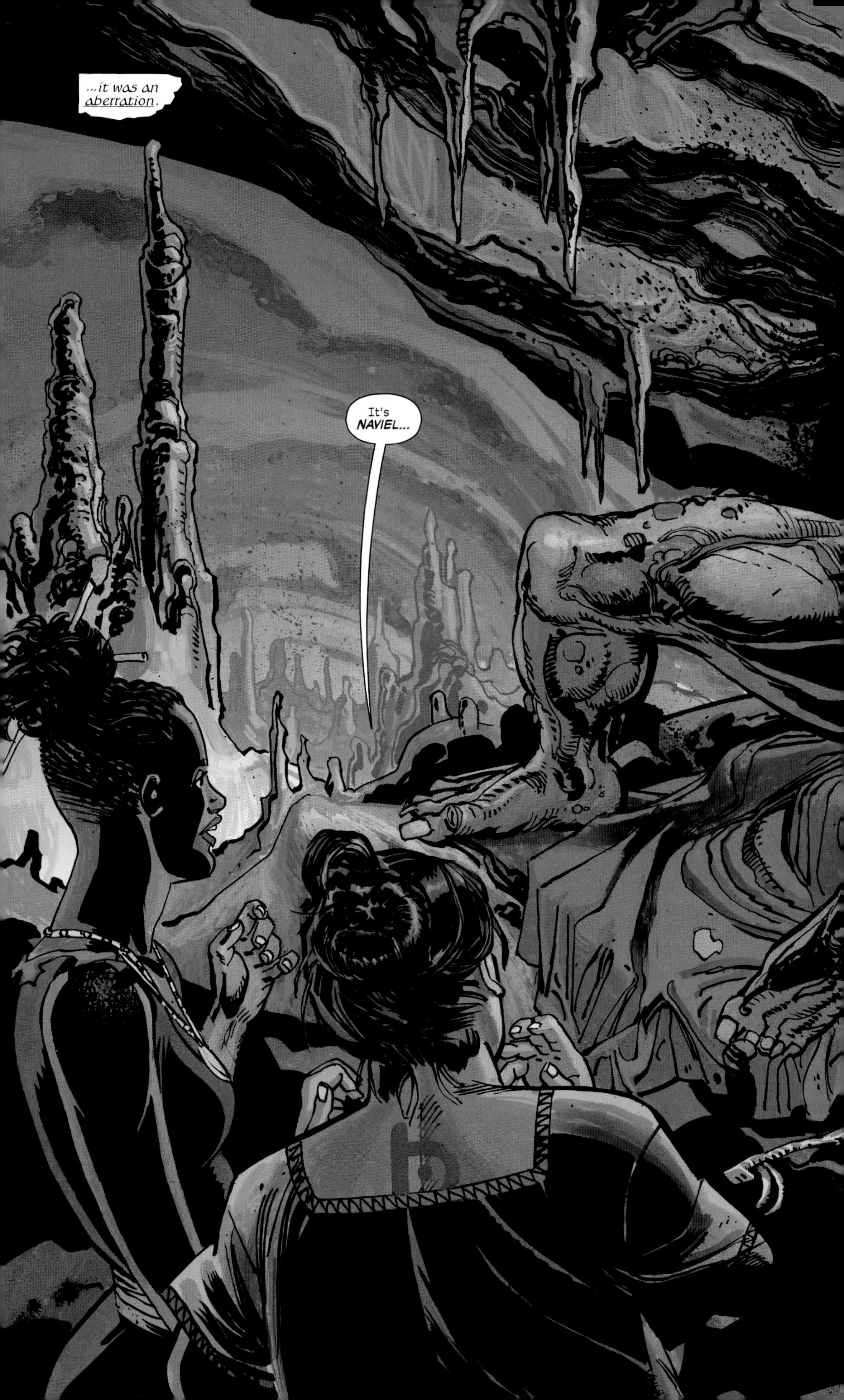
...it was an aberration.
It's NAVIEL...

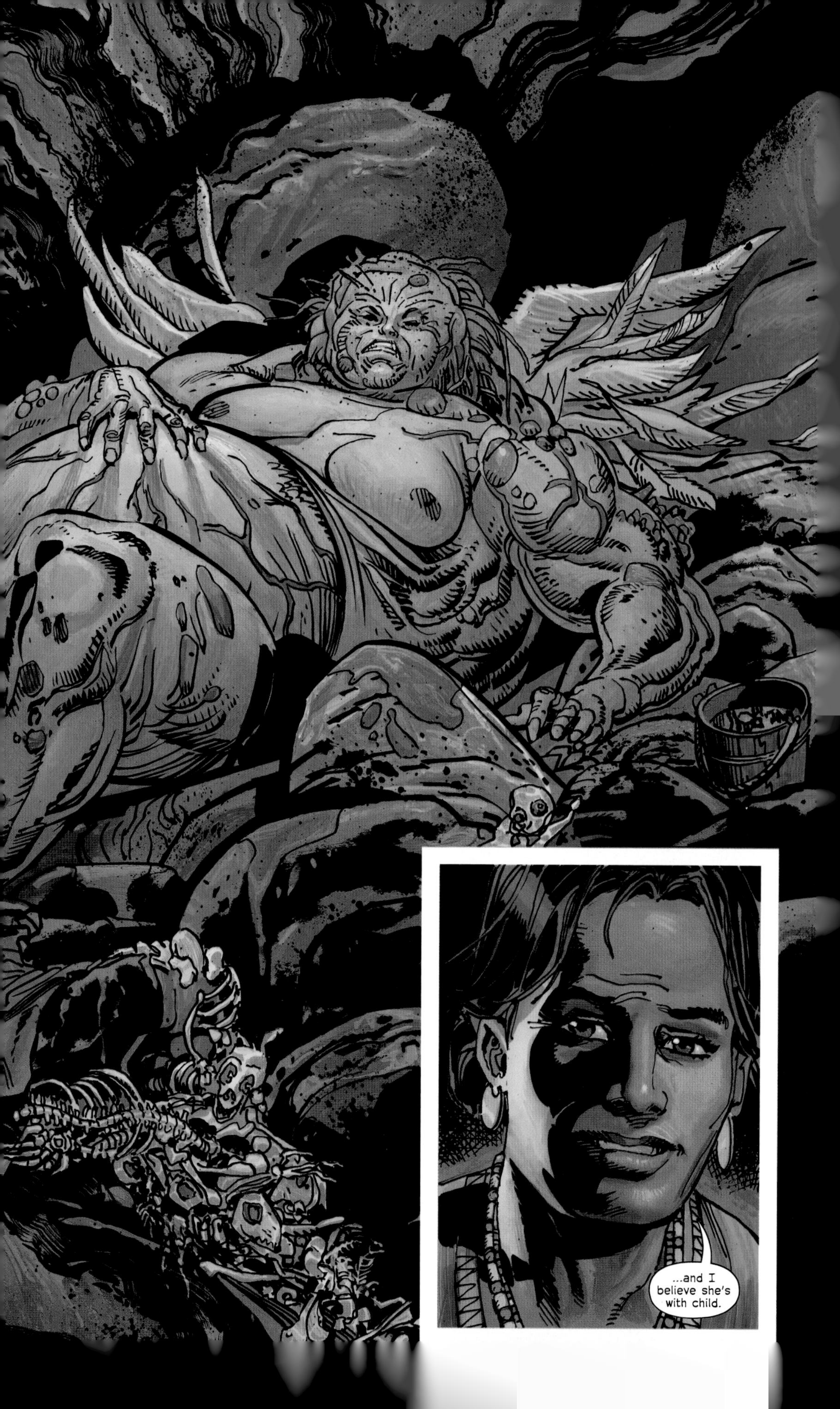
...and I
believe she's
with child.

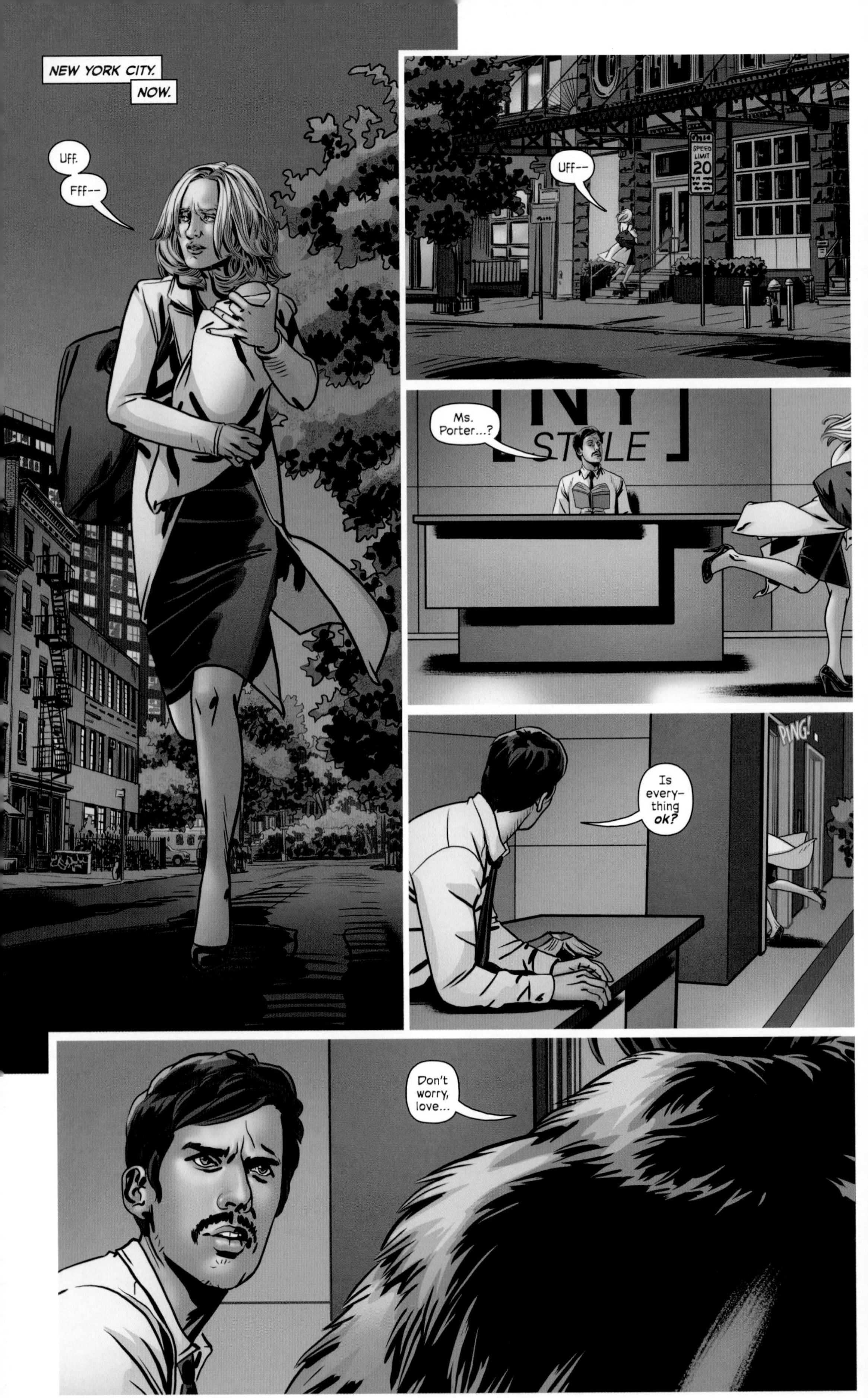

NEW YORK CITY.
NOW.
UFF.
FFF--
UFF--
Ms. Porter...?
NY STYLE
Is every-thing ***ok?***
PING!
Don't worry, love...

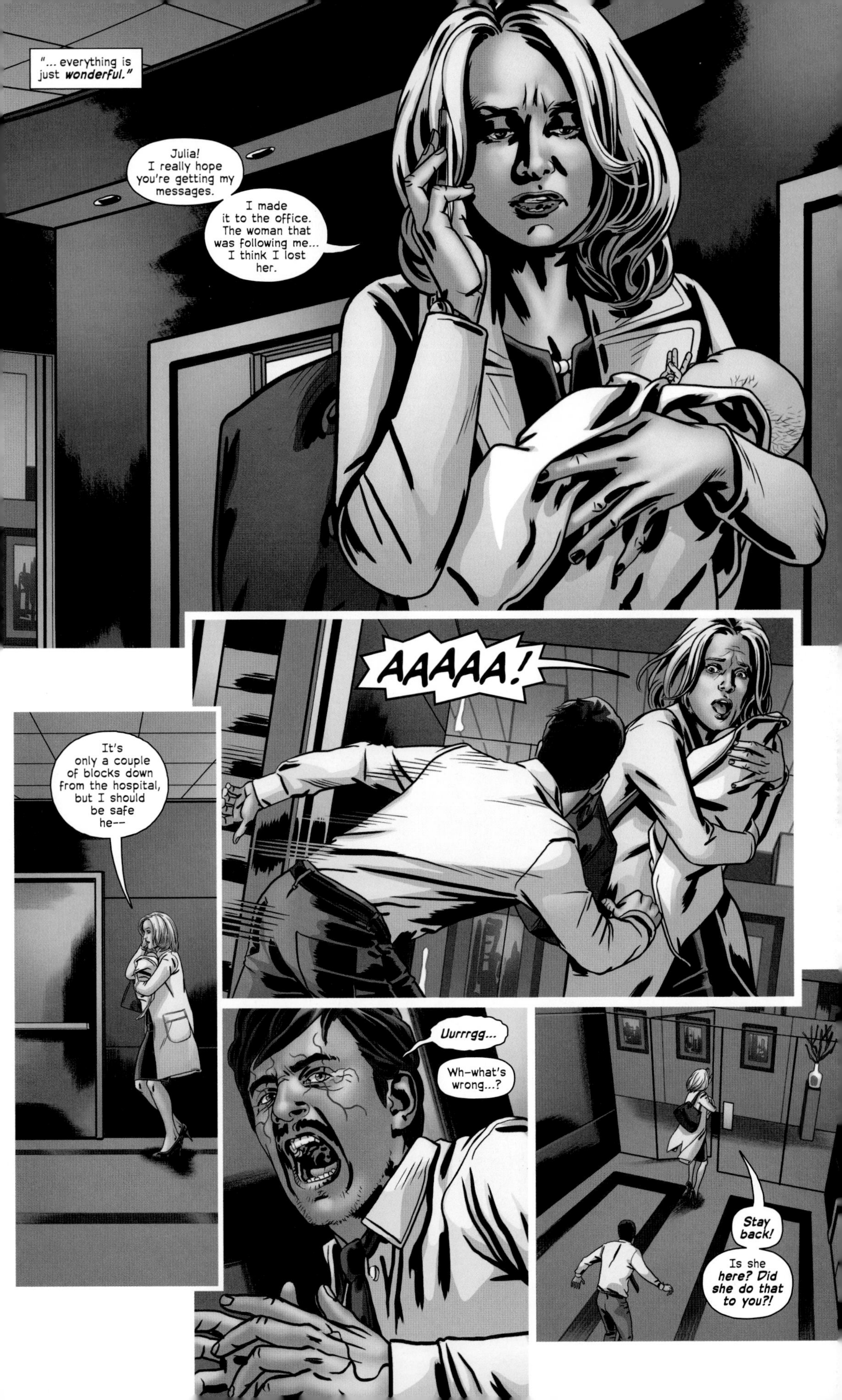
"... everything is just *wonderful.*"
Julia! I really hope you're getting my messages.
I made it to the office. The woman that was following me... I think I lost her.
It's only a couple of blocks down from the hospital, but I should be safe he--
AAAAA!
Uurrrgg...
Wh-what's wrong...?
Stay back!
Is she *here? Did she do that to you?!*

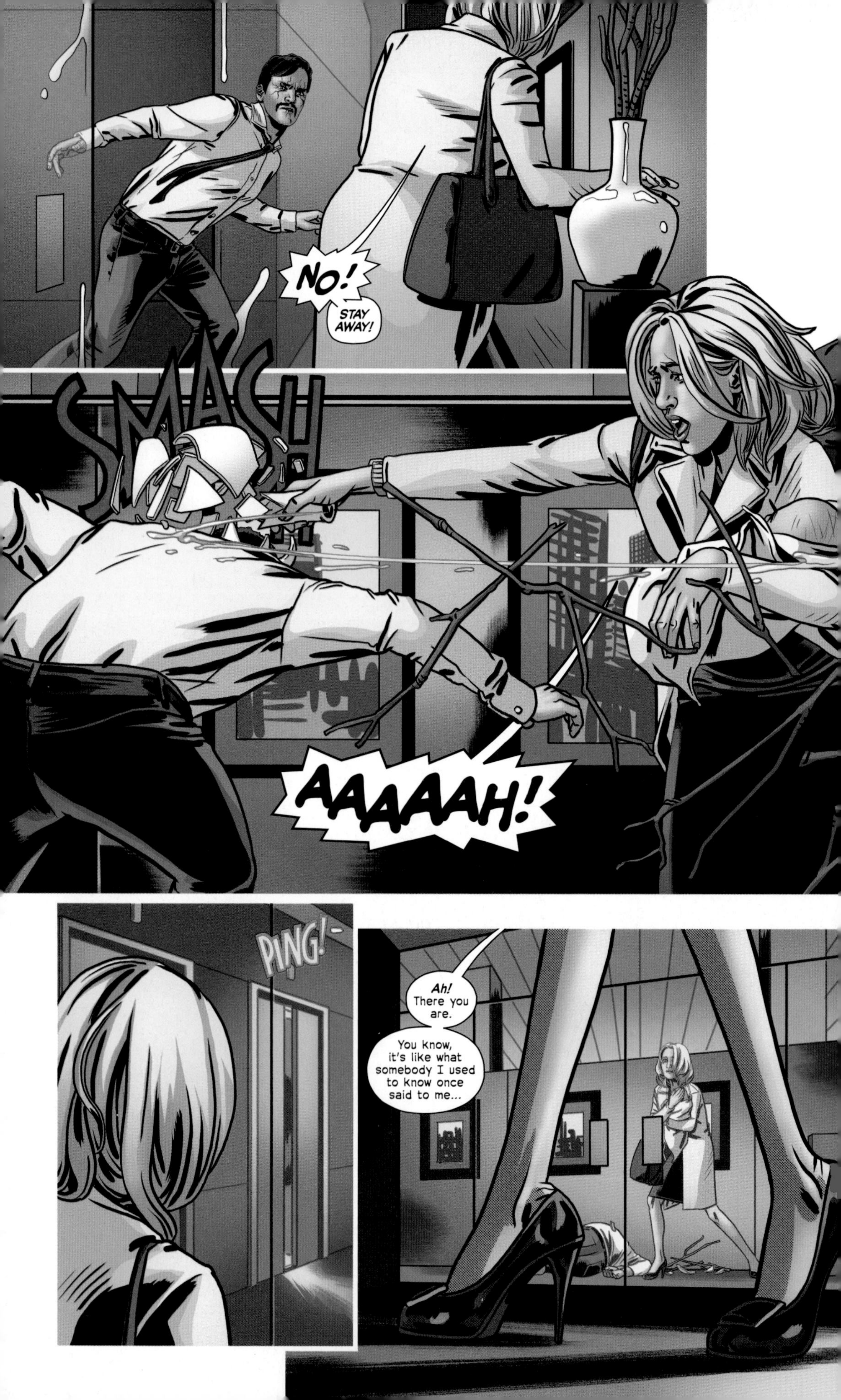
NO!
STAY AWAY!
SMASH
AAAAAH!
PING!
Ah! There you are.
You know, it's like what somebody I used to know once said to me...

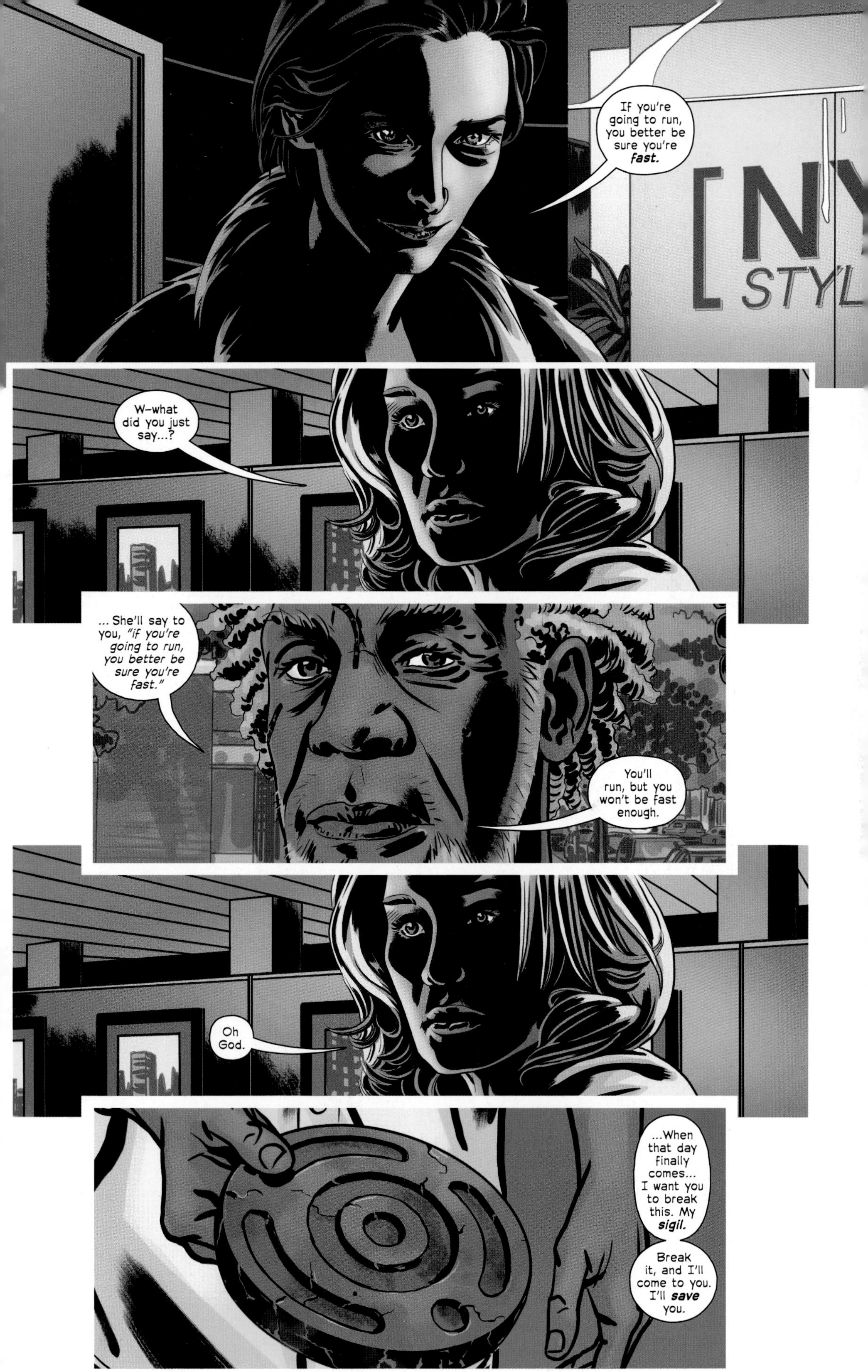
If you're going to run, you better be sure you're **fast.**
[NY
STYL
W-what did you just say...?
... She'll say to you, *"if you're going to run, you better be sure you're fast."*
You'll run, but you won't be fast enough.
Oh God.
...When that day finally comes... I want you to break this. My ***sigil.***
Break it, and I'll come to you. I'll ***save*** you.

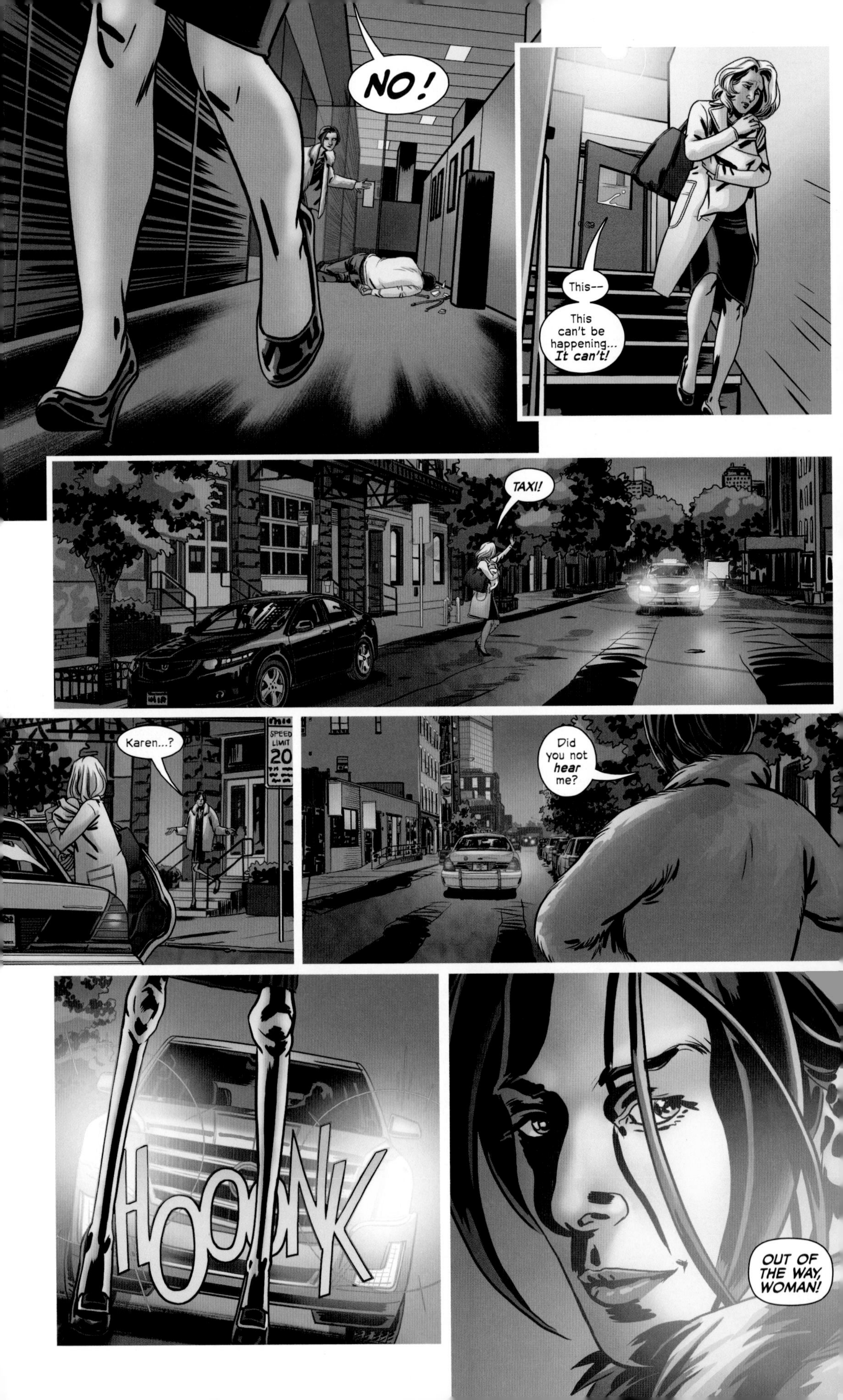
NO!
This--
This can't be happening... It can't!
TAXI!
Karen...?
SPEED LIMIT 20
Did you not hear me?
HOOONK
OUT OF THE WAY, WOMAN!

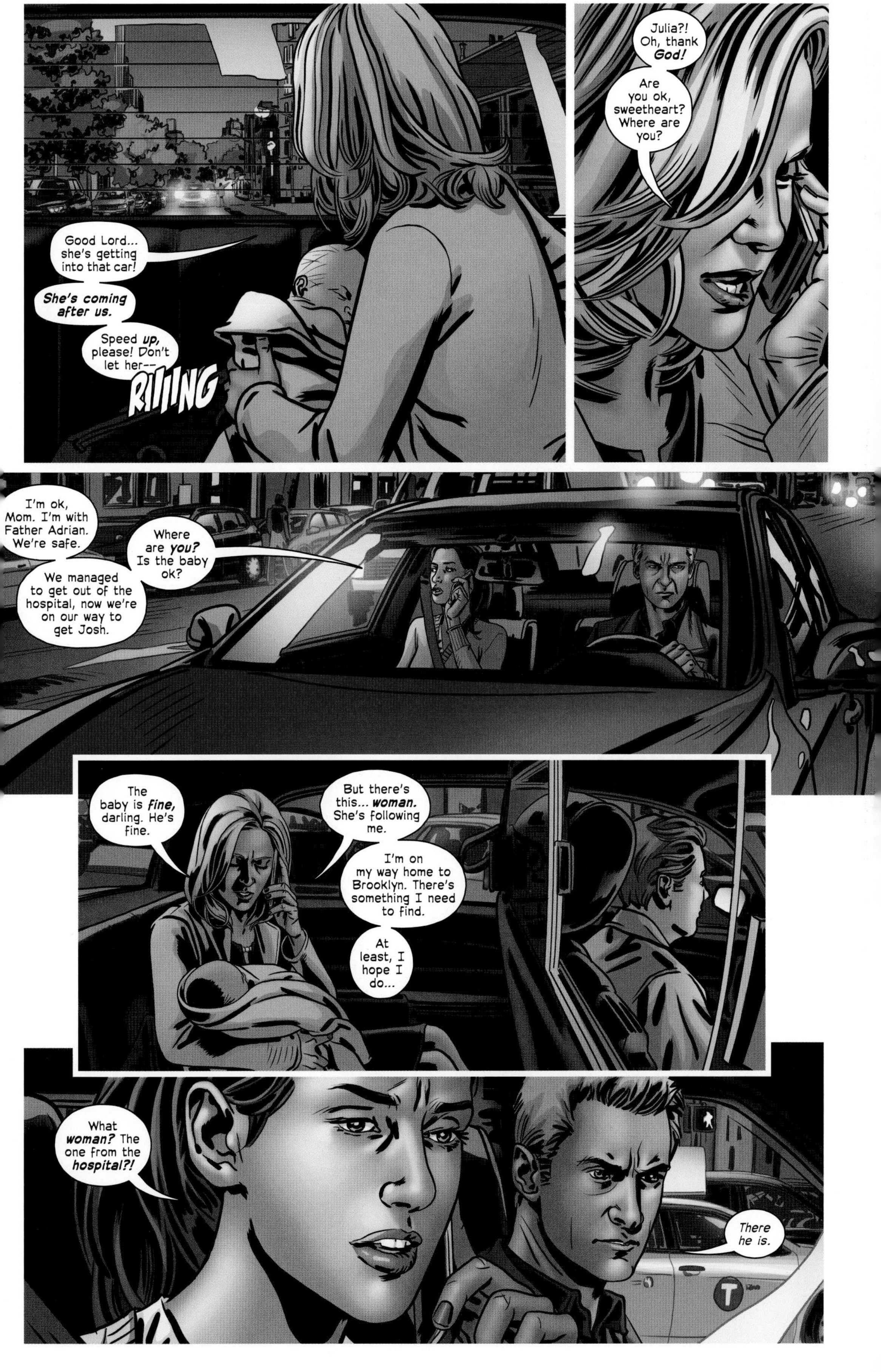
Good Lord... she's getting into that car!
She's coming after us.
Speed up, please! Don't let her--
RIIIING
Julia?! Oh, thank God!
Are you ok, sweetheart? Where are you?
I'm ok, Mom. I'm with Father Adrian. We're safe.
We managed to get out of the hospital, now we're on our way to get Josh.
Where are you? Is the baby ok?
The baby is fine, darling. He's fine.
But there's this... woman. She's following me.
I'm on my way home to Brooklyn. There's something I need to find.
At least, I hope I do...
What woman? The one from the hospital?!
There he is.

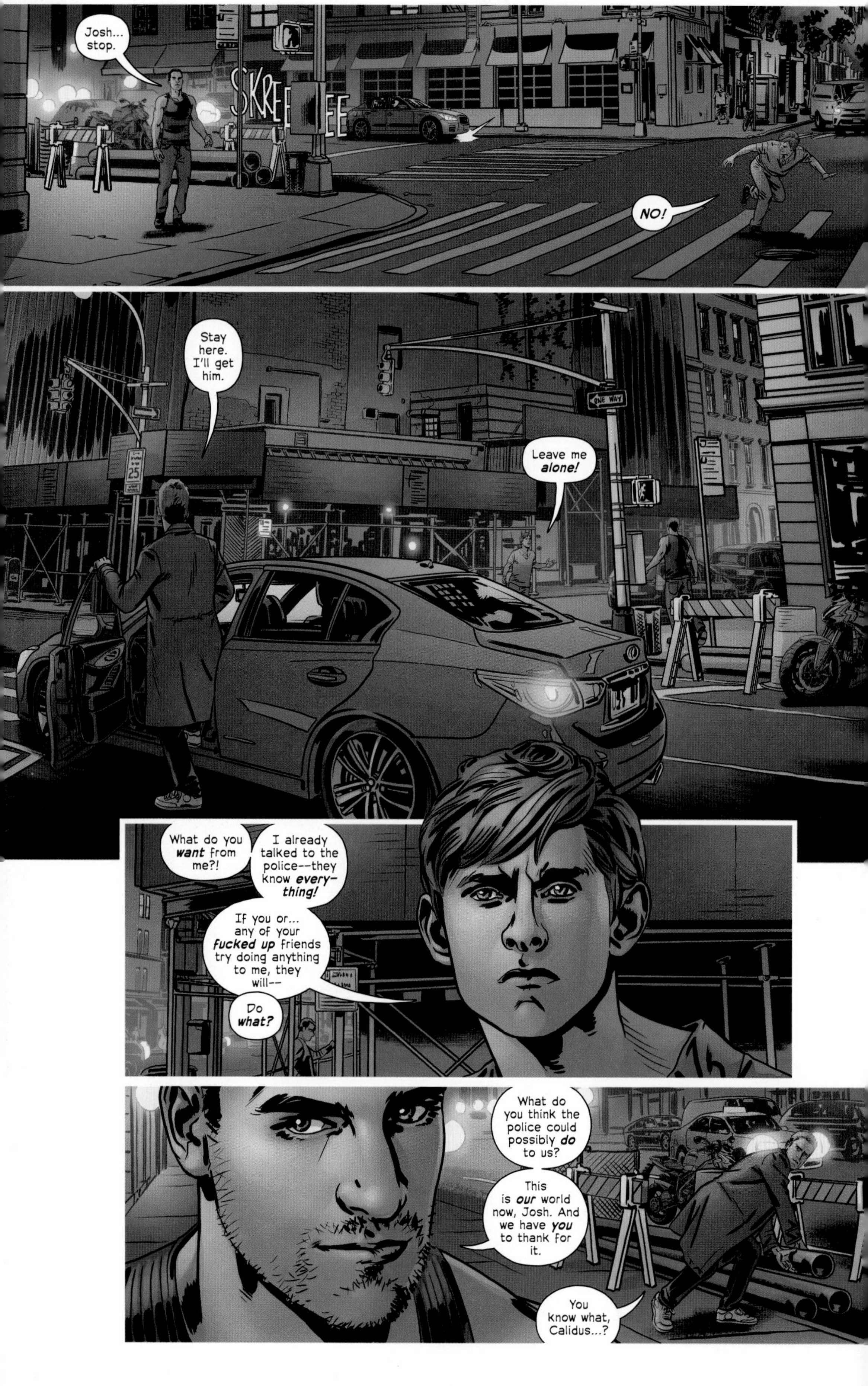
Josh... stop.
SKREEEEEE
NO!
Stay here. I'll get him.
ONE WAY
Leave me *alone!*
What do you *want* from me?!
I already talked to the police--they know *every-thing!*
If you or... any of your *fucked up* friends try doing anything to me, they will--
Do *what?*
What do you think the police could possibly *do* to us?
This is *our* world now, Josh. And we have *you* to thank for it.
You know what, Calidus...?

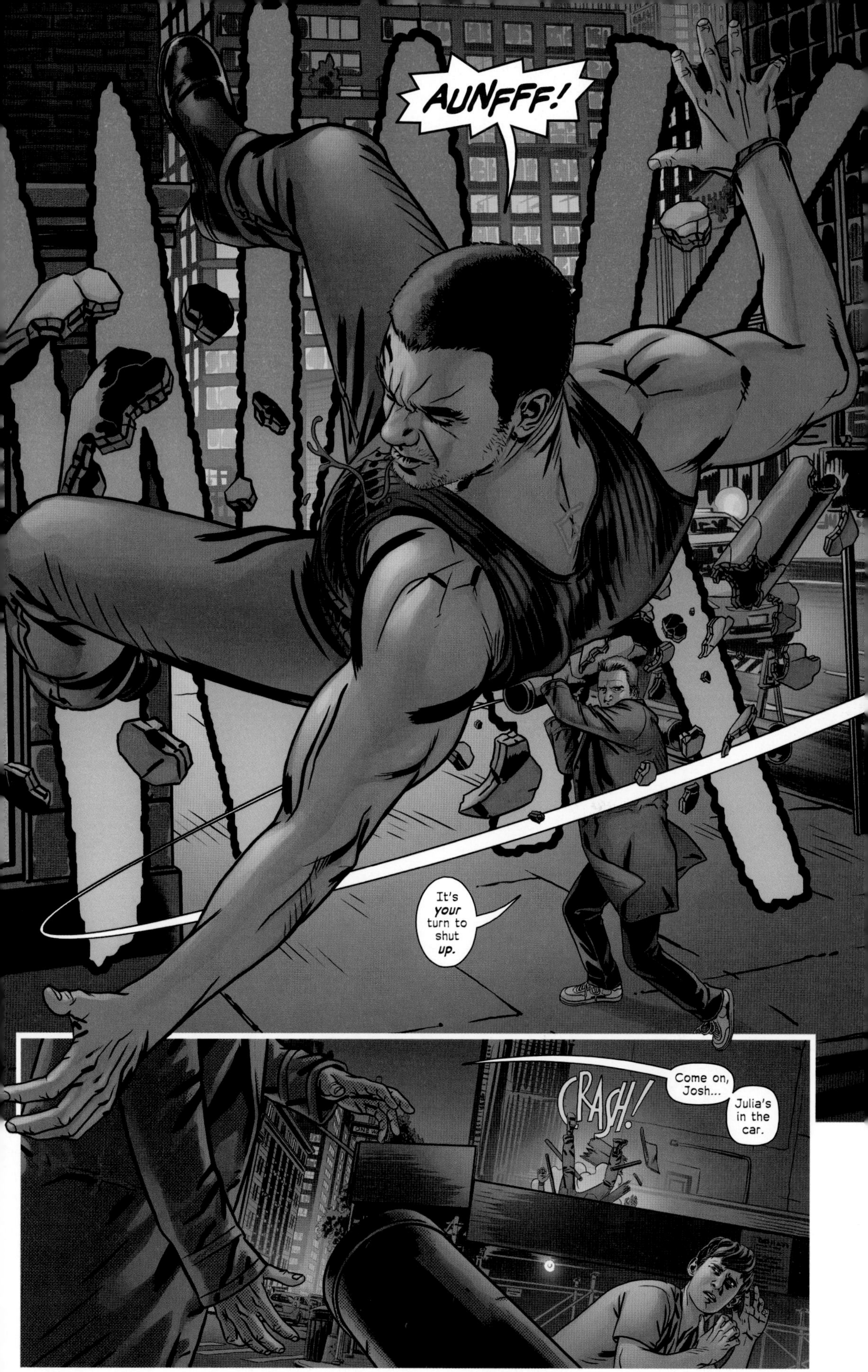
AUNFFF!
It's *your* turn to shut *up.*
CRASH!
Come on, Josh...
Julia's in the car.

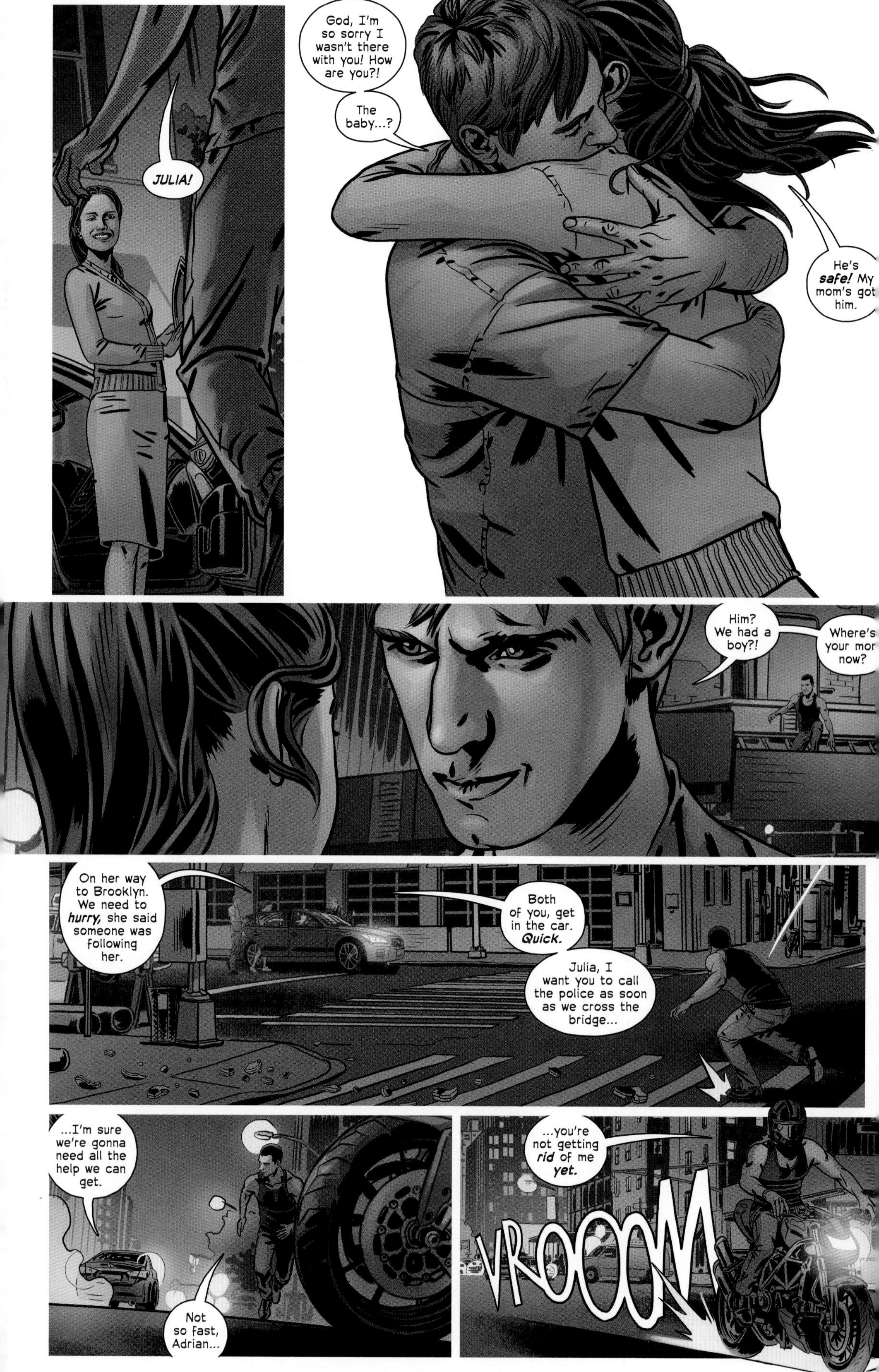
JULIA!
God, I'm so sorry I wasn't there with you! How are you?!
The baby...?
He's safe! My mom's got him.
Him? We had a boy?!
Where's your mom now?
On her way to Brooklyn. We need to hurry, she said someone was following her.
Both of you, get in the car. Quick.
Julia, I want you to call the police as soon as we cross the bridge...
...I'm sure we're gonna need all the help we can get.
Not so fast, Adrian...
...you're not getting rid of me yet.
VROOOM

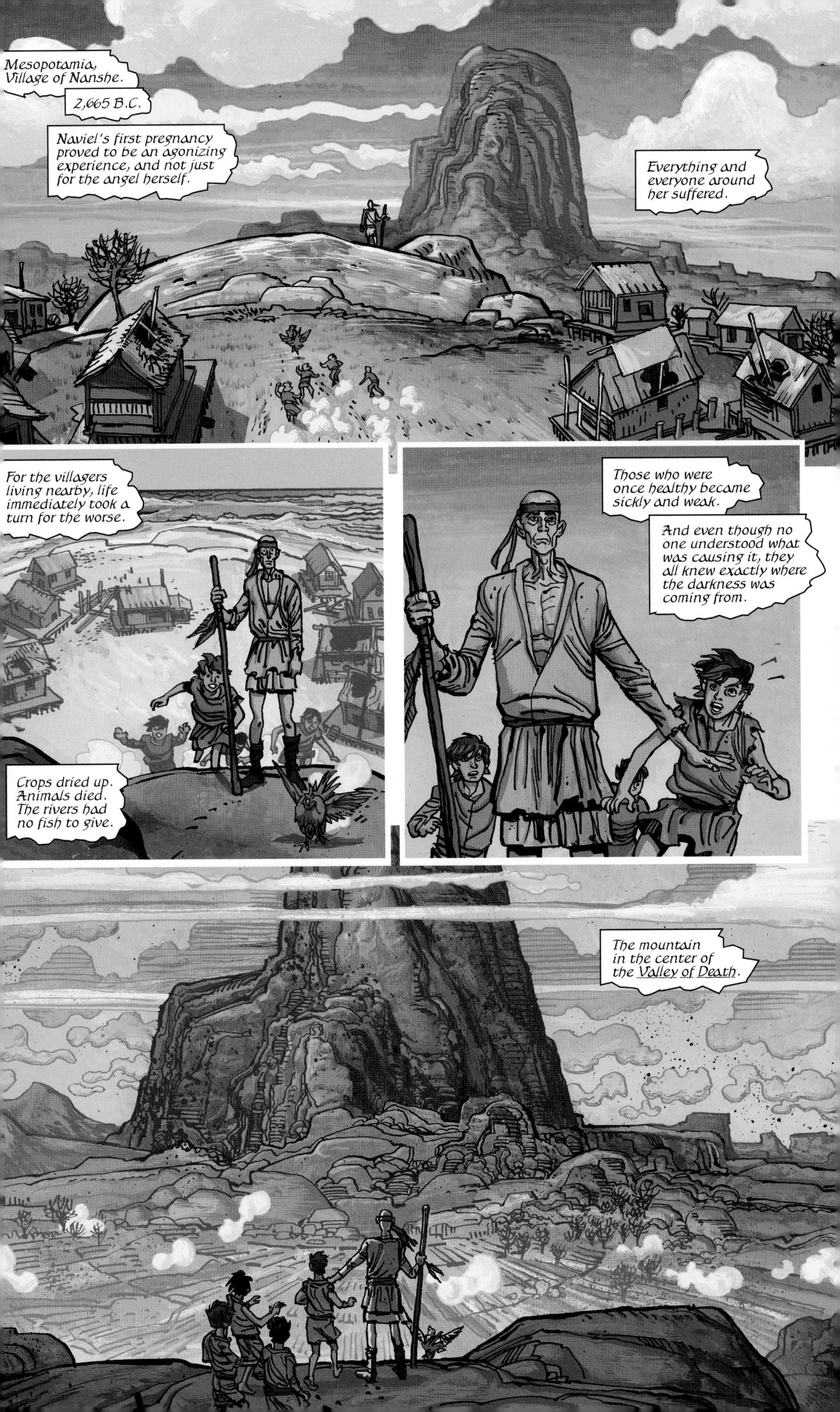
Mesopotamia, Village of Nanshe.
2,665 B.C.
Naviel's first pregnancy proved to be an agonizing experience, and not just for the angel herself.
Everything and everyone around her suffered.
For the villagers living nearby, life immediately took a turn for the worse.
Crops dried up. Animals died. The rivers had no fish to give.
Those who were once healthy became sickly and weak.
And even though no one understood what was causing it, they all knew exactly where the darkness was coming from.
The mountain in the center of the Valley of Death.

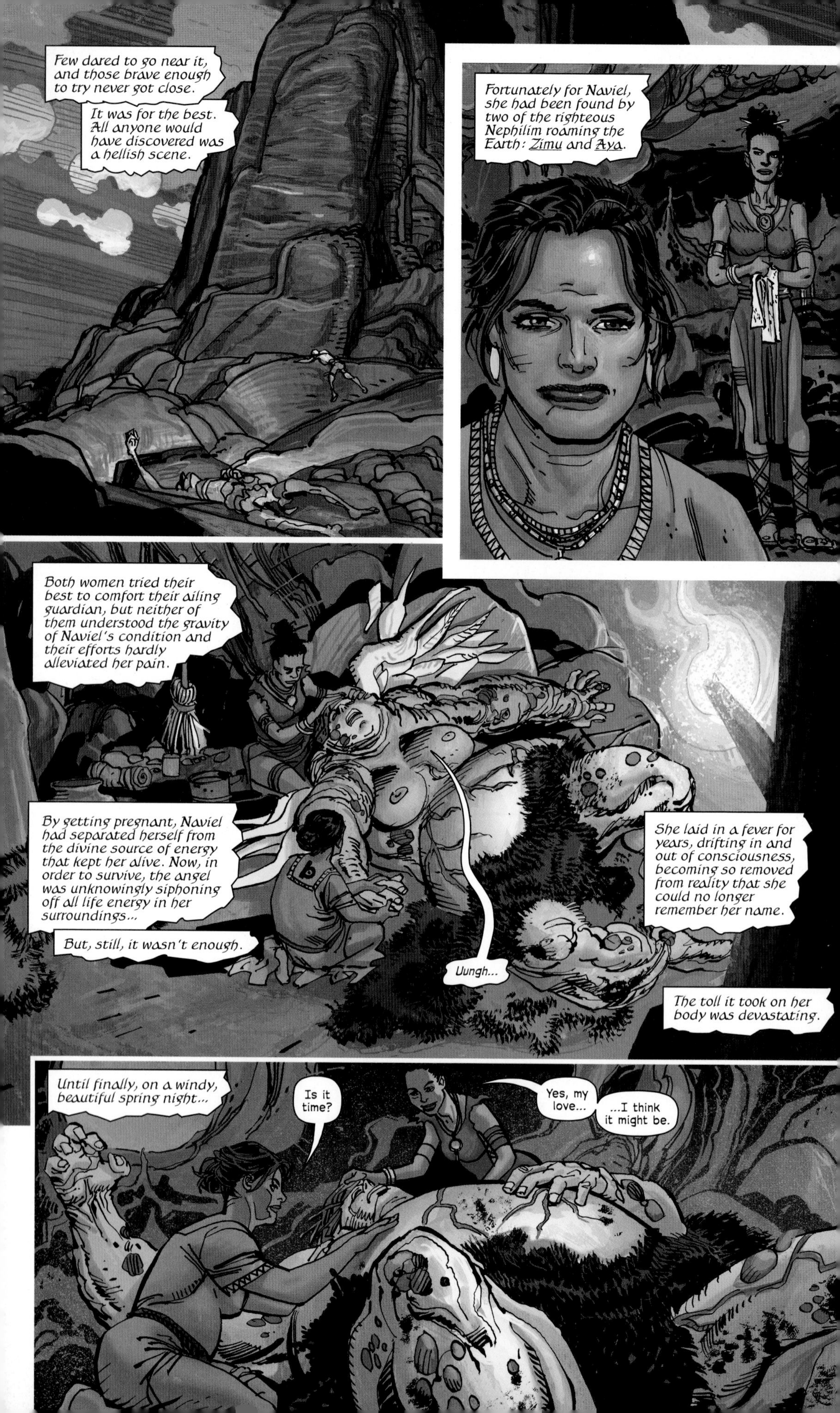
Few dared to go near it, and those brave enough to try never got close.
It was for the best. All anyone would have discovered was a hellish scene.
Fortunately for Naviel, she had been found by two of the righteous Nephilim roaming the Earth: Zimu and Aya.
Both women tried their best to comfort their ailing guardian, but neither of them understood the gravity of Naviel's condition and their efforts hardly alleviated her pain.
By getting pregnant, Naviel had separated herself from the divine source of energy that kept her alive. Now, in order to survive, the angel was unknowingly siphoning off all life energy in her surroundings...
But, still, it wasn't enough.
Uungh...
She laid in a fever for years, drifting in and out of consciousness, becoming so removed from reality that she could no longer remember her name.
The toll it took on her body was devastating.
Until finally, on a windy, beautiful spring night...
Is it time?
Yes, my love...
...I think it might be.

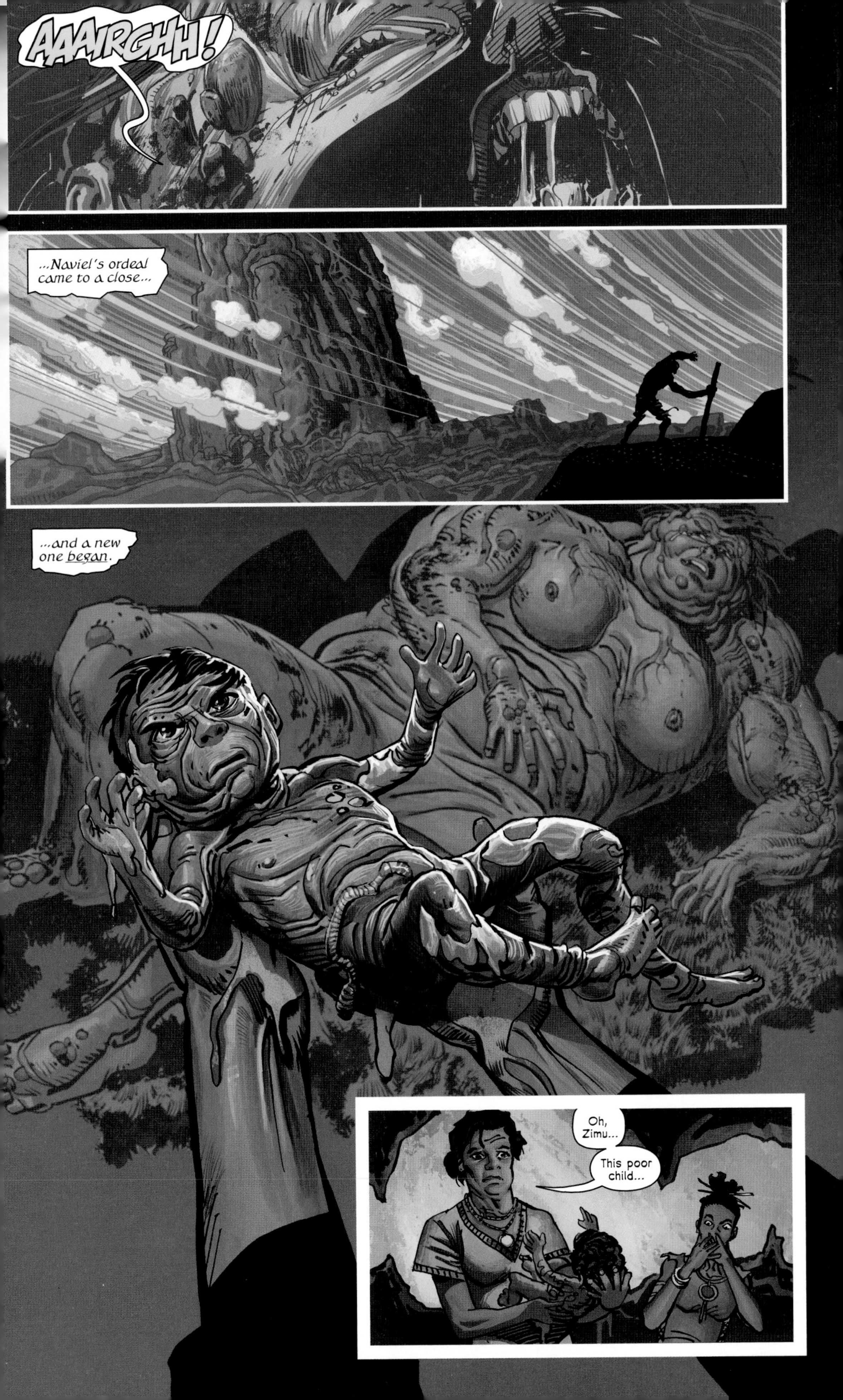

AAAIRGHH!
...Naviel's ordeal came to a close...
...and a new one began.
Oh, Zimu...
This poor child...

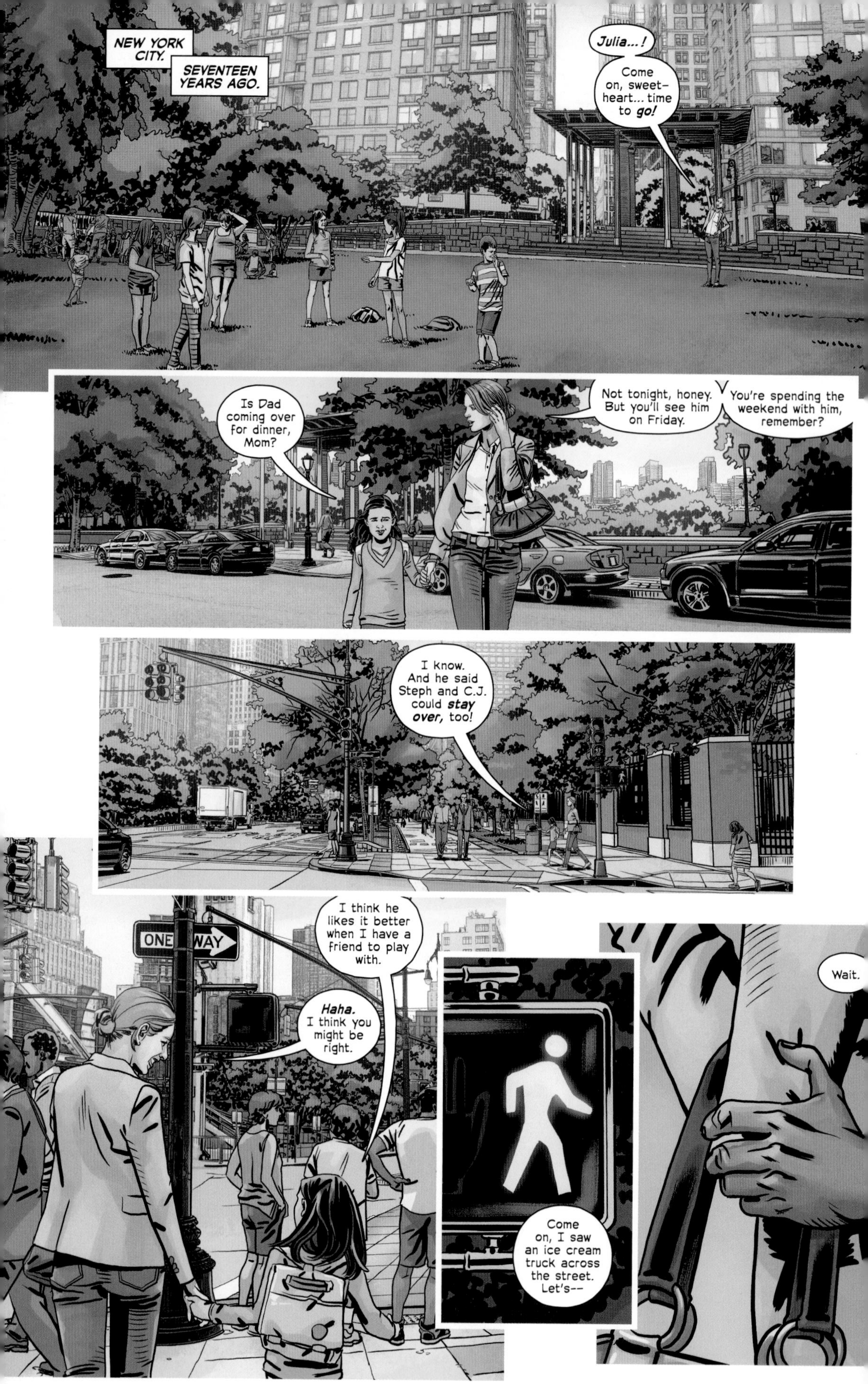

NEW YORK CITY.
SEVENTEEN YEARS AGO.
Julia...!
Come on, sweet-heart... time to go!
Is Dad coming over for dinner, Mom?
Not tonight, honey. But you'll see him on Friday.
You're spending the weekend with him, remember?
I know. And he said Steph and C.J. could stay over, too!
ONE WAY
I think he likes it better when I have a friend to play with.
Haha. I think you might be right.
Come on, I saw an ice cream truck across the street. Let's--
Wait.

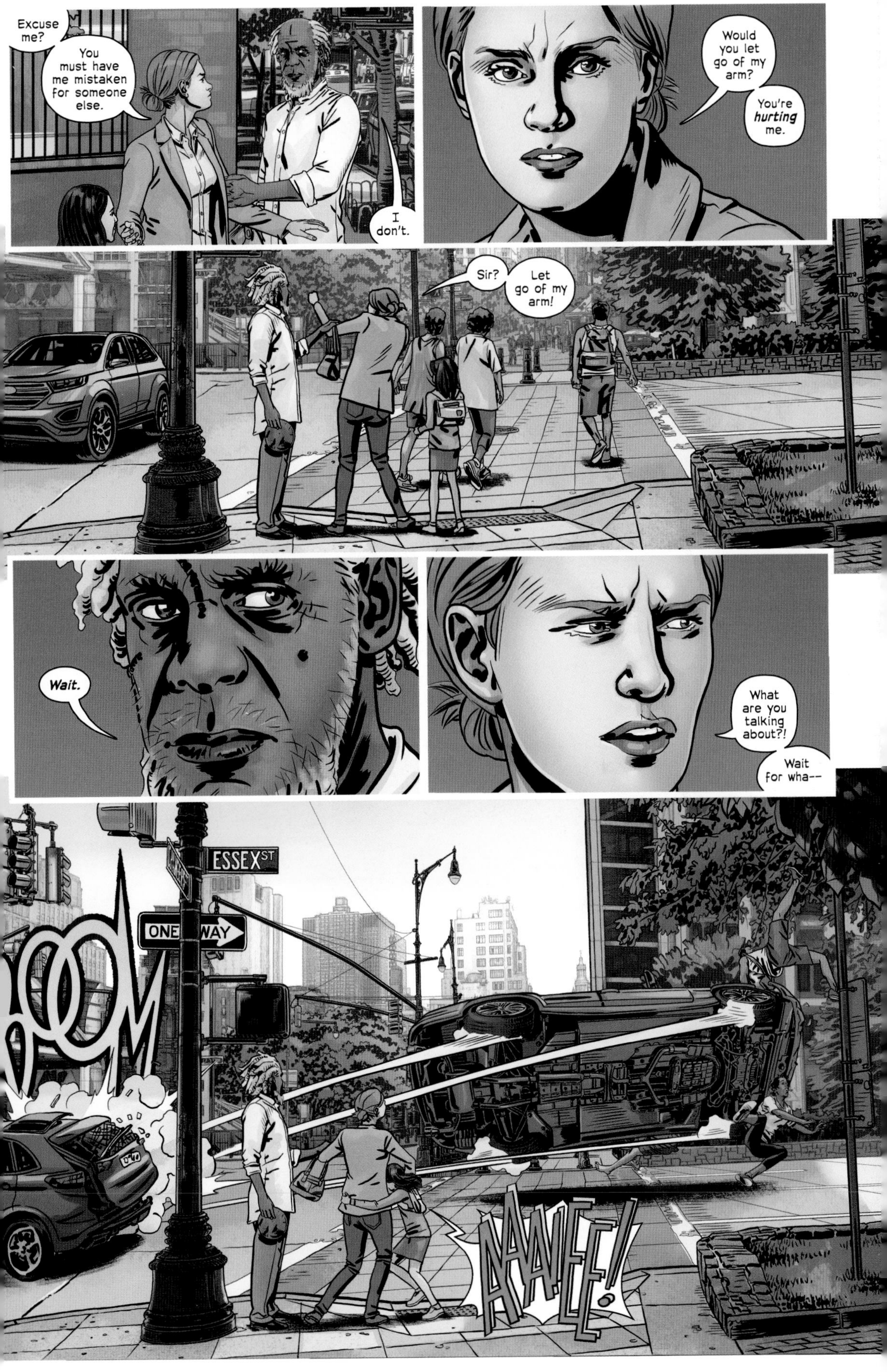
Excuse me?
You must have me mistaken for someone else.
I don't.
Would you let go of my arm?
You're *hurting* me.
Sir?
Let go of my arm!
Wait.
What are you talking about?!
Wait for wha--
ESSEX ST
ONE WAY
BOOM
AAAIEE!

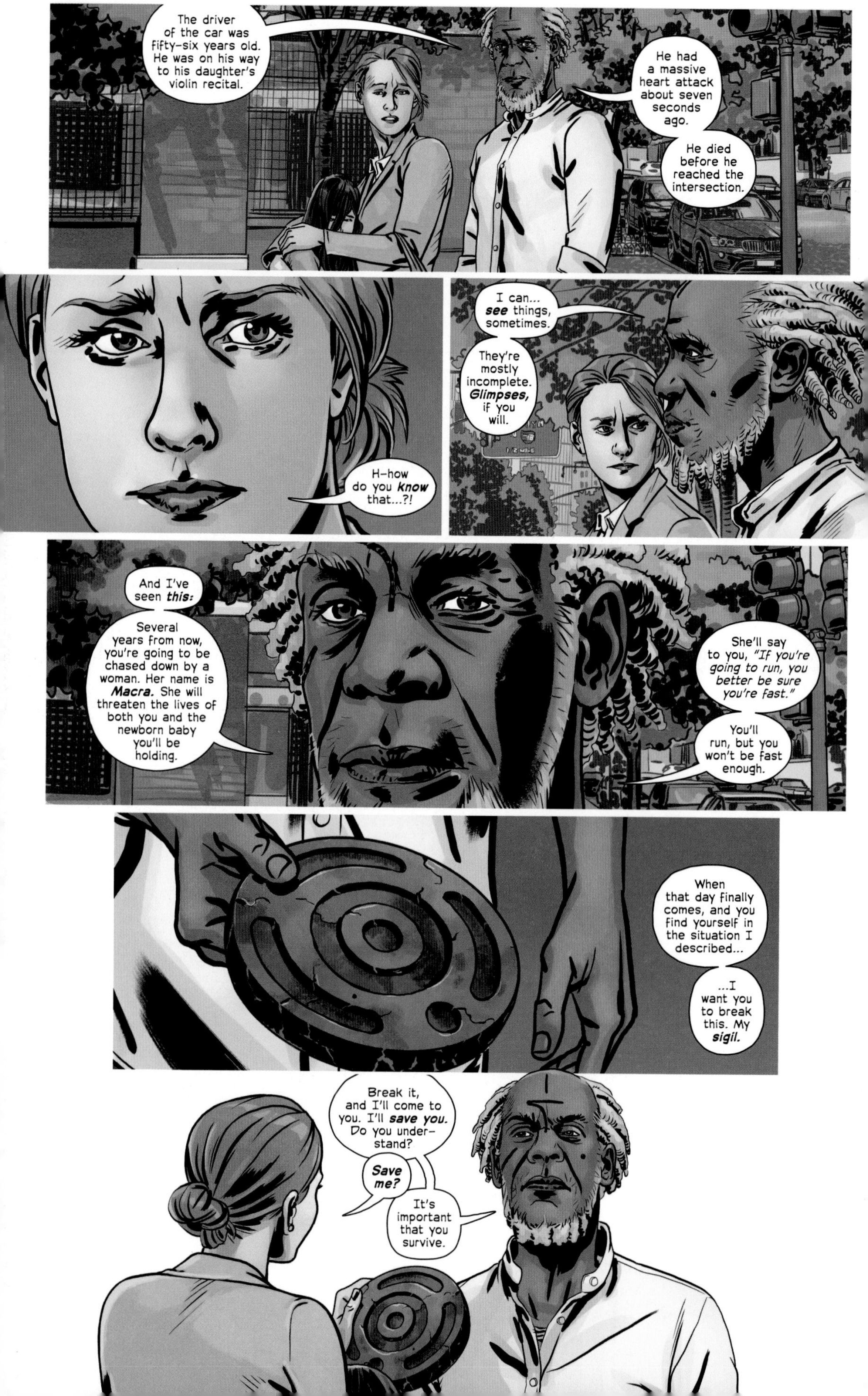

The driver of the car was fifty-six years old. He was on his way to his daughter's violin recital.
He had a massive heart attack about seven seconds ago.
He died before he reached the intersection.
H-how do you *know* that...?!
I can... *see* things, sometimes.
They're mostly incomplete. *Glimpses,* if you will.
And I've seen *this:*
Several years from now, you're going to be chased down by a woman. Her name is *Macra.* She will threaten the lives of both you and the newborn baby you'll be holding.
She'll say to you, *"If you're going to run, you better be sure you're fast."*
You'll run, but you won't be fast enough.
When that day finally comes, and you find yourself in the situation I described...
...I want you to break this. My *sigil.*
Break it, and I'll come to you. I'll *save you.* Do you under-stand?
Save me?
It's important that you survive.

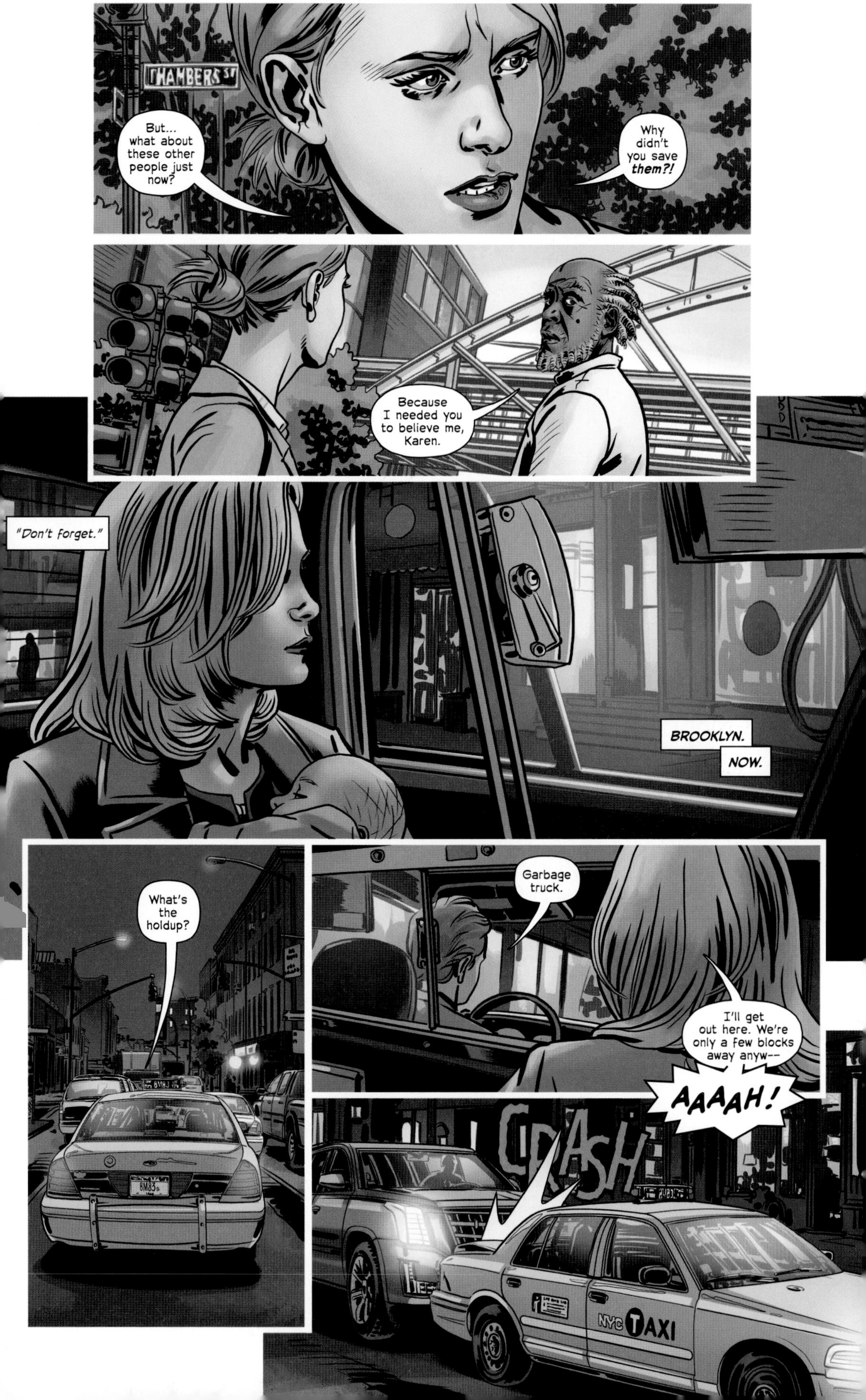
CHAMBERS ST
But... what about these other people just now?
Why didn't you save *them?!*
Because I needed you to believe me, Karen.
"Don't forget."
BROOKLYN.
NOW.
What's the holdup?
Garbage truck.
I'll get out here. We're only a few blocks away anyw--
AAAAH!
CRASH
NYC TAXI

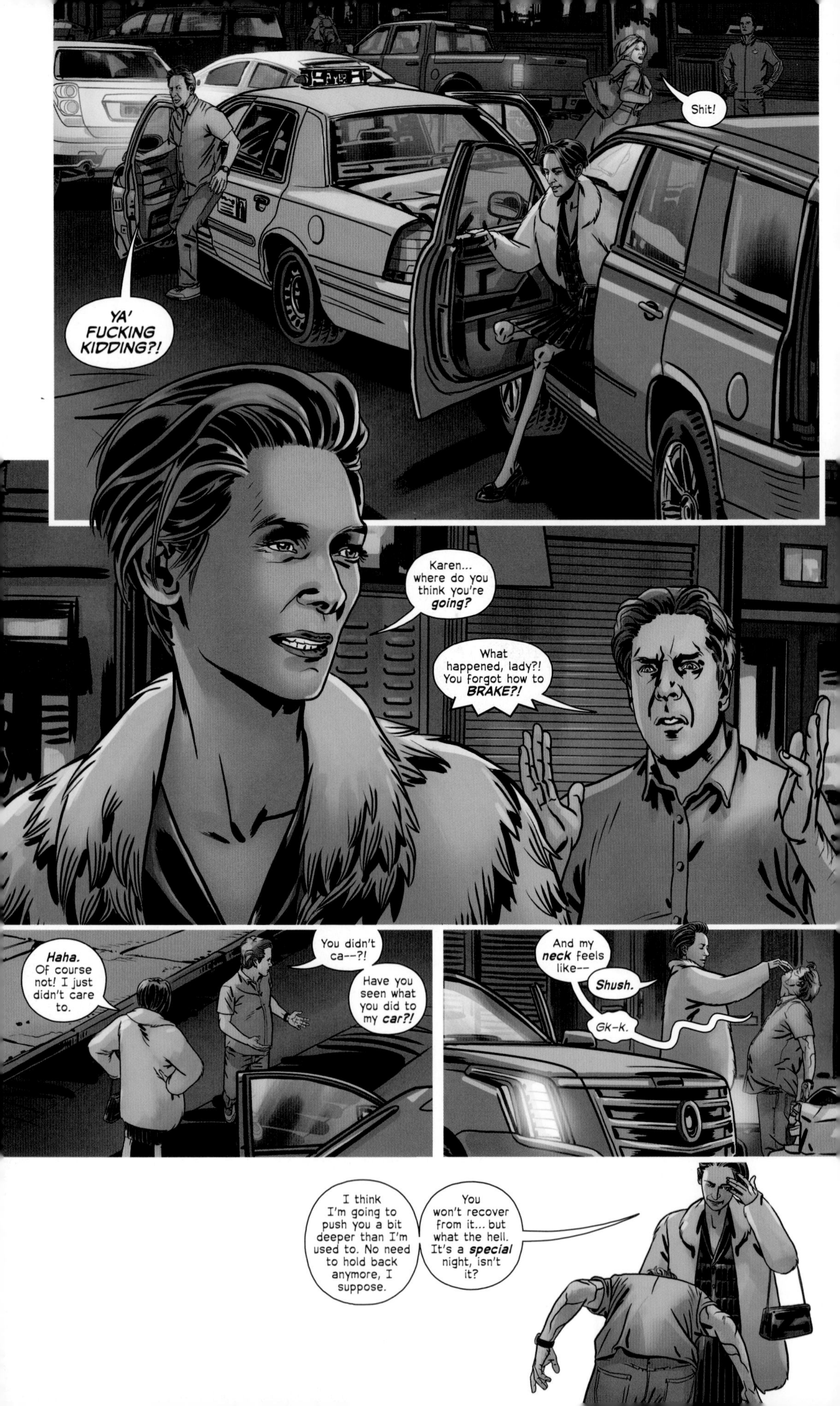
Shit!
YA' FUCKING KIDDING?!
Karen... where do you think you're *going?*
What happened, lady?! You forgot how to *BRAKE?!*
Haha. Of course not! I just didn't care to.
You didn't ca--?!
Have you seen what you did to my ***car?!***
And my ***neck*** feels like--
Shush.
Gk-k.
I think I'm going to push you a bit deeper than I'm used to. No need to hold back anymore, I suppose.
You won't recover from it... but what the hell. It's a ***special*** night, isn't it?

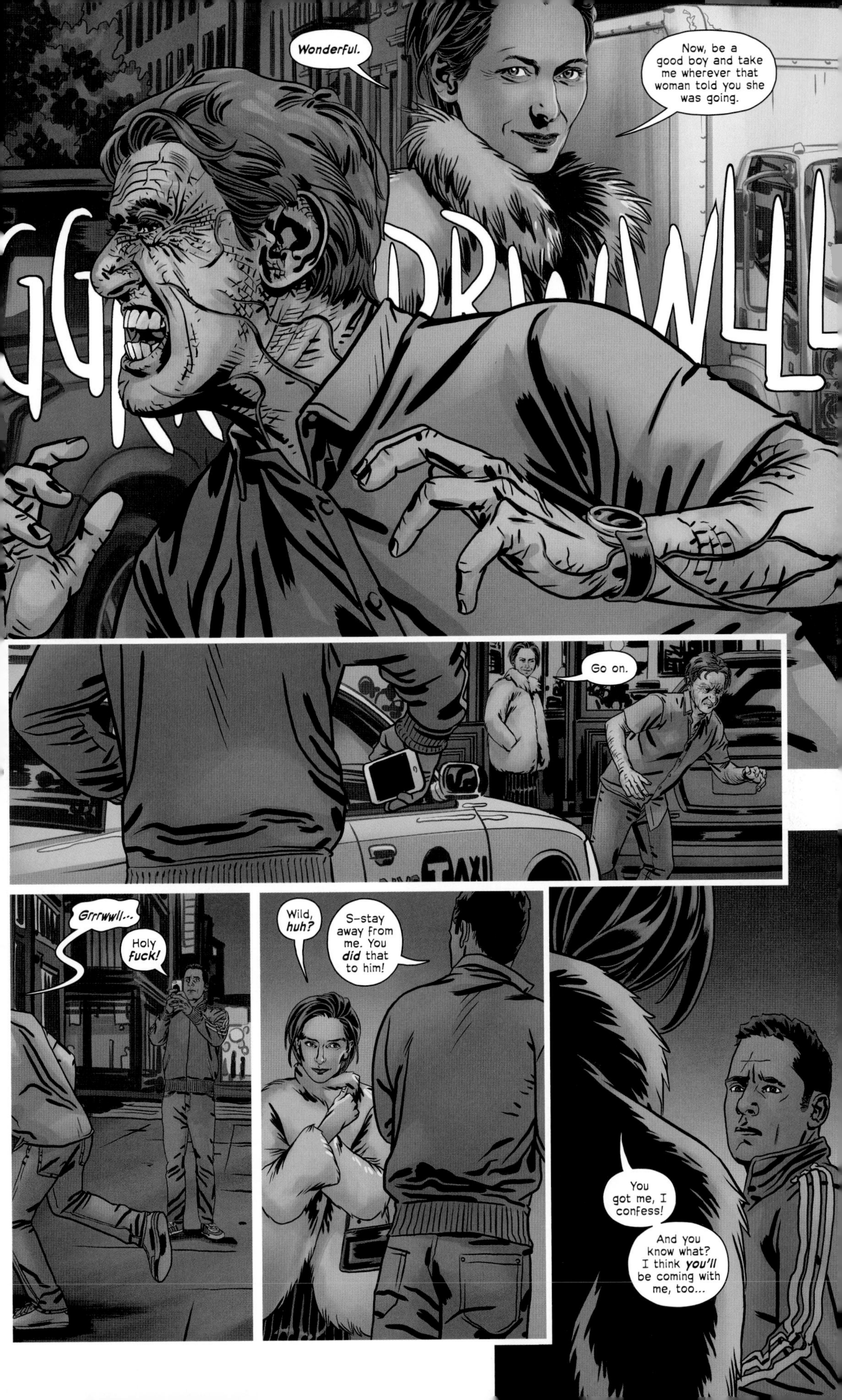
Wonderful.
Now, be a good boy and take me wherever that woman told you she was going.
Go on.
Grrrwwll...
Holy *fuck!*
Wild, *huh?*
S-stay away from me. You *did* that to him!
You got me, I confess!
And you know what? I think *you'll* be coming with me, too...

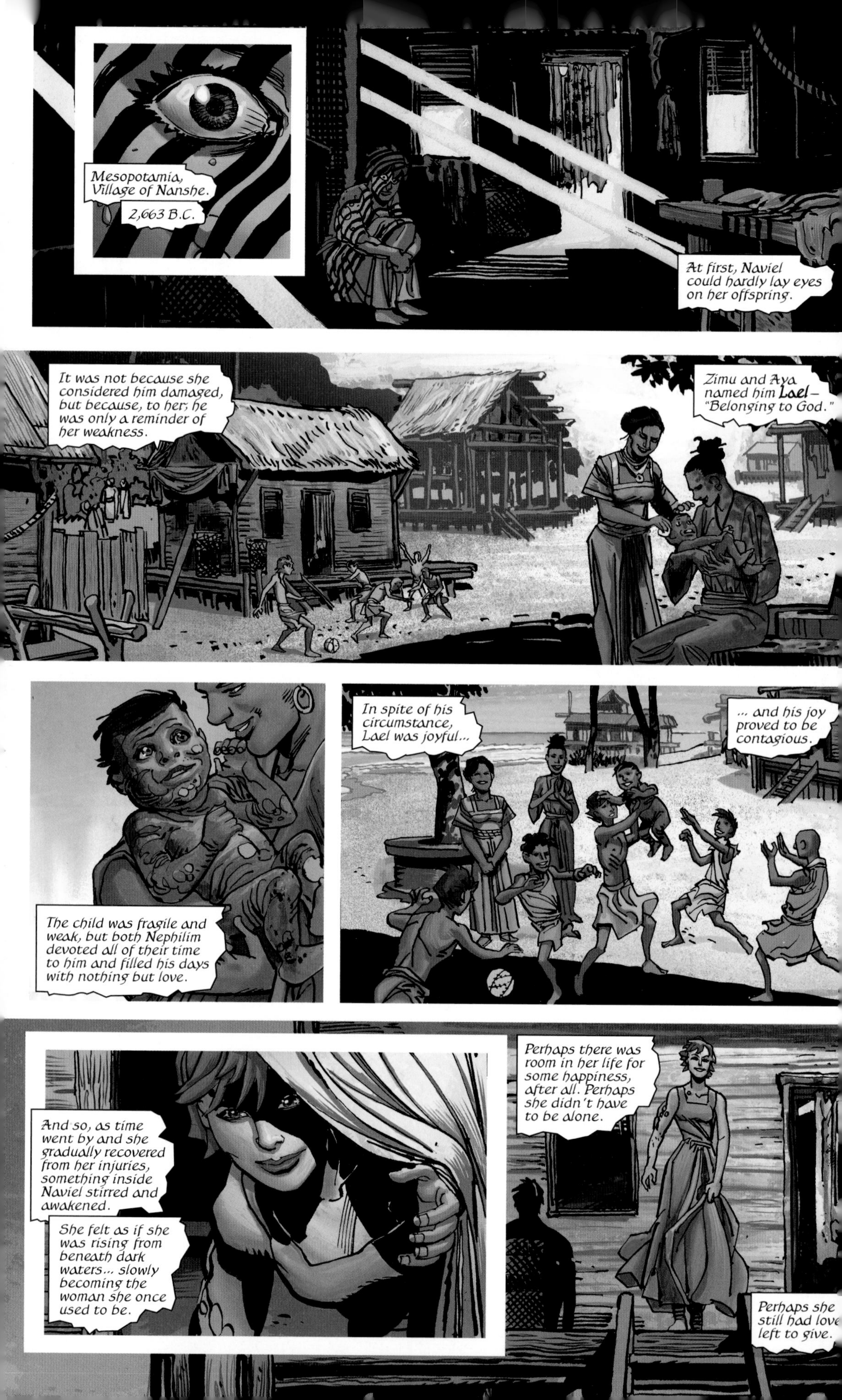

Mesopotamia, Village of Nanshe.
2,663 B.C.
At first, Naviel could hardly lay eyes on her offspring.
It was not because she considered him damaged, but because, to her, he was only a reminder of her weakness.
Zimu and Aya named him Lael— "Belonging to God."
The child was fragile and weak, but both Nephilim devoted all of their time to him and filled his days with nothing but love.
In spite of his circumstance, Lael was joyful...
... and his joy proved to be contagious.
And so, as time went by and she gradually recovered from her injuries, something inside Naviel stirred and awakened.
She felt as if she was rising from beneath dark waters... slowly becoming the woman she once used to be.
Perhaps there was room in her life for some happiness, after all. Perhaps she didn't have to be alone.
Perhaps she still had love left to give.

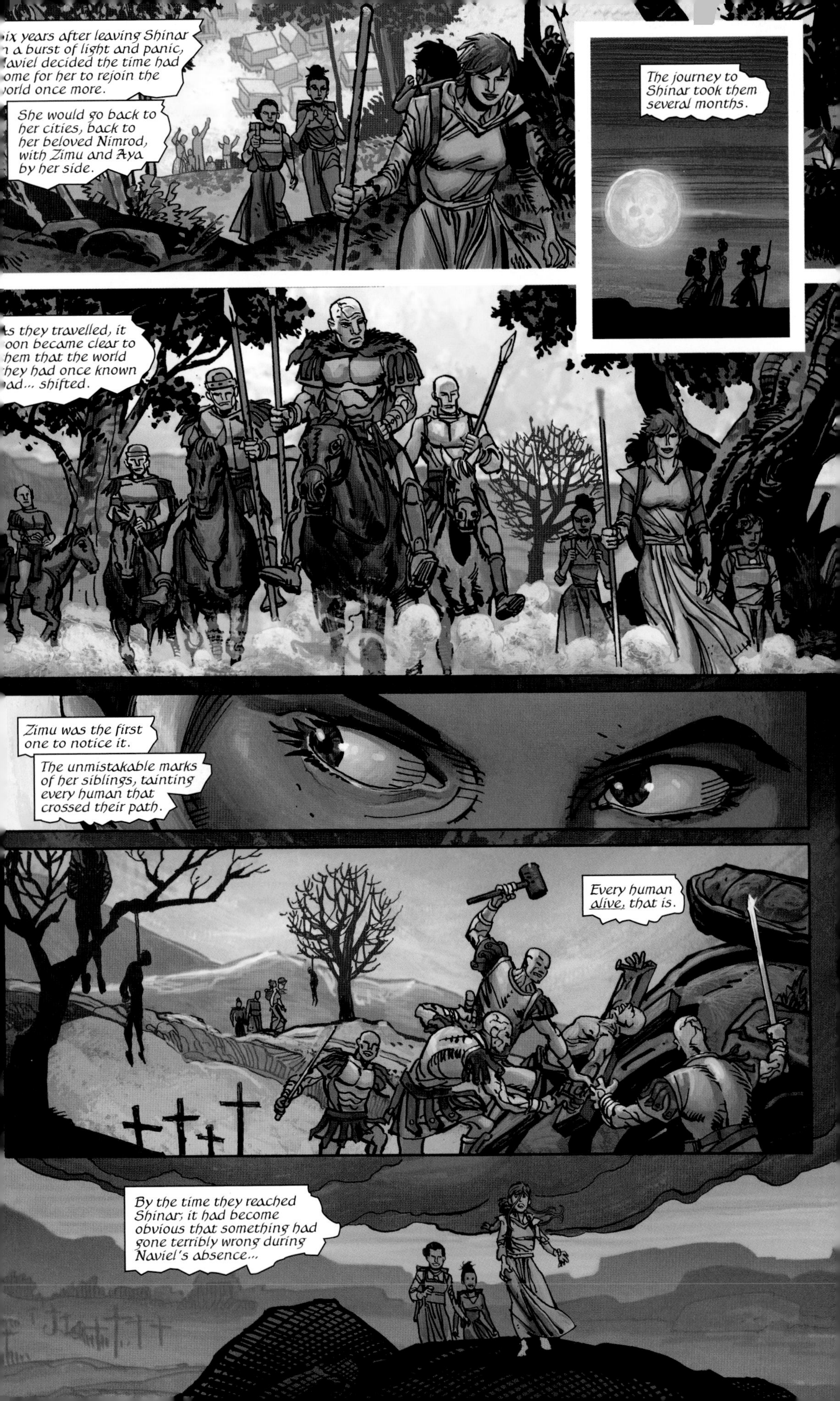

ix years after leaving Shinar
n a burst of light and panic,
aviel decided the time had
ome for her to rejoin the
orld once more.
She would go back to her cities, back to her beloved Nimrod, with Zimu and Aya by her side.
The journey to Shinar took them several months.
s they travelled, it
oon became clear to
hem that the world
hey had once known
ad... shifted.
Zimu was the first one to notice it.
The unmistakable marks of her siblings, tainting every human that crossed their path.
Every human alive, that is.
By the time they reached Shinar, it had become obvious that something had gone terribly wrong during Naviel's absence...

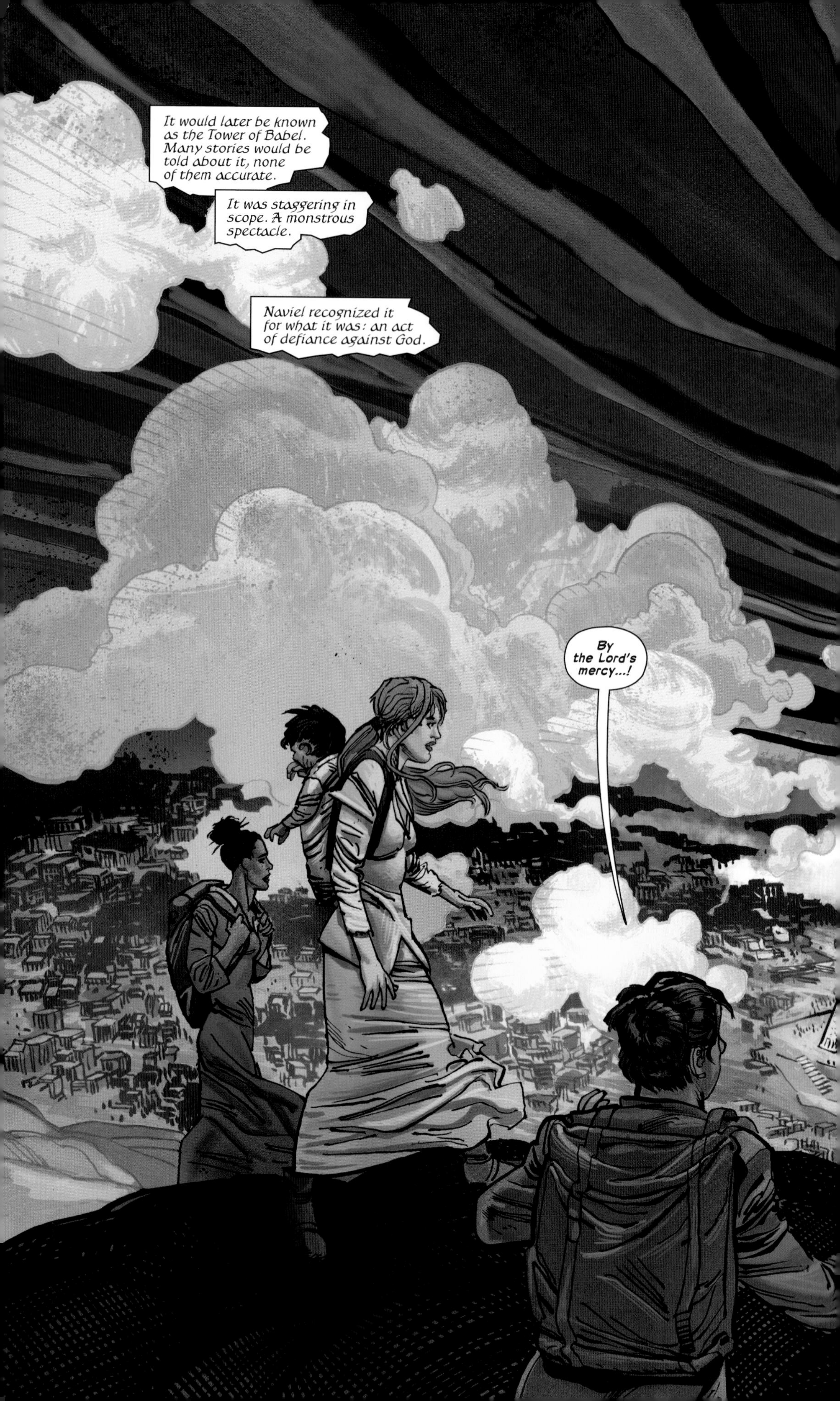
It would later be known as the Tower of Babel. Many stories would be told about it, none of them accurate.
It was staggering in scope. A monstrous spectacle.
Naviel recognized it for what it was: an act of defiance against God.
By the Lord's mercy...!

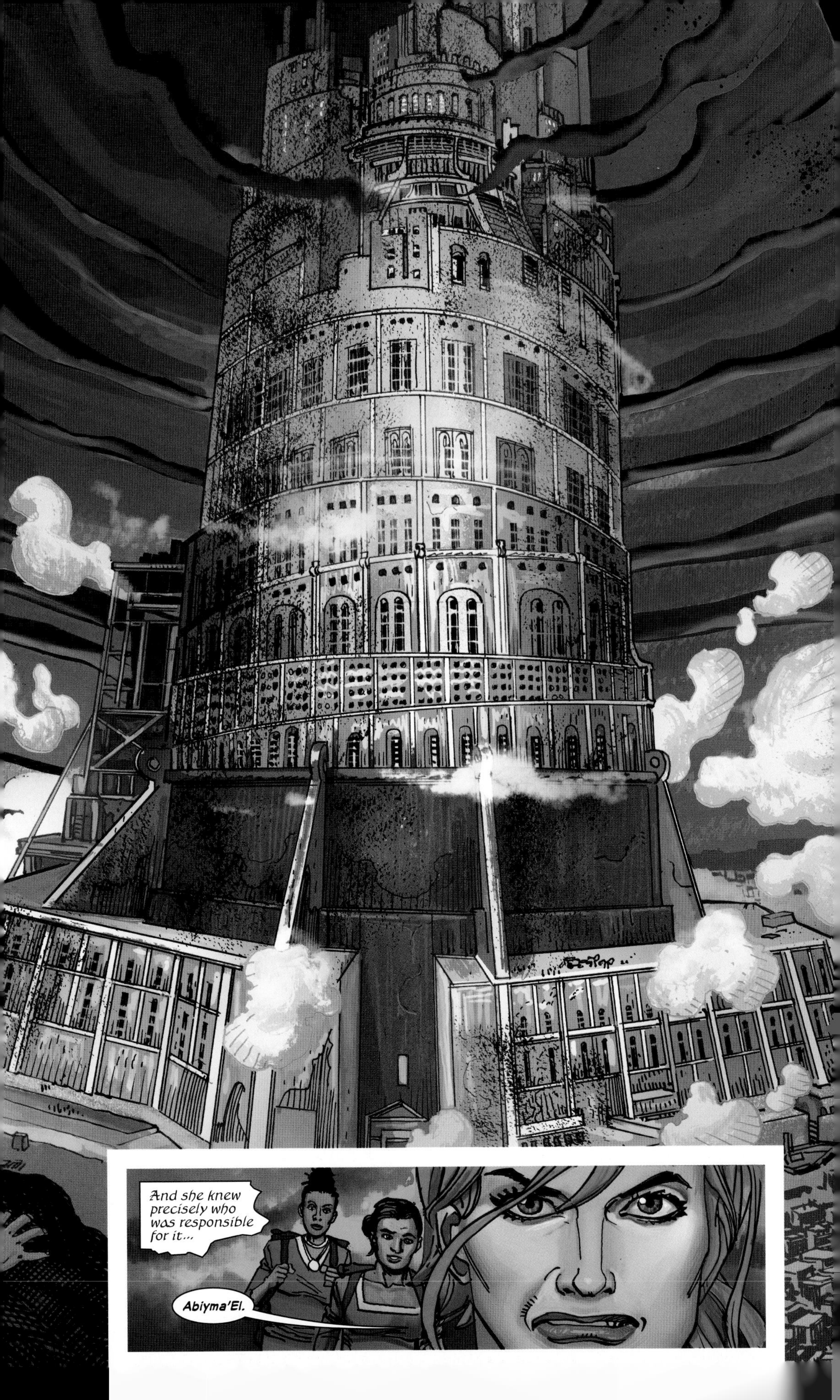

And she knew precisely who was responsible for it...
Abiyma'El.

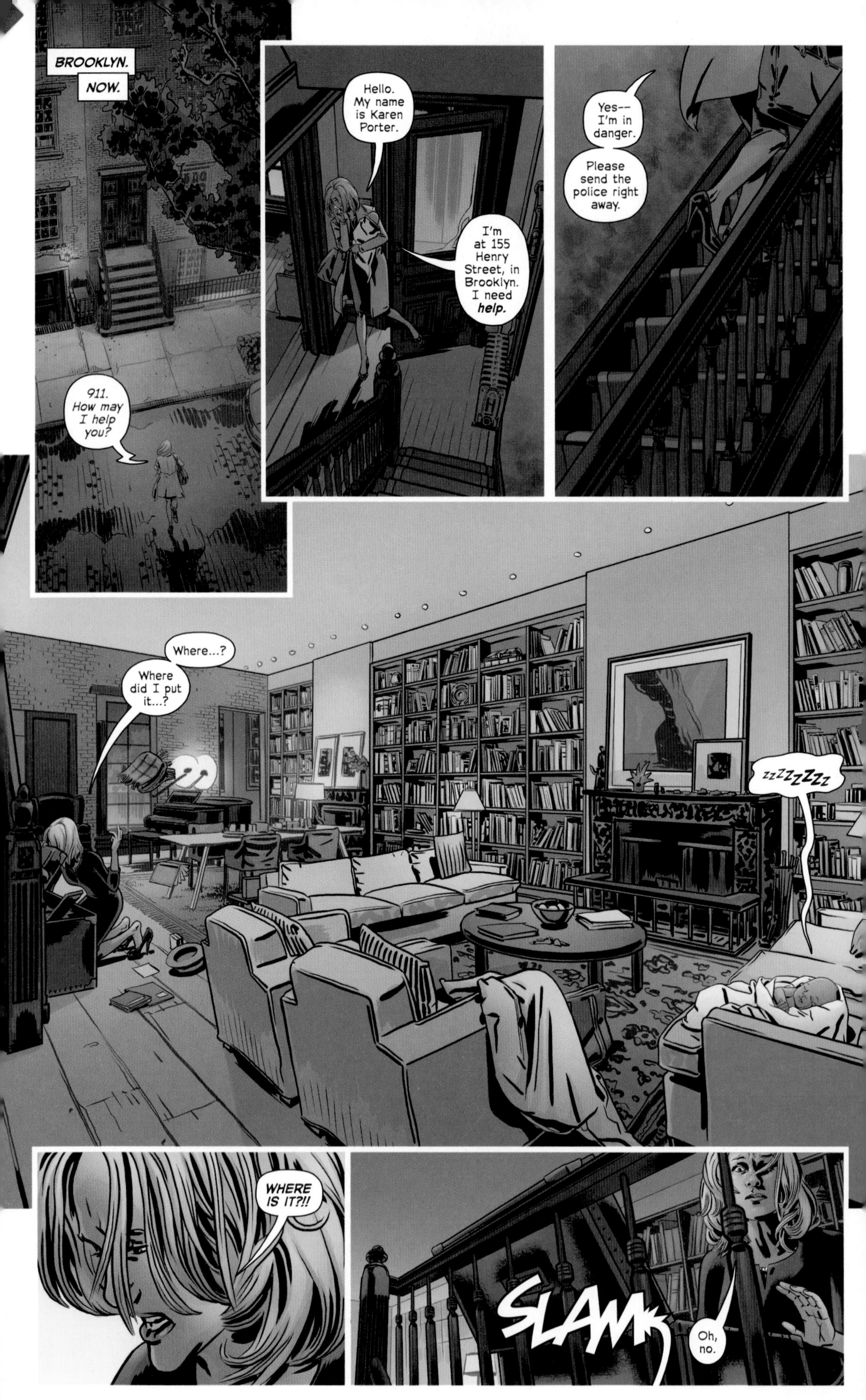

BROOKLYN.
NOW.
911. How may I help you?
Hello. My name is Karen Porter.
I'm at 155 Henry Street, in Brooklyn. I need help.
Yes-- I'm in danger.
Please send the police right away.
Where...?
Where did I put it...?
zzZZZZZz
WHERE IS IT?!!
SLAM
Oh, no.

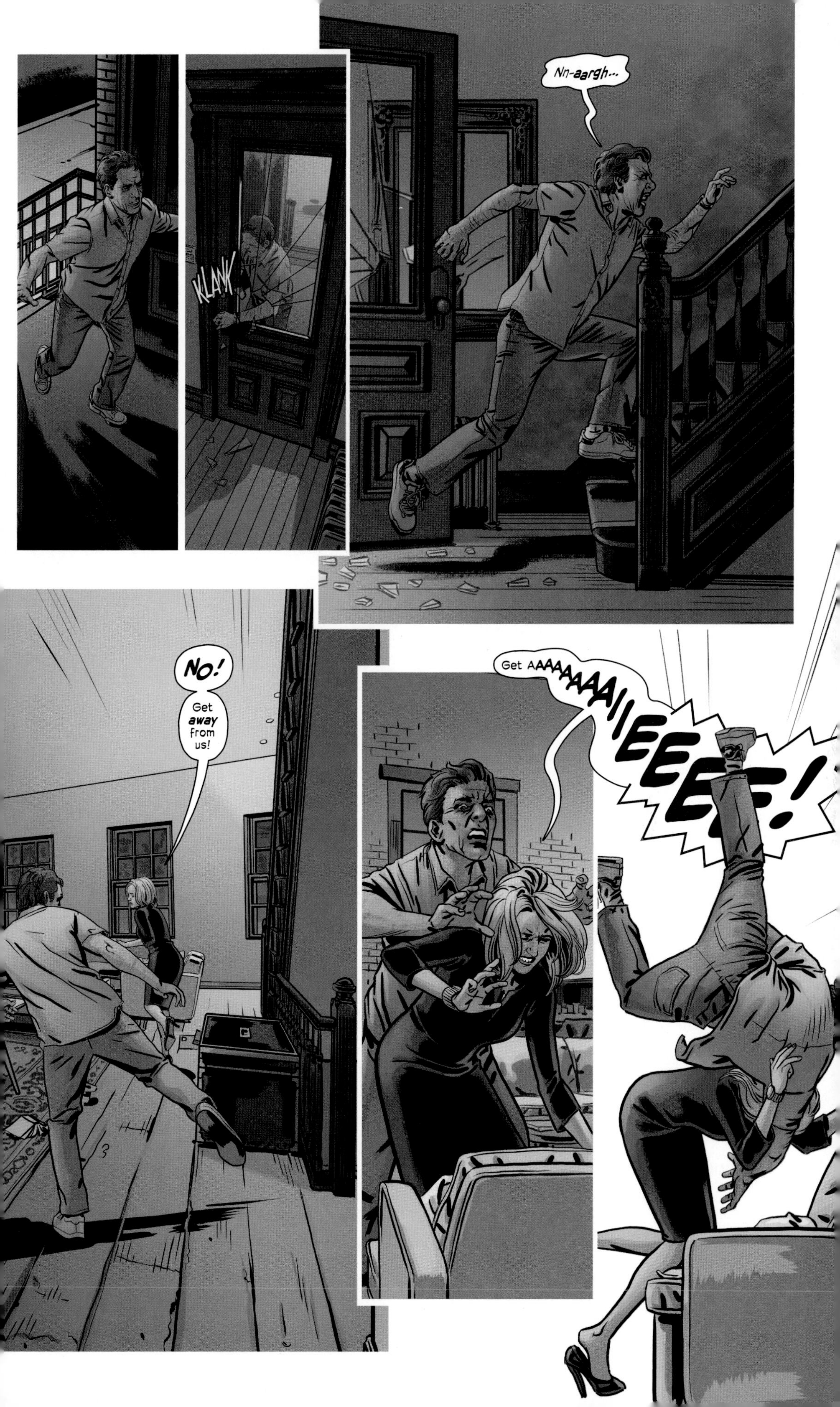
KLANK
Nn-aargh...
NO!
Get away from us!
Get AAAAAAAAIIEEEEE!

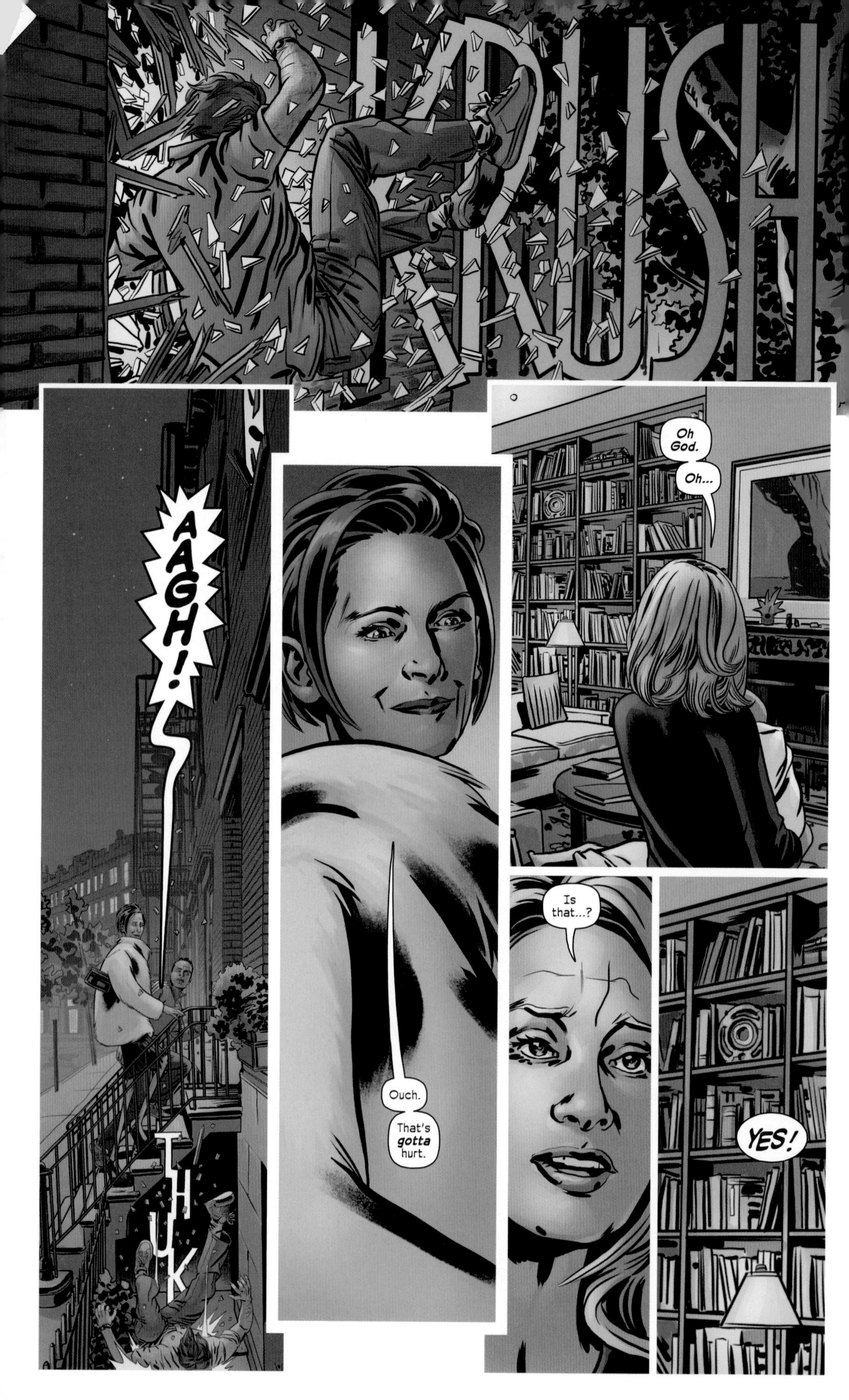
KRUSH
AAGH!
THUK
Ouch.
That's ***gotta*** hurt.
Oh God.
Oh...
Is that...?
YES!

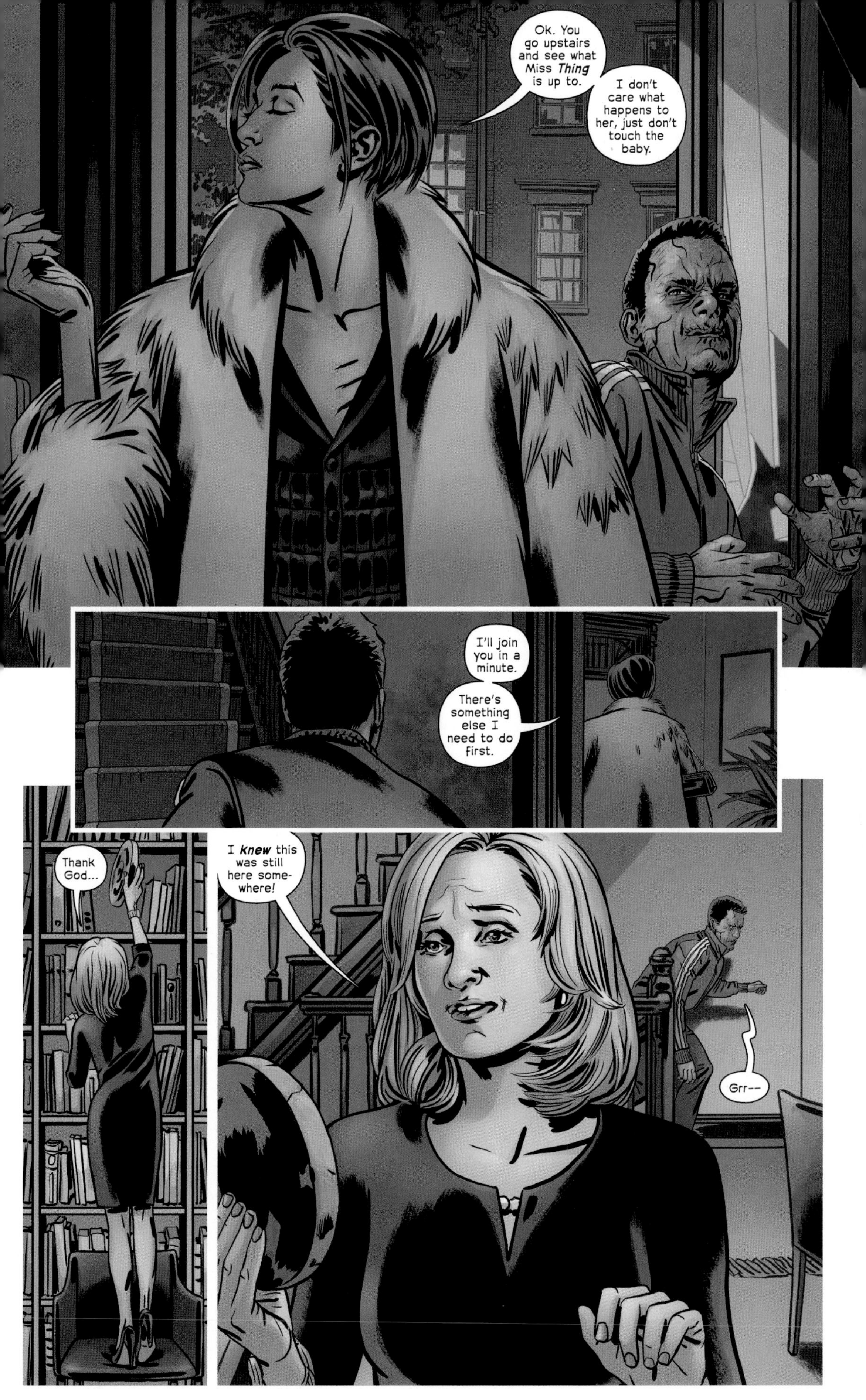

Ok. You go upstairs and see what Miss *Thing* is up to.
I don't care what happens to her, just don't touch the baby.
I'll join you in a minute.
There's something else I need to do first.
Thank God...
I ***knew*** this was still here some-where!
Grr--

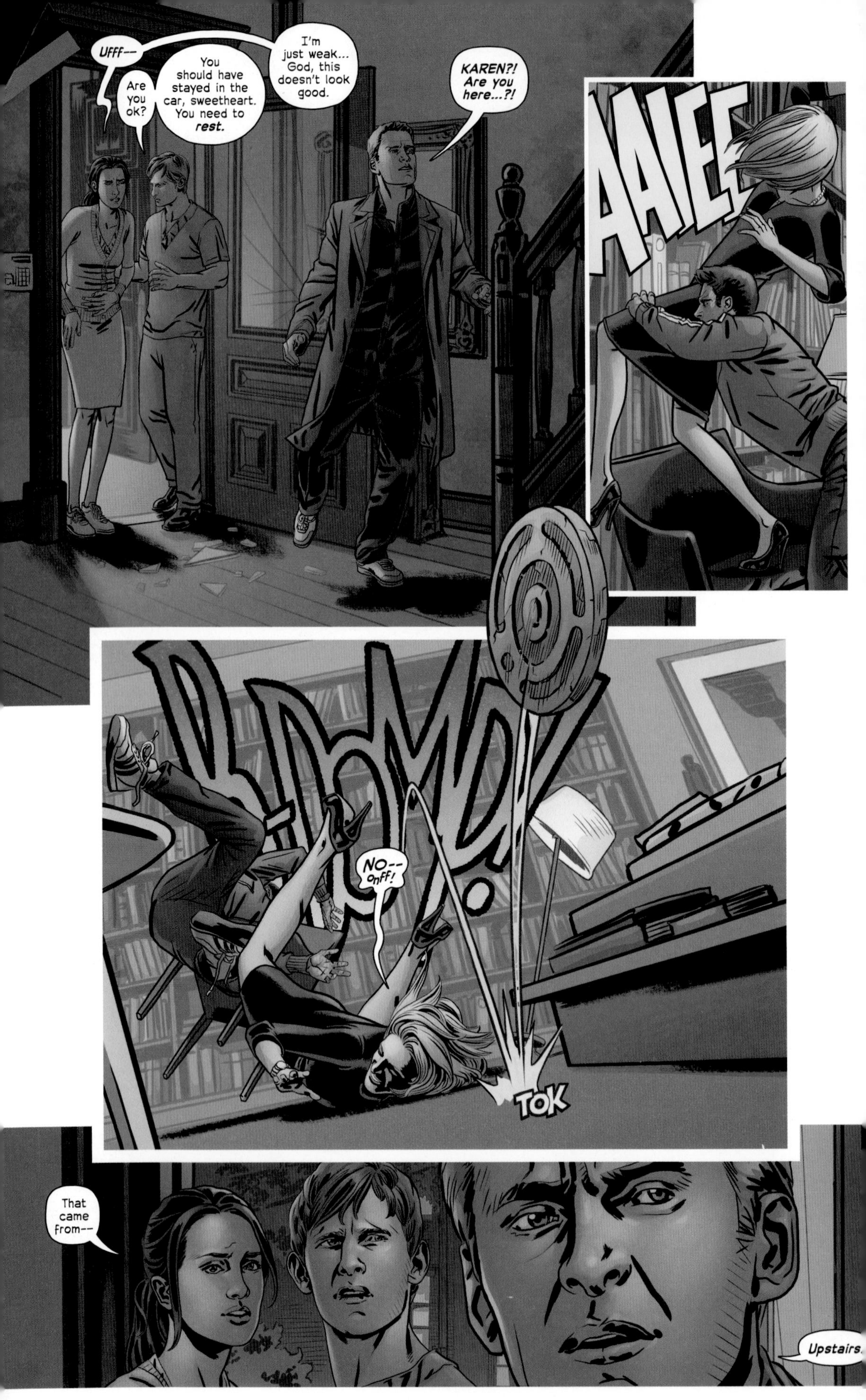
UFFF--
Are you ok?
You should have stayed in the car, sweetheart. You need to *rest.*
I'm just weak... God, this doesn't look good.
KAREN?! Are you here...?!
AAIEE
BOOM!
NO-- onff!
TOK
That came from--
Upstairs.

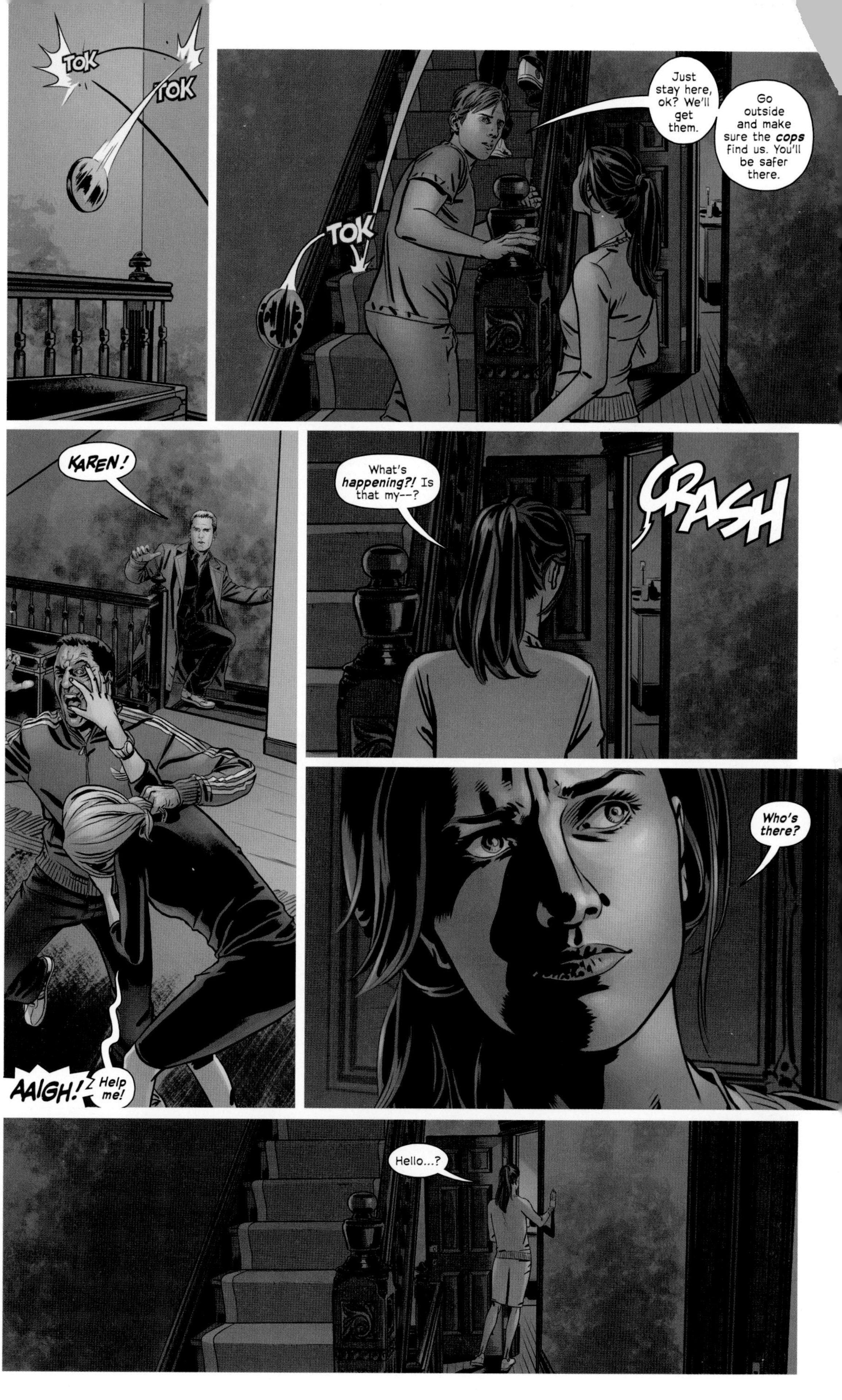
TOK
TOK
Just stay here, ok? We'll get them.
Go outside and make sure the *cops* find us. You'll be safer there.
TOK
KAREN!
AAIGH!
Help me!
What's *happening?!* Is that my--?
CRASH
Who's there?
Hello...?

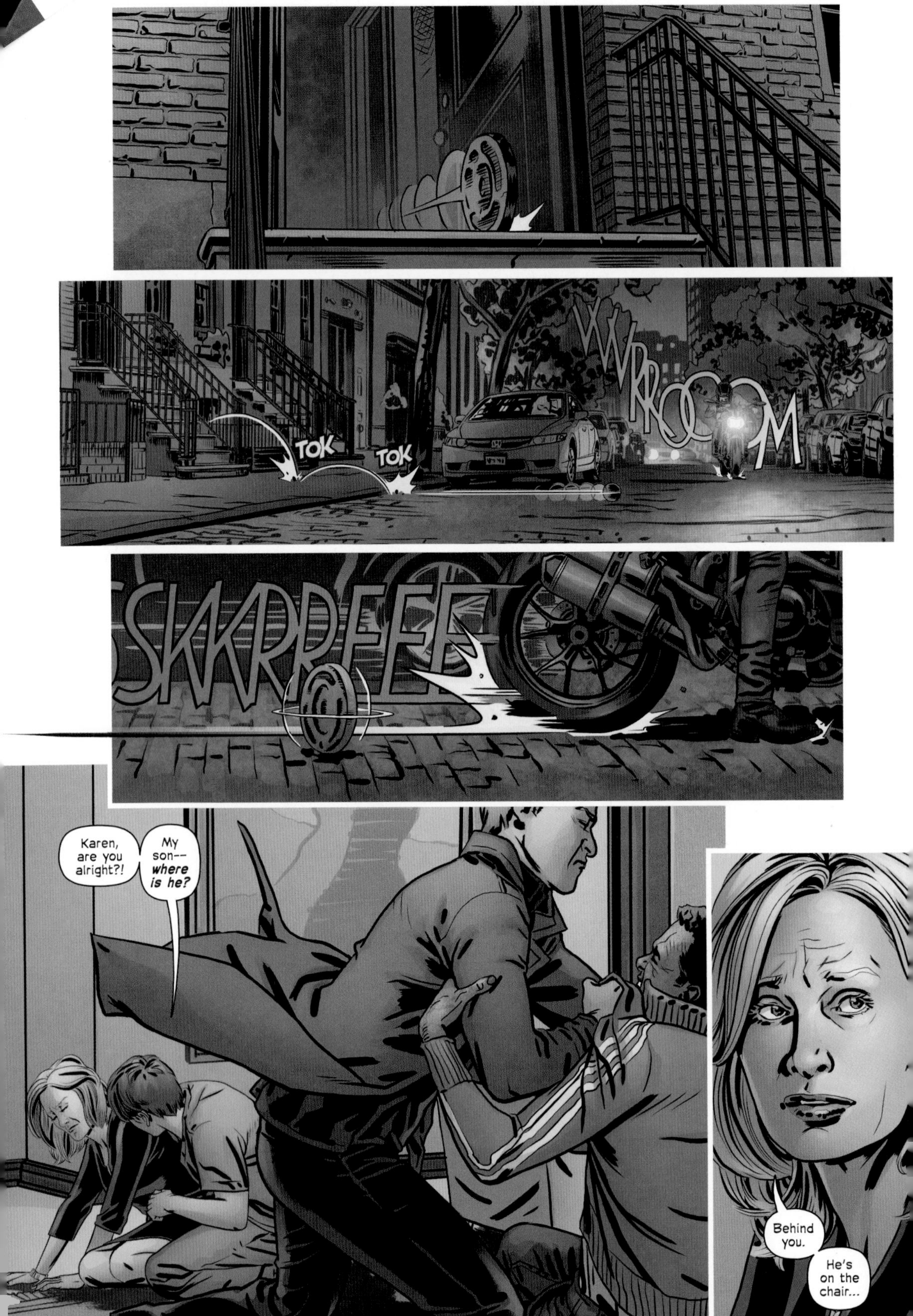
TOK
TOK
VVVRRROOOOM
SKKRRFFFF
Karen, are you alright?!
My son-- *where is he?*
Behind you.
He's on the chair...

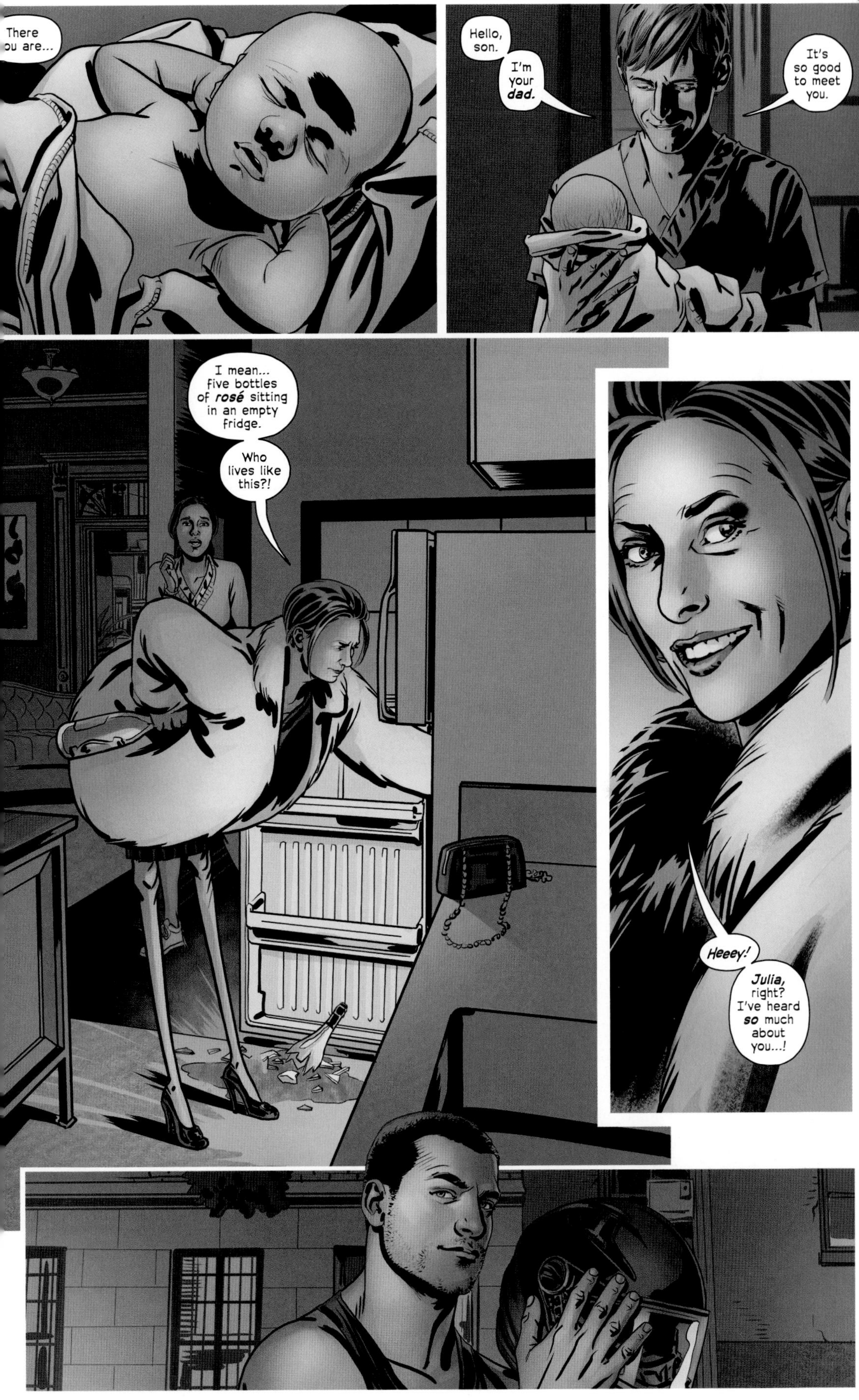

There
ou are...
Hello,
son.
I'm
your
dad.
It's
so good
to meet
you.
I mean...
five bottles
of *rosé* sitting
in an empty
fridge.
Who
lives like
this?!
Heeey!
Julia,
right?
I've heard
so much
about
you...!

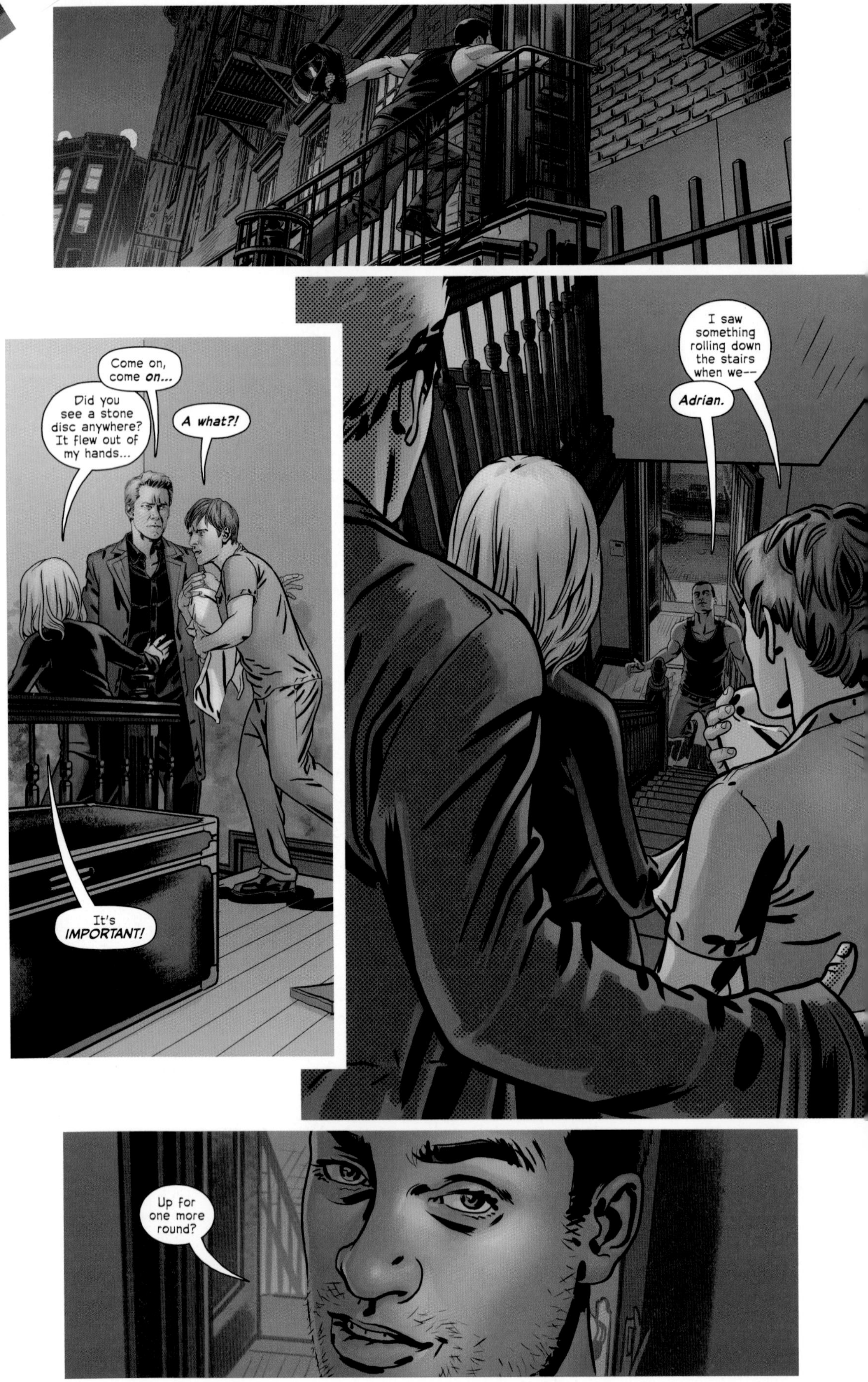
Come on, come on...
Did you see a stone disc anywhere? It flew out of my hands...
A what?!
It's IMPORTANT!
I saw something rolling down the stairs when we--
Adrian.
Up for one more round?

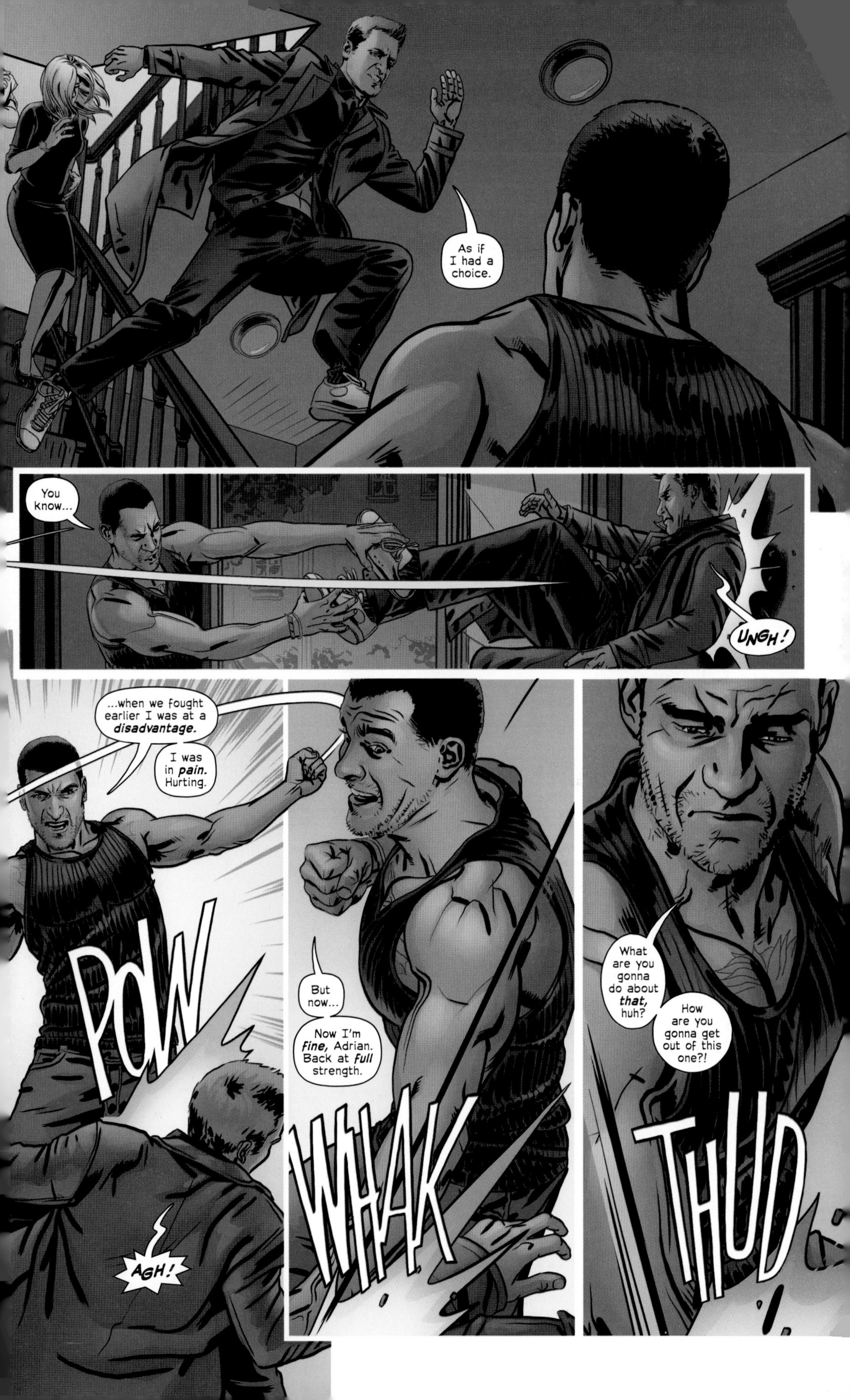
As if I had a choice.
You know...
UNGH!
...when we fought earlier I was at a ***disadvantage.***
I was in ***pain.*** Hurting.
POW
AGH!
But now...
Now I'm ***fine,*** Adrian. Back at ***full*** strength.
WHAK
What are you gonna do about ***that,*** huh?
How are you gonna get out of this one?!
THUD

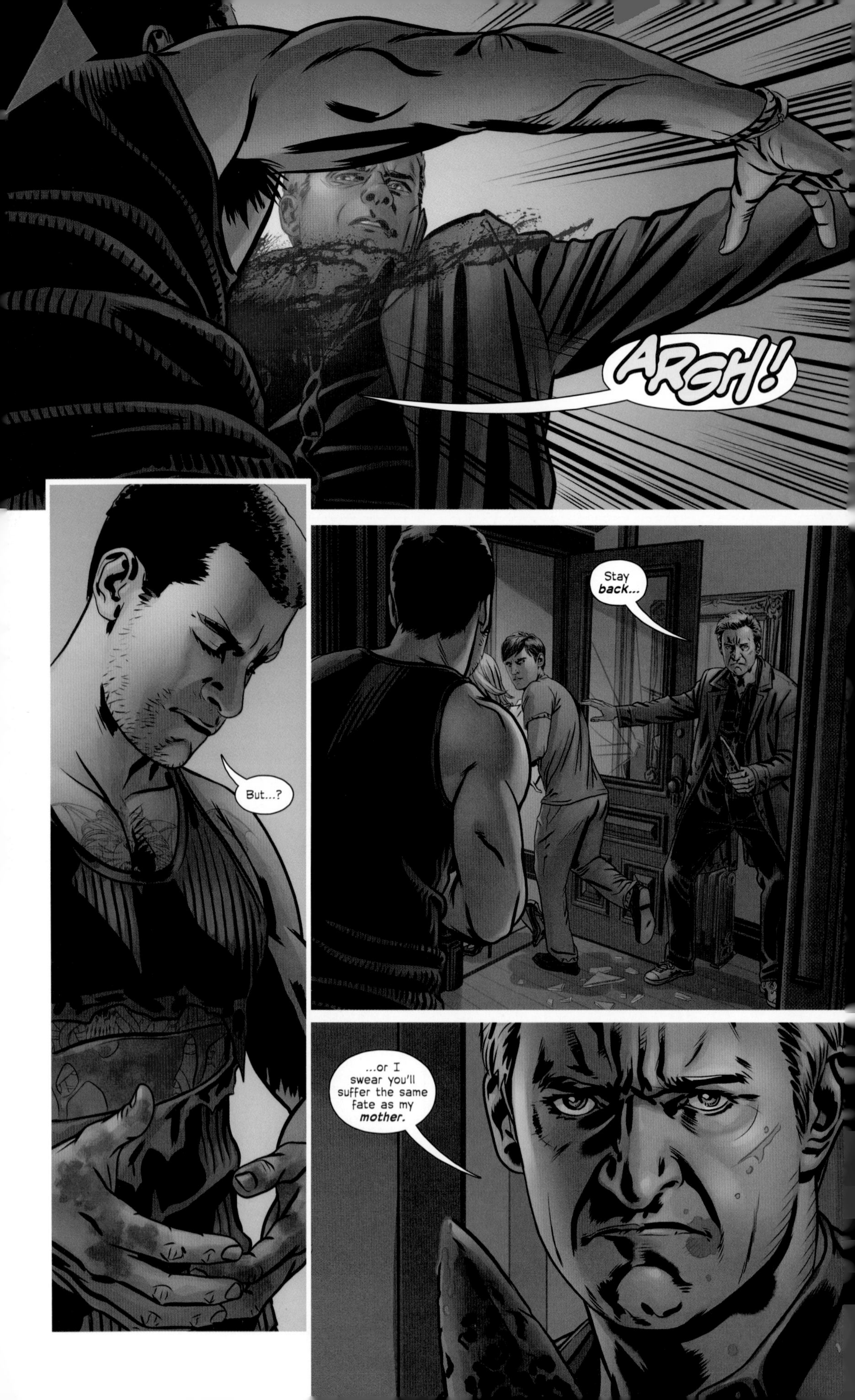
ARGH!
But...?
Stay back...
...or I swear you'll suffer the same fate as my mother.

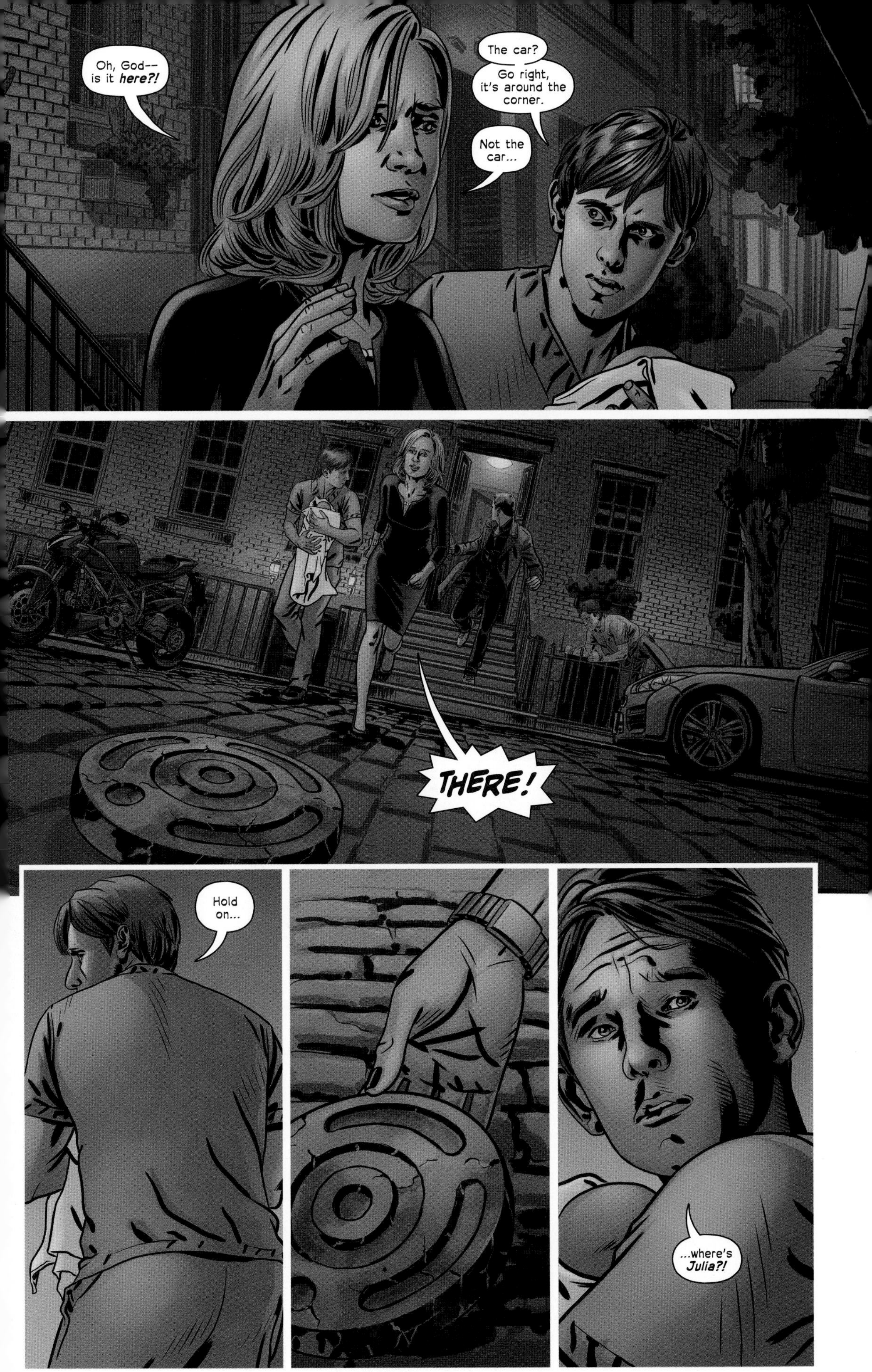
Oh, God--
is it here?!
The car?
Go right, it's around the corner.
Not the car...
THERE!
Hold on...
...where's Julia?!

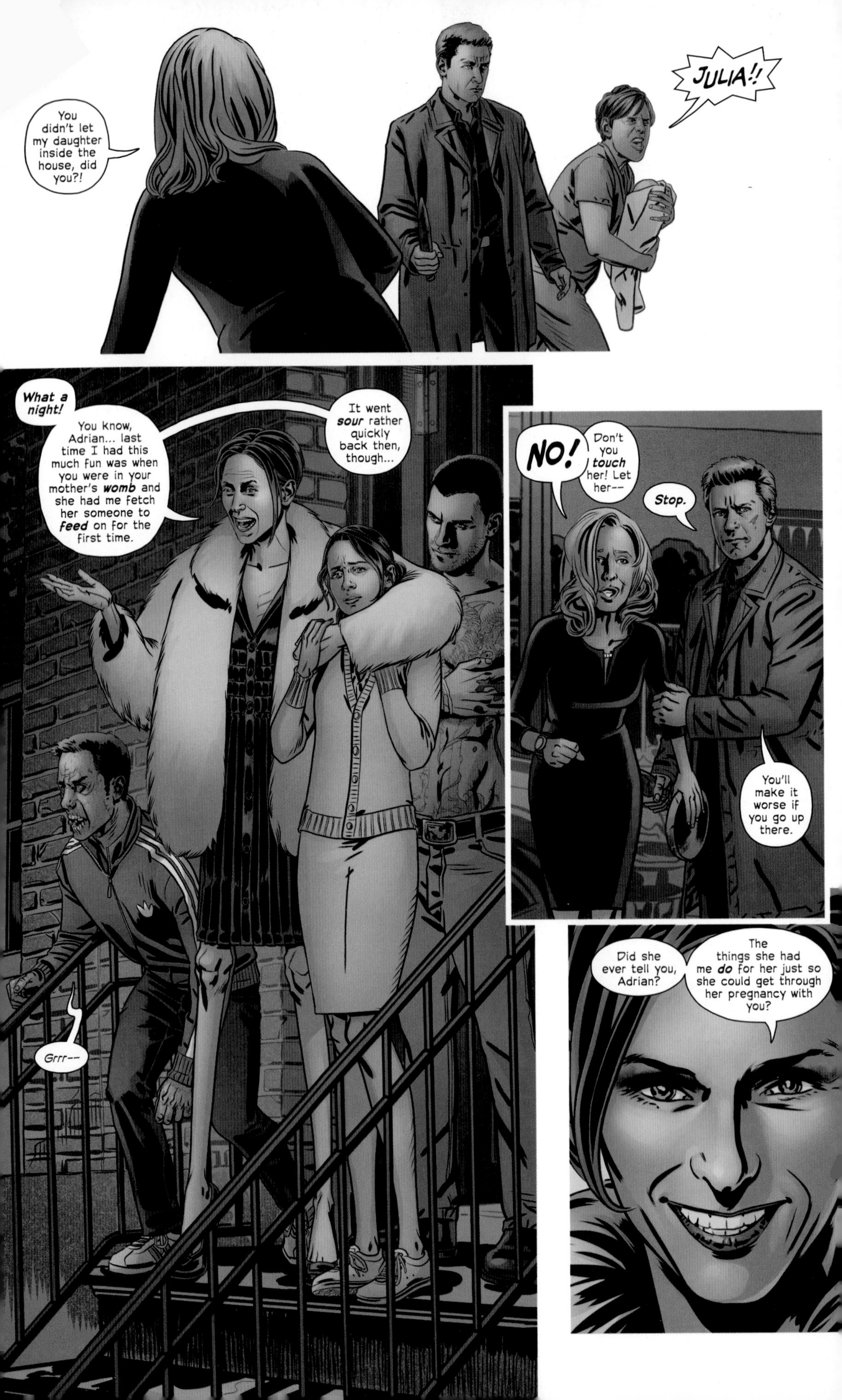
You didn't let my daughter inside the house, did you?!
JULIA!!
What a night!
You know, Adrian... last time I had this much fun was when you were in your mother's **womb** and she had me fetch her someone to **feed** on for the first time.
It went **sour** rather quickly back then, though...
Grrr--
NO!
Don't you **touch** her! Let her--
Stop.
You'll make it worse if you go up there.
Did she ever tell you, Adrian?
The things she had me **do** for her just so she could get through her pregnancy with you?

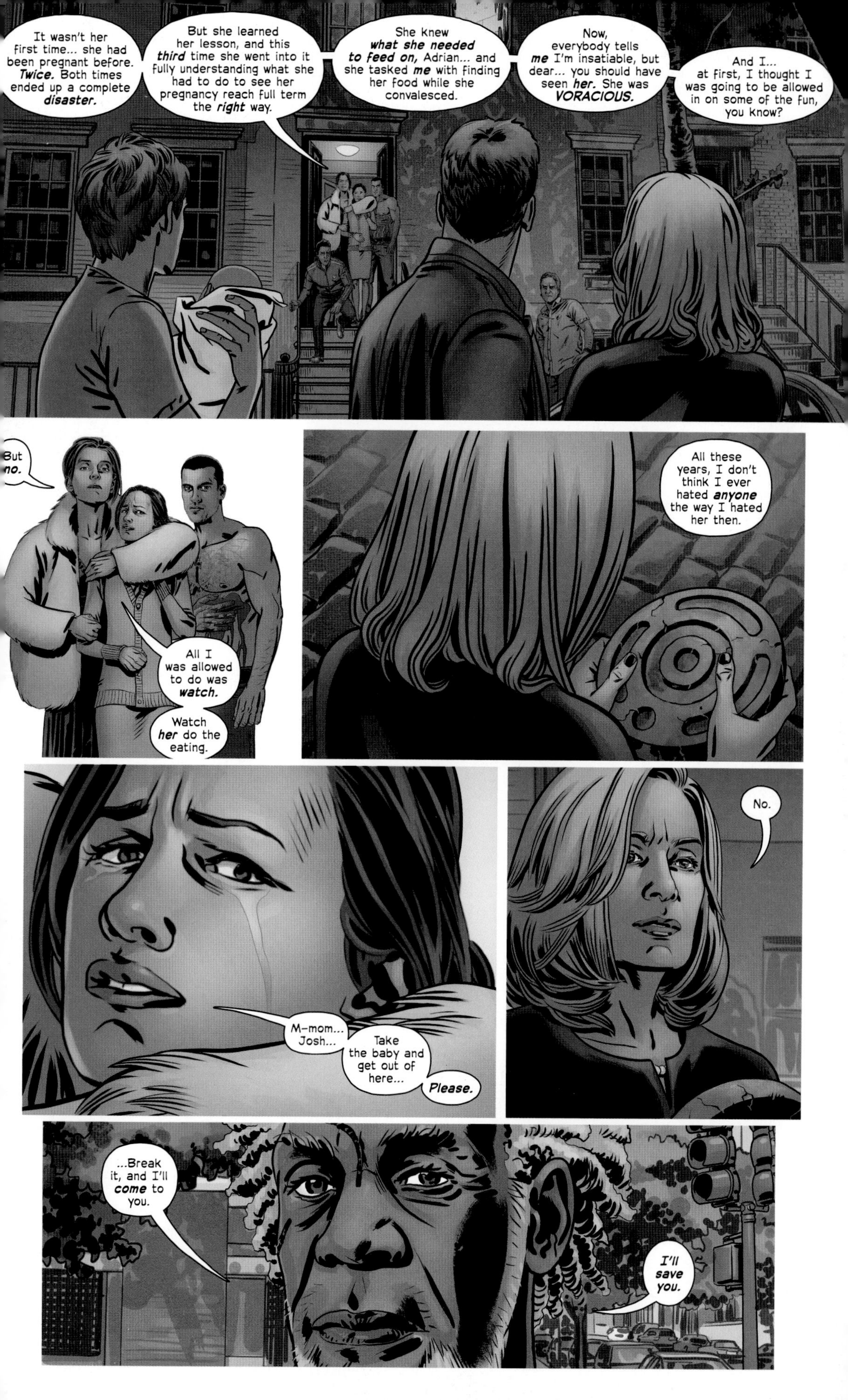
It wasn't her first time... she had been pregnant before. *Twice.* Both times ended up a complete *disaster.*
But she learned her lesson, and this *third* time she went into it fully understanding what she had to do to see her pregnancy reach full term the *right* way.
She knew *what she needed to feed on,* Adrian... and she tasked *me* with finding her food while she convalesced.
Now, everybody tells *me* I'm insatiable, but dear... you should have seen *her.* She was *VORACIOUS.*
And I... at first, I thought I was going to be allowed in on some of the fun, you know?
But *no.*
All I was allowed to do was *watch.*
Watch *her* do the eating.
All these years, I don't think I ever hated *anyone* the way I hated her then.
M-mom... Josh...
Take the baby and get out of here...
Please.
No.
...Break it, and I'll *come* to you.
I'll save you.

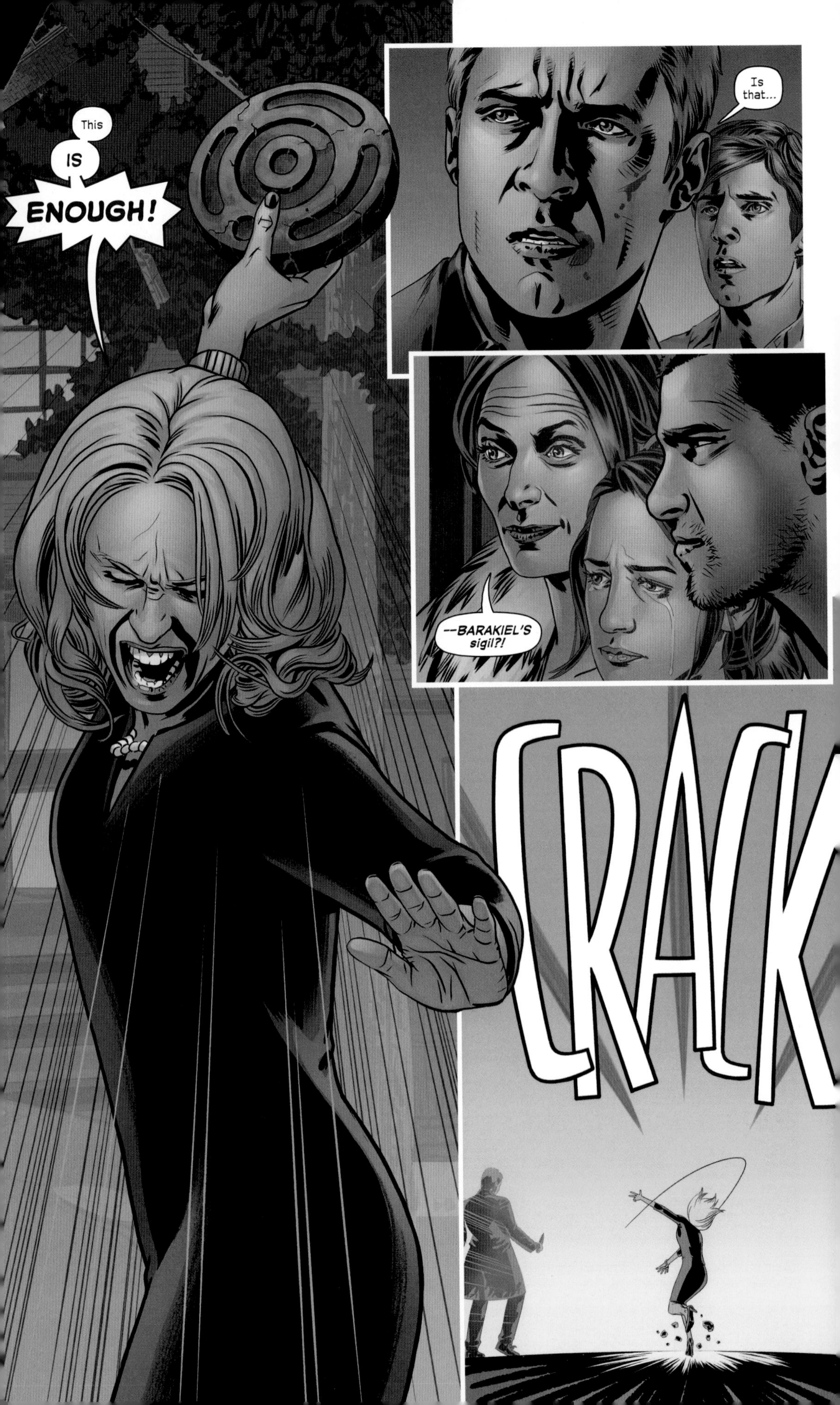
This
IS
ENOUGH!
Is that...
--BARAKIEL'S sigil?!
CRACK

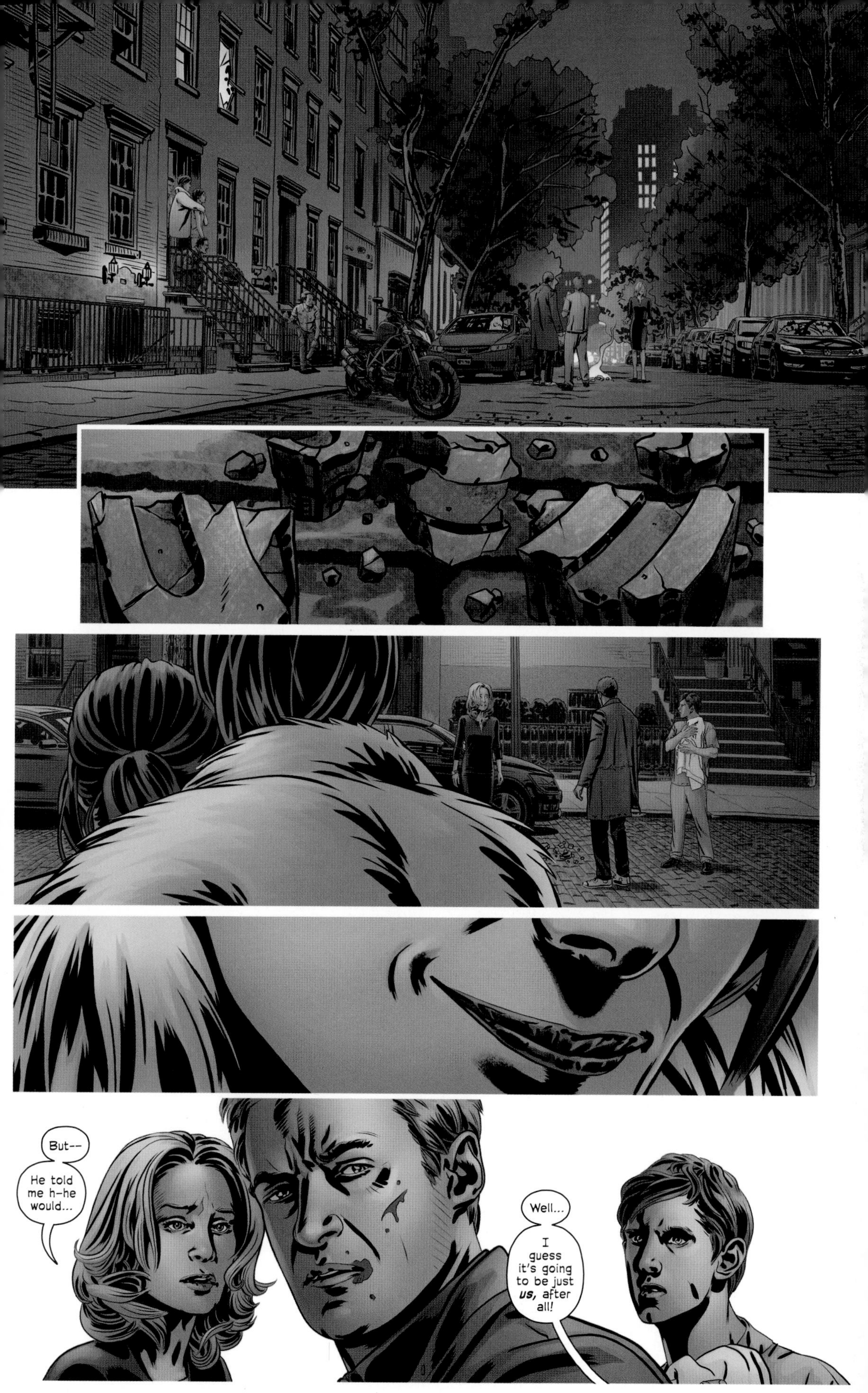

But--
He told me h-he would...
Well...
I guess it's going to be just *us,* after all!

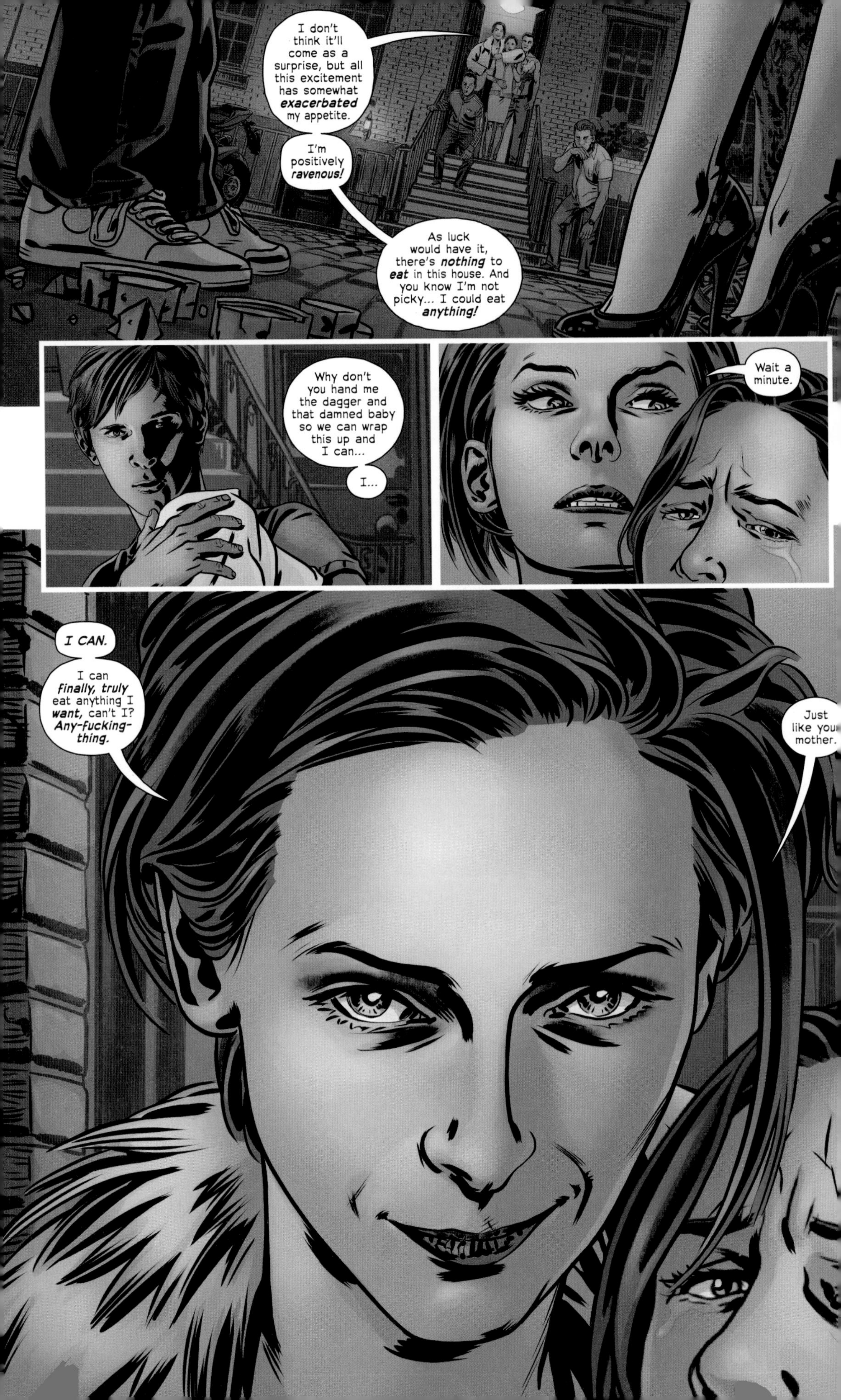
I don't think it'll come as a surprise, but all this excitement has somewhat *exacerbated* my appetite.
I'm positively *ravenous!*
As luck would have it, there's *nothing* to *eat* in this house. And you know I'm not picky... I could eat *anything!*
Why don't you hand me the dagger and that damned baby so we can wrap this up and I can...
I...
Wait a minute.
I CAN.
I can *finally, truly* eat anything I *want,* can't I? *Any-fucking-thing.*
Just like you mother.

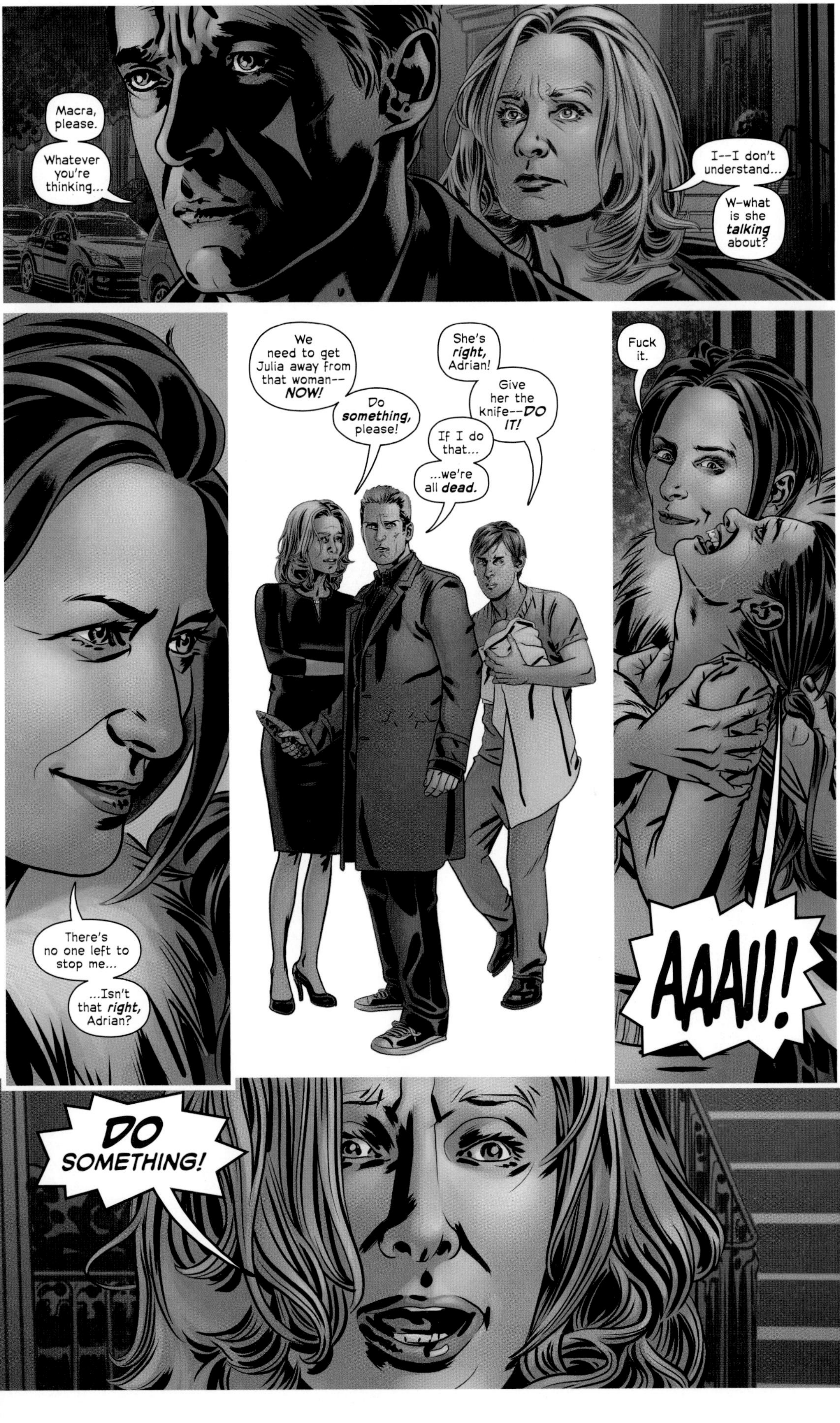
Macra, please.
Whatever you're thinking...
I--I don't understand...
W-what is she *talking* about?
There's no one left to stop me...
...Isn't that *right,* Adrian?
We need to get Julia away from that woman-- *NOW!*
Do *something,* please!
She's *right,* Adrian!
Give her the knife--*DO IT!*
If I do that...
...we're all *dead.*
Fuck it.
AAAII!
DO SOMETHING!

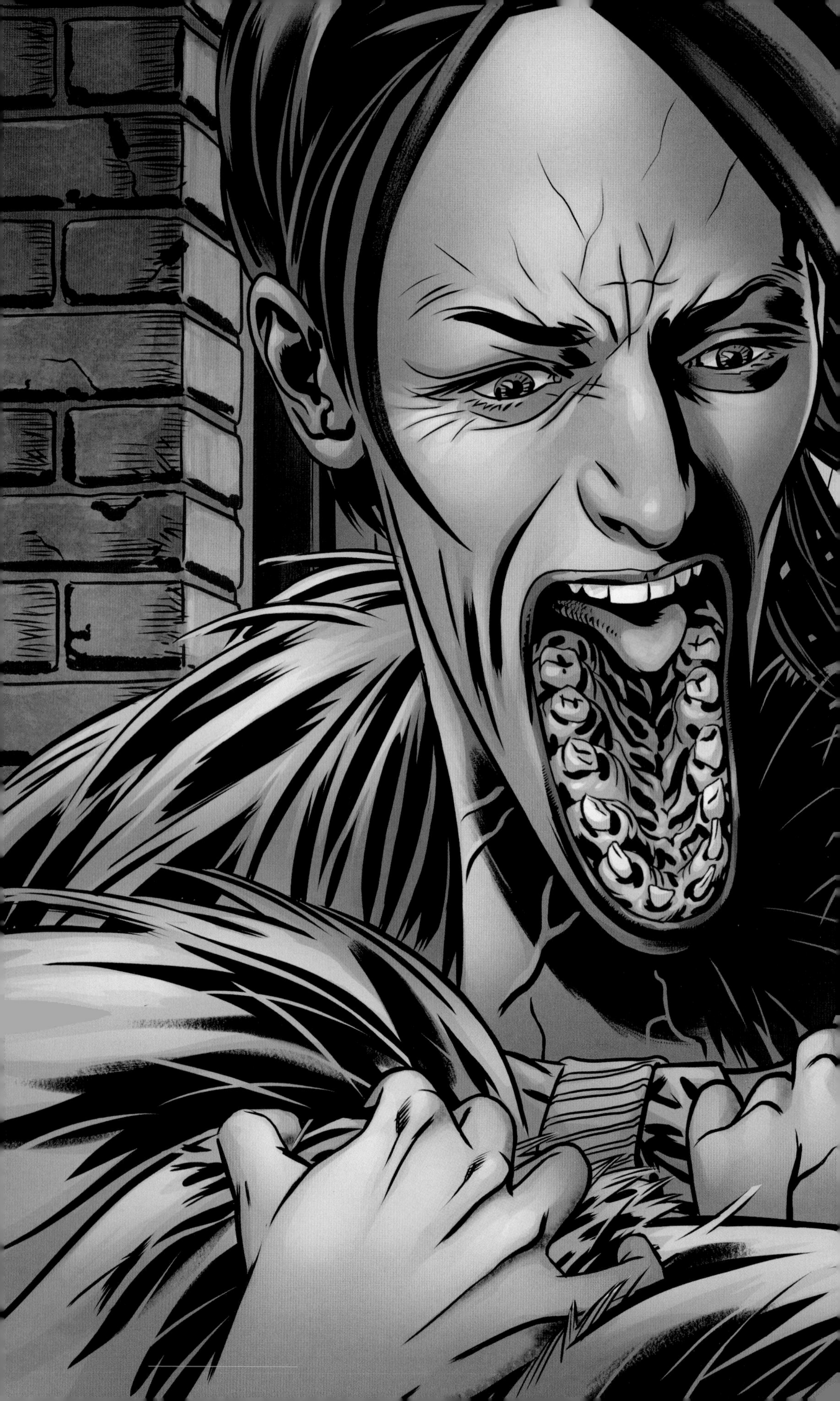

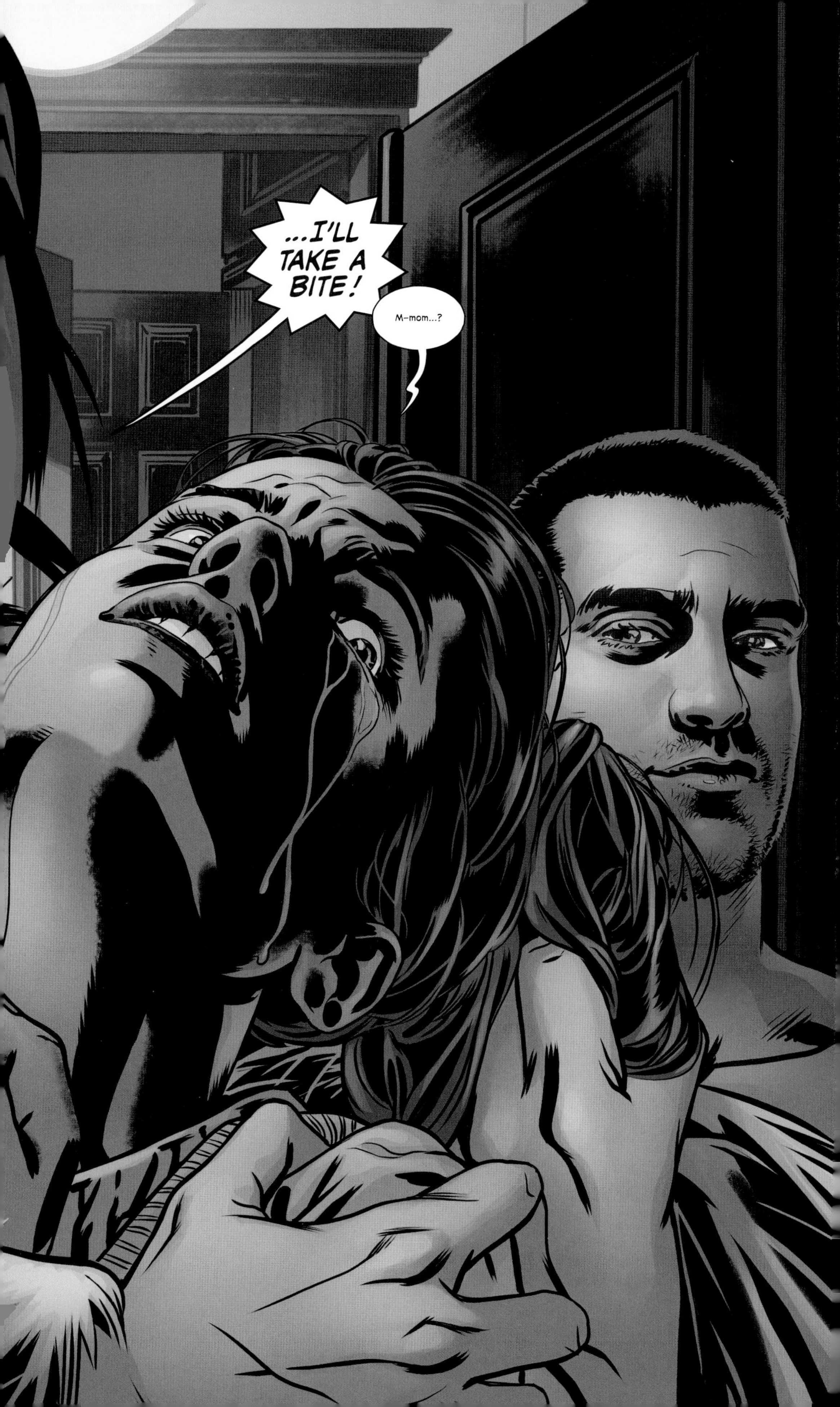
...I'LL TAKE A BITE!
M-mom...?

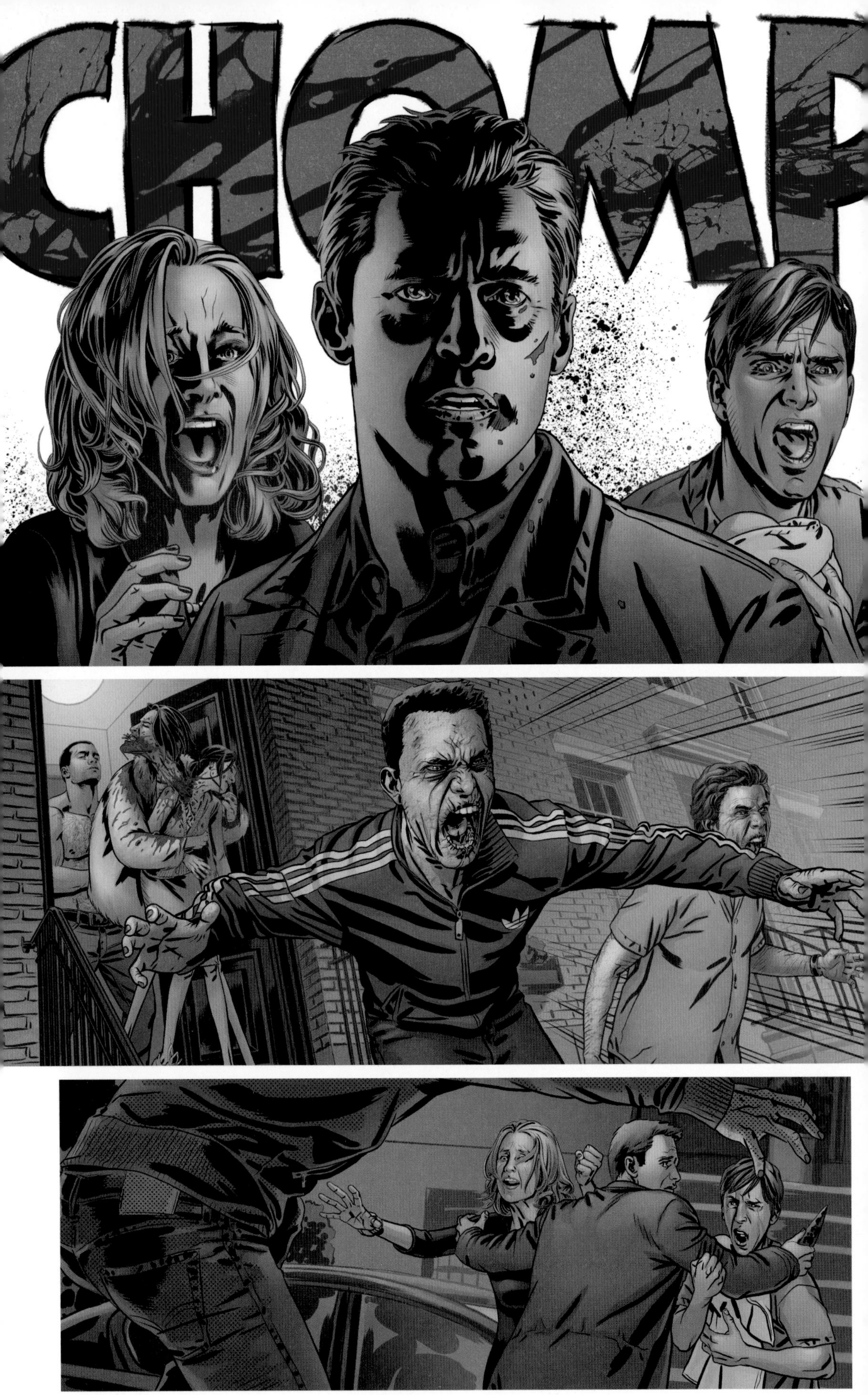
CHOMP

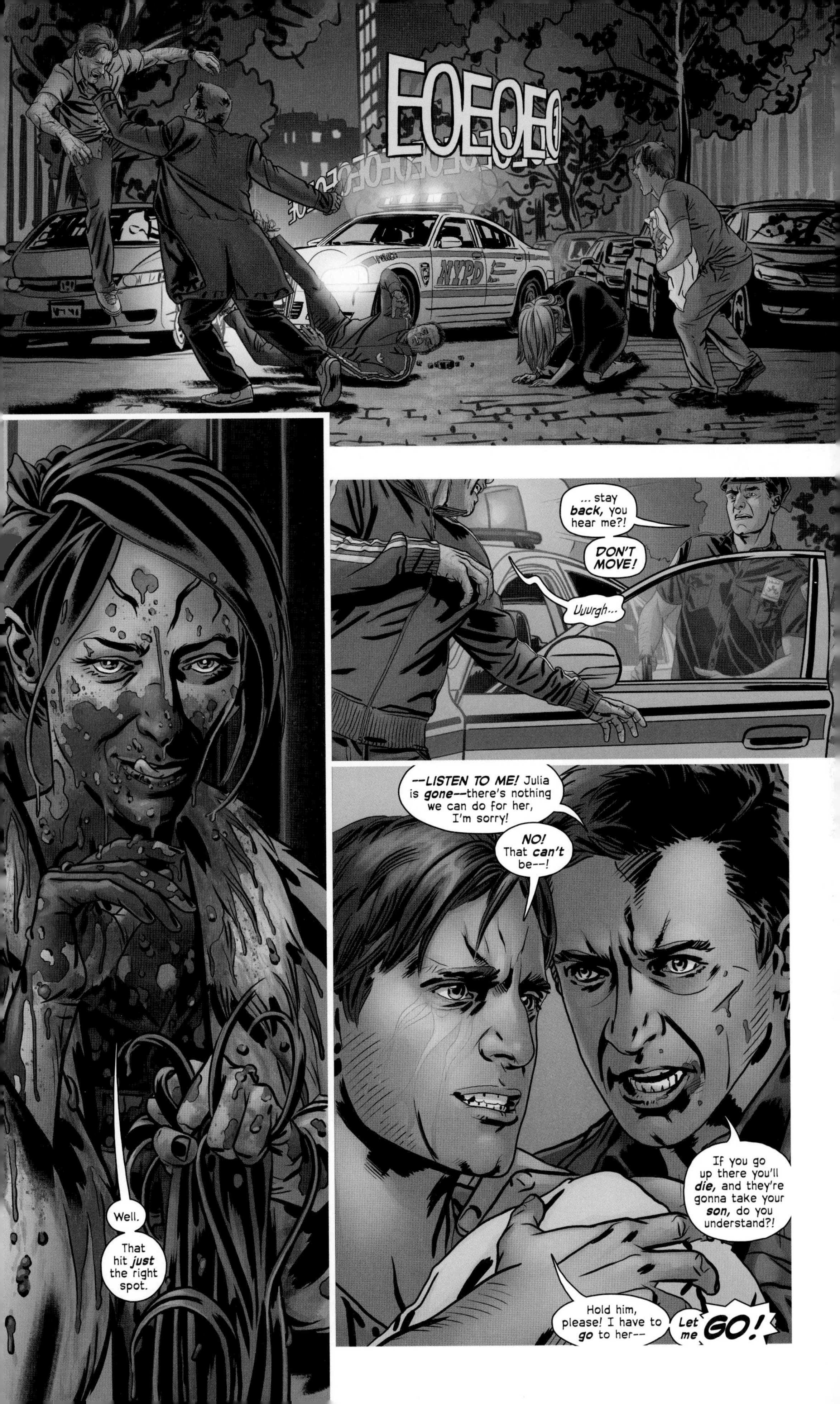
EOEOEO
EOEOEOEOEO
... stay back, you hear me?!
DON'T MOVE!
Uuurgh...
Well.
That hit just the right spot.
--LISTEN TO ME! Julia is gone--there's nothing we can do for her, I'm sorry!
NO! That can't be--!
If you go up there you'll die, and they're gonna take your son, do you understand?!
Hold him, please! I have to go to her--
Let me GO!

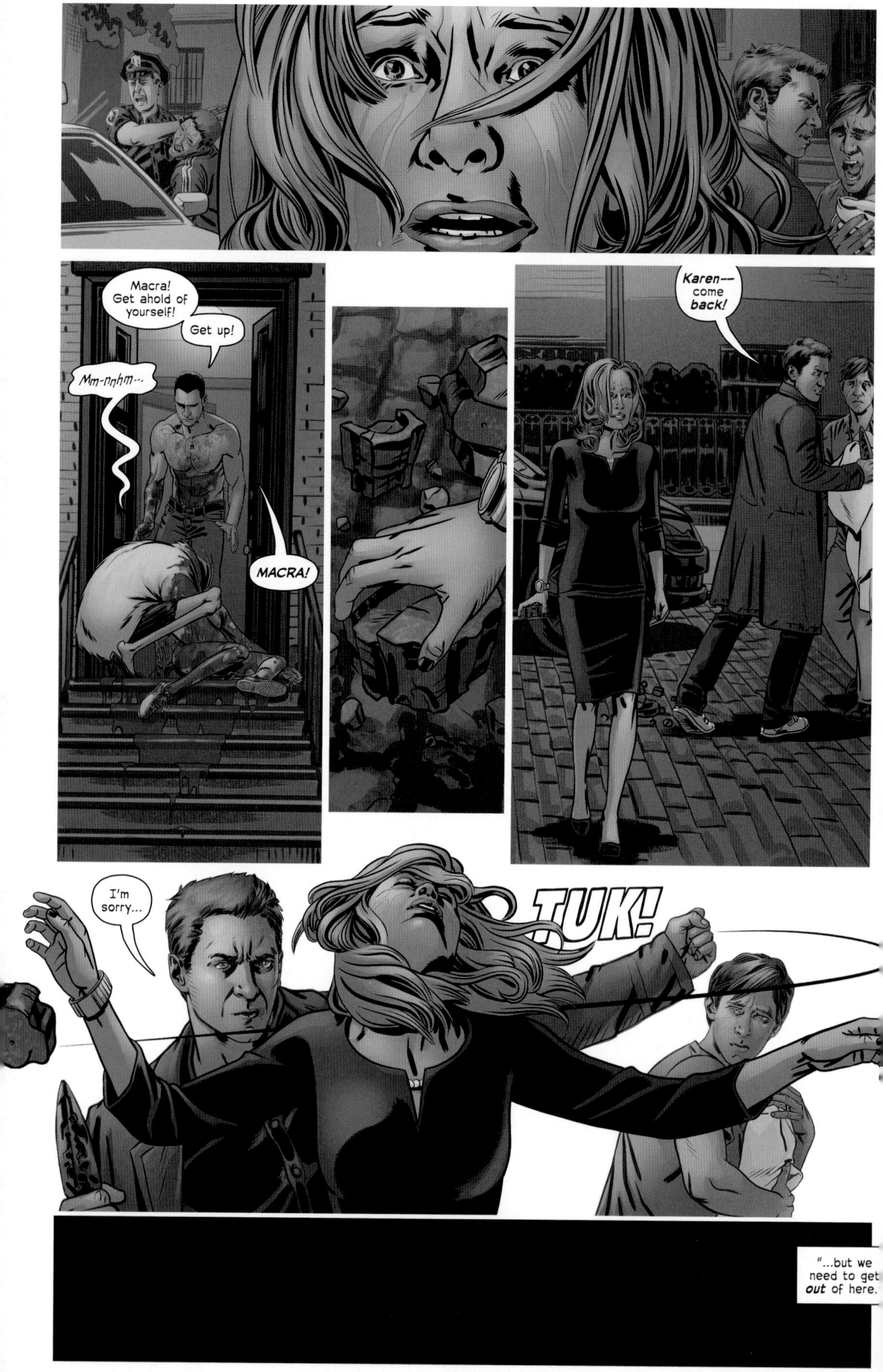
Macra! Get ahold of yourself!
Get up!
Mm-nnhm...
MACRA!
Karen-- come back!
I'm sorry...
TUK!
"...but we need to get out of here.

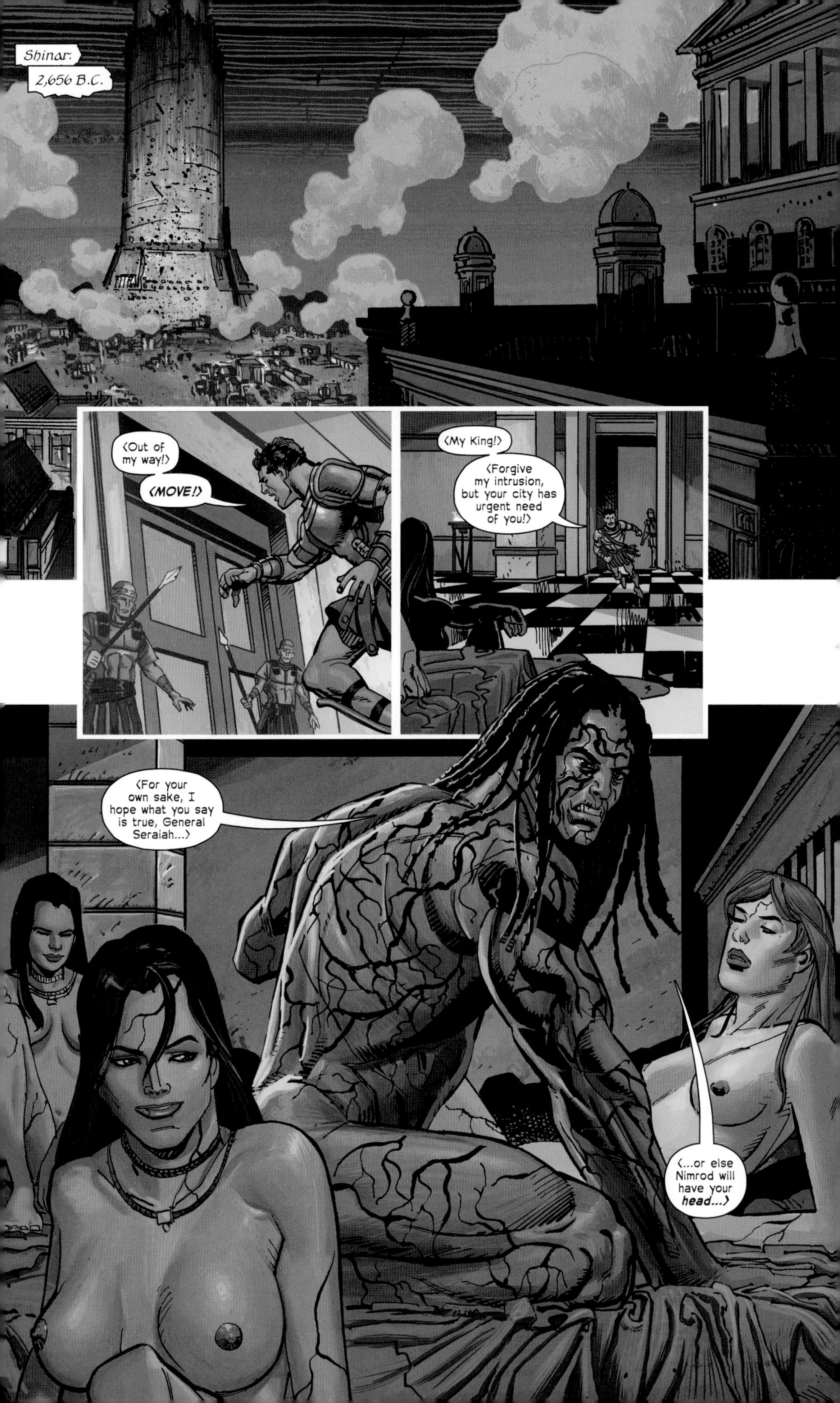
Shinar.
2,656 B.C.
‹Out of my way!›
‹MOVE!›
‹My King!›
‹Forgive my intrusion, but your city has urgent need of you!›
‹For your own sake, I hope what you say is true, General Seraiah...›
‹...or else Nimrod will have your head...›

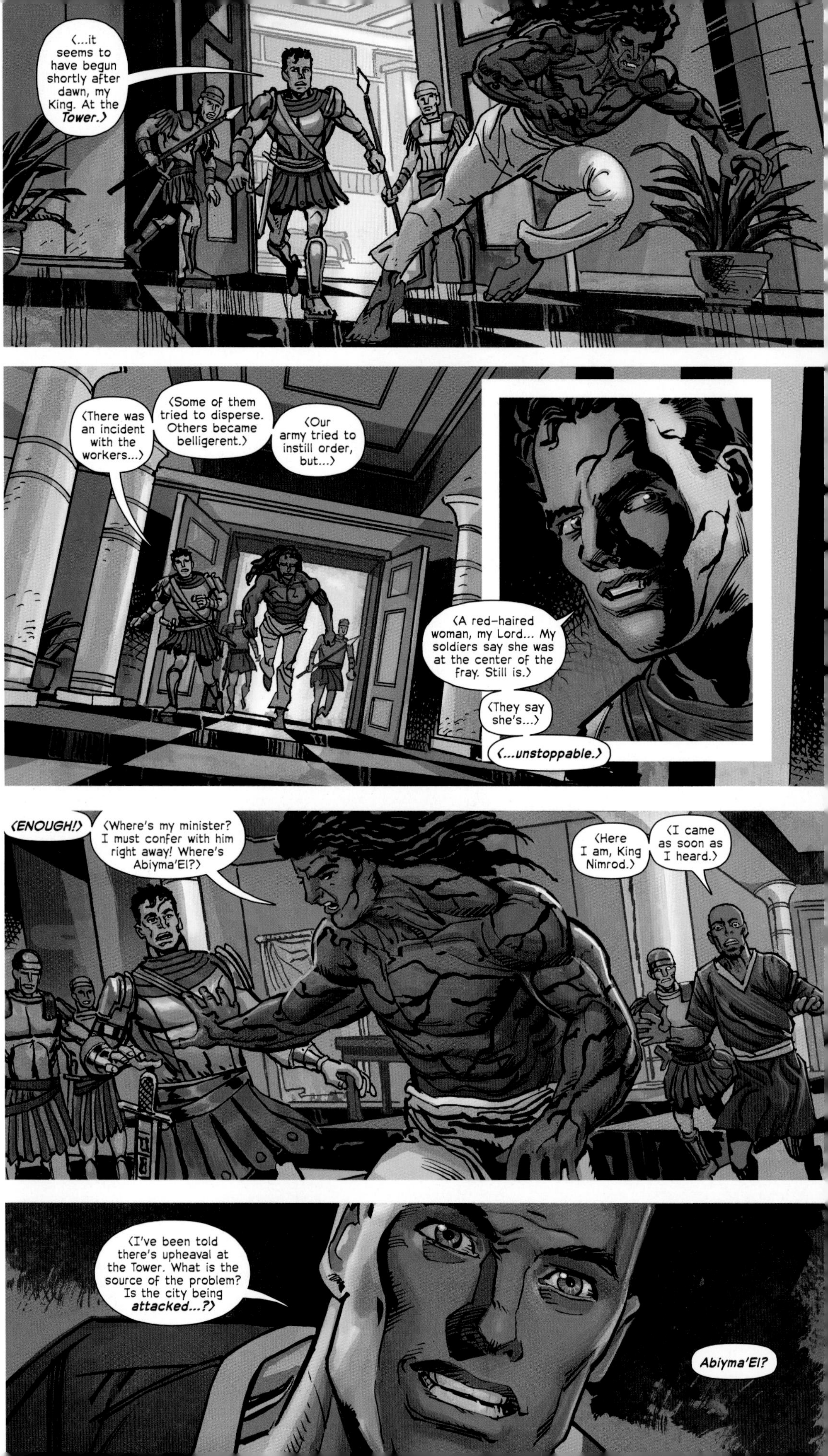
‹...it seems to have begun shortly after dawn, my King. At the *Tower.*›
‹There was an incident with the workers...›
‹Some of them tried to disperse. Others became belligerent.›
‹Our army tried to instill order, but...›
‹A red-haired woman, my Lord... My soldiers say she was at the center of the fray. Still is.›
‹They say she's...›
‹*...unstoppable.*›
‹*ENOUGH!*›
‹Where's my minister? I must confer with him right away! Where's Abiyma'El?›
‹Here I am, King Nimrod.›
‹I came as soon as I heard.›
‹I've been told there's upheaval at the Tower. What is the source of the problem? Is the city being *attacked...?*›
Abiyma'El?

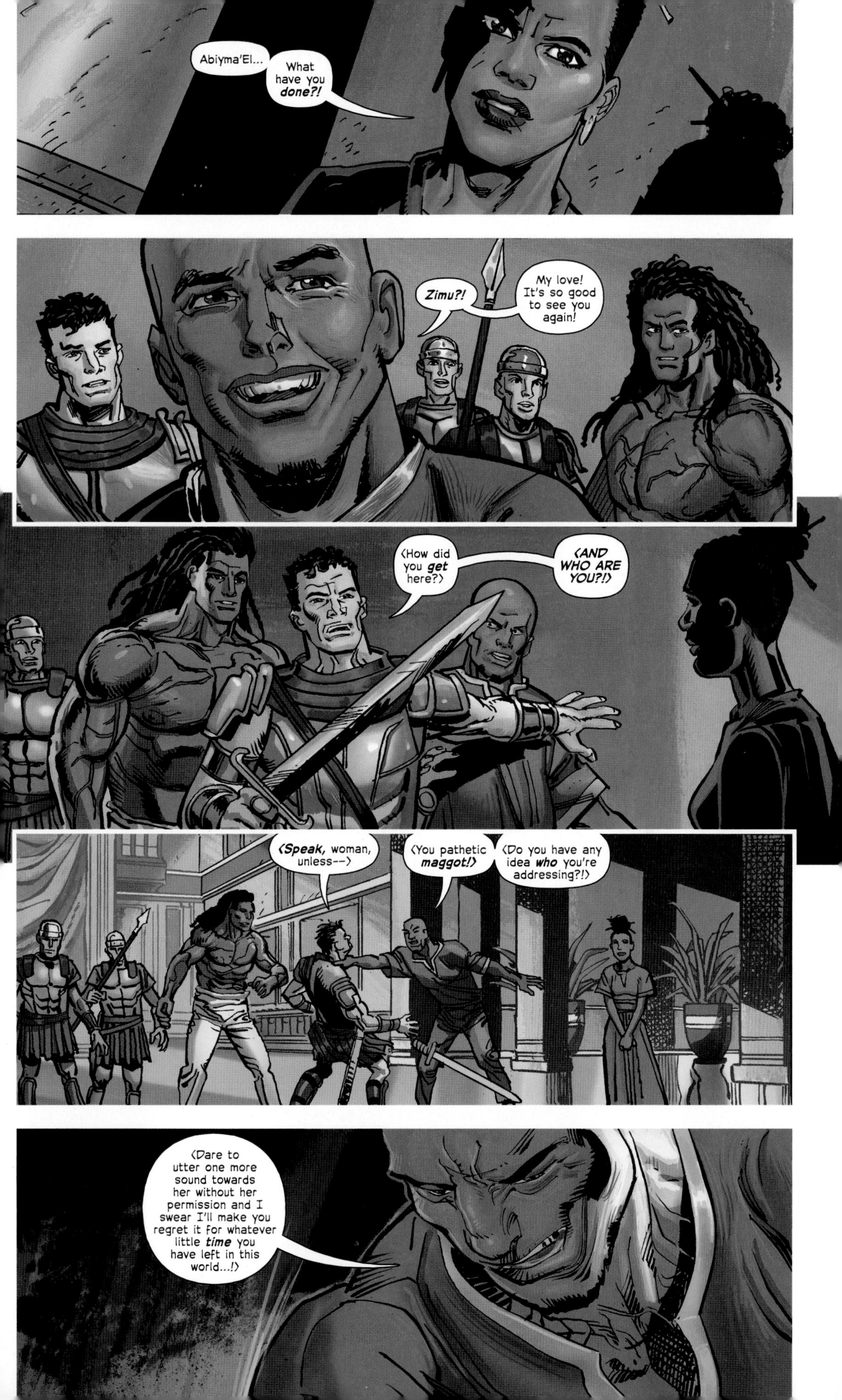
Abiyma'El...
What have you *done?!*
Zimu?!
My love! It's so good to see you again!
‹How did you *get* here?›
‹AND WHO ARE YOU?!›
‹*Speak,* woman, unless--›
‹You pathetic *maggot!*›
‹Do you have any idea *who* you're addressing?!›
‹Dare to utter one more sound towards her without her permission and I swear I'll make you regret it for whatever little *time* you have left in this world...!›

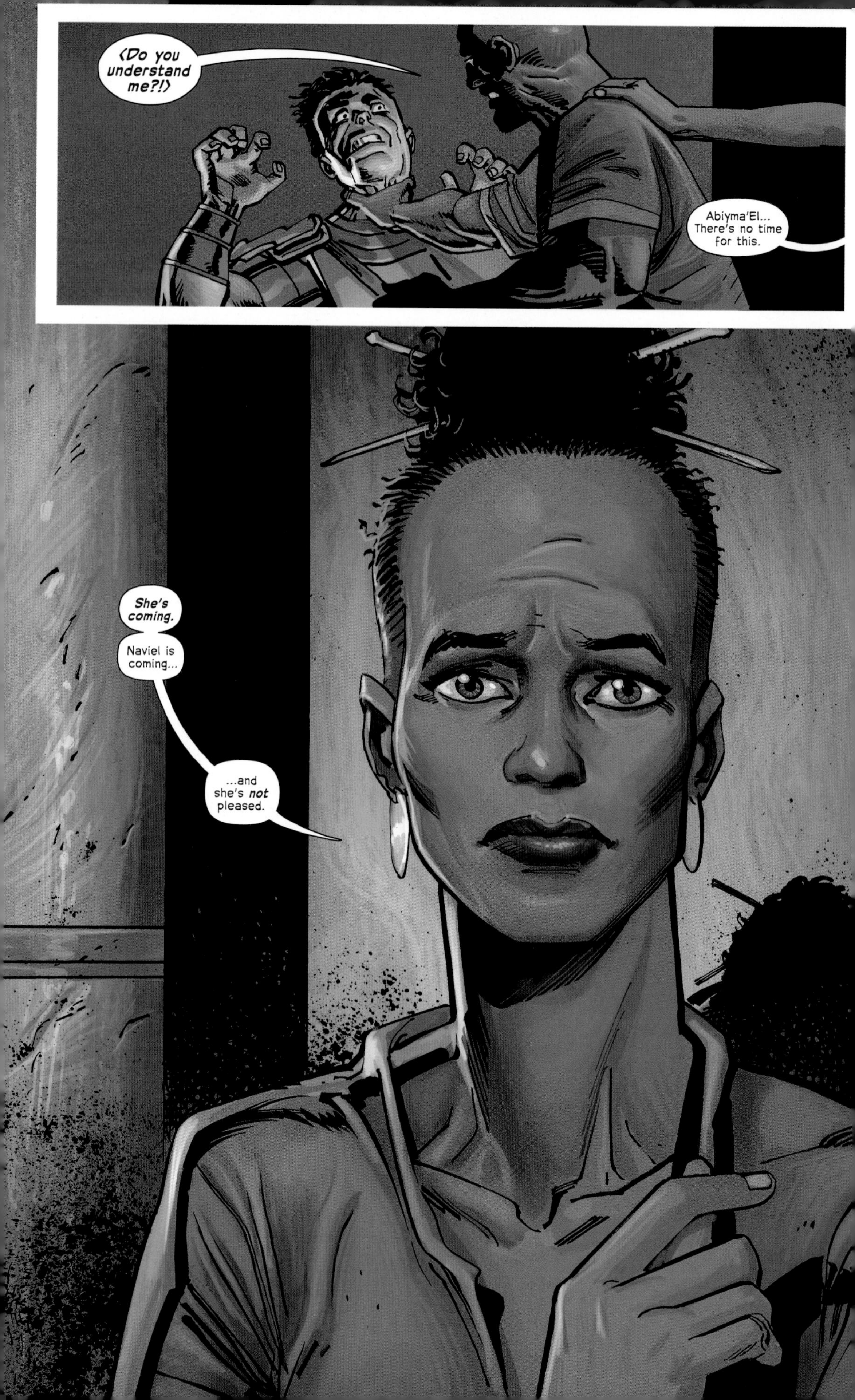

‹Do you understand me?!›
Abiyma'El... There's no time for this.
She's coming.
Naviel is coming...
...and she's not pleased.

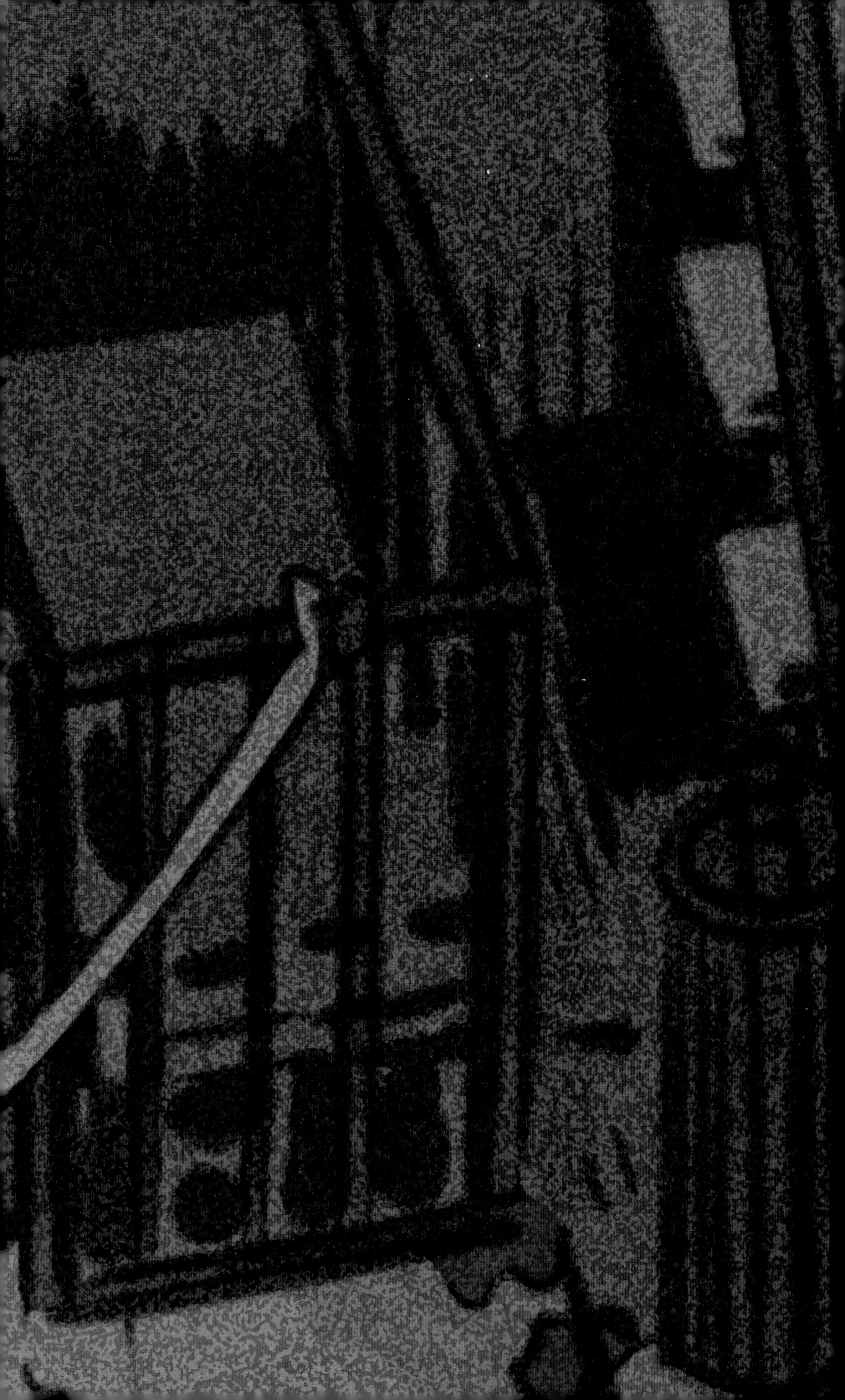

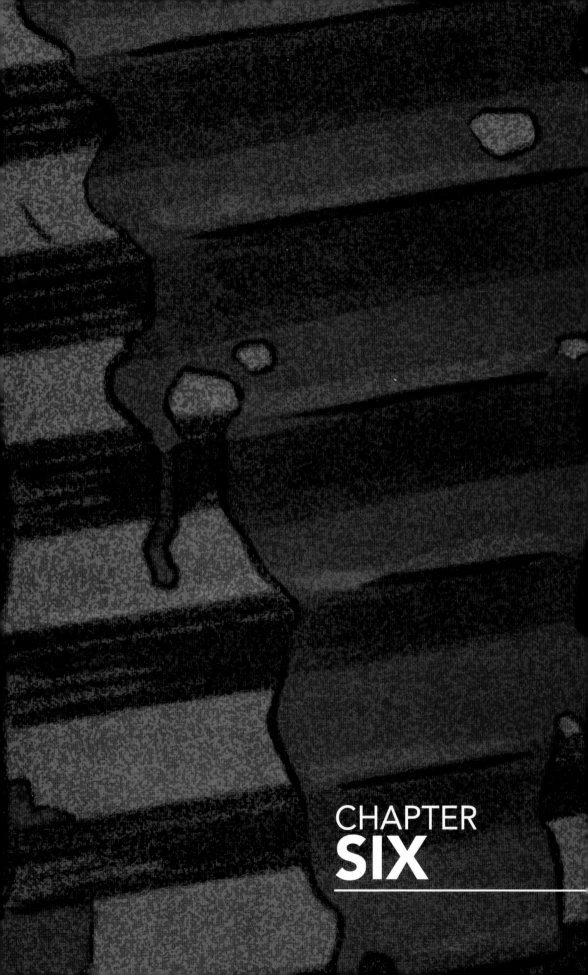

CHAPTER
SIX

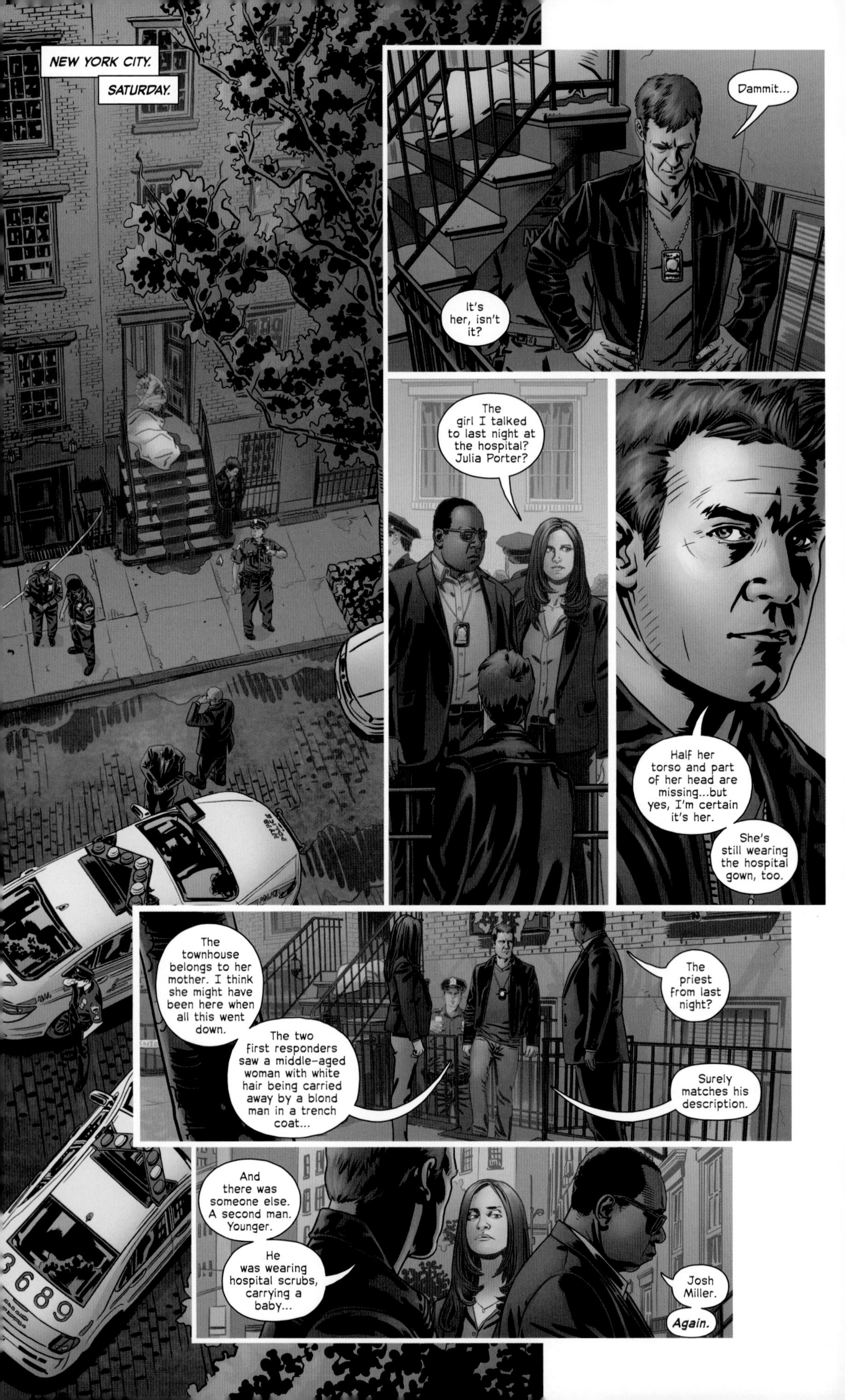
NEW YORK CITY.
SATURDAY.
Dammit...
It's her, isn't it?
The girl I talked to last night at the hospital? Julia Porter?
Half her torso and part of her head are missing...but yes, I'm certain it's her.
She's still wearing the hospital gown, too.
The townhouse belongs to her mother. I think she might have been here when all this went down.
The two first responders saw a middle-aged woman with white hair being carried away by a blond man in a trench coat...
The priest from last night?
Surely matches his description.
And there was someone else. A second man. Younger.
He was wearing hospital scrubs, carrying a baby...
Josh Miller.
Again.

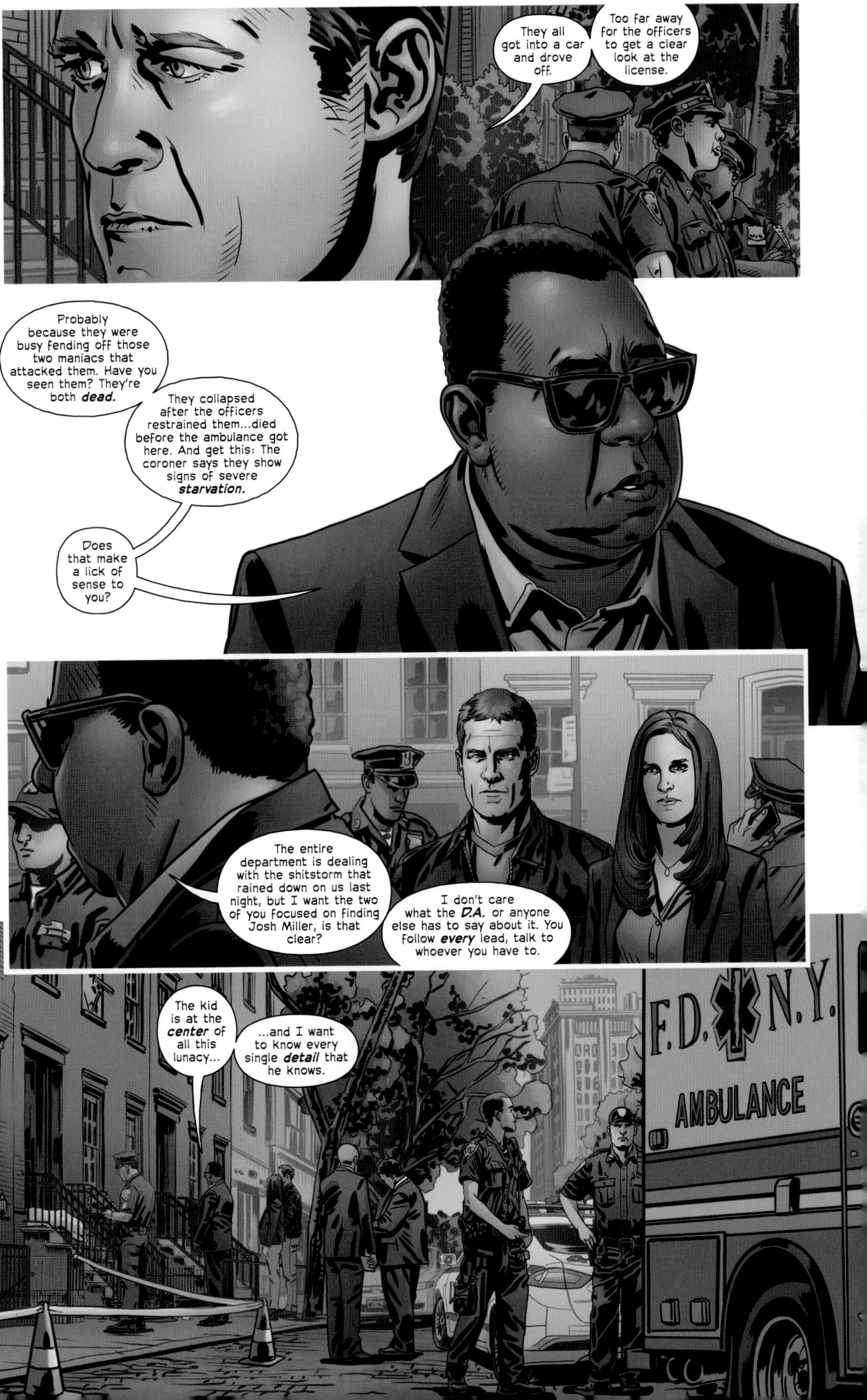
They all got into a car and drove off.
Too far away for the officers to get a clear look at the license.
Probably because they were busy fending off those two maniacs that attacked them. Have you seen them? They're both *dead.*
They collapsed after the officers restrained them...died before the ambulance got here. And get this: The coroner says they show signs of severe *starvation.*
Does that make a lick of sense to you?
The entire department is dealing with the shitstorm that rained down on us last night, but I want the two of you focused on finding Josh Miller, is that clear?
I don't care what the *D.A.* or anyone else has to say about it. You follow *every* lead, talk to whoever you have to.
The kid is at the *center* of all this lunacy...
...and I want to know every single *detail* that he knows.
F.D. N.Y.
AMBULANCE

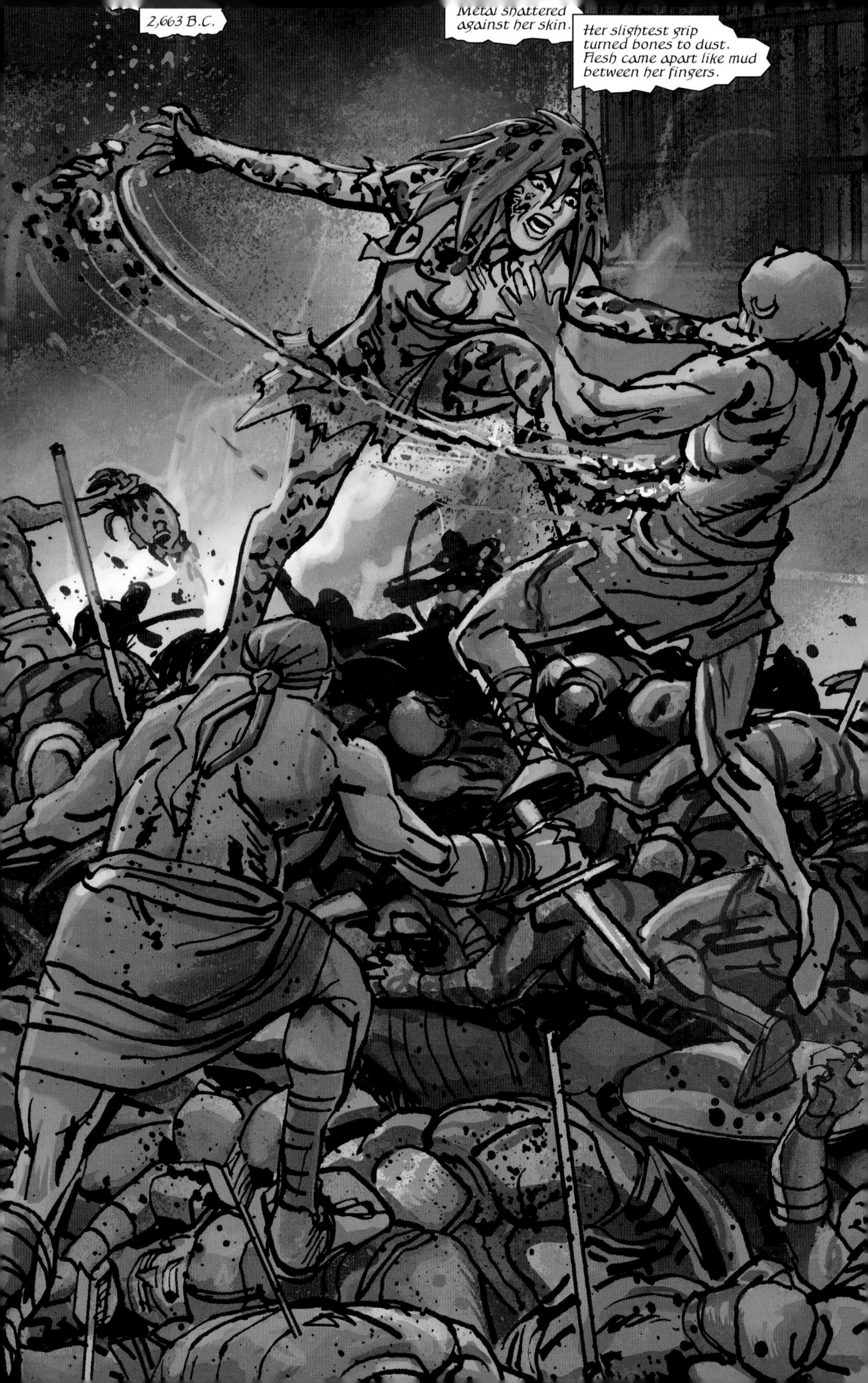
2,663 B.C.
Metal shattered against her skin.
Her slightest grip turned bones to dust. Flesh came apart like mud between her fingers.

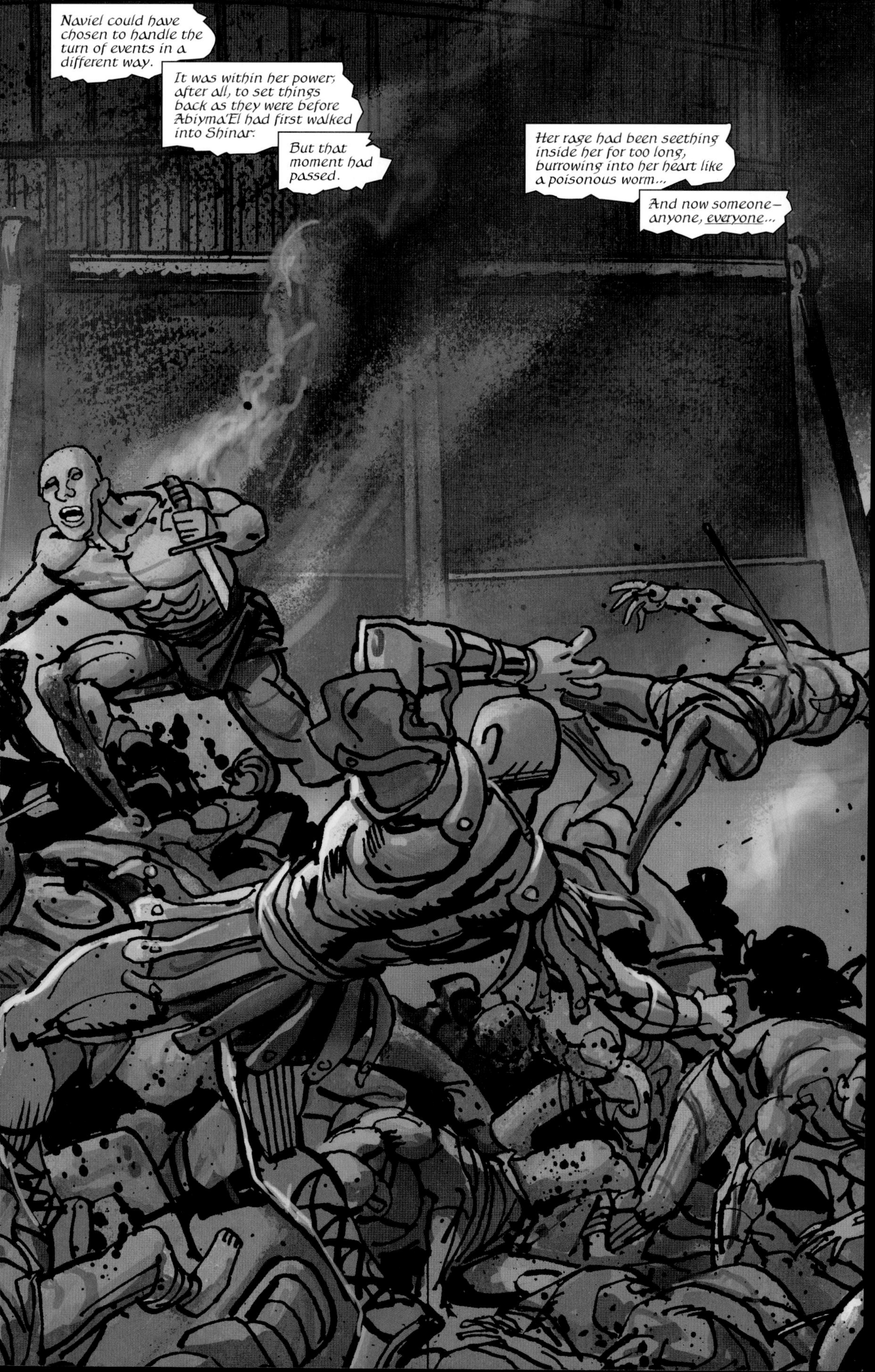
Naviel could have chosen to handle the turn of events in a different way.
It was within her power, after all, to set things back as they were before Abiyma'El had first walked into Shinar.
But that moment had passed.
Her rage had been seething inside her for too long, burrowing into her heart like a poisonous worm...
And now someone— anyone, everyone...

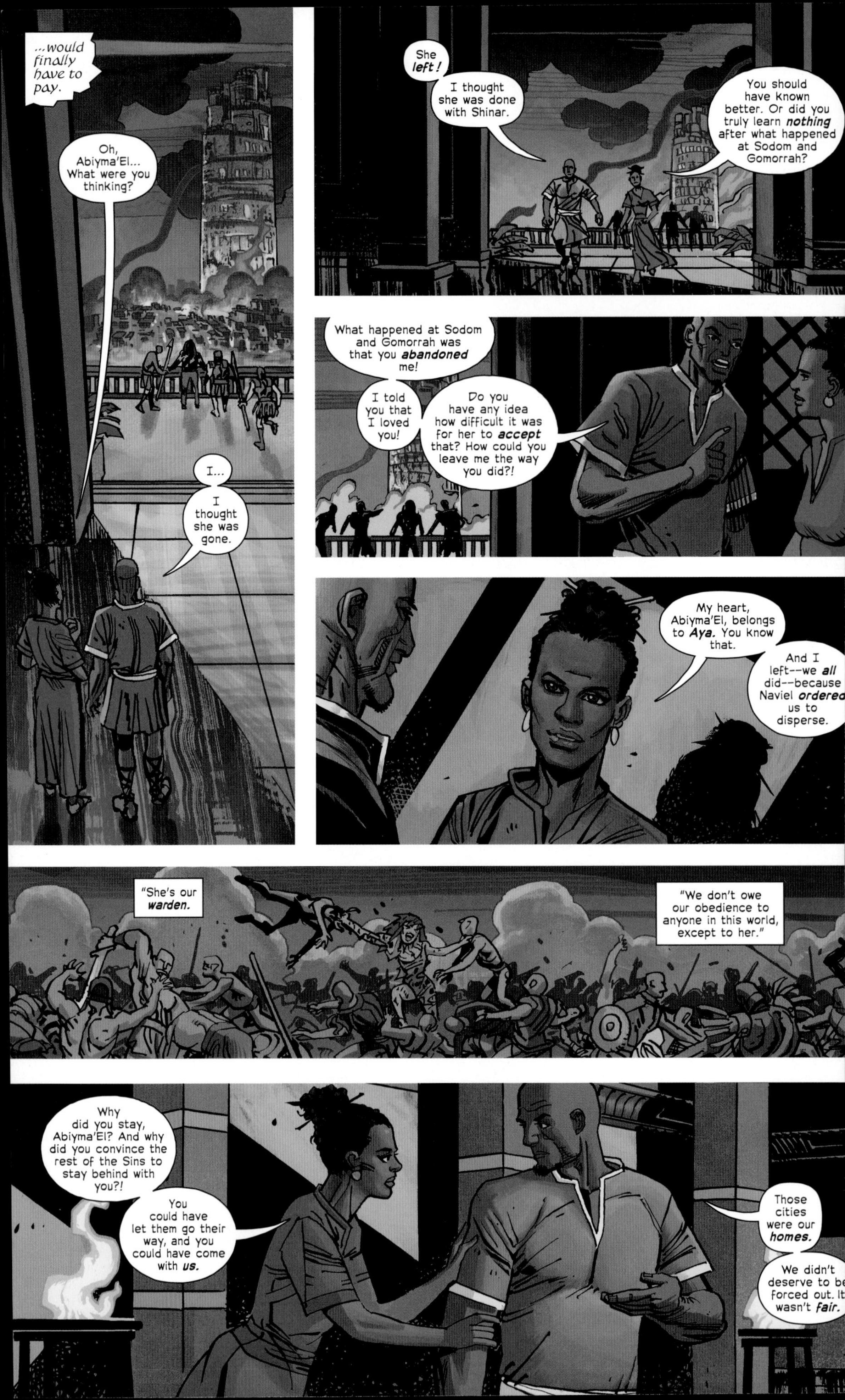
...would finally have to pay.
Oh, Abiyma'El... What were you thinking?
I...
I thought she was gone.
She left!
I thought she was done with Shinar.
You should have known better. Or did you truly learn nothing after what happened at Sodom and Gomorrah?
What happened at Sodom and Gomorrah was that you abandoned me!
I told you that I loved you!
Do you have any idea how difficult it was for her to accept that? How could you leave me the way you did?!
My heart, Abiyma'El, belongs to Aya. You know that.
And I left--we all did--because Naviel ordered us to disperse.
"She's our warden.
"We don't owe our obedience to anyone in this world, except to her."
Why did you stay, Abiyma'El? And why did you convince the rest of the Sins to stay behind with you?!
You could have let them go their way, and you could have come with us.
Those cities were our homes.
We didn't deserve to be forced out. It wasn't fair.

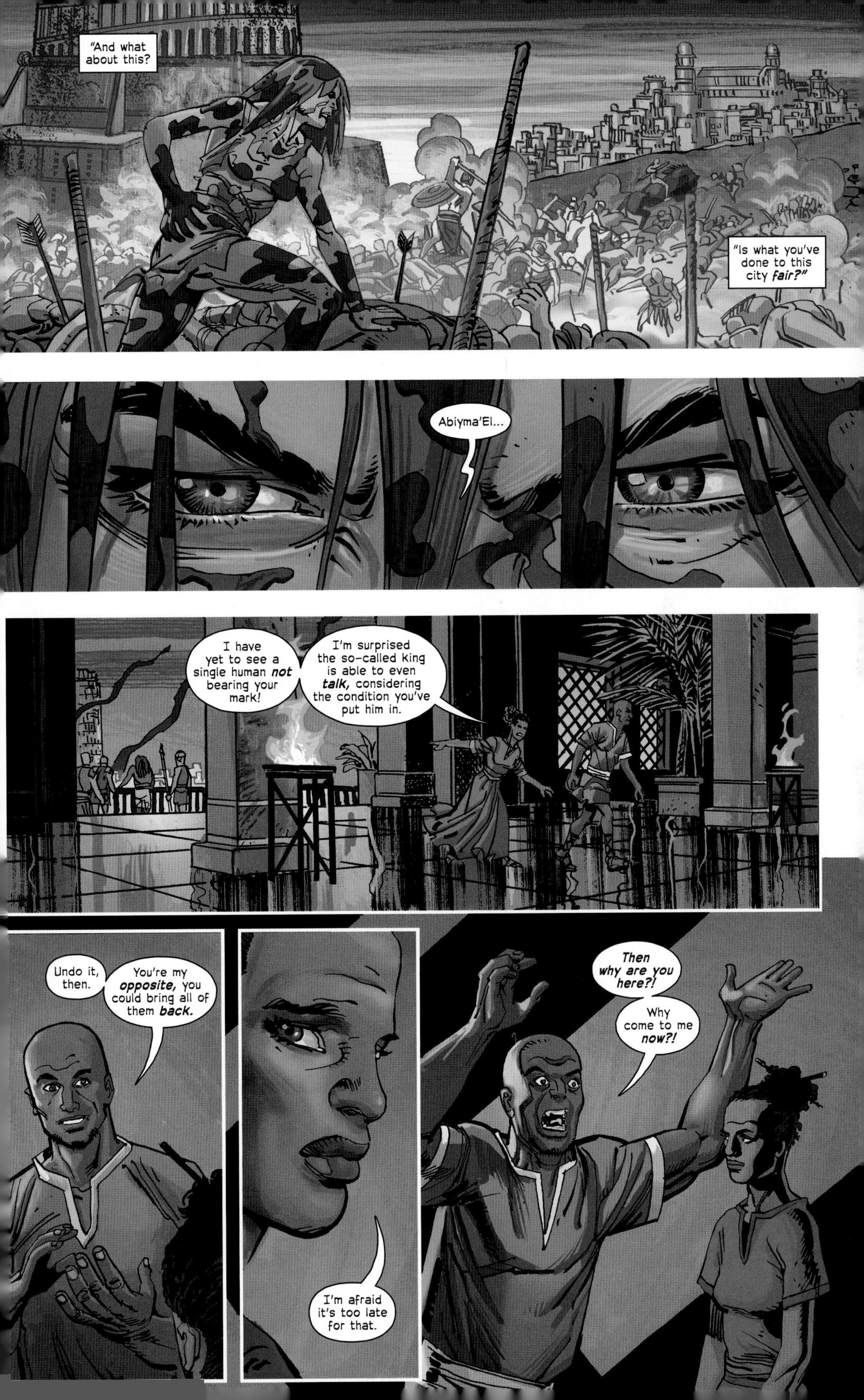
"And what about this?
"Is what you've done to this city *fair?"*
Abiyma'El...
I have yet to see a single human ***not*** bearing your mark!
I'm surprised the so-called king is able to even ***talk,*** considering the condition you've put him in.
Undo it, then.
You're my ***opposite,*** you could bring all of them ***back.***
I'm afraid it's too late for that.
Then why are you here?!
Why come to me ***now?!***

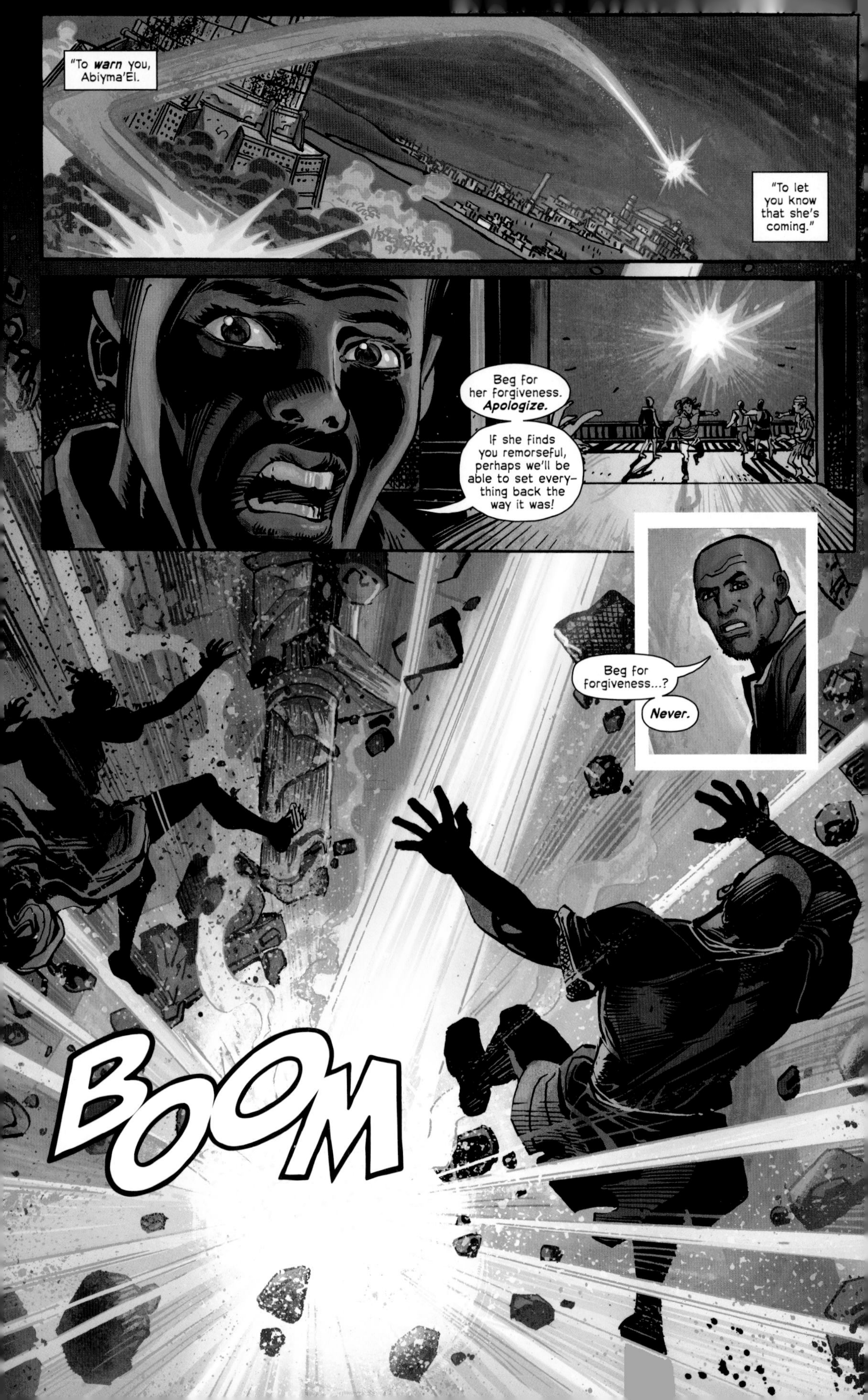
"To warn you, Abiyma'El.
"To let you know that she's coming."
Beg for her forgiveness. Apologize.
If she finds you remorseful, perhaps we'll be able to set everything back the way it was!
Beg for forgiveness...?
Never.
BOOM

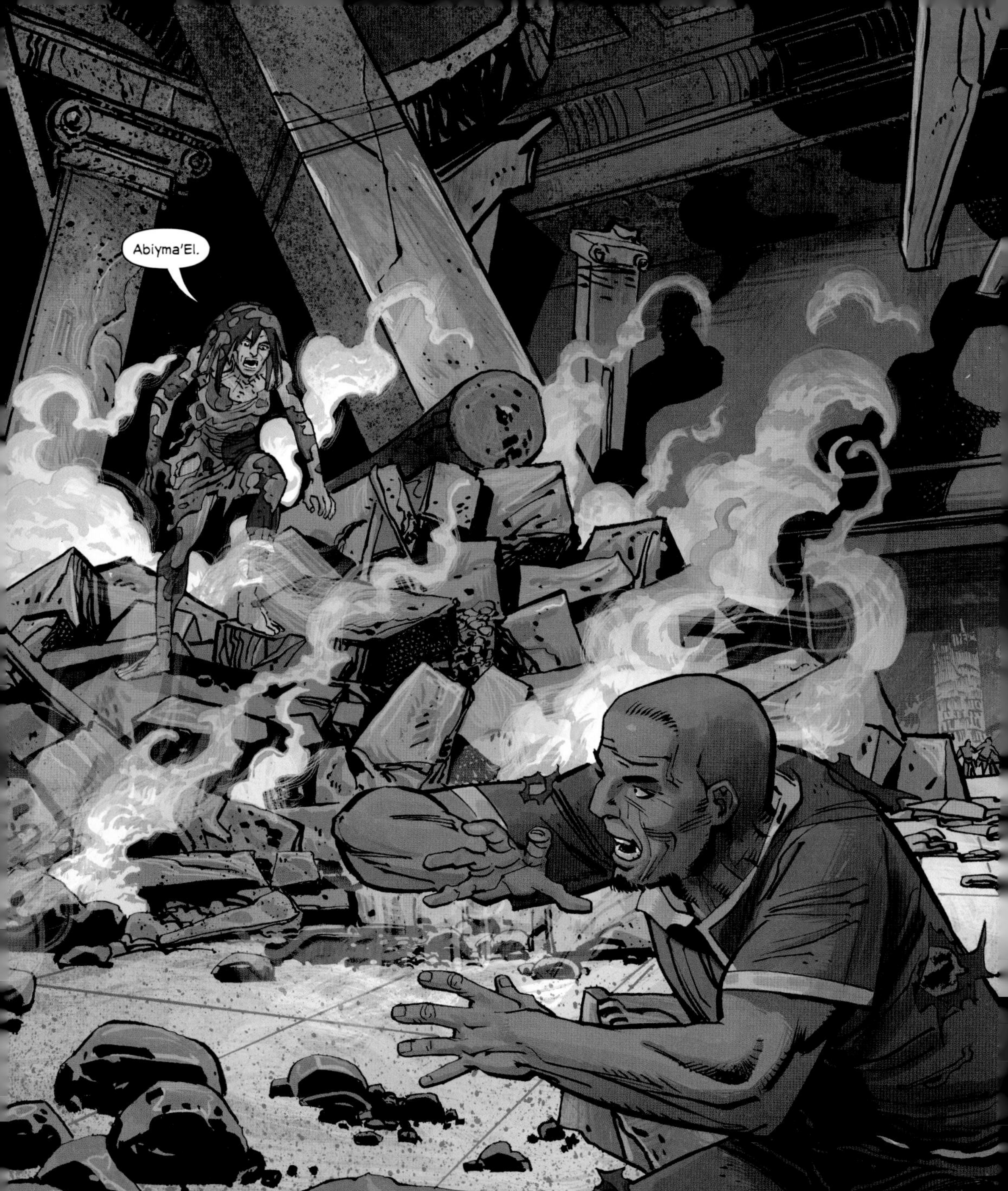
Abiyma'El.

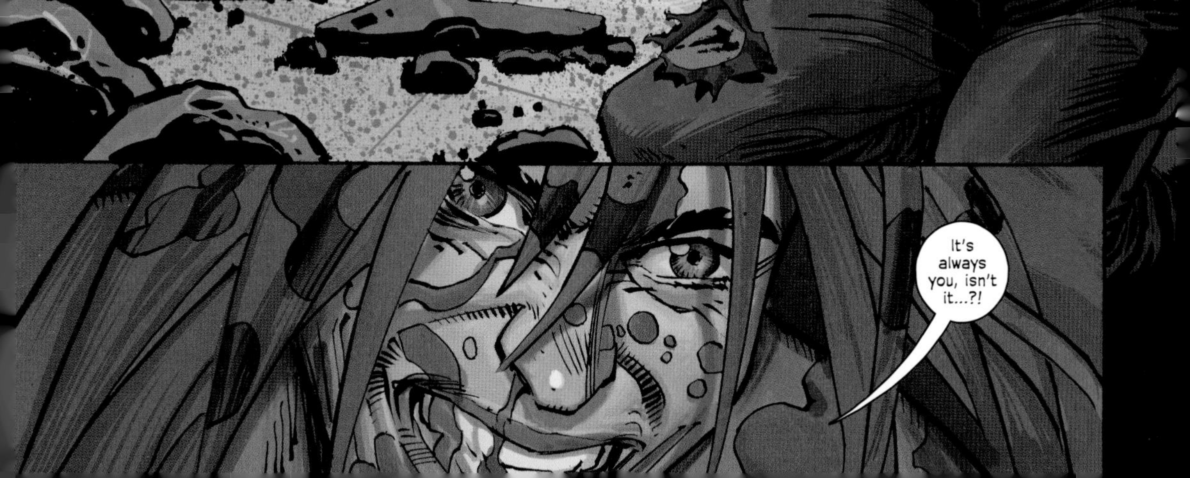
It's always you, isn't it...?!

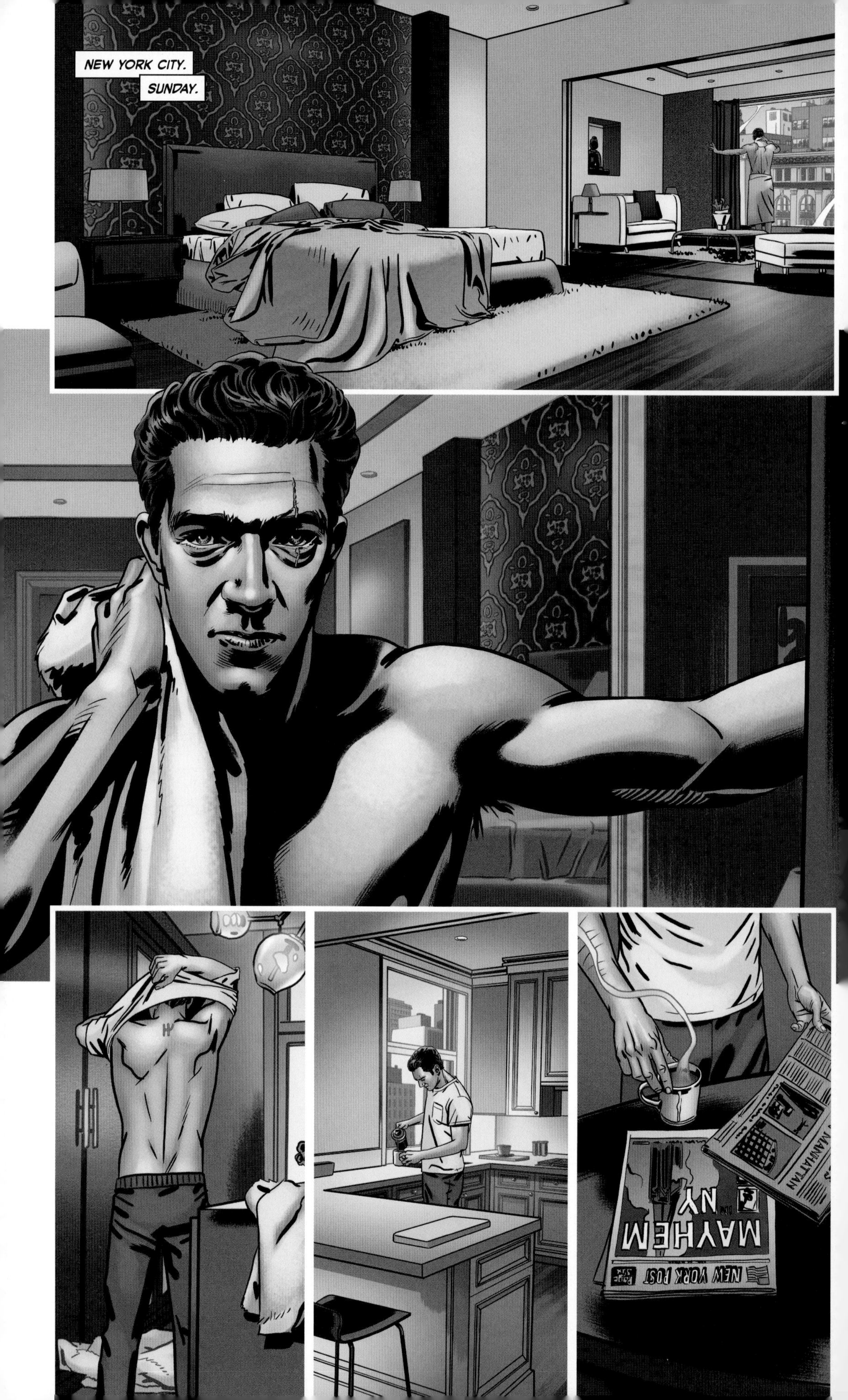
NEW YORK CITY.
SUNDAY.
NEW YORK POST
MAYHEM
NY

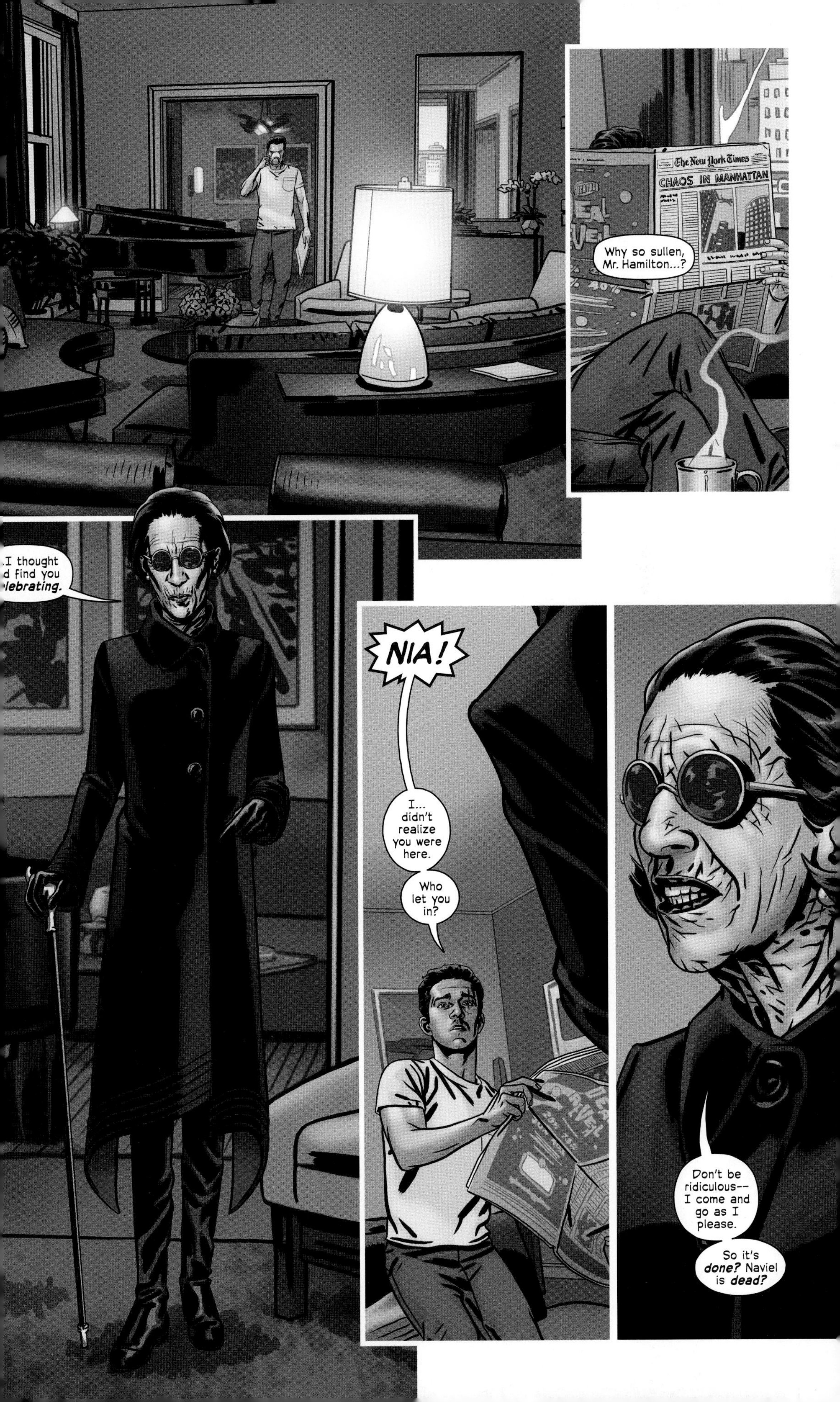
Why so sullen, Mr. Hamilton...?
The New York Times
CHAOS IN MANHATTAN
...I thought I'd find you celebrating.
NIA!
I... didn't realize you were here.
Who let you in?
Don't be ridiculous-- I come and go as I please.
So it's done? Naviel is dead?

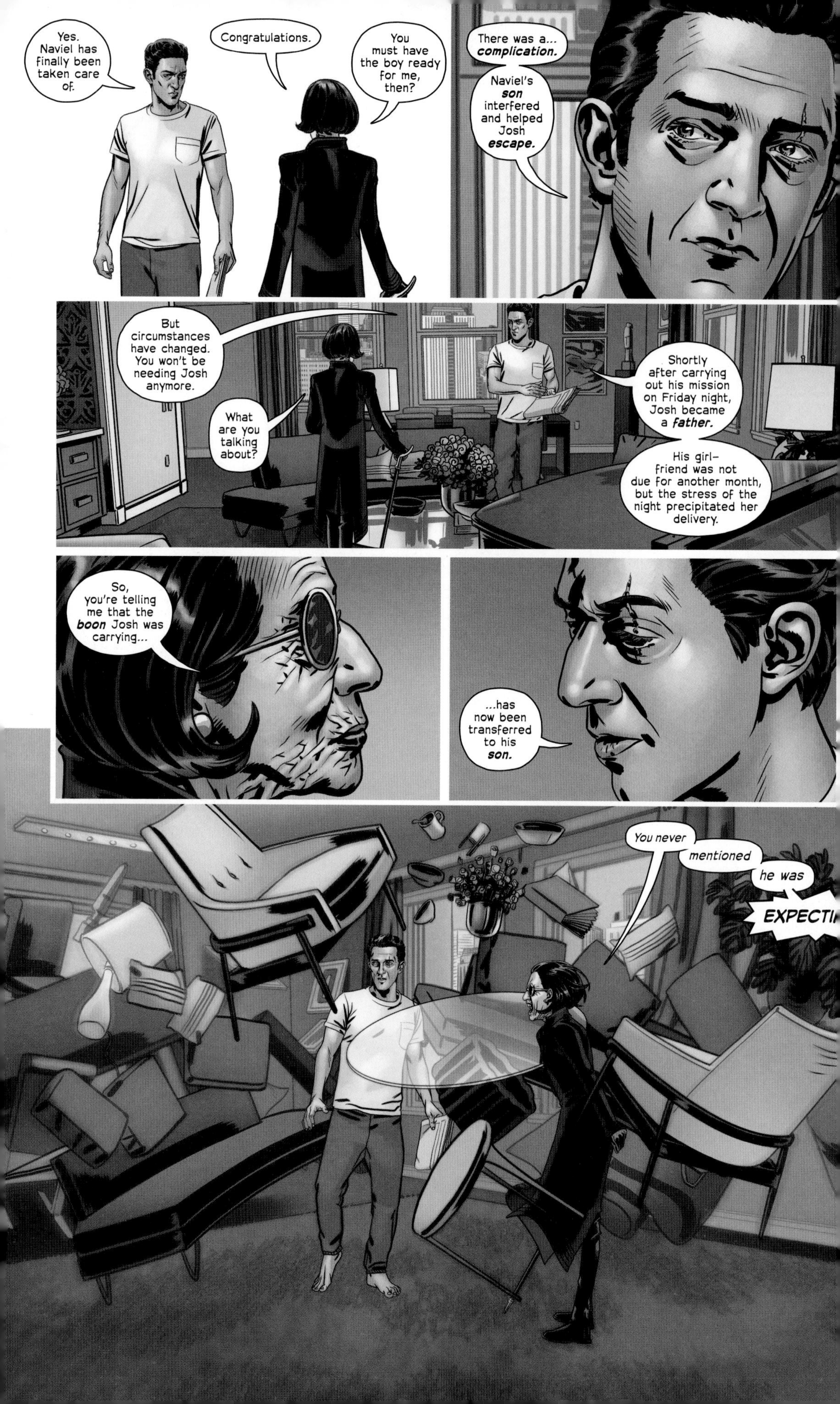
Yes. Naviel has finally been taken care of.
Congratulations.
You must have the boy ready for me, then?
There was a... **complication.**
Naviel's **son** interfered and helped Josh **escape.**
But circumstances have changed. You won't be needing Josh anymore.
What are you talking about?
Shortly after carrying out his mission on Friday night, Josh became a **father.**
His girl-friend was not due for another month, but the stress of the night precipitated her delivery.
So, you're telling me that the **boon** Josh was carrying...
...has now been transferred to his **son.**
You never
mentioned
he was
EXPECTI

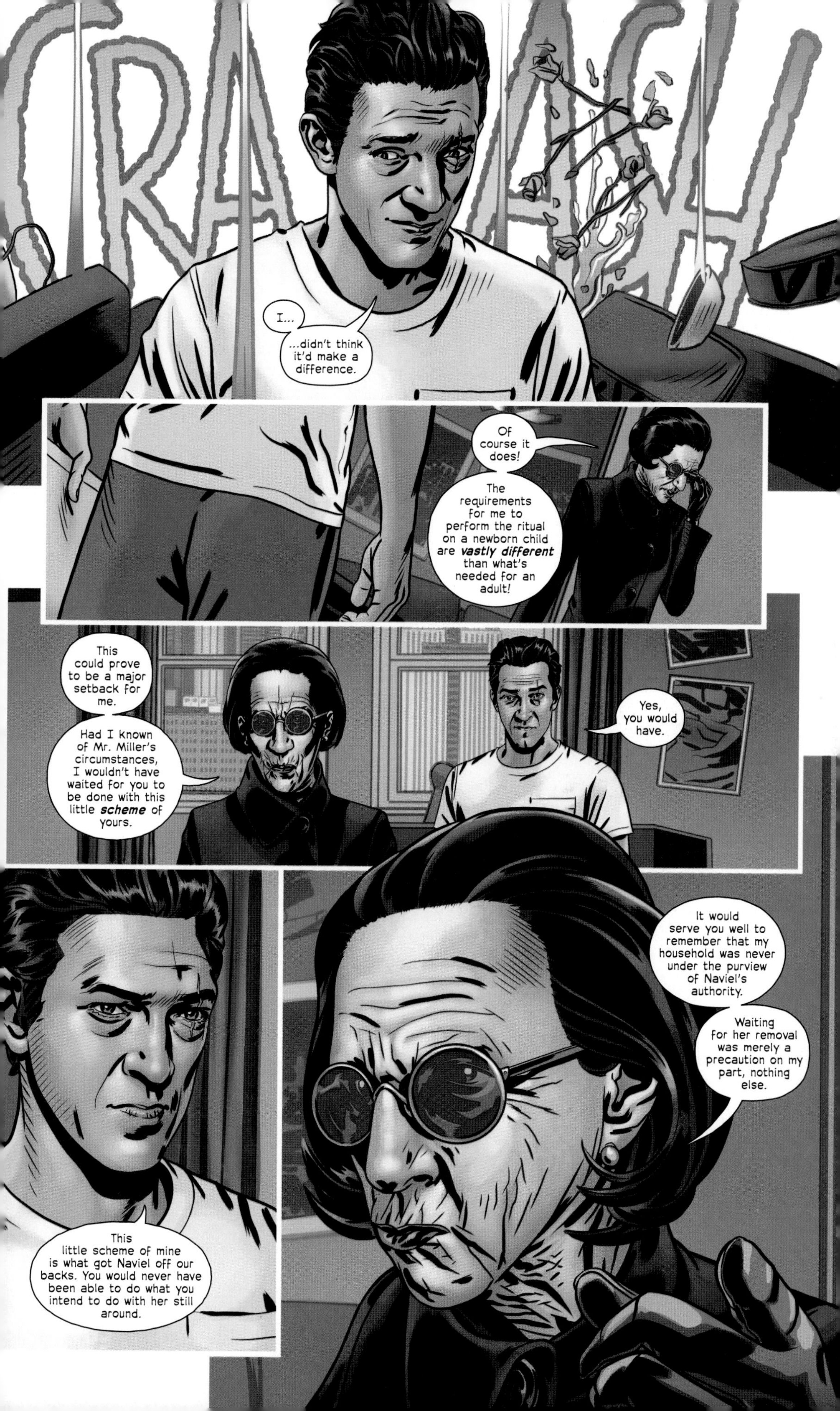
CRASH
I...
...didn't think it'd make a difference.
Of course it does!
The requirements for me to perform the ritual on a newborn child are *vastly different* than what's needed for an adult!
This could prove to be a major setback for me.
Had I known of Mr. Miller's circumstances, I wouldn't have waited for you to be done with this little *scheme* of yours.
Yes, you would have.
It would serve you well to remember that my household was never under the purview of Naviel's authority.
Waiting for her removal was merely a precaution on my part, nothing else.
This little scheme of mine is what got Naviel off our backs. You would never have been able to do what you intend to do with her still around.

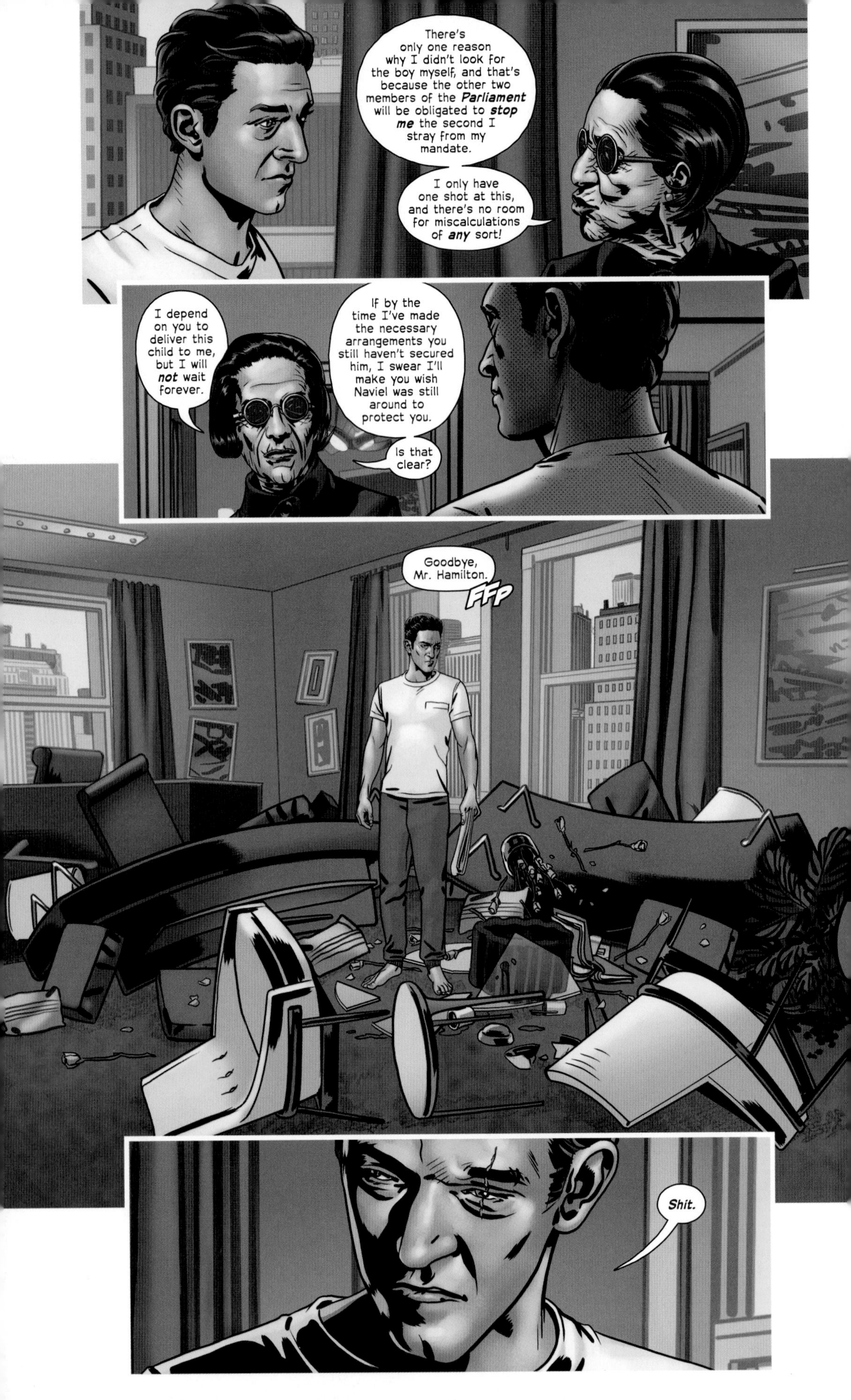

There's only one reason why I didn't look for the boy myself, and that's because the other two members of the *Parliament* will be obligated to ***stop me*** the second I stray from my mandate.
I only have one shot at this, and there's no room for miscalculations of ***any*** sort!
I depend on you to deliver this child to me, but I will ***not*** wait forever.
If by the time I've made the necessary arrangements you still haven't secured him, I swear I'll make you wish Naviel was still around to protect you.
Is that clear?
Goodbye, Mr. Hamilton.
FFP
Shit.

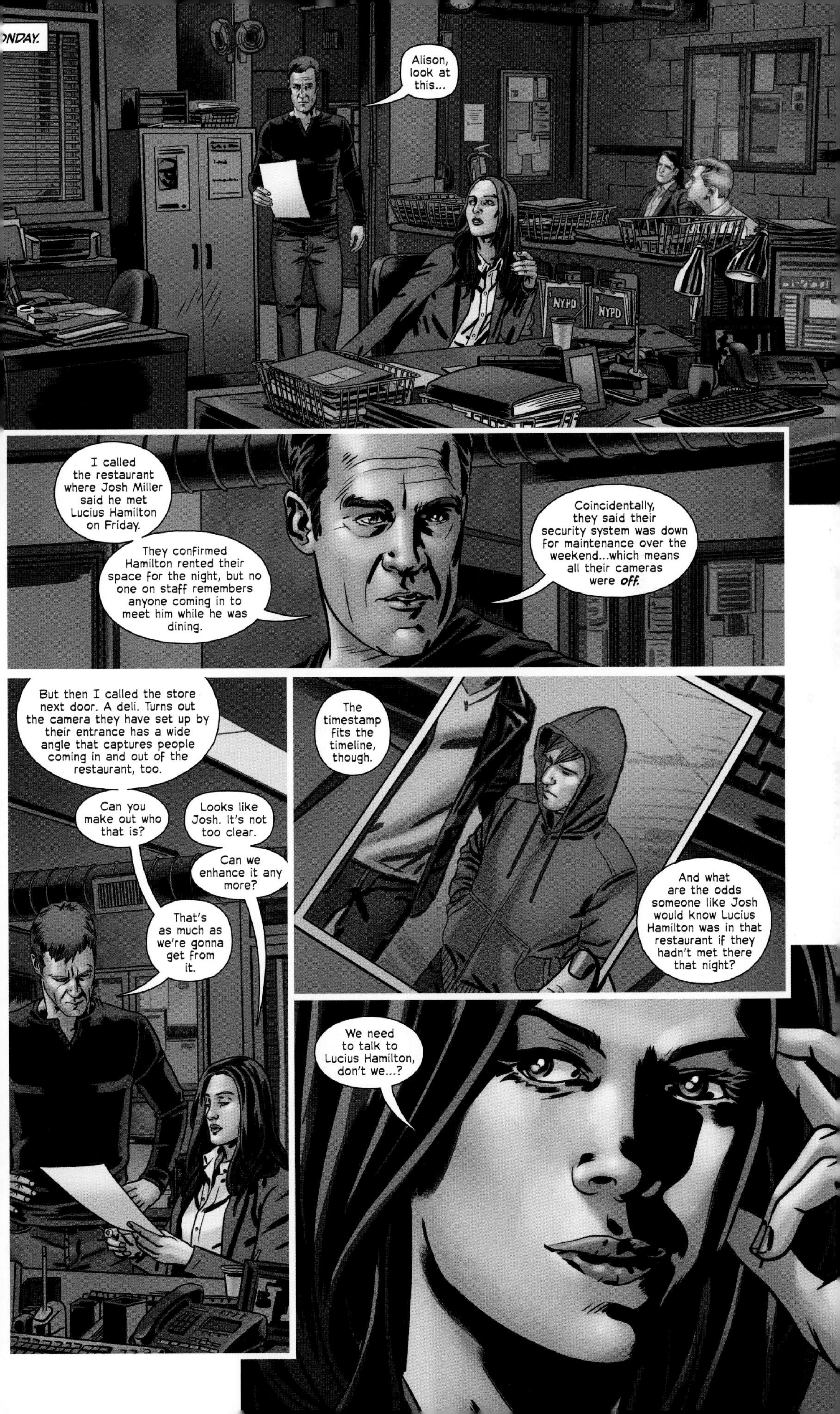

ONDAY.
Alison, look at this...
I called the restaurant where Josh Miller said he met Lucius Hamilton on Friday.
They confirmed Hamilton rented their space for the night, but no one on staff remembers anyone coming in to meet him while he was dining.
Coincidentally, they said their security system was down for maintenance over the weekend...which means all their cameras were *off.*
But then I called the store next door. A deli. Turns out the camera they have set up by their entrance has a wide angle that captures people coming in and out of the restaurant, too.
Can you make out who that is?
Looks like Josh. It's not too clear.
Can we enhance it any more?
That's as much as we're gonna get from it.
The timestamp fits the timeline, though.
And what are the odds someone like Josh would know Lucius Hamilton was in that restaurant if they hadn't met there that night?
We need to talk to Lucius Hamilton, don't we...?
NYPD
NYPD

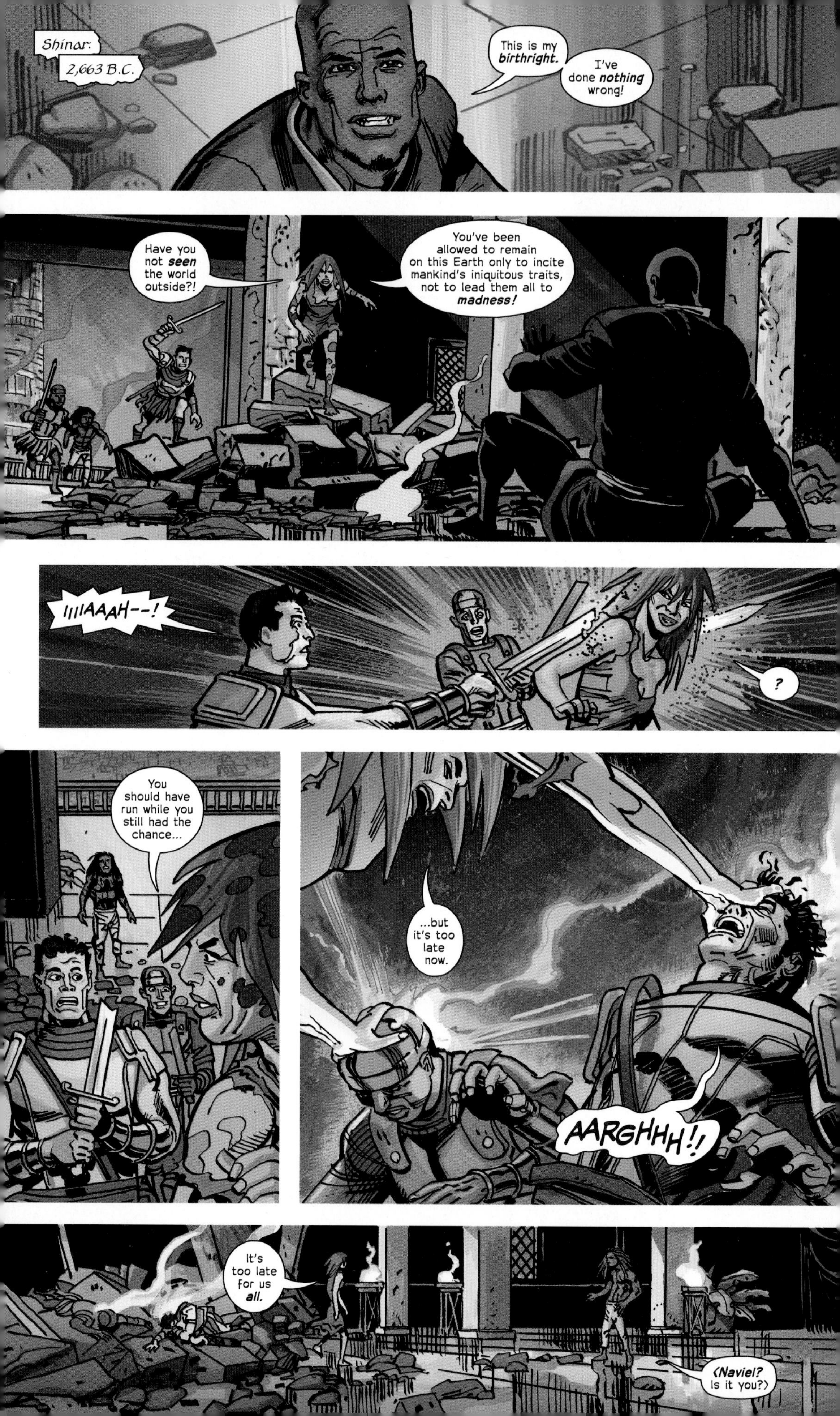
Shinar.
2,663 B.C.
This is my birthright.
I've done nothing wrong!
Have you not seen the world outside?!
You've been allowed to remain on this Earth only to incite mankind's iniquitous traits, not to lead them all to madness!
IIIIAAAH--!
?
You should have run while you still had the chance...
...but it's too late now.
AARGHHH!!
It's too late for us all.
⟨Naviel? Is it you?⟩

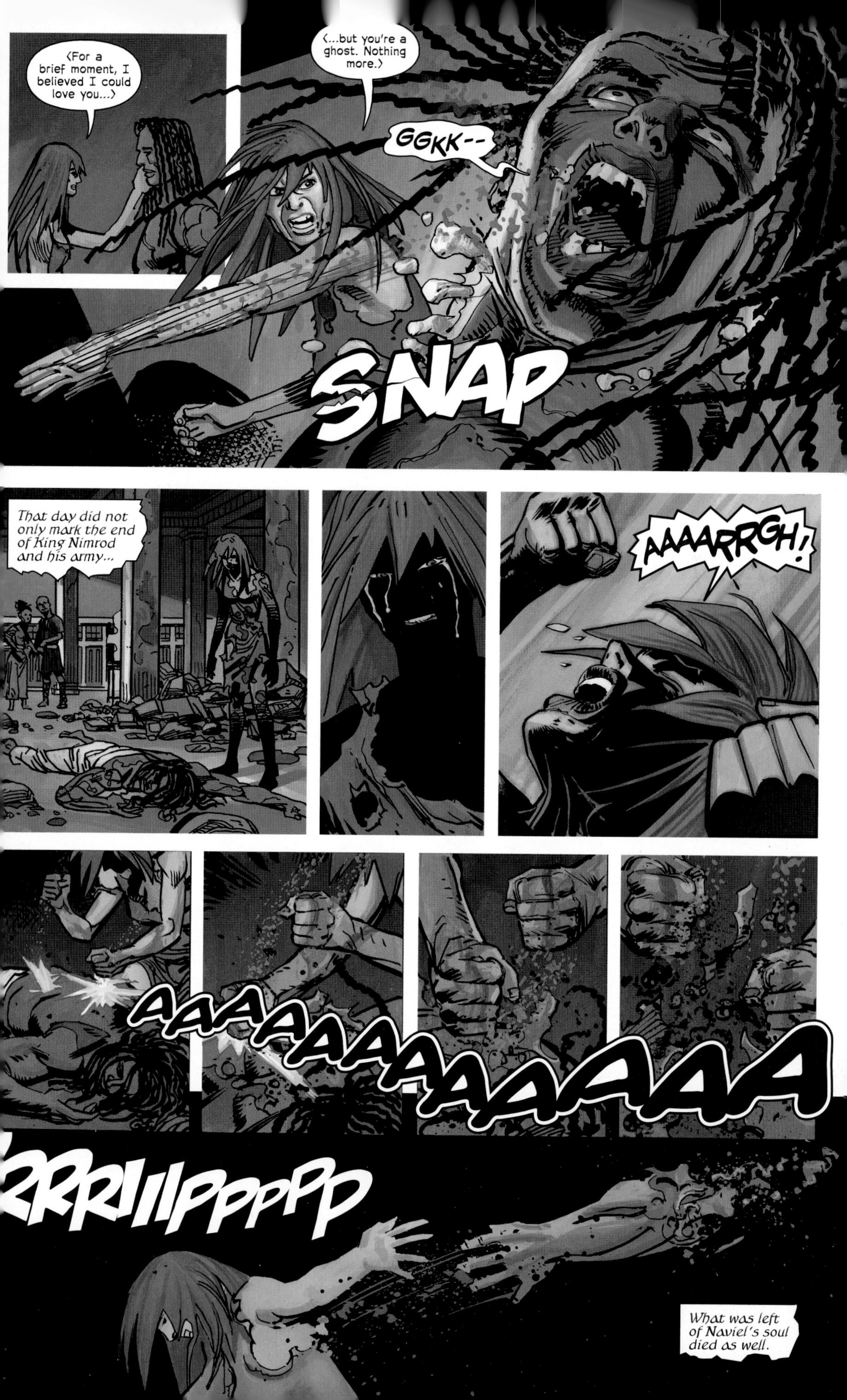

‹For a brief moment, I believed I could love you...›
‹...but you're a ghost. Nothing more.›
GGKK--
SNAP
That day did not only mark the end of King Nimrod and his army...
AAAARRGH!
AAAAAAAAAAAAA
RRRIIIPPPPP
What was left of Naviel's soul died as well.

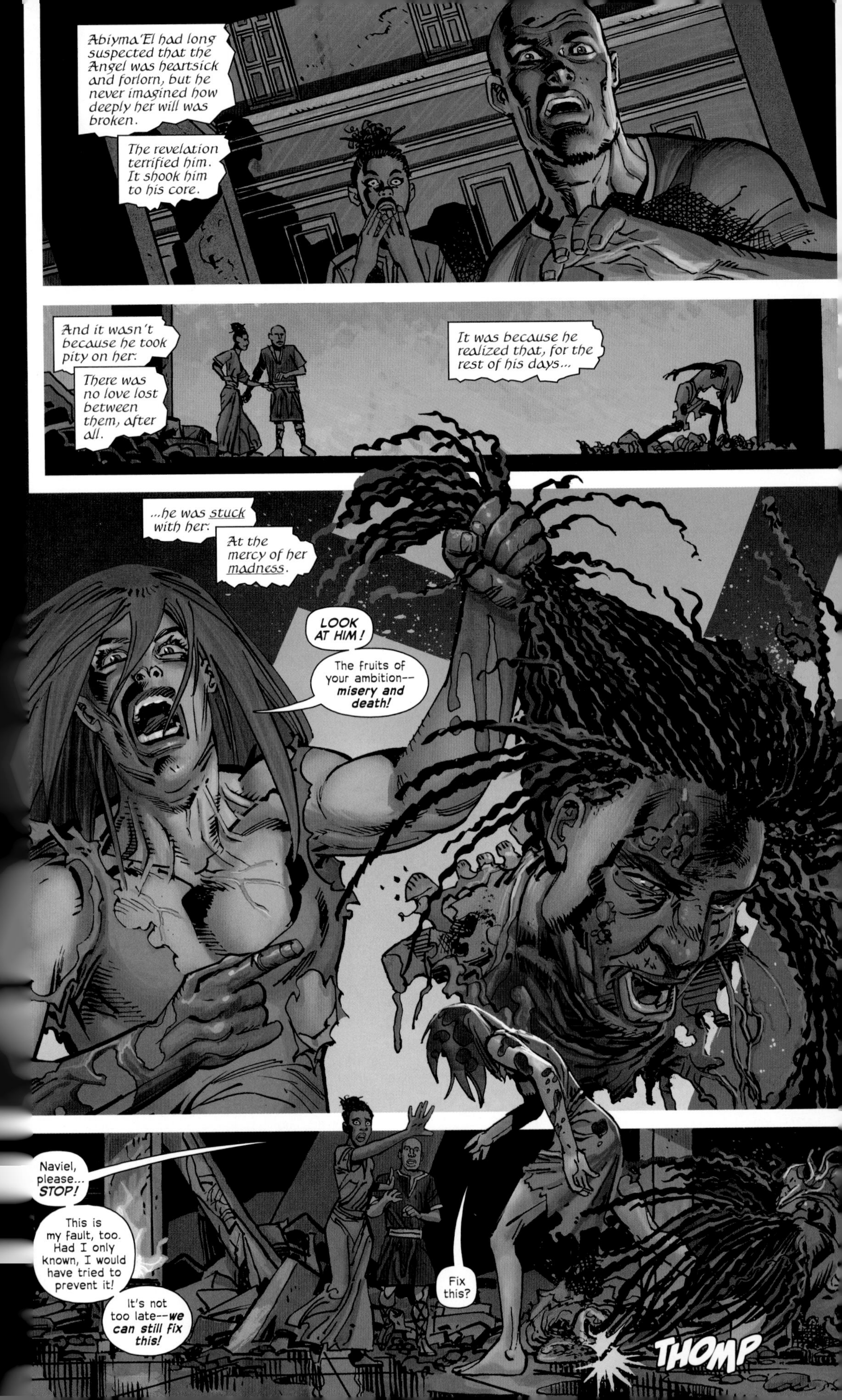
Abiyma'El had long suspected that the Angel was heartsick and forlorn, but he never imagined how deeply her will was broken.
The revelation terrified him. It shook him to his core.
And it wasn't because he took pity on her.
There was no love lost between them, after all.
It was because he realized that, for the rest of his days...
...he was stuck with her.
At the mercy of her madness.
LOOK AT HIM!
The fruits of your ambition--misery and death!
Naviel, please... STOP!
This is my fault, too. Had I only known, I would have tried to prevent it!
It's not too late--we can still fix this!
Fix this?
THOMP

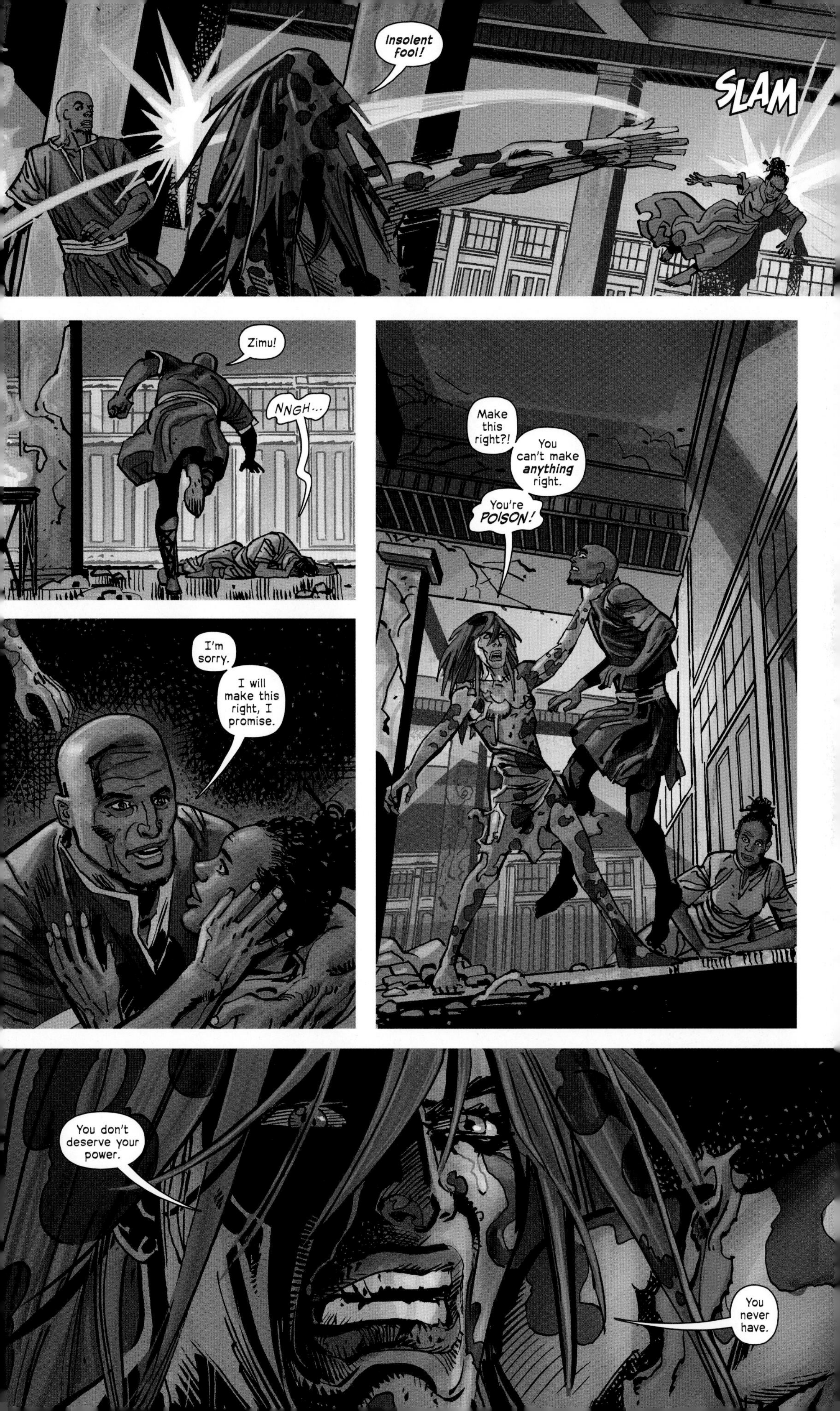

Insolent fool!
SLAM
Zimu!
NNGH...
I'm sorry.
I will make this right, I promise.
Make this right?!
You can't make *anything* right.
You're POISON!
You don't deserve your power.
You never have.

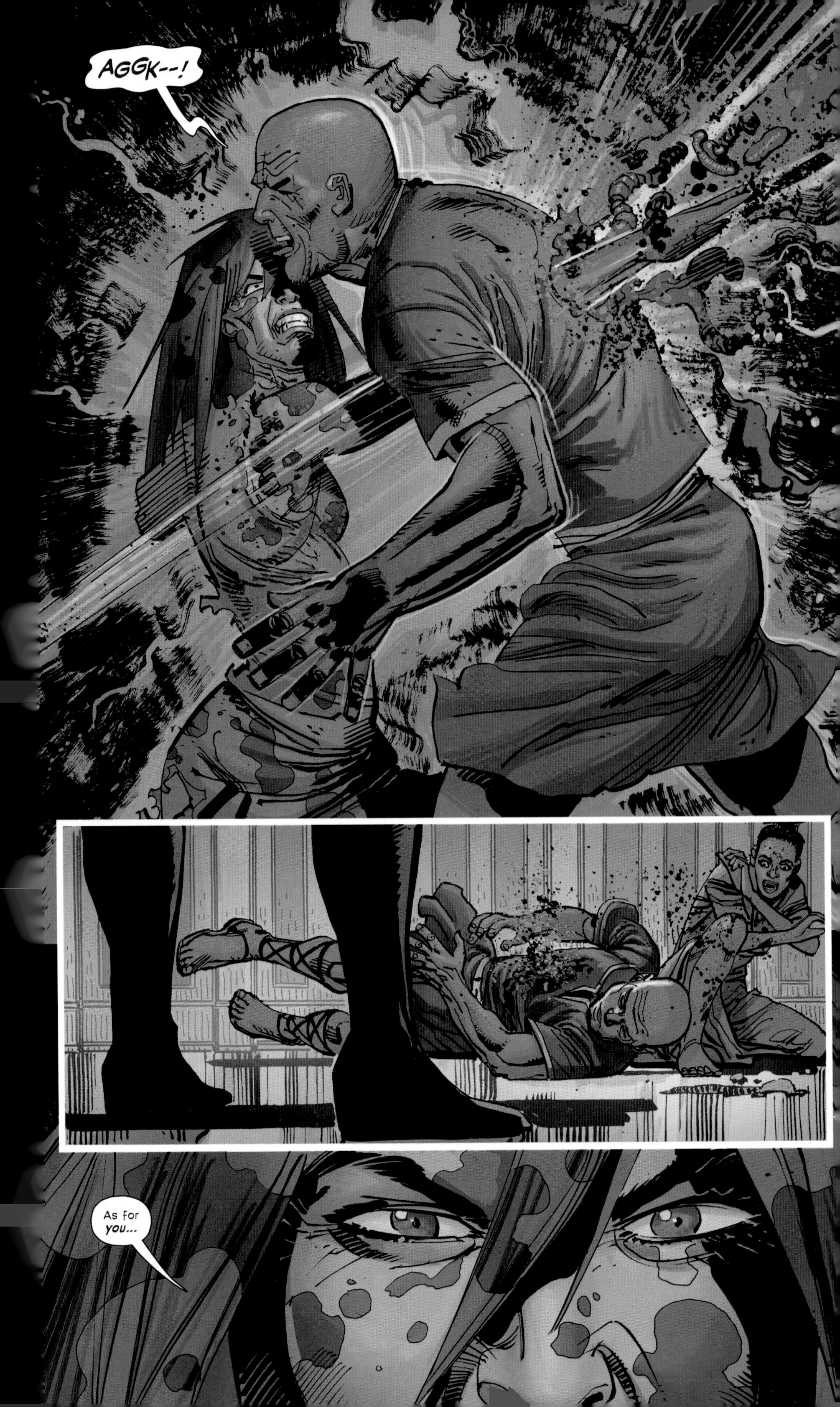
AGGK--!
As for you...

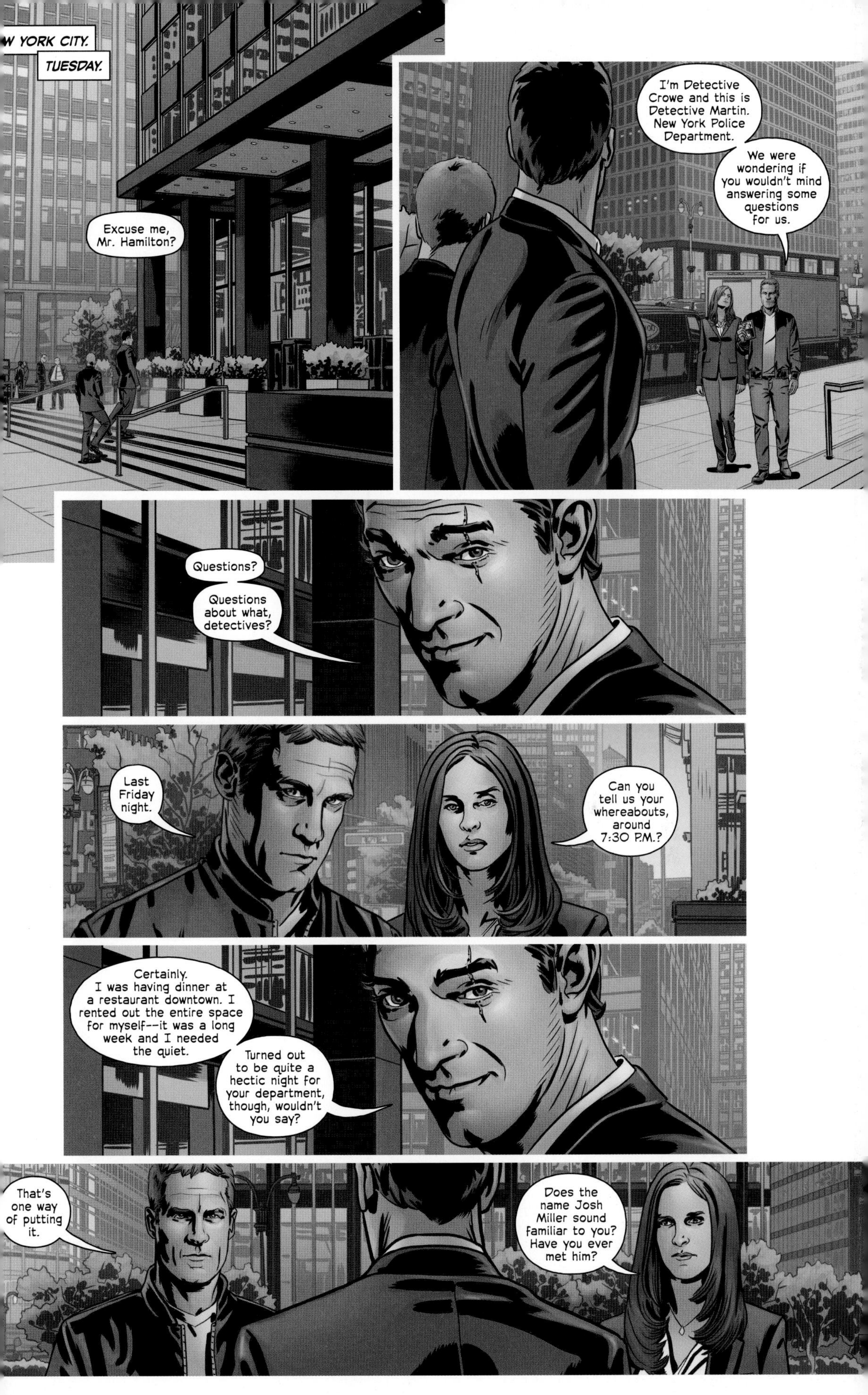
W YORK CITY.
TUESDAY.
Excuse me, Mr. Hamilton?
I'm Detective Crowe and this is Detective Martin. New York Police Department.
We were wondering if you wouldn't mind answering some questions for us.
Questions?
Questions about what, detectives?
Last Friday night.
Can you tell us your whereabouts, around 7:30 P.M.?
Certainly. I was having dinner at a restaurant downtown. I rented out the entire space for myself--it was a long week and I needed the quiet.
Turned out to be quite a hectic night for your department, though, wouldn't you say?
That's one way of putting it.
Does the name Josh Miller sound familiar to you? Have you ever met him?

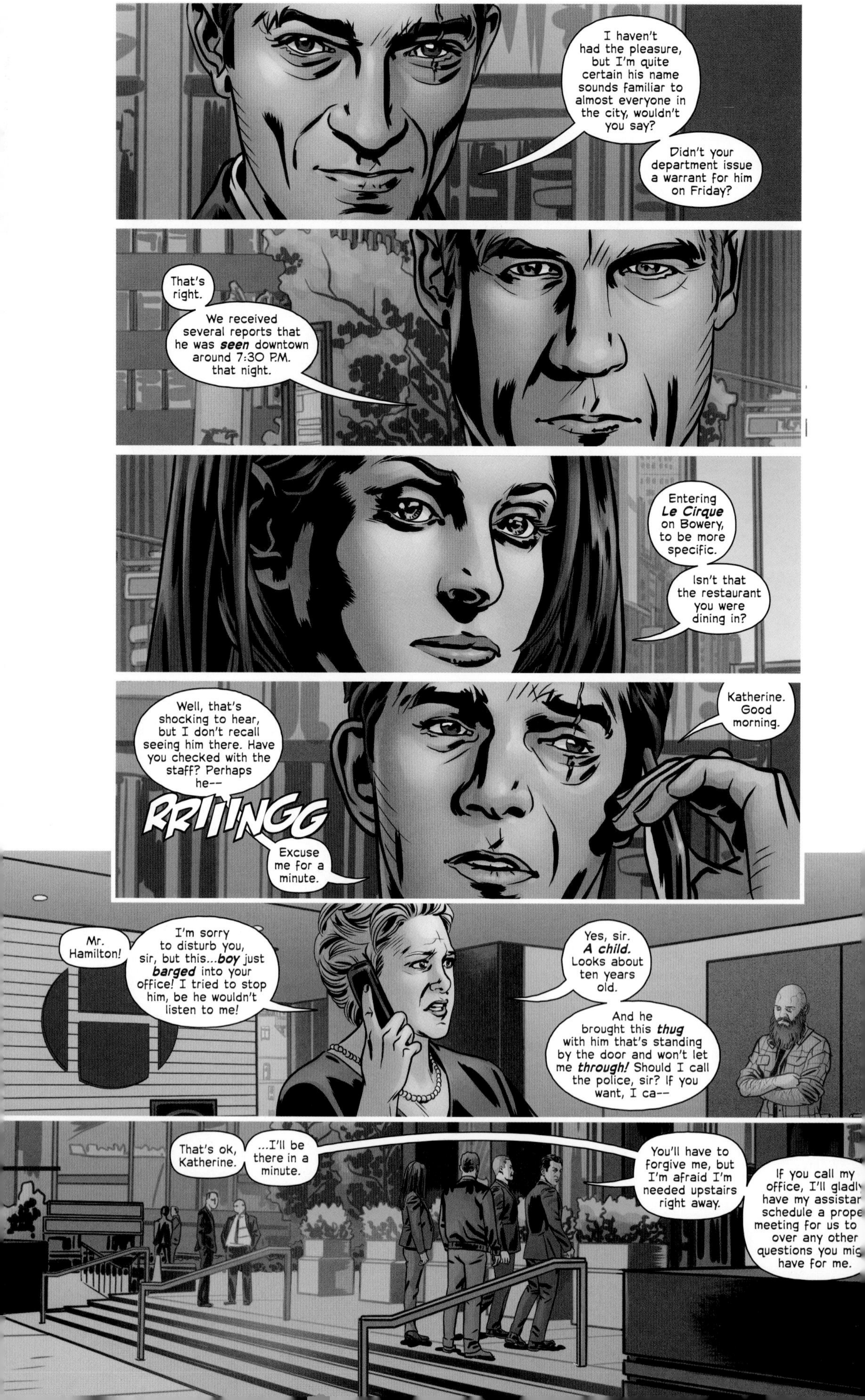
I haven't had the pleasure, but I'm quite certain his name sounds familiar to almost everyone in the city, wouldn't you say?
Didn't your department issue a warrant for him on Friday?
That's right.
We received several reports that he was *seen* downtown around 7:30 P.M. that night.
Entering *Le Cirque* on Bowery, to be more specific.
Isn't that the restaurant you were dining in?
Well, that's shocking to hear, but I don't recall seeing him there. Have you checked with the staff? Perhaps he--
RRIIINGG
Excuse me for a minute.
Katherine. Good morning.
Mr. Hamilton!
I'm sorry to disturb you, sir, but this...*boy* just *barged* into your office! I tried to stop him, be he wouldn't listen to me!
Yes, sir. *A child.* Looks about ten years old.
And he brought this *thug* with him that's standing by the door and won't let me *through!* Should I call the police, sir? If you want, I ca--
That's ok, Katherine.
...I'll be there in a minute.
You'll have to forgive me, but I'm afraid I'm needed upstairs right away.

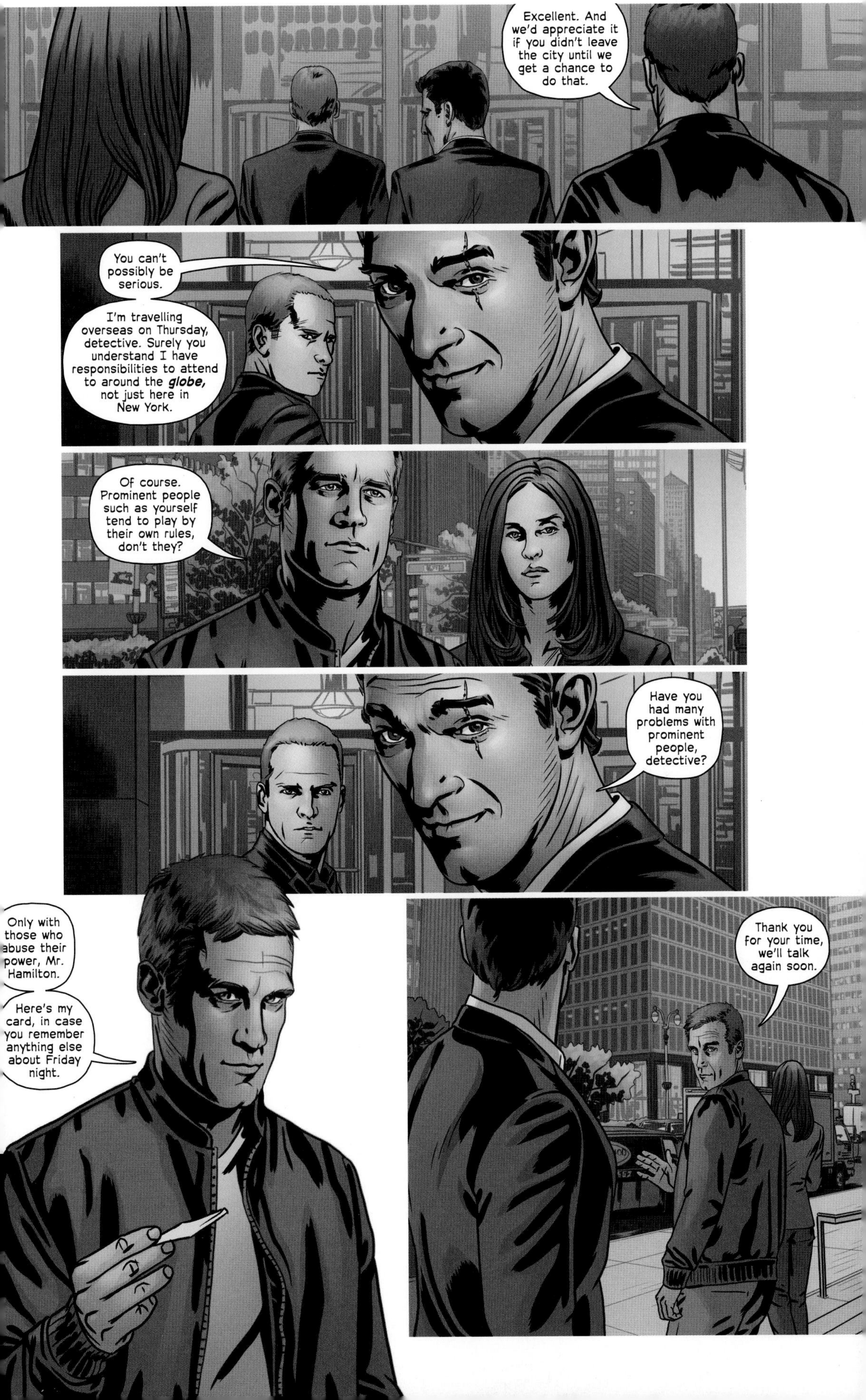
Excellent. And we'd appreciate it if you didn't leave the city until we get a chance to do that.
You can't possibly be serious.
I'm travelling overseas on Thursday, detective. Surely you understand I have responsibilities to attend to around the ***globe,*** not just here in New York.
Of course. Prominent people such as yourself tend to play by their own rules, don't they?
Have you had many problems with prominent people, detective?
Only with those who abuse their power, Mr. Hamilton.
Here's my card, in case you remember anything else about Friday night.
Thank you for your time, we'll talk again soon.

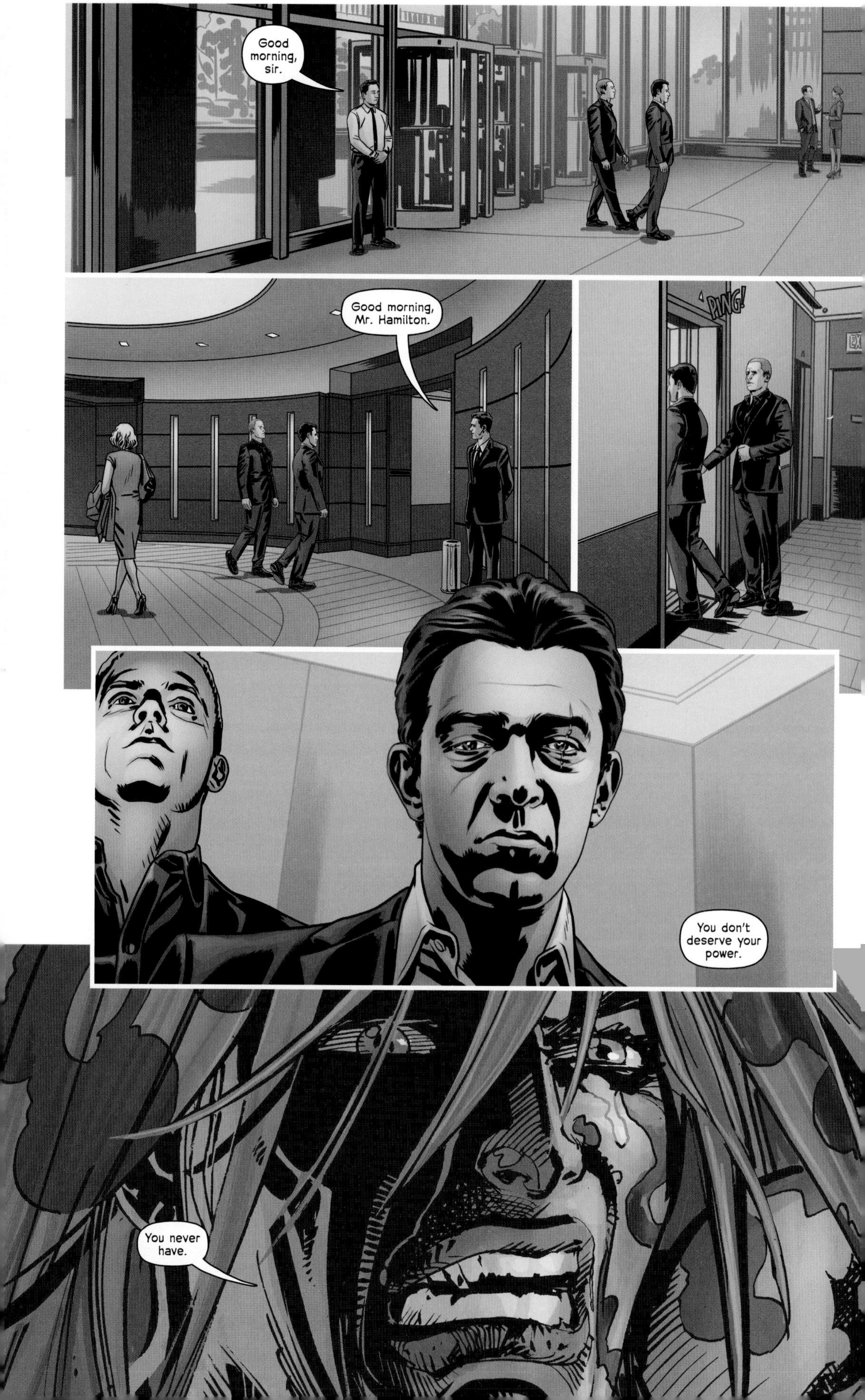
Good morning, sir.
Good morning, Mr. Hamilton.
PING!
You don't deserve your power.
You never have.

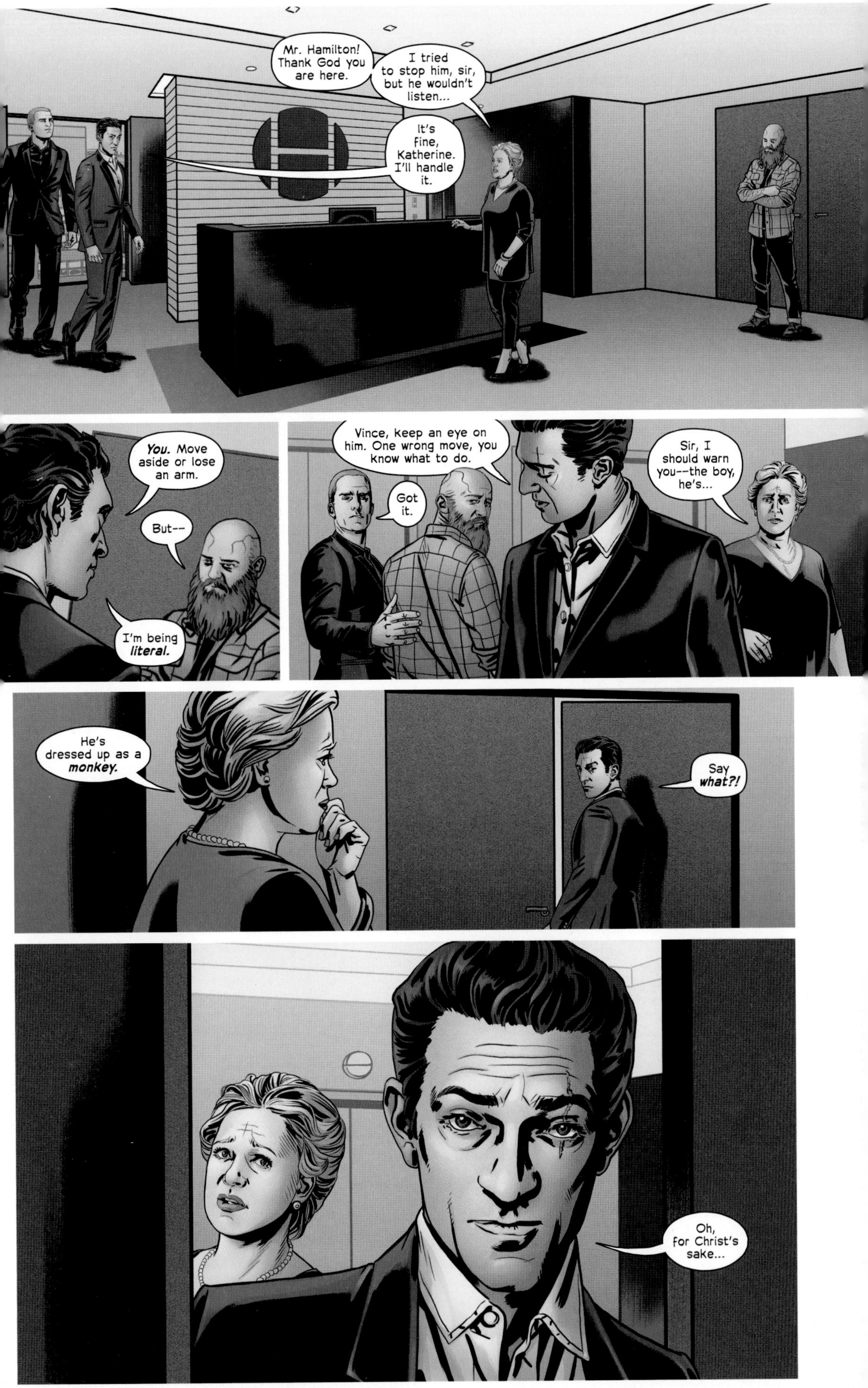

Mr. Hamilton! Thank God you are here.
I tried to stop him, sir, but he wouldn't listen...
It's fine, Katherine. I'll handle it.
You. Move aside or lose an arm.
But--
I'm being literal.
Vince, keep an eye on him. One wrong move, you know what to do.
Got it.
Sir, I should warn you--the boy, he's...
He's dressed up as a monkey.
Say what?!
Oh, for Christ's sake...

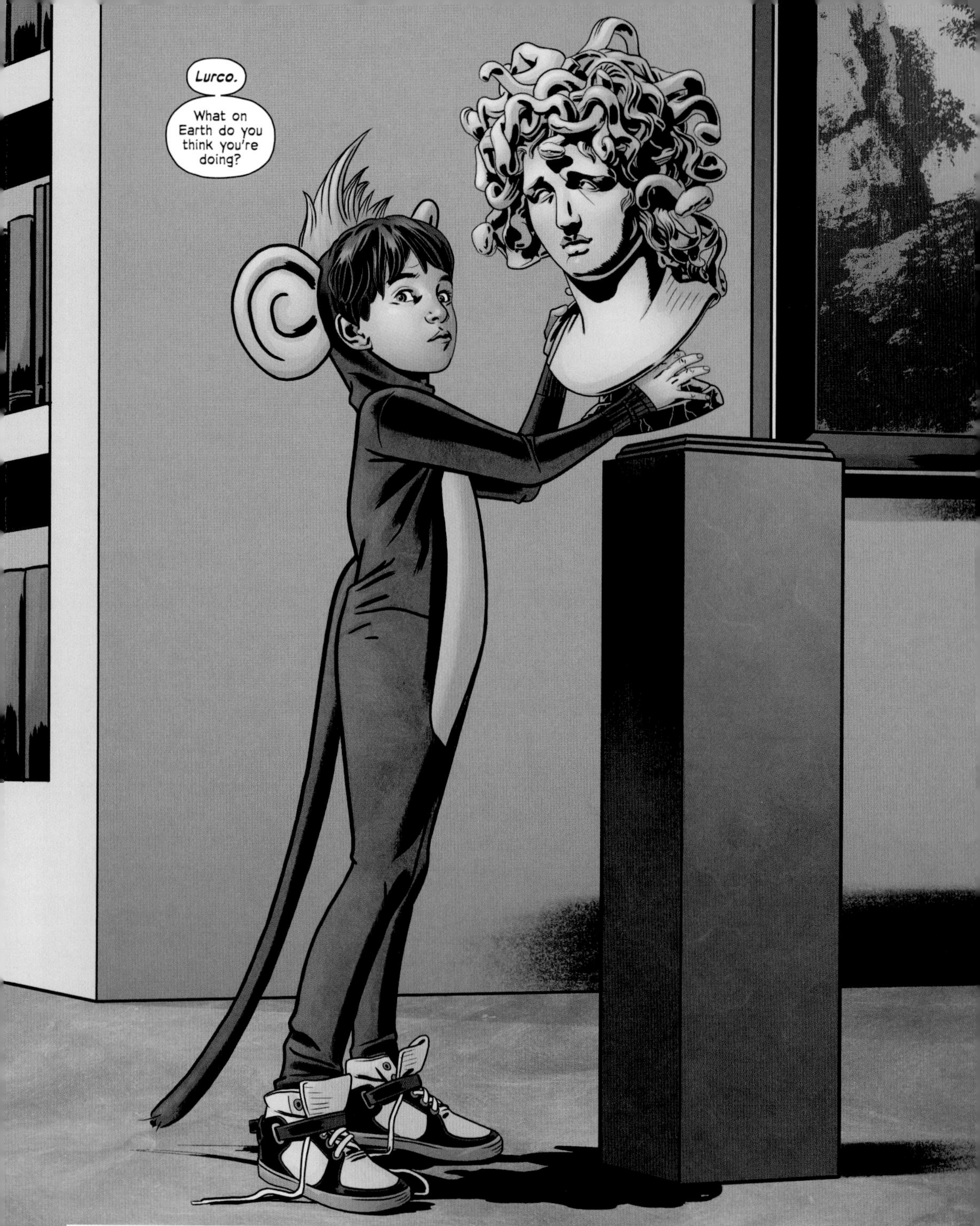
Lurco.
What on Earth do you think you're doing?

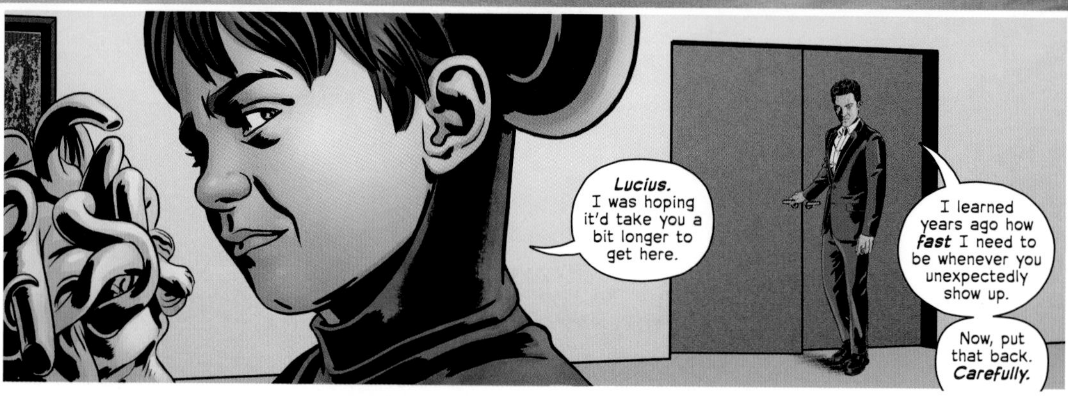
Lucius. I was hoping it'd take you a bit longer to get here.
I learned years ago how ***fast*** I need to be whenever you unexpectedly show up.
Now, put that back. ***Carefully.***

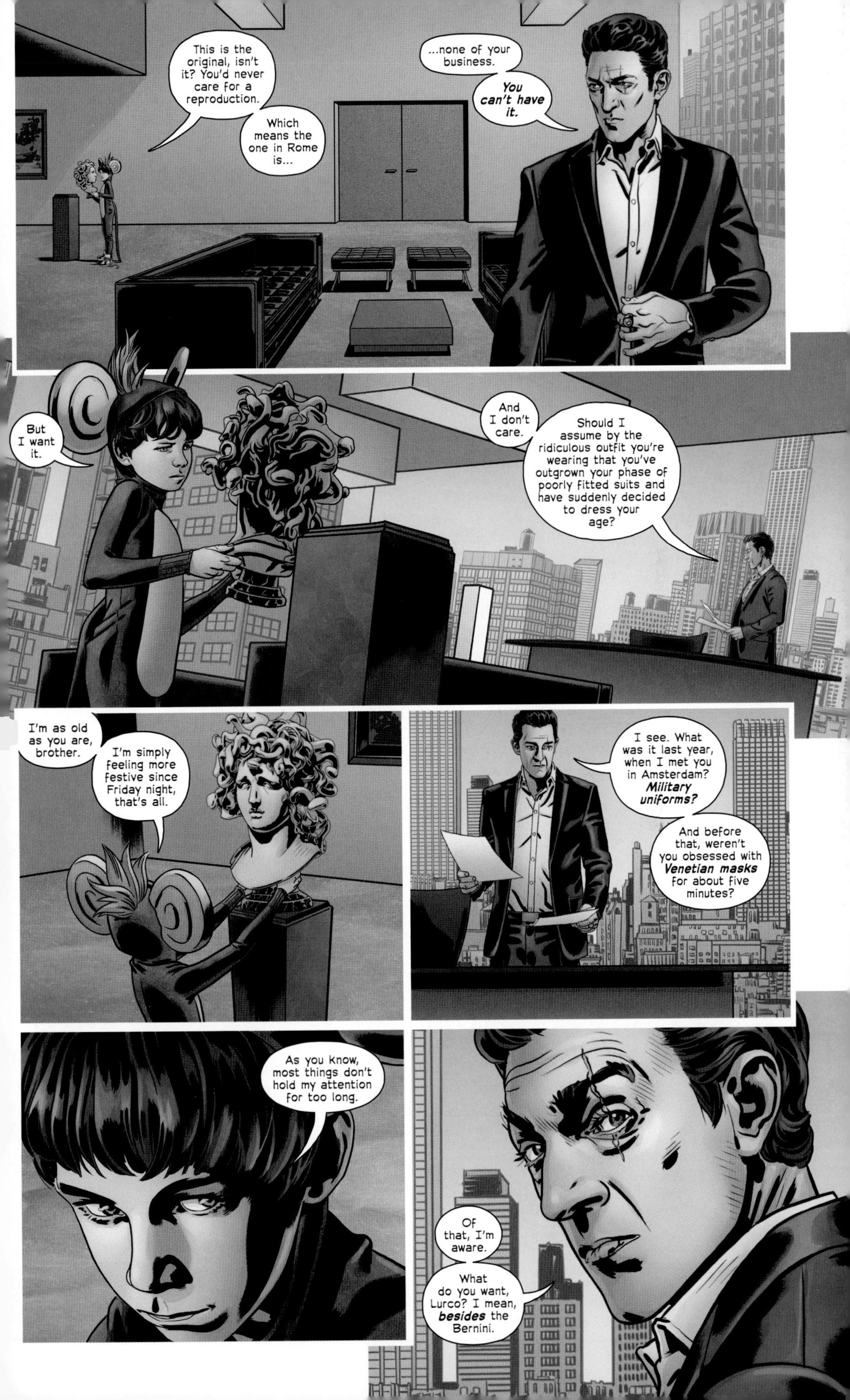
This is the original, isn't it? You'd never care for a reproduction.
Which means the one in Rome is...
...none of your business.
You can't have it.
But I want it.
And I don't care.
Should I assume by the ridiculous outfit you're wearing that you've outgrown your phase of poorly fitted suits and have suddenly decided to dress your age?
I'm as old as you are, brother.
I'm simply feeling more festive since Friday night, that's all.
I see. What was it last year, when I met you in Amsterdam? Military uniforms?
And before that, weren't you obsessed with Venetian masks for about five minutes?
As you know, most things don't hold my attention for too long.
Of that, I'm aware.
What do you want, Lurco? I mean, besides the Bernini.

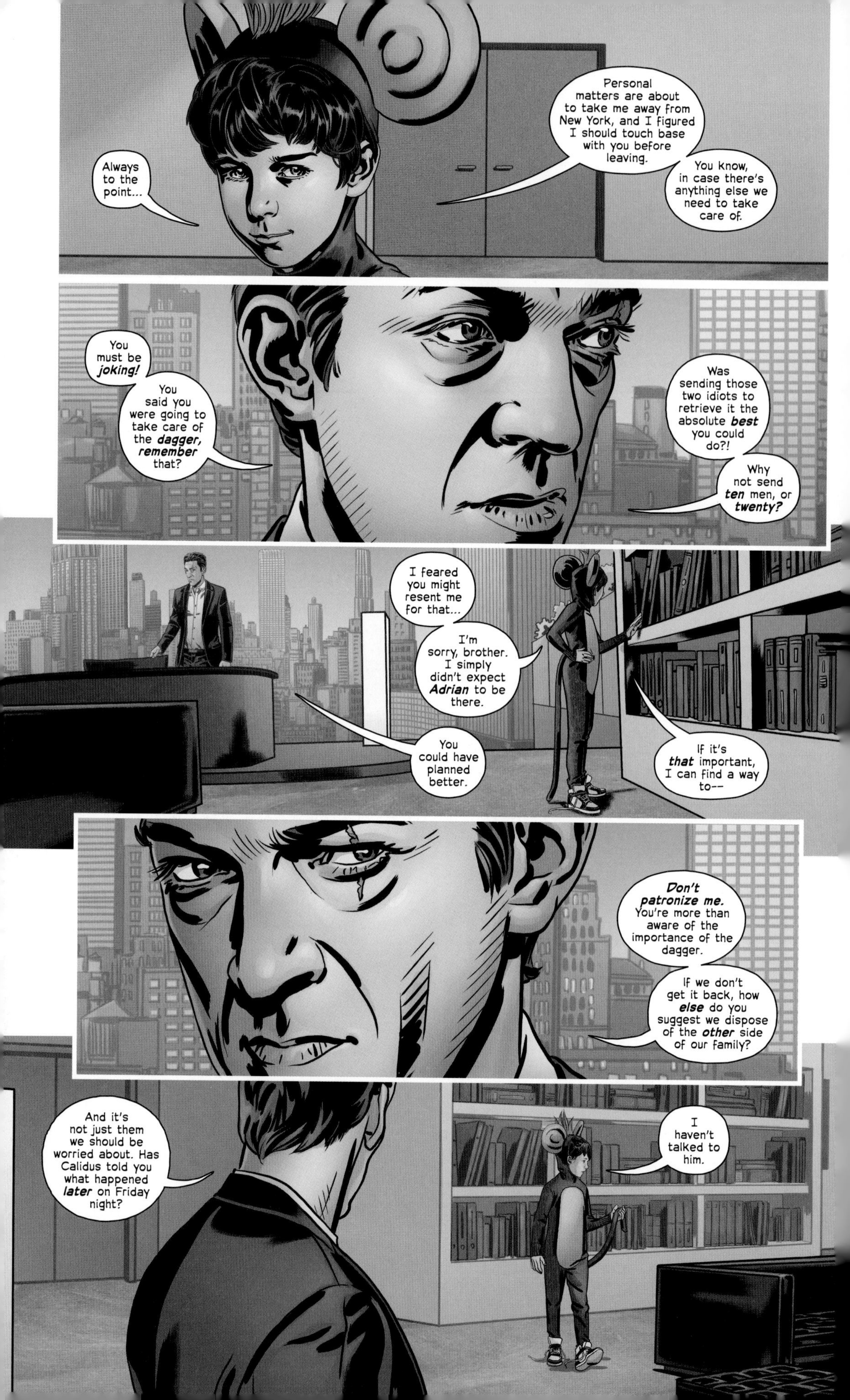
Always to the point...
Personal matters are about to take me away from New York, and I figured I should touch base with you before leaving.
You know, in case there's anything else we need to take care of.
You must be *joking!*
You said you were going to take care of the *dagger, remember* that?
Was sending those two idiots to retrieve it the absolute *best* you could do?!
Why not send *ten* men, or *twenty?*
I feared you might resent me for that...
I'm sorry, brother. I simply didn't expect *Adrian* to be there.
You could have planned better.
If it's *that* important, I can find a way to--
Don't patronize me. You're more than aware of the importance of the dagger.
If we don't get it back, how *else* do you suggest we dispose of the *other* side of our family?
And it's not just them we should be worried about. Has Calidus told you what happened *later* on Friday night?
I haven't talked to him.

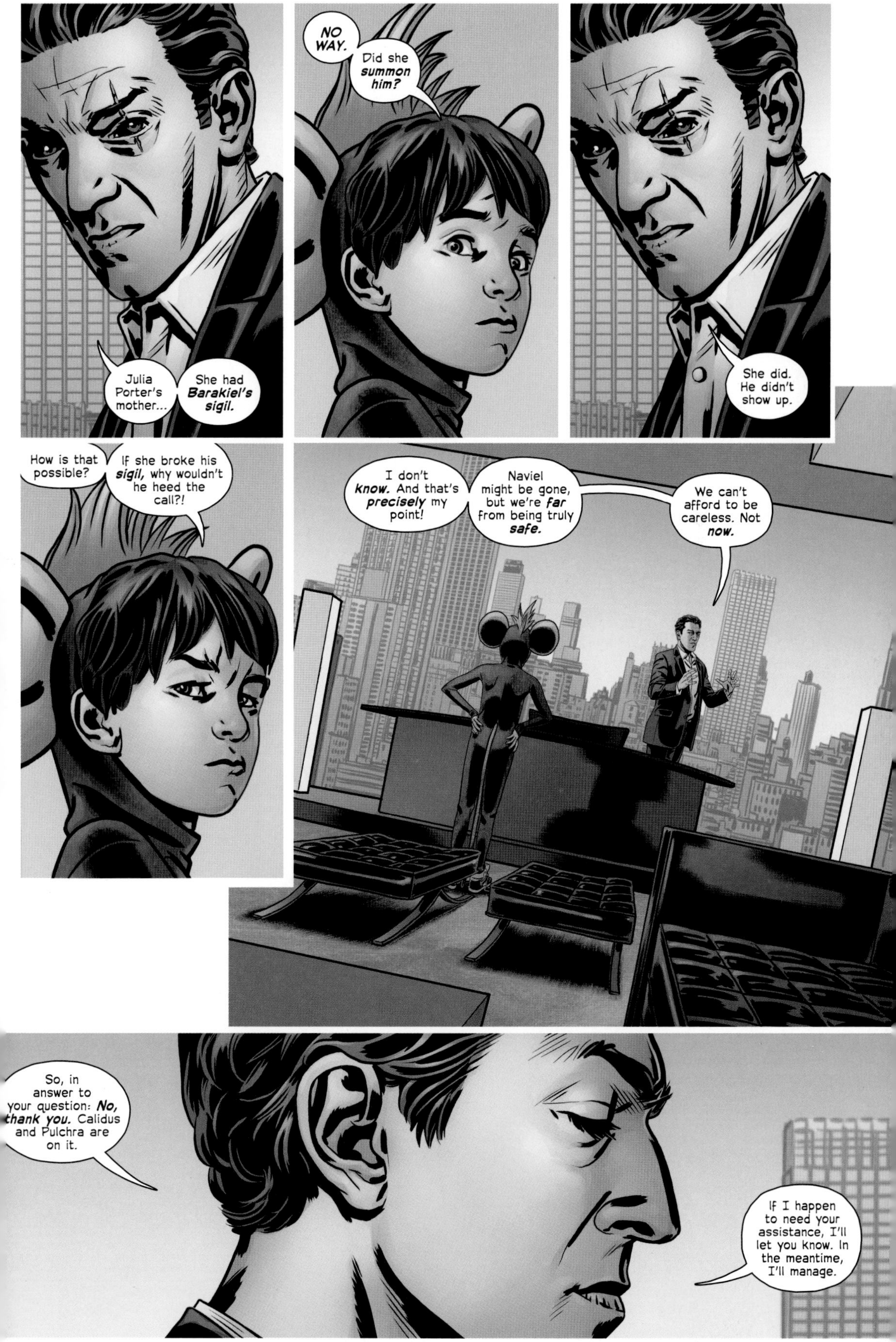
Julia Porter's mother...
She had *Barakiel's sigil.*
NO WAY.
Did she *summon him?*
She did. He didn't show up.
How is that possible?
If she broke his *sigil,* why wouldn't he heed the call?!
I don't *know.* And that's *precisely* my point!
Naviel might be gone, but we're *far* from being truly *safe.*
We can't afford to be careless. Not *now.*
So, in answer to your question: *No, thank you.* Calidus and Pulchra are on it.
If I happen to need your assistance, I'll let you know. In the meantime, I'll manage.

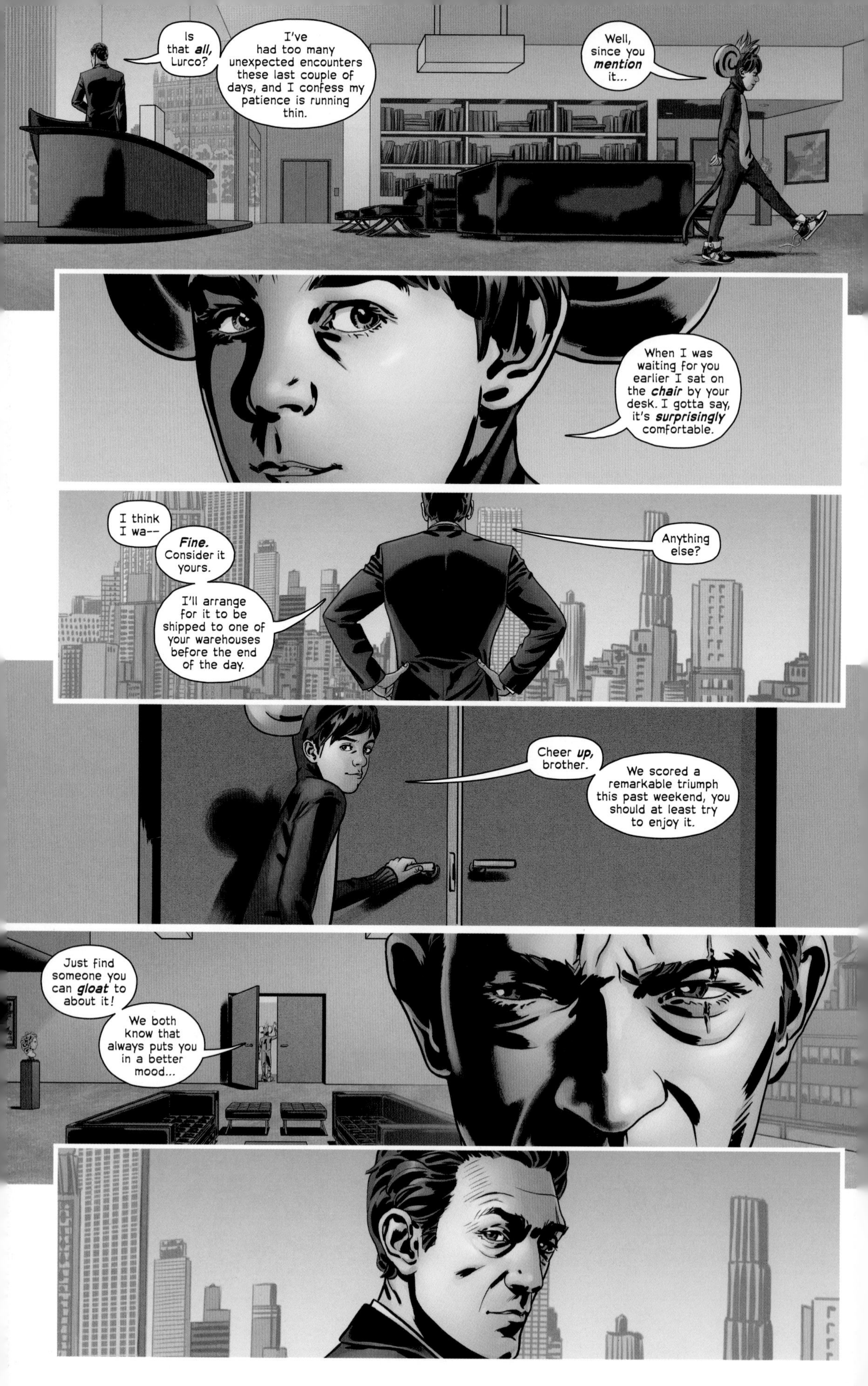
Is that *all,* Lurco?
I've had too many unexpected encounters these last couple of days, and I confess my patience is running thin.
Well, since you *mention* it...
When I was waiting for you earlier I sat on the *chair* by your desk. I gotta say, it's *surprisingly* comfortable.
I think I wa--
Fine. Consider it yours.
I'll arrange for it to be shipped to one of your warehouses before the end of the day.
Anything else?
Cheer *up,* brother.
We scored a remarkable triumph this past weekend, you should at least try to enjoy it.
Just find someone you can *gloat* to about it!
We both know that always puts you in a better mood...

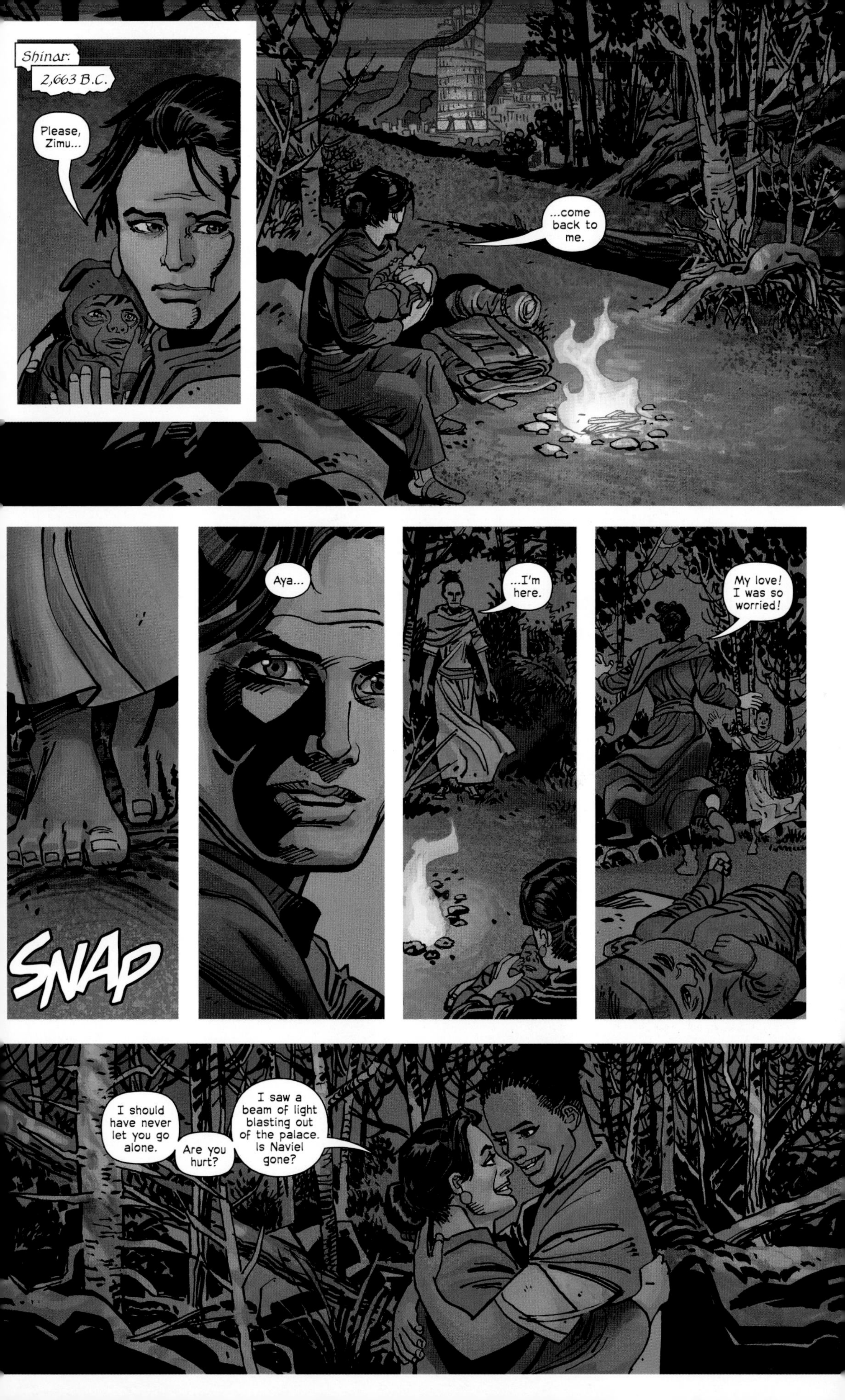
Shinar.
2,663 B.C.
Please, Zimu...
...come back to me.
SNAP
Aya...
...I'm here.
My love! I was so worried!
I should have never let you go alone.
Are you hurt?
I saw a beam of light blasting out of the palace. Is Naviel gone?

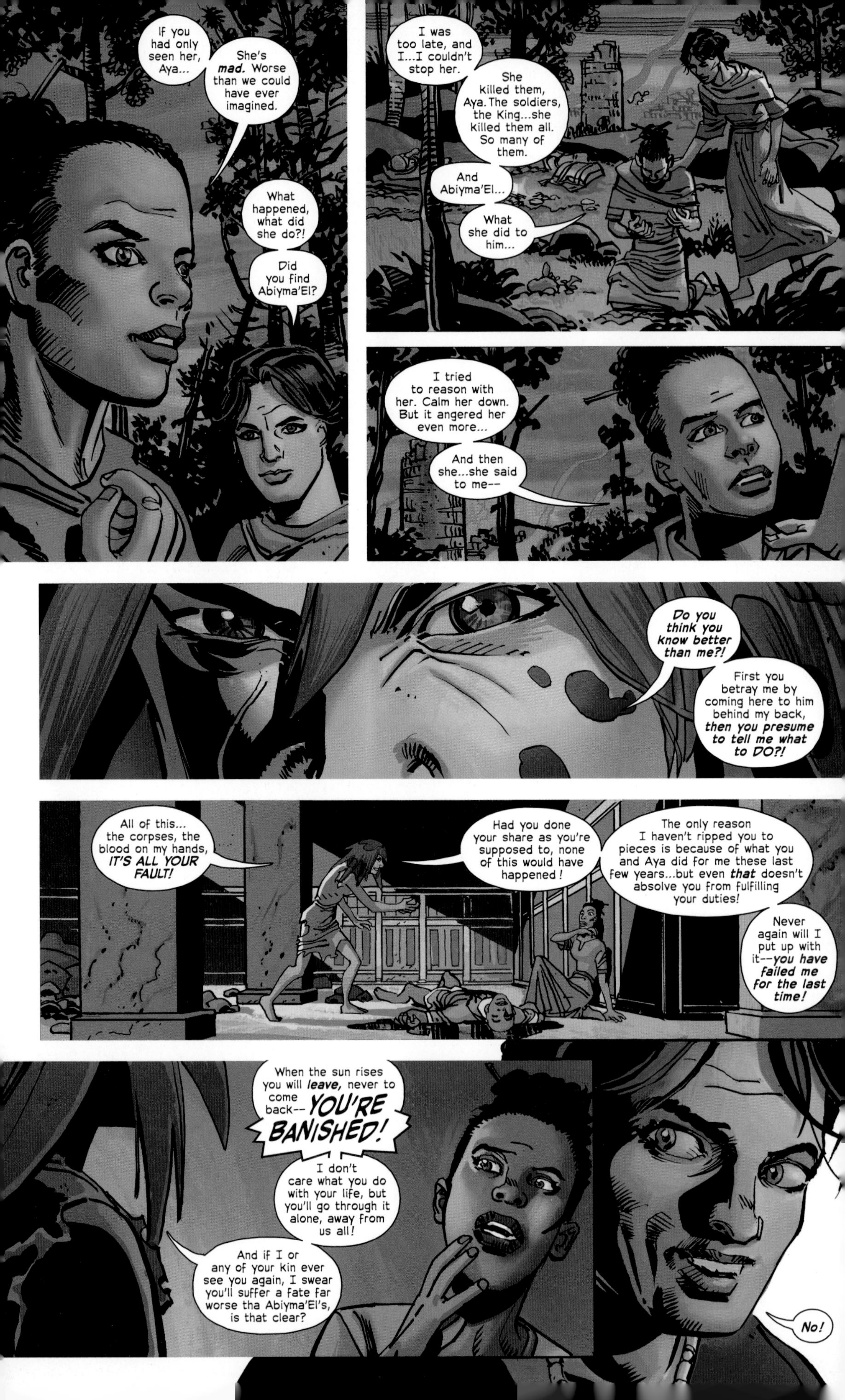

If you had only seen her, Aya...
She's *mad.* Worse than we could have ever imagined.
What happened, what did she do?!
Did you find Abiyma'El?
I was too late, and I...I couldn't stop her.
She killed them, Aya. The soldiers, the King...she killed them all. So many of them.
And Abiyma'El...
What she did to him...
I tried to reason with her. Calm her down. But it angered her even more...
And then she...she said to me--
Do you think you know better than me?!
First you betray me by coming here to him behind my back, ***then you presume to tell me what to DO?!***
All of this... the corpses, the blood on my hands, ***IT'S ALL YOUR FAULT!***
Had you done your share as you're supposed to, none of this would have happened!
The only reason I haven't ripped you to pieces is because of what you and Aya did for me these last few years...but even *that* doesn't absolve you from fulfilling your duties!
Never again will I put up with it--***you have failed me for the last time!***
When the sun rises you will *leave,* never to come back-- YOU'RE BANISHED!
I don't care what you do with your life, but you'll go through it alone, away from us all!
And if I or any of your kin ever see you again, I swear you'll suffer a fate far worse tha Abiyma'El's, is that clear?
No!

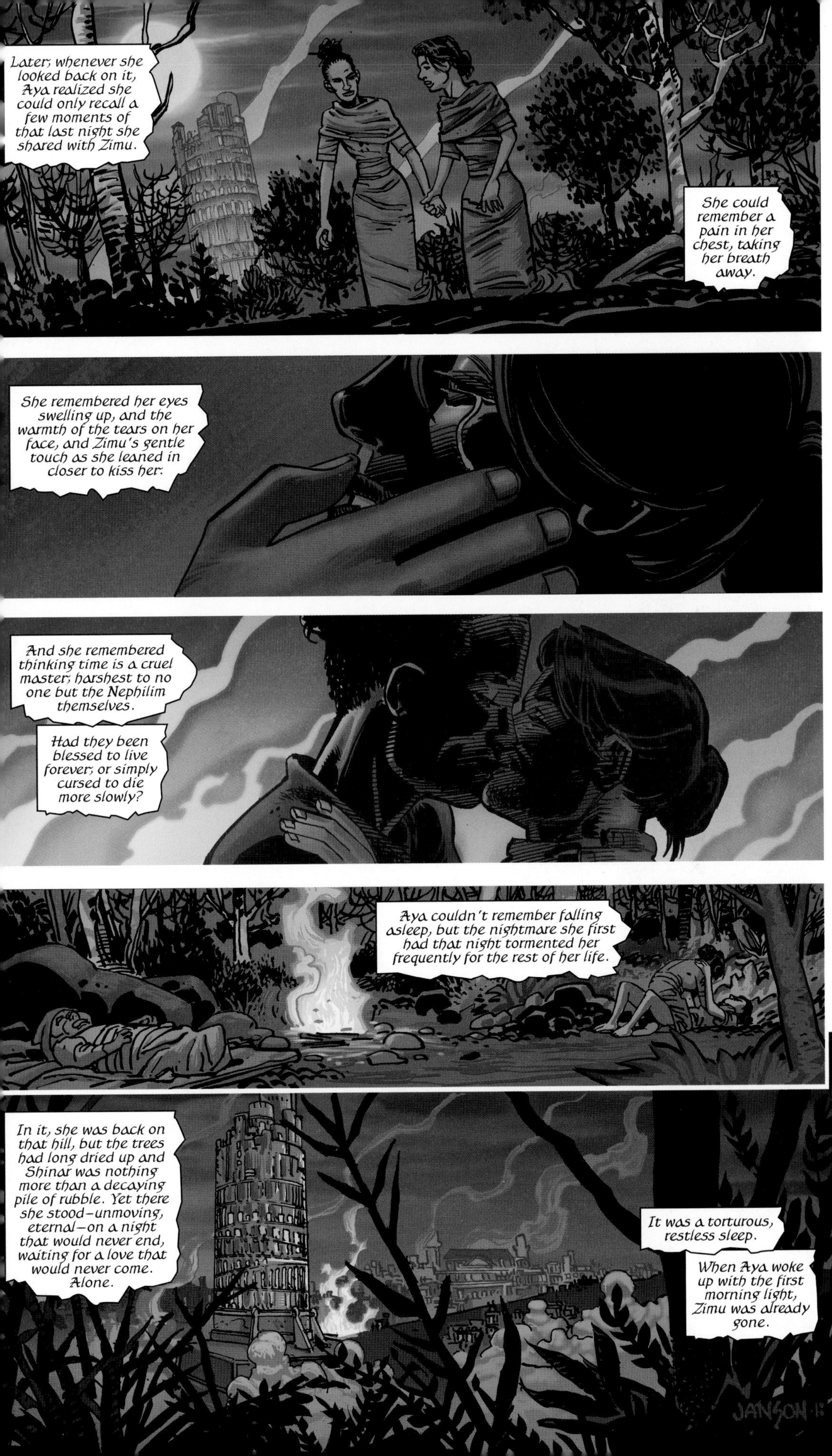

Later, whenever she looked back on it, Aya realized she could only recall a few moments of that last night she shared with Zimu.
She could remember a pain in her chest, taking her breath away.
She remembered her eyes swelling up, and the warmth of the tears on her face, and Zimu's gentle touch as she leaned in closer to kiss her.
And she remembered thinking time is a cruel master, harshest to no one but the Nephilim themselves.
Had they been blessed to live forever, or simply cursed to die more slowly?
Aya couldn't remember falling asleep, but the nightmare she first had that night tormented her frequently for the rest of her life.
In it, she was back on that hill, but the trees had long dried up and Shinar was nothing more than a decaying pile of rubble. Yet there she stood–unmoving, eternal–on a night that would never end, waiting for a love that would never come. Alone.
It was a torturous, restless sleep.
When Aya woke up with the first morning light, Zimu was already gone.
JANSON

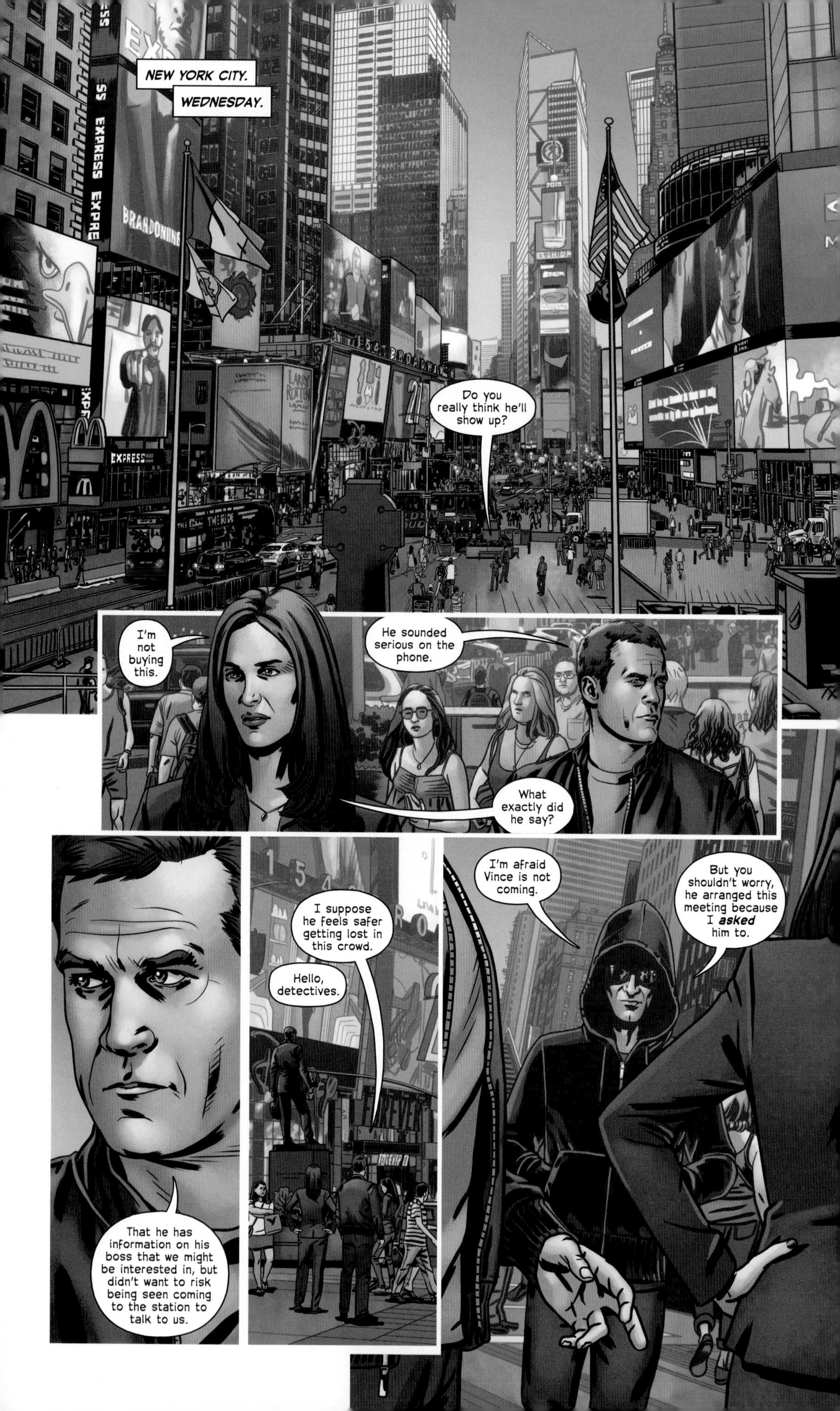

NEW YORK CITY.
WEDNESDAY.
Do you really think he'll show up?
I'm not buying this.
He sounded serious on the phone.
What exactly did he say?
That he has information on his boss that we might be interested in, but didn't want to risk being seen coming to the station to talk to us.
I suppose he feels safer getting lost in this crowd.
Hello, detectives.
I'm afraid Vince is not coming.
But you shouldn't worry, he arranged this meeting because I *asked* him to.

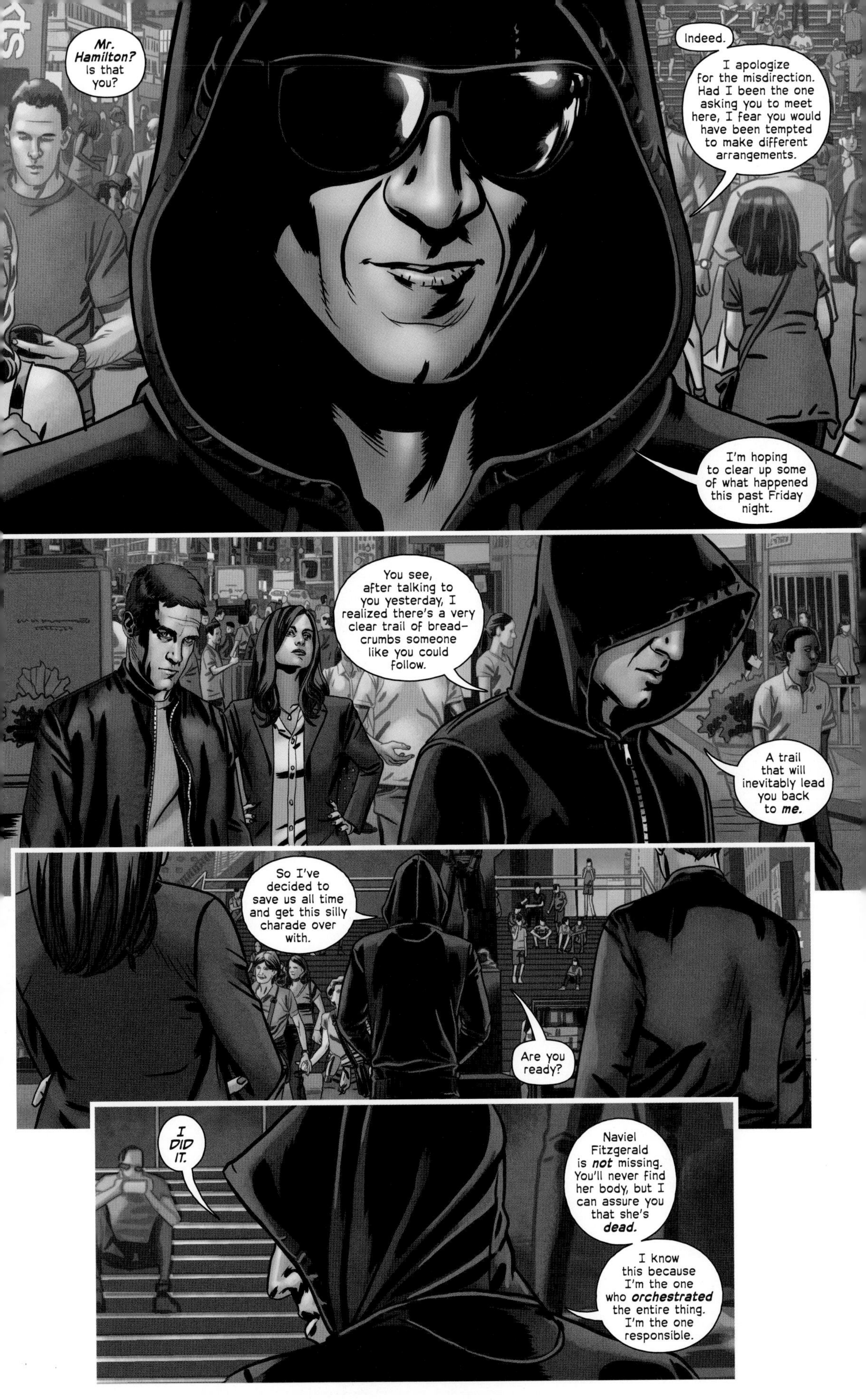

Mr. Hamilton? Is that you?
Indeed.
I apologize for the misdirection. Had I been the one asking you to meet here, I fear you would have been tempted to make different arrangements.
I'm hoping to clear up some of what happened this past Friday night.
You see, after talking to you yesterday, I realized there's a very clear trail of bread-crumbs someone like you could follow.
A trail that will inevitably lead you back to *me.*
So I've decided to save us all time and get this silly charade over with.
Are you ready?
I DID IT.
Naviel Fitzgerald is ***not*** missing. You'll never find her body, but I can assure you that she's ***dead.***
I know this because I'm the one who ***orchestrated*** the entire thing. I'm the one responsible.

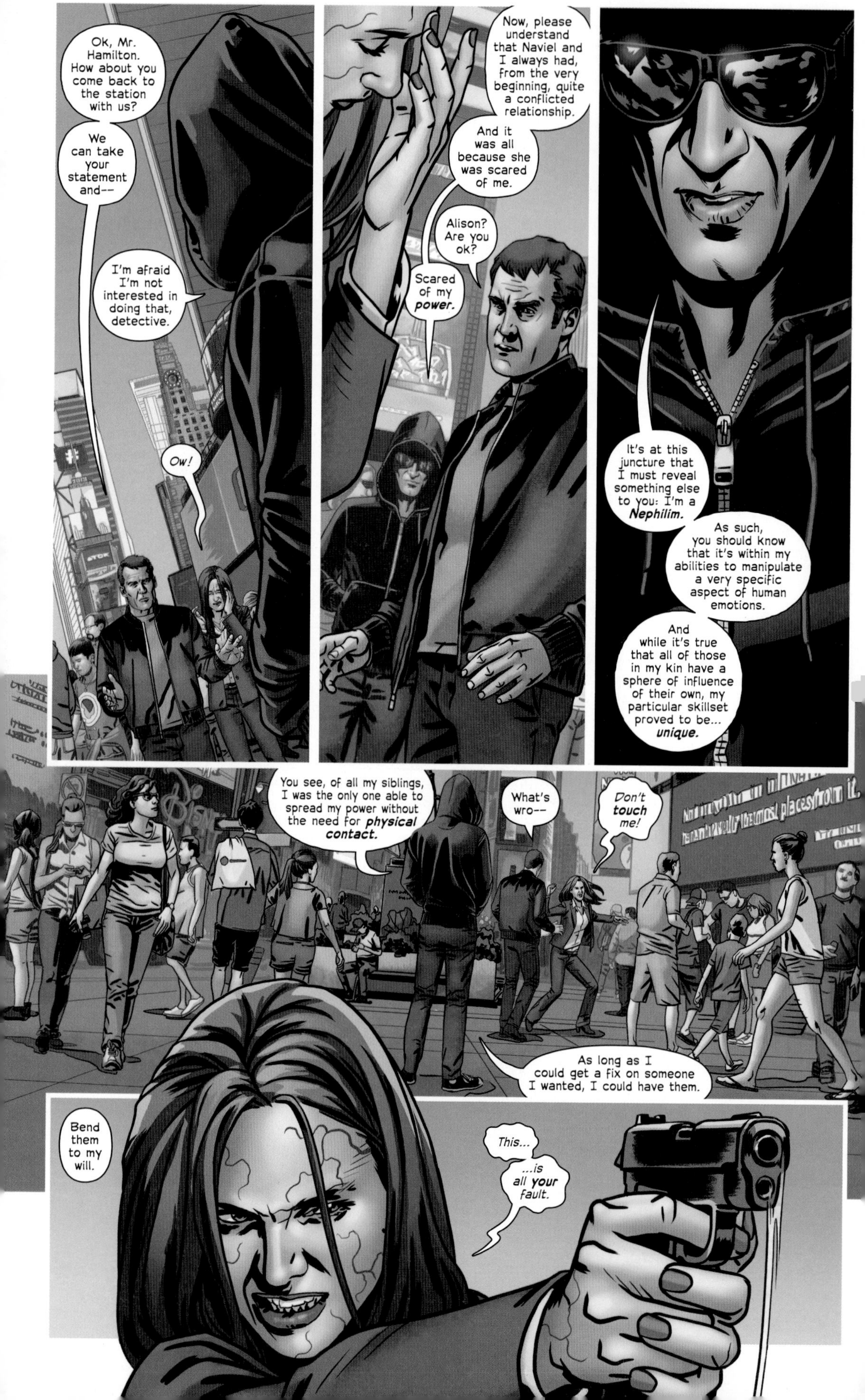
Ok, Mr. Hamilton. How about you come back to the station with us?
We can take your statement and--
I'm afraid I'm not interested in doing that, detective.
Ow!
Now, please understand that Naviel and I always had, from the very beginning, quite a conflicted relationship.
And it was all because she was scared of me.
Alison? Are you ok?
Scared of my *power.*
It's at this juncture that I must reveal something else to you: I'm a ***Nephilim.***
As such, you should know that it's within my abilities to manipulate a very specific aspect of human emotions.
And while it's true that all of those in my kin have a sphere of influence of their own, my particular skillset proved to be... ***unique.***
You see, of all my siblings, I was the only one able to spread my power without the need for ***physical contact.***
What's wro--
Don't ***touch*** *me!*
As long as I could get a fix on someone I wanted, I could have them.
Bend them to my will.
This...
...is all ***your*** *fault.*

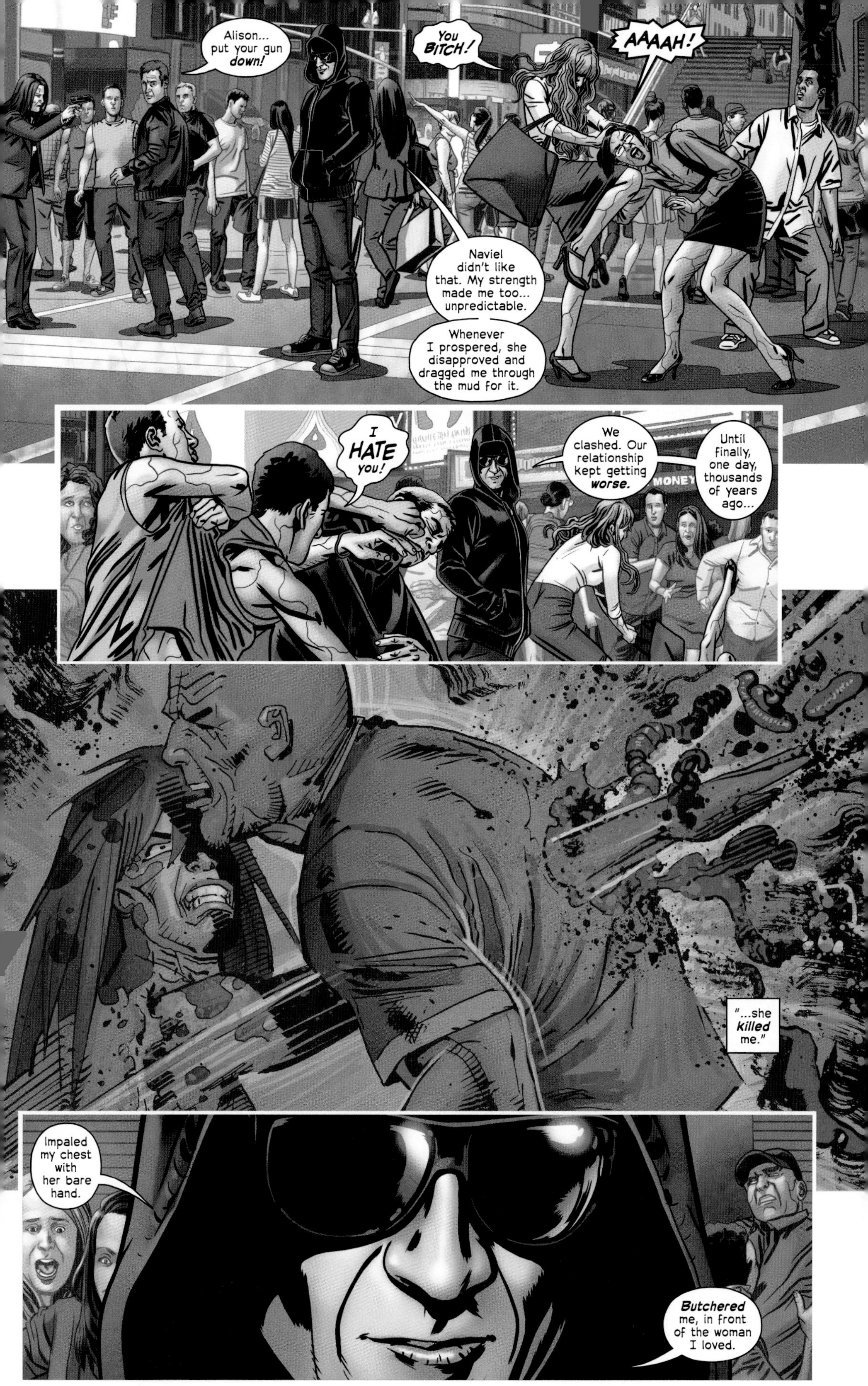

Alison... put your gun *down!*
You *BITCH!*
AAAAH!
Naviel didn't like that. My strength made me too... unpredictable.
Whenever I prospered, she disapproved and dragged me through the mud for it.
I *HATE* you!
We clashed. Our relationship kept getting *worse.*
Until finally, one day, thousands of years ago...
"...she *killed* me."
Impaled my chest with her bare hand.
Butchered me, in front of the woman I loved.

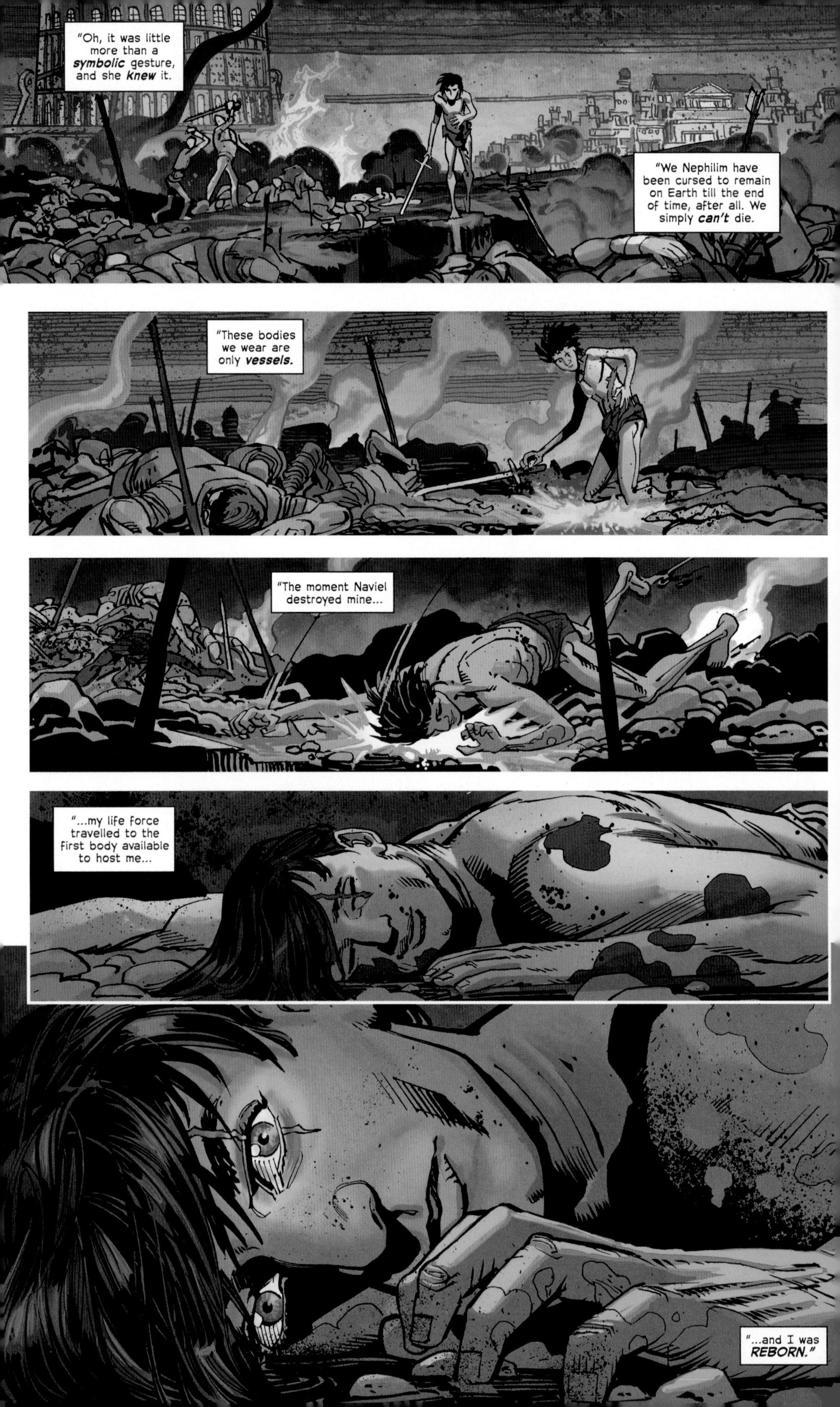
"Oh, it was little more than a *symbolic* gesture, and she *knew* it.
"We Nephilim have been cursed to remain on Earth till the end of time, after all. We simply *can't* die.
"These bodies we wear are only *vessels.*
"The moment Naviel destroyed mine...
"...my life force travelled to the first body available to host me...
"...and I was *REBORN.*"

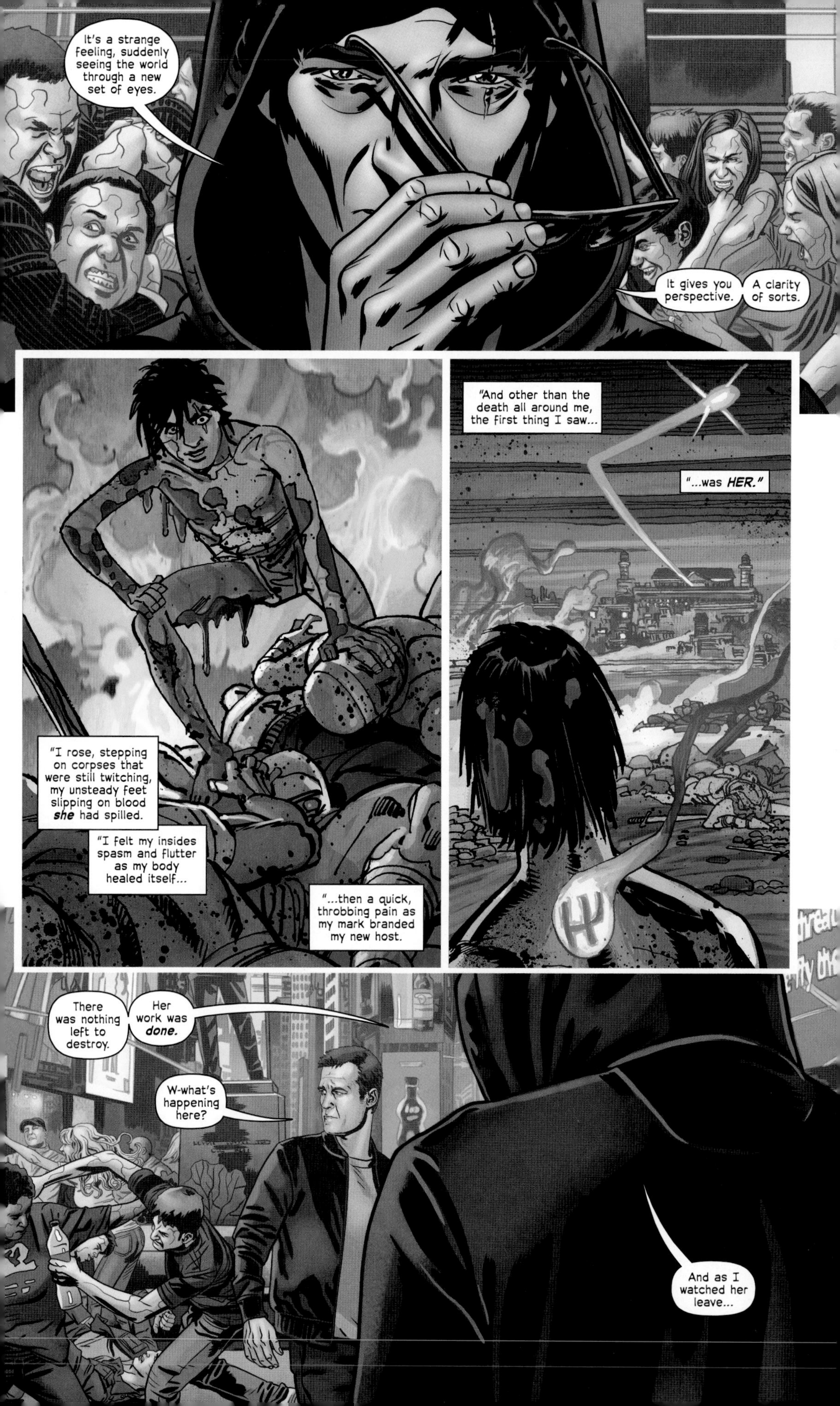

It's a strange feeling, suddenly seeing the world through a new set of eyes.
It gives you perspective.
A clarity of sorts.
"I rose, stepping on corpses that were still twitching, my unsteady feet slipping on blood *she* had spilled.
"I felt my insides spasm and flutter as my body healed itself...
"...then a quick, throbbing pain as my mark branded my new host.
"And other than the death all around me, the first thing I saw...
"...was ***HER.***"
There was nothing left to destroy.
Her work was ***done.***
W-what's happening here?
And as I watched her leave...

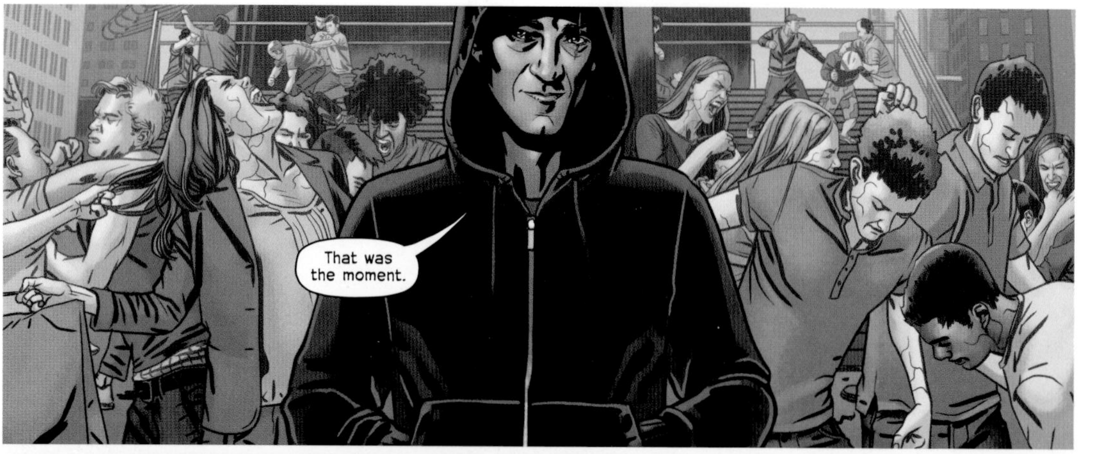
That was the moment.

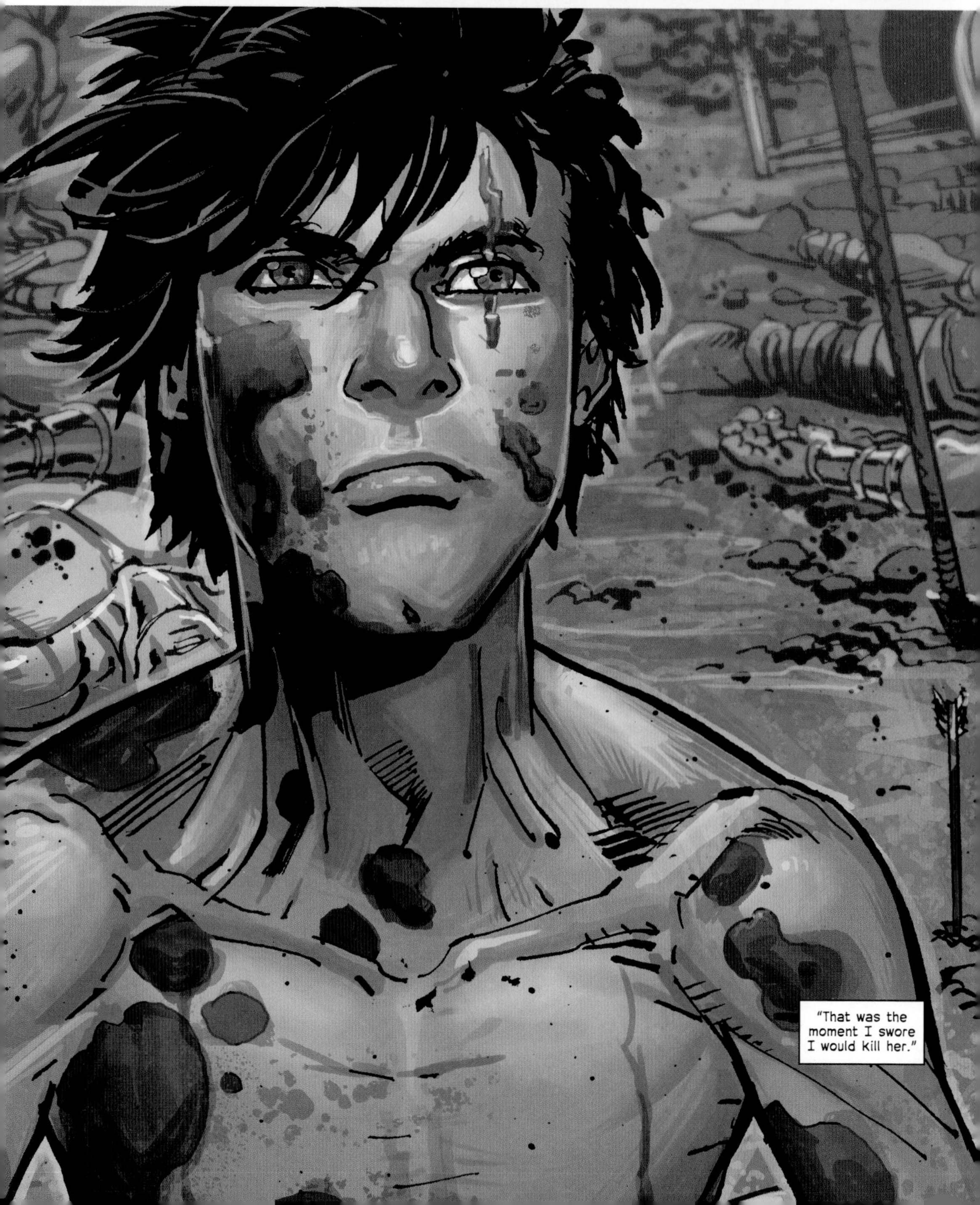
"That was the moment I swore I would kill her."

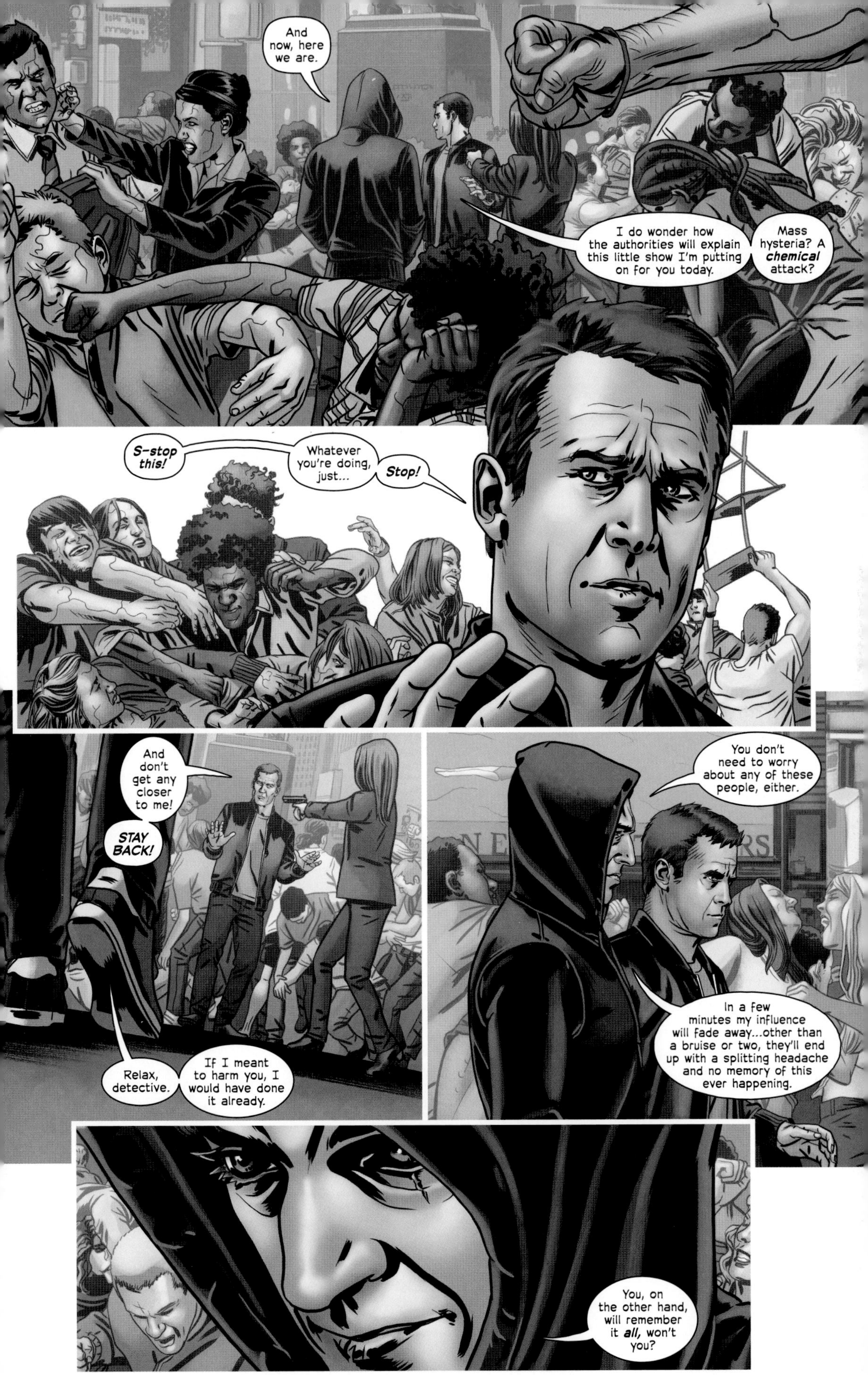
And now, here we are.
I do wonder how the authorities will explain this little show I'm putting on for you today.
Mass hysteria? A *chemical* attack?
S–stop this!
Whatever you're doing, just...
Stop!
And don't get any closer to me!
STAY BACK!
Relax, detective.
If I meant to harm you, I would have done it already.
You don't need to worry about any of these people, either.
In a few minutes my influence will fade away...other than a bruise or two, they'll end up with a splitting headache and no memory of this ever happening.
You, on the other hand, will remember it *all,* won't you?

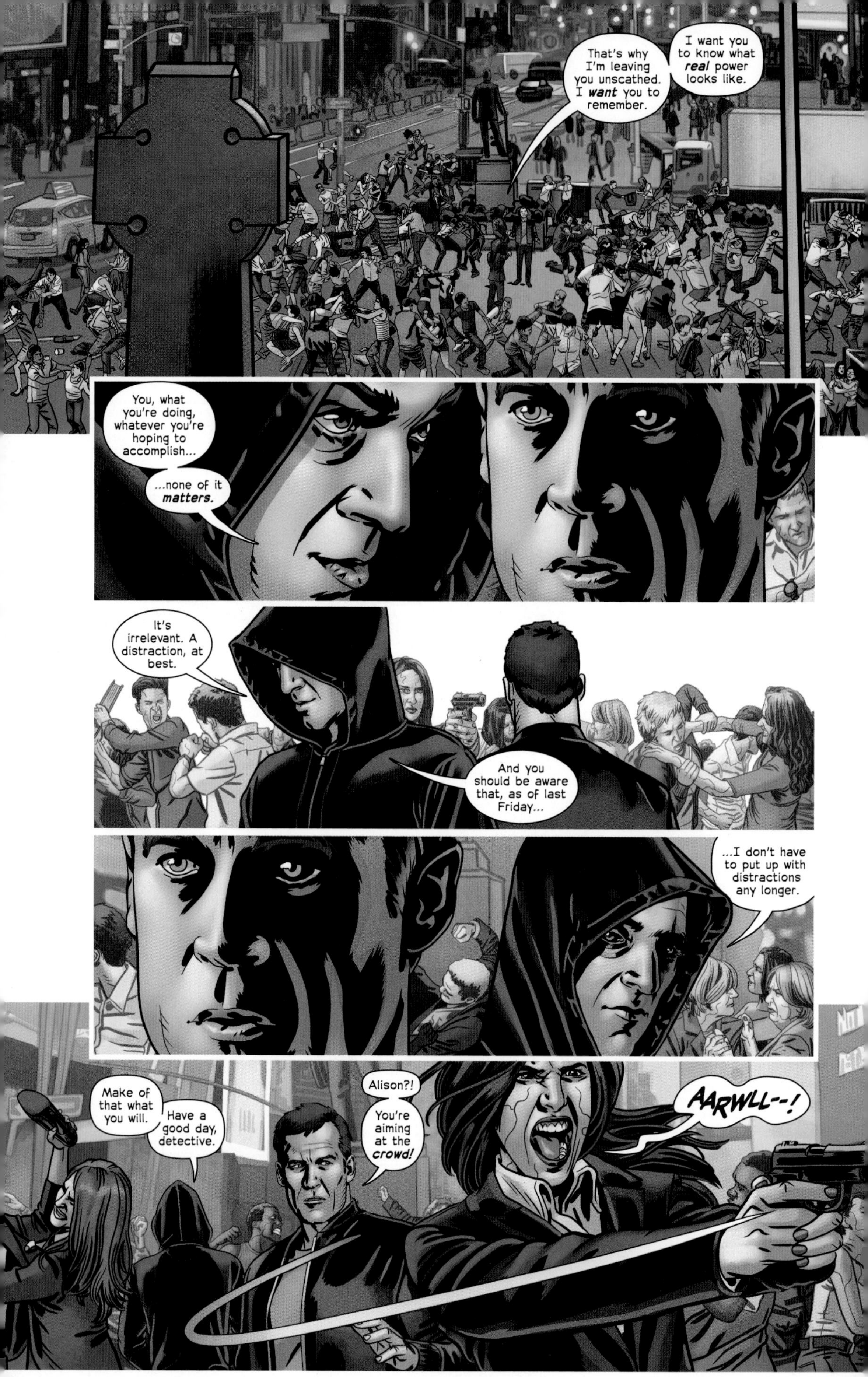

That's why I'm leaving you unscathed. I *want* you to remember.
I want you to know what *real* power looks like.
You, what you're doing, whatever you're hoping to accomplish...
...none of it *matters.*
It's irrelevant. A distraction, at best.
And you should be aware that, as of last Friday...
...I don't have to put up with distractions any longer.
Make of that what you will.
Have a good day, detective.
Alison?!
You're aiming at the *crowd!*
AARWLL--!

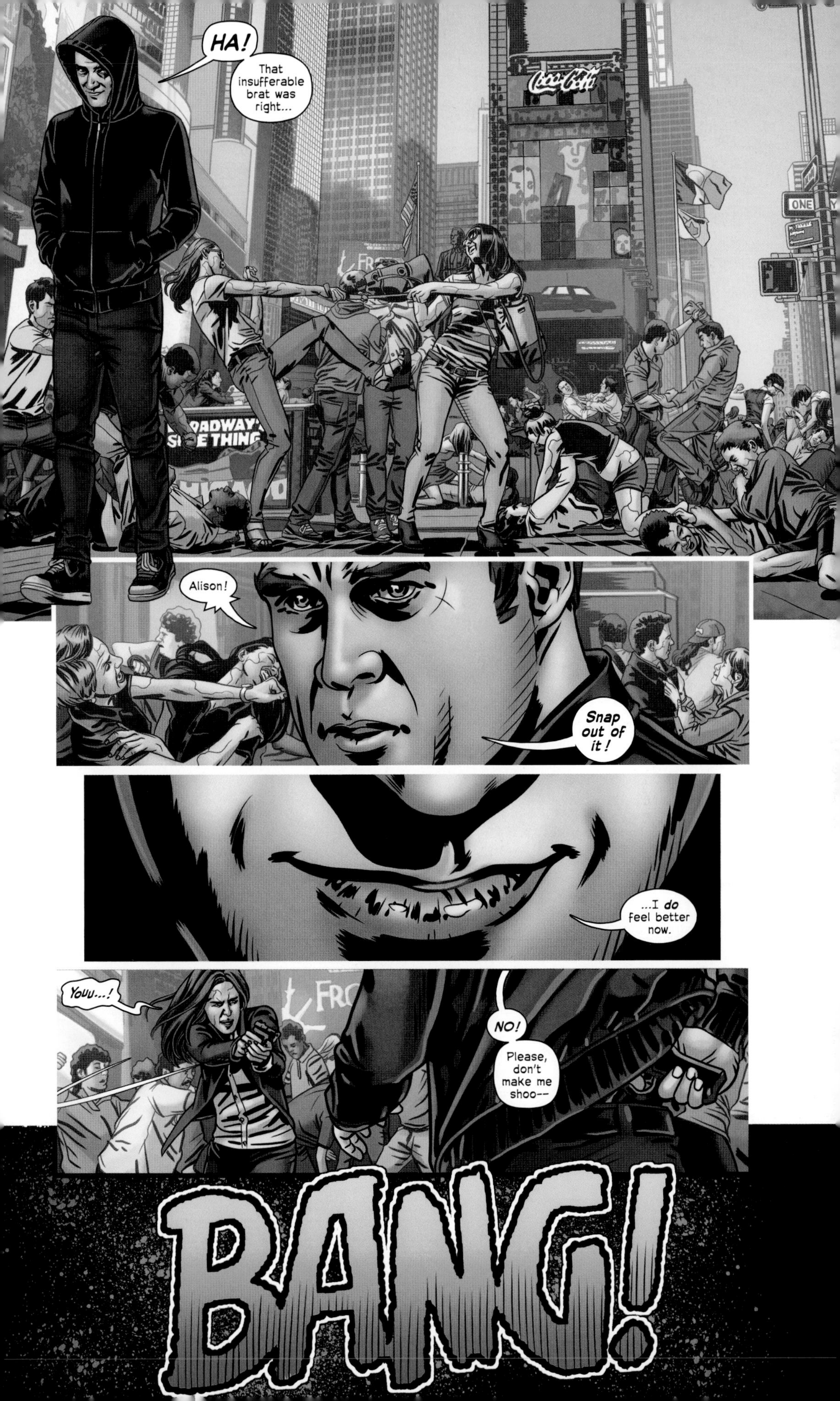
HA!
That insufferable brat was right...
ONE
PADWAY'S
S E THING
Alison!
Snap out of it!
...I do feel better now.
Youu...!
NO!
Please, don't make me shoo--
BANG!

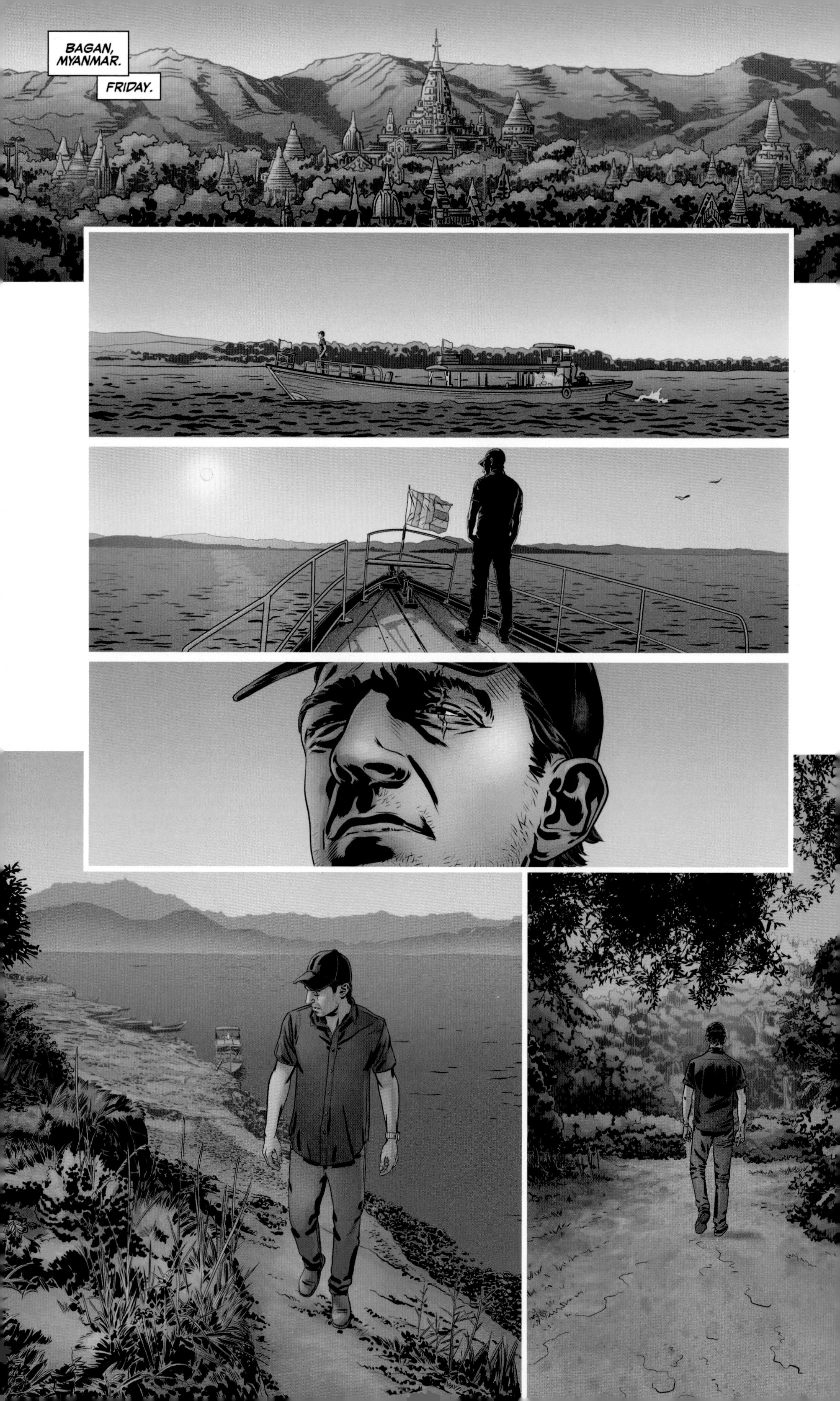
BAGAN, MYANMAR.
FRIDAY.

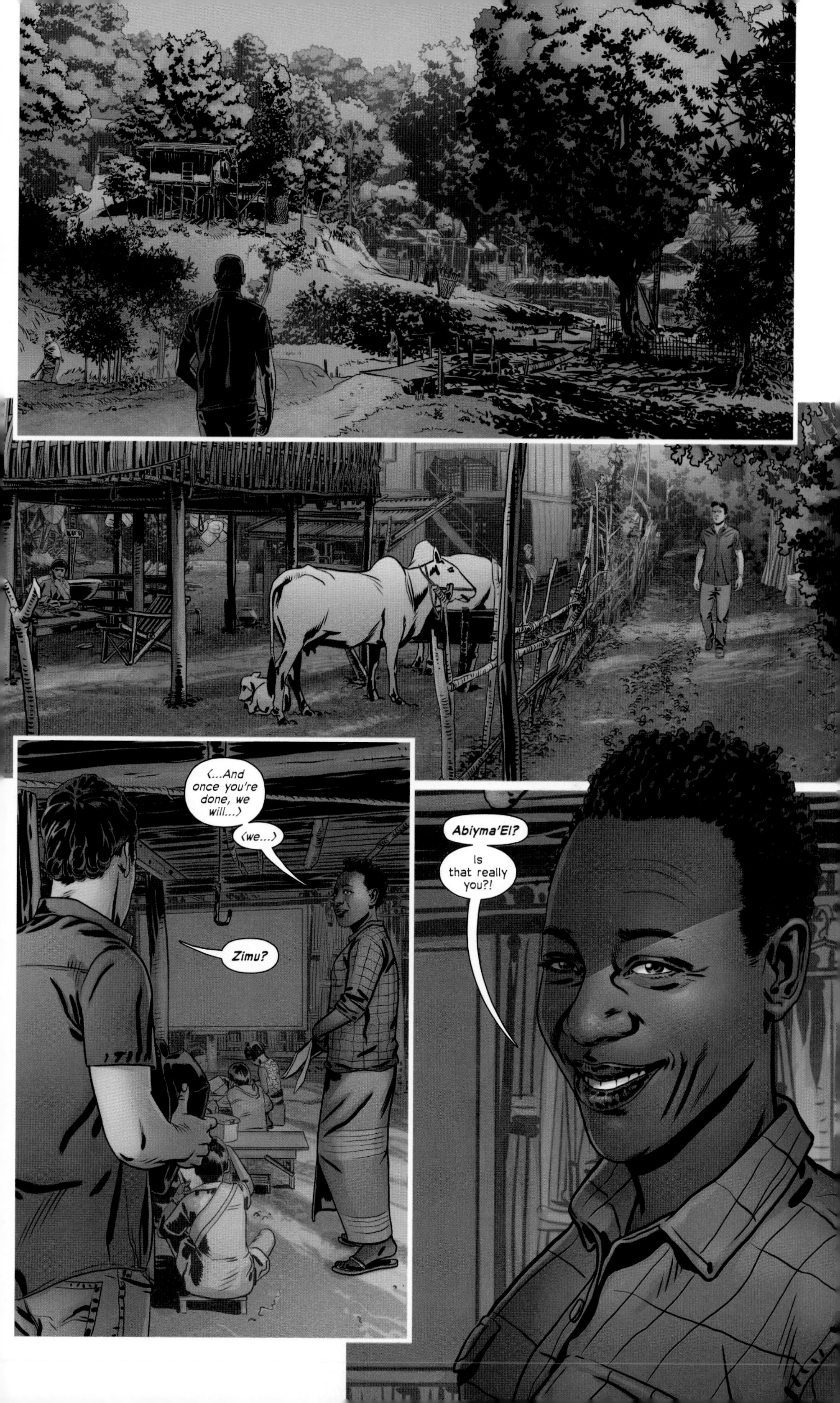

〈...And once you're done, we will...〉
〈we...〉
Zimu?
Abiyma'El?
Is that really you?!

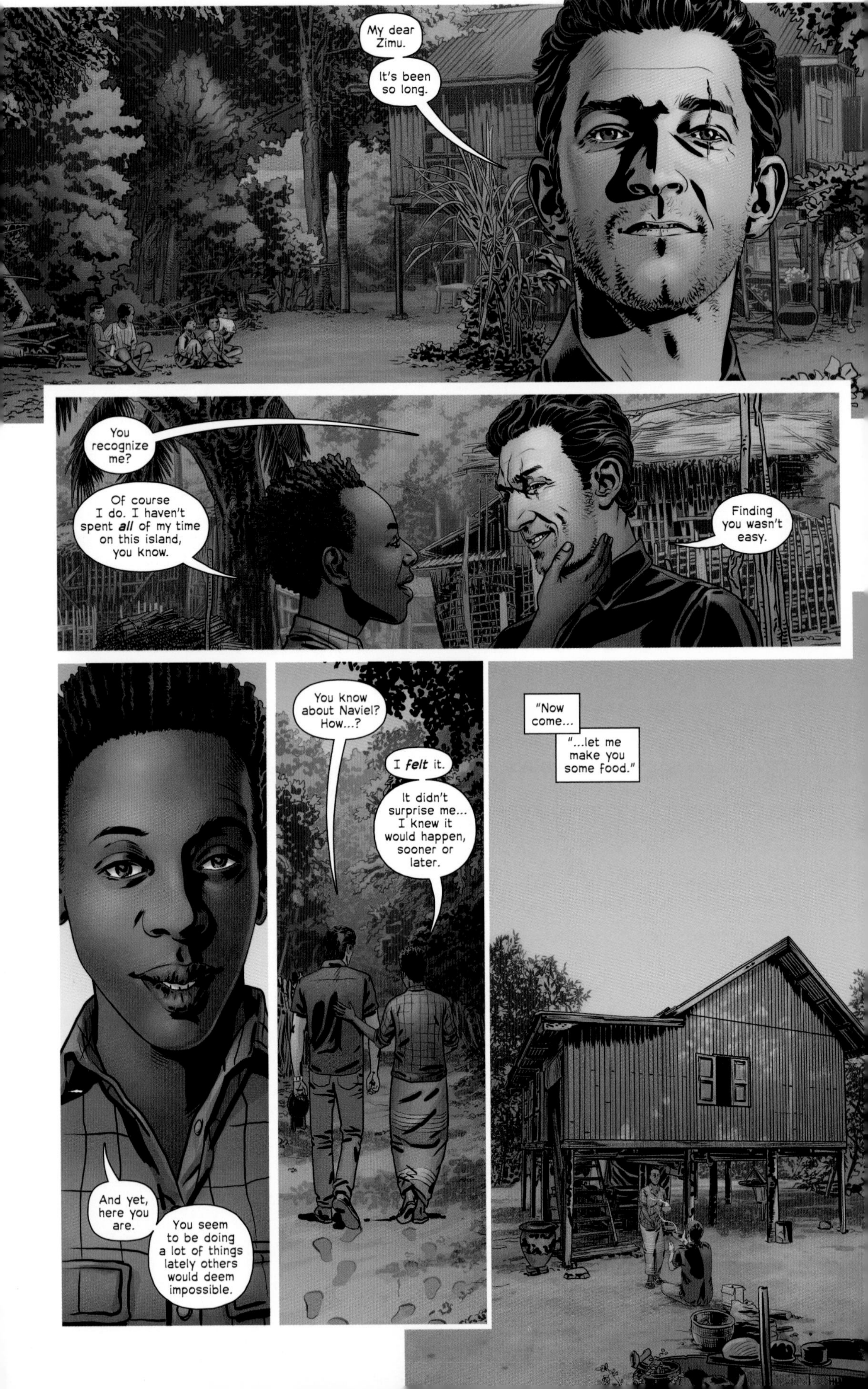
My dear Zimu.
It's been so long.
You recognize me?
Of course I do. I haven't spent *all* of my time on this island, you know.
Finding you wasn't easy.
And yet, here you are.
You seem to be doing a lot of things lately others would deem impossible.
You know about Naviel? How...?
I *felt* it.
It didn't surprise me... I knew it would happen, sooner or later.
"Now come...
"...let me make you some food."

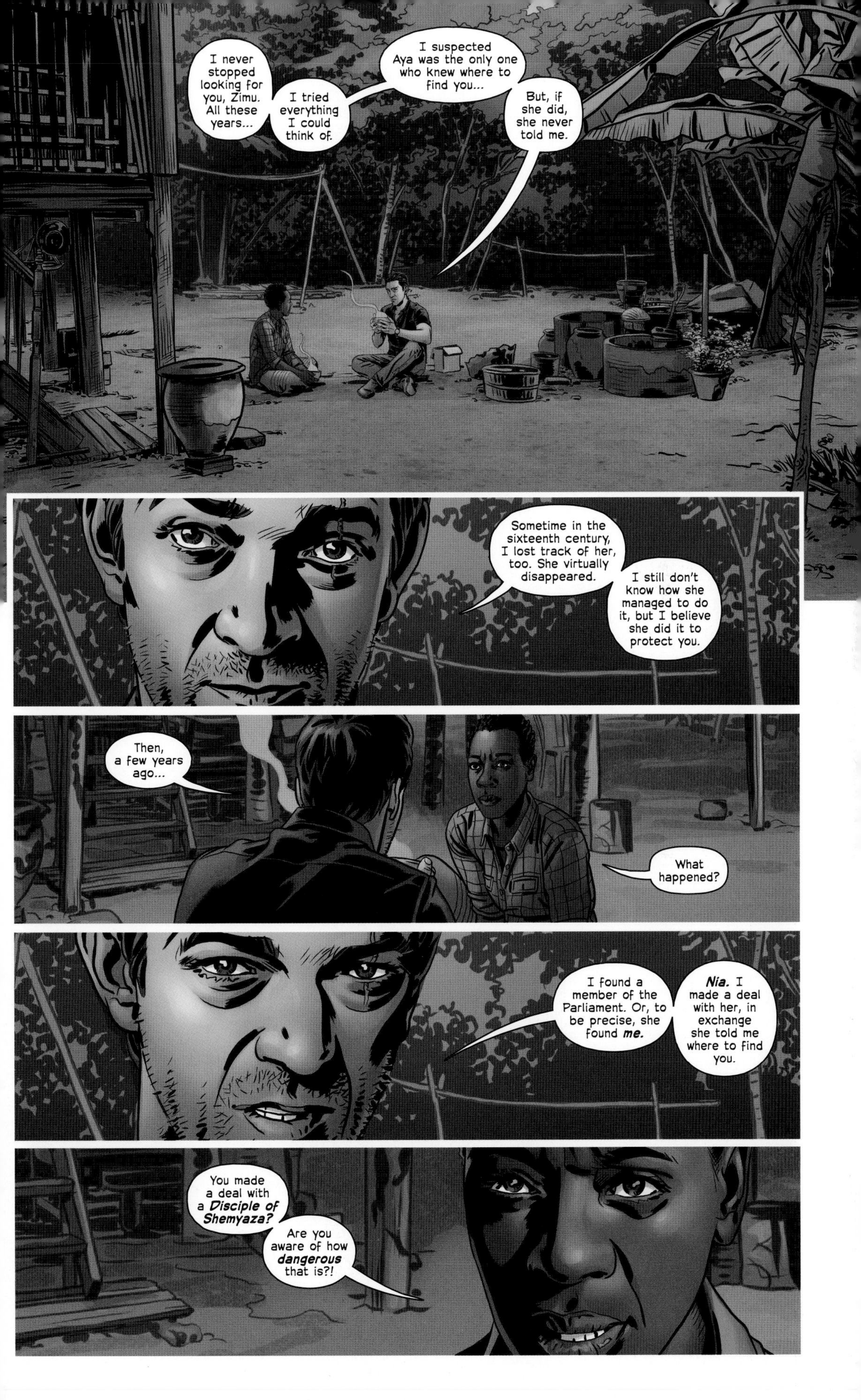
I never stopped looking for you, Zimu. All these years...
I tried everything I could think of.
I suspected Aya was the only one who knew where to find you...
But, if she did, she never told me.
Sometime in the sixteenth century, I lost track of her, too. She virtually disappeared.
I still don't know how she managed to do it, but I believe she did it to protect you.
Then, a few years ago...
What happened?
I found a member of the Parliament. Or, to be precise, she found *me.*
Nia. I made a deal with her, in exchange she told me where to find you.
You made a deal with a *Disciple of Shemyaza?*
Are you aware of how *dangerous* that is?!

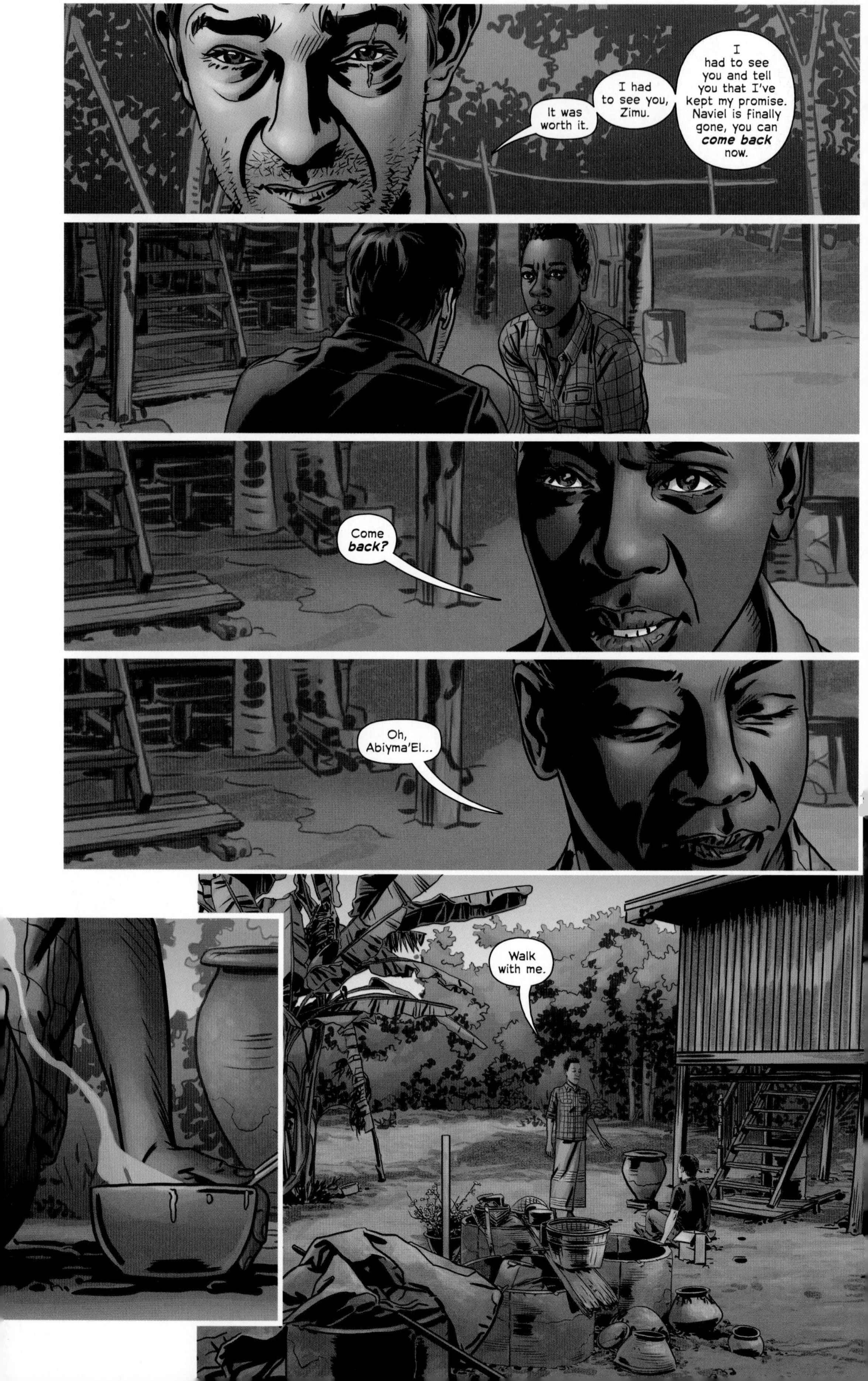
It was worth it.
I had to see you, Zimu.
I had to see you and tell you that I've kept my promise. Naviel is finally gone, you can *come back* now.
Come *back?*
Oh, Abiyma'El...
Walk with me.

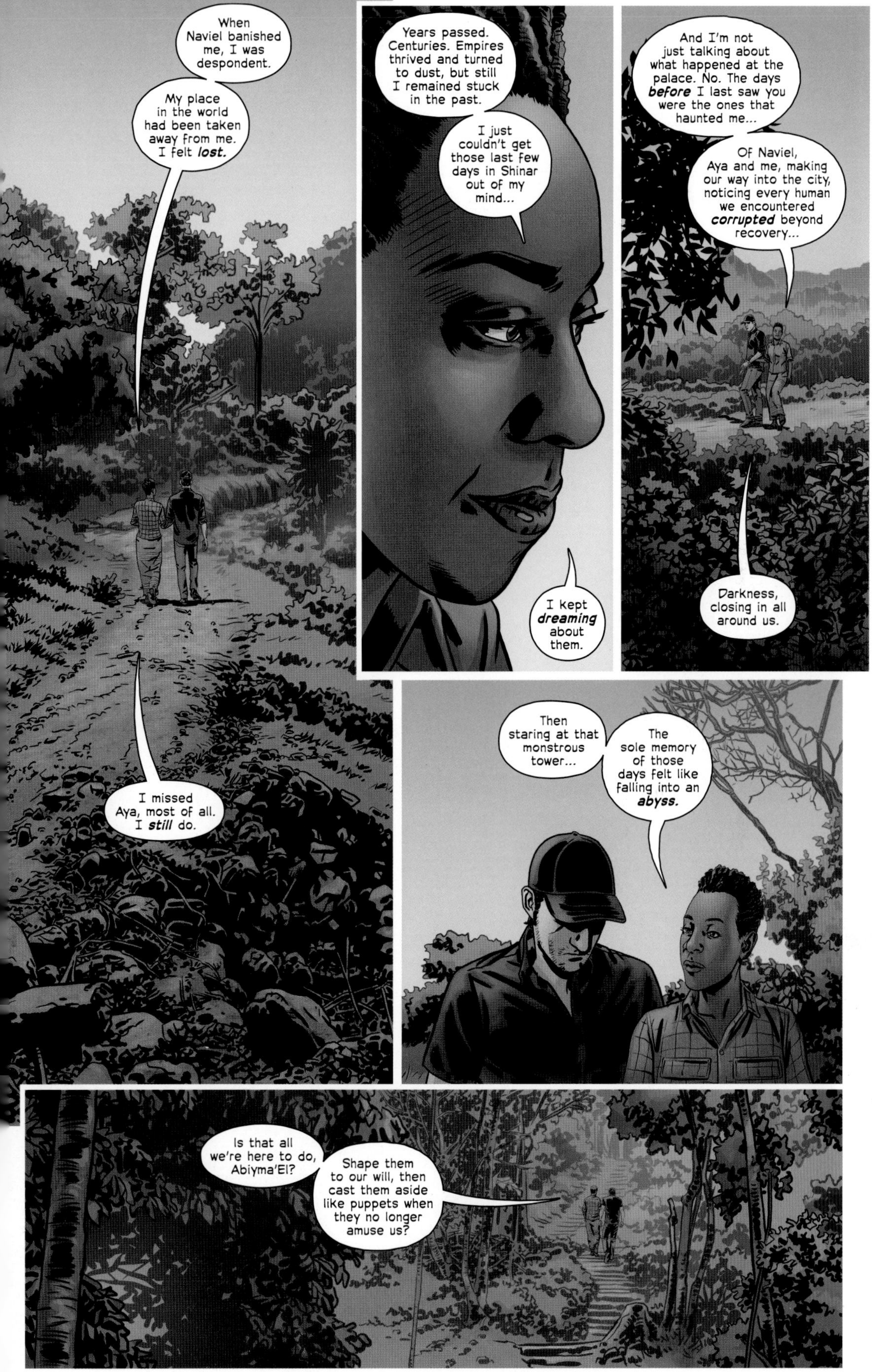
When Naviel banished me, I was despondent.
My place in the world had been taken away from me. I felt *lost.*
I missed Aya, most of all. I *still* do.
Years passed. Centuries. Empires thrived and turned to dust, but still I remained stuck in the past.
I just couldn't get those last few days in Shinar out of my mind...
I kept *dreaming* about them.
And I'm not just talking about what happened at the palace. No. The days *before* I last saw you were the ones that haunted me...
Of Naviel, Aya and me, making our way into the city, noticing every human we encountered *corrupted* beyond recovery...
Darkness, closing in all around us.
Then staring at that monstrous tower...
The sole memory of those days felt like falling into an *abyss.*
Is that all we're here to do, Abiyma'El?
Shape them to our will, then cast them aside like puppets when they no longer amuse us?

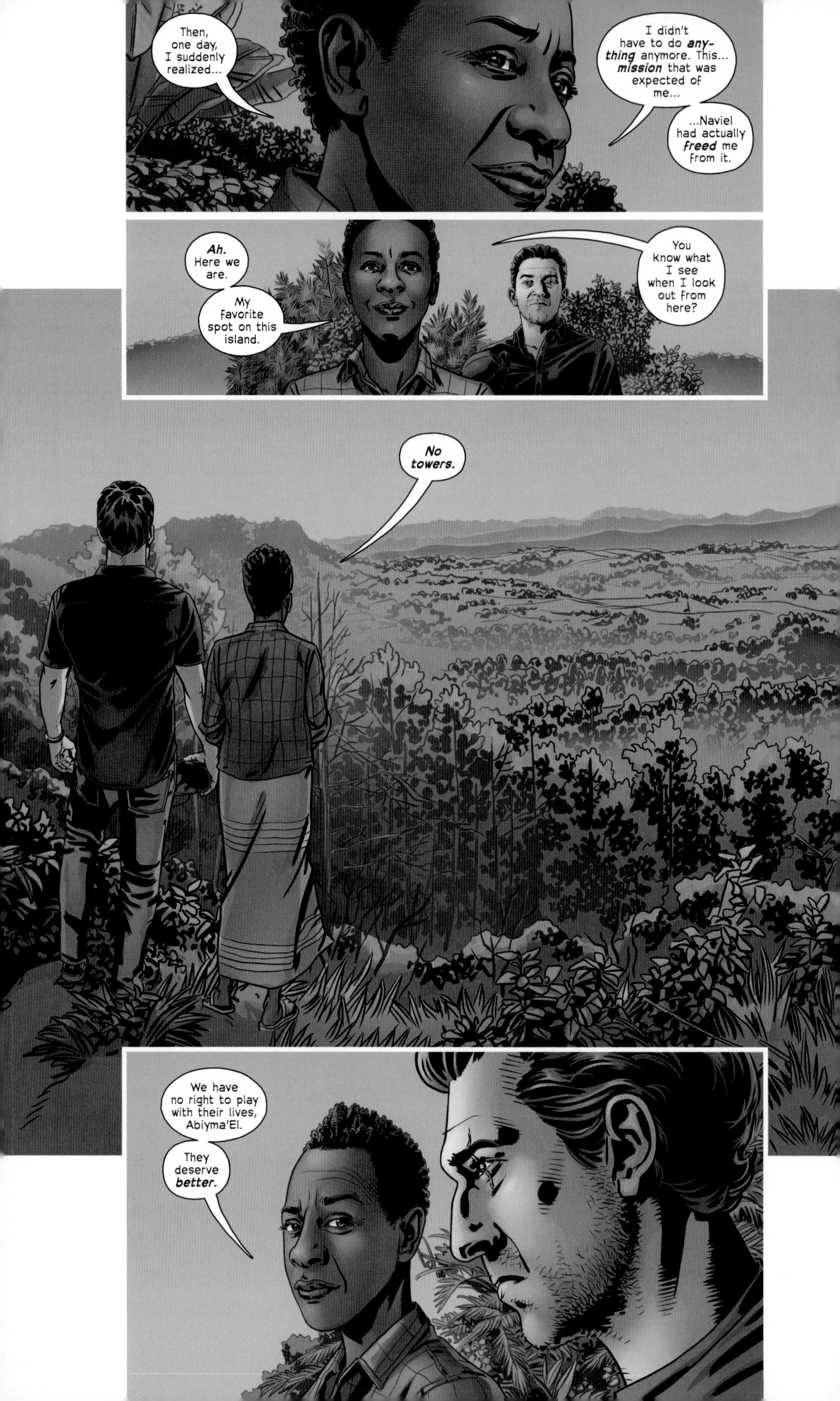
Then, one day, I suddenly realized...
I didn't have to do *anything* anymore. This... *mission* that was expected of me...
...Naviel had actually *freed* me from it.
Ah. Here we are.
My favorite spot on this island.
You know what I see when I look out from here?
No towers.
We have no right to play with their lives, Abiyma'El.
They deserve *better.*

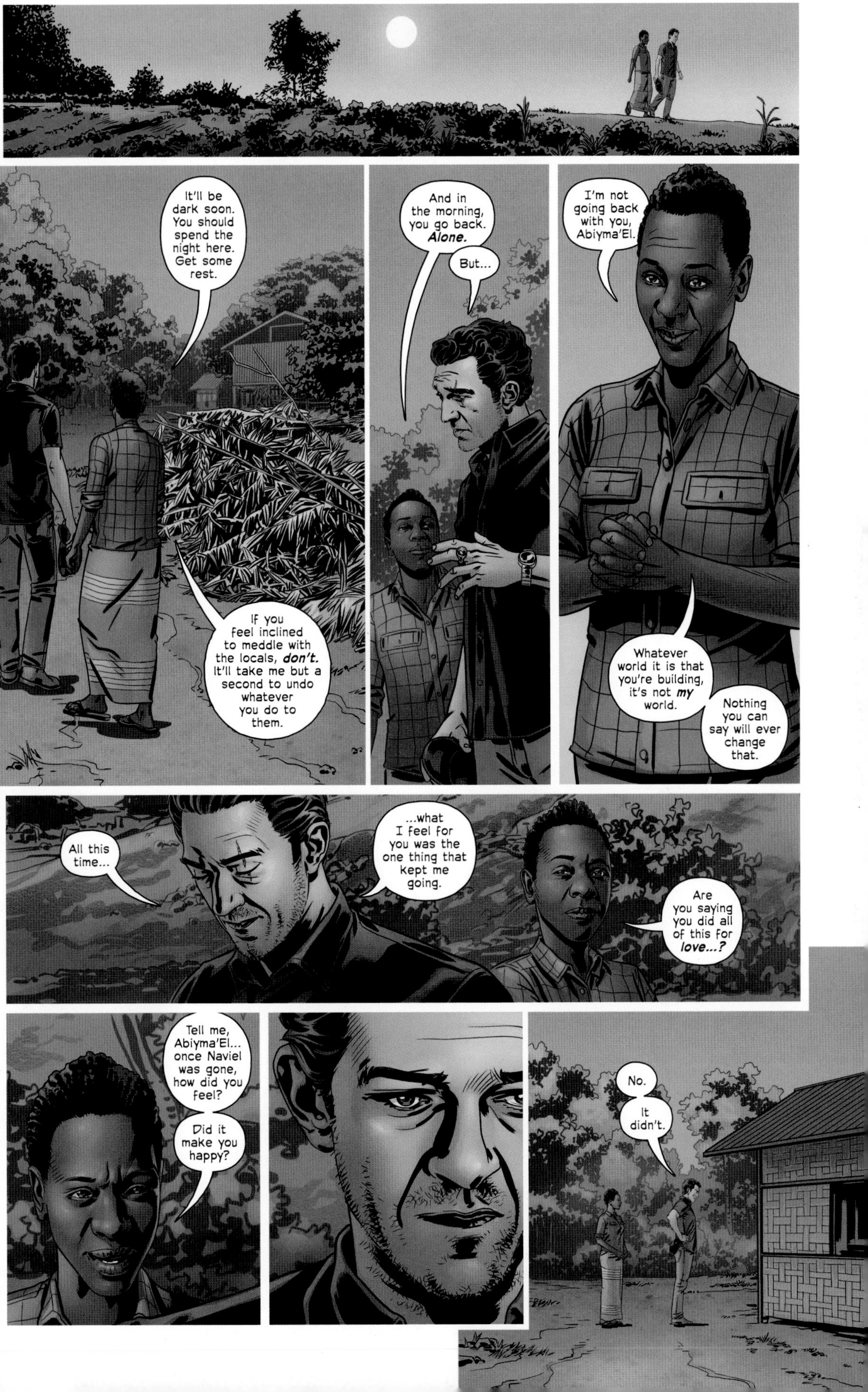
It'll be dark soon. You should spend the night here. Get some rest.
If you feel inclined to meddle with the locals, *don't.* It'll take me but a second to undo whatever you do to them.
And in the morning, you go back. ***Alone.***
But...
I'm not going back with you, Abiyma'El.
Whatever world it is that you're building, it's not *my* world.
Nothing you can say will ever change that.
All this time...
...what I feel for you was the one thing that kept me going.
Are you saying you did all of this for *love...?*
Tell me, Abiyma'El... once Naviel was gone, how did you feel?
Did it make you happy?
No.
It didn't.

And do you understand *why?*

It's because happiness is antithetical to who you *are,* Abiyma'El. It's simply not in your nature.

To be envious is to be unhappy, and you, my dear, are the embodiment of envy itself.

You will never be *content.* You can't escape it.

Believing that you did all of this for love is what, in your mind, gave you the right to go through with it. *A story you told yourself.*

But the truth is that it had nothing to do with love...just like it had nothing to do with fairness.

You did what you did out of *hatred.*

And I want *no part* of it.

I don't blame you. It's who you *are.*

If you ever acce— that, perha— one day, yo— be able t— walk a les— burdensom— path.

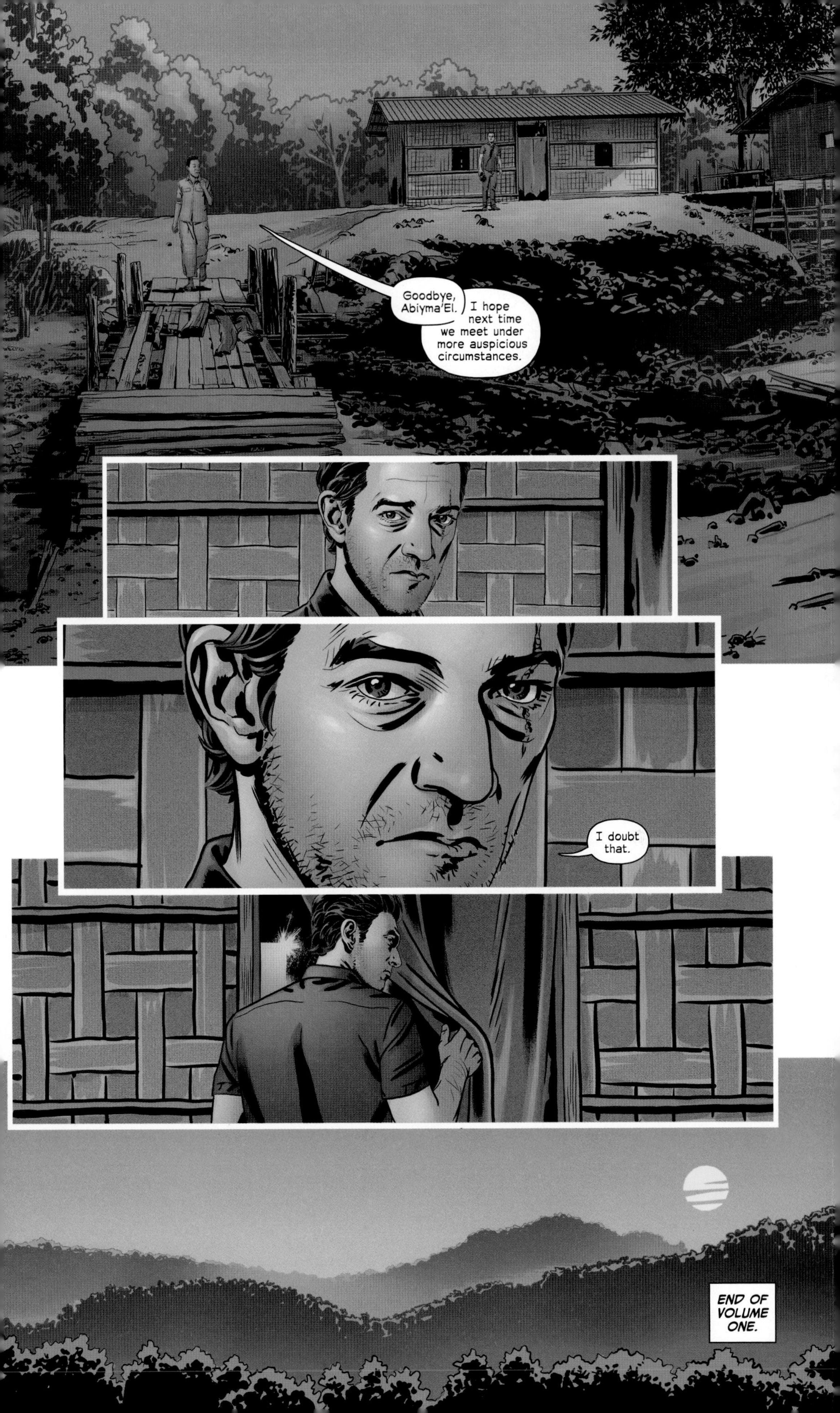
Goodbye, Abiyma'El.
I hope next time we meet under more auspicious circumstances.
I doubt that.
END OF VOLUME ONE.

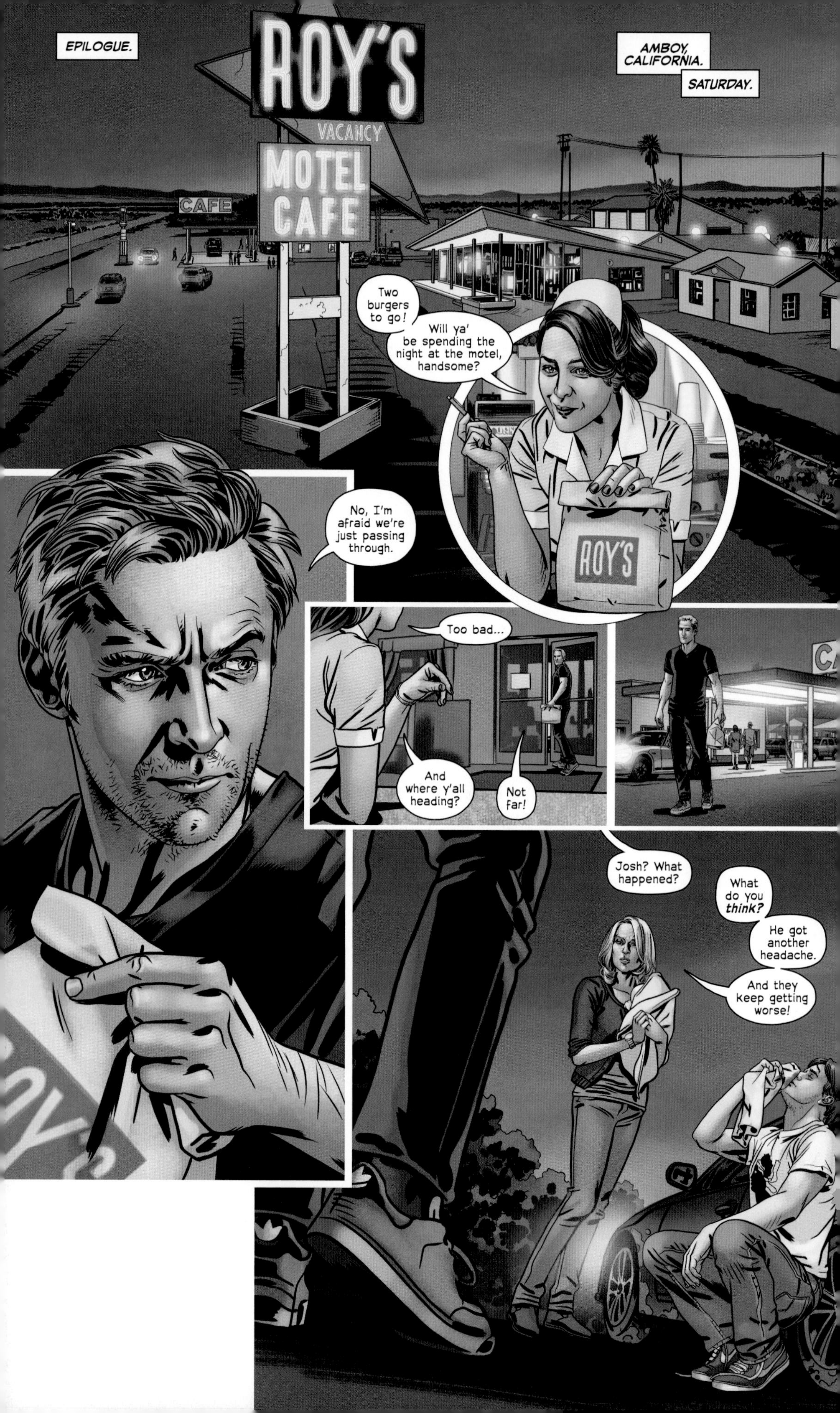
EPILOGUE.
ROY'S
VACANCY
MOTEL
CAFE
CAFE
AMBOY, CALIFORNIA.
SATURDAY.
Two burgers to go!
Will ya' be spending the night at the motel, handsome?
ROY'S
No, I'm afraid we're just passing through.
Too bad...
And where y'all heading?
Not far!
Josh? What happened?
What do you *think?*
He got another headache.
And they keep getting worse!

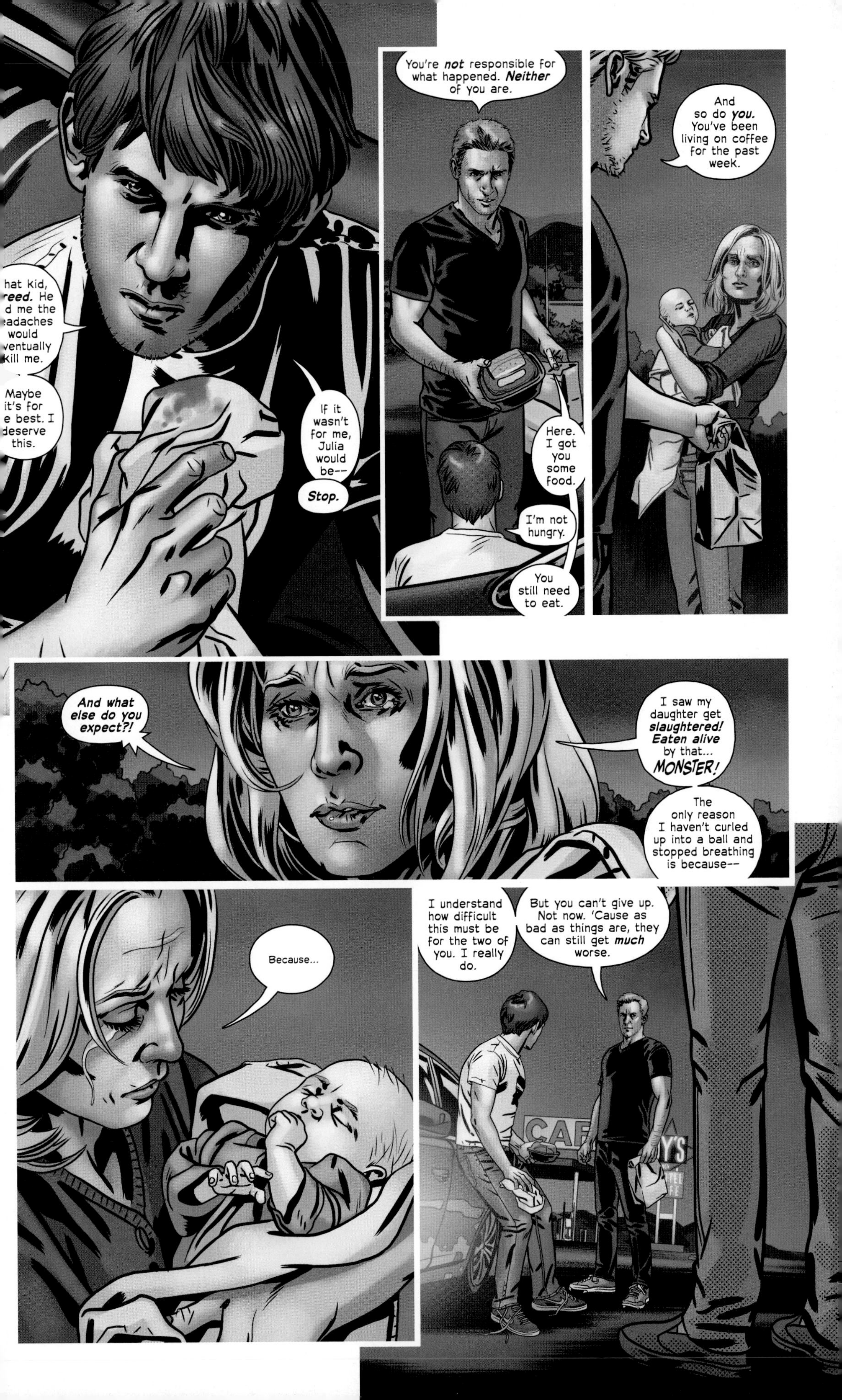

hat kid, reed. He d me the adaches would ventually kill me.
Maybe it's for e best. I deserve this.
If it wasn't for me, Julia would be--
Stop.
You're not responsible for what happened. Neither of you are.
Here. I got you some food.
I'm not hungry.
You still need to eat.
And so do you. You've been living on coffee for the past week.
And what else do you expect?!
I saw my daughter get slaughtered! Eaten alive by that... MONSTER!
The only reason I haven't curled up into a ball and stopped breathing is because--
Because...
I understand how difficult this must be for the two of you. I really do.
But you can't give up. Not now. 'Cause as bad as things are, they can still get much worse.

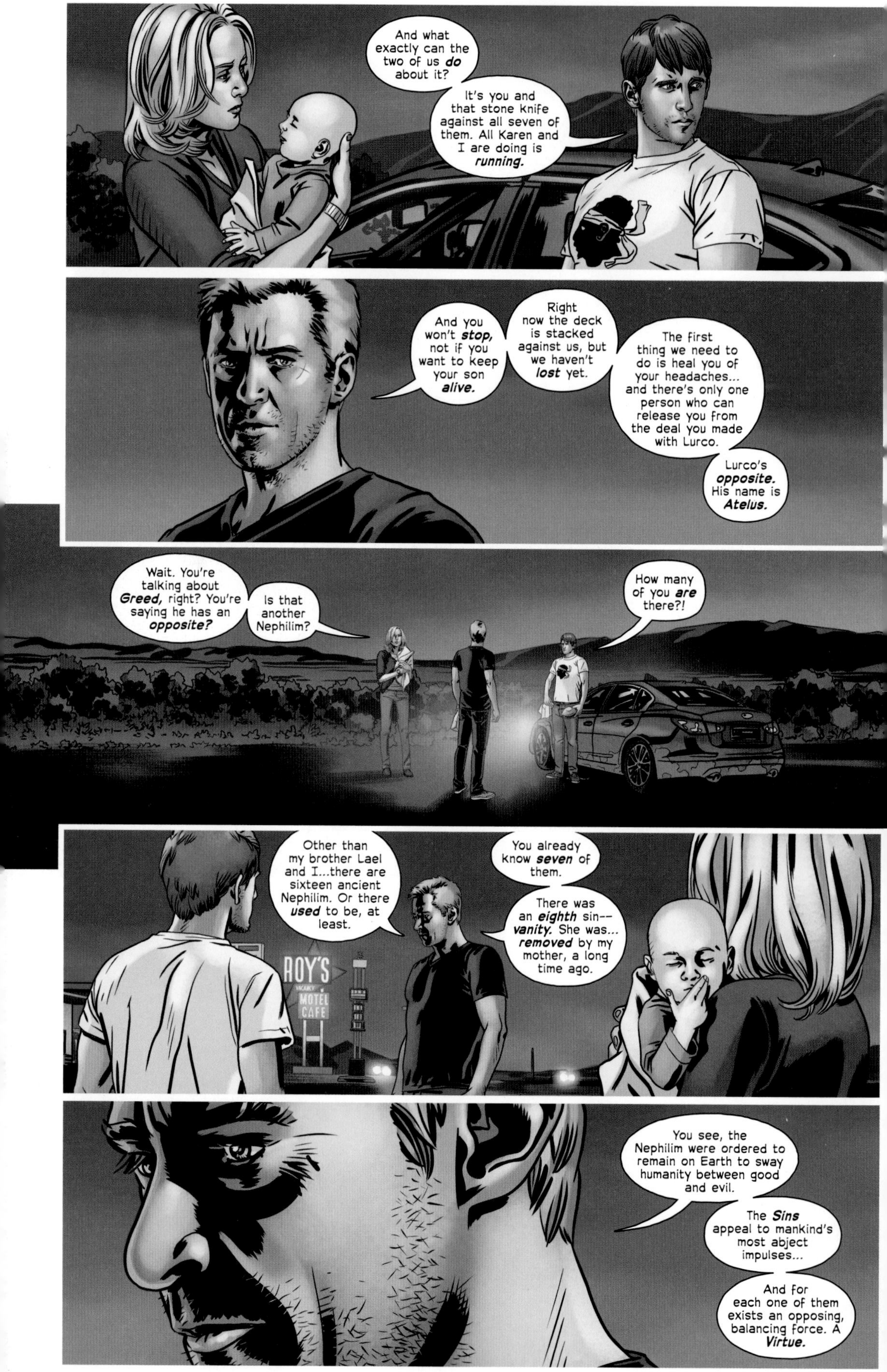
And what exactly can the two of us do about it?
It's you and that stone knife against all seven of them. All Karen and I are doing is running.
And you won't stop, not if you want to keep your son alive.
Right now the deck is stacked against us, but we haven't lost yet.
The first thing we need to do is heal you of your headaches... and there's only one person who can release you from the deal you made with Lurco.
Lurco's opposite. His name is Atelus.
Wait. You're talking about Greed, right? You're saying he has an opposite?
Is that another Nephilim?
How many of you are there?!
Other than my brother Lael and I...there are sixteen ancient Nephilim. Or there used to be, at least.
ROY'S
MOTEL
CAFE
You already know seven of them.
There was an eighth sin-- vanity. She was... removed by my mother, a long time ago.
You see, the Nephilim were ordered to remain on Earth to sway humanity between good and evil.
The Sins appeal to mankind's most abject impulses...
And for each one of them exists an opposing, balancing force. A Virtue.

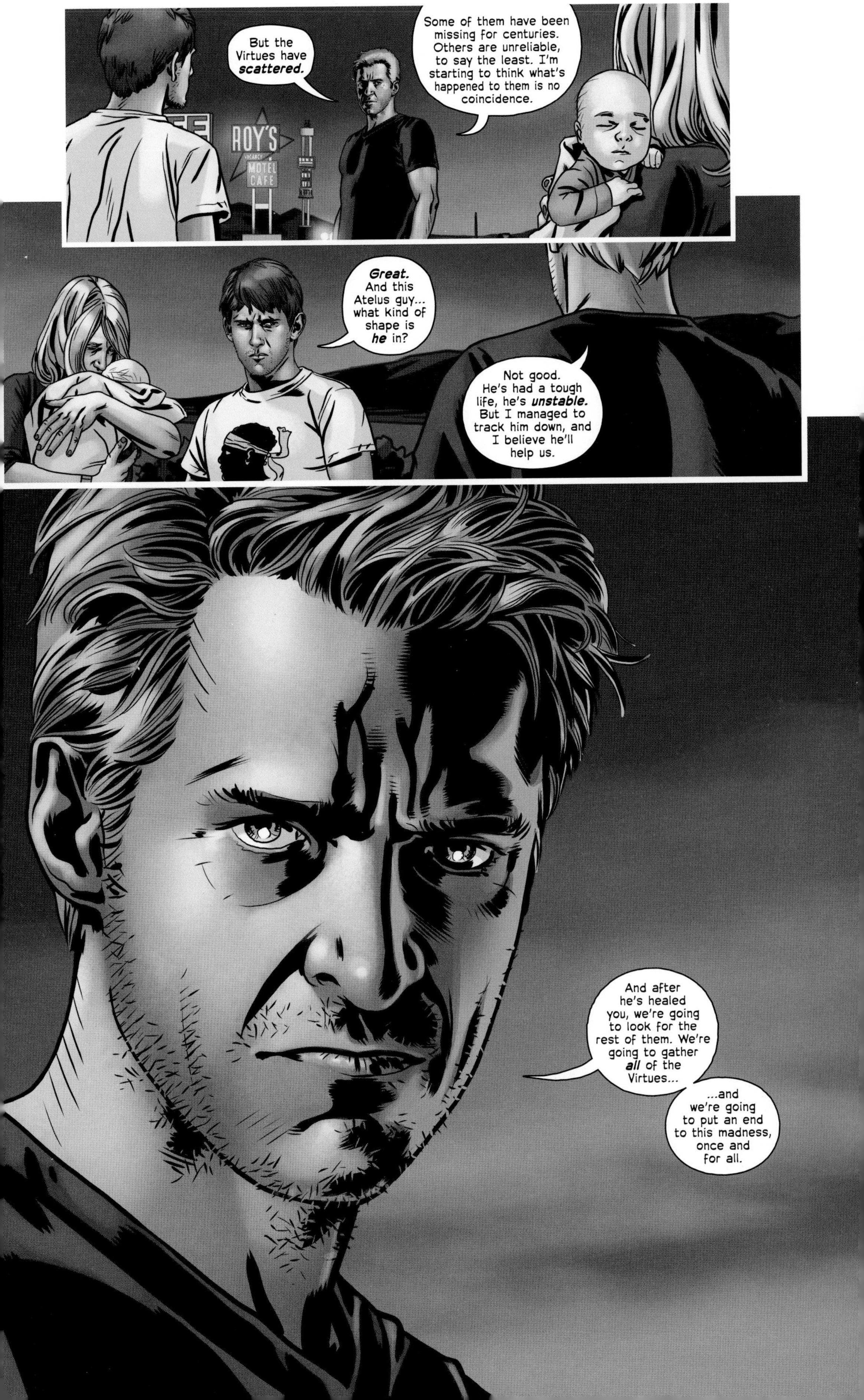
But the Virtues have *scattered.*
Some of them have been missing for centuries. Others are unreliable, to say the least. I'm starting to think what's happened to them is no coincidence.
ROY'S
MOTEL
CAFE
Great. And this Atelus guy... what kind of shape is *he* in?
Not good. He's had a tough life, he's *unstable.* But I managed to track him down, and I believe he'll help us.
And after he's healed you, we're going to look for the rest of them. We're going to gather *all* of the Virtues...
...and we're going to put an end to this madness, once and for all.

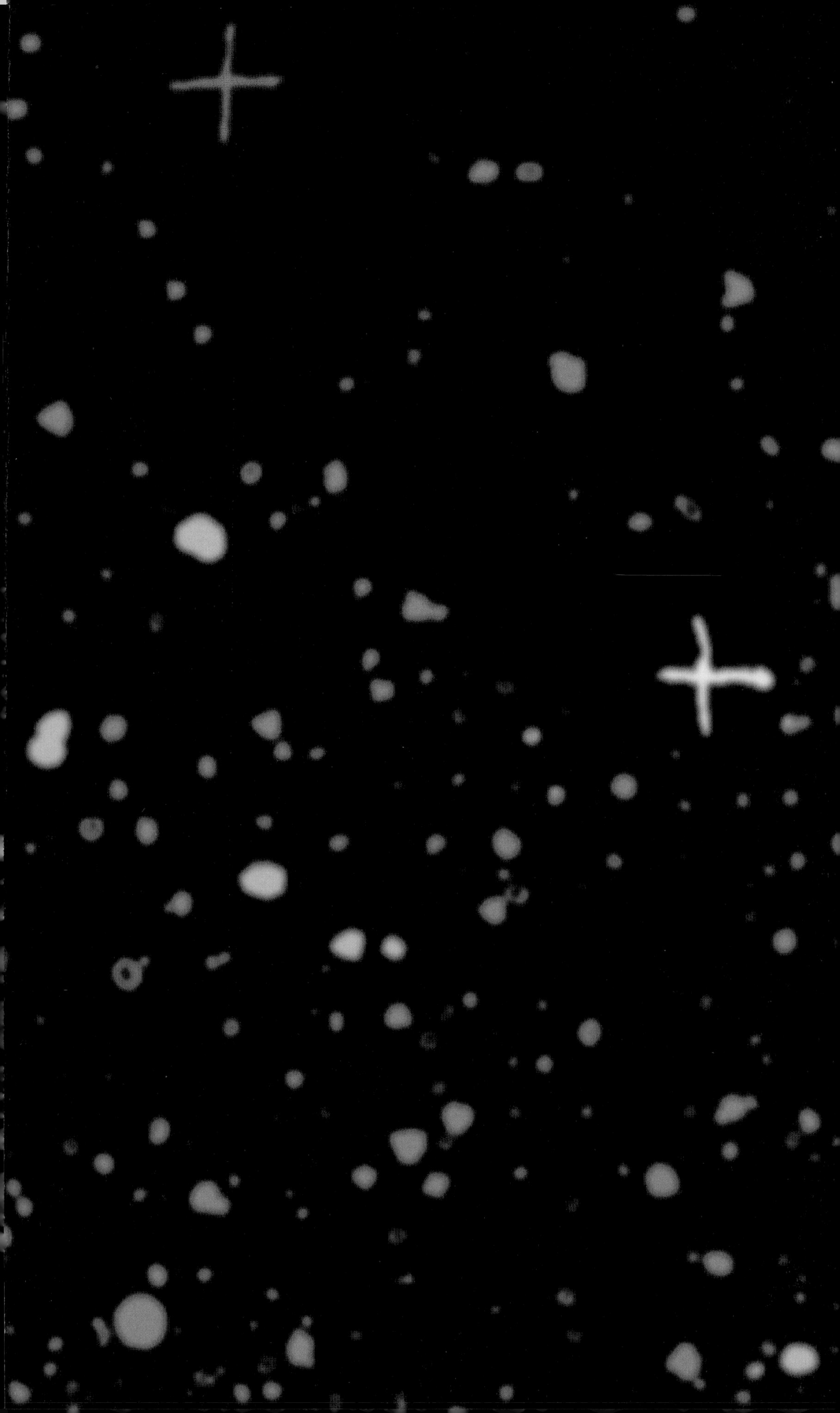

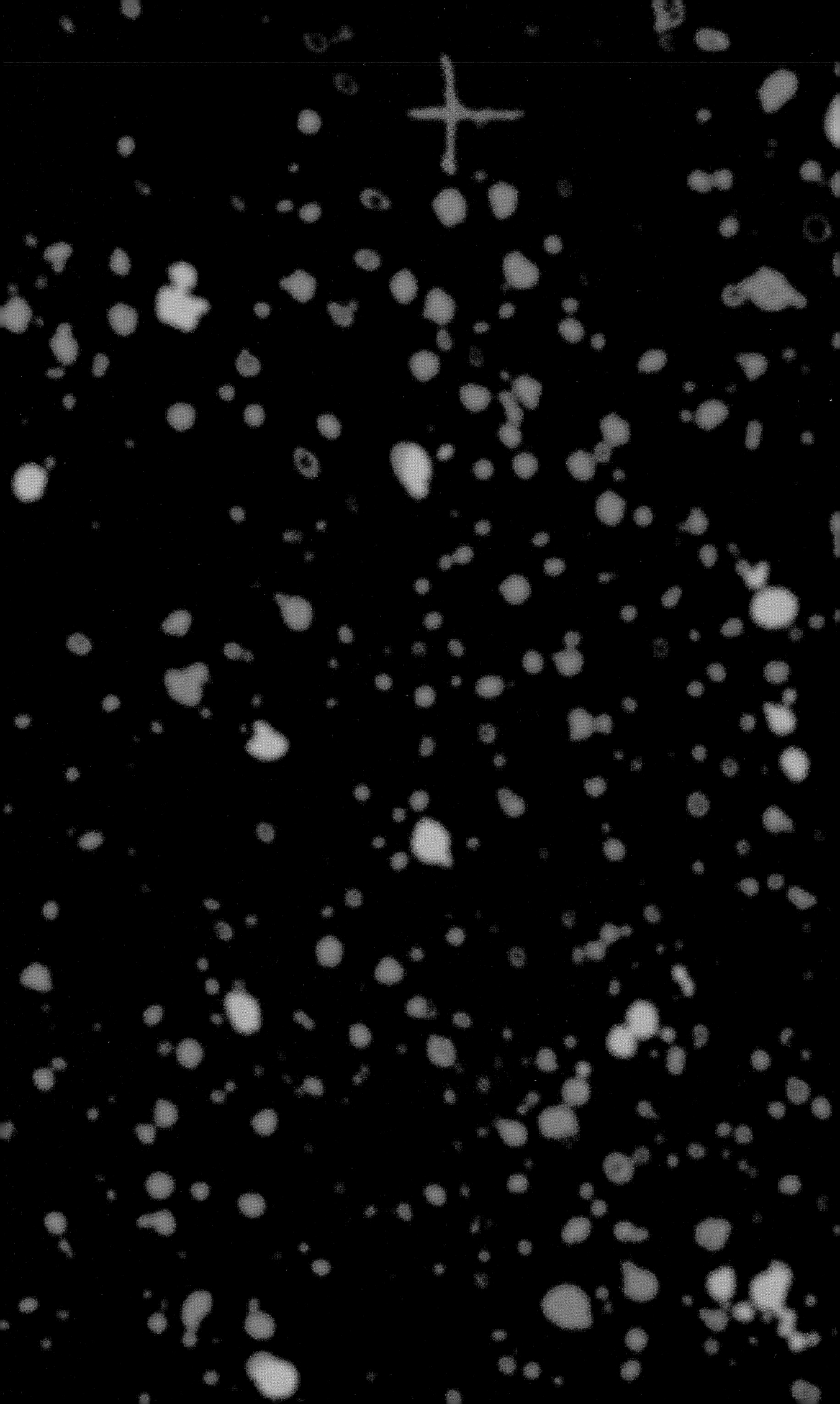

CAST

NEPHILIM

S
I
N
S

ENVY
Abiyma'El
A.K.A. Gurges,
Lucius Hamilton.

GLUTTONY
Claire
A.K.A. Macra.

PRIDE
Ian Whitaker
A.K.A. Aculeo.

SLOTH
Beatrice
A.K.A. Seneca.

V
I
R
T
U
E
S

KINDNESS
A.K.A. Zimu,
Aberash.

TEMPERANCE
A.K.A. Titus.

HUMILITY
A.K.A. Bilhan,
Marinus.

DILIGENCE
A.K.A. Valeria.

LAEL
First son of Naviel.

ADRIAN
Third son of Naviel.

BARAKIEL
Oracle.

(Missing)

NAVIEL
A.K.A. Naviel
Fitzgerald.
Keeper Of The Nephilim.

(Deceased In
Contemporary Times)

GUARDIANS

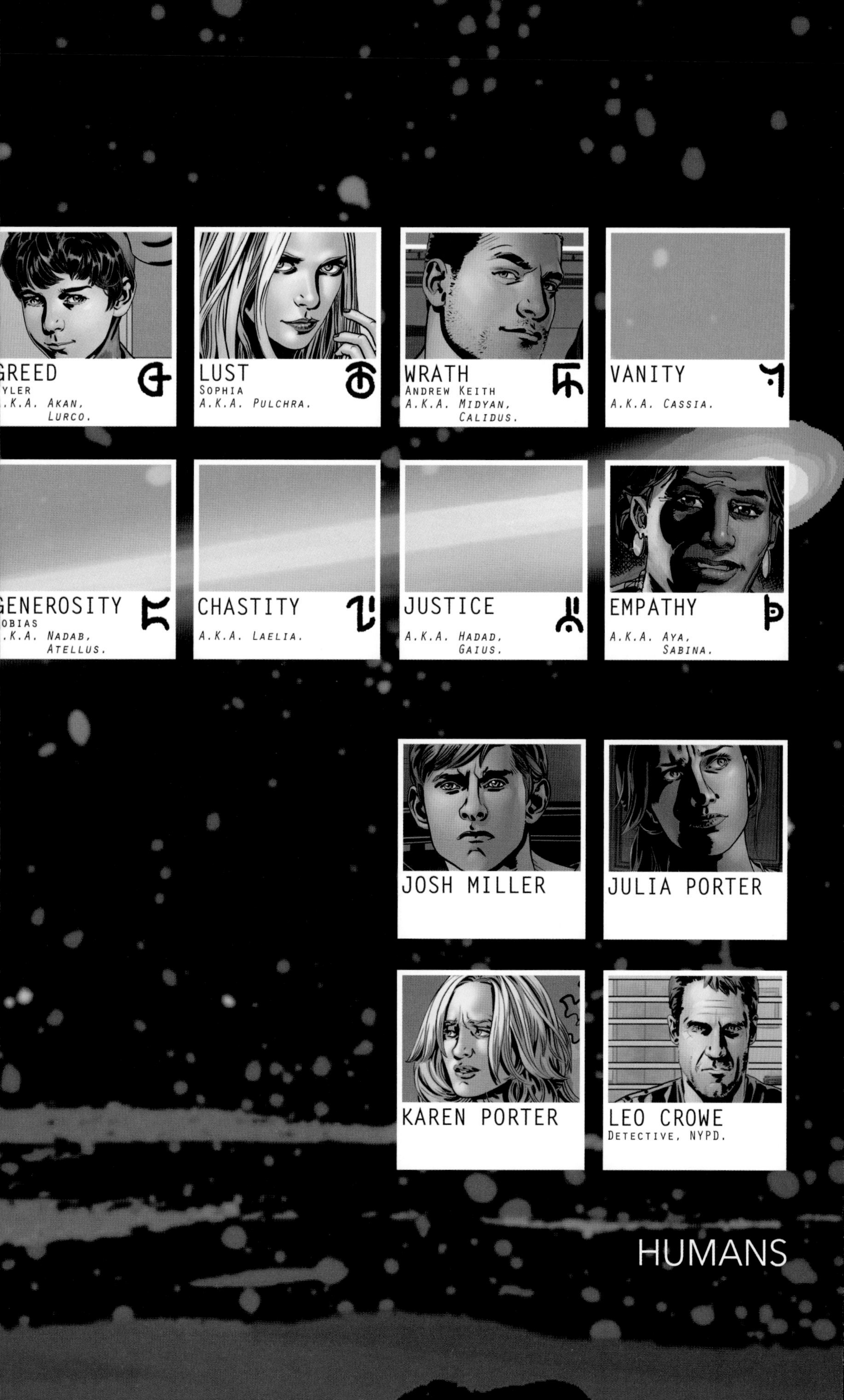

GREED
...YLER
...K.A. AKAN,
LURCO.

LUST
SOPHIA
A.K.A. PULCHRA.

WRATH
ANDREW KEITH
A.K.A. MIDYAN,
CALIDUS.

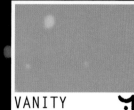

VANITY
A.K.A. CASSIA.

GENEROSITY
...OBIAS
...K.A. NADAB,
ATELLUS.

CHASTITY
A.K.A. LAELIA.

JUSTICE
A.K.A. HADAD,
GAIUS.

EMPATHY
A.K.A. AYA,
SABINA.

JOSH MILLER

JULIA PORTER

KAREN PORTER

LEO CROWE
DETECTIVE, NYPD.

HUMANS

COVER GALLERY

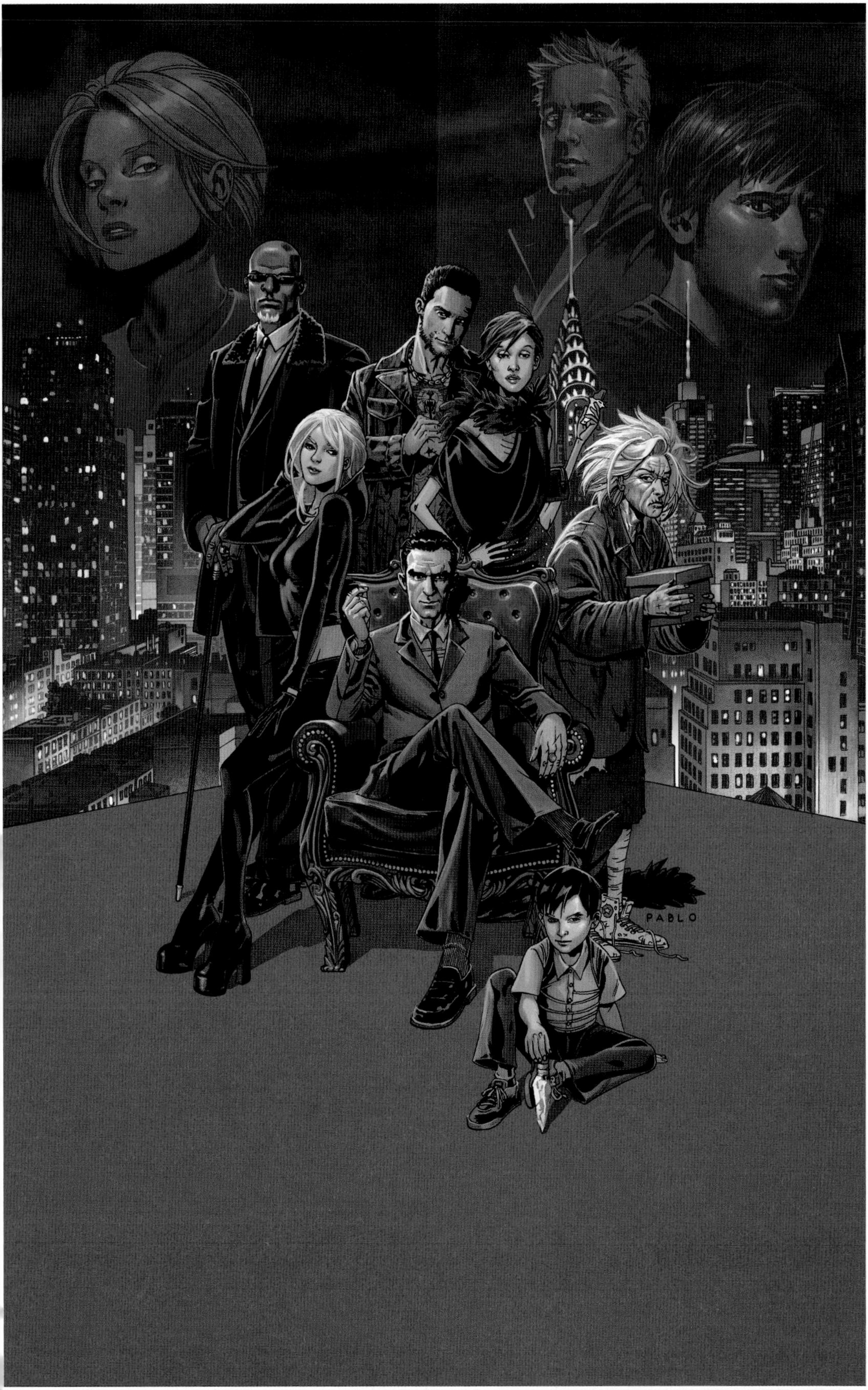

PABLO

SSUE #1, Cover A. Art by PABLO RAIMONDI, colors by DEAN WHITE.

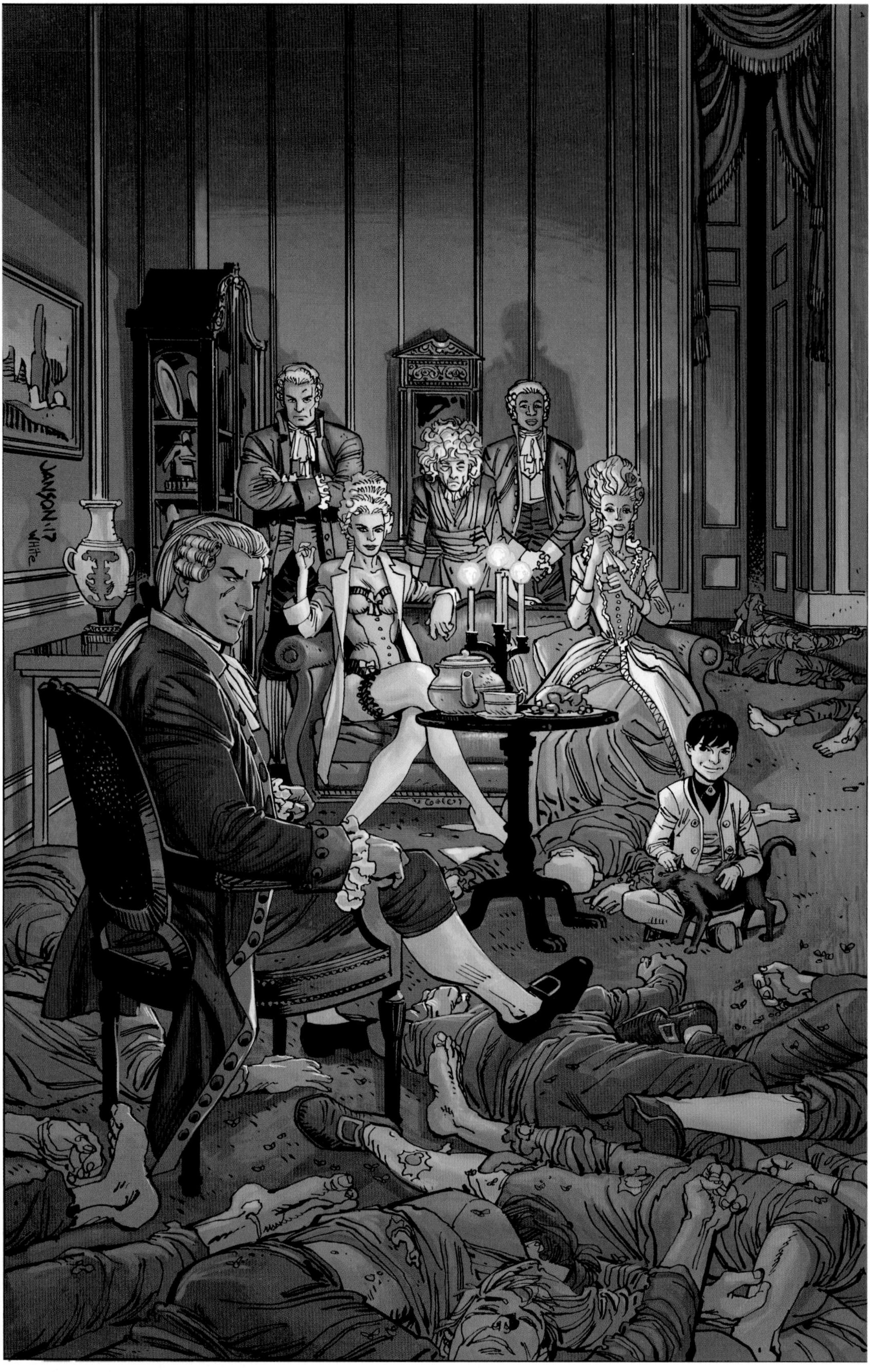
JANSON '17
White

ISSUE #1, Cover B. Art by KLAUS JANSON, colors by DEAN WHITE

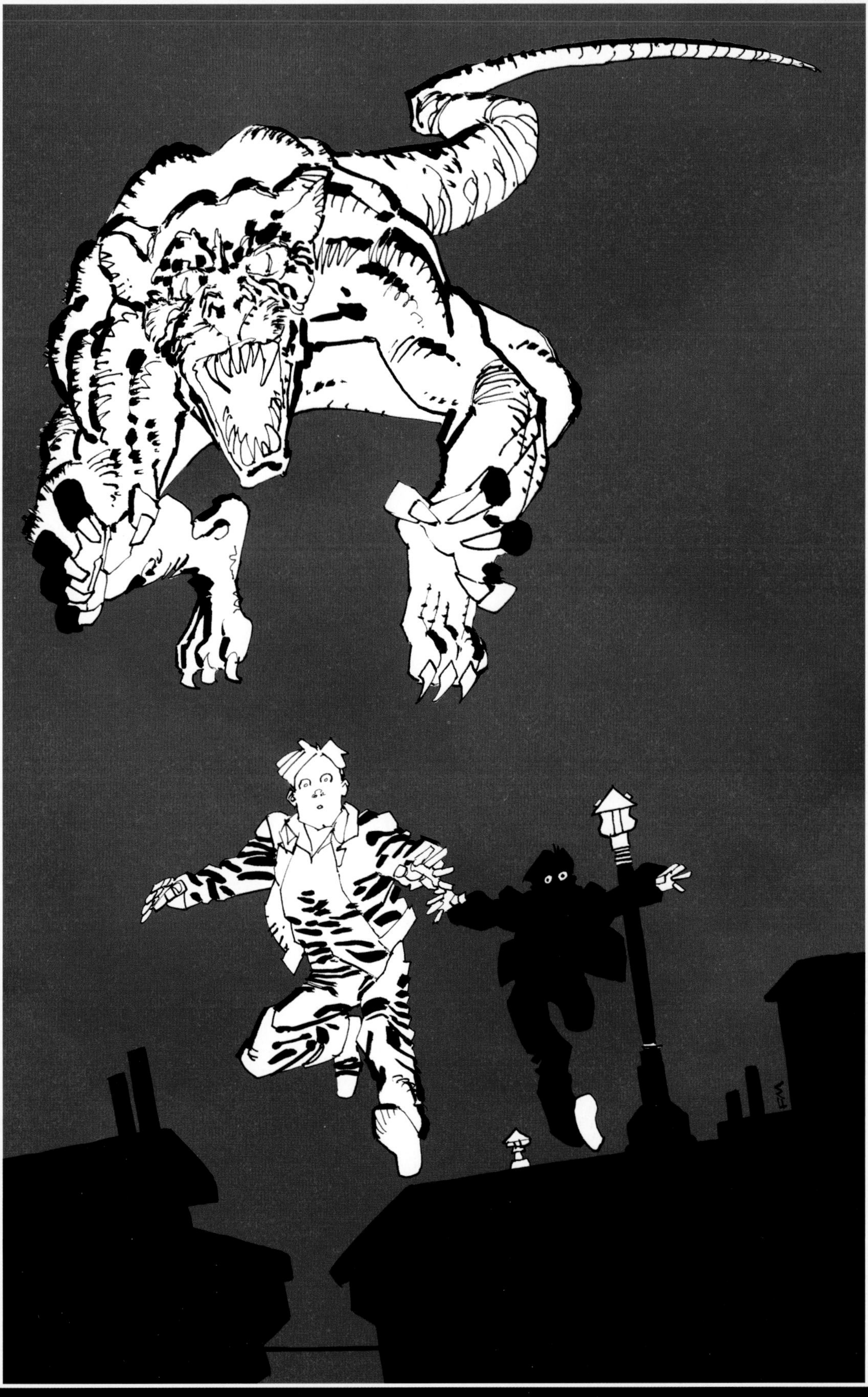
FM

ISSUE #1, Cover C. Art by FRANK MILLER, colors by PABLO RAIMONDI.

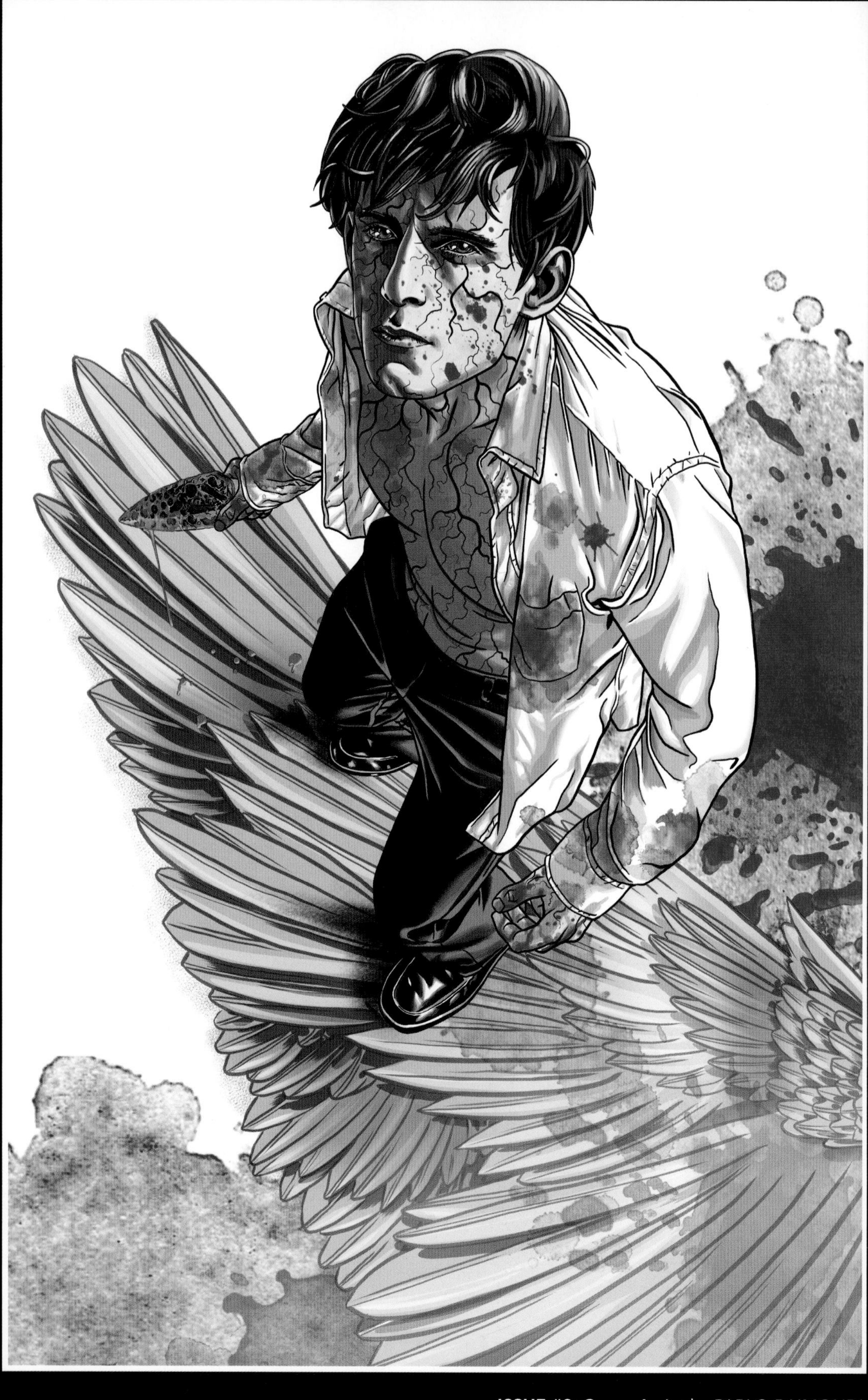

ISSUE #2, Cover A. Art by PABLO RAIMONDI.

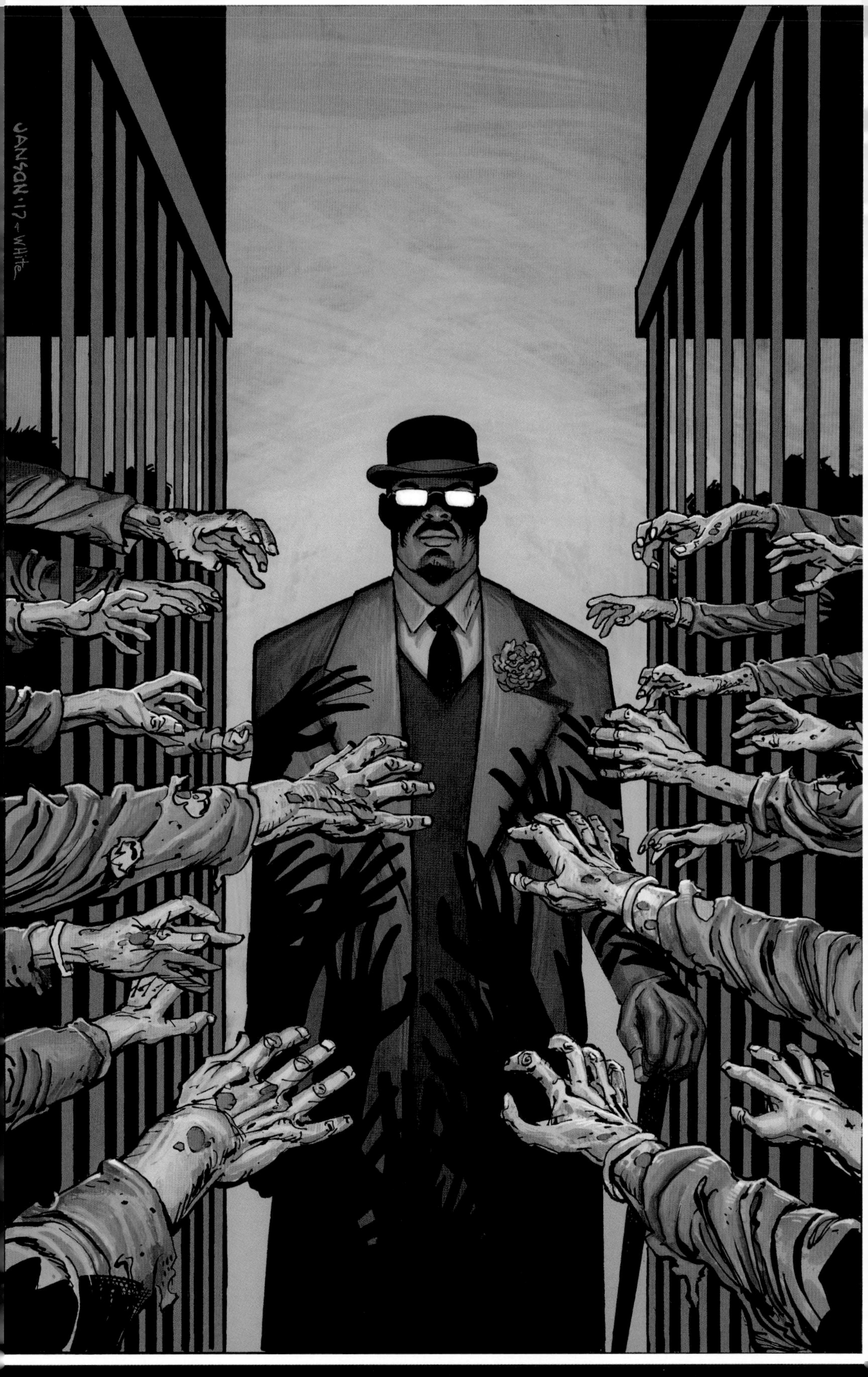
JANSON '17 - White

SSUE #2, Cover B. Art by KLAUS JANSON, colors by DEAN WHITE.

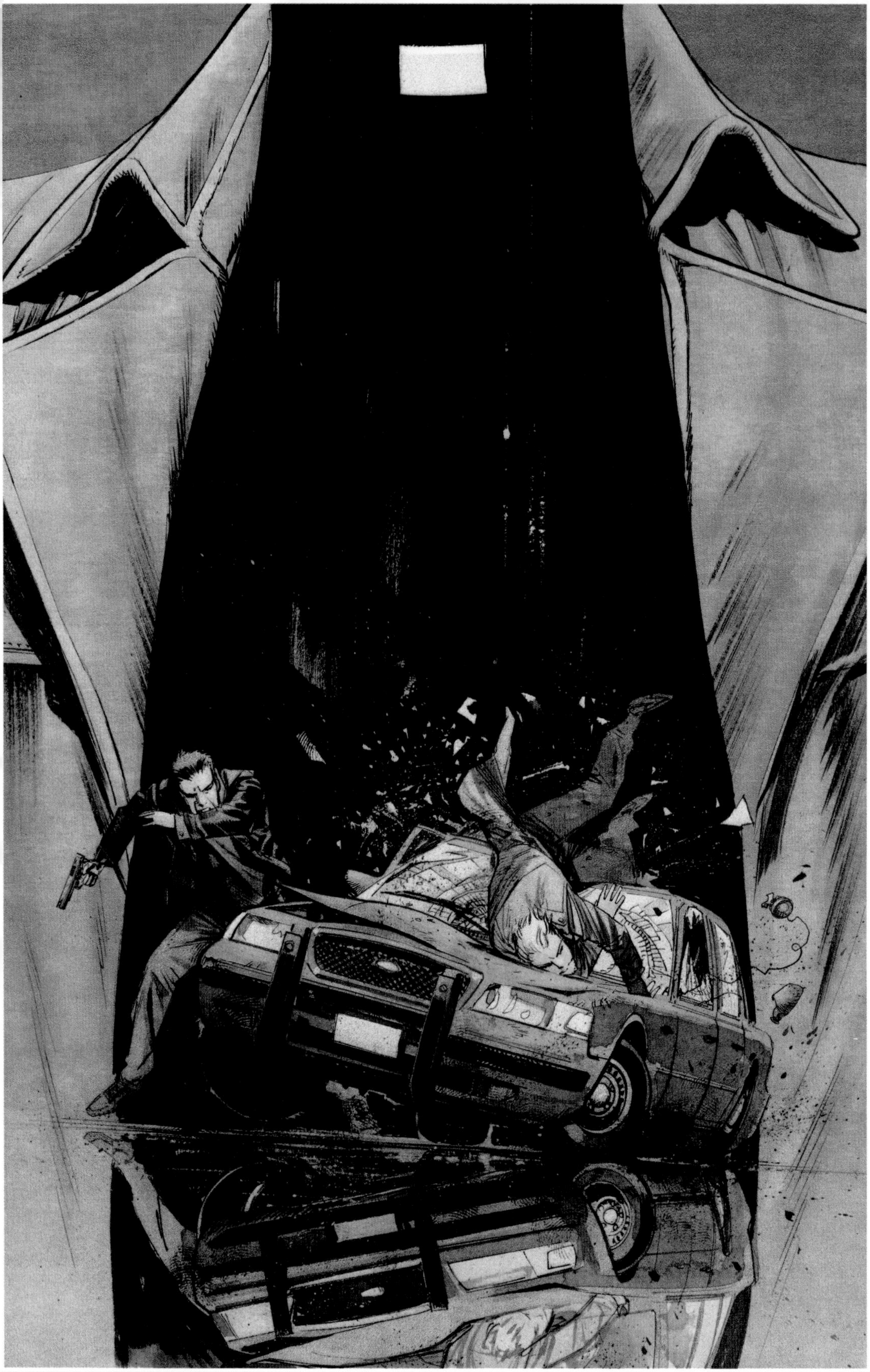

ISSUE #2, Cover C. Art by SEAN MURPHY, colors by MATT HOLLINGSWORTH

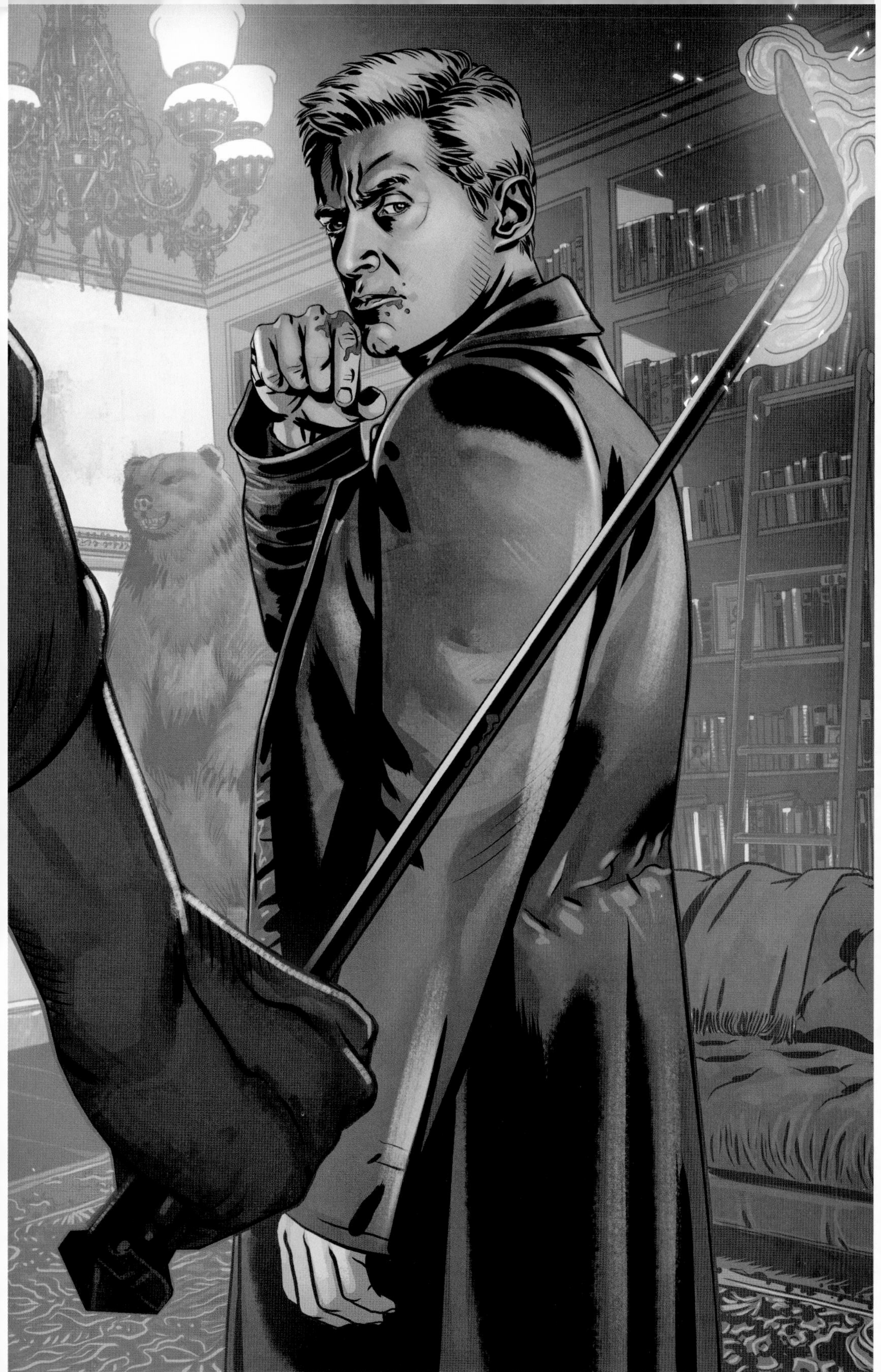

ISSUE #3, Cover A. Art by PA r.

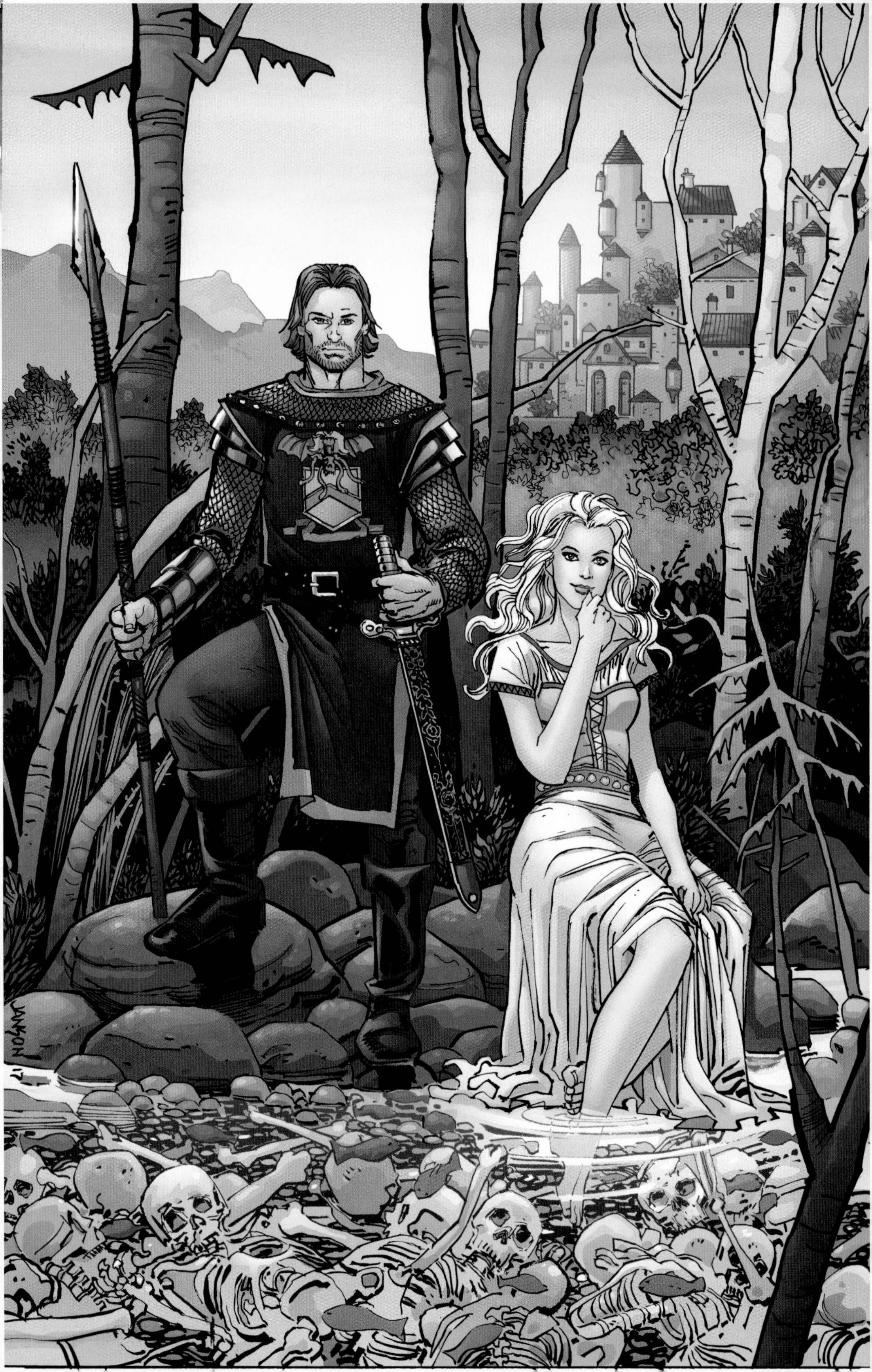

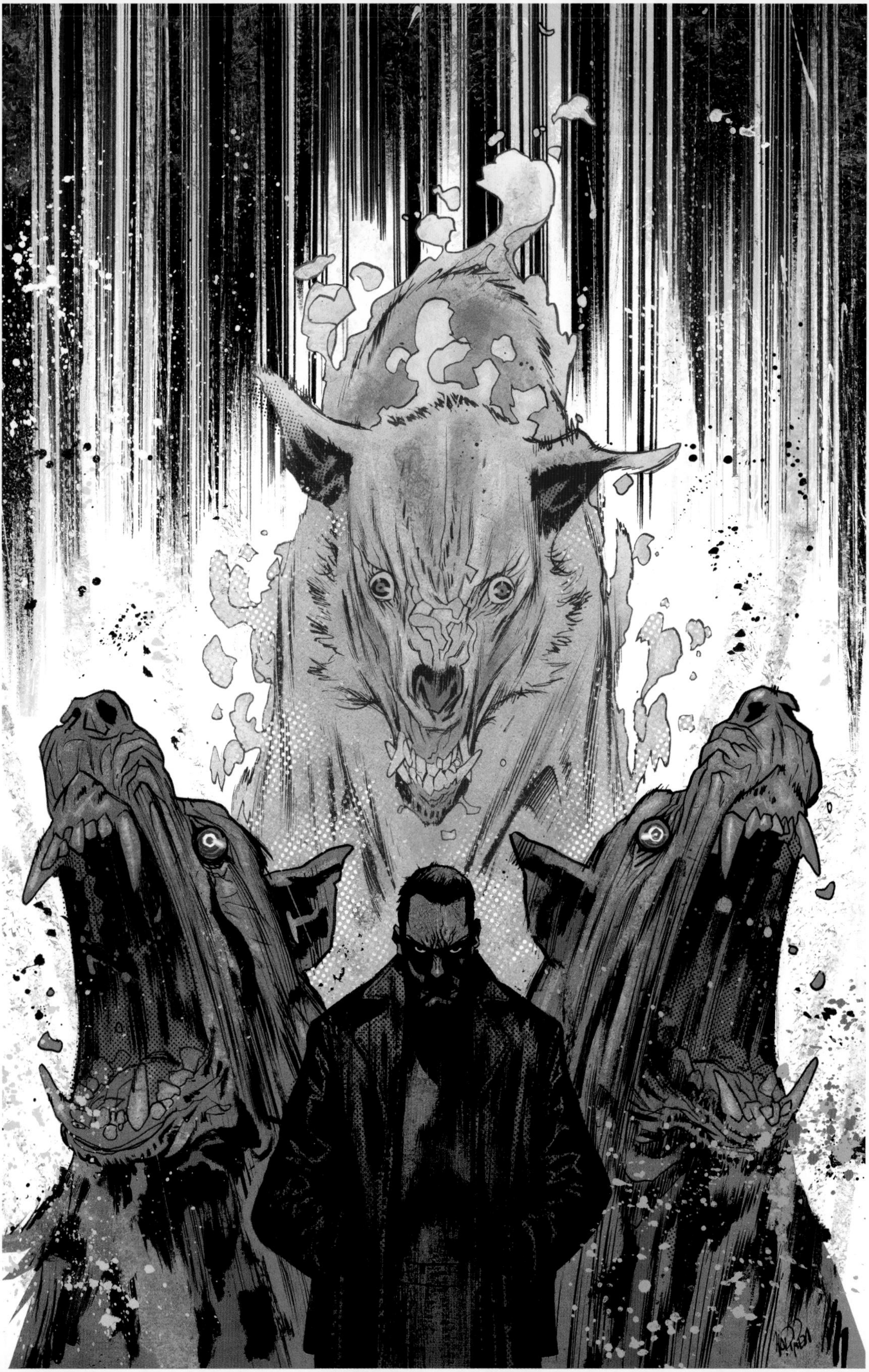

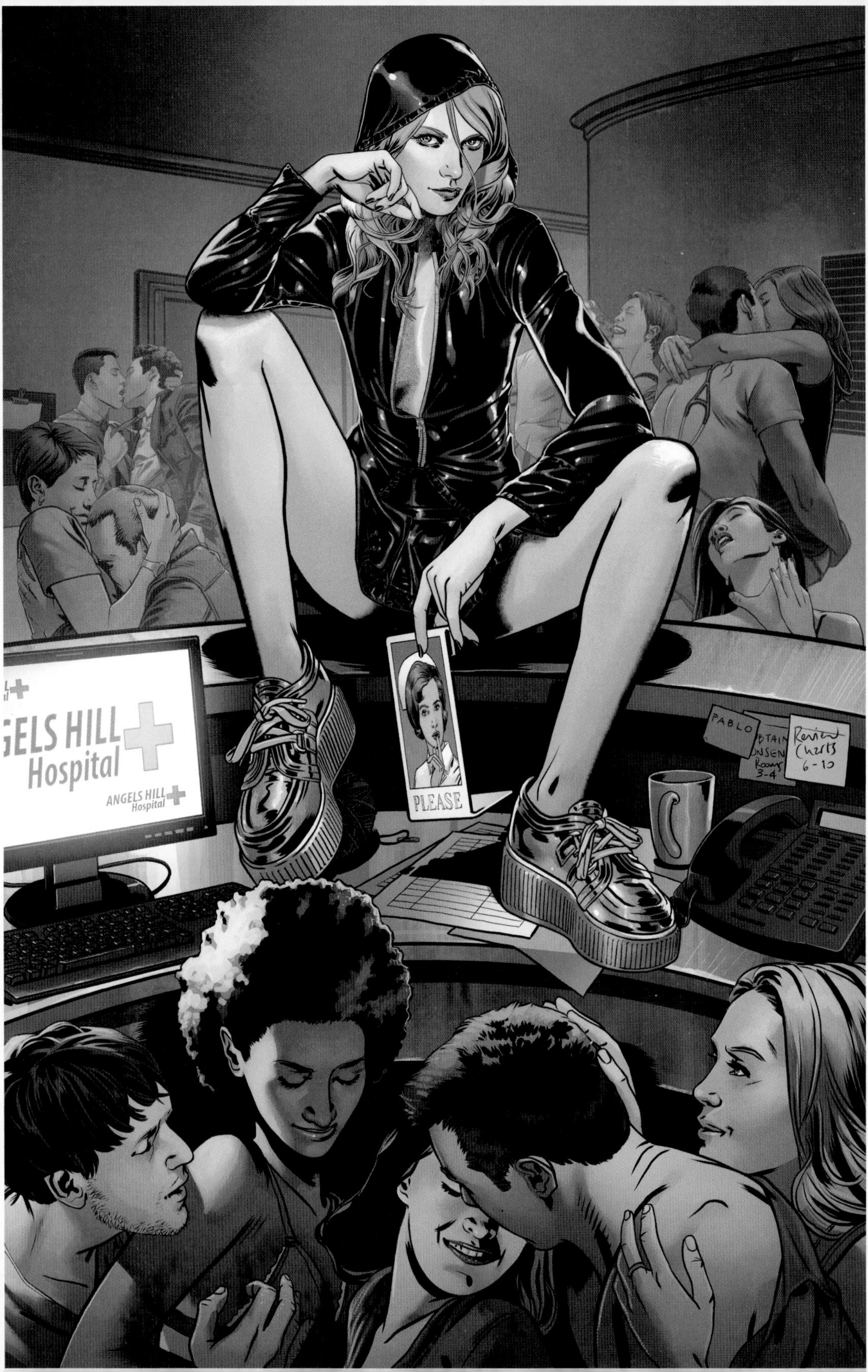
GELS HILL
Hospital
ANGELS HILL
Hospital
PLEASE
PABLO
Review Charts
6-10

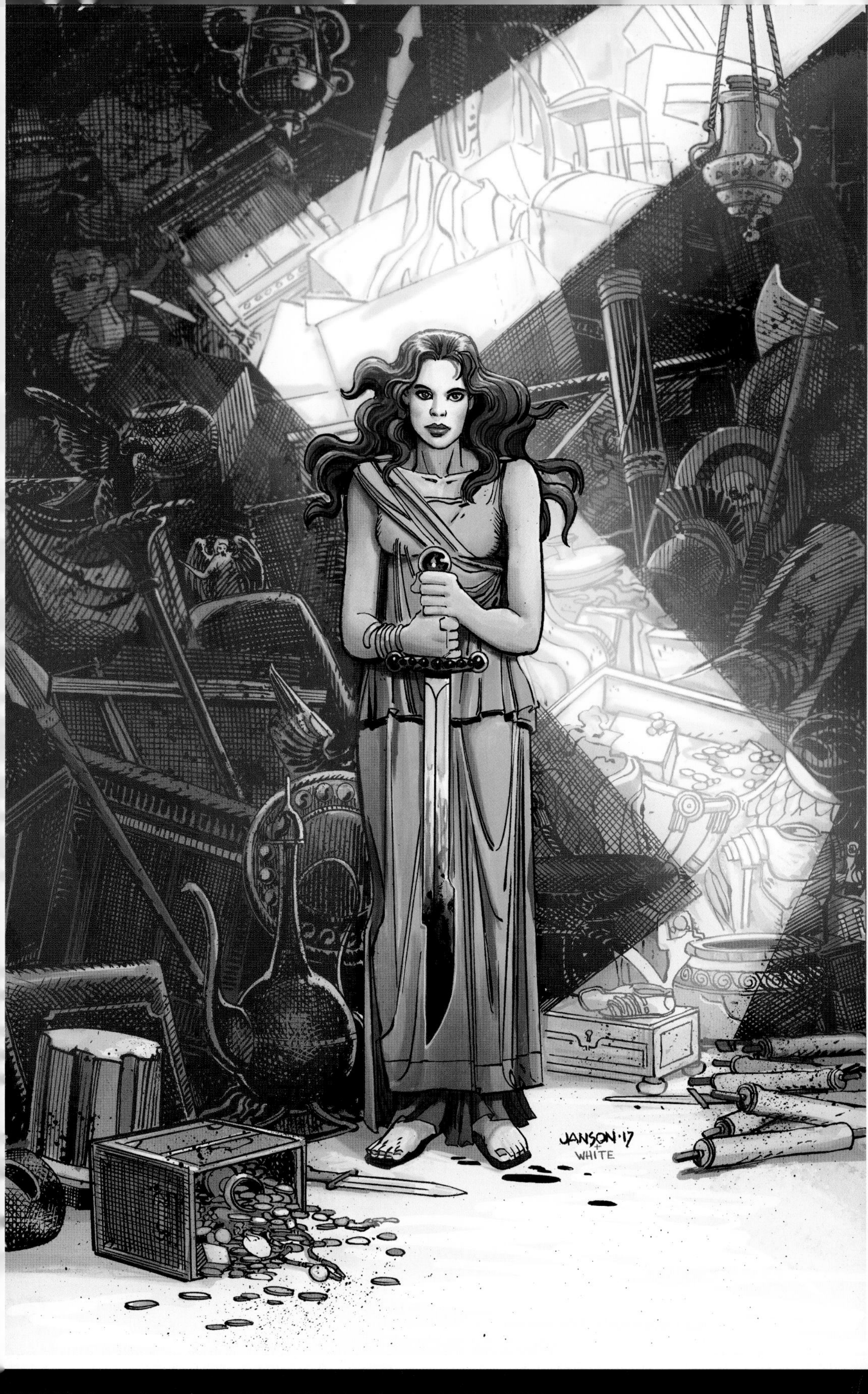
JANSON·17
+
WHITE

ISSUE #4, Cover B. Art by KLAUS JANSON, colors by DEAN WHITE.

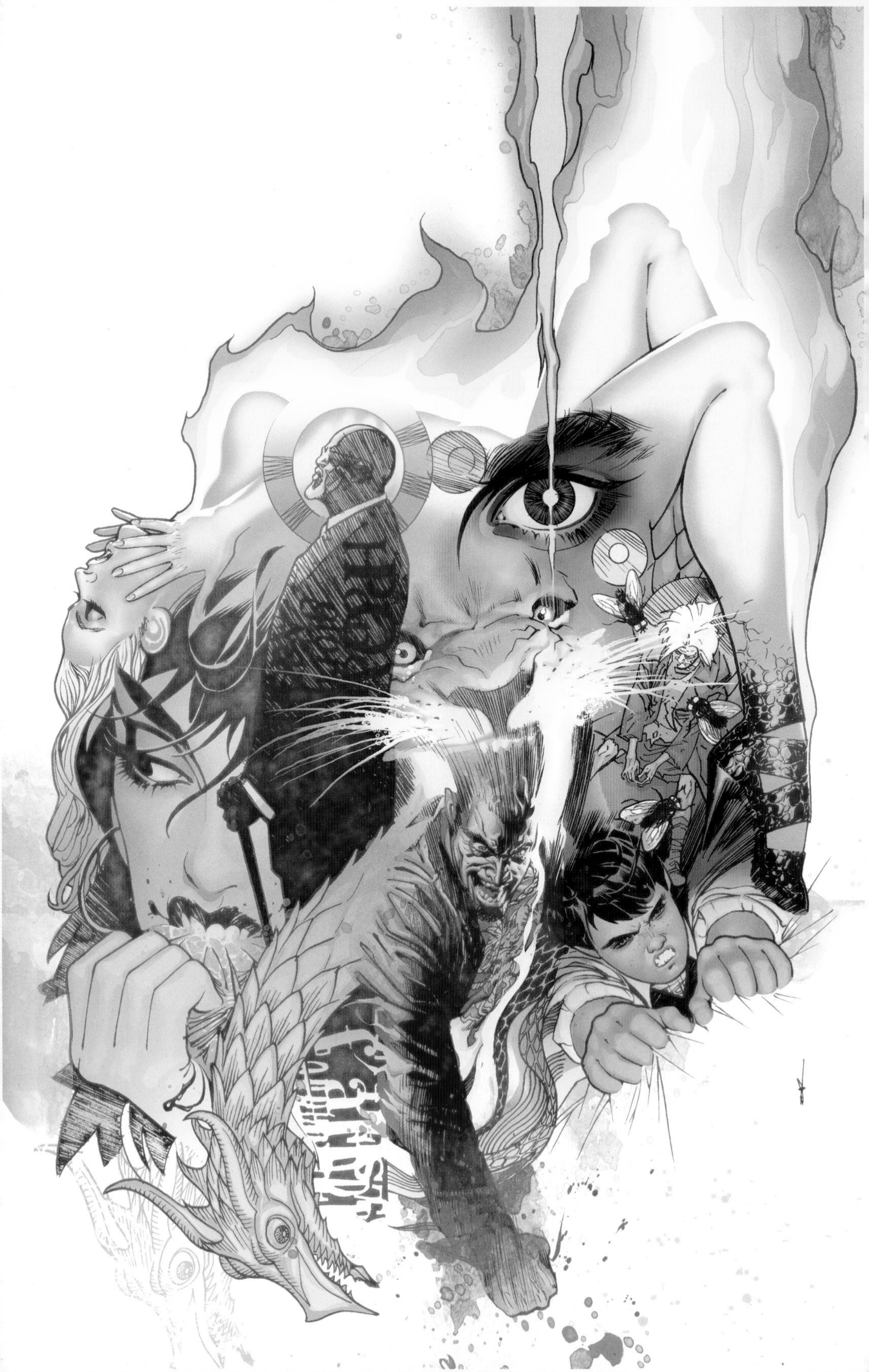

ISSUE #4, Cover C. Art by RYAN SOOK

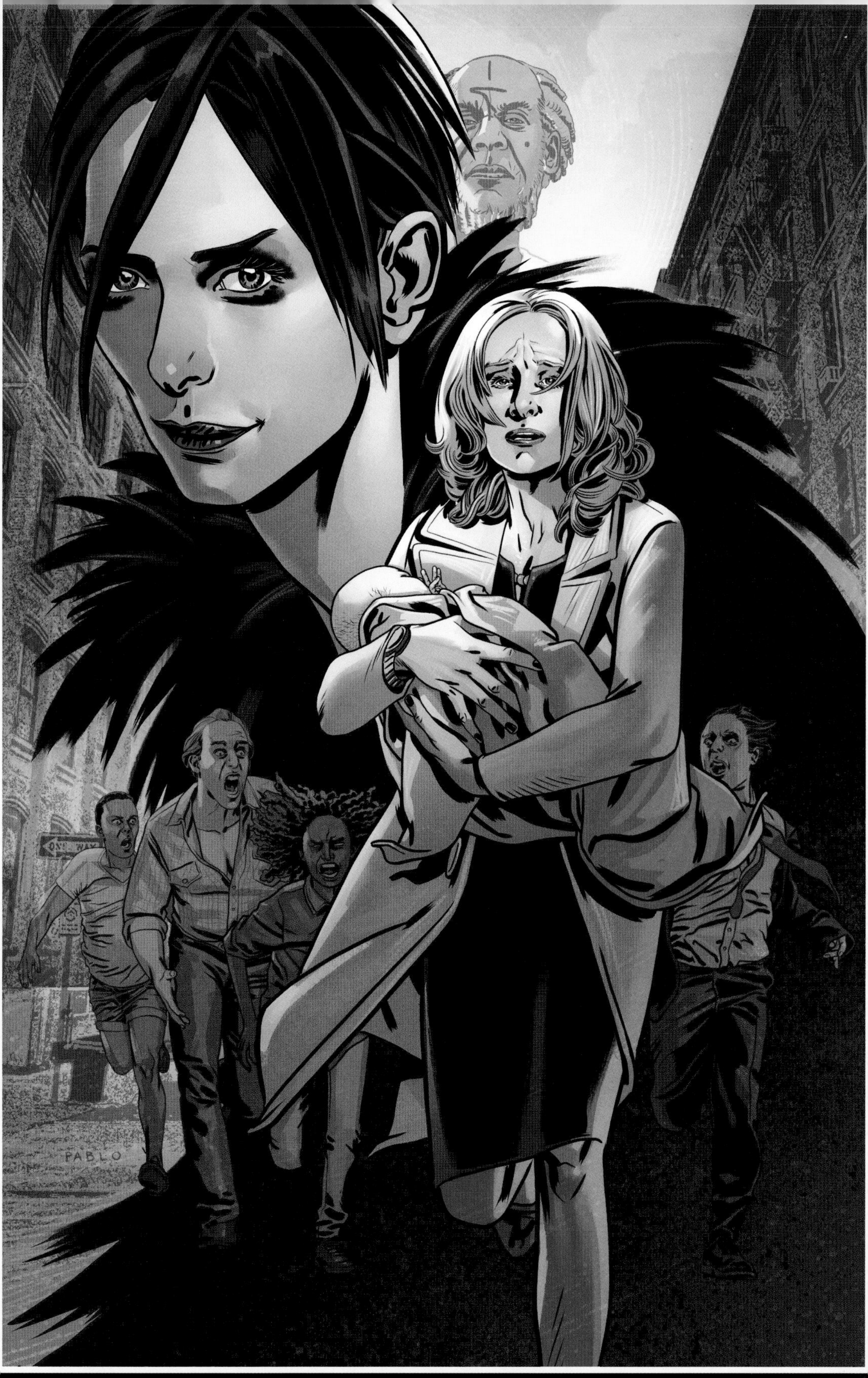
ONE WAY
PABLO

SSUE #5, Cover A. Art by PABLO RAIMONDI, colors by ROMULO FAJARDO Jr.

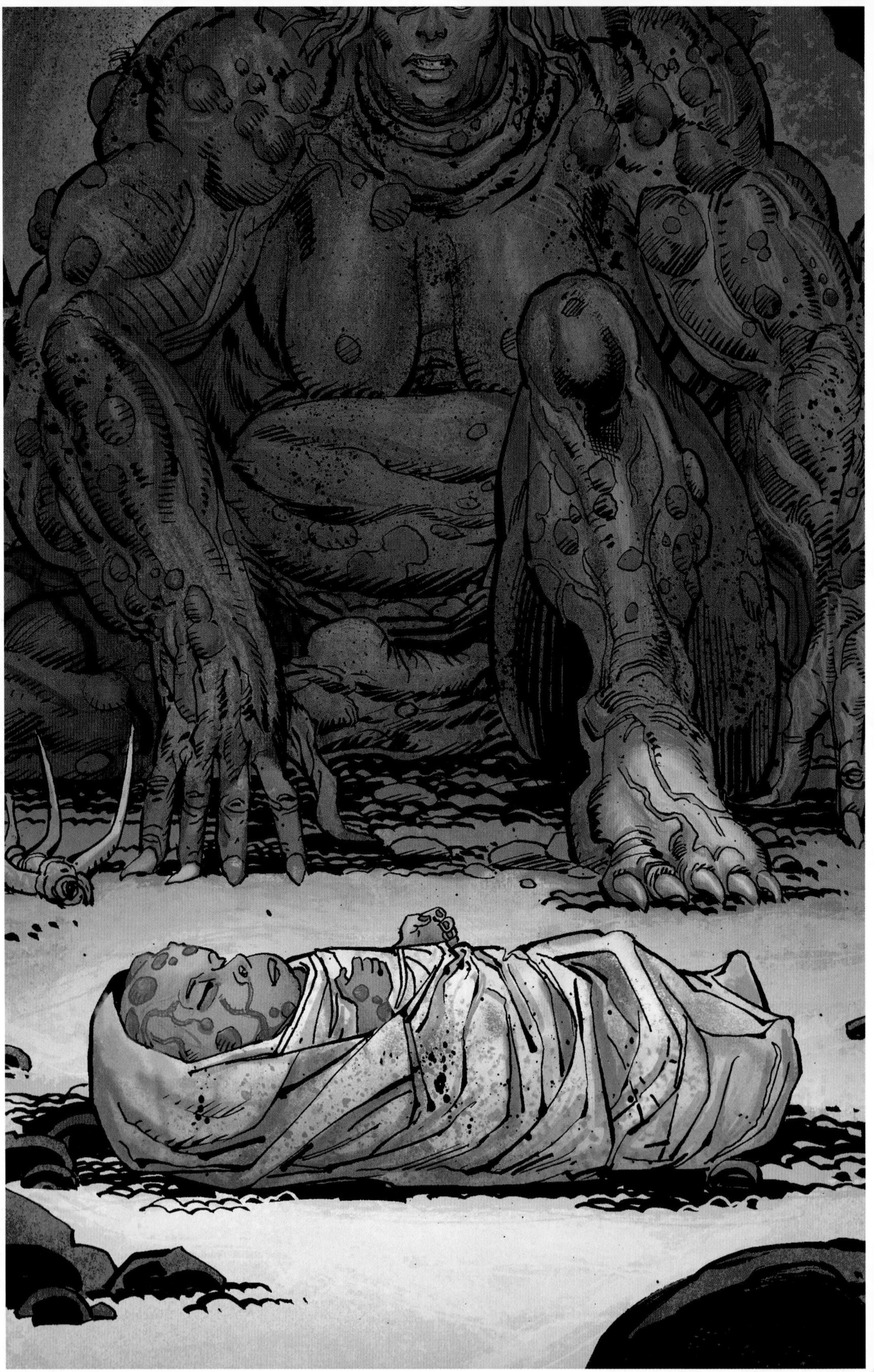

ISSUE #5, Cover B. Art by KLAUS JANSON, colors by DEAN WHITE

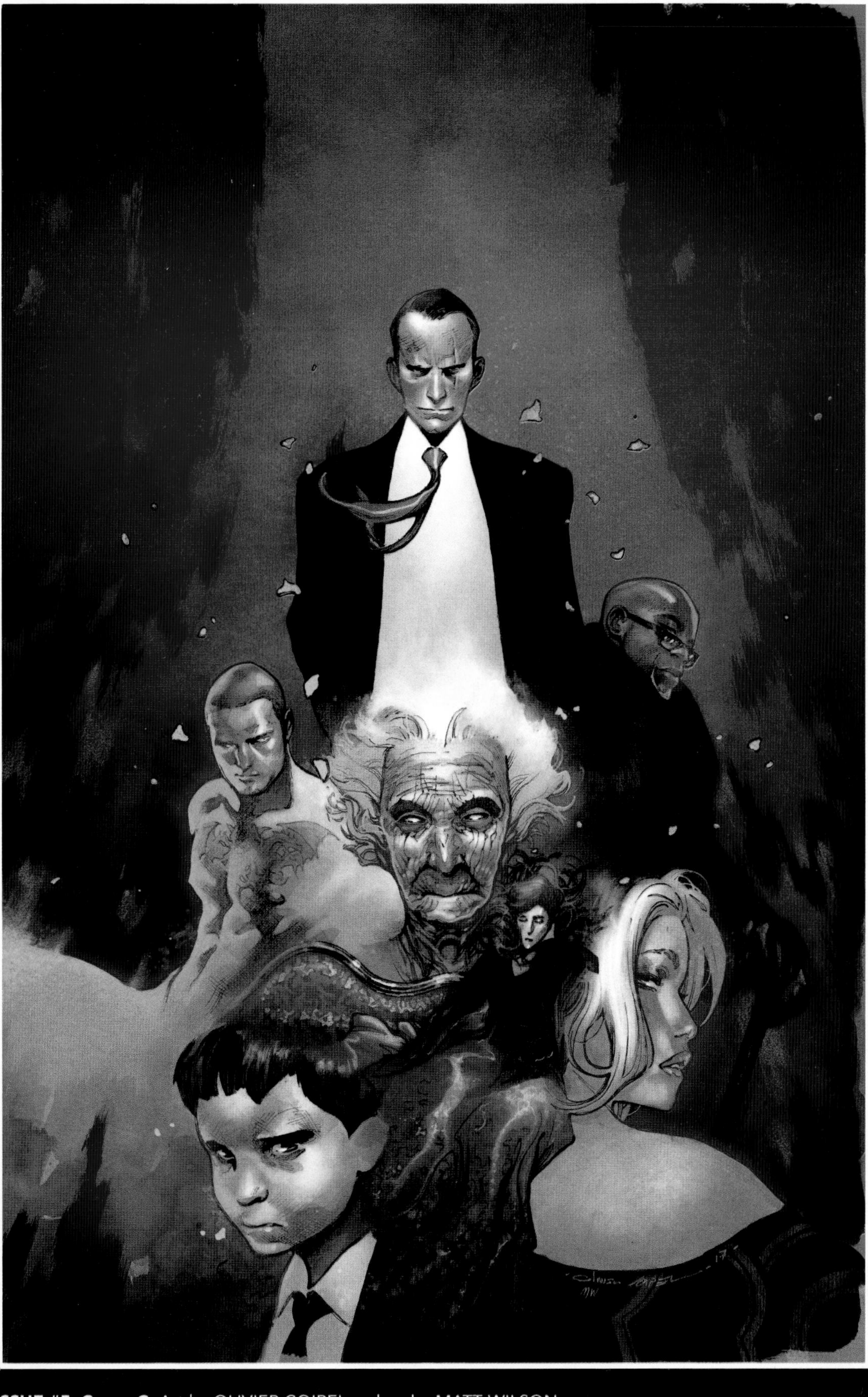

SSUE #5, Cover C. Art by OLIVIER COIPEL, colors by MATT WILSON.

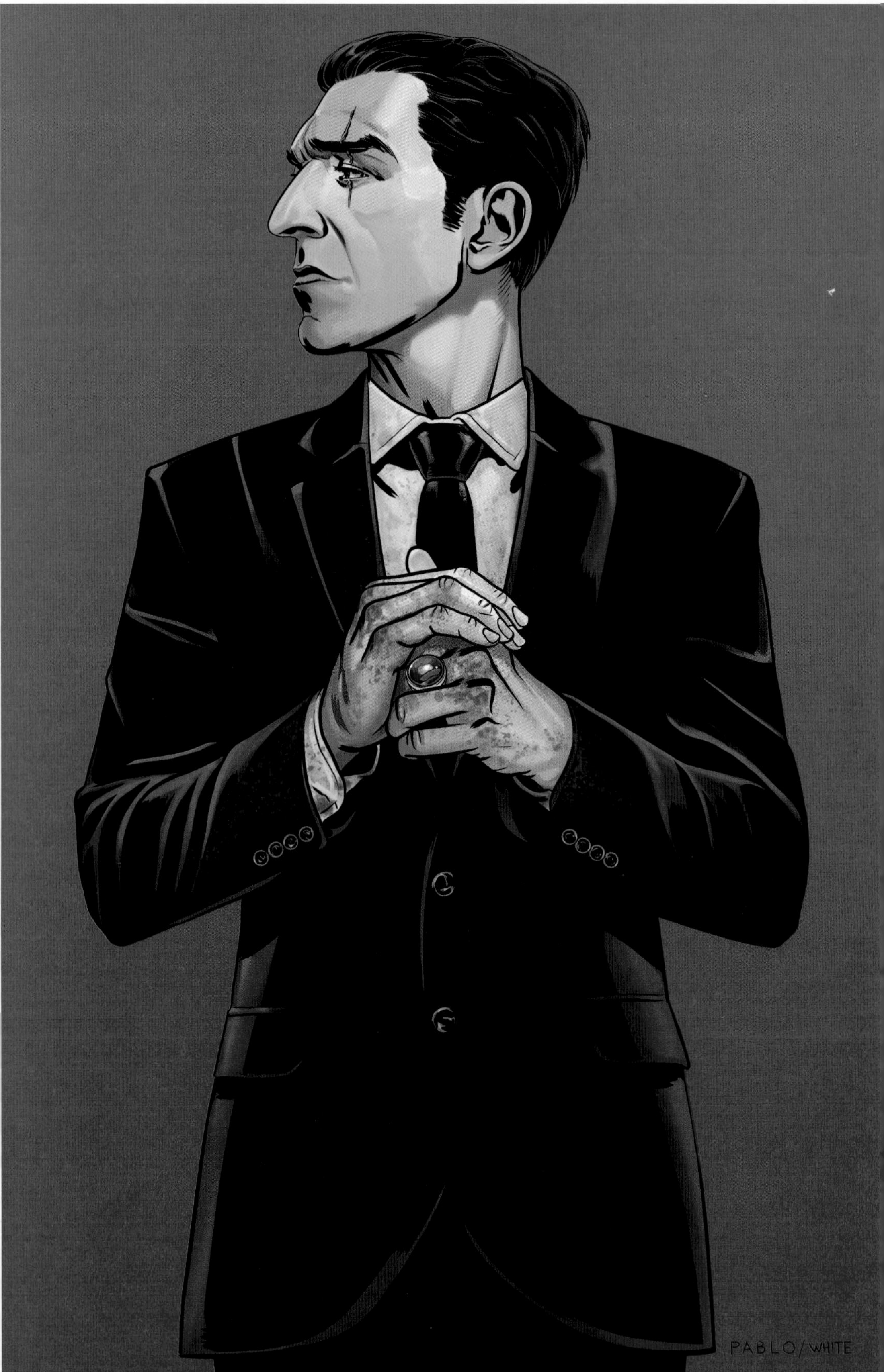
PABLO/WHITE

ISSUE #6, Cover A. Art by PABLO RAIMONDI, colors by DEAN WHITE

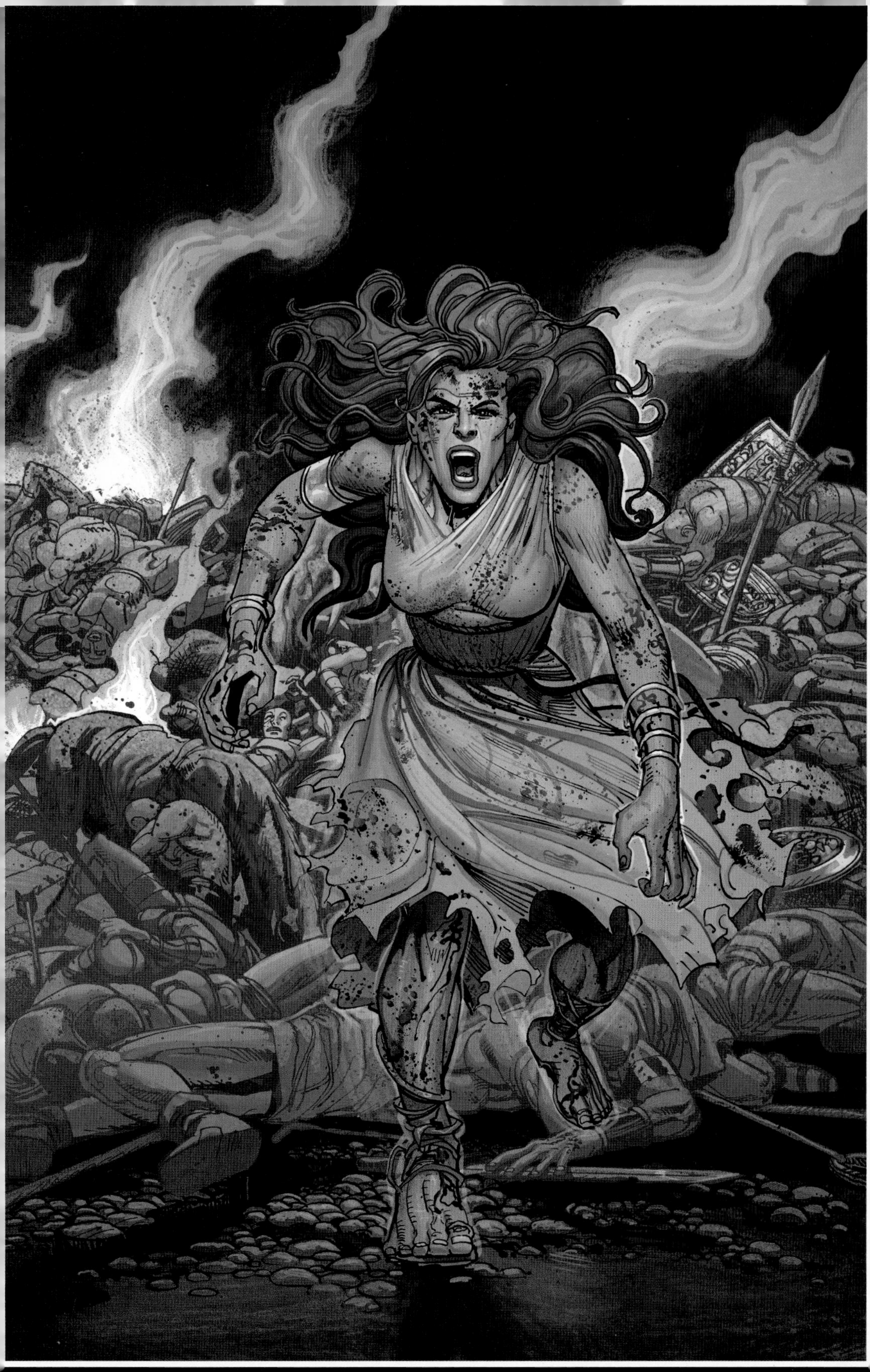

SSUE #6, Cover B. Art by KLAUS JANSON, colors by DEAN WHITE.

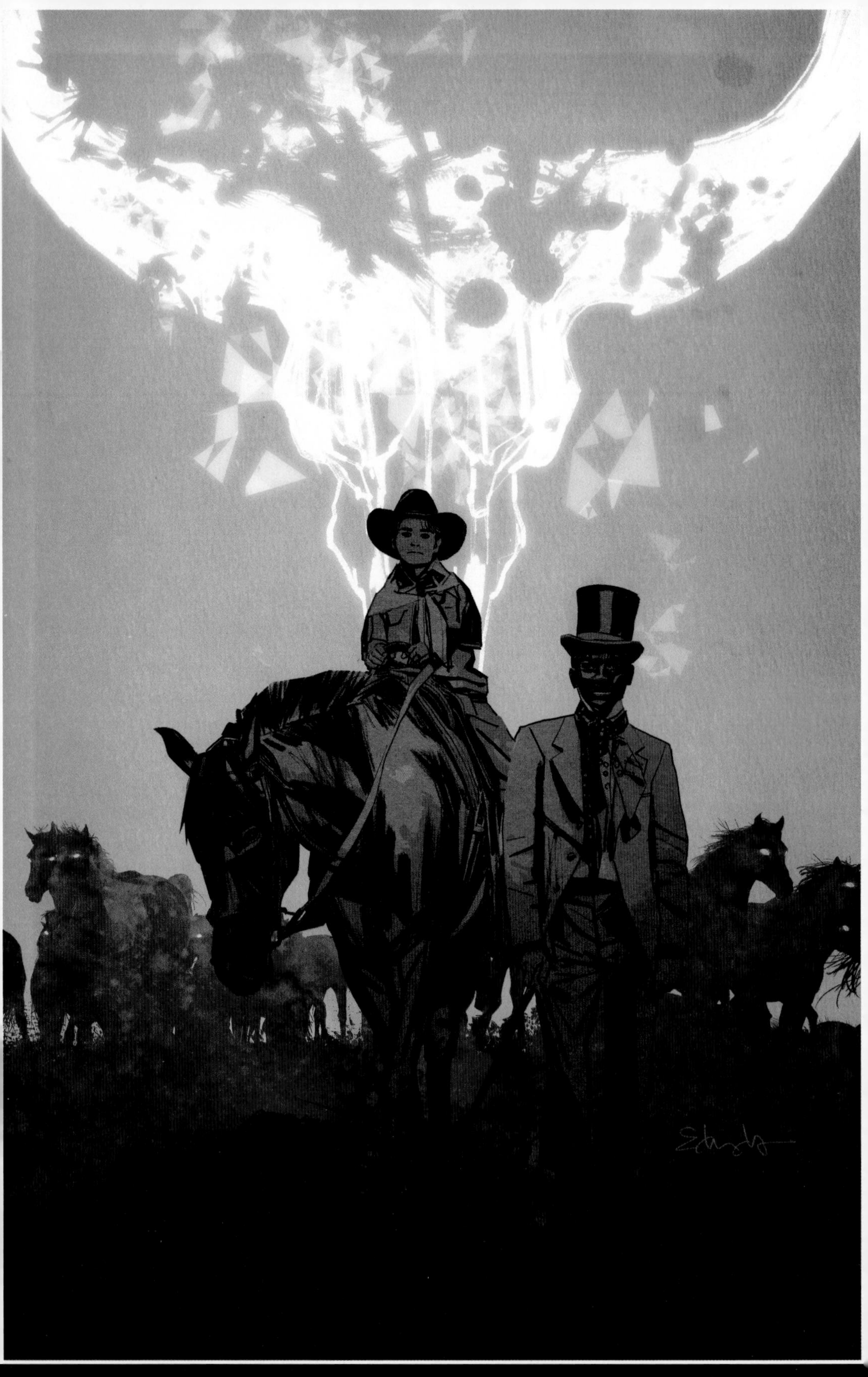

ISSUE #6, Cover C. Art by TOMMY LEE EDWARDS